Adventure Series

Enid Blyton, who died in 1968, is one of the most popular and prolific children's authors of all time. She wrote over seven hundred books which have been translated into many languages throughout the world. She also found time to write numerous songs, poems, and plays, and ran magazines and clubs.

She was always very concerned for the welfare of children in need, and the Enid Blyton Trust, set up after her death, is very active in raising funds for sick and handicapped children.

All eight titles in the Adventure series
are also available individually
from Piper Books:

Enid Blyton

Adventure Series

including

The Island of Adventure
The Castle of Adventure
The Valley of Adventure

PIPER

MACMILLAN
CHILDREN'S BOOKS

The Island of Adventure first published 1944 by Macmillan and Co. Ltd
Revised edition published 1988 by Pan Books Ltd
© Darrell Waters Ltd 1944
The Castle of Adventure first published 1946 by Macmillan and Co. Ltd
Revised edition published 1988 by Pan Books Ltd
© Darrell Waters Ltd 1946
The Valley of Adventure first published 1947 by Macmillan and Co. Ltd
Revised edition published 1988 by Pan Books Ltd
© Darrell Waters Ltd 1947

Omnibus edition first published 1989 by Pan Books Ltd
This revised omnibus edition published 1994 by Macmillan Children's Books
a division of Macmillan Publishers Limited
Cavaye Place London SW10 9PG
and Basingstoke
9
ISBN 0 330 31012 7

Printed and bound in Great Britain by
Cox & Wyman Ltd, Reading, Berkshire

The Enid Blyton Trust for Children

We hope you will enjoy the adventures of the children in this book. Please think for a moment about those children who are too ill to do the exciting things you and your friends do. Help them by sending a donation, large or small, to the ENID BLYTON TRUST FOR SICK CHILDREN. The trust will use all your gifts to help children who are sick or handicapped and need to be made happy or comfortable.

Please send your postal orders or cheques to:
The Enid Blyton Trust for Children
International House
1 St. Katharine's Way
London E1 9UN

Thank you very much for your help

Enid Blyton

The Island of Adventure

Contents

1

The beginning of things

It was really most extraordinary.

There was Philip Mannering, doing his best to puzzle out algebra problems, lying full-length under a tree with nobody near him at all – and yet he could hear a voice speaking to him most distinctly.

'Can't you shut the door, idiot?' said the voice, in a most impatient tone. 'And how many times have I told you to wipe your feet?'

Philip sat up straight and took a good look round for the third time – but the hillside stretched above and below him, completely empty of any boy, girl, man or woman.

'It's so silly,' said Philip to himself. 'Because there is no door to shut, and no mat to wipe my feet on. Whoever is speaking must be perfectly mad. Anyway, I don't like it. A voice without a body is too odd for anything.'

A small brown nose poked up out of Philip's jersey collar. It belonged to a little brown mouse, one of the boy's many pets. Philip put up a gentle hand and rubbed the tiny creature's head. Its nose twitched in delight.

'Shut the door, idiot!' roared the voice from nowhere, 'and don't sniff. Where's your handkerchief?'

This was too much for Philip. He roared back.

'Shut up! I'm not sniffing. Who are you, anyway?'

There was no answer. Philip felt very puzzled. It was uncanny and peculiar. Where did that extraordinary voice with its rude commands come from, on this bright, sunny but completely empty hillside? He shouted again.

'I'm working. If you want to talk, come out and show yourself.'

'All right, Uncle,' said the voice, speaking unexpectedly in a very different tone, apologetic and quiet.

'Gosh!' said Philip. 'I can't stand this. I'll have to solve the mystery. If I can find out where the voice comes from, I may find its owner.' He shouted again. 'Where are you? Come out and let me see you.'

'If I've told you once I've told you a dozen times not to whistle,' answered the voice fiercely. Philip was silent with astonishment. He hadn't been whistling. Evidently the owner of the voice must be completely mad. Philip suddenly felt that he didn't want to meet this strange person. He would rather go home without seeing him.

He looked carefully round. He had no idea at all where the voice came from, but he rather thought it must be somewhere to the left of him. All right, he would go quietly down the hill to the right, keeping to the trees if he could, so that they might hide him a little.

He picked up his books, put his pencil into his pocket and stood up cautiously. He almost jumped out of his skin as the voice broke out into cackles of laughter. Philip forgot to be cautious and darted down the hillside to the shelter of a clump of trees. The laughter stopped suddenly.

Philip stood under a big tree and listened. His heart beat fast. He wished he was back at the house with the others. Then, just above his head, the voice spoke again.

'How many times have I told you to wipe your feet?'

Then there came a most unearthly screech that made poor Philip drop his books in terror. He looked up into the tree near by, and saw a beautiful white parrot, with a yellow crest on its head that it worked up and down. It gazed at Philip with bright black eyes, its head on one side, its curved beak making a grating noise.

Philip stared at the parrot and the parrot stared back. Then the bird lifted up a clawed foot and scratched its head very thoughtfully, still raising and lowering its crest. Then it spoke.

'Don't sniff,' it said, in a conversational tone. 'Can't you shut the door, idiot? Where are your manners?'

'Golly!' said Philip, in amazement. 'So it was *you* talking

8

and shouting and laughing! Well – you gave me an awful fright.'

The parrot gave a most realistic sneeze. 'Where's your handkerchief?' it said.

Philip laughed. 'You really are a most extraordinary bird,' he said. 'The cleverest I ever saw. Where have you escaped from?'

'Wipe your feet,' answered the parrot sternly. Philip laughed again. Then he heard the sound of a boy's voice, calling loudly from the bottom of the hill.

'Kiki, Kiki, Kiki! Where have you got to?'

The parrot spread out its wings, gave a hideous screech, and sailed away down the hillside towards a house set at the foot. Philip watched it go.

'That was a boy calling it,' he thought. 'And he was in the garden of Hillfoot House, where I'm staying. I wonder if he's come there to be crammed too. I jolly well hope he has. It would be fine to have a parrot like that living with us. It's dull enough having to do lessons in the hols – a parrot would liven things up a bit.'

Philip had had scarlet fever the term before, and measles immediately afterwards, so that he had missed most of his school-work. His headmaster had written to his uncle and aunt suggesting that he should go and stay at the home of one of the teachers for a few weeks, to make up a little of what he had missed. And, much to Philip's disgust, his uncle had at once agreed – so there was Philip, in the summer holidays, having to work at algebra and geography and history, instead of having a fine time with his sister Dinah at his home, Craggy-Tops, by the sea.

He liked the master, Mr Roy, but he was bored with the other two boys there, who, also owing to illness, were being crammed or coached by Mr Roy. One was much older than Philip, and the other was a poor whining creature who was simply terrified of the various insects and animals that Philip always seemed to be collecting or rescuing. The boy was intensely fond of all creatures and had an amazing knack of

9

making them trust him.

Now he hurried down the hillside, eager to see if another pupil had joined the little holiday collection of boys to be coached. If the new boy owned the parrot, he would be somebody interesting – more interesting than that big lout of a Sam, and better fun than poor whining Oliver.

He opened the garden gate and then stared in surprise. A girl was in the garden, not a very big girl – perhaps about eleven. She had red hair, rather curly, and green eyes, a fair skin and hundreds of freckles. She stared at Philip.

'Hallo,' said Philip, rather liking the look of the girl, who was dressed in shorts and a jersey. 'Have you come here?'

'Looks like it,' said the girl, with a grin. 'But I haven't come to work. Only to be with Jack.'

'Who's Jack?' asked Philip.

'My brother,' said the girl. 'He's got to be coached. You should have seen his report last term. He was bottom in everything. He's very clever really, but he just doesn't bother. He says he's going to be an ornithologist, so what's the good of learning dates and capes and poems and things?'

'What's an— an— whatever it was you said?' said Philip, wondering how anyone could possibly have so many freckles on her nose as this girl had.

'Ornithologist? Oh, it's someone who loves and studies birds,' said the girl. 'Didn't you know that? Jack's mad on birds.'

'He ought to come and live where *I* live then,' said Philip at once. 'I live on a very wild, lonely part of the sea-coast, and there are heaps of rare sea-birds there. I like birds too, but I don't know much about them. I say – does that parrot belong to Jack?'

'Yes,' said the girl. 'He's had her for four years. Her name is Kiki.'

'Did he teach it to say all those things?' said Philip, thinking that though Jack might be bottom in all school subjects he would certainly get top marks for teaching parrots to talk!

10

'Oh no,' said the girl, smiling, so that her green eyes twinkled and crinkled. 'Kiki just picked up those sayings of hers — picked them up from our old uncle, who is the crossest old man in the world, I should think. Our mother and father are dead, so Uncle Geoffrey has us in the hols, and doesn't he just hate it! His housekeeper hates us too, so we don't have much of a time, but so long as I have Jack, and so long as Jack has his beloved birds, we are happy enough.'

'I suppose Jack got sent here to learn a few things, like me,' said Philip. 'You'll be lucky — you'll be able to play, go for walks, do what you like, whilst we are stewing in lessons.'

'No, I shan't,' said the girl. 'I shall be with Jack. I don't have him in the school term, so I'm jolly well going to have him in the hols. I think he's marvellous.'

'Well, that's more than *my* sister, Dinah, thinks of me,' said Philip. 'We're always quarrelling. Hallo — is this Jack?'

A boy came up the path towards Philip. On his left shoulder sat the parrot, Kiki, rubbing her beak softly against Jack's ear, and saying something in a low voice. The boy scratched the parrot's head and gazed at Philip with the same green eyes as his sister had. His hair was even redder, and his face so freckled that it would have been impossible to find a clear space anywhere, for there seemed to be freckles on top of freckles.

'Hallo, Freckles,' said Philip, and grinned.

'Hallo, Tufty,' said Jack, and grinned too. Philip put up his hand and felt his front bit of hair, which always rose up in a sort of tuft. No amount of water and brushing would make it lie down for long.

'Wipe your feet,' said Kiki severely.

'I'm glad you found Kiki all right,' said the girl. 'She didn't like coming to a strange place, and that's why she flew off, I expect.'

'She wasn't far away, Lucy-Ann,' said Jack. 'I bet old Tufty here got a fright if he heard her up on the hillside.'

'I did,' said Philip, and began telling the two what had

11

happened. They laughed loudly, and Kiki joined in, cackling in a most human manner.

'Golly, I'm glad you and Lucy-Ann have come here,' said Philip, feeling much happier than he had felt for some days. He liked the look of the red-haired, green-eyed brother and sister very much. They would be friends. He would show them the animals he had as pets. They could go for walks together. Jack was some years older than Lucy-Ann, about fourteen, Philip thought, just a little older than he himself was. It was a pity Dinah wasn't there too, then there would be four of them. Dinah was twelve. She would fit in nicely – only, perhaps, with her quick impatience and quarrelsome nature, it might not be peaceful!

'How different Lucy-Ann and Jack are from me and Dinah,' thought Philip. It was quite plain that Lucy-Ann adored Jack, and Philip could not imagine Dinah hanging on to his words, eager to do his bidding, fetching and carrying for him, as Lucy-Ann did for Jack.

'Oh, well – people are different,' thought the boy. 'Dinah's a good sort, even if we do quarrel and fight. She must be having a pretty awful time at Craggy-Tops without me. I bet Aunt Polly is working her hard.'

It was pleasant at tea-time that day to sit and watch Jack's parrot on his shoulder, making remarks from time to time. It was good to see the glint in Lucy-Ann's green eyes as she teased big, slow Sam, and ticked off the smaller, peevish Oliver. Things would liven up a bit now.

They certainly did. Holiday coaching was *much* more fun with Jack and Lucy-Ann there too.

2

Making friends

Mr Roy, the holiday master, worked the children hard, because that was his job. He coached them the whole of the morning, going over and over everything patiently, making sure it was understood, demanding, and usually getting, close attention.

At least he got it from everyone except Jack. Jack gave close attention to nothing unless it had feathers.

'If you studied your geometry as closely as you study that book on birds, you'd be top of any class,' complained Mr Roy. 'You exasperate me, Jack Trent. You exasperate me more than I can say.'

'Use your handkerchief,' said the parrot impertinently.

Mr Roy made a clicking noise of annoyance with his tongue. 'I shall wring that bird's neck one day. What with you saying you can't work unless Kiki is on your shoulder, and Philip harbouring all kinds of unpleasant creatures about his person, this holiday class is rapidly getting unbearable. The only one that appears to do any work at all is Lucy-Ann, and she hasn't come here to work.'

Lucy-Ann liked work. She enjoyed sitting beside Jack, trying to do the same work as he had been set. Jack mooned over it, thinking of gannets and cormorants which he had just been reading about, whilst Lucy-Ann tried her hand at solving the problems set out in his book. She liked, too, watching Philip, because she never knew what animal or creature would walk out of his sleeve or collar or pocket. The day before, a very large and peculiarly coloured caterpillar had crawled from his sleeve, to Mr Roy's intense annoyance. And that morning a young rat had left Philip's sleeve on a journey of exploration and had gone up Mr Roy's trouser-leg in a most determined manner.

This had upset the whole class for ten minutes whilst Mr Roy had tried to dislodge the rat. It was no wonder he was in a bad temper. He was usually a patient and amiable man, but two boys like Jack and Philip were disturbing to any class.

The mornings were always passed in hard work. The afternoons were given to preparation for the next day, and to the writing-out of answers on the morning's work. The evenings were completely free. As there were only four boys to coach, Mr Roy could give them each individual attention, and try to fill in the gaps in their knowledge. Usually he was a most successful coach, but these holidays were not showing as much good work as he had hoped.

Sam, the big boy, was stupid and slow. Oliver was peevish, sorry for himself, and resented having to work at all. Jack was impossible, so inattentive at times that it seemed a waste of time to try and teach him. He seemed to think of nothing but birds. 'If I grew feathers, he would probably do everything I told him,' thought Mr Roy. 'I never knew anyone so mad on birds before. I believe he knows the eggs of every bird in the world. He's got good brains, but he won't use them for anything that he's not really interested in.'

Philip was the only boy who showed much improvement, though he was a trial too, with his different and peculiar pets. That rat! Mr Roy shuddered when he thought of how it had felt, climbing up his leg. Really, Lucy-Ann was the only one who worked properly, and she didn't need to. She had only come because she would not be separated from her brother, Jack.

Jack, Philip and Lucy-Ann soon became firm friends. The love for all living things that both Jack and Philip had drew them together. Jack had never had a real friend before, and he enjoyed Philip's jokes and teasing. Lucy-Ann liked Philip too, though she was sometimes jealous when Jack showed his liking for him. Kiki loved Philip, and made funny crooning noises when the boy scratched her head.

Kiki had been a great annoyance to Mr Roy at first. She had interrupted the mornings constantly with her remarks. It was unfortunate that the master had a sniff, because Kiki spoke about it whenever he sniffed.

'Don't sniff!' the parrot would say in a reproving tone, and the five children would begin to giggle. So Mr Roy forbade Kiki to be brought into the classroom.

But matters only became worse, because Kiki, furious at being shut away outside in the garden, unable to sit on her beloved master's shoulder, sat in a bush outside the half-open window, and made loud and piercing remarks that seemed to be directed at poor Mr Roy.

'Don't talk nonsense,' said the parrot, when Mr Roy was in the middle of explaining some fact of history.

Mr Roy sniffed in exasperation. 'Where's your handkerchief?' asked Kiki at once. Mr Roy went to the window and shouted and waved at Kiki to frighten her away.

'Naughty boy,' said Kiki, not budging an inch. 'I'll send you to bed. You're a naughty boy.'

You couldn't do anything with a bird like that. So Mr Roy gave it up and allowed the parrot to sit on Jack's shoulder once more. Jack worked better with the bird near him, and Kiki was not so disturbing indoors as out-of-doors. All the same, Mr Roy felt he would be very glad when the little holiday school came to an end, and the four boys and one girl went home, together with the parrot and the various creatures owned by Philip.

Philip, Jack and Lucy-Ann left the big slow-witted Sam and the peevish little Oliver to be company for one another each day after tea, and went off on their own together. The boys talked of all the birds and animals they had known, and Lucy-Ann listened, stumbling to keep up with them as they walked. No matter how far they walked, or what steep hills they climbed, the little girl followed. She did not mean to let her beloved brother out of sight.

Philip felt impatient with Lucy-Ann sometimes. 'Golly, I'm glad Dinah doesn't tag after me like Lucy-Ann tags after

Jack,' he thought. 'I wonder Jack puts up with it.'

But Jack did. Although he often did not appear to notice Lucy-Ann and did not even speak to her for some time, he was never impatient with her, never irritable or cross. Next to his birds, he cared for Lucy-Ann, thought Philip. Well, it was a good thing somebody cared for her. She didn't seem to have much of a life.

The three children had exchanged news about themselves. 'Our mother and father are both dead,' Jack said, 'We don't remember them. They were killed in an aeroplane crash. We were sent to live with our only relation, Uncle Geoffrey. He's old and cross, always nagging at us. His housekeeper, Mrs Miggles, hates us to go home for the holidays – and you can tell what our life is like by listening to old Kiki. Wipe your feet! Don't sniff! Change your shoes at once! Where's your handkerchief? How many times have I told you not to whistle? Can't you shut the door, idiot?'

Philip laughed. 'Well, if Kiki echoes what she hears in your home, you must have a pretty mouldy time,' he said. 'We don't have too grand a time either – but it's better than you and Lucy-Ann have.'

'Are your father and mother dead too?' asked Lucy-Ann, her green eyes staring at Philip as unblinkingly as a cat's.

'Our father's dead – and he left no money,' said Philip. 'But we've got a mother. She doesn't live with us, though.'

'Why not?' asked Lucy-Ann in surprise.

'Well, she has a job,' said Philip. 'She makes enough money at her job for our schooling and our keep in the hols. She runs an art agency – you know, takes orders for posters and pictures and things, gets artists to do them for her, and then takes a commission on the sales. She's a very good business woman – but we don't see much of her.'

'Is she nice?' asked Jack. Never having had a mother that he could remember, he was always interested in other people's. Philip nodded.

'She's fine,' he said, thinking of his keen-eyed, pretty mother, feeling proud of her cleverness, but secretly sad

16

when he remembered how tired she had seemed sometimes when she had paid them a flying visit. One day, thought Philip, one day *he* would be the clever one – earn the money, keep things going, and make things easy for his hard-working mother.

'And you live with an uncle, like we do?' said Lucy-Ann, stroking a tiny grey squirrel that had suddenly popped its head out of one of Philip's pockets.

'Yes. Dinah and I spend all our hols with Uncle Jocelyn and Aunt Polly,' said Philip. 'Uncle Jocelyn is quite impossible. He's always buying old papers and books and documents, studying them and filing them. He's making it his life-work to work out the history of the part of the coast where we live – there were battles there in the old days, and burnings and killings – all most exciting. He's writing a whole history – but as it seems to take him a year to make certain of a fact or two, he'll have to live to be four or five hundred years old before he gets a quarter of the book done, it seems to me.'

The others laughed. They pictured a cross and learned old man poring over yellow, musty papers. What a waste of time, thought Lucy-Ann. She wondered what Aunt Polly was like.

'What's your aunt like?' she said. Philip screwed up his nose.

'A bit sour,' he said. 'Not too bad, really. Too hard-worked, no money, no help in the old house except for old Joe, the sort of handyman helper we've got. She makes poor Dinah slave – I won't, so she's given me up, but Dinah's afraid of her and does what she is told more than I do.'

'What's your home like?' asked Lucy-Ann.

'A funny old place, hundreds of years old, half in ruins, awfully big and draughty, set half-way up a steep cliff, and almost drowned in spray in a storm,' said Philip. 'But I love it. It's wild and lonely and strange, and there's the cry of the sea-birds always round it. You'd love it, Freckles.'

Jack thought he would. It sounded exciting to him. His

17

home was ordinary, a house in a row in a small-sized town. But Philip's house sounded really exciting. The wind and the waves and the sea-birds – he felt as if he could almost hear them clamouring together, when he shut his eyes.

'Wake up, wake up, sleepy-head,' said Kiki, pecking gently at Jack's ear. He opened his eyes and laughed. The parrot had an extraordinary way of saying the right thing sometimes.

'I wish I could see that home of yours – Craggy-Tops,' he said to Philip. 'It sounds as if things could happen there – real, live, exciting things, thrilling adventures. Nothing ever happens in Lippinton, where we live.'

'Well, nothing much happens at Craggy-Tops either,' said Philip, putting the little squirrel back into his pocket, and taking a hedgehog out of another pocket. It was a baby one, whose prickles were not yet hardened and set. It seemed quite happy to live in Philip's pocket, along with a very large snail, who was careful to keep inside his shell.

'I wish we were all going home together,' said Jack. 'I'd like to see your sister Dinah, though she does sound a bit of a wild-cat to me. And I'd love to see all those rare birds on the coast. I'd like to see your old half-ruined house too. Fancy living in a house so old that it's almost a ruin. You don't know how lucky you are.'

'Not so lucky when you have to carry hot water for miles to the only bath in the house,' said Philip, getting up from the grass where he had been sitting with the others. 'Come on – it's time to get back. You're never likely to see Craggy-Tops, and you wouldn't like it if you did – so what's the good of talking about it?'

3

Two letters — and a plan

The next day Philip had a letter from Dinah. He showed it to the others.

'Old Dinah's having a rough time,' he said. 'It's a good thing I leave here soon. It's better for her when I'm there.'

Dear Phil [said Dinah in her letter],
Aren't you ever coming back? Not that you're much good for anything except quarrelling with, but still it's pretty lonely here with nobody but Uncle and Aunt and Joe, who's even more strange than before. He told me yesterday not to go out at night down the cliff, because there are 'things' wandering about. He's quite mad. The only 'things' wandering about besides me are the sea-birds. There are thousands of them here this year.

Don't, for goodness' sake, bring any creatures home these holidays. You know how I hate them. I shall die if you bring a bat again, and if you dare to try and train earwigs like you did last year, I'll throw a chair at your head!

Aunt Polly is making me work awfully hard. We wash and scrub and clean all day, goodness knows what for, because nobody ever comes. I shall be glad when it's time to go off to school again. When do you come back? I wish we could earn some money somehow. Aunt Polly is worrying herself to death because she can't pay some bill or other, and Uncle swears he hasn't got the money, and wouldn't give it to her if he had. I suppose Mother would send more money if we asked her, but it's pretty awful to have her slaving away as she does, anyhow. Tell me more about Freckles and Lucy-Ann. I like the sound of them.
Your loving sister,
Dinah

Dinah sounded rather fun, Jack thought, as he read the letter and gave it back to Philip. 'Here you are, Tufty,' he said. 'Dinah sounds lonely. Hallo – there's Mr Roy beckoning me. I'll see what he wants. More work, I suppose.'

By the same post had come a letter for Mr Roy, from the housekeeper who looked after Jack's Uncle Geoffrey. It was short and to the point.

Mr Roy had read it with dismay, and then called Jack in to show him the letter. Jack read it, also filled with dismay.

Dear Mr Roy [said the letter]
Mr Trent has broken his leg, and he doesn't want the children back these holidays. He wants to know if you will keep them with you, and he sends a cheque to cover the rest of the time. They can come back two days before school begins, to help me to sort out their clothes.
Yours faithfully,
Elspeth Miggles

'Oh, Mr Roy!' groaned Jack who, much as he disliked his home, disliked the thought of staying on with Mr Roy, and with the peevish Oliver, who was also staying on, even more than the thought of returning to his irritable uncle. 'I don't see why Lucy-Ann and I can't go back – we shan't go near Uncle.'

Mr Roy did not want Jack to stay on any more than the boy himself did. The thought of having that parrot for one day longer than he needed to filled him with horror. He had never in his life disliked anything so much as he disliked Kiki. Rude boys he could deal with, and did – but rude parrots were beyond him.

'Well,' said Mr Roy, pursing up his lips and looking at Kiki with dislike, 'well – I'm sure I don't want to keep you any longer, because it's pure waste of your time to be here – you haven't learnt a thing – but I don't see what else to do. It's quite plain that your uncle doesn't want you back – you can see he has sent quite a generous cheque to cover the rest of your stay here – but I had other plans. With only Oliver here, I intended to do a little visiting. I wish we could find some place for you to go to, you and Lucy-Ann.'

Jack went back to his sister and to Philip, looking so dismayed that Lucy-Ann slipped her arm into his at once.

'What is it? What's the matter?'

'Uncle doesn't want us back' said Jack, and explained about the letter. 'And Mr Roy doesn't want us here – so it looks as if nobody loves us at the moment, Lucy-Ann.'

The three children looked at one another. And then Philip had his brain-wave. He clutched at Jack, almost knocking Kiki off her balance.

'Jack! Come back home with me! You and Lucy-Ann can come to Craggy-Tops! Dinah would be thrilled. You could have a fine time with the sea-birds. What about it?'

Jack and Lucy-Ann stared in excitement and delight. Go to Craggy-Tops? Live in an old half-ruined house, with a learned uncle, an impatient aunt, a strange handyman and the sound of the sea all the time? Now that really would be thrilling!

Jack sighed and shook his head. He knew that the plans of children seldom came to anything when grown-ups had to be consulted about them.

'It's no good,' he said. 'Uncle Geoffrey would probably say no – and Mr Roy would anyway – and your uncle and aunt would just hate to have extra children on their hands.'

'They wouldn't,' said Philip. 'You could give them the cheque that your Uncle Geoffrey sent to Mr Roy, and I bet my aunt would be thrilled. It would pay that bill Dinah talked about in her letter.'

'Oh, Philip – oh, Jack – do let's go to Craggy-Tops!' begged Lucy-Ann, her green eyes shining. 'I'd like it more than anything in the world. We'll be in the way here, Jack, if we stay on, you know we will – and I'm sure Mr Roy will kill Kiki one day if she says any more rude things to him.'

Kiki gave a hideous screech and stuck her head hard into Jack's neck. 'It's all right, Kiki,' said Jack. 'I won't let anyone hurt you. Lucy-Ann, honestly it's no good asking Mr Roy to see if we can go to Craggy-Tops. He thinks it's his duty to have us here, and we'll have to stay.'

'Well, let's go without asking him, then,' said Lucy-Ann recklessly. The boys stared at her without speaking. That was an idea. Go without asking! Well – why not?

'It would be all right if we all turned up at Craggy-Tops together, really it would,' said Philip, though he was by no means certain that it would be all right at all. 'You see, once you were there, my uncle and aunt couldn't very well turn you out, and I could get Aunt Polly to telephone to Mr Roy and explain things to him, and get him to send her the cheque your Uncle Geoffrey sent for you.'

'Mr Roy would be glad to think we had gone,' said Lucy-Ann, thinking what fun it would be to know Dinah. 'Uncle Geoff wouldn't care anyhow. So let's, Jack, do let's.'

'All right,' said Jack, giving way suddenly. 'We'll all go off together. When is your train, Tufty? We'll go down to the station saying that we'll see you off – and we'll hop into the carriage at the last minute and go with you.'

'Oooh!' said Lucy-Ann, thrilled.

'Where's your handkerchief? said Kiki sensing the excitement, and rocking herself to and fro on Jack's shoulder. Nobody took any notice of her. 'Poor old Kiki,' said the parrot sorrowfully. 'Poor old Kiki.'

Jack put up a hand and fondled the parrot, thinking out ways and means of escape. 'We could wheel my trunk and Lucy-Ann's down to the station the night before, when we take yours,' he said. 'Nobody would notice ours was gone out of the loft. We could buy our tickets then, too. Has anyone any money?'

The three of them put their money together. It would probably just buy the tickets. They simply must go off together! Now that they had made up their minds, it was quite unthinkable that anything should be allowed to prevent it.

So they made their plans. The day before Philip was due to

leave, his trunk was taken from the loft, and Jack managed to get his down unobserved too. He pushed it into a big cupboard in his room, and Lucy-Ann helped him pack it when no one was about.

'I'll wheel my trunk down to the station on the barrow, sir,' said Philip to Mr Roy. It was the custom to do this, and the master nodded, not taking much notice. He wished Jack and that parrot were going too.

The boys managed to get both trunks on to the barrow without being seen, and set off to the station in great spirits. Escape seemed quite easy, after all. Sam and Oliver did not seem to notice anything. Sam was too excited at leaving for home himself, and Oliver too miserable at the idea of being left behind to bother about anyone else.

The next morning Philip said a polite goodbye to Mr Roy. 'Thank you for all your help and coaching, sir,' he said. 'I think I shall get on well next term now. Goodbye, sir.'

'Goodbye, Philip. You've not done badly,' said Mr Roy.

Philip shook hands with Mr Roy, who drew back a little as a mouse ran out of the boy's sleeve. Philip tucked it back again.

'How can you have those creatures running about you like that?' said Mr Roy, and sniffed loudly.

'Where's your handkerchief?' said the parrot at once, and Mr Roy glared at it. As usual it was on Jack's shoulder.

'Could I go down to the station with Lucy-Ann and see Philip off?' asked Jack. Kiki gave a squawk of laughter, and Jack gave her a little slap. 'Be quiet! There's nothing to laugh at.'

'Naughty boy!' said Kiki, just as if she knew what mischief was in Jack's mind.

'Yes, you can go down and see Philip off,' said Mr Roy, thinking that it would be nice to get rid of the parrot for a little while. So the children went off together, grinning secretly at each other. Kiki had the last word with Mr Roy.

'Can't you shut the door?' she bawled. Mr Roy gave an exasperated click, and banged the door. He heard the parrot's cackle of laughter as the children went down the road.

'If only I need never see that bird again,' he thought to himself, little knowing that his wish was about to come true.

Jack, Lucy-Ann and Philip arrived at the station in plenty of time. They found their luggage and gave it to the porter to put on the train. When the engine steamed in they found an empty carriage and got in. No one stopped them. No one guessed that two of the children were running away. They all felt thrilled and rather nervous.

'I do hope your uncle and aunt won't send us back,' said Jack, stroking Kiki to quieten her. She did not like the noise of the trains, and had already told one to stop whistling. An old lady looked as if she were about to get into their carriage, but when Kiki gave one of her appalling screeches, she thought again and hurried a good way up the train.

At last the train moved off, with many snorts that caused the excited parrot to tell it to use its handkerchief, much to the children's amusement. It steamed out of the station, and, in the distance, the children saw the house where they had lived for the past few weeks, sitting at the bottom of the hill.

'Well – we're off,' said Philip, pleased. 'And it was perfectly easy for you to escape, wasn't it? Golly, what fun it will be to have you and Lucy-Ann at Craggy-Tops! Dinah will be thrilled to bits when we arrive.'

'Off to Craggy-Tops!' sang Lucy-Ann. 'Off to the sea and the wind and the waves! Off to Craggy-Tops!'

Yes – off to Craggy-Tops – and to a wild and astonishing time that not one of the children could possibly have imagined. Off to Craggy-Tops – and off to Adventure.

4

Craggy-Tops

The train sped on through the countryside, passing many stations, and stopping at very few. On towards the coast it went, through high mountains that towered up, over silver rivers, through big, straggling towns.

And then it came to wilder country. The sea-wind came in at the window. 'I can smell the sea already,' said Jack, who had only once before been to the sea, and scarcely remembered it.

The train stopped at last at a lonely little station. 'Here we are,' said Philip. 'Tumble out. Hi, Joe! Here I am. Have you got the old car handy?'

Jack and Lucy-Ann saw a strange man coming towards them. His skin was lined, his teeth were very white, and his eyes darted from side to side as he looked at them. Running behind him was a girl a little older than Lucy-Ann, but tall for her age. She had the same brown, wavy hair that Philip had, and the same tuft in front.

'Another Tufty,' thought Jack, 'but a fiercer one. It must be Dinah.'

It *was* Dinah. She had come with Joe to meet Philip, in the ramshackle old car. She stopped short in the greatest surprise when she saw Lucy-Ann and Jack. Jack grinned, but Lucy-Ann, suddenly feeling shy of this strapping, confident-looking girl, hid behind her brother. Dinah stared in even greater amazement at Kiki, who was telling Joe to wipe his feet at once.

'You mind your manners,' said Joe roughly, talking to the bird as if it was a human being. Kiki put up her crest and growled angrily, like a dog. Joe looked startled.

'That a bird?' he enquired of Philip.

'Yes,' said Philip. 'Joe, that trunk should go in the car too.

It belongs to my two friends.'

'They coming to Craggy-Tops?' said Joe in the greatest surprise. 'Miss Polly, she didn't say nothing about any friends, no, she didn't.'

'Philip, who are they?' asked Dinah, coming up and joining the little group.

'Two friends from Mr Roy's,' said Philip. 'I'll tell you all about it afterwards.' He winked at Dinah to make her understand that he would explain when Joe was not there. 'This is Freckles – I told you about him, you know – and Lucy-Ann too.'

The three children solemnly shook hands. Then they all got into the jerky, jumpy old car, with the two trunks at the back, and Joe drove off in a manner that seemed most dangerous to Lucy-Ann. She clutched the side of the car, half frightened.

They drove through wild hills, rocky and bare. Soon they saw the sea in the distance. High cliffs bounded it except for breaks here and there. It certainly was a wild and desolate coast. They passed ruined mansions and cottages on their way.

'They were burnt in the battle I told you about,' said Philip. 'And no one has rebuilt them. Craggy-Tops more or less escaped.'

'That's the cliff behind which Craggy-Tops is built,' said Dinah, pointing. The others saw a high, rocky cliff, and just jutting up they could see a small round tower, which they imagined was part of Craggy-Tops.

'Craggy-Tops is built out of reach of the waves,' said Philip, 'but on stormy nights the spray dashes against the window almost as strongly as the waves pound the shore.'

Lucy-Ann and Jack thought it all sounded very thrilling. It would be fun to stay in a house that had spray dashed against its windows. They did hope there would be a terrific storm whilst they were there.

'Is Miss Polly expecting you all?' asked Joe suddenly. He was plainly puzzled by the two extra children. 'She didn't say nothing to me about them.'

'Didn't she? How strange!' said Philip. Kiki screeched with laughter, and Joe wrinkled up his nose in dislike of the noise. He was not going to fall in love with Kiki, that was certain. Jack didn't like the way the man looked at his pet bird.

Dinah suddenly gave a shriek and pushed Philip away from her. 'Oh! You've got a mouse down your neck! I saw its nose peeping out. Take it away, Philip; you know I can't bear mice.'

'Oh, shut up and don't be an idiot,' said Philip crossly. Dinah at once flew into one of her tempers. She clutched Philip's collar and shook him, trying to dislodge the mouse and frighten it away. Philip gave Dinah a push, and she banged her head against the side of the car. She at once slapped him hard. Jack and Lucy-Ann stared in surprise.

'Beast!' said Dinah. 'I wish you hadn't come back. Take your two horrid friends and go off again to Mr Roy.'

'They're not horrid,' said Philip, in a mild tone. 'They're fun.' He put his mouth to Dinah's ear, after seeing that Joe was paying no attention, and whispered: 'They've escaped from Mr Roy. I asked them to. Their uncle will pay Aunt Polly for them to stay with us, and she can pay that bill you told me about. See?'

Dinah forgot her temper as quickly as it had come. She stared with interest at the brother and sister, rubbing her bruised head as she did so. What would Aunt Polly say? Where would they sleep? This was going to be exciting.

Joe drove headlong over the bumpy, stony road. Jack wondered that any car could stand such driving. They drove up the cliff, then down a hidden way that sloped round to Craggy-Tops.

And there, suddenly, was the roaring sea and Craggy-Tops standing sullenly above it, built half-way down the cliff. The car stopped, and the children got out. Jack gazed at the strange house. It was a strange place. Once it had two towers, but one had fallen in. The other still stood. The house was built of great grey stones, and was massive and ugly, but somehow rather grand. It faced the sea with a proud and angry look, as if defying the strong gale and the restless ocean. Jack looked down at the water. On it, and circling above it, were hundreds of wild sea-birds of all kinds. It was a perfect paradise of birds. The boy's heart sang for joy. Birds by the hundred, birds by the thousand. He would be able to study them to his heart's content, find their nests, photograph them at his leisure. What a time he would have!

A woman came to the door, and looked down at the four children in surprise. She was thin, and her hair was sandy-coloured and wispy. She looked tired and faded.

'Hallo, Aunt Polly!' cried Philip, running up the stone steps, 'I'm back!'

'So I see,' said his aunt, giving him a peck of a kiss on his cheek. 'But who are these?'

'Aunt Polly, they're friends of mine,' said Philip earnestly. 'They couldn't go home because their uncle broke his leg. So I brought them here. Their uncle will pay you for having them.'

'Philip! How can you do a thing like this? Springing people on me without telling me!' said Aunt Polly sharply. 'Where will they sleep? You know we've no room.'

'They can sleep in the tower-room,' said Philip. The tower-room! How lovely! Jack and Lucy-Ann were thrilled.

'There are no beds there,' said Aunt Polly, in a disagreeable tone. 'They'll have to go back. They can stay the night and then go back.'

Lucy-Ann looked ready to cry. There was a harshness in Aunt Polly's tone that she could not bear. She felt unwelcome and miserable. Jack put his arm round her and gave her a squeeze.

He was determined that he would not go back. The sight of those gliding, circling, soaring birds had filled his heart with joy. Oh, to lie on the cliff and watch them! He would *not* go back!

They all went in, Joe carrying the trunks. Aunt Polly looked with much disfavour on Kiki.

'A parrot too!' she said. 'Nasty, squawking, screeching bird! I never liked parrots. It's bad enough to have all the creatures you collect, Philip, without a parrot coming too.'

'Poor Polly, poor old Polly,' said Kiki unexpectedly. Aunt Polly looked at the bird, startled.

'How does it know my name?' she asked in astonishment.

Kiki didn't. It was a name she herself was often called, and she often said 'Poor old Polly!' or 'Poor old Kiki!' She saw that she had made an impression on this sharp-voiced woman, and she repeated the words softly, as if she was about to burst into tears.

'Poor Polly! Dear Polly! Poor, dear old Polly!'

'Well I never!' said Aunt Polly, and looked at the parrot more kindly. Aunt Polly felt ill, tired and harassed, but no one ever said they were sorry, or seemed to notice it. Now here was a bird pitying her and speaking to her more kindly than anyone had for years! Aunt Polly felt strange about it, but quite pleased.

'You can take a mattress up to the tower-room, and sleep there tonight with the boy — what's his name?' said Aunt Polly to Philip. 'The girl can sleep with Dinah. It's a small bed, but I can't help that. If you bring people here without telling me, I can't prepare for them.'

The children sat down to a good meal. Aunt Polly was a good cook. It was a mixture of tea and supper, and the children tucked into it well. All they had had that day, since their breakfast, were the sandwiches that Mr Roy had packed for Philip — and one packet of sandwiches did not go far between three hungry children.

Dinah gave a sneeze, and the parrot spoke to her sternly. 'Where's your handkerchief?'

Aunt Polly looked at the bird in surprised admiration. 'Well, I'm always saying that to Dinah,' she said. 'That bird seems to be a most sensible creature.'

Kiki was pleased at Aunt Polly's admiration. 'Poor Polly,

poor dear Polly,' she said, her head coyly on one side, her bright eye glinting at Aunt Polly.

'Aunt Polly likes your parrot better than she likes *you*,' whispered Philip to Jack, with a grin.

After the meal, Aunt Polly took Philip to his uncle's study. He knocked and went in. His Uncle Jocelyn was bent over a sheaf of yellow papers, examining them with a magnifying-glass. He grunted at Philip.

'So you're back again. Behave yourself and keep out of my way. I shall be very busy these holidays.'

'Jocelyn, Philip has brought two children back with him – and a parrot,' said Aunt Polly.

'A parrot?' said Uncle Jocelyn. 'Why a parrot?'

'Jocelyn, that parrot belongs to one of the children that Philip brought home,' said Aunt Polly. 'Philip wants these children to stay here.'

'Can't have them. Don't mind the parrot,' said Uncle Jocelyn, 'Keep the parrot if you want it. Send it away if you don't. I'm busy.'

He bent over his papers again. Aunt Polly gave a sigh and shut the door. 'He's so interested in the past that he forgets all about the present,' she said, half to herself. 'Well – I suppose I must ring up Mr Roy myself. He'll be wondering about those children.'

She went to the telephone. Philip followed close behind her, longing to know what Mr Roy would say. Dinah peeped out from the sitting-room and Philip nodded towards the telephone. If only Mr Roy was cross and said he would not have Jack and Lucy-Ann back! If only Aunt Polly would think the cheque was big enough to make it worth while letting them stay!

5

Settling in at Craggy-Tops

It seemed ages before Aunt Polly got through to Mr Roy. The master was worried and puzzled. Jack and Lucy-Ann had not returned, of course, and at first he had thought they had gone off for one of their walks, and that Jack had found some unusual bird and had forgotten all about time.

But as the hours went by and still the children had not come back, he became seriously worried. It did not occur to him that they might have gone with Philip, or he would have telephoned to the boy's aunt at once.

He was most relieved to hear Mrs Sullivan, Philip's aunt, speaking, giving him the news that the children were safe.

'They arrived here with Philip,' she said, with some sharpness. 'I cannot think how it was that they were allowed to do this. I cannot possibly keep them.'

Mr Roy's heart sank. He had hoped for one wild moment that his problem concerning Jack and Lucy-Ann, and that tiresome parrot, was solved. Now it seemed as if it wasn't.

'Well, Mrs Sullivan,' said Mr Roy politely, though he did not feel at all civil, 'I'm sorry about it. The children went down to see Philip off, and I suppose the boy persuaded them to go with him. It's a pity you could not keep them for the rest of the holidays, as they would probably be happier with you and Philip. No doubt they have told you that their uncle cannot have them back these holidays. He sent me a cheque for a large sum of money, hoping that I could have them. But I should be pleased to hand this over to you if you felt that you could take charge of them, and we could get Mr Trent's consent to it.'

There was a pause. 'How much was the cheque?' asked Mrs Sullivan.

There was another pause after Mr Roy told her the sum of

31

money that had been sent. It certainly was a very generous amount. Mrs Sullivan thought quickly. The children would not cost much to keep. She could see that they kept out of Jocelyn's way. That girl Lucy-Ann could help Dinah with the housework. And she would be able to pay off a few bills, which would be a great relief to her.

Mr Roy waited hopefully at the other end of the wire. He could not bear the thought of having the parrot back again. Jack was bearable, Lucy-Ann was nice – but Kiki was impossible.

'Well,' said Mrs Sullivan, in the sort of voice that meant she was prepared to give in. 'Well – let me think now. It's going to be difficult – because we've so little room here. I mean, though the house is enormous, half of it is in ruins and most of it is too draughty to live in. But perhaps we could manage. If I use the tower-room again . . . '

Philip and the others, who could hear everything that was being said by Mrs Sullivan, looked at one another in delight. 'Aunt Polly's giving in!' whispered Philip. 'And oh, Jack – I bet we'll have the old tower-room for our own. I've always wanted to sleep there and have it for my room, but Aunt Polly would never let me.'

'Mrs Sullivan, you would be doing me a great kindness if you could manage to take the children off my hands,' said Mr Roy earnestly. 'I will telephone at once to Mr Trent. Leave it all to me. I will send you the cheque at once. And if you should need any more money, let me know. I really cannot tell you how obliged I should be to you if you could manage this for me. The children are quite easy to manage. Lucy-Ann is sweet. It's only that awful parrot – so rude – but you could get a cage for it, perhaps.'

'Oh, I don't mind the parrot,' said Mrs Sullivan, which surprised Mr Roy very much. Kiki gave a loud squawk, which Mr Roy heard down the telephone. Well – Mrs Sullivan must be a remarkable woman if she liked Kiki!

Not much more was said. Mrs Sullivan said she would write to Mr Trent, after she had heard again from Mr Roy.

In the meantime she undertook to look after the children for the rest of the holidays.

The receiver clicked as she put it down. The children heaved a sigh of relief. Philip went up to his aunt.

'Oh, thanks, Aunt Polly,' he said. 'It will be fine for me and Dinah to have friends with us. We'll try and keep out of Uncle's way, and help you all we can.'

'Dear Polly,' said Kiki affectionately, and actually left Jack's shoulder to hop on to Aunt Polly's! The children stared in astonishment. Good old Kiki! She was playing up to Aunt Polly properly.

'Silly bird!' said Aunt Polly, hardly liking to show how pleased she was.

'God save the Queen,' said Kiki unexpectedly, and everyone laughed.

'Philip, you and Jack must have the tower-room for your own,' said Aunt Polly. 'Come with me, and I'll see what can be arranged. Dinah, go to your room and see if you would rather share it with Lucy-Ann, or whether she would rather have Philip's old room. They open out of one another, so perhaps you would like to have the two rooms.'

Dinah went off happily with Lucy-Ann to examine the room. Lucy-Ann wished she was sleeping nearer to Jack. The tower-room was a good way from where she herself would sleep. Jack took Kiki and went to a high window, settling on the window seat to watch the sea-birds in their restless soaring and gliding outside.

Philip went to the tower-room with his aunt. He felt very happy. He had become very fond of Jack and Lucy-Ann, and it was almost too good to be true to think they had come to stay with him for some weeks.

The two of them went down a cold stone passage. They came to a narrow, winding stone stairway, and climbed up the steep steps. The stairway wound round and round, and at last came out into the tower-room. This was a perfectly round room whose walls were very thick. It had three narrow windows, one facing the sea. There was no glass in it at all, and the room was draughty, and full of the sound of the crying of birds, and the roaring of the waves below.

'I'm afraid this room will be cold for you two boys,' said Aunt Polly, but Philip shook his head at once.

'We shan't mind that. We should have the windows wide open if there *was* any glass, Aunt Polly. We'll be all right. We shall love it up here. Look – there's an old oak chest to put our things in – and a wooden stool – and we can bring a rug up from downstairs. We only need a mattress.'

'Well – we can't possibly get a bed up those narrow stairs,' said Aunt Polly. 'So you will have to have a mattress to sleep on. I've got an old double one that must do for you. I will send Dinah up with a broom and a cloth to clean the room a bit.'

'Aunt Polly, thanks awfully again for arranging all this,' said Philip, half shyly, for he was afraid of his hard-working aunt, and although he spent all his holidays with her, he felt that he did not really know her very well. 'I hope Mr Trent's cheque will cover all your expenses – but I'm sure Jack and Lucy-Ann won't cost much.'

'Well, Philip,' said Aunt Polly, shutting the lid of the old chest and turning to the boy with a troubled face, 'Well, my boy, you mustn't think I am making too much fuss – but the fact is, your mother hasn't been at all well, and hasn't been able to send nearly as much money for you as usual – and, you see, your school fees are rather high – and I've been a bit worried to know what to do. You are old enough now to realise that dear old Uncle Jocelyn is not much use in bearing responsibility for a household – and the bit of money I have soon goes.'

Philip listened in alarm. His mother was ill! Aunt Polly hadn't been getting the money as usual – it all sounded very worrying to him.

'What's the matter with Mother?' he asked.

'Well – she's very thin and run-down, and she's got a dreadful cough, she says,' answered Aunt Polly. 'The doctors say she must have a long rest – by the sea if possible

– but how can she give up her job?'

'I shan't go back to school,' said Philip at once. 'I shall find a job myself somehow. I can't have mother working herself to death for us.'

'You can't do that,' said Aunt Polly. 'Why, you are not even fourteen yet. No – now that I have a little money coming in from Mr Trent for these two children, it will ease things a good deal.'

'This house is too big for you,' said Philip, suddenly noticing how tired his aunt looked. 'Aunt Polly, why do we have to live here? Why can't we leave and take a nice little house somewhere, where you wouldn't have to work so hard, and which wouldn't be so lonely?'

'I'd like to,' said Aunt Polly, with a sigh, 'but who would buy a place like this, half ruined and in such a wind-swept, desolate spot? And I should never be able to get your uncle to move. He loves this place, he loves this whole coast, and knows more about it than anyone else in the world. Well, well – it's no good wishing this and that. We must just go on until you and Dinah are old enough to earn your living.'

'Then I shall make a home for Mother, and she and Dinah and I will live together happily,' thought Philip, as he followed his aunt downstairs to fetch the old mattress. He called to Jack, and the two boys, with much puffing and panting, got the awkward mattress up the narrow stairway. Kiki encouraged them with shrieks and squawks. Joe, the handyman, frowned at the noise. He seemed to think Kiki was directing her screeches at him, and, when she found that her noises annoyed him, she did her best to make him jump by unexpected squawks in his ear.

Joe was taking up a small table and Jack's trunk. He set them down in the tower-room and looked out of the window. He seemed very bad-tempered, Philip thought. Not that he was good-tempered at any time – but he looked even sulkier than usual.

'What's up, Joe?' said Philip, who was not in the least afraid of the sullen man. 'Seeing things?'

The children had laughed over Joe's idea that there were 'things' wandering about at night. Joe frowned.

'Miss Polly shouldn't use this room,' he said. 'No, that she shouldn't, and I've told her so. It's a bad room. And you can see the Isle of Gloom from it too, when the mists lift – and it's bad to look on the Isle of Gloom.'

'Don't be silly, Joe,' said Philip, laughing.

'Don't be silly, Joe,' repeated Kiki, in an exact imitation of Philip's voice. Joe scowled at both boy and bird.

'Well, you take my word, Master Philip, and don't you go looking at the Isle of Gloom more than you can help. This is the only room you can see it from, and that's why it's a bad room. No good ever came from the Isle of Gloom. Bad men lived there, and bad deeds were done there, and wickedness came from the isle as long as anyone remembers.'

With this very weird warning the man departed down the stairs, his eyes angry, as he gazed back at the two boys with a scowl.

'Pleasant fellow, isn't he?' said Philip, as he and Jack unrolled the mattress. 'Half mad, I think. He must be daft to stay on here and do the work he does. He could get much more money anywhere else.'

'What's this Isle of Gloom he talks about?' said Jack, going to the window. 'What a weird name! I can't see any island, Tufty.'

'You hardly ever can see it,' said Philip. 'It lies right out there, to the west, and there is a reef of rocks round it over which waves continually break, flinging up spray. It seems always to have a mist hanging over it. No one lives there, though people used to, years and years ago.'

'I'd like to go there,' said Jack. 'There must be hundreds of birds on that island – quite tame and friendly. It would be marvellous to see them.'

'Tame and friendly. What do you mean, Freckles?' said Philip, in surprise. 'Look at the birds here – afraid even of Kiki!'

'Ah, but the birds on the Isle of Gloom would not have

known man at all,' said Jack. 'They would not have learnt to be wary or cautious. I could get some simply marvellous photographs. Gosh, I'd like to go there!'

'Well, you can't,' said Philip. 'I've never been myself, and no one has, as far as I know. Look – will this be the best place for the mattress? We don't want it too near the window because the rain would wet it – and it often rains here.'

'Put it where you like,' said Jack, lost in dreams about the misty island and its unknown birds. He might see birds there that he had never seen at all – he might find rare nests and eggs. He might take the most wonderful bird-photographs in the world. Jack was quite determined to go to the Isle of Gloom if he could, in spite of all Joe's frightening tales.

'Come on down to the others,' said Philip at last, putting the last of their clothes into the chest. 'I can't say you've been much help, Jack. Come on, Kiki.'

They went down the narrow, winding stair to find the others. It was good to think of the weeks ahead, with no work, no lessons – just bathing, climbing, rowing. They certainly would have fun!

6

The days go by

The girls had decided to have the two rooms. They were such small rooms, and it would be easier to keep two rooms tidier than one, if two people were to have them.

'There would never be room for anything if we tried to keep all our things in one room,' said Dinah, and Lucy-Ann agreed. She had been up to see the tower-room and liked it very much. She would have liked a room without glass panes too. It was almost as good as sleeping out-of-doors, thought the little girl, as she leaned out of one of the windows, and felt the sea-breeze streaming through her hair.

The girls' two rooms looked out over the sea, but in a different direction from the boys'. The Isle of Gloom could never be seen from there. Jack told Lucy-Ann what Joe had said, and Lucy-Ann looked rather alarmed.

'You needn't worry. Joe's full of strange beliefs and strange stories,' said Philip with a laugh. 'There's nothing in his stories, really – I believe he just likes frightening people.'

It was strange to sleep for the first time at Craggy-Tops. Lucy-Ann lay awake for a long time, listening to the muffled roar of the waves breaking on the rocks below. She heard the wind whistling, too, and liked it. How different it all was from the quiet little town Uncle Geoffrey lived in! There everything seemed half dead – but here there was noise and movement, the taste of salt on her lips, the feel of the wind through her hair. It was exciting. Anything might happen at lonely Craggy-Tops.

Jack lay awake in the tower-room too. Philip was asleep on the mattress beside him. Jack got up and went to the window. The room was full of the wind, sweeping in at the sea-windows. Jack put his head out, and looked down.

There was a little moon rushing through the clouds. Down below was the swirling water, for the tide was in, beating over the black rocks. Spray flew up on the wind, and Jack felt sure he could feel a little on his cheek, high though his room was. He licked his lips. They tasted deliciously salty.

A bird cried in the night. It sounded sad and mournful, but Jack liked it. What bird was it? One he didn't know? The sea pounded away below and the wind swept up in gusts. Jack shivered. It was summer time, but Craggy-Tops was built in such a wind-driven spot that there were always draughts blowing around.

Then he jumped violently, for something touched his shoulder. His heart thumped, and then he laughed. It was only Kiki.

Kiki always slept with Jack, wherever he was. Usually she sat on the rail at the head of his bed, her big head tucked under her wing, but there was no rail this time, only a flat mattress laid on the floor.

So Kiki had found an uncomfortable perch on the edge of the chest – but when she heard Jack at the window she had flown to her usual perch, on his shoulder, making him jump violently. She nestled against him.

'Go to bed, naughty boy,' she said. 'Go to bed.'

Jack grinned. It was funny when Kiki by chance hit on the right sentences. He scratched her poll, talking in a low voice to her, so as not to wake Philip.

'I'll rig you up a perch of some sort tomorrow, Kiki,' he said. 'You can't sleep properly on the edge of that chest, I know. Now I'm going to bed. It's a wild night, isn't it? But I like it.'

He went back to bed, cold and shivering. But he soon got warm, cuddled up against Philip's back, and fell asleep, to dream of thousands of sea-birds walking tamely up to be photographed.

Life at Craggy-Tops was strange to Jack and Lucy-Ann at first, after all the years they had spent in an ordinary little house in an ordinary little town.

There was no electric light. There was no hot or cold water coming out of taps. There were no shops round the corner. There was no garden.

There were oil lamps to clean and trim each day, and candles to be put into candlesticks. There was water to be pumped up from a deep, deep well. Jack was interested in the well.

There was a small yard behind the house, backing on to the rocky cliff, and in it was the well that gave the household their water. Jack and Lucy-Ann were surprised that the water was not salty.

'No, it's pure drinking water all right,' said Dinah, lifting a heavy bucket from the chain. 'The well goes right down in the rocks, far below the sea bed, to pure water, crystal clear and icy cold. Taste it.'

It was good to drink – as good as any iced water the children had drunk on hot summer days. Jack peered down the dark, deep well.

'I'd like to go down in that bucket and find out how deep the well-bottom is,' he said.

'You'd feel funny if you got stuck and couldn't get up again,' said Dinah, with a giggle. 'Come on, help me, Jack. Don't stand dreaming there. You're always dreaming.'

'And you're always so quick and impatient,' said Philip, near by. Dinah gave him an angry look. She flared up very quickly, and it was easy to provoke her.

'Well, if you had to do as much as Lucy-Ann and I have been told to do, you'd be a bit quicker too,' she snapped back. 'Come on, Lucy-Ann. Let's leave the boys to get on with their jobs. Boys aren't much good, anyway.'

'Yes, you'd better go, before I slap you,' yelled Philip after her, and then darted away before the angry Dinah could come after him. Lucy-Ann was puzzled and rather shocked at their continual quarrels, but she soon saw that they were over as quickly as they arose, and got used to them.

Shopping was quite a business. It meant that Joe had to get out the old car, and go off with a long list to the nearest village twice a week. If anything was forgotten, it had to be done without till the next visit. Vegetables were got from a small allotment that Joe worked at himself, in a sheltered dip of the cliff away behind the house.

'Let's go with Joe and have a ride in the car,' suggested Lucy-Ann one morning. But Philip shook his head.

'No good,' he said. 'We've asked Joe heaps of times, but he won't take us. He just refuses, and says he'll push us out of the car if we get in it to go with him. I did get in once, and he kept his word and pushed me out.'

'The old beast!' said Jack, astonished. 'I wonder you put up with him.'

'Well, who else would come here and work for us in this desolate place?' said Dinah, 'Nobody else. Joe wouldn't either if he wasn't so strange.'

Still, Lucy-Ann did ask Joe if she could go with him when he went shopping.

'No,' snapped the man, and scowled.

'Please, Joe,' said Lucy-Ann, looking at him pleadingly. Usually she got her own way when she badly wanted it – but not with Joe.

'I said no,' repeated the man, and walked off, his powerful arms swinging by his sides. Lucy-Ann stared after him. How horrid he was! Why wouldn't he take any of them in the car when he went shopping? Just bad temper, she supposed.

It was fun being at Craggy-Tops, in spite of so many things being difficult. Hot baths, for instance, could only be had once a week. At least, they *could* be taken every day, if someone lighted the copper fire, and was willing to carry pails of hot water down miles of stone passages to the one and only bath, set in a small room called the bathroom.

After doing this once, Jack decided that he didn't really care whether he had any more hot baths or not whilst he was at Craggy-Tops. He'd bathe in the sea two or three times a day, and make that do instead.

The girls were given household tasks to do, and did them as best they could. Aunt Polly did the cooking. Uncle Jocelyn did not appear even for meals. Aunt Polly took them to him in his study, and the children hardly remembered he was in the house.

The boys had to get in the water from the well, bring the wood in for the kitchen fire, and fill the burners in the oil stove with oil. They took it in turns with the girls to clean and trim the lamps. Nobody liked doing that, it was such a messy job.

Joe looked after the car and the allotment, did rough scrubbing, cleaned the windows when they became clogged up with salty spray, and did all kinds of other jobs. He had a boat of his own, a sound and good one with a small sail.

'Would he let us use it?' asked Jack.

'Of course not,' said Philip scornfully. 'And you'd better

not try, without permission. He'd beat you if you did. That boat is the apple of his eye. We are not allowed to set foot in it.'

Jack went to have a look at it. It was a very good boat indeed, and must have cost a lot of money. It had recently been painted and was in first-class order. There were oars, mast and sail, and a good deal of fishing tackle. Jack would dearly have loved to go out in it.

But even as he stood looking at it, wondering if he dared to put his foot into it and feel the boat rocking gently beneath him, the handyman appeared, his usual scowl even deeper.

'What are you doing?' he demanded, his eyes roving, so the whites showed plainly. 'That's *my* boat.'

'All right, all right,' said Jack impatiently. 'Can't I look at it?'

'No,' said Joe and scowled again.

'Naughty boy,' said Kiki, and screeched at Joe, who looked as if he would like to wring the bird's neck.

'Well, you certainly are a pleasant fellow,' said Jack, stepping away from the boat, feeling suddenly afraid of the unfriendly man. 'But let me tell you this – I'm going out in a boat, *somehow*, and *you* can't stop me.'

Joe looked after Jack with eyes half closed and his mouth turned in angrily. That interfering boy! Joe would certainly stop him doing anything if he could!

7

An odd discovery

If it had not been for Joe, life at Craggy-Tops, once the children had settled down to their daily tasks, would have been very pleasant. There seemed so much to do that was fun – swimming in the sheltered cove, where the water was calm, was simply lovely. Exploring the damp dark caves in the cliffs was fun. Fishing from the rocks with a line was also very exciting, because quite big fish could be caught that way.

But Joe seemed to spoil everything, with his scowls and continued interference. He always seemed to appear where-ever the children were. If they bathed, his sour face appeared round the rocks. If they fished, he came scowling out on the rocks and told them they were wasting their time.

'Oh, leave us alone, Joe,' said Philip impatiently. 'You act as if you were our keeper! For goodness' sake leave us to do what we want to do. We're not doing any harm.'

'Miss Polly said to me to keep an eye on you all,' said Joe sulkily. 'She said to me not to let you get into danger, see.'

'No, I don't see,' said Philip crossly. 'All I can see is that you keep popping up wherever we are and spoiling things for us. Don't keep prying on us. We don't like it.'

Lucy-Ann giggled. She thought it was brave of Philip to talk to the big man like that. He certainly *was* a nuisance. What fun they would have had if he had been jolly and good-tempered! They could have gone fishing and sailing in his boat. They could have fished properly with him. They could have gone out in the car and picnicked.

'But all because he's so sour and bad-tempered we can't do any of those things,' said Lucy-Ann. 'Why, we might even have tried to sail out to the Isle of Gloom to see if there were many birds there, as Jack so badly wants to do, if only Joe had been nice.'

'Well, he's not nice, and we'll never go to Gloom, and if we did get there, I bet there wouldn't be any birds on such a desolate place,' said Philip. 'Come on – let's explore that big cave we found yesterday.'

It really was fun exploring the caves on the shore. Some of them ran very far back into the cliff. Others had holes in the roofs, that led to upper caves. Philip said that in olden times men had used the caves for hiding in, or for storing smug-gled goods. But there was nothing to be seen in them now except seaweed and empty shells.

'I wish we had a good torch,' said Jack, as his candle was blown out for the sixth time that morning. 'I shall soon have no candles left. If only there was a shop round the corner where we could slip along and buy a torch! I asked Joe to get me one when he went shopping in the car, but he wouldn't.'

'Oooh – here's a most enormous starfish!' said Philip, holding his candle down to the floor of the damp cave. 'Do look – it's a giant one, I'm sure.'

Dinah gave a shriek. She hated creepy-crawly things as much as Philip liked them. 'Don't touch it, And don't bring it near me.'

But Philip was a tease, and he picked up the great starfish, with its long five fingers, and walked over to Dinah with it. She flew into a furious rage.

'You beast! I told you not to bring it near me. I'll kill it if you do.'

'You can't kill starfish,' said Philip. 'If you cut one in half it grows new fingers, and, hey presto, it is two starfishes instead of one. So there! Have a look at it, Dinah – smell it – feel it.'

Philip pushed the great clammy thing near to his sister's face. Really alarmed, Dinah hit out, and gave Philip such a push that he reeled, overbalanced and fell headlong to the floor of the cave. His candle went out. There was a shout from Philip, then a curious slithering noise – and silence.

'Hi, Tufty! Are you all right?' called Jack, and held his candle high. To his enormous astonishment, Philip had completely disappeared. There was the starfish on the sea-weedy ground – but no Philip was beside it.

The three children stared in the greatest amazement at clumps of seaweed hanging from the walls of the cave, spreading over the ground. Wherever had Philip gone?

Dinah was scared. She had certainly meant to give Philip a hard blow – but she hadn't meant him to disappear off the face of the earth. She gave a yell.

'Philip! Are you hiding? Come out, idiot!'

A muffled voice came from somewhere. 'Hi! – where am I?'

'That's Tufty's voice,' said Jack. 'But where is he? He's nowhere in this cave.'

The children put their three candles together and looked round the small, low-roofed, seaweedy cave. It smelt very dank and musty. Philip's voice came again from somewhere, sounding rather frightened.

'I say! Where am I?'

Jack advanced cautiously over the slippery seaweed to where Philip had fallen when Dinah had struck him. Then suddenly he seemed to lose his footing, and, to the surprise of the watching girls, he too disappeared, seeming to sink down into the floor of the seaweedy cave.

By the wavering light of their two candles the girls tried to see what had happened to Jack. Then they saw the explanation of the mystery. The fronds of seaweed hid an opening in the floor of the cave, and when the boys had put their weight on to the seaweed covering the hole, they had slipped between the fronds down into some cave below. How strange!

'That's where they went,' said Dinah, pointing to a dark space between the seaweed covering that part of the floor. 'I hope they haven't broken their legs. However shall we get them out?'

Jack had fallen on top of poor Philip, almost squashing him. Kiki, left behind in the cave above, let out an ear-piercing screech. She hated these dark caves, but always came with Jack. Now he had suddenly gone, and the parrot was alarmed.

'Shut up, Kiki,' said Dinah, jumping in fright at the screech. 'Look, Lucy-Ann, there's a hole in the cave floor there, just between that thick seaweed. Walk carefully, or you'll disappear too. Hold up my candle as well as your own and I'll see if I can make out exactly what has happened.'

What had happened was really quite simple. First Philip had gone down the hole into a cave below, and then Jack had fallen on top of him. Philip was feeling frightened and bruised. He clutched Jack and wouldn't let go.

'What's happened?' he said.

'Hole in the cave floor,' said Jack, putting out his hands and feeling round to see how big the cave was they had fallen into. He touched rocky walls on each side of him at once. 'I say – this is a mighty small cave. Hi, girls, put the candles over the hole so that we can see something.'

A lighted candle now appeared above the boys and they were able to see a little.

'We're not in a cave. We're in a passage,' said Jack, astonished. 'At least, we're at the beginning of a passage. I wonder where it goes to . . . right into the cliff, I suppose.'

'Hand us down a candle,' called Philip, feeling better now. 'Oh, goodness – here's Kiki.'

'Can't you shut the door?' said Kiki, in a sharp voice, sitting hard on Jack's shoulder, glad to be with her master again. She began to whistle, and then told herself not to.

'Shut up, Kiki,' said Jack. 'Look, Philip – there really *is* a passage leading up there – awfully dark and narrow. And what a smell there is! Dinah, pass that candle down quickly, do!'

Dinah at last managed to hand down a lighted candle. She lay flat on the seaweedy cave floor, and just managed to pass the candle down through the hole. Jack held it up. The dark passage looked mysterious and strange.

'What about exploring it?' said Philip, feeling excited. 'It looks as if it ought to go below Craggy-Tops itself. It's a secret passage.'

'More likely a short crack in the cliff rocks that leads nowhere at all,' said Jack. 'Kiki, don't peck my ear so hard. We'll go into the open air soon. Hi, you girls! We think we'll go up this funny passage. Are you coming?'

'No, thanks,' said Lucy-Ann at once, who didn't at all like the sound of a seaweedy passage that ran, dark and narrow, through the cliffs. 'We'll stay here till you come back. Don't be long. We've only got one candle now. Have you some matches in case your candle goes out?'

'Yes,' said Jack, feeling in his pocket. 'Well, goodbye for the present. Don't fall down the hole.'

The boys left the dark hole under which they stood and began to make their way up the damp passage. The girls could no longer hear their voices or footsteps. They waited patiently in the cave above, lighted by one flickering candle. It was cold and they shivered, glad of their warm jerseys.

The boys were a very long time. The two girls became impatient and then alarmed. What could have happened to them? They peered down the hole between the great fronds of seaweed and listened. Not a sound could be heard.

'Oh dear – do you think we ought to go after them?' said Lucy-Ann desperately. She would be frightened to death going up that dark secret passage, she was sure, and yet if Jack was in need of help she would have no hesitation in jumping down and following him.

'Better go and tell Joe and get him to come and help,' said Dinah. 'He'd better bring a rope, I should think. The boys would never be able to climb up through the hole back into this cave without help.'

'No, don't let's tell Joe,' said Lucy-Ann, who disliked the man thoroughly, and was afraid of him. 'We'll wait a bit longer. Maybe the passage was a very long one.'

It was – far longer than the boys expected. It twisted and turned as it went through the cliff, going upwards all the time. It was pitch-dark, and the candle did not seem to light it very much. The boys bumped their heads against the roof every now and again, for it was sometimes only shoulder-high.

It grew drier as it went up. Soon there was no seaweedy smell at all, but the air felt stale and musty. It was rather difficult to breathe.

'I believe the air is bad here,' panted Philip, as they went on. 'I can hardly breathe. Once or twice I thought our candle was going out, Freckles. That would mean the air was very bad. Surely we shall come to the end of this passage soon.'

As he spoke, the passage went steeply upwards and was cut into rough steps. It ended abruptly in a rocky wall. The boys were puzzled.

'It's not a real passage, then,' said Philip, disappointed. 'Just a crack in the cliff rocks, as you said. But these do look like rough steps, don't they?'

The light of the candle shone down on to the steps. Yes – someone had hewn out those steps at one time – but why?

Jack held the candle above his head – and gave a shout.

'Look! Isn't that a trap-door above our heads? That's where the passage led to – that trap-door! I say – let's get it open if we can.'

Sure enough, there was an old wooden trap-door, closing the exit of the passage, above their heads. If only they could lift it! Wherever would they find themselves?

8

In the cellars

'Let's push at it together,' said Philip, in excitement. 'I'll put the candle down on this ledge.'

He stuck the candle firmly into a crack on the ledge. Then he and Jack pushed hard at the trap-door just above their heads. A shower of dust fell down, and Philip blinked his eyes, half blinded. Jack had closed his.

'Blow!' said Philip, rubbing his eyes. 'Come on, let's try again. I felt it move.'

They tried again, and this time the trap-door suddenly gave way. It lifted a few inches, and then fell back again, setting free another cloud of dust.

'Get a rock or big stone and we'll stand on it,' said Jack, red with excitement. 'A bit more of a push and we'll get the thing right open.'

They found three or four flattish stones, put them in a

stout pile, and stood on them. They pushed against the trap-door, and to their delight it lifted right up, and fell backwards with a thud on the floor above, leaving a square opening above the heads of the boys.

'Give me a heave up, Jack,' said Philip. He got such a shove that he shot out through the trap-door opening and landed on a rocky floor above. It was dark there and he could see nothing.

'Hand up the candles, Freckles, and then I'll haul you up,' said Philip. The candle was handed up, but went out suddenly.

'Blow!' said Philip. 'Oh glory, what's that?'

'Kiki, I expect,' said Jack. 'She's flown up.'

Kiki had not made a sound or said a word all through the secret passage. She had been alarmed at the dark strange place, and had clung hard to Jack all the way.

Philip hauled Jack up, and then groped in his pocket for the matches to light the candle again. 'Where do you suppose we are?' he said. 'I simply can't imagine.'

'Feels like the other end of the world,' said Jack. 'Ah – that's better, Now we can see.'

He held up the lighted candle and the two boys looked round.

'*I* know where we are,' said Philip suddenly. 'In one of the cellars at Craggy-Tops. Look – there are boxes of stores over there. Tins of food and stuff.'

'So there are,' said Jack. 'My word, what a fine store your aunt keeps down here! Golly, this is quite an adventure. Do you suppose your aunt and uncle know about the secret passage?'

'I shouldn't think so,' said Philip. 'Aunt Polly would be sure to have mentioned it to us, I should think. I don't seem to know this part of the cellars very well. Let me see – where is the cellar door now?'

The boys wandered down the cellar, trying to find the way out. They came to a stout wooden door, but, to their surprise, it was locked.

'Blow!' said Philip, annoyed. 'Now we shall have to creep all the way back down that passage again, I don't feel like doing that, somehow. Anyway, this isn't the door that leads out of the cellars into the kitchen. You have to go up steps to that one. This must be a door that shuts off one part of the cellars from the other. I don't remember seeing it before.'

'Listen – isn't that somebody coming?' said Jack suddenly, his sharp ears hearing footsteps.

'Yes – it's Joe,' said Philip, hearing the familiar cough he knew so well. 'Let's hide. I'm not going to tell Joe about that passage. We'll keep it to ourselves. Shut the trap-door down quickly, Jack, and then we'll hide behind this archway here. We could slip out quietly when Joe opens the door. Blow out the candle.'

They shut the trap-door quietly and then, in the pitch darkness, hid behind the stone archway near the door. They heard Joe putting a key into the lock. The door swung open, and the man appeared, looking huge in the flickering light of his lantern. He left the door open, and went towards the back of the cellar, where the stores lay.

The boys had on rubber shoes, and could have slipped out without Joe knowing anything at all – but Kiki chose that moment to imitate Joe's hollow cough. It filled the cellar with mournful echoes, and Joe dropped his lantern with a crash. The glass splintered and the light went out. Joe gave a howl of terror and fled out of the door at once, not even pausing to lock it. He brushed against the two boys as he went, and gave another screech of fright, feeling their warm bodies as he passed.

Kiki, thrilled at the result of her coughing imitation, gave an unearthly screech that sent Joe headlong through the other part of the cellar, up the steps and through the cellar door. He almost fell as he appeared in the kitchen, and Aunt Polly jumped in astonishment.

'What's the matter? What has happened?'

'There's things down there!' panted Joe, his face looking as scared as it ever could look.

'Things! What do you mean?' said Aunt Polly severely.

'Things that screech and yell and clutch at me,' said Joe, sinking into a chair, and closing his eyes till nothing but the thinnest slits could be seen.

'Nonsense!' said Aunt Polly, stirring a saucepan vigorously. 'I don't know why you wanted to go down there anyway. We don't need anything from the cellars this morning. I've plenty of potatoes up here. Pull yourself together. Joe. You'll frighten the children if you behave like this.'

The two boys had collapsed into helpless laughter when they had seen poor Joe running in alarm from the cellar, yelling for all he was worth. They clutched each other and laughed till they ached. 'Well, Joe is always trying to frighten us by tales of peculiar "things" that wander about at night,' said Jack, 'and now he's been caught by his own silly stories – and been almost frightened out of his wits.'

'I say – he's left the key in the door,' said Philip, who had now lighted his candle again. 'Let's take it. Then, if ever we want to use that passage again, we can always get out this way if we want to, by unlocking the door.'

He put the big key into his pocket, grinning. Maybe the jumpy man would think it was one of the 'things' he was always talking about had gone off with his key.

The boys went into the part of the cellar they knew. Philip looked with interest at the door through which they had come.

'I never knew there was another cellar beyond this first one,' he said, looking round the vast underground room. 'How did I never notice that door before, I wonder?'

'Those boxes must have been piled in front of it to hide it,' said Jack. There were empty boxes by the door, and now that he thought of it, Philip had remembered seeing them in a big pile every time he had gone into the cellar. They had been neatly piled in front of that door. A trick of Joe's, no doubt, to stop the children going into the second cellar, where all those stores were kept. How silly and childish!

Well, he couldn't stop them going there now.

'We can go there through the secret passage, or we could go there through the door, because I've got the key now,' thought Philip, pleased at the idea of being able to outwit the man if he wanted to.

'I suppose those steps lead up to the kitchen, don't they?' said Jack, pointing to them. 'Is it safe to go up, do you think? 'We don't want anyone to see us, or they'd ask awkward questions.'

'I'll slip up to the top, open the door a crack, and listen to see if anyone is about,' said Philip. So up he went. But Joe had gone out and his aunt was no longer there, so the big kitchen was empty and silent. The boys were able to slip out, go to the outer door, and run down the cliff path without anyone seeing them at all.

'The girls will wonder whatever had become of us,' said Jack, suddenly remembering Dinah and Lucy-Ann, waiting patiently for them in the cave where the hole was that led into the passage. 'Come on – let's give them a surprise, shall we? They'll be expecting us to come back through the secret passage – they'll never expect us to come back this way.'

They made their way down to the rocky shore. They went to the caves they had explored that morning and found the one that had the hole. The two girls were sitting by the hole, anxiously discussing what they ought to do.

'We really *must* go and get help now,' said Lucy-Ann. 'I'm sure something had happened to the boys. Really I am.'

Philip suddenly spotted the giant starfish again, the one that had caused all the trouble. Very silently he picked it up. Without making a sound, he crept over the seaweedy cave floor to poor Dinah. He placed the starfish on her bare arm, where it silthered down in a horrible manner.

Dinah leapt up with a shriek that was even worse tham Kiki's loudest one. 'Oh-oh-Philip's back again, the beast! Wait till I get hold of you, Philip! I'll pull all your hair out of your head! You hateful boy!'

In one of her furious rages Dinah leapt at Philip, who ran

out of the caves and on to the sandy shore in glee. Lucy-Ann threw her arms round Jack. She had been very anxious about him.

'Jack! Oh, Jack, what happened to you? I waited so long. How did you come back this way? Where did the passage lead to?'

Shrieks and yells and shouts from Dinah and Philip made it impossible for Jack to answer, especially as Kiki now joined in the row, screeching like an express train in a tunnel.

There was a fine fight going on between Philip and Dinah. The angry girl had caught her brother, and was hitting out at him for all she was worth.

'I'll teach you to throw starfish at me. You mean pig! You know I hate those things. I'll pull all your hair out.'

Philip got free and ran off, leaving a few of his hairs in Dinah's fingers. Dinah turned a furious face to the others.

'He's a beast. I shan't talk to him for days. I wish he wasn't my brother.'

'It was only a bit of fun,' began Jack, but this made matters worse. Dinah flew into a temper with him too, and looked so fierce that Lucy-Ann was quite alarmed, and thought she would have to defend Jack if Dinah rushed to slap him.

'I won't have anything to do with any of you,' stormed Dinah, and walked off angrily.

'Now she won't hear all we've found this morning,' said Jack. 'What a spitfire she is! Well, we'll have to tell *you*, Lucy-Ann. We've had a real adventure.'

Dinah, walking off in a fury, suddenly remembered that she had not heard the story of the secret passage and where it came out. Forgetting her rage, she turned back at once.

She saw Lucy-Ann and the two boys together. Philip turned his back on her as she came up. But Dinah could be as sudden in her good tempers as she was in her bad ones. She put her arm on Philip's.

'Sorry, Philip,' she said. 'What happened to you and Jack

in that secret passage? I'm longing to know.'

So peace was restored again, and soon the two girls were listening in the greatest excitement to all that the boys had to tell.

'It was an adventure, I can tell you,' said Jack. So it was — and there were more to come!

9

A strange boat

The girls would not go up the secret passage, no matter how much the boys urged them to. They shuddered to think of the dark, narrow, winding tunnel, and although they agreed that it was very exciting, they did not want to feel the thrill of creeping along it by themselves.

'I suppose Dinah's afraid of giant starfish jumping out at her, or something,' said Philip in disgust. 'And Lucy-Ann takes her side.'

But even teasing would not make the girls try the passage, thought they never tired of hearing about it. The boys slipped down into the cellar the next day, and found that Joe had once again piled up the boxes in front of the second door, so that it was quite hidden. It was puzzling, but he often did silly spiteful things. Anyway, they had the key of the door. That was something.

The weather became fine and hot. The sun shone down out of a cloudless sky and the children went about in bathing-suits. They were soon burnt as brown as toast. Philip, Dinah and Lucy-Ann spent more time than Jack in the water. The boy was quite mad over the wild birds that infested the coast in such numbers. He was for ever identifying terns and skuas, cormorants, gulls and others. He did not want Lucy-Ann with him, much to her dismay.

'The birds are learning to know me,' he explained to his sister. 'But they don't know you, Lucy-Ann. You keep with the others, there's a good girl. Anyway, we can't both leave Tufty and Dinah, it would be rude.'

So for once Lucy-Ann was not Jack's shadow, and spent most of her time with the others. But she usually knew where Jack was, and, when it was about time for him to return, she would always watch for him.

Dinah thought she was silly. She would never have dreamt of watching for Philip. 'I'm only too glad when he gets out of the way,' she said to Lucy-Ann. 'Horrid tease! He nearly made me go mad last year when he put earwigs under my pillow, and they all crawled out in the middle of the night.'

Lucy-Ann thought that sounded horrid. But by now she was used to Philip and his peculiar ways. Even when he was only wearing swimming trunks he seemed able to secrete some kind of creature about his body. Yesterday it had been a couple of friendly crabs. But when he had accidentally sat down on one, and it had nipped him, he had come to the conclusion that crabs were better in the sea than out of it.

'Anyway, I'm glad Freckles takes Kiki with him when he goes bird-watching,' said Dinah. 'I quite like Kiki, but now that she has taken to imitating all the birds around here, it is rather sickening. I'm surprised Aunt Polly puts up with her as well as she does.'

Aunt Polly had become fond of the parrot. It was an artful bird and knew that it had only to murmur 'Poor dear Polly' to get anything it liked out of Aunt Polly. Joe had been well and truly ticked off by Aunt Polly the day he had gone shopping in the car and had forgotten the parrot's sunflower seeds. The children had been delighted to hear the man so well scolded.

Uncle Jocelyn's experience of Kiki was definitely not so good. One hot afternoon the parrot had flown silently in at the open window of the study, where Uncle Jocelyn sat, as usual, bent double over his old papers and books. Kiki flew to the book-shelf and perched there, looking round her with interest.

'How many times have I told you not to whistle?' she said in a stern voice.

Uncle Jocelyn, lost in his books, came out of them with a start. He had never seen the parrot and had forgotten that one had come to the house. He sat puzzling his head to know where such an extraordinary speech came from.

Kiki said nothing more for a time. Uncle Jocelyn came to the conclusion that he had been mistaken, and he dropped his head to study his papers once more.

'Where's your handkerchief?' asked Kiki sternly.

Uncle Jocelyn felt sure that his wife was somewhere in the room, for Kiki imitated Aunt Polly's voice very well. He groped in his pocket for a handkerchief.

'Good boy,' said the parrot. 'Don't forget to wipe your feet now.'

'They're not dirty, Polly,' said Uncle Jocelyn in surprise, thinking that he was speaking to his wife. He was puzzled and annoyed. Aunt Polly did not usually come and disturb him like this by giving him unnecessary orders. He turned round to tell her to go, but could not see her.

Kiki gave a hollow cough, exactly like Joe's. Uncle Jocelyn, now certain that the man was also in the room, felt most irritable. Why must everyone walk in and disturb him today? Really, it was unbearable.

'Get out,' he said, thinking that he was speaking to Joe. 'I'm busy.'

'Oh, you naughty boy,' said the parrot, in a reproving tone. Then it coughed again, and gave a realistic sneeze. Then, for a while, there was complete silence.

Uncle Jocelyn settled down again, forgetting all about the interruption at once. Kiki did not like being ignored like that. She flew from the book-shelf on to Uncle Jocelyn's grey head, giving one of her railway-engine screams as she did so.

Poor Uncle Jocelyn leapt to his feet, clutched at his head,

dislodged Kiki, and gave a yell that brought Aunt Polly into the room at once. Kiki sailed out of the window, making a cackling sound that sounded just like laughter.

'What's the matter, Jocelyn?' asked Aunt Polly, alarmed.

Uncle Jocelyn was in a rage. 'People have been in and out of this room all the morning, telling me to wipe my feet and not to whistle, and somebody threw something at my head,' he fumed.

'Oh – that was only Kiki,' said Aunt Polly, beginning to smile.

'Only Kiki! And who on earth is Kiki?' shouted Uncle Jocelyn, furious at seeing his wife smile at his troubles instead of sympathising with them.

'The parrot,' said Aunt Polly. 'The boy's parrot, you know.'

Uncle Jocelyn had forgotten all about Jack and Lucy-Ann. He stared at his wife as if she had gone mad.

'What boy – and what parrot?' he demanded. 'Have you gone crazy, Polly?'

'Oh dear,' sighed Aunt Polly. 'How you do forget things, Jocelyn!' She reminded him of the two children who had come for the holidays, and explained about Kiki. 'She's the cleverest parrot you ever saw,' said Aunt Polly, who had now completely lost her heart to Kiki.

'Well,' said Uncle Jocelyn grimly, 'all I can say is that if that parrot is as clever as you think it is, it will keep out of my way – because I shall throw all my paperweights at it if it comes in here again.'

Aunt Polly, thinking of her husband's very bad aim whenever he threw anything, gave a glance at the window. She thought she had better keep it closed, or she might find everything in the room smashed by paperweights one day. Dear, dear, what annoying things did happen, to be sure! If it wasn't children clamouring for more to eat, it was Joe worrying her; and if it wasn't Joe, it was the parrot; and if it wasn't the parrot, it was Uncle Jocelyn threatening to throw his paperweights about. Aunt Polly closed the window firmly, went out of the room, and shut the door sharply.

'Don't slam the door,' came Kiki's voice from the passage. 'And how many times have I . . . '

But for once Aunt Polly had no kind word for Kiki. 'You're a bad bird,' she said sternly to the parrot. 'A very bad bird.'

Kiki sailed down the passage with an indignant screech. She would find Jack. Jack was always good and kind to her. Where was Jack?

Jack was not with the others. He had gone with his field-glasses to the top of the cliff, and was lying on his back, looking with pleasure at the birds soaring above his head. Kiki landed on his middle and made him jump.

'Oh – it's you, Kiki. Be careful with your claws, for goodness' sake. I've only got my bathing-suit on. Now keep quiet, or you'll frighten away the birds. I've already seen five different kinds of gulls today.'

Jack got tired of lying on his back at last. He sat up, pushed Kiki off his middle, and blinked round. He put his field-glasses to his eyes again, and looked out over the sea in the direction of the Isle of Gloom. He had not seen it properly yet.

But today, though most of the distant hills behind him were lost in the heat-haze, for some reason or other the island could be quite plainly seen, jutting up from the sea to the west. 'Gosh!' said Jack, in surprise, 'there's that mystery island that Joe says is a bad island. How clearly it can be seen today! I can see hills jutting up – and I can even see the waves dashing spray over the rocks that go round it!'

Jack could not see any birds on the island, for his glasses were not strong enough to show him anything more than the island itself and its hills. But the boy felt certain that it was full of birds.

'Rare birds,' he said to himself. 'Birds that people don't know any more. Birds that might nest there undisturbed year after year, and be as tame as cats. Golly, I wish I could

58

go there. What a tiresome nuisance Joe is not to let us use his boat! We could get to the island in it quite easily if the sea was as calm as it is today. Blow Joe!'

The boy swept his glasses around the jagged coast, and then stared hard in surprise at something. It couldn't be somebody rowing a boat along the coast, about a mile or so away. Surely it couldn't. Joe had said that nobody but himself had a boat for miles and miles – and Aunt Polly had said that nobody lived anywhere near Craggy-Tops at all – not nearer than six or seven miles, anyway.

'And yet there's someone in a boat out there on the sea to the west of this cliff,' said Jack, puzzled. 'Who is it? I suppose it *must* be Joe.'

The man in the boat was too far away to make out. It might be Joe and it might not. Jack came to the conclusion that it must be. He glanced at the sun. It was pretty high, so it must be dinner-time. He'd go back, and on the way he would look and see if Joe's boat was tied up in the usual place. If it was gone, then the man in the boat must be Joe.

But the boat was not gone. It was in its usual place, firmly tied to its post, rocking gently in the little harbour near the house. And there was Joe too, collecting driftwood from the beach for the kitchen fire. Then there *must* be someone else not far away who had a boat of his own.

Jack ran to tell the others. They were surprised and pleased. 'We'll go and find out who he is, and pal up with him, and maybe he'll take us out fishing in the boat,' said Philip at once. 'Good for you, Freckles. Your old field-glasses have found out something besides birds for you.'

'We'll go and see him tomorrow,' said Jack. 'What I really want is a chance to go out to the Isle of Gloom and see if there are any rare birds there. I just feel I *must* go there! I really have got a sort of hunch about it.'

'We won't tell Joe we've seen someone else with a boat,' said Dinah. 'He'd only try to stop us. He hates us doing anything we like.'

So nothing was said to Joe or to Aunt Polly about the stranger in the boat. The next day they would find him and talk to him.

But something was to happen before the next day came.

10

Night adventure

That night Jack could not sleep. The moon was full and shone in at his window. The moonlight fell on his face and he lay there, staring at the big silvery moon, thinking of the gulls he had seen gliding and circling on the wind, and the big black cormorants that stood on the rocks, their beaks wide open as they digested the fish they had caught.

He remembered the Isle of Gloom, as he had seen it that morning. It looked mysterious and exciting – so far away, and lonely and desolate. Yet people had lived there once. Why did no one live there now? Was it so desolate that no one could make a living there? What was it like?

'I wonder if I could possibly see it tonight, in the light of the full moon,' thought Jack. He slipped off the mattress without waking Philip, and went to the window. He stared out.

The sea was silvery bright in the moonlight. Where rocks cast shadows, deep black patches lay on the sea. The waters were calmer than usual, and the wind had dropped. Only a murmur came up to Jack as he stood at the window.

Then he stared in surprise. A sailing boat was coming over the water. It was still a good way out, but it was making for the shore. Whose boat was it? Jack strained his eyes but could not make out. A sailing boat making for Craggy-Tops in the middle of the night! It was odd.

'I'll wake Tufty,' he thought, and went to the mattress. 'Tufty! Philip! Wake up and come to the window.'

In half a minute Philip was wide awake, leaning out of the narrow window with Jack. He too saw the sailing boat, and gave a low whistle that awoke Kiki and brought her to Jack's shoulder in surprise.

'Is it Joe in the boat?' wondered Philip. 'I can't tell if it's his boat or not from here. Anyway, let's get down to the shore and watch it come in, Freckles. Come on. I'm surprised that he should be out at night, when he's always telling us about "things" that wander around the cliff in the dark – but it probably isn't him.'

They put on shorts and jerseys, and their rubber shoes, and made their way down the spiral stair. They were soon climbing down the steep cliff path. Under the moon the sailing boat came steadily in, the night wind behind it.

'It *is* Joe's boat,' said Philip at last. 'We can see it plainly now. And there's Joe in it. He's alone, but he's got a cargo of some sort.'

'Maybe he's been fishing,' said Jack. 'Let's give him a fright, Philip.'

The boys crept up to where the boat was heading. Joe was furling the sail. Then he began to row to the shore, towards the little harbour where he always tied up his boat. The boys crouched down behind a rock. Joe brought the big boat safely in, and then tied the rope to the post. He turned to pull out whatever cargo he had – and at that very moment the boys jumped out at him, giving Red Indian whoops and rocking the boat violently.

The man was taken unawares, lost his balance and fell into the water, going overboard with a terrific splash. He came up at once, his face gleaming in the moonlight. The boys did not like the expression on it. Joe climbed out of the water, shook himself like a dog, and came towards the boys determinedly.

'Golly – he's going to lick us,' said Jack to Philip. 'Come on – we must run for it.'

But the way to the house was barred by the big powerful body of the angry man.

'Now I'll show you what happens to boys who come spying around at night,' he said between his teeth. Jack tried to dodge by, but Joe caught hold of him. He swung his big fist into the air and Jack gave a yell. At the same moment Philip charged Joe full in the middle, and the winded man gasped for breath, and let go of Jack. The boys sped off over the beach at once, heading away from the steep cliff path that led to the house. Joe was after them immediately.

'The tide's coming in,' gasped Jack, as he felt water running over his ankles. 'We must turn back. We'll be caught by the tide and pounded against the rocks.'

'We can't turn back. We shall be licked black and blue by Joe,' panted Philip. 'Jack – make for that cave. We can perhaps creep up that secret passage. We simply must. I really don't know what he mightn't do if he was in a rage. He might even kill us.'

Quite terrified now, the boys floundered into the cave, the waves running round their ankles. Joe came splashing behind them. Ah – he had got those boys now! Wait till he had done with them! They wouldn't leave their beds again at night!

The boys found the hole in the floor of the cave they were looking for and disappeared down it into the darkness of the secret passage. They heard Joe breathing heavily outside in the upper cave. They hoped and prayed he would not slip down the hole too.

He didn't. He stood outside by the entrance, waiting for the boys to come out. He had no idea there was a secret passage there. He stood, panting heavily, clenching his fist hard. A big wave covered his knees. Joe muttered something. The tide was coming in rapidly. If those boys didn't come out immediately they would be trapped there for the night.

Another wave ran up, almost as high as the angry man's waist. It was such a powerful wave that he at once left the cave entrance and tried to make his way back across the beach. He could not risk being dashed to pieces against the cliff by the incoming tide.

'Those boys can spend the night in the caves, and I'll deal with them tomorrow morning early,' thought Joe grimly. 'As soon as the tide goes down in the morning I'll be there — and they'll be mighty sorry for themselves when I've finished with them.'

But the boys were not shivering inside the cave. They were once more climbing up the secret passage, this time in complete darkness. The passage was terrifying enough — but not nearly so alarming as Joe.

They came at last to the trap-door and pushed it open. They clambered out on to the rocky cellar floor, and shut the trap-door.

'Take my hand,' said Jack, shivering as much with cold as with fright. 'We'll make our way towards the door as best we can. Come on. You know the direction, don't you? I don't.'

Philip thought he did, but he found that he didn't. It took the boys some time to find the cellar door. They felt all round the rocky walls of the cellar, and at long last, after falling over boxes of all kinds, they came to the door. It was not locked. Thank goodness they had taken away the key. Philip pushed at the door and it opened.

The pile of boxes on the other side fell over with a terrific crash that echoed all round the cellar. The boys stood listening to see if anyone would hear and come. But nobody did. They piled up the boxes again as best they could and crept up the cellar steps and into the moonlit kitchen.

They wondered where Joe was. Was he still waiting for them at the entrance to the caves?

He was not. He had made fast his boat, removed several things from it, and then had climbed the cliff path to the house. He had gone to his bedroom, just off the kitchen, gloating over the thought of the two boys shivering in the caves, when a terrific noise came to his ears.

It was the pile of boxes overturning down in the cellar, but Joe did not know that. He stood in his bedroom, rooted to the ground. What was that noise? He did not dare to go and find out. If he had, he would have seen two figures stealing through the moonlit kitchen towards the hall. He would have seen them scurrying up the stairs as quietly as mice.

Soon the boys were on their mattress, glad to be there safe and sound. They chuckled when they thought of Joe waiting in vain for them. And, down in his bedroom, Joe chuckled to think of how he would wait outside the cave the next morning, armed with a rope, and give those two boys a good hiding.

They all fell asleep at last.

Joe was up first, piling driftwood on the kitchen fire. He did his jobs, and then tied the rope-end round his waist. It was time he went down to the beach and caught those boys. The tide would soon be down low enough for them to come out.

Then he stopped still in the greatest astonishment – for into the kitchen, as bold as brass, came all four children, chattering away loudly.

'What's for breakfast? Golly, I'm hungry.'

'Did you have a good night boys? We did.'

'Fine. We must have slept all the night through.' These words were from Philip. Jack joined in, delighted to see amazement and wonder appear on Joe's face. 'Yes, we slept like logs. Even if Kiki had done her imitation of a railway express, I don't think we'd have woken up.'

'What's for breakfast, Joe?' asked Dinah. Both the girls knew about the boys' adventure the night before, and were entering into the fun of teasing Joe. He evidently still thought the boys were down in the caves.

'You two boys been asleep in your room all night?' asked Joe at last, hardly able to believe his eyes and ears.

'Where else should we sleep?' said Philip impudently. 'On the Isle of Gloom?'

Joe turned away, puzzled and taken aback. It couldn't have been these two boys last night. It was true he had not seen their faces clearly, but he had felt certain they were Philip and Jack. But now that was plainly impossible. No one could have got out of those caves at high tide – and yet here were the boys. It was disturbing and puzzling. Joe didn't like it.

'I'll go down to those caves now and watch to see who comes out,' he thought at last. 'Then I'll know who it was spying on me last night.'

So down he went – but though he watched for two hours, nobody came from the caves. Which was not very surprising, because there was nobody there.

'He just simply can't understand it,' said Jack, grinning, as he watched the tall man from the cliff path. 'What a good thing we didn't tell anyone about the secret passage! It came in mighty useful last night.'

'He'll think you and Philip were two of the "things" he's always trying to frighten us with,' said Dinah. 'Silly old Joe! He must think we are babies to be frightened of anything *he* would say.'

'What are we going to do today when we've finished our jobs?' asked Lucy-Ann, polishing the lamp she had been cleaning. 'It's such a fine day. Can't we go for a picnic – walk over the cliff and along the coast?'

'Oh yes – and we'll see if we can find that man I saw in a boat yesterday,' said Jack, remembering. 'That would be fine. Maybe he'll let us go in his boat. Dinah, ask your Aunt Polly if we can take our dinner with us.'

Aunt Polly said yes, and in about half an hour they set off, passing Joe on the way. He was now working on his allotment, over the edge of the cliff, behind the house.

'Did you have a good night, Joe?' yelled Philip. 'Did you sleep all night long, like a good boy?'

The man scowled and made a threatening noise. Kiki imitated him, and he bent down to pick up a stone to throw at her.

'Naughty boy!' screeched Kiki, flying high into the air. 'Naughty, naughty boy! Go to bed at once, naughty boy!'

11

Bill Smugs

'Whereabouts did you see the strange boat, Freckles?' asked Philip, as they went over the cliffs.

'Over there, beyond those rocks that jut out,' said Jack, pointing. 'Quite a big boat, really. I wonder where it's kept when it's not in use. Somebody must live fairly near it – but I couldn't see any houses.'

'There aren't any proper houses near,' said Philip. 'People used to live about here ages ago, but there was fighting and burning, and now there are only ruined places. But there might be a tumbledown shack of some sort, all right for a man who wants a lonely kind of holiday.'

They walked on over the cliffs, Kiki sailing up into the air every now and again to join a surprised gull, and making noises exactly like the sea-birds, but more piercing.

Philip collected a large and unusual caterpillar from a bush, much to Dinah's dismay, and put a lizard into his pocket. After that Dinah walked a good distance from him, and even Lucy-Ann was a bit wary. Lucy-Ann did not mind live creatures as Dinah did, but she wasn't particularly anxious to be asked to carry lizards or caterpillars, as she might quite well be requested to do if Philip decided to take home some other creature that, if put in his pocket, might eat the caterpillar or lizard already there!

They all walked on happily, enjoying the rough sea-breeze, the salty smell of the sea, and the sound of the waves against the rocks below. The grass was springy beneath their feet, and the air was full of gliding birds. This was a lovely holiday, lovely, lovely!

They came to a jutting part of the cliff and walked out almost to the edge. 'I can't see signs of any boat on the water at all,' said Jack.

'You're sure you didn't imagine it?' said Philip. 'It's funny there's not a thing to be seen today – a boat is not an easy thing to hide.'

'There's a sort of cove down there,' said Lucy-Ann, pointing to where the cliff turned in a little, and there was a small beach of shining sand. 'Let's go down and picnic there, shall we? We can bathe first. It's awfully windy up here; I can hardly get my breath to talk.'

They began to climb down the steep and rocky cliff. The boys went first and the girls followed, slipping a little now and again. But they were all good climbers, and reached the bottom of the cliff in safety.

Here it was sheltered from the rushing wind and was warm and quiet. The children slipped off their jerseys and shorts and went into the water to bathe. Philip, who was a good swimmer, swam right out to some black rocks that stuck out from the water, high and forbidding. He reached them, and climbed up to rest for a while.

And then he suddenly saw a boat, on the other side of the rocks! There was a flat stretch there, and on it, pulled up out of reach of the waves, was the boat that Jack had seen on the sea the day before. No one could possibly see the boat unless he, like Philip, was on those particular rocks, for, from the shore, the high rocks hid the flat stretch facing seawards, where the boat lay.

'Whew!' whistled Philip in surprise. He got up and went over to the boat. It was a fine boat with a sail, and was almost as big as Joe's. It was called *The Albatross*. There were two pairs of oars in it.

'Well!' said Philip, surprised, 'what a strange place to keep a boat – right out here on these rocks! Whoever owns it would have to swim out whenever he wanted to get it. Funny!'

He shouted to the others. 'The boat's here – on these rocks. Come and see it.'

Soon all the children were examining the boat. 'That's the one I saw,' said Jack. 'But where's the owner? There's no sign of him anywhere.'

'We'll have our lunch and then we'll have a good look-see,' said Philip. 'Come on – back to the shore we'll go. Then we'll separate after our picnic and hunt round properly for the man who owns this boat.'

They swam back to the shore, took off their wet things, set them out to dry in the sun and put on their dry clothes. Then they sat down to enjoy the sandwiches, chocolate and fruit that Aunt Polly had prepared for them. They lolled in the sun, tired with their swim, hungry and thirsty, enjoying the food immensely.

'Food's gorgeous when you're really hungry,' said Lucy-Ann, taking a huge bite at her sandwich.

'I always am hungry,' said Jack. 'Shut up, Kiki – that's the best part of my apple you've pecked. I've got some sunflower seeds for you in my pocket. Can't you wait?'

'What a pity, what a pity!' said Kiki, imitating Aunt Polly when something went wrong. 'What a pity, what a pity, what a . . . '

'Oh, stop her,' said Dinah, who knew that the parrot was quite capable of repeating a brand-new sentence a hundred times without stopping. 'Here, Kiki – have a bite of my apple, do.'

That stopped Kiki, and she ran her beak into the apple in delight, pecking out a bit that kept her busy for some time.

A quarrel nearly blew up between Dinah and Philip over the large caterpillar which made its way out of the boy's pocket, over the sand, towards Dinah. She gave a shriek, and was about to hurl a large shell at Philip when Jack picked up the caterpillar and put it back into Philip's pocket.

'No harm done, Dinah,' he said. 'Keep you hair on! Don't let's start a free fight now. Let's have a peaceful day.'

They finished up every crumb of the lunch. 'The gulls won't get much,' said Philip lazily, shaking out the papers, then folding them up and putting them into his pocket. 'Look at that young gull – it's as tame as anything.'

'I wish I had my camera here,' said Jack longingly, watching the enormous young gull walking very near. 'I could get a marvellous snap of him. I haven't taken any bird pictures yet. I really must. I'll find my camera tomorrow.'

'Come on,' said Dinah, jumping up. 'If we're going to do a spot of man-hunting, we'd better begin. I bet I find the strange boatman first.'

They separated, Jack and Philip going one way and the girls going the other. They walked on the sandy little beach, keeping close to the rocky cliffs. The girls found that they could not get very far, because steep rocks barred their way after a bit, and they had to turn back.

But the boys managed to get past the piece of cliff that jutted out and sheltered the little cove they had been picnicking in. On the other side of the cliff was another cove, with no beach at all, merely flattish rocks that shelved upwards to the cliff. The boys clambered over these rocks, examining the creatures in the pools as they went. Philip added a sea snail to the collection in his pocket.

'There's a break in the cliff just over there,' said Jack. 'Let's explore it.'

They made their way towards the gap in the cliff. It was much wider than they expected when they got there. A stream trickled over the rocks towards the sea, running down from somewhere halfway up the cliff.

'Must be spring water,' said Jack, and tasted it. 'Yes, it is. Hallo – look, Tufty!'

Philip looked to where Jack pointed, and saw floating in a pool a cigarette end, almost falling to pieces.

'Someone's been here, and quite recently too,' said Jack, 'else the tide would have carried that cigarette end away. This is exciting.'

With the cigarette end as a proof of someone's nearness, the boys went on more eagerly still. They came to the wide crack in the cliff – and there, a little way up, built close against the rocky slope, was a tumbledown hut. The back of it was made of the cliff itself. The roof had been roughly mended. The walls were falling to pieces here and there, and, in winter, it would have been quite impossible to live in it. But someone was certainly living there now, for outside, spread over a stunted bush, was a shirt set out to dry.

'Look,' said Jack, in a whisper. 'That's where our boatman lives. What a lovely hidiehole he's found!'

The boys went quietly up to the tumbledown hut. It was very, very old, and had probably once belonged to a lonely fisherman. A whistling came from inside the hut.

'Do we knock at the door?' said Philip, with a nervous giggle. But at that moment someone came out of the open doorway and caught sight of the boys. He stood gaping in great surprise.

The boys stared back without a word. They rather liked the look of the stranger. He wore shorts and a rough shirt, open at the neck. He had a red, jolly face, twinkling eyes, and a head that was bald on the top, but had plenty of hair round the sides. He was tall and strong-looking, and his chin jutted out below his clean-shaven mouth.

'Hallo,' he said. 'Coming visiting? How nice!'

'I saw you out in your boat yesterday,' said Jack. 'So we came to see if we could find you.'

'Very friendly of you,' said the man. 'Who are you?'

'We're from Craggy-Tops, the house about a mile and a half away,' said Philip. 'I don't expect you know it.'

'Yes, I do,' said the man unexpectedly. 'But I thought only grown-ups lived there – a man and a woman – and an odd-job man.'

'Well, usually only grown-ups *do* live there,' said Philip. 'But in the hols my sister and I come there too, to stay with our Aunt Polly and Uncle Jocelyn. And these hols two friends of ours came too. This is one of them – Jack Trent. His sister Lucy-Ann is somewhere about. I'm Philip Mannering and my sister is Dinah – she's with Lucy-Ann.'

'I'm Bill Smugs,' said the man, smiling at all this sudden information. 'And I live here alone.'

'Have you just suddenly come here?' asked Jack, in curiosity.

'Quite suddenly,' said the man. 'Just an idea of mine, you know.'

'Not much to come for here,' said Philip. 'Why did you come?'

The man hesitated for a moment. 'Well,' he said, 'I'm a bird-watcher. Interested in birds, you know. And there are a great many unusual birds here.'

'Oh!' cried Jack, in the greatest delight, 'do you like birds too? I'm mad on them. Always have been. I've seen crowds here that I've only seen in books before.'

And then the boy plunged into a list of the unusual birds he had seen, making Philip yawn. Bill Smugs listened, but did not say very much. He seemed amused at Jack's enthusiasm.

'What particular bird did you hope to see here, Mr Smugs?' asked Jack, stopping at last.

Bill Smugs seemed to consider. 'Well,' he said, 'I rather hoped I might see a Great Auk.'

Jack looked at him in astonished silence that changed to awe. 'The Great Auk!' he said, in a voice mixed with surprise and wonder. 'But—but isn't it extinct? Surely there are no Great Auks left now? Golly – did you really think you might see one?'

'You never know,' said Bill Smugs. 'There might be one or two left somewhere – and think what a scoop it would be to discover them!'

Jack went brick-red with excitement. He looked out over the sea towards the west, where the Isle of Gloom lay hidden in a haze.

'I bet you thought there might be a chance of them on a desolate island like that,' he said, pointing to the west. 'You know – the Isle of Gloom. You've heard about it, I expect.'

'Yes, I have,' said Bill Smugs. 'I certainly have. I'd like to go there. But it's impossible, I believe.'

'Would you take us out in your boat sometimes?' asked Philip. 'Joe, the odd-job man, has a fine boat, but he won't let us use it, and we'd love to go fishing sometimes, and sailing too. Do you think it's awful cheek to ask you? But I expect you find it a bit lonely here, don't you?'

'Sometimes,' said Bill Smugs. 'Yes, we'll go fishing and sailing together – you and your sisters too. It would be fun. We'll see how near we can go to the Isle of Gloom too, shall we?'

The boys were thrilled. At last they could sail a boat. They went off to call the girls.

'Hi, Dinah! Hi, Lucy-Ann!' yelled Jack. 'Come and be introduced to our new friend – Bill Smugs!'

12

A treat – and a surprise for Joe

Bill Smugs proved to be a fine friend. He was a jolly fellow, always ready for a joke, patient with Kiki, and even more patient with Philip's ever-changing collection of strange pets. He did not even say anything when Philip's latest possession, an extra large spider, ran up the leg of his shorts. He merely put his hand up, took hold of the wriggling spider, and deposited it on Philip's knee.

Dinah, of course, was nearly in hysterics, but mercifully the spider decided that captivity was boring, ran into a rock crevice and disappeared.

The children visited Bill Smugs nearly every day. They went fishing in his boat and brought home marvellous catches that made Joe's mouth fall open in amazement. Bill showed them how to sail the boat too, and soon the four children could manage it perfectly well themselves. It was great fun sailing about in a good strong breeze.

'Almost as fast as a motor-boat,' said Philip in glee. 'Bill, I *am* glad we found you.'

To Jack's disappointment Bill Smugs did not seem to want to talk endlessly about birds, nor did he want to go off with Jack and watch the birds on the cliffs or on the sea. He was quite willing to listen to Jack raving about birds, though, and produced many fine new bird books for him, which he said Jack could keep for himself.

'But they're new,' protested Jack. 'Look, the pages of this one haven't even been cut – you've not read them yourself, sir. You read them first.'

'No, you can have them,' said Bill Smugs, lighting his cigarette. 'There's a bit about the Great Auk in one of them. I'm afraid we shall never find that bird after all. No one has seen it for about a hundred years.'

'It *might* be on the Isle of Gloom – or on some equally deserted, desolate island,' said Jack hopefully. 'I do wish we could go there and see. I bet there would be thousands of frightfully tame birds there, sir.'

This eternal talk about birds always bored Dinah. She changed the subject.

'You should have seen Joe's face when we brought in our catch of fish yesterday,' she said, with a grin. 'He said, "You never caught those from the rocks. You've been out in a boat".'

'You didn't tell him you had?' said Bill Smugs at once. Dinah shook her head.

'No,' she said. 'He'd try to spoil our pleasure if he knew we used your boat.'

'Do your uncle and aunt know you've met me?' asked Bill. Dinah shook her head again.

'Why?' she asked. 'Don't you want them to know? What does it matter whether they do or not?'

'Well,' said Bill Smugs, scratching the bald top of his head. 'I came here to be alone – and to watch the birds – and I don't want people coming round spoiling things for me. I don't mind you children, of course. You're fun.'

Bill Smugs lived all alone in the tumbledown hut. He had a comfortable car, which he kept under a tarpaulin at the top of the cliff, in as sheltered a place as possible. He went into the nearest town to do his shopping whenever he wanted to. He had brought a mattress and other things to the hut, to make it as comfortable as he could.

The children were thrilled when they knew he had a car as well as a boat. They begged him to take them out in it next time he went.

'I want to buy a torch,' said Jack. 'You remember that secret passage we told you about, Bill? Well, it's difficult to go up it carrying a candle – a torch would be much handier. I could buy one if you'd take me in your car.'

'I'd like one too,' said Philip. 'And, Jack – you said you wanted some camera film, because you'd left yours behind at Mr Roy's. You can't take photographs of birds unless we get some. You could get that too.'

The girls wanted things as well, so Bill Smugs agreed to take them the next day. They all crowded into the car in excitement the following morning.

'Joe's going into the town as well today,' said Dinah, with a giggle. 'It would be funny if we saw him, wouldn't it? He *would* get a surprise.'

Bill Smugs' car was really a beauty. The boys, who knew about cars, examined it in delight.

'It's new,' said Jack. 'This year's, and a jolly fast one. Bill, are you very rich? This car must have cost a lot of money. You must be awfully well-off.'

'Not very,' said Bill, with a grin. 'Now – off we go.'

And off they went, cruising very swiftly, once they left the bad coast road behind. The car was well-sprung, and seemed to surge along.

'Golly, isn't it different from Aunt Polly's old car!' said Dinah, enjoying herself. 'It won't take us any time to get to the town.'

They were very soon there. Bill Smugs parked the car, and then went off by himself, after arranging with the children to meet them for lunch at a very grand hotel.

'I wonder where he's gone,' said Jack, staring after him. 'We might just as well have kept all together. I wanted to go to that stuffed animal shop with him, and see some of the stuffed birds there.'

'Well, you could see he didn't want us,' said Dinah, who was disappointed too. She was very fond of Bill Smugs now and had saved up some money to buy him an ice cream. 'I expect he has got business of his own to do.'

'What is his business?' asked Lucy-Ann. 'He must do something besides bird-watching, I should think. Not that he does much of that, now that he knows us.'

'He never said what his work was,' said Jack. 'Anyway, why should he? He's not like us, always wanting to blurt out everything. Grown-ups are different. Come on – let's find a shop that sells torches.'

They found one that had extremely nice pocket torches, small and neat. The beam was strong, and the boys could well imagine how the dark secret passage would be lighted up, once they turned on their torches. They each bought a torch.

'Now we needn't light our bedroom candles at night,' said Dinah. 'We can use torches.'

They went to buy rolls of film to fit Jack's camera. They bought sweets and biscuits, and a small bottle of strong-smelling scent for Aunt Polly.

'Now we'd better get some sunflower seeds for Kiki,' said Jack. Kiki gave a squawk. She was on Jack's shoulder as usual, behaving very well for once. Every passer-by stared at her in surprise, of course, and the parrot enjoyed this very much. But, except for sternly telling a surprised errand-boy to stop whistling at once, Kiki hardly said a word. She was pleased with the sunflower seeds, which she adored, and gobbled up a few in the shop.

The children looked in the shops for a time, waiting for one o'clock to come, so that they might join Bill Smugs at the hotel. And then, quite suddenly, they saw Joe.

He was coming along the street in the old car, hooting at a woman crossing the road. The children clutched one another, wondering if he would see them, half hoping that he would.

And he did. He caught sight of Philip first, then saw Jack with Kiki on his shoulder, and then the two girls behind. He was so overcome with amazement that he let the car swerve across the road, almost knocking down a policeman.

'Here, you! What do you think you're doing?' yelled the policeman angrily. Joe muttered an apology, and then looked for the children again.

'Don't run away,' said Jack to the others. 'He can't chase us in the car. Just walk along and take no notice of him.'

So they walked down the street, talking together, pretending not to see Joe and taking no notice at all of his shouts.

Joe simply could not believe his eyes. How did the children get here? There was no bus, no train, no coach they could take. They had no bicycles. It was too far for them to have walked there in the time. Then how was it they were here?

The man hurried to park his car, meaning to go after the children and question them. He parked it and jumped out. He ran after the four children, but at that moment they reached the very grand hotel where they had arranged to meet Bill Smugs, and ran up the steps.

Joe did not dare to follow the children into the grand hotel. He stood at the bottom of the big flight of steps, looking after them in annoyed surprise. It was astonishing enough to find them in the town – but even more astonishing to find them disappearing into the most expensive hotel in the place.

Joe sat down at the bottom of the steps. He meant to wait till they came out. Then he would pack them into his car and take them home, and tell Miss Polly where he'd found them. She wouldn't be best pleased to hear they were wasting hard-earned money at expensive hotels, when they could easily take a packet of sandwiches with them.

The children giggled as they ran up the steps. Bill Smugs was waiting for them in the lounge. He showed them where to wash and comb their hair. They all met together again in a few minutes and went into the restaurant to have lunch.

It was a magnificent lunch. The children ate everything put in front of them, and finished up with the biggest ice creams they had ever seen.

'Oh, Bill, that was grand,' said Dinah, sinking back into her comfortable chair with a sigh. 'Simply marvellous. A real treat. Thanks awfully.'

'I think you must be a millionaire,' said Lucy-Ann, watching Bill count out notes to the waiter in payment of the bill. 'Golly, I've eaten so much that I feel I really can't get up and walk.'

Jack remembered Joe, and wondered if the man was watching for them. He got up to see.

He peeped out of a window that looked on to the hotel's main entrance. He saw Joe sitting patiently down at the bottom of the steps. Jack went back to the others, grinning.

'Is there a back entrance to this hotel?' he asked Bill Smugs. Bill looked surprised.

'Yes,' he said. 'Why?'

'Because Joe is sitting outside the hotel entrance waiting for us,' said Jack. Bill nodded, understanding.

'Well, we'll depart quietly by the back entrance,' he said. 'Come on. It's time we went, anyway. Got all you wanted from the shops?'

'Yes,' said the children, and trooped out after him. He led them to the back of the hotel, and out of a door there into a quiet street. He took them to where he had parked his car, and they all got in, happy at having had such a lovely day.

They sped back to the coast, and got out of the car at the nearest point to Craggy-Tops. They hurried over the cliff, eager to get back before Joe did.

He did not arrive until about an hour later, looking dour and grim. He put away the car and went to the house. The first thing he saw was the group of four children playing down on the rocks. He stood and stared in angry astonishment.

There was a mystery somewhere. And Joe meant to find out what it was. He wasn't going to be puzzled and defeated by four children. Not he!

13

Joe is tricked again

Joe thought about the mystery of the children being in the town, with, as far as he knew, no possible way of getting there – except by walking, and this they had not had time to do. He came to the conclusion that they must know someone who gave them a lift there.

So he set himself to watch the children closely. He managed to find jobs that always took him near them. If they went down to the shore, he would be there, collecting driftwood. If they stayed in the house, he stayed too. If they went up on the cliff, Joe followed. It was most annoying for the children.

'He'll follow us and find out about Bill Smugs and his boat and car,' said Lucy-Ann. 'We haven't been able to go and see him at all today – and if he goes on like this we shan't be able to go tomorrow either.'

It was impossible to give Joe the slip. He was very clever at keeping a watch on the children, and soon they grew angry. The two girls went up into the tower-room with the boys that night and discussed the matter together.

'*I* know,' said Jack suddenly. 'I know how we can give him the slip properly, and puzzle him terribly.'

'How?' asked the others.

'Why, we'll all go into the caves,' said Jack. 'And we'll slip down the hole into the secret passage, and go up to Craggy-Tops cellar, slip out of there whilst Joe is waiting down on the beach for us, and go over the cliffs to Bill.'

'Oooh, that *is* a good idea,' said Philip. The girls were doubtful about it, for they neither of them liked the idea of the secret passage very much. Still – they all had torches now, and it would be a good chance to use them.

So next day, with Joe close on their heels, the four children and Kiki went down to the beach.

'Joe, for goodness' sake leave us alone,' said Philip. 'We're going into the caves, and no harm can come to us there. Go away!'

'Miss Polly said I was to keep an eye on you,' repeated Joe. He had told the children this times without number, but they knew it wasn't the real reason. Joe enjoyed making himself a nuisance. He wanted to poke his nose into everything they did.

They went into the caves. Joe wandered outside, putting driftwood into his sack. The children all slipped down the hole that led to the secret passage, and then, with their torches switched on, they made their way along it.

The girls didn't like it at all. They hated the smell, and when they found that in one part it was difficult to breathe, they stopped.

'Well, it's no good going back,' said Philip, giving Dinah a shove to make her go on. 'We've come more than halfway now. Do go on, Dinah. You're holding us up.'

'Don't push!' said Dinah. 'I shall stop if I want to.'

'Oh, shut up arguing, you two,' groaned Jack. 'I believe you'd start a quarrel if you were in a ship that was just about to sink, or an aeroplane about to crash. Get on, Dinah, we'll be out soon.'

Dinah was about to start an argument with Jack too, when Kiki gave a mournful cough, so exactly like Joe's that the children at first thought the man must have found the passage, and all of them, Dinah as well, hurried forward at once.

'It's all right – it was only that wretch Kiki,' said Jack, relieved, as Kiki coughed again. They pushed on, and at last came to the end of the passage. They all stared at the trap-door above their heads, brightly lit by the light of their four torches.

Up it went, and over with a crash. The boys climbed up to the cellar floor and then helped the girls up. They shut the trap-door, went to the cellar door, which was shut, and pushed it open. The boxes on the other side fell over again with a familiar crashing noise.

The children went through the door, shut it, piled the boxes up again, and then went up the cellar steps to the big kitchen. No one was there. That was lucky.

Out they went, and up to the cliff. Keeping to the path, where they were well hidden from the shore below, they hurried off to find their friend Bill Smugs. They grinned to think of Joe waiting down on the beach for them to come out of the caves.

Bill Smugs was tinkering with his boat. He waved cheerily as they came up.

'Hallo,' he said, 'why didn't you come and see me yesterday? I missed you.'

'It was because of Joe,' said Jack. 'He keeps following us around like a shadow. I think he probably suspects we have a friend who has a car, and he means to find out who it is.'

'Well, don't tell him anything,' said Bill quickly. 'Keep things to yourself. I don't want him prying around here. He doesn't sound at all a nice person.'

'What are you doing to your boat?' asked Jack. 'Are you going out in it?'

'I thought I would,' said Bill. 'It's a fine day, the sea is fairly calm, yet there's a nice breeze – and I half thought I might sail near to the Isle of Gloom.'

There was an excited silence. The Isle of Gloom! All the children wanted to see it close to – and Jack badly wanted to land there. If only Bill would take them with him!

Jack looked out to the west. He could not see the island, for once again there was a low heat haze on the sea. But he knew exactly where it was. His heart beat fast. The Great

Auk might be there. Anyway, even if it wasn't, all kinds of other sea-birds would be there – and probably as tame as anything. He could take his camera – he could . . .

'Bill—please, please take us with you!' begged Lucy-Ann. 'Oh, do! We'll be very good, and you know, now that you have taught us how to sail a boat, we can really help.'

'Well – I meant to take you,' said Bill, lighting a cigarette, and smiling round at the children. 'I wanted to go yesterday, and when you didn't come, I put the trip off till today. We'll go this afternoon, and take our tea with us. You'll have to give Joe the slip again. He mustn't see you sailing in my boat or he'd probably try to stop you.'

'Oh, Bill! We'll be along first thing this afternoon,' said Jack, his eyes gleaming very green.

'Thanks most *awfully*,' said Philip.

'Shall we really see the Isle of Gloom close to?' asked Lucy-Ann, in excitement.

'Can't we land there?' said Dinah.

'I don't think so,' said Bill. 'You see, there is a ring of dangerous rocks around it, and although there may once have been a passage somewhere through them, and possibly is now, for all I know, I don't know where it is. I'm not going to risk drowning you all.'

'Oh,' said the children, disappointed. They would have been quite willing to run the risk of being drowned, for the sake of trying to land on the bad isle.

'You'd better go back and have an early lunch, if your aunt will let you have it,' said Bill. 'I don't want to be too late in starting. The tide will help us, if we get off fairly early.'

'All right,' said the four, jumping up from the rocks at once. 'Goodbye till this afternoon, Bill. We'll bring tea with us – as nice as we can, to reward you for waiting for us.'

They set off home again, talking eagerly of the coming trip. Joe had said so many frightening things about the desolate island that the children couldn't help feeling excited at the idea of seeing it.

'I wonder if Joe is still on the beach, watching for us

outside the caves,' said Jack. The children went cautiously to the edge of the cliff and peeped over. Yes – he was still down there. What a sell for him!

They went to Craggy-Tops and found Aunt Polly. 'Aunt, could we possibly have an early lunch, and then go off and take our tea with us?' asked Philip. 'Will it be any trouble? We'll help to get the lunch, and we don't mind what we have.'

'There's a cold pie in the larder,' said Aunt Polly considering. 'And some tomatoes. And there are some stewed plums. Dinah, you lay the table, and the others can set out the food. I'll make you some sandwiches for your tea, and there's a ginger cake you can have too. Lucy-Ann, can you put the kettle on to boil? You can have some tea in a thermos flask if you like.'

'Oh, thank you,' said the children, and set to work at once. They laid a place for Aunt Polly, but she shook her head.

'I don't feel very well today,' she said. 'I've got a bad headache. I shan't want anything. I shall have a good long rest while you are out this afternoon.'

The children were sorry. Certainly Aunt Polly did look tired out. Philip wondered if his mother had sent any more money to help things along a bit, or whether Aunt Polly was finding things very difficult. He didn't like to ask her in front of the others. Soon the children were having their dinner, and then, the tea being packed up and ready, they set off over the cliff.

They had not seen Joe. The man was still down on the beach, now feeling puzzled, and most annoyed with the vanished children. He felt certain they were in the caves. He went in himself and called to them.

There was no answer, of course. He called again and again. 'Well, if they've lost themselves in the caves, it will be good riddance of bad rubbish,' he said to himself. He decided to go up and report the matter to Miss Polly.

So up he went. The children had gone, and Aunt Polly was

washing up. She glanced sharply at Joe.

'Where have you been all the morning?' she asked. 'I wanted you, and you were nowhere to be found.'

'Looking for them children,' said Joe. 'It's my belief they've gone into the caves down there, and got lost. I been calling and calling for them.'

'Don't be so silly, Joe,' said Aunt Polly. 'You're just making the children an excuse for your laziness. You know quite well they are not in the caves.'

'Miss Polly, I seed them go in, and I didn't seed them come out,' began Joe indignantly. 'I was on the beach all the time, wasn't I? Well, I tells you, Miss Polly, them children went into the caves, and they're there still.'

'No, they're not,' said Aunt Polly firmly. 'They have just gone off for a picnic. They came in, had an early lunch and went out again. So don't come to me anymore with silly stories about them being lost in the caves.'

Joe's mouth dropped open. He simply could not believe his ears. Hadn't he been on the beach by the caves all the morning? He would have seen the children as soon as they came out.

'Don't pretend to be so surprised,' said Aunt Polly sharply. 'Just stir yourself and do a few jobs quickly. You will have to do this afternoon all the things you didn't do this morning. I expect the children did go into the caves – but they must have slipped out when you were not looking. Don't just stand there! Get on with some of your work.'

Joe shook himself, shut his mouth and went off silently to do some jobs in the house. He was full of amazement. He remembered how one night he had chased two boys into the caves, thinking they were Philip and Jack – and the tide had come up and imprisoned them in the caves – but they were not there the next morning.

And now the four children had done the same thing. Joe thought it was decidedly uncanny. He didn't like it. Now those children had given him the slip again. Where had they gone? Well, it wasn't much good trying to find out that afternoon – not with Miss Polly in such a bad temper anyway!

14

A glimpse of the Isle of Gloom

The children hurried over the cliffs to Bill Smugs and his boat. He was ready for them. He put their packet of sandwiches and cake, their thermos, and a packet of biscuits and chocolate of his own, into the boat. Then they all got in.

Bill had brought the boat to shore, instead of hiding it out by the rocks. He pushed off, wading in the water till the boat floated. Then in he jumped, and took the oars till they were away from the rocks.

'Now then,' he said, in a little while, when they were well beyond the rocks and out at sea, 'now then, boys, up with that sail and let's see how you do it!'

The boys put up the sail easily. Then they took turns at the tiller, and Bill was pleased with them. 'You are good pupils,' he said approvingly. 'I believe you could take this boat out alone now.'

'Oh, Bill – would you let us?' asked Jack eagerly. 'You could trust us, really you could.'

'I might, one day,' said Bill. 'You would have to promise not to sail out very far, that's all.'

'Oh yes, we'd promise anything,' said the children earnestly. How thrilling it would be to set off in Bill's boat all by themselves!

There was a good wind and the boat sped along smoothly, rocking a little every now and again as she came to a swell. The sea was really very calm.

'It's lovely,' said Jack. 'I do like the flapping noise the sail makes – and the sound of the water slapping against the boat, and the steady whistling of the wind . . . '

Dinah and Lucy-Ann let their hands trail in the cool, silky water. Kiki watched with interest from her perch on the big sail. She could hardly keep her balance there, and had to half-spread her wings to help her. She seemed to be enjoying the trip as much as the children.

'Wipe your feet and shut the door,' she said to Bill Smugs, catching his eye. 'How many times have I . . . '

'Shut up, Kiki!' cried everyone at once. 'Don't be rude to Bill, or he'll throw you overboard.'

Kiki cackled with laughter, rose into the air and joined a couple of startled sea-gulls, announcing to them that they had better use their handkerchiefs. Then she gave an ear-piercing shriek that made the gulls sheer off in alarm. Kiki returned to her perch, pleased with herself. She did enjoy creating a sensation, whether it was among human beings, birds or animals.

'I still can't see the Isle of Gloom,' said Jack, who was keeping a sharp look-out for it. 'Whereabouts is it, Bill? I seem to have lost my sense of direction now I'm right out at sea.'

'Over there,' said Bill pointing. The children followed his finger, but could see nothing. Still, it was exciting that the 'bad island,' as Joe called it, was coming nearer and nearer.

The sailing boat sped on, and the wind freshened a little as they got further out. The girls' hair streamed out behind them, or blew all over their faces, and Bill gave an exclamation of annoyance as the wind neatly whipped his cigarette from his fingers and swept it away.

'Now, if Kiki was any use at all, she would fly after that and bring it back to me,' said Bill, cocking an eye at the parrot.

'Poor Kiki,' said the parrot, sorrowfully shaking her head. 'Poor old Kiki. What a pity, what a pity, what . . . '

Jack aimed an old shell at her and she stopped with a cackle of laughter. Bill tried to light another cigarette, which the wind made rather difficult.

After a while Jack gave a sudden cry. 'Look! Land ho!

Isn't that the Isle of Gloom? It must be.'

They all looked hard. Looming up out of the heat haze was land, there was no doubt about it.

'Yes – that's the island all right,' said Bill, with great interest. 'It's fairly big, too.'

The boat drew nearer. The island became clearer and the children could see how rocky and hilly it was. Round it was a continual turmoil of water. Surf and spray were flung high into the air, and here and there the children could see jagged rocks sticking up from the sea.

They went nearer in. The water was rough and choppy now, and Lucy-Ann began to look a little green. She was the only one who was not a first-rate sailor. But she bravely said nothing, and soon the seasick feeling began to pass off a little.

'Now you can see the wide ring of rocks running round the island,' said Bill Smugs. 'My word, aren't they wicked! I guess many a boat has been wrecked on them at some time or another. We'll cruise round a bit, and see if we can spot any entry. But – we don't go any nearer, so it's no use begging me to.'

The Albatross was now in a very choppy sea indeed and poor Lucy-Ann went green again. 'Have a dry biscuit, Lucy-Ann,' said Bill Smugs, noticing her looks. 'Nibble it. It may keep off that sick feeling.'

It did. Lucy-Ann nibbled the dry biscuit gratefully and was soon able to take an interest in the trip once more. The Isle of Gloom certainly lived up to its name. It was a most desolate place, as far as the children could see. It seemed to be made of jagged rocks that rose into high hills in the middle of the island. A few stunted trees grew here and there, and grass showed green in some places. The rocks were a curious red colour on the seaweed side of the island, but black everywhere else.

'There are heaps and heaps of birds there, just as I thought,' said Jack, looking through his field-glasses in excitement. 'Golly – just look at them, Bill!'

But Bill would not leave the tiller. It was dangerous work cruising near to the ring of rocks in such a choppy sea. He nodded to Jack. 'I'll take your word for it,' he said. 'Tell me if you recognise any birds.'

Jack reeled off a list of names. 'Bill, there are thousands and thousands of birds!' he cried. 'Oh, do, do let's land on the island. Find a way through this ring of rocks somehow. Please, please do.'

'No,' said Bill firmly. 'I said not. It would be a dangerous business to get to the island even if we knew the way, and I don't. I'm not risking all our lives for the sake of seeing a few birds at close quarters – birds you can see at Craggy-Tops any day.'

The sailing boat went on its way round the island, keeping well outside the wicked ring of rocks over which waves broke continually, sending spray high into the air. The children watched them, and noticed how they raced over the treacherous rocks, making a roaring noise that never stopped. It was somehow very thrilling, and the children felt exultant and wanted to shout.

Jack could see the island most clearly because of his field-glasses. He kept them glued to his eyes, looking at the hundreds of birds, both flying and sitting, that he could see. Philip tapped his arm.

'Let someone else have a look too,' he said. 'Hand over the glasses.'

Jack didn't want to, because he was afraid of missing seeing a Great Auk, but he did at last give them to Philip. Philip was not so interested in the birds – he swept the coast of the island with the glasses – and then gave an exclamation.

'Hallo! There are still houses or something on the island. Surely people don't live there now.'

'Of course not,' said Bill Smugs. 'It's been deserted for ages. I can't imagine why anyone ever *did* live on it. They could not have farmed it or used it for fishing – it's a desolate, impossible sort of place.'

'I suppose what I can see are only ruins,' said Philip. 'They seem to be in the hills. I can't make them out really.'

'Anyone walking about – any of Joe's "things"?' asked Dinah, with a laugh.

'No nobody at all,' said Philip. 'Have a look through the glasses, Dinah – and then Lucy-Ann. I don't wonder it's called the Isle of Gloom. It certainly is a terribly gloomy-looking place – nothing alive on it except the sea-birds.'

The girls had a turn of looking through the glasses too. They didn't like the look of the island at all. It was ugly and bare, and had an extraordinary air of forlornness about it.

The sailing boat went all round the island, keeping well outside the rocks that guarded it. The only place where there might conceivably be an entrance between the rocks was a spot to the west. Here the sea became less choppy, and although spray was flung up high, the children could see no rocks on the surface. The spray was flung by waves racing over rocks near by.

'I bet that's the only entrance to the island,' said Jack.

'Well, we're not going to try it,' said Bill Smugs at once. 'I'm going to leave the island now, and head for calmer water. Then we'll take down the sail and have our tea, bobbing gently about instead of tossing and pitching like this. Poor Lucy-Ann keeps on turning green.'

Jack took a last look through his glasses – and gave such a shout that Dinah nearly over-balanced, and Kiki fell off her perch above.

'Whatever is it?' said Bill Smugs, startled.

'A Great Auk!' yelled Jack, the glasses glued to his eyes. 'It is, it is – an enormous bird – with small wings close to its sides – and a big razor-like bill. It's a Great Auk!'

Bill gave the tiller to Jack for a moment and took the glasses. But he could see no Great Auk, and he handed them back to the excited boy, whose green eyes were gleaming with joy.

'I expect it's one of the razorbills,' he said. 'The Great Auk is much like a big razorbill, you know – you've let your wish be father to the thought, old man. That wasn't a Great Auk, I'll be bound.'

But Jack was absolutely convinced that it was. He could not see it any longer, but, as they left the island behind, the boy sat looking longingly backwards at it. The Great Auk was there. He was sure it was. He was certain he had seen one. How could Bill suggest it was a razorbill?

'Bill—Bill—do go back,' begged Jack, hardly able to contain himself. 'I know it was an auk – a Great Auk. I suddenly saw it. Imagine it! What will the world say if they know I've found a Great Auk, a bird that's been extinct for years!'

'The world wouldn't care much,' said Bill Smugs drily. 'Only a few people keen on birds would be excited. Calm yourself a bit – I'm afraid it certainly wasn't the bird you thought.'

Jack couldn't calm himself. He sat looking terribly excited, his eyes glowing, his face red, his hair blown about in the wind. Kiki felt the excitement and came down to his shoulder, pecking at his ear to get his attention.

'It was a Great Auk, it was, it was,' said Jack, and Lucy-Ann slipped a hand in his arm and squeezed it. She too was sure it was a Great Auk – and anyway she wasn't going to spoil her brother's pleasure by saying that it wasn't. Neither Philip nor Dinah believed that it was.

They had their tea on calmer water, with the sail down and the boat drifting where it pleased. Jack could eat nothing, though he drank his tea. Lucy-Ann, hungry now after her seasickness, ate Jack's share of the tea, and enjoyed it. The others enjoyed themselves too. It had been an exciting afternoon.

'Can we sail your boat by ourselves sometime, as you promised?' asked Jack suddenly. Bill Smugs looked at him sharply.

'Only if you promise not to go very far out,' he said. 'No rushing off to find the Great Auk on the Isle of Gloom, you know.'

As this was the idea at the back of Jack's mind, the boy went red at once. 'All right,' he said at last. 'I promise not to go to the Isle of Gloom in your boat, Bill. But may we really go out by ourselves other days?'

'Yes, you may,' said Bill. 'I think you really know how to manage the boat all right – and you can't come to much harm if you choose a calm day.'

Jack looked pleased. A dreamy expression came over his face. He knew what he meant to do. He would keep his word to Bill Smugs – he would not go to the Isle of Gloom in Bill's boat – but he would go in someone else's. He would practise sailing and rowing in *Bill's* boat – and as soon as he was absolutely sure of handling it, he would borrow Joe's boat, and go to the island in that.

This was a bold and daring plan – but Jack was so thrilled at the idea of finding a Great Auk, when everyone else thought it was extinct, that he was willing to run any risk to get to the island. He was sure he could find the entrance to the ring of rocks. He would furl the sail when he got near the rocks and do some rowing. Joe's boat was big and heavy, but Jack thought he could manage it well enough.

He said nothing to the others whilst Bill was there. Bill mustn't know. He was jolly and kind and a good friend – but he was a grown-up, and grown-ups always stopped children doing anything risky. So Jack sat in the rocking boat and thought out his daring plan, not hearing the others' remarks or teasing.

'He's gone off to the island to see his Great Auk,' said Dinah, with a laugh.

'Poor old Jack – that bird has quite taken his appetite away,' said Philip.

'Wake up!' said Bill, giving Jack a nudge. 'Be a little sociable.'

After tea they decided to row back, taking it in turns. Bill thought it would be good for them to have some exercise, and the children enjoyed handling the oars. Jack rowed vigorously, thinking that it was good practice for the time when he would go to the island.

'Well – here we are, safely back again,' said Bill, as the boat came to shore. The boys jumped out and pulled it in. The girls got out, bringing the thermos flask with them. Bill pulled the boat up the shore.

'Well, goodbye,' he said. 'We've had a fine time. Come along tomorrow, if you like, and I'll let you have a shot at taking the boat out by yourselves.'

'Oh, thanks!' cried the children, and Kiki echoed the words too. 'Oh, thanks!' she said, 'oh, thanks; oh, thanks; oh thanks!'

'Be quiet,' said Philip, with a laugh, but Kiki chanted the words all the way home. 'Oh, thanks; oh, thanks; oh, thanks; oh, thanks!'

'Did you have a nice afternoon?' asked Aunt Polly, when they went into the house.

'Lovely,' said Dinah. 'Is your headache better, Aunt Polly?'

'Not much,' said her aunt, who looked pale and tired. 'I think I'll go to bed early tonight, if you'll take your uncle's supper in to him, instead of me, Dinah.'

'Yes, I will,' said Dinah, not liking the task very much, for she was rather afraid of her learned and peculiar uncle.

Joe came in at that moment and stared at the four children. 'Where you been?' he asked roughly. 'And where did you go this morning, after you went into the caves?'

'We came up to the house,' said Philip, putting on a surprised expression that infuriated Joe. 'Didn't you see us? And we've just come back from a picnic, Joe. Why all this concern for our whereabouts? Did you want to come with us?'

Joe made an angry noise, at once copied by Kiki, who then cackled out her maddening laughter. Joe gave the parrot a look of hatred and stalked out.

'Don't tease him,' said Aunt Polly wearily. 'He's really getting lazy. He never came near the house all the morning. Well – I'm going to bed.'

'Jack, you help me with Uncle Jocelyn's tray,' said Dinah, when the supper was ready. 'It's heavy. Philip's gone off somewhere as usual. He always disappears when there's any job to be done.'

Jack took the heavy tray and followed Dinah as she led the way to her uncle's study. She knocked on the door. A voice grunted, and Dinah imagined it said 'Come in.'

They went in, Kiki on Jack's shoulder as usual. 'Your supper, Uncle,' said Dinah. 'Aunt Polly's gone to bed. She's tired.'

'Poor Polly, poor dear Polly,' said Kiki, in a pitying tone. Uncle Jocelyn looked up, startled. He saw the parrot and picked up a paperweight.

Kiki at once flew out of the door, and Uncle Jocelyn put the paperweight down again. 'Keep that parrot out,' he said grumpily. 'Interfering bird. Put the tray down there. Who are you, young man?'

'I'm Jack Trent,' said Jack, surprised that anyone could be so forgetful. 'You saw me and my sister Lucy-Ann the day we came here, sir. Don't you remember?'

'Too many children in this house,' said Uncle Jocelyn, in a grumbling tone. 'Can't get any work done at all.'

'Oh, Uncle – you know we never disturb you,' said Dinah indignantly.

Uncle Jocelyn was bending over a big and very old map. Jack glanced at it.

'Oh,' he said, 'that's a map of part of this coast – and that's the Isle of Gloom, isn't it, sir?'

He pointed to the outline of the island, drawn carefully on the big map. Uncle Jocelyn nodded.

'Have you ever been there?' asked Jack eagerly. 'We saw it this afternoon, sir.'

'Never been there, and don't want to go either,' said Uncle Jocelyn surlily.

'I saw a Great Auk there this afternoon,' said Jack proudly.

This did not impress Uncle Jocelyn at all. 'Nonsense,' he said. 'Bird's been extinct for ages. You saw a razorbill. Don't be foolish, boy.'

Jack was annoyed. Only Lucy-Ann paid any attention to

his great discovery, and she, he knew, would have believed him if he had said he had seen Santa Claus on the island. He stared sulkily at the untidy, frowning old man.

Uncle Jocelyn stared back. 'Could I see the map, please?' asked Jack suddenly, thinking that he might possibly see marked on it the entrance between the rocks.

'Why? Are you interested in that sort of thing?' asked Uncle Jocelyn, surprised.

'I'm very interested in the Isle of Gloom,' said Jack. 'Please – may I see the map, sir?'

'I've got a bigger one somewhere – showing only the island, in great detail,' said Uncle Jocelyn, quite pleased now to think that anyone should be interested in his maps. 'Let me see – where is it?'

Whilst he went to look for it, Jack and Dinah had a good look at the big map of the coast. There, lying off it, ringed by rocks, was the Isle of Gloom. It had a queer shape, rather like an egg with a bulge in the middle of one side, and its coast was very much indented. It lay almost due west of Craggy-Tops.

Jack pored over the map, feeling terribly excited. If only Uncle Jocelyn would lend it to him!

'Look,' he said to Dinah, in a low voice. 'Look. The ring of rocks is broken just there. See? I bet it's where I imagined the entrance was this afternoon. See that hill shown in the map? The entrance to the rocks is just about opposite. If ever we wanted to go there – and goodness knows I do – we need only look for that hill – it's the highest on the island, I should think – and then watch for the entrance to the rocks just opposite to the hill. Easy!'

'It looks easy on the map, but I bet it's a jolly sight more difficult when you get out on the sea,' said Dinah. 'You sound as if you mean to go there, Jack – but you know what we promised Bill Smugs. We can't break our promise.'

'I know that, idiot,' said Jack, who had never broken a promise in his life. 'I've got another plan. I'll tell you later.'

Much to the children's disappointment, Uncle Jocelyn could not find the large map of the island. He would not lend the other to Jack.

'Certainly not,' he said, looking quite shocked. 'It's a very, very old map – hundreds of years old. I wouldn't dream of handing it out to you. You'd damage it, or lose it or something. I know what children are.'

'You don't, Uncle,' said Dinah. 'You don't know what we are like a bit. Why, we hardly ever see you. Do lend us the map.'

But nothing would persuade the old man to part with his precious map. So, taking one last glance at the drawing of the island, with its curious ring of protecting rocks, and the one break in them, Jack and Dinah left the untidy, book-lined study.

'Don't forget your supper, Uncle,' called back Dinah as she shut the door. Uncle Jocelyn gave a grunt. He was already lost in his work again. The supper-tray stood unheeded beside him.

'I bet he'll forget all about it,' said Dinah. And she was right. When Aunt Polly went into the study the next day to tidy it as usual, there was the supper-tray standing on the table, complete with plate of meat and vegetables, and piece of pie and custard.

'You're worse than a child,' scolded Aunt Polly. 'Yes, you really are, Jocelyn.'

15

A peculiar happening – and a fine trip

That night Jack told the others his plan, and they were at first doubtful, and then thrilled and excited.

'Could we really find the entrance?' said Lucy-Ann, scared.

'Easily,' said Jack, who, once he had made up his mind about anything, would not recognise any difficulties at all. 'I saw the entrance this afternoon, I'm sure, and I certainly saw it on the map. So did Dinah.'

'So did Dinah, so did Dinah, so did Dinah,' chanted Kiki. Nobody took any notice of her. They all went on talking excitedly.

'You see, once I feel absolutely at home in handling Bill's boat, I shan't be a bit afraid of taking Joe's,' said Jack.

'He'll half kill you if he finds out,' said Philip. 'How are you going to manage it without his knowing?'

'I shall wait till he takes the old car and goes shopping,' said Jack at once. 'I'd thought of that. As soon as he goes off in the car, I shall take out the boat, and hope to come back before he returns. If I don't – well, it just can't be helped. You'll have to distract his attention somehow – or lock him up in the cellar – or something.'

The others giggled. The idea of locking Joe up amused them.

'But look here,' said Philip, 'aren't we coming with you? You can't go alone.'

'I'm not taking the girls,' said Jack firmly. 'I don't mind any risk myself – but I won't risk everyone. I'd better take you, Philip.'

'I don't want you to take risks,' said poor Lucy-Ann, with tears in her eyes.

'Don't be such a baby,' said Jack. Why can't you be like Dinah, and not worry about me when I want to do something? Dinah doesn't bother about Philip taking risks, do you, Dinah?'

'No,' said Dinah, well aware that Philip could take very good care of himself. 'All the same – I wish we could come.'

Lucy-Ann blinked back her tears. She didn't want to spoil things for Jack – but really, it was awful to think he might be wrecked or drowned. She wished with all her heart that Great Auks had never existed. If they hadn't existed they couldn't be extinct, and if they hadn't been extinct there wouldn't be all this excitement about finding one again.

Jack did not sleep much that night. He lay and thought

about the island and its birds, and could hardly wait to sail off and see whether it really was a Great Auk or not he had spotted through his glasses that afternoon. He might get a lot of money if he caught the Great Auk. It couldn't fly, it could only swim. It might be so tame that it would let itself be caught. There might be three or four Great Auks. It would be simply wonderful to find out.

Jack got up and went to the window. He looked out to the west where the island lay. There was no moon that night, and he could see nothing at first. But, as he gazed earnestly to the west, thinking hard of the island, he was astonished to see something distinctly unusual.

He blinked his eyes and looked again. It seemed as if a light was shining out there, over to the west where the island was. It went out slowly as he watched, and then came again. 'It *can't* be a real light,' said Jack. 'Anyway, it can't be a light on the island. It must be some ship a good way out, signalling.'

The light to the west faded again, and did not reappear. Jack pulled his head back, meaning to go to bed again, feeling sure that it must have been a ship's light he had seen.

But, before he could go back to his bed, something else attracted him. The narrow window on the opposite side, the one looking over the top of the cliff, was outlined in a soft light. Jack stared in amazement.

He ran to the window and looked out. The light came from the top of the rocky cliff. Someone had either built a fire there or had a bright lantern. Who could it be? And why show a light at night? Was it to signal to the ship out at sea?

Jack's room was the highest in Craggy-Tops, and the tower in which it was built jutted above the cliff-top. But though he craned his neck to look out as far as he could, he could not see what the light was on the top of the cliff, nor exactly where. He decided to find out.

He did not wake Philip. He put on shorts and coat and shoes and ran silently down the stairs. He was soon climbing the path to the top of the cliff. But when he got there, there was no light to be seen at all – no smell, even, of a fire. It was very puzzling.

The boy stumbled along the cliff – and suddenly he got the fright of his life. Someone clutched at him and held him fast.

'What you doing up here?' said Joe's voice, and he shook the boy till he had no breath left in his body. 'Go on – you tell me what you doing up here.'

Too frightened to think of anything but the truth, Jack blurted it out.

'I saw a light from the tower-room – and I came to see what it was.'

'I told you there was "things" on the cliff at night, didn't I?' said Joe, in a frightening voice. 'Well, those things show lights, and they wail and yell sometimes, and lord knows what else they do. Didn't I tell you not to wander out at night?'

'What are *you* out for?' asked Jack, beginning to recover from his fright.

Joe shook him again, glad to have got one of the children in his power. 'I come out to see what the light was too,' he growled. 'See? That's what I was out for, of course. But it's always those "things" making a disturbance and a trouble. Now, you promise me you'll never leave your bedroom no more at nights.'

'I shan't promise you anything,' said Jack, beginning to struggle. 'Let me go, you beast. You're hurting me.'

'I'll hurt you a mighty lot more, less you tell me you won't go out at nights,' threatened the man. 'I got a rope-end here, see? I been keeping it for you and Philip.'

Jack was afraid. Joe was immensely strong, spiteful and cruel. He struggled hard again, feeling Joe untying the rope he had around his waist.

It was Kiki that saved him. The parrot, missing Jack suddenly from the tower-room, where she had been sleeping peacefully on the perch that the boy had rigged up for her, had come in search of her master. She would not be separated from him for long, if she could help it.

Just as Jack was wondering whether it would be a good idea to bite Joe hard or not, Kiki swooped down with a glad screech. 'Kiki! Kiki! Bite him! Bite him!' yelled Jack.

The parrot gladly fastened her sharp curved beak into a very fleshy part of the man's arm. He let Jack go and gave an agonised yell. He hit out at Kiki, who was now well beyond reach, watching for a chance to attack again.

This time she tore at Joe's ear, and he yelled loudly. 'Call that bird off! I'll wring her neck!'

Jack disappeared down the cliff path. When he was safely out of reach, he called Kiki.

'Kiki! Come on. You're a very good bird.'

Kiki took a last bite at Joe's other ear and then flew off with a screech. She flew to Jack's shoulder and made soft noises in his ear. He scratched her head gently as he made his way back to the house, his heart beating fast.

'Keep out of Joe's way, Kiki,' he said. 'He certainly *will* wring your neck now, if he can. I don't know what you did to him – but it must have been something very painful.'

Jack woke up Philip and told him what had happened. 'I expect the light was from a ship at sea,' he said, 'but I don't know what the other light was. Joe said he went up to see too, but he thought it was made by the "things" he is always talking about. Golly, I nearly got tanned by him, Philip. If it hadn't been for Kiki, I guess I'd have had a bad time.'

'Good old Kiki,' said Philip, and Kiki repeated his words in delight.

'Good old Kiki, good old Kiki, good old . . .'

'That's enough,' said Jack, and Kiki stopped. Jack snuggled deep into bed. 'I'm tired,' he said. 'I hope I soon go to sleep. I simply couldn't doze off before. I kept thinking and thinking of the Isle of Gloom.'

But it was not long before he was asleep, dreaming of a large map that had the island marked on it, then of a boat that was trying to get to the isle, and then of Joe clutching him and trying to pull back both him and the boat.

The children felt pleased the next morning when they

remembered that Bill Smugs had said they could try out the boat by themselves. They set off early, having done all their jobs very quickly. Joe was in a bad temper that day. He slouched about, frowning, glaring at Jack and Kiki as if he would like to get hold of both of them.

For once in a way he did not follow them about or try to track them where they went. Aunt Polly was determined that he was going to do some work that morning, and she set him all kinds of tasks. He saw that it would be no good trying to evade them, so, very sulkily, he set to work, and the children were able to escape easily without being seen.

'I'm going to the town today,' said Bill, when they arrived at his tumbledown shack. 'I simply must get hammer and nails and wood, and mend up my house a bit. Some more bits of wall have fallen down, and I spent last night with a gale rushing all round me — or what seemed like a gale in this small place. I must do a spot of mending. Do you want to come with me and do some shopping again too?'

'No, thank you,' said Jack at once. 'We would rather go out in the boat, please, Bill. It's quite a calm day. We will be very careful.'

'You'll remember your promise, of course,' said Bill, and looked at Jack sharply. The boy nodded.

'I won't go far out,' he said, and the others said the same. They saw Bill off in his car, and watched him going carefully down the bumpy way to join the rough-and-ready road that led to the town.

Then they went to get the boat. Bill had left it out on the rocks, in its hiding place. The children had not discovered why he liked to keep it there, but they imagined that he did not want it stolen when he was away from the place. They had to swim out to it, wrapping their dry clothes in an oilskin bag that Bill lent them for the purpose. Philip towed it behind him.

They reached the rocks and made their way over them to the flattish stretch where the boat was hauled up, well out of reach of the waves. They undid the oilskin bag and changed into dry things. They threw their bathing-suits into the boat and then pulled her down to the water.

The sea was deep around the rocks, and the boat slid neatly in, with hardly a splash. The children piled into her, and the two boys took the oars.

With a little trouble they rowed the big boat away from the rocks and out into open water. Then they faced the task of putting up the sail without Bill Smugs to help them.

'It ought to be easy enough to us,' panted Jack, tugging at various ropes. 'We did it yesterday by ourselves.'

But yesterday Bill had shouted directions at them. Now there was no one to help them if they got into a muddle. Still, they did get the sail up after a time. Dinah was nearly knocked overboard, but just managed to save herself. She was very angry.

'You did that on purpose, Philip,' she said to her brother, who was still struggling with different ropes. 'Just you apologise! Bill said there wasn't to be any hanky-panky or silly tricks on board.'

'Shut up,' said Philip, getting suddenly caught in a rope that seemed determined to hang him, 'Jack, help me.'

'Take the tiller, Dinah,' said Jack. 'I'll help old Tufty.'

But it was Dinah who, suddenly seeing that Philip was indeed in difficulties, came to his rescue and untangled him.

'Thanks,' said Philip. 'Blow these ropes! I seem to have undone too many. Is the sail all right?'

It seemed to be. The wind filled it and the boat began to rush along. It was fun. The children felt important at being alone, managing the boat all by themselves. It was, after all, a very big boat for children to sail. Jack looked across the water to where the Isle of Gloom loomed up. One day he would go there – land on it – look around – and goodness knows what he might find! A picture of the Great Auk rose in his mind and in his excitement he gybed the boat round and the sail swung across, almost knocking off the heads of the crouching children.

'Idiot!' said Philip indignantly. 'Here, let *me* take the

tiller. We shall all be in the water if you play about like that.'

'Sorry,' said Jack. 'I was just thinking of something – how I'd go off in Joe's boat. When do you think we could, Philip? In two or three days' time?'

'I should think we could sail Joe's boat all right by then,' said Philip. 'It's easy enough once you've got the knack and are quick enough. I'm getting to know the feel of the wind, and its strength – really feeling at home in the boat. Poor Lucy-Ann never will, though. Look how green she's gone.'

'I'm all right,' said Lucy-Ann valiantly. They had run into a choppy patch, and poor Lucy-Ann's tummy didn't like it. But nothing would ever persuade her to let the others go without her, even if she knew she was going to feel sick all the time. Lucy-Ann had plenty of pluck.

The children furled the sail after a time and got out the oars. They carefully remembered their promise and did not go very far away. They thought it would be a good thing to practise rowing for a while, too.

So all of them took turns, and soon they could pull the boat along well, and make it go any way they liked, even without the rudder.

Then they put up the sail once more and sailed to shore, feeling very proud of themselves. When they came near the shore they saw Bill Smugs waving to them. He had already come back.

They sailed in to the beach, and pulled in the boat. 'Good!' said Bill. 'I was watching you out at sea. You did very well. Have another go tomorrow.'

'Oh, thanks,' said Jack. 'I suppose we couldn't have a try this afternoon too, could we? Dinah and Lucy-Ann wouldn't be able to, because they've got to do something for Aunt Polly. But Philip and I could come.'

The girls knew that Jack wanted to see if he and Philip were able to manage the boat by themselves, in preparation for going out alone in Joe's boat. So they said nothing, much as they would have liked to join in, and Bill Smugs said yes, the boys could go along that afternoon if they liked.

'I shan't come,' he said. 'I'm going to have a go at my radio set. It's gone wrong.'

Bill had a marvellous radio, the finest the boys had ever seen. It was set at the back of the old hut, and there was no station that Bill could not get. He would not allow the boys to tamper with it at all.

'Well, we'll be along this afternoon, then,' said Jack, pleased. 'It's awfully nice of you to lend us your boat like this, Bill. Really it is.'

'It's a pleasure,' said Bill Smugs, and grinned. Kiki imitated him.

'It's a pleasure, it's a pleasure, it's a pleasure, poor old Kiki, wipe your feet, never mind, never mind, it's a pleasure.'

'Oh – that reminds me,' said Jack, remembering his strange experience of the night before. 'Bill, listen to this.' He went off into a long account of his adventure on the cliff with Joe, and Bill Smugs listened with the greatest attention.

'So you saw lights?' he said. 'Out at sea – and on the cliff. Very interesting. I don't wonder you wanted to look into the matter. Joe apparently had the same curiosity about them. Well, if I may give you a bit of advice, it's this – don't get up against Joe more than you can help. I don't much like the sound of him. He sounds a dangerous sort of fellow.'

'Oh, he's just a bit grumpy and hates children and their games, but I don't think he'd really do us much harm,' said Philip. 'He's been with us for years.'

'Really?' said Bill, interested. 'Well, well – I expect your people would have a hard job to get anyone in Joe's place if he went. All the same – beware of him.'

The boys went off with the two girls. Philip was rather inclined to laugh at Bill's warning, but Jack took it to heart. He had not forgotten his fear the night before when the handyman had caught him.

'I think Bill's right, somehow,' thought Jack, with a little shiver. 'Joe could be a very dangerous sort of fellow.'

16

Strange discoveries

The next three days the children worked hard at rowing and sailing, until they were perfectly at home in Bill's boat, and could handle it almost as well as Bill. He was pleased with them.

'I must say I do like to see children sticking to things, even if it means hard work,' he said. 'Even old Kiki has stuck to it too, sitting on the sail, over-balancing half the time, but not dreaming of letting you go by yourselves. And as for Lucy-Ann, she's the best of the lot, because she has had to fight seasickness a good part of the time.'

That afternoon, having first seen that Joe was safely in the yard at the back of the house, pumping up water from the deep well there, the children went to examine Joe's boat carefully, to see if they could possibly handle it themselves.

They stood and looked at it bobbing on the water. It was bigger than Bill's, but not very much. They felt certain they would be all right in it.

'It's a pity Kiki can't row,' said Jack. 'She could take the third pair of oars and we could get along fine.'

'Fine,' said Kiki. 'Fine. God save the Queen.'

'Idiot,' said Philip affectionately. He was as fond of Kiki as Jack and Lucy-Ann were, and the bird went to him readily. 'I say, Freckles – I wonder when Joe is going to town again. I'm longing to try my hand at the boat; aren't you?'

'I should just think so,' said Jack. 'I keep on and on thinking of that Great Auk I saw. I shan't be happy till I've seen it close to.'

'Bet you won't find it,' said Philip. 'It would be awfully funny if you did, though – and came back with it cradled in your arms. Wouldn't Kiki be jealous?'

To the children's delight, Aunt Polly announced that Joe

was going shopping the next day 'So if you want anything, you must tell him,' she said. 'He has a long list of things to get for me – you can add anything you want to it, and give him the money.'

They put down a new torch battery on the list. Dinah had left her torch on one night and the battery was now no use. She must have a new one. Jack added another roll of film. He had been taking photographs of the sea-birds round Craggy-Tops, and now wanted a new film to take to the Isle of Gloom with him.

They waited anxiously for Joe to depart the next day. He seemed irritatingly slow. He started up the car at last and backed it out of the tumbledown shed where it lived. 'Now don't you children get into mischief while I'm gone,' he said, his sharp eyes watching them suspiciously. Perhaps he sensed that they were wishing him to be gone for reasons of their own.

'We never get into mischief,' said Philip. 'Have a good time – and don't hurry back.'

Joe scowled, put his foot on the accelerator and shot off at his usual breakneck speed. 'Can't think how the old car stands those bumps and jerks,' said Philip, watching it go across the cliff and disappear down to the road on the other side. 'Well – he's gone. Now, what about it? Our chance has come.'

In great excitement the children ran down to the beach, and made their way to the big boat. The boys got in. Dinah untied the rope and gave it a push.

'Take care of yourselves,' called Lucy-Ann anxiously, longing to jump into the boat with them. 'Do take care of yourselves.'

'Okay!' yelled back Jack, and Kiki echoed the word. 'Okay, okay, okay, shut the door and wipe your feet!'

The girls watched the boys rowing hard, and then they saw them put up the sail as soon as they were out on the open sea. There was a good wind and they were soon moving along at a fine speed.

'Off to the Isle of Gloom,' said Lucy-Ann. 'Well, I hope Jack brings back the Great Auk.'

'He won't,' said Dinah, whose common sense told her that it would indeed be a miracle if he did. 'Well, I hope they find the entrance to those awful rocks all right. They seem to be managing the boat well, don't they?'

'Yes,' said Lucy-Ann, straining her eyes to follow the boat, which was now becoming difficult to see, owing to a haze over the water. The Isle of Gloom could not be seen at all. 'Oh dear – I do hope they'll get on well.'

The boys were having a fine time. They found that although Joe's boat was heavier and more awkward to manage than Bill's, it was not really difficult. There was quite enough wind and they were simply rushing through the water. It was most exhilarating to feel the up-and-down movement, and to hear the wind in the taut sail, and see the waves racing by.

'Nothing like a boat,' said Jack happily. 'One day I'll have one of my own.'

'They cost a lot of money,' said Philip.

'Well, I'll make a lot, then,' said Jack. 'Then I'll buy a fine boat of my own, and go sailing off to distant islands inhabited by nothing but birds, and won't I have a marvellous time!'

'I wish we could see the island,' said Philip. 'This haze is a nuisance. I hope we're going in the right direction.'

Before they saw the island, they heard the thundering of the waves on the ring of rocks around it. Then quite suddenly, after what seemed a very long time, the island loomed up, and the boys felt the spray from the breaking waves falling finely around them.

'Look out – we're heading straight for the rocks!' cried Philip in alarm. 'Take down the sail. We'll have to row. We can't manage the boat in this wind – it's got too strong. She's going too fast.'

They took down the sail, got out the oars and began to row. Jack tried to see the high hill. But it was much more difficult to spot the hill in reality than it had been to see it on the map. The hills seemed more or less the same size. The boys rowed round the ring of rocks, keeping well out of reach of the current that swept towards the island.

'There's a high hill – see, to the left,' suddenly said Jack. 'Pull towards there, Tufty. That's right. I believe that's the one we want.'

They pulled hard at their oars, panting and perspiring. Then, as the hill came right into view, the boys saw, to their delight, a gap in the ring of rocks – a narrow gap, it is true, but decidedly an opening through which a boat might pass.

'Now – careful,' warned Philip. 'This is the tricky bit. Watch out. We may get swung off our course and run into the rocks. And anyway, although there are none showing just there, in the gap, there might be some just below the water that would rip the bottom from our boat. Careful, Freckles, careful!'

Jack was very careful. Everything depended on getting safely through the gap. The boys, their faces strained and anxious, rowed cautiously. Kiki didn't say a word. She knew that the boys were worried.

The gap or passage was narrow but long. It was anxious work getting the boat through. Various strong currents seemed to be doing their best to drive her to this side or that, and once the boys felt the bottom being scraped by some rock that was not far below the water.

'That was a narrow shave,' said Philip, in a low voice. 'Did you hear that nasty scrape?'

'I felt it too,' said Jack. 'Hallo – we seem to be all right now. I say, how marvellous, Tufty – we're in a channel of perfectly calm water!'

Beyond the rim of rocks was a channel or moat of brilliant blue, calm water, gleaming in the summer sun. It was strange to see it after the turbulence of the waves that raced over the rocks. They could hear the thunder of these still.

'Not far to the island now,' said Philip, thrilled. 'Come on – I'm frightfully tired – at least my arms are – but we simply *must* get to land. I'm longing to explore.'

They looked about for a good landing place. The island was very rocky indeed, but in one place there was a tiny cove where sand gleamed. The boys decided to land there.

It was quite easy to land and haul the boat a little way up the beach, though it took all the boys' strength to pull it up. But Bill had shown them the knack of hauling, and soon they were free to explore the deserted island.

They climbed the rocky cliff behind the little cover, and gazed over that side of the Isle of Gloom.

It was the number of birds that first took the boys' attention. There were thousands upon thousands, all kinds, all sizes, all shapes. The noise they made was tremendous. They took little notice of the boys, who stood watching them in wonder.

But they were not as tame as they had hoped. Sitting birds flew away as soon as the boys went near. They seemed as wild as those at Craggy-Tops. Jack was disappointed.

'Funny!' he said. 'I always thought that birds on a deserted island, where no men ever came, were completely tame. It says so in all my books, anyway. These are quite wild. They won't let us go really near them.'

There were a few tress to be seen, and what there were grew in sheltered spots, bent over sideways by the wind that blew across the island. Underfoot was a kind of wiry grass which grew in tufted patches here and there. But even that did not grow everywhere, and the bare rock thrust up in many places.

The boys left the cliff and walked inland, the cries of the thousands of birds in their ears. They made their way towards the hill that towered up in the centre of the isle.

'I want to see what those funny buildings are that I saw through the glasses,' said Jack, remembering. 'And oh dear, I do want to find a Great Auk. I haven't seen a sign of one yet. I keep on looking and looking.'

Poor Jack was in a terrible state of excitement, expecting to see a Great Auk at any moment, and, instead, seeing all kinds of birds he had already seen at Craggy-Tops. It *was* disappointing. He hadn't expected to see a procession of Great Auks – but one, just one, would have been marvellous.

There were plenty of big razorbills with their curiously-shaped beaks, plenty of skuas, gulls, cormorants and other birds. It was a paradise of sea-birds, and Jack was lost in wonder at the number of them. How he would like to spend a few days on this island, watching and taking photographs!

They came to the hills, and found a pass between them. Here there was more grass and a few tiny wild flowers, sea-pinks and others. One or two stunted birches grew on the hillsides.

Between the hills lay a small valley, and in it was a stream, running off the the sea on the other side of the island. The boys went to have a look at it because it seemed rather a curious colour.

It certainly was a strange colour. 'Sort of bright bluey-green,' said Jack, puzzled. 'I wonder why. I say, look! – there are those queer buildings, up on that hill. And do you notice, Tufty, how the rocks change in colour here? They are not black any more, but green. And some of them look like sandstone. It's queer, isn't it?'

'I don't think I like this island much,' said Philip, with a shudder. 'It feels lonely and odd – and sort of bad.'

'You've been listening to old Joe's tales too much,' said Jack, with a laugh, though he himself did not like the 'feel' of the island either. It was so mournful and desolate, and the only sounds to be heard so far inland were the incessant cries of the sea birds circling overhead.

They climbed halfway up a hill to see the 'buildings'. It was difficult to make out what they were, they were so old and broken down – not much more than heaps of stones or rocks. They did not look as if they ever could have been places to live in.

And then, close to one of these 'buildings', Philip discovered something strange. He called Jack in excitement.

'I say! Come and look here! There's a terrific hole going right down into the earth – simply terrifically deep!'

Jack ran over to the hole and peered down it. It was a large hole, about six feet round, and it went so far down into the earth that the boys could not possibly see the bottom of it.

'What's it for?' said Philip. 'Is it a well, do you think?'

The boys dropped a stone down to see if they could hear a splash. But none came. Either it was not a well, or it was so deep that the sound of the splash could not be heard.

'I shouldn't like to fall down there,' said Philip. 'Look! – there's a ladder going down – awfully old and broken – but still, a ladder.'

'It's a mystery,' said Jack, puzzled. 'Let's go and look around a bit. We might find something to help us to clear up such a peculiar problem. A shaft going down into the depths of the earth, in a lonely island like this! Whatever was it made for?'

17

Joe is angry

To the boys' intense surprise, they found more of the deep narrow holes, all of them near the curious old 'buildings'. 'They can't be wells,' said Jack. 'That's impossible. No one would want so many. They must be shafts, sunk down deep into the earth here, for some good reason.'

'Do you think there were mines?' asked Philip, remembering that coal mines always had shafts bored down through the earth, so that men might go down and get the coal. 'Do you think there are old mines here? Coal mines, for instance?'

'No, not coal,' said Jack. 'I can't imagine what. We'll have to find out. I expect your uncle knows. Wouldn't it be exciting if it was a *gold* mine! You never know.'

'Well, it must have been worked out hundreds of years ago,' said Philip. 'There wouldn't be any gold left now, or it would still be worked. I say — shall we go down and see what there is to be seen?'

'I don't know,' said Jack doubtfully. 'The old ladders aren't much good, are they? We might fall hundreds of feet down — and that would be the end of us.'

'What a pity, what a pity!' remarked Kiki.

'Yes, it *would* be a pity,' said Philip, with a grin. 'Well, perhaps we'd better not. Hallo! — here's another shaft, Jack — a bit bigger one.'

The boys peered down this big one. It had a much better ladder than the others. They went down it a little way, feeling very daring. They soon came up again, for they did not like the darkness and the shut-in feeling.

And then they made a discovery that surprised them even more than the shafts. Not far off, piled under an over-hanging bit of rock, were some empty meat and fruit tins.

This was such an extraordinary find that the boys could hardly believe their eyes. They stood and stared at the tins, and Kiki flew down to inspect them to see if there was anything left to eat.

'Where *do* you suppose those came from?' asked Jack at last. 'What a queer thing! Some are very rusty — but others seem quite new. Who could come to this island — and why — and where do they live?'

'It's a mystery,' said Philip. 'Let's have a jolly good look all round whilst we're here, and see if we can find anyone. Better go carefully, because it's quite plain that whoever lives here doesn't want it known.'

So the boys made a careful tour of the island, but saw nothing and nobody that could explain the mystery of the pile of tins. They wondered at the green rocks on the south-ward side of the island, and again puzzled over the green colour of the stream that ran into the sea there. There were many more birds on the seaward side, and Jack kept a sharp look-out for the Great Auk. But he did not see one, which was very disappointing.

'Aren't you going to take any photos?' asked Philip. 'You said you were. Hurry up, because we oughtn't to be much longer.'

'Yes – I'll take a few,' said Jack, and hid behind a convenient rock to snap a few young birds. Then, having one more film left, a thought struck him.

'I'll take a snap of that pile of tins,' he said. 'The girls mightn't believe us if we bring home such a queer tale, but they'll believe it all right if we show them the photo.'

So he snapped the pile of tins too, and then, with one last look down the big, silent shaft, the boys made their way back to the boat. There it lay, just out of reach of the water.

'Well, let's hope we make as good a trip home as we did coming out,' said Jack. 'I wonder if Joe is back yet. I hope to goodness that the girls have dealt with him somehow if he is.'

They pulled the boat into the water and got in. They rowed over the smooth moat to the exit between the rocks, where spray was being sent high into the air from waves breaking on either side. They managed to avoid the rock that had scraped the bottom of the boat before, and rowed quite easily out of the passage.

They had some trouble just outside, where the sea was very choppy indeed. The wind had changed a little, and the sea was rougher. They put up the sail and ran home in great style, exulting in the feel of the wind on their cheeks and the spray on their faces.

As they got near the shore after their long run, they saw the two girls waiting for them, and they waved. Dinah and Lucy-Ann waved back. Soon the boat slid to its mooring-place and the boys got out and tied it up.

'Did you find the Great Auk?' cried Lucy-Ann.

'Is Joe back?' asked Philip.

'You've been ages,' said Dinah, impatient to hear everything.

'We've had a fine adventure,' said Philip. 'Is Joe back?'

All these questions were asked at the same moment. The most important one was – was Joe back?

'Yes,' said Dinah, with a giggle. 'He came back about an hour ago. We were watching for him. Luckily, he went straight down into the cellar with some boxes he brought back in the car, and we followed him. He opened that inner door and went into the back cellar with the boxes – and the cellar where the trap-door is – and we remembered where you'd put the key of that door, got in, and locked him in. He's banging away there like anything.'

'Good for you!' said the boys, pleased. 'Now he won't know we've been out in his boat. But how on earth are we going to let him out without his knowing we've locked him in?'

'You'll have to think of something,' said Dinah. The boys walked up to the house, thinking hard.

'We'd better slip down quietly and unlock the door when he's having a rest,' said Philip at last. 'He can't keep banging at the door for ever. As soon as he stops for a bit of rest, I'll quietly put the key in the lock and unlock the door. Then I'll slip upstairs again. The next time he tries the door, it will open – but he won't know why.'

'Good!' said the others, pleased. It seemed a very simple way of setting Joe free without his guessing that it had anything to do with them.

Philip took the key and went down into the cellar as quietly as he could. As soon as he got down there he heard Joe hammering on the door. The boy waited till he had stopped for breath, and then pushed the big key quietly into the lock. He heard Joe coughing, and turned the key at the same moment, and then withdrew it. The door was unlocked now – and Joe could come out when he wanted to. Philip shot across the cellar to the steps, ran up them, out into the kitchen, and joined the others.

'He'll be out in a minute,' he panted. 'Let's slip up on to the cliff, and as soon as we see Joe again, we'll walk down to the house, pretending we are just back from a walk. That will puzzle him properly.'

So they all ran up to the cliff, lay down on the top, and

peeped over to see when Joe appeared. In low voices the boys told the girls all they had found on the Isle of Gloom.

The two girls listened in amazement. Deep holes in the earth – a stream that was bright green – a pile of food tins – how very strange! No one had expected anything like that. It was birds they had gone to see.

'We simply must go back again and find out what those shafts lead down to,' said Jack. 'We'll find out, too, if there were once mines of some sort there. Perhaps your Uncle Jocelyn would know, Dinah.'

'Yes, he would,' said Dinah. 'Golly, I wish we could get hold of that old map of the island he spoke about – the one he couldn't find. It might show us all kinds of interesting things, mightn't it?'

Kiki suddenly gave one of her express train screeches, which meant she had sighted her enemy, Joe. The children saw him down below, looking all round, evidently for them. They scrambled to their feet and walked jauntily down the path to the house.

Joe saw them and came to meet them, fury in his face. 'You locked me in,' he said. 'I'll tell Miss Polly of you. You ought to be whipped.'

'Locked you in!' said Philip, putting a look of sheer amazement on his face. 'Where did we lock you in? Into your room?'

'Down in the cellar,' said Joe, in a furious voice. 'Here's Miss Polly. I'll tell of you. Miss Polly, these children locked me into the cellar.'

'Don't talk nonsense,' said Aunt Polly. 'You know there is no lock on the cellar door. The children have been for a walk – look at them just coming back to the house – how can you say they locked you in? You must be imagining things.'

'They locked me in,' said Joe sulkily, suddenly remembering that the inner cellar was his own secret place and that he had better not go into any details, or Aunt Polly would go down and discover the door he had so carefully hidden.

'I didn't lock him in, Aunt Polly,' said Philip earnestly.

'I've been ever so far away all morning.'

'So have I,' said Jack, quite truthfully. Aunt Polly believed them, and as she knew that the four children were always together, she imagined that the girls had been with them. So how could any of them have played a trick on Joe? And anyway, thought Aunt Polly, there *was* no lock on the door to the cellar, so what in the wide world did Joe mean? He really must be getting confused

'Go and do your work, Joe,' she said sharply. 'You always seem to have your knife into the children, accusing them of this and that. Leave them alone. They're good children.'

Joe thought otherwise. He gave one of his famous scowls, made an angry noise, beautifully copied by Kiki and returned to the kitchen.

'Don't take any notice of him,' said Aunt Polly. 'He's very bad-tempered, but he's quite harmless.'

The children went back into the house, winking at one another. It was nice to have Aunt Polly on their side. All the same, Joe was piling up grievances against them. They must look out.

'Funny,' thought Jack. 'Aunt Polly says Joe is quite harmless — and Bill Smugs says he's a dangerous fellow. One of them is certainly wrong.'

18

Off to the island again

What should be done next? Should they tell Bill Smugs of their adventure? Would he be angry because they had evaded their promise, without actually breaking it, and gone out to the island in someone else's boat? The children decided that he might be very angry. He had great ideas of honour and promises and keeping one's word.

'Well, so have we,' said Jack. 'I wouldn't have broken my

promise. I didn't. I just found a way round it.'

'Well, you know what grown-ups are,' said Dinah. 'They don't think the same way as we do. I expect when we grow up, we shall think like them — but let's hope we remember what it was like to think in the way children do, and understand the boys and girls that are growing up when *we're* men and women.'

'You're talking like a grown-up already,' said Philip in disgust. 'Stop it.'

'Don't talk to me like that,' flared Dinah. 'Just because I was talking a bit of sense.'

'Shut up,' said Philip, and got a box on the ear from Dinah immediately. He gave her a slap that sounded like a pistol-shot and she yelled.

'Beast!' she said. 'You know boys shouldn't hit girls.'

'I shouldn't hit ordinary decent girls, like Lucy-Ann,' said Philip. 'But you're just too bad-tempered for words. You ought to know by now that if you box my ears you'll get a jolly good slap. Serves you right.'

'Jack, tell him he's a beast,' said Dinah; but Jack couldn't help giving Dinah some advice.

'You should keep your hands to yourself,' he said to her. 'You're so quick at dishing out ear-boxes, and you ought to know by now that Philip won't stand for it.'

Lucy-Ann looked distressed. She hated these quarrels between the brother and sister. Philip put his hand into his pocket and pulled out a box in which he had kept an extraordinary tame beetle for days. Dinah knew he meant to open the box and put the beetle close to her. She gave a scream and rushed out of the room.

Philip put the box back into his pocket, after letting the enormous beetle have a run on the table. Wherever he held out his finger the beetle ran to it in delight. It really was amazing the way all creatures liked Philip.

'You oughtn't to keep it in a box,' said Lucy-Ann. 'I'm sure it hates it.'

'Well, watch then,' said Philip, and put the box out on the

115

table again. He opened it, took out the beetle, and put it at the other end of the big table. He put the box, with its lid a little way open, on to the middle of the table. The beetle, having explored the top of the table thoroughly, made its way to the box, examined it, and then climbed into it and settled down peacefully.

'There you are!' said Philip, shutting the box and putting it back into his pocket. 'It wouldn't go deliberately back into its box if it hated it, would it?'

'Well – it must be because it likes being with you,' said Lucy-Ann. 'Most beetles would hate it.'

'Philip is a friend to everything,' said Jack, with a grin. 'I believe he could train fleas and keep a circus of them.'

'I shouldn't like that,' said Lucy-Ann, looking disgusted. 'Oh dear, I wonder where Dinah has gone off to. I wish you wouldn't quarrel like this. We were having such a nice talk about what to do next.'

Dinah had left the room in a rage, her arm stinging from Philip's slap. She wandered down the passage that led to her uncle's room, thinking up horrid things to do to her brother. Suddenly her uncle's door opened and he peered out.

'Oh, Dinah – is that you? The ink pot here is empty,' he said, in a peevish voice. 'Why doesn't somebody fill it?'

'I'll get the ink bottle for you,' said Dinah, and went to get it from her aunt's cupboard. She took it to the study and filled her uncle's ink pot. As she turned to go, she noticed a map on a chair near by. It was the one that her uncle could not find before – the large one of the Isle of Gloom. The little girl looked at it with interest.

'Oh, Uncle – here's that map you told us about. Uncle, do tell me – used there to be mines on the island?'

'Now, where did you hear that?' said her uncle, astonished. 'That's old history. Yes, there used to be mines, hundreds of years ago. Copper-mines – rich ones too. But they were all worked out years ago. There's no copper there now.'

Dinah pored over the map. To her delight it showed

116

where the shafts were, that ran deep down into the earth. How the boys would like to see that map!

Her uncle turned to his work, forgetting all about Dinah. She picked up the map and slipped out of the room very quietly. How pleased Philip would be with the map!

She had forgotten all her anger. That was the best part about Dinah – she bore no malice, and her furies were soon over. She ran down the passage to the room where she had left the others. She flung open the door and burst in.

The others were amazed to see her smiling and excited face. Lucy-Ann could never get used to the quick changes in Dinah's moods. Philip looked at her doubtfully, not smiling.

Dinah remembered the quarrel. 'Oh,' she said, 'I'm sorry I boxed your ears, Philip. Look here – I've got that old map of the island. What do you think of that? And Uncle Jocelyn told me there *were* mines there, once – copper ones – very rich. But they are worked out now. So those shafts must once have led down to the mines.'

'Golly!' said Philip, taking the map from Dinah's hands and spreading it out. 'What a map! Oh, Dinah, you *are* clever!'

He gave his sister a squeeze and Dinah glowed. She quarrelled with her brother continually, but she loved getting a word of praise from him. The four children bent over the map.

'There's the gap in the rocks – as plain as anything,' said Dinah. The boys nodded.

'It must have always been there,' said Jack. 'I suppose that's the only way the old miners could use to go to and from the island. How thrilling to think of their boats going and coming – taking food there, bringing back copper! Golly, I'd like to go down and see what they are like.'

'Look, all the old shafts are marked,' said Philip, and he placed his finger on them. 'There's the one we must have found those tins near, Freckles, look! – and here's the stream. And now I know why it's green. It's coloured by the copper deposits still in the hills, I bet.'

117

'Well, perhaps there is still copper there then,' said Dinah, in great excitement. 'Copper nuggets! Oooh, I wish we could find some.'

'Copper is found in veins,' said Philip, 'but I think it's found whole, in nuggets too. They might be valuable. I say – shall we, just for a lark, go across to the island, go down to the mines, and hunt about a bit? Who knows, we *might* find nuggets of copper.'

'There won't be any,' said Jack. 'No one would leave a mine if there were still copper to be worked. It's been deserted for hundreds of years.'

'There's something stuck on to the back of the map,' said Lucy-Ann suddenly. The children turned it over, and saw a smaller map fastened to the larger one. They smoothed it out to look at it – and then Philip gave an exclamation.

'Of course! It's an underground map of the island – a map of the mines. Look at these passages and galleries and these draining-channels to take away water. Golly, part of these mines are below the level of the sea.'

It was weird to look at a map that showed the maze of tunnels under the surface of the island. There had evidently been a vast area mined, some of it under the sea itself.

'This section is right under the bed of the sea,' said Jack, pointing. 'How queer to work there, and know that all the time the sea is heaving above the rocky ceiling over your head!'

'I shouldn't like it,' said Lucy-Ann, shivering. 'I'd be afraid it would break through and flood where I was working.'

'Look here, we simply must go over to the island again,' said Philip excitedly. 'Do you know what I think? I think that people are working in those mines now.'

'Whatever makes you think that?' said Dinah.

'Well, those food tins,' said Philip. 'Someone eats food there, out of tins. And we couldn't see them anywhere, could we? So it must be that they were down in the mines, working. I bet you that's the solution of the mystery.'

'Let's go over to Bill and tell him all about it tomorrow, and take this map to show him,' said Dinah, thrilled. 'He will tell us what to do. I don't feel like exploring the mines by ourselves. I somehow feel I'd like Bill with us.'

'No,' said Jack suddenly. 'We won't tell Bill.'

The others looked at him in surprise.

'Why ever not?' demanded Dinah.

'Well – because I've suddenly got an idea,' said Jack. 'I believe it's a friend of Bill's – or friends – working in those mines. I believe Bill's come here to be near them – to take food over – and that sort of thing. I bet he uses his boat for that. It must be a secret, I should think. Well – he wouldn't be too pleased if we knew his secret. He'd never let us go out in his boat again.'

'But, Jack – you're exaggerating. Bill's only come for a holiday. He's bird-watching,' said Philip.

'He doesn't *really* do much bird-watching,' said Jack. 'And though he listens to me when I rave about the birds here, he doesn't talk much about them himself – not like I would if someone gave me the chance. And we don't know what his business is. He's never told us. I bet you anything you like that he and his friends are trying to work a copper-mine over on the island. I don't know who the mines belong to – if they *do* belong to anyone – but I guess if it was suspected that there was still copper there, the people who made the discovery would keep it secret on the chance of mining some good copper nuggets themselves.'

Jack paused, quite out of breath. Kiki murmured the new word she had heard.

'Copper, copper, copper. Spare a copper, copper, copper.'

'Isn't she clever?' said Lucy-Ann; but no one paid any attention to Kiki. The matters being discussed were far too important to be interrupted by a parrot.

'Let's ask Bill Smugs straight out,' suggested Dinah, who always liked to get things clear. She disliked mysteries that couldn't be solved.

119

'Don't be an ass,' said Philip. 'Jack's already told you why it would be best not to let Bill know we know his secret. Maybe he'll tell us himself one day – and won't he be surprised to know that we guessed it!'

'We'll go over in Joe's boat again soon,' said Jack. 'We'll go down that big shaft and explore a bit. We'll soon find out if anyone is there. We'll take this map with us so that we don't lose our way. It shows the underground passages and galleries very clearly.'

It was exciting to talk over these secrets. When could they go off to the island again? Should they take the girls this time – or not?

'Well, I think we shall manage even better this time,' said Philip. 'There wasn't much danger really last time, once we found the passage through the ring of rocks. I'm pretty certain we shall get to the island easily next time. We can take the girls as well.'

Dinah and Lucy-Ann were thrilled. They longed for a chance to go at once, but Joe did not leave Craggy-Tops long enough for them to take his boat. However, he went out in it himself two or three times.

'Are you going fishing?' asked Philip. 'Why don't you take us with you?'

'Not going to bother myself with children like you,' said the man, in his surly way, and set off in his boat. He sailed out such a long way that his boat disappeared into the haze that always seemed to hang about the western horizon.

'He may have gone to the island, for all we can see,' said Jack. 'He just disappears. I hope he brings some fish back for supper tonight.'

He did. His boat returned after tea and the children helped to take in a fine catch of fish. 'You might have taken us too, you mean thing,' said Dinah. 'We could have let lines down as well.'

The next day Joe departed to the town again, much to the children's joy. 'He's got the day off,' said Aunt Polly. 'You will have to do some of his jobs. You boys can pump up the water for the day.'

The boys went off to the well and let down the heavy bucket, unwinding the chain till the bucket reached the water. Jack peered over the edge.

'Just like one of those shafts over in the island,' he said. 'Wind up, wind up, Tufty – here goes!'

The children hurried over all the work that Aunt Polly set them to do. Then, making certain that the car was gone out of the garage, they begged a picnic lunch from Aunt Polly and raced down to Joe's boat.

They undid the rope and pushed off, the two boys rowing hard. As soon as they were out on the open sea, up went the sail. 'Off we go to the Isle of Gloom,' said Dinah, in delight. 'Gosh, I'm glad we're coming with you this time, Jack. It was hateful being left behind last time.'

'Did you bring the torches?' asked Philip of Lucy-Ann. She nodded. 'Yes. They're over there with the lunch.'

'We shall need them down the mines,' said Philip, with an air of excitement. What an adventure this was – to be going down old, old mines, where possibly men might be secretly hunting for copper. Philip shivered deliciously with excitement.

The sailing-boat, handled most expertly by the four children, went along well and they made very good time indeed. It did not seem to be very long before the island loomed up out of the usual haze.

'Hear the waves banging on the rocks?' said Jack. The girls nodded. This was the dangerous part. They hoped the boys would find the rock passage as easily as before, and go in safely.

'There's the big hill,' said Jack suddenly. 'Down with the sail. That's right – easy does it. Look out for that rope, Lucy-Ann. No, not that one – that's right.'

The sail was down. The boys took the oars and began to row cautiously towards the gap in the rocks. They knew where it was now. Into it they went, looking out for the rock that lay near the surface, ready to avoid it. It did scrape the bottom slightly and Lucy-Ann looked frightened. But soon they were in the calm moat of water that ran gleaming all round the island, between the shore and the ring of rocks.

Lucy-Ann heaved a sigh of relief. What with feeling a bit seasick and scared, she had gone quite pale. But now she recovered quickly as she saw the island itself so near.

They landed safely and pulled the boat up on to the shore. 'Now we make for the hills,' said Jack. 'My word, look at the thousands of birds again! I never in my life saw such a lot. If only I could see that Great Auk!'

'Perhaps I'll see one for you,' said Lucy-Ann, wishing with all her heart that she could. 'Philip, where's that green-coloured stream – and the pile of tins? Anywhere near here?'

'You'll see soon,' said Philip, striding ahead. 'We go through this little pass in the hills.'

Soon they could see the bright green stream running in the valley among the hills. Jack paused and took his bearings. 'Wait a bit. Where exactly was that big shaft?'

The girls had already exclaimed over the other holes in the ground, and the queer tumble-down erections beside them. 'There must have been some sort of shaft-head,' said Jack, considering. 'Now, where's that pile of tins? It was some-where near here. Oh – there's the shaft, girls!'

Everyone hurried to the big round hole and peered down it. There was no doubt but that the ladder leading down it was in very good condition. 'This is the shaft the men are using,' said Philip. 'It's the only one whose ladder is safe.'

'Don't talk too loudly,' said Jack, in a low voice. 'You don't know how sound might carry down this shaft.'

'Where are those tins you told us about?' said Lucy-Ann.

'Over there – by that rock,' said Philip, pointing. 'Go and see them if you want to.'

He shone his torch down the shaft, but could see very little. It looked rather sinister and forbidding. What was it like down there? Were there really men down there? The children mustn't be discovered by them – grown-ups were always angry when children poked their noses into matters that didn't concern them.

'Jack – I can't find the tins,' said Lucy-Ann. Philip made an impatient noise. He strode over to show them the pile.

Then he stopped in astonishment. The place under the rock was empty. There was nothing there at all. The tins had been removed.

'Look at that, Jack,' said Philip, forgetting to speak softly. 'All those tins have gone. Who took them? Well – that just *shows* there are people on this island – people who have been here since we last came too. I say – isn't this exciting!'

19

Down in the copper-mines

Lucy-Ann looked round her fearfully as if she half expected to see somebody hiding behind a rock.

'I don't like to think there may be people here we don't know anything about,' she said.

'Don't be silly,' said Jack. 'They're down in the mines. Shall we go down this shaft now, and see what we can discover?'

The girls didn't like the look of it, but Lucy-Ann felt that it would be worse to stay up above ground than it would be to go down and keep with the boys. So she said she would go, and Dinah, who wasn't going to be left all alone, promptly said she would go too.

Philip spread the map of the underground mines out on the ground, and they all knelt down and studied it. 'See – this shaft goes down to the centre of a perfect maze of passages and galleries,' said Philip. 'Shall we take this passage here? – it's a sort of main road, and leads to the mines that were worked right under the sea.'

'Oh no, don't let's go there,' said Lucy-Ann, in alarm. But the other three voted to go there, so the matter was decided.

'Now, Kiki, if you come with us, you are *not* to make a noise,' warned Jack. 'Else, if we go anywhere near the miners, they will hear you, and we shall be discovered. See?'

'Eena meena mina mo,' said Kiki solemnly, and scratched her poll hard.

'You're a silly bird,' said Jack. 'Now mind what I've told you – don't you dare to screech or shout.'

They went to the head of the shaft. They all peered down, feeling rather solemn. An adventure was exciting, but somehow this one seemed a bit frightening, all of a sudden.

'Come on,' said Philip, beginning to go down the ladder. 'Nothing can happen to us really, even if we *are* discovered. After all, we first came to this island to see if we could find a Great Auk for Freckles. Even if we were caught we could say that we'd keep our mouths shut. If the men are friends of Bill Smugs, they must be decent fellows. We can always say we are his friends.'

They all began to climb down the long, long shaft. Before they were halfway down they wished they had never begun their descent. They had not guessed they would have to go so far. It was like climbing down to the middle of the earth, down, down, down in the darkness, which was lit now by the beams from four torch lights.

'Everyone all right?' asked Philip, rather anxiously. 'I should think we must be near the bottom now.'

'My arms are terribly tired,' said poor Lucy-Ann, who was not so strong as the others. Dinah was as big and strong as any boy, but Lucy-Ann was not.

'Stop a little and rest,' said Jack. 'Golly, Kiki feels heavy on my shoulder. That's because my arms are a bit tired too, I expect, with holding on to the ladder-rungs.'

They rested a little and then went on downwards. Then Philip gave a low exclamation.

'I say! I'm at the bottom!'

With great thankfulness the others joined him. Lucy-Ann

promptly sat down on the ground, for her knees were aching now, as well as her arms. Philip flashed his torch around.

They were in a fairly wide passage. The walls and ceiling were of rock, gleaming a coppery colour in the light of the torches. From the main passage branched many galleries or smaller passages.

'We'll do as we said and keep to this main passage, which looks like a sort of main road of the mines,' said Philip.

Jack flashed his torch down a smaller passage. 'Look!' he said. 'The roof has fallen in there. We couldn't go down that way if we wanted to.'

'Golly, I hope the roof of *this* passage won't fall in on top of us,' said Lucy-Ann, looking up at it in alarm. In places it was propped up by big timbers, but mostly it was of hard rock.

'Come on – we're safe enough,' said Jack impatiently. 'I say – isn't it thrilling to be hundreds of feet below the earth, down in a copper mine as old as the hills!'

'It's funny that the air is quite good here, isn't it?' said Dinah, remembering the musty-smelling air in the secret passage at Craggy-Tops.

'There must be good airways in these mines,' said Philip, trying to remember how the airways in coal mines worked. 'That's one of the first things that men think about when they begin to work mines underground – how to get draughts of air moving down the tunnels they make – and channels to drain off any water that might collect and flood the mine.'

'I'd hate to work in a mine,' said Lucy-Ann, shivering. 'Philip, are we under the sea yet?'

'Not yet,' said Philip. 'About halfway there, I should think. Hallo, here's a well-worked piece – quite a big cave!'

The passage suddenly opened out into a vast open cave that showed many signs of being worked by men. Marks of tools stood out here and there in the rock, and Jack, with a delighted exclamation, darted to a corner and picked up

125

what looked like a small hammer-top made of bronze.

'Look,' he said proudly to the others. 'This must be part of a broken tool used by the ancient miners – it's made of bronze – a mixture of copper and tin. My word, won't the boys at school envy me this!'

That made the others look around eagerly as well, and Lucy-Ann made a discovery that interested everybody very much. It was not an ancient bronze tool – it was a stub of pencil, bright yellow in colour.

'Do you know who this belongs to?' said Lucy-Ann, her green eyes gleaming in the torchlight like a cat's. 'It belongs to Bill Smugs. I saw him writing notes with it the other day. I know it's Bill's.'

'Then he must have been down here and dropped it by accident,' said Philip, thrilled. 'Golly, our guess was right then! He's no bird-watcher – he's living on the coast with his car and his boat because he's friends with the men working this old mine, and brings them food and stuff. Artful old Bill – he never told us a word about it.'

'Well, you don't go blabbing everything out to children you meet,' said Dinah. 'Well, well – how surprised he would be if he knew we knew his secret! I wonder if he's down here now?'

''Course not, silly,' said Philip, at once. 'His boat wasn't on the shore, was it? And there's no other way of getting here except by boat.'

'I forgot that,' said Dinah. 'Anyway – I don't feel afraid of meeting the secret miners now that we know they are friends of Bill's. All the same, we won't let them know we're here if we can help it. They might think that children couldn't be trusted, and be rather cross about it.'

They examined the big cave closely. The ceiling was propped up with big old timbers, some of them broken now, so that the roof was gradually falling in. A number of hewn out steps led to a cave above, but the roof of that had fallen in and the children could not get into it.

'Do you know what I think?' said Jack suddenly, stopping

to face the others behind him, as they examined the cave. 'I believe that light I saw out to sea the other night *wasn't* from a ship at all – it was from this island. The miners were giving a signal to say that they had finished their food and wanted more – and the light from the cliff was flashed by Bill to say he was bringing more.'

'Yes – but the light came from *our* cliff, not from Bill's cliff,' objected Philip.

'I know – but you know jolly well that it's only from the highest part of the cliff that anyone signalling from the cove side of the island could be seen,' said Jack. 'If somebody stood on that hill in the middle of the island and made a bonfire or waved a powerful lamp, it could only be seen from our cliff, and not from Bill's. So Bill must have gone to our cliff that night and answered the signal.'

'I believe you're right,' said Philip. 'Old Bill must have been wandering about that night, behind Craggy-Tops – and you saw his signalling light and so did Joe. No wonder old Joe says there are "things" wandering about at night and is scared of them! He must often have heard Bill and seen lights, and not known what they were.'

'I expect Bill went off to the island in his boat, as soon as he could, with fresh food,' said Jack. 'And he took away the pile of old tins. That explains why it is they are gone. Artful old Bill! What a fine secret he has – and we are the only people who know it!'

'I do wish we could tell him we know it,' said Lucy-Ann. 'I don't see why we can't. I'm sure he'd rather know that we knew it.'

'Well – we could sort of say a few things that will make him guess we know it, perhaps,' said Philip. 'Then if he guesses, he'll own up, and we'll have a good talk about the mines, and Bill will tell us all kinds of exciting things.'

'Yes, that's what we'll do,' said Jack. 'Come on – let's explore a bit further. I feel as if I know this cave by heart.'

The passage swerved suddenly to the left after a bit, and Philip's heart gave a thump. He knew, by the map, that when the main passage swerved left, they were going under the sea-bed itself. It was somehow very thrilling to be walking under the deep sea.

'What's that funny noise?' asked Dinah. They all listened. There was a curious, far-off booming noise that never stopped.

'Miners with machines?' said Philip. Then he suddenly knew what it was. 'No – it's the sea booming away above our heads! That's what it is!'

So it was. The children stood and listened to the muffled, faraway noise. Boom-boooom, boom. That was the sea, moving restlessly over the rocky bed, maybe pounding over rocks in its way, talking with its continual, rhythmical voice.

'It's funny to be under the sea itself,' said Lucy-Ann, half frightened. She shivered. It was so dark, and the noise was so strange.

'Isn't it awfully warm down here?' she said, and the others agreed with her. It certainly was hot down in the old copper mines.

They went on their way down the passage, keeping to the main one, and avoiding all the many galleries that spread out continually sideways, which probably led to other workings of the big mines.

'If we don't keep to this main road, we'll lose ourselves,' said Philip, and Lucy-Ann gave a gasp. It had not occurred to her that they might get lost. How awful to go wandering about miles of mine-workings, and never find the shaft that led them upwards!

They came to a place where, quite suddenly, a brilliant light shone. The children had rounded a corner, noticing, as they came to it, that a glimmer of light seemed to show there. As they turned the corner of the passage they came into a cave lighted by a powerful lamp. They stopped in the greatest surprise.

Then a noise came to their ears – a queer noise, not the muffled boom of the sea, but a clattering noise that they

128

couldn't recognise – then a bang, then a clattering noise again.

'We've found where the miners work,' said Jack, in an excited whisper. 'Keep back a bit. We may see them – but we don't want them to see us!'

20

Prisoners underground

The children huddled against the wall, trying to see what was in the cave before them, blinking their eyes in the brilliant light.

There were boxes and crates in the cave, but nothing else. No man was there. But in the near distance was somebody at work, making that queer clattering, banging noise.

'Let's go back,' said Lucy-Ann, frightened.

'No. But look – there's a passage going off just here,' whispered Philip, flashing his torch into a dark tunnel near by. 'We'll creep down there and see if we come across the miners working somewhere near.'

So they all crept down the tunnel. As they went down it, pressing themselves closely against the rocky sides, a rock fell from the roof. It gave Kiki such a fright that she gave a squawk and flew off Jack's shoulder.

'Here, Kiki!' said Jack, afraid of losing her. But Kiki did not come back to his shoulder. The boy stumbled back up the passage to look for her, whistling softly in the way he did when he wanted to call her to him. The others did not realise that he was no longer with them, but went on down the tunnel, slowly and painfully.

And then things happened very quickly. Someone came swiftly up the tunnel with a lantern, whose light picked out the three children at once. They cowered back against the wall and tried not to be dazzled by the lantern. The man carrying it paused in the greatest astonishment.

'Well,' he said, in a deep, rather hoarse voice. 'Well – if this doesn't beat everything!' He held his lantern up high to see the children more clearly. Then he called over his shoulder.

'Jake! Come and take a look-see here. I've got something here that'll make your eyes drop out.'

Another man came swiftly up, tall and dark in the shadows. He gave a loud exclamation as he saw the three children.

'Well, what do you think of that!' he said. 'Children! How did *they* come here? Are they real? Or am I dreaming?'

'It's children all right,' said the first man. He spoke to the three, and his voice was rough and harsh.

'What are you doing here? Who are you with?'

'We're by ourselves,' said Philip.

The man laughed loudly. 'Oh no, you're not. It's no good spinning that kind of tale to us. Who brought you here, and why?'

'We came ourselves in a boat,' said Lucy-Ann indignantly. 'We know the gap in the rocks, and we came to see the island.'

'Why did you come down here?' demanded Jake, coming nearer. Now the children could see what he was like, and they didn't like the look of him at all. He had a black patch over one eye, and the other eye gleamed wickedly at them. His mouth was so tight-lipped that it almost seemed as if he had no lips at all. Lucy-Ann cowered away.

'Go on – why did you come down here?' demanded Jake.

'Well – we found the shaft hole – and we climbed down to see the old mines,' said Philip. 'We shan't split on you, don't be afraid.'

'Split on us? What do you mean? What do you know, boy?' asked Jake roughly.

Philip said nothing. He didn't really know what to say. Jake nodded his head to the first man, who went behind the children. Now they could not go forward or backward to escape.

Lucy-Ann began to cry. Philip put his arm round her, and wondered, for the first time, where Jack was. Lucy-Ann looked round for him too. She began to cry more loudly when she saw he was not there.

'Lucy-Ann, don't tell these men that Jack is gone,' whispered Philip. 'If they take us prisoner, Jack will be able to escape and bring help. So don't say a word about him.'

'What are you whispering about?' asked Jake. 'Now, look here, my boy – you don't want any harm to come to your sisters, do you? Well – you just tell us what you know, and maybe we'll let you go.'

Philip was alarmed at the man's tone. For the first time it dawned on the boy that there might be danger. These men were fierce – they wouldn't let three children share their secrets willingly. Suppose they kept them prisoner underground – starved them – beat them? Who knew what might happen? Philip made up his mind to tell a little of what he guessed.

'Look here,' he said to Jake, 'we know who you are working with, see? And he's a friend of ours. He'll be mighty angry if you do us any harm.'

'Oh, really!' said Jake, in a mocking tone. 'And who is this wonderful friend of yours?'

'Bill Smugs,' said Philip, feeling certain that everything would be all right at the mention of Bill's name.

'Bill Smugs?' said the man, with a jeering note in his voice. 'And who may *he* be? I've never heard of him in my life.'

'But you must have,' said Philip desperately. 'He brings you food, and signals to you. You know he does. You *must* know Bill Smugs and his boat, *The Albatross*.'

The two men stared intently at the children. Then they spoke together quickly in a foreign language. They seemed puzzled.

'Bill Smugs is no friend of ours,' Jake said, after a pause. 'Did he tell you that he knew us?'

'Oh no,' said Philip. 'We only guessed it.'

'Then you guessed wrong,' said the man. 'Come along – we're going to make you comfortable somewhere till we decide what to do with children who poke their noses into things that don't concern them.'

Philip guessed that they were going to be kept prisoners somewhere underground, and he was alarmed and angry. The girls were frightened. Dinah didn't cry, but Lucy-Ann, forlorn because Jack was not by her, cried without stopping.

Jake prodded Philip to make him go along in front of him. He turned the children off into a narrow passage running at right angles from the tunnel they were in. A door was set across this passage and Jake unbolted it. He pushed the children inside the cave there, which looked almost like a small room, for it had benches and a small table. Jake set his lantern down on the table.

'You'll be safe here,' he said, with a horrid crooked grin. 'Quite safe. I shan't starve you, don't be afraid of that.'

The children were left alone. They heard the door bolted firmly and footsteps dying away. Lucy-Ann still wept.

'What a bit of bad luck!' said Philip, trying to speak cheerfully. 'Don't cry, Lucy-Ann.'

'Why didn't those men know Bill Smugs?' said Dinah, puzzled. 'We know he must bring them food, and probably take away the copper they mine.'

'Easy to guess,' said Philip gloomily. 'I bet old Bill gave us a wrong name. It sounds pretty peculiar, anyway – Bill *Smugs* – I never heard a name like that before, now I come to think of it.'

'Oh – you think it isn't his real name?' said Dinah. 'So of course those men don't know it. Dash! If only we knew his real name, everything would be all right.'

'What are we going to do?' wept Lucy-Ann. 'I don't like being a prisoner in a copper mine under the sea. It's horrid.'

'But it's a very thrilling adventure, Lucy-Ann,' said Philip, trying to comfort her.

'I don't like a thrilling adventure when I'm in the middle

of it,' wept Lucy-Ann. Neither did the others, very much. Philip wondered about Jack.

'What can have happened to him?' he said. 'I hope he's safe. He'll be able to rescue us if he is.'

But at that moment Jack was anything but safe. He had wandered up the tunnel looking for Kiki, had turned into another passage, found Kiki, turned to go back – and then had lost his way. He had no idea that the others had been caught. Kiki was on his shoulder, talking softly to herself.

Philip had the map, not Jack. So, once the boy had lost his way, he had no means of discovering how to get back to the main passage. He turned into one tunnel after another, found some of them blocked, turned back, and began wandering helplessly here and there.

'Kiki, we're lost,' said Jack. He shouted again and again, as loudly as he could, and his voice went echoing through the ancient tunnels very weirdly, coming back to him time and time again. Kiki screeched too, but there was no answering call.

The children shut up in the cell-like cave fell silent after a time. There was nothing to do, nothing to say. Lucy-Ann put her head down on her arms, which she rested on the table, and fell fast asleep, tired out. Dinah and Philip stretched themselves out on the benches and tried to sleep too. But they couldn't.

'Philip, we'll just *have* to escape from here,' said Dinah desperately.

'Easy to say that,' said Philip sarcastically. 'Not so easy to do. How would you suggest that we escape from a cave set deep in a copper mine under the sea, a cave which has a stout wooden door to it well bolted on the outside? Don't be foolish.'

'I've got an idea, Philip,' said Dinah at last. Philip grunted. Dinah's ideas were rather farfetched as a rule.

'Now, do listen, Philip,' said Dinah earnestly. 'It's quite a good idea.'

'What is it?' said Philip grumpily.

'Well, Jake or that other man will be sure to come back here sooner or later with food,' began Dinah. 'And when he comes, let's all be gasping and holding our breaths and groaning.'

'Whatever for?' asked Philip in astonishment.

'So as to make him think the air is very bad in here, and we can't breathe, and we're almost dying,' said Dinah. 'Then maybe he'll let us go out into the passage for a breath of air – and you can reel towards him, kick out his light – and we'll all escape as quickly as we can.'

Philip sat up and looked at his sister with admiration. 'I really do think you've got an idea there,' he said, and Dinah glowed with pleasure. 'Yes, I really do. We'll have to wake Lucy-Ann and tell her. She must play her part too.'

So Lucy-Ann was awakened and told the plan. She thought it was very good. She began to gasp and hold her head and moan in a most realistic way. Philip nodded his head.

'That's fine,' he said. 'We'll all do that when we hear Jake or the other fellow coming. Now, whilst there's still time, I'd better find where we are on the underground map, and see exactly what direction to take as soon as we've kicked the man's light out.'

He spread the map out on the table and studied it. 'Yes,' he said at last. 'I see where we are. There's the big cave that was lighted up – see? And the little passage off it where we were caught – and here's the passage we were taken down – and here's the little cave we're in now. Now, listen, girls – as soon as I've kicked out the man's light, take my hand and keep close by me. I'll lead you the right way, and find the shaft-hole again. Then up we'll go, join up with old Jack somewhere and get to the boat.'

'Good,' said Dinah, thrilled – and at that very moment they heard footsteps coming to the wooden door.

21

Escape – but what about Jack?

The bolts were shot back. The door opened and Jake appeared, carrying a tin plate of biscuits, and a big open tin of sardines. He also put on the table a jug of water.

Then he stared in amazement at the three children. Philip seemed to be choking, and he rolled off his bench on the floor. Dinah was making the most extraordinary noises, and holding her head tightly in her hands. Lucy-Ann appeared to be on the point of being sick, and made the most alarming groans.

'What's up?' asked Jake.

'Air! We want air!' gasped Philip. 'We're choking! Air! Air!'

Dinah rolled on to the ground as well. Jake pulled her up and hustled her to the door. He pushed the others out into the passage. He thought they must really be on the point of choking – the air in the cell must be used up.

Philip watched his chance and reeled towards Jake as if he could not stand straight. As he came towards him he lifted his right foot, and aimed a mighty kick at the lantern in Jake's hand. It fell and smashed at once, and the light went out. There was a tinkling of glass, a shout from Jake – and then Philip sought for the hands of the two frightened girls. He found them and pushed the two hurriedly in front of him towards a passage on the left. Jake, left in the darkness, began to grope about, shouting for the other man.

'Olly! Hi, Olly! Bring a lamp! Quick! These dratted kids have fooled me. Hi, *Olly!*'

Philip, trying hard to keep his sense of direction correct, hurried the girls along. Their hearts were beating painfully, and Lucy-Ann really did feel as if she was going to choke now. Soon they had left Jake's shouts behind and were in the wide main passage down which they had come not many hours before. Philip was now using his torch, and it was pleasant to see the thin, bright beam of light.

'Thank goodness – we're in the right tunnel,' said Philip, pausing to listen. He could hear nothing but the boom of the sea far above their heads. He swung his torch around. Yes – they were on the right road. Good!

'Can we have a little rest?' panted Lucy-Ann.

'No,' said Philip. 'Those men will be after us almost at once – as soon as they get another lamp. They will guess we are making for the shaft. Come on. There's no time to be lost.'

The children hurried on again – but after a time, to their great dismay, they heard shouts behind them. That meant that the men were after them – and what was more, were catching them up. Lucy-Ann felt so alarmed that she could hardly run.

They came at last to the big shaft-hole. It was so deep that the children could not see the entrance to it, far above. The daylight was not to be seen.

'Up you go,' said Philip anxiously. 'You first, Lucy-Ann. Be as quick as you can.'

Lucy-Ann began to climb. Dinah followed her, Philip came last. He could hear the men's voices even more clearly now. And then – quite suddenly, they stopped, and Philip could hear them no more. What had happened?

An extraordinary thing had happened. Kiki the parrot, hearing the tumult in the distance, had become excited and was shouting. She and Jack were still wandering about, quite lost, in the maze of passages and galleries. Kiki's sharp ears heard the men and she began to screech and yell.

'Wipe your feet! Shut the door! Hi, hi, hi, Polly put the kettle on!'

The men heard the shouting voice and thought it belonged to the children. 'They've lost themselves,' said Jake, stopping. 'They don't know the way back to the shaft. They're lost and are shouting for help.'

'Let them shout,' said Olly sourly. 'They'll never find the way to the shaft. I told you they wouldn't. Let them get lost and starve.'

'No,' said Jake. 'We can't do that. We don't want to have to explain half-starving children to search-parties, do we? We'd better go and get them. They are over in that direction.'

They went off the main passage, meaning to try and find the children where the shouts had come from. Kiki's voice came again to them. 'Wipe your feet, idiot, wipe your feet!'

This astonished the two men. They went on towards the voice, but even as they went, Jack and Kiki wandered into a passage that the two men missed. Kiki fell silent, and the men paused.

'Can't hear them any more,' said Jake. 'Better go to the shaft. They may have found their way there after all. We can't afford to let them escape till we've decided what to do about all this.'

So they retraced their steps to the shaft, and looked up it. A shower of stones came down and hit them.

'Gosh! The children *are* up there!' cried Jake, and started up the ladder at once.

The children were almost at the top. Lucy-Ann felt as if her arms and legs could not climb one more rung – but they held out, and at last the tired girl reached the top, climbed out, and rolled over on the ground, exhausted. Dinah came next, and sat down with a long sigh. And then Philip, tired too, but determined not to rest for one moment.

'I'm sure those men will come up the shaft after us,' he said. 'We haven't a minute to lose. Do come on, girls. We must get to the boat and be off before anyone stops us.'

It was getting dark. What a long time they must have been underground! Philip dragged the girls to their feet and they set off to the shore. The boat was there, thank goodness.

'I don't want to go without Jack,' said Lucy-Ann obstinately, her heart wrung with anxiety for her beloved brother. But Philip bundled her into the boat at once.

'No time to lose,' he said. 'Come on. We'll send help back for Jack as soon as ever we can. I can't bear leaving him behind either – but I've got to get you girls away safely.'

Dinah took one pair of oars and Philip the other. Soon the two were rowing the boat away quickly, across the calm channel of water to where, in the distance, the waves thundered over the reef of rocks. Philip felt anxious. It was one thing to get through the gap safely when he could see where he was going, but quite another when it was almost dark.

He heard shouting, but he was too far away from the shore to see the men there. Jake and Olly had climbed up the shaft, raced over the island to the shore, and were looking for a boat. But there was none. The tide was coming in and there was not even a mark on the sand to show where the boat had rested. In fact, it had been almost afloat when the children had got in, and it was lucky that it had not floated away.

'No boat here,' said Olly. 'How did those kids come? It's strange. They *must* have escaped by boat. They can't still be underground. We'd better signal tonight and get someone over here. We must warn them that kids have found us underground.'

They went back to the shaft and climbed down it, not knowing that one of the children was still wandering about in the mines. Poor Jack was still making his way down a maze of tunnels, all looking exactly alike to him.

In the meantime Philip, Lucy-Ann and Dinah had, by great good luck, just struck the gap in the rocks. It was really because of Lucy-Ann's sharp ears that they had been so lucky. She had listened to the pounding of the water over the rocks, and her ears had noticed a softening of the thunder. 'That's where the gap must be,' she thought. 'The noise dies away a little there.' So, sitting at the tiller, she tried to guide the boat to where she guessed the gap to be, and by good chance she found it. The boat slipped through, scraping its keel once more on the rock just below the surface – and then it was in the open sea, rocking up and down.

How Philip put up the sail in the half darkness, and sailed the boat home, he never quite knew. He was desperate; they must get back safely, so with great courage he went about his task. When at last he reached the mooring-place, under the cliff, he could not get out of the boat. Quite suddenly his knees seemed to give way, and he could not walk.

'I'll have to wait a minute or two,' he said to Dinah. 'My legs have gone funny. I'll be all right soon.'

'You've been awfully clever,' said Dinah, and from her those words meant a lot.

They tied up the boat at last and went up to the house. Aunt Polly met them at the door, in a great state of alarm.

'Wherever have you been? I've been so worried about you. I've been nearly off my head with anxiety. I really feel faint.'

She looked very white and ill. Even as she spoke, she tottered a little, and Philip bounded forward and caught her as she fell.

'Poor Aunt Polly,' he said, dragging her indoors as gently as he could and putting her on the sofa. 'We're so sorry we upset you. I'll get some water – no, Dinah, you get some.'

Soon Aunt Polly said she felt a little better, but it was quite plain that she was ill. 'She never could stand any worry of this sort,' Dinah said to Lucy-Ann. 'Once Philip nearly fell down the cliff, she was ill for days. It seems to make her heart bad. I'll get her to bed.'

'Don't say a word about Jack being missing,' Philip warned Dinah in a low voice. 'That really will give her a heart attack.'

Dinah went off upstairs with her aunt, supporting her as firmly as she could. Philip went to look for Joe. He wasn't back yet. Good! Then he wouldn't have missed the boat. He looked at Lucy-Ann's white little face, its green tired eyes and worried expression. He felt sorry for her.

'What are we going to do about Jack?' said Lucy-Ann, with a gulp. 'We've got to rescue him, Philip.'

'I know,' said Philip. 'Well – we can't tell Aunt Polly – and

Uncle Jocelyn wouldn't be any good – and we'd be idiots to tell Joe. So there is no one left but Bill, I'm afraid.'

'But – you said we'd better not tell Bill we knew his secret,' said Lucy-Ann.

'I know. But we've got to, now that Jack is alone on the island,' said Philip. 'Bill will have to go and tell those fierce friends of his that Jack is a pal, and he'll find him and bring him back safely. So don't worry, Lucy-Ann.'

'Will you go and tell him now, straight away?' asked Lucy-Ann tearfully.

'I'll go just as soon as ever I've had something to eat,' said Philip, suddenly feeling so hungry that he felt he could eat a whole loaf, a pound of butter, and a jar of jam. 'You'd better have something too, Lucy-Ann – you look as white as a sheet. Cheer up! Jack will soon be safe here, and we'll all be laughing and talking like anything.'

Dinah came down then, and set about getting some food. They were all very hungry, even Lucy-Ann. Dinah agreed that the only thing to do was to go to Bill Smugs and get him to go and rescue Jack before the men found him.

'They'll be so wild that we've escaped that they may be really tough with Jack,' said Dinah, and then wished she hadn't spoken the words, for Lucy-Ann looked scared to death.

'Please go, Philip,' begged the little girl. 'Go now. If you don't, I shall.'

'Don't be silly,' said Philip, getting up. 'You don't want to make your way across the cliff on a dark night. You'd fall over the edge! Well – so long! I'll be back.'

Off went the boy, climbing the steep path to the top of the cliff. Then he set off to find Bill. He saw the lights of Joe's car in the distance, coming home, and heard the noise of the engine. He hurried so that he would not be seen.

'Bill *will* be surprised to see me,' he thought. 'He'll wonder whoever it is, knocking at his door in the middle of the night.'

But alas – Bill wasn't there when Philip at last arrived at the shack. *Now* what was he to do?

22

A talk with Bill – and a shock

Philip was filled with dismay. It had never occurred to him that Bill might not be at home. How awful! Philip sat down on a stool and tried to think – but he was tired out, and his brain wouldn't seem to work.

'What shall I do now? What shall I do now?' he thought, and could not seem to think of anything else. 'What shall I do now?'

It was dark in the little shack. Philip sat on the stool, his hands hanging limply between his legs. Then he became aware of something at the back of the shack, and he turned to see what it was.

To his great amazement he saw a red light there, glowing deeply. Then it disappeared. Then it came back again, went out, reappeared. It went on doing this for a few minutes, whilst Philip tried to think what it was, and why it seemed to be signalling. At last he got up and went over to the light. It came from a small bulb beside the radio. Philip had a look at it. He twiddled one or two knobs. A Morse code came from it when he twiddled another. Then by chance he saw, at the back of the set, a small telephone receiver, smaller than any he had seen before – almost a pocket size, he thought.

He picked it up – and immediately he heard a voice crackling in the receiver. He lifted it to his ear

'Y2 calling,' said the voice. 'Y2. Y2 calling.'

Philip listened in, astonished. He decided to speak to the voice.

'Hallo!' he said. 'Who are you?'

There was a moment's silence. Evidently Y2, whoever he might be, was surprised. A cautious voice came over the phone again.

'Who is there?'

'A boy called Philip Mannering,' said Philip. 'I came to find Bill Smugs, but he isn't here.'

'Who did you say?' said the voice.

'Bill Smugs. But he's not here,' repeated Philip. 'I say, who are you? Do you want me to leave a message for Bill? I expect he'll be back some time.'

'How long has he been gone?' asked Y2.

'Don't know,' said Philip. 'Wait – I can hear someone. Here he comes, I do believe.'

Joyfully the boy put down the tiny telephone receiver. He had heard the low sound of whistling outside, and footsteps. It must be Bill.

It was. He came in, shining his torch – and he was so surprised when he saw Philip there that he stood stockstill without saying a word.

'Oh, Bill!' said Philip joyfully. 'I'm so glad you've come. Quick! – somebody wants you on the phone – Y2 he says he is.'

'Did you speak to him?' said Bill, his voice sounding astonished. He picked up the tiny phone and spoke curtly.

'Is that Y2? L4 speaking.'

The voice evidently asked him who Philip was.

'Boy that lives round here,' said Bill. 'What's the news, please?'

Then all that was said by Bill was 'Yes. Of course. I'll let you know. Thanks. No, nothing yet. Goodbye.'

He turned to Philip when he had finished talking. 'Look here, my boy,' he said, 'please understand that if you come paying calls here when I am out, you must on no account tamper with my possessions or meddle with my affairs.'

Bill had never spoken so sternly before, and Philip's heart sank. What would Bill say when he knew that the children had guessed his secret? He would think they had been

142

meddling more than ever.

'Sorry, Bill,' he said awkwardly. 'I didn't mean to interfere at all.'

'Why have you come at this time of night?' asked Bill.

'Bill — is this your pencil?' asked Philip, taking it out. He hoped that when Bill saw it he would remember that he had dropped it down in the copper mines, and would guess, without Philip saying any more, that the children knew his secret. Bill stared at the yellow pencil stub.

'Yes, that's mine,' he said. 'But you didn't come here at night to give me back my pencil. What have you come for?'

'Oh, Bill — don't be so cross,' said poor Philip. 'You see — we know your secret. We know what you are doing here. We know why you go to the island — we know everything.'

Bill listened to all this as if he simply could not believe his ears. He stared at Philip in the utmost amazement. His eyes grew narrow, and his mouth hardened into a thin line. For a moment he looked very frightening.

'You are going to tell me exactly what you mean by all this,' said Bill, in a horrid sort of voice. 'What *is* my secret? What is the "everything" that you know?'

'Well,' said Philip desperately, 'we know that you and your friends are trying to work the copper mines again — and we know that you are here, with your boat and your car, to provide them with food — and to take away any copper they find. We know you've been down the mines, visiting the men there. We know you've given us a false name. But, please, Bill, we wouldn't dream of giving you away — we hope you'll get lots of copper.'

Bill listened, his eyes still narrow — but as Philip went on talking, the twinkle came back into them, and his mouth looked like Bill's again.

'Well, well, well — so you know all that,' said Bill. 'And what else to you know? How did *you* get to the island? Not in my boat, I hope?'

'Oh no,' said Philip, relieved to see Bill looking friendly again. 'We took Joe's when he was out. We went right down

143

into the mines, too – that was where we found your pencil. But we don't like your friends there, Bill. They took us prisoner – they're horrid – and even when we mentioned your name to them and said we were friends of yours, they said they didn't know it and wouldn't let us go free.'

'You told them you knew Bill Smugs?' said Bill. Philip nodded.

'What men did you see?' asked Bill. His voice had become sharp again, and he snapped out his questions in rather a frightening manner.

'Two – one call Jake and one Olly,' said Philip. Bill made a note in his notebook. 'What were they like?' he asked sharply.

'Well – but you must know them,' said Philip in astonishment. 'Anyway, I couldn't really see much – either it was dark – or the light dazzled me. I just saw that Jake was tall and dark, with a patch over one eye, that's all. But you must know what they are like yourself, Bill.'

'See anyone or anything else?' asked Bill.

Philip shook his head. 'No. We heard other miners at work, though – a terrific clattering, banging sort of noise, you know – they must have found some part of the mine that was still rich in copper. Bill, are you finding much copper there? Will it make you rich?'

'Look here, you didn't come here tonight to tell me all this,' said Bill suddenly. 'What *did* you come for?'

'I came to say that although Dinah and Lucy-Ann and I managed to fool Jake and get away – we had to leave Jack behind – with Kiki,' said Philip. 'And we are worried about him. You see, he might get lost for ever in those workings under the sea – or those friends of yours might find him and ill-treat him because they are angry at our tricking them as we did.'

'Jack's still there – on the island – in the mines!' said Bill, looking quite shocked. 'Good heavens! This is serious. Why didn't you tell me that at first? My word, it looks as if everything's going to be ruined by you kids.'

Bill looked angry and upset. He went to his radio, fiddled about with the knobs, and then, to Philip's amazement, began to talk in short, sharp tones, in a language the boy did not know.

'It's a transmitter as well as receiving set,' thought Philip. 'This is all very mysterious. Who is Bill talking to now? Have they all got a boss who is directing this copper mine affair? I suppose there's very big money in it. Oh dear, I hope we haven't really ruined things for them. What does Bill mean? How could we have spoilt anything? He's only got to go over to the island, see his friends, tell them to set Jack free, and that would finish it. He might know he can trust us not to split on him.'

Bill turned round. 'We must get the boat at once,' he said. 'Come on.'

With their torches throwing beams of light before them they went down to where the boat was kept. Bill began to push it out – and then he suddenly gave such a shout that Philip's heart nearly jumped out of his body.

'Who's done that?'

Bill shone his torch into the boat – and Philip saw, with a shock of dismay and fear, that someone had chopped viciously at the bottom of the boat – chopped so hard that there were holes there through which the water was even now pouring.

Bill pulled her back on the beach again, his face very grim. 'Do you know anything about that?' he asked Philip.

'Of course not,' said the boy. 'Golly – who did it, Bill? This is awful.'

'Well – the boat is no use at all till she's repaired,' said Bill. 'But somehow we've got to get over to the Isle of Gloom. We'll have to take Joe's boat. Come on. But mind – he mustn't know a thing about it. There's too much known about everything already – and too many people nosing about for my liking.'

They set off over the cliffs, poor Philip so tired that he could hardly keep up with Bill. They came to Craggy-Tops, climbed down the cliff path and made their way to where Joe's boat was always tied.

But, to their intense surprise and despair, Joe's boat was not there. It was gone.

23

Another secret passage

After Philip had left, Lucy-Ann and Dinah tried to settle down to some sewing. But Lucy-Ann's hands trembled so much that she kept pricking her finger.

'I'd better go and tell Uncle Jocelyn that Aunt Polly has gone to bed, feeling ill,' said Dinah. 'Come with me, Lucy-Ann.'

The two girls went off to the study and knocked at the door. They went in, and Dinah told her uncle about her aunt. He nodded, hardly seeming to hear.

'Uncle Jocelyn,' said Dinah, 'have you any more maps of the Isle of Gloom? Or any books about it?'

'No,' said her uncle. 'But wait – there's a book about this house, Craggy-Tops, I think. You know that it was a great place for illegal goings-on and secret doings two or three hundred years ago? I believe there was a secret passage to it from the beach.'

'Yes, there is,' said Dinah. 'We know it.'

Her uncle became quite excited. He made her tell him all about it. 'Dear me,' he said, 'I thought it had fallen in long ago. But these secret passages hewn out of the rock last for years. Still, I should think the one that goes under the sea to the Isle of Gloom has been flooded long since.'

The two girls stared at the old man in amazement. Dinah found her tongue at last.

'Uncle Jocelyn, do you mean to say there was *another*

secret passage here – under the sea to the island? Why, it's ever so far away!'

'Well, there was supposed to be,' said her uncle. 'There's something about it in that book. Now – where is it?'

The girls waited in the greatest impatience whilst he found the book. He put his hand on it at last and Dinah almost snatched if from him.

'Thank you, Uncle,' she said, and before he could say she must not take it out of the room, she and Lucy-Ann rushed out of the door and sped to the sitting room as fast as they could. *Another passage* . . . this time to the island itself! What a thrill! Surely Uncle Jocelyn must be mistaken.

'It's quite likely it's true, though,' said Dinah excitedly. 'I know this whole coast is honeycombed with caves and passages – it's noted for that. Some districts are, you know, Lucy-Ann. I expect the passage joins up with the mine-workings that extend right under the sea bed. We know there are miles of them.'

The girls opened the funny old book. They could not read the printing, partly because it was so faded and partly because the letters were shaped differently from the ones they knew. They turned over page after page, looking for maps or pictures.

The book was apparently a history of Craggy-Tops, which was hundreds of years old. In those days it must have been almost a castle, built securely on the cliff rock, protected by the sea in front, and the cliff behind. Now, of course, it was half ruined, and the family lived only in the few rooms that were still habitable.

'Look,' said Dinah, pointing to a queer old map, 'that's what Craggy-Tops was like in the old days. What a fine place! Look at the towers – and what a grand front it had!'

They turned over the pages. They came to one that had a kind of diagram on it. The girls studied it closely. Then Lucy-Ann gave a shout. 'I know what this is – it's the secret passage from the cellar to the beach. Isn't it?'

It was. There was no doubt about that. The girls felt excited. Perhaps the book would show the other passage too.

There were two or three more diagram-like maps, some of them so faded that it was impossible to see what they were meant to represent. Dinah gave a sigh.

'I wish I could read this old printing. If I could, I might be able to find out whether any of these maps are meant to show the other secret passage – the one to the island. It would be so exciting to discover that. What a thrill if we did! What will the boys say when we tell them there's actually a way to the island under the sea itself?'

That made Lucy-Ann think of Jack, and her face clouded over. Where was Jack? Had Philip got Bill Smugs to go out in his boat and rescue him? Were they even now bringing Jack safely back again?

As she thought about this, she heard Philip's voice in the passage outside the sitting-room. She jumped up in delight. Had Philip and Bill brought back Jack already? How marvellously quick they had been! She ran to the door joyfully.

But outside there were only Bill and Philip – no Jack. Lucy-Ann called out to them.

'Where's Jack? Haven't you rescued him? Where is he?'

'Bill's boat has been smashed up by someone,' said Philip, going into the room. 'So we came to get Joe's. And that's gone too. I suppose Joe is doing some of his usual night fishing. So we're stumped – don't know what to do.'

The girls stared at the two in dismay. No boat – no way of rescuing poor Jack? Lucy-Ann's eyes filled with tears as she thought of Jack lost in those dark endless caves, with those fierce men ready to catch him and imprison him. She felt glad he had Kiki with him.

'Oh, Philip,' said Dinah, suddenly remembering, 'do you know what Uncle Jocelyn told us tonight? He said there used to be a way under the sea to the copper mines – to the island! He knew about the other secret passage, but he didn't think it was still usable. He was surprised. Oh, Philip, do you suppose the secret passage to the island is still there? Do you think it has been flooded by the sea – or fallen in? Oh, how I wish we could find it!'

Bill looked suddenly interested. He picked up the book Dinah held. 'This is a book about the old house?' he asked, Dinah nodded.

'Yes – our own secret passage is in it, the one we found ourselves – and I expect the other is too, only we can't understand the old maps and the printing.'

'Well, I can,' said Bill, and became lost in the book, turning over the pages slowly, skipping a few here and there, looking for details of the way to the Isle of Gloom.

He suddenly began to look excited, and turned over one or two pages very quickly. He looked hard at first one queer map and then another. Then he asked a peculiar question.

'How deep is your well here?'

'The well?' said Philip, in amazement. 'Ooooh – awfully deep – deep as the shaft hole in the island, I should think. It goes down below sea-level, anyway, but there's not a trace of salt in it, of course.'

'Look here,' said Bill, and spelt out a few words in the book to make them clear to the children, and then he turned to a map. It showed a deep shaft going down into the earth. 'See?' said Bill. 'The beginning of the passage to the island is down at the bottom of your well. It's quite obvious that that would be the place, anyway, if I'd thought about it – you see, to go under the sea bed to the mines means that the entrance must be below sea level – and that's the only spot here below sea level – the well, of course!'

'Gosh!' said all three children at once. The well! They hadn't thought of that. How extraordinary!

'But – there's water at the bottom of the well,' said Philip. 'You can't go through the water, surely.'

'No – look,' said Bill Smugs, and he pointed to the map. 'The entrance to the passage is above the water-line of the well. See? These must be steps, I should think, cut in an opening of the shaft, leading upwards a little way, and then through a passage in the rock itself – a natural crack, I imagine, such as this coast is full of – which someone discovered, followed up, and by means of pickaxes or blasting, made into a usable passage.'

'I see,' said Philip excitedly. 'I suppose when they sank the shaft for the well, someone discovered the hole deep down, explored it, found it was a sort of natural passage, and, as you say, followed it up, and made use of it. Bill – could we get down there and find out?'

'Not now, in the middle of the night,' said Bill at once. 'You've all had enough adventure for this one day – we must go to bed.'

'But—but what about Jack?' asked Lucy-Ann, her green eyes wide with anxiety.

'We can't do anything about him tonight,' said Bill, firmly but kindly. 'Anyway, if he's caught, he's caught, and if he's not, we may be able to do something about him tomorrow. But we are *not* going to go down wells in buckets in the dead of night, so that's that. Philip, I'll sleep with you in the tower-room tonight.'

Philip was glad. He did not want to sleep alone that night. The girls were sent off to bed, in spite of their protests that they were not tired, and Philip and Bill climbed the spiral stairway to the little tower-room. Philip showed Bill the window from which they could see the island at times.

Then he sat down on the bed to take off his shoes. But he was so tired that even the effort of undoing the laces was too much for him. He rolled over on the bed, shut his eyes and fell fast asleep, fully dressed as he was. Bill looked at him and smiled. He drew a cover over him, and sat at the window to think.

Tomorrow would show whether or not there was still a way from Craggy-Tops to the island. Bill felt certain there would not be. True, the other passage was still usable, but that was very short compared with the other – and this second one had had the sea pounding on top of it for many, many years. A crack in it – a trickle of water down – and the passage would be flooded in a very few weeks. Then it would be impassable.

Bill went to bed at last, stretched himself out beside the sleeping boy, and fell asleep himself. He was awakened by Philip, who was shaking him.

'Bill! It's morning! Let's have breakfast and try and find that well passage. Hurry!'

They were soon downstairs, to find the girls there, already cooking bacon and eggs for breakfast. 'Where's Joe?' asked Philip, in surprise.

'Hasn't come back from fishing yet,' said Dinah, getting a fried egg deftly out of the pan. 'Here you are, Bill, I'll do an egg for you now, Philip. It's a good thing Joe isn't back, isn't it – or he'd wonder what on earth Bill was doing here. He would think it all mighty suspicious.'

'Joe may be back at any minute,' said Lucy-Ann. 'So let's hurry before he comes. I'd just hate him to stand glowering at the head of the well whilst we explore it all that way below.'

They finished their breakfast quickly. Dinah had already taken some to her aunt in her bedroom, and to her uncle in his study. She said Aunt Polly was feeling a bit better and would be down later. She didn't think Uncle Jocelyn had gone to bed at all.

'I really believe he works all night long,' said Dinah. 'Now – have we all finished? I'll leave the washing-up till I get back.'

They all went out into the little yard that lay behind the house, backing on to the sheer rise of the cliff. Bill leaned over the well. It certainly was very, very deep.

'Do we go down in the bucket?' asked Philip.

'We could if there was a really big one,' said Dinah. 'But we can't possible go down in this. Not even Lucy-Ann could get into it.'

'You know,' said Bill, taking his big torch from his pocket, 'You know, if this well-shaft is really the only way down to the entrance of the island passage, there should be a ladder. I can't imagine people going up and down in buckets.'

'Well – there isn't a ladder,' said Philip. 'I should have seen it if there was.'

Bill flashed his torch down the well, examining the sides carefully. 'Look,' he said to Philip, 'it is true there is no ladder – but do you see those iron staples jutting out from the wall down there? Well, those are what would be used to help anyone wanting to descend this well-hole. They would use them as steps, holding on to the ones above with their hands, and going down bit by bit – feeling with their feet for the next one.'

'Yes!' said Philip, in excitement. 'You're right! That's the way that people went down in the olden days. I bet when there was fighting round about here, many refugees used this old well as a hiding-place, even if they didn't know of the passage entrance down below. Come on, Bill – let's go down. I'm simply longing to get going.'

'Well, it's time we did,' said Bill. 'I'll go first. Keep a watch out for Joe, Dinah.'

24

A journey under the sea

Bill couldn't reach the first iron staples, so Philip had to fetch a rope. It was tied tightly to an iron post by the well, and then Bill slipped down it, and placed his feet on the first staples.

'I'm all right,' he said. 'You come along as soon as you can, Philip – let me get down a few steps first – and for goodness' sake don't slip.'

The girls did not go – and, indeed, neither of them liked the thought of going down the steep, cold well-shaft with only insecure staples for a foot- and hand-hold. They watched the two disappearing down into the dark, and shivered.

'It's beastly to be left behind, but I honestly think it's beastlier to go down there,' said Dinah. 'Come on – we can't see or hear Bill and Philip now – we'd better go back to the kitchen and do a few jobs. Isn't Joe late!'

They went back, wondering how Bill and Philip were getting on down the well. They were climbing down slowly but surely; the staples seemed to be as firmly in the wall as when they were first driven in.

It was tiring work, and would have been utterly impossible to tackle if it had not been for unexpected resting-places let into the well-wall every now and again. The first one puzzled Bill, till he guessed what it was. It was an opening in the well-wall, going back a few feet, big enough to crouch in and rest. At first Bill had half thought the first one to be the entrance to the passage and he was surprised to come to it so soon. But he soon realised what it was, and very thankfully he rested there a few minutes. Then Philip had a rest there, whilst Bill went slowly downwards, his feet always feeling for the next staple.

It seemed ages going down the well-shaft, and, in fact it took the two of them nearly an hour. They used each resting-place, but in spite of that they became very tired. Then suddenly Bill's torch, which he had stuck into his belt alight, gleamed on to dark water. They were at the bottom.

'We're there!' Bill yelled up to Philip. 'I'm just going to look about for the entrance.'

It was easy to find, for there, in the well-wall, was a round, gaping hole like a small tunnel. Bill slipped into it. It was dark, slimy and evil-smelling. 'Funny that the air is still fresh,' thought Bill. 'But all the way down the well I could feel a current of air blowing round me – so there must be some sort of through-draught to keep it pure.'

He waited for Philip. Then the two of them set out on what must surely have been one of the strangest roads in the world – a path under the bed of the sea itself. At first the tunnel was narrow and led upwards a little by means of steps, and the two had to crouch down to get along. But after a bit it widened out and became higher. It was still slimy and evil-smelling, but they got used to that.

Then the passage led downwards, at times rather steeply. There were rough steps made in the steepest part so that travellers might not slip too much. But they were so slimy that even a goat would have slipped. Bill came down with a bump, and Philip followed almost immediately.

'Take your foot out of my neck,' said Bill, trying to get up. 'My word, I am in a nice old mess!'

They went on and on. Soon the passage stopped descending, and kept level. It was enclosed in the solid rock. There was no earth, no sand, no chalk – all rock, quite black, and glinting with strange lights now and again.

Once or twice the passage narrowed so much that it was almost impossible to squeeze through. 'Good thing we're not fat,' said Philip, squeezing in his tummy to get by. 'Golly, that was a tight fit! Have the rocks come closer together during the years, Bill – or do you suppose the passage was always narrow there?'

'Always, I should think,' said Bill. 'It's a perfectly natural fissure in the rocky bed under the sea – an amazing one – though I have heard of others like this in different parts of the world. I believe this coast has a good many.'

It was warm in the passage. Here and there the air was not good and the man and the boy began to pant. There seemed to be pockets of airlessness. But on went the two, on and on, their torches gleaming on black, slimy walls, out of which still shone queer phosphorescent lights now and again. Philip began to feel as if he was in a dream. He said so.

'Well, you're not,' came Bill's reassuring voice. 'We're in a peculiar place, but a perfectly real one. It's no dream. Like me to pinch you?'

'Well, I think I would,' said Philip, who really did feel rather odd after so much time in the dark narrow way. So Bill pinched him – and it was a very hard pinch that made Philip yell.

'All right!' he said. 'I'm awake and not dreaming. No-body would be silly enough to dream *that* pinch.'

Suddenly Bill felt something running by his feet, and he looked down in great astonishment, swinging his torch downwards too. To his enormous surprise he saw a small mouse looking up at him. Bill stopped in astonishment.

'Look here,' he said. 'A mouse. A mouse down *here*! What does it live on? It's a most incredible thing. I simply cannot imagine any animal living down in this passage under the sea.'

Philip chuckled. 'It's all right! It's only Woffly, my pet mouse. It must have run down my sleeve and hopped out.'

'Well, it had better hop in again, if it wants to live,' said Bill. 'No animal could last down here for long.'

'Oh, it will come back when it wants to,' said Philip. 'It won't leave me for long.'

They had to have two or three rests, for the way was tiring and difficult. It went curiously straight for a time and then seemed to go in jerks, having little bits that went off at right angles for a few feet, only to come to the straight again. Philip began to wonder how long his torch would last. He felt suddenly frightened at the thought of being left in the dark down there. Supposing Bill's torch gave out as well?

But Bill reassured him. 'I've got another battery in my pocket,' he told Philip, 'so don't worry. We shall be all right. And that reminds me – I've got a packet of boiled sweets somewhere. I can't help feeling it would make this awful journey easier if we sucked one or two.'

There was a pause whilst Bill searched his pockets. He found the sweets, and soon the two of them were sucking away hard. Certainly it made things easier, somehow, to have a nice big boiled sweet tucked away in his mouth, Philip thought.

'How far do you think we've gone?' asked Philip. 'Half-way?'

'Can't tell,' said Bill. 'Hallo – what's this?'

He paused and shone his torch in front of him. The way appeared to be blocked. 'Gosh! – it looks like a roof-fall,' said Bill. 'Well, if it is, we're done. We've got nothing to clear up the mess with, to see if we can get by.'

But, to their great relief, the fall was very slight, and with the combined strength of both of them, the main rock that stopped their progress was removed to one side, and they managed to clear it.

'I say,' said Philip, after a long time of groping along the passage, 'do you notice that the rocks are changing colour, Bill? They're not black any longer. They're greenish. Do you think that means we are nearing the mines?'

'Yes, I think it probably does,' said Bill. 'It's distinctly hopeful. I don't know how many hours we have been so far – it seems about a hundred at least – but I do think it's about time we were nearing that wretched island.'

'I'm glad we had such a good breakfast,' said Philip. 'I'm beginning to feel very hungry again now, though. I wish we had brought some food with us.'

'I've got plenty of chocolate,' said Bill. 'I'll give you some presently – if it hasn't melted. It's so hot down here now that I shouldn't be surprised if it has.'

It had certainly got very soft, but it hadn't melted. It was good chocolate – slightly bitter, but really delicious to the hungry boy. He went on the dreary way, feeling the slimy walls, noticing the coppery gleams in them, wondering how much longer it would be before the end came.

'Have you by any chance got that map on you?' called Bill suddenly. 'I forgot to tell you to take it. We shall need it soon.'

'Yes. It's in my pocket,' said Philip. 'Hallo, look – the passage is widening out tremendously!'

It was. It suddenly ended and came out into a big open space, evidently the end of the mine-workings. It must have been here that the copper had run out, thought Philip. What big mines they must have been – and how rich at one time!

'Well – here we are at last,' said Bill, in a low voice. 'And remember that from now on we don't make any noise, Philip. We must find Jack, if we can, without attracting any attention at all.'

Philip felt astonished. 'But, Bill,' he said, 'why can't you just go to the part of the mine where your friends are working and ask them where old Freckles is? Why all the hush-hush, mustn't-talk-loudly business? I don't understand.'

'Well, I have my reasons,' said Bill. 'So please respect them, Philip, even if you don't know what they are. Come on – where's that map?'

Philip pulled it from his pocket. Bill took it, opened it, spread it on a conveniently flat rock, shone his torch on it and studied it very carefully. At last he put his finger on a certain place.

'Look,' he said. 'That's where we are – see? Right at the end of the workings. I think this bit here shows the beginning of the under-sea passage, but I'm not sure. Now, tell me – which of these many ways did you take when you came into the mines from the shaft-hole?'

'Well – there's the shaft we went down,' said Philip, pointing to where it was marked on the map. 'And here's the main passage we kept to – and there is the cave with the bright light – and it was somewhere about there we heard the clattering, banging noise of men at work.'

'Good,' said Bill, pleased. 'I have quite a clear idea of where to go now. Come along – as quietly as possible. We will make for the main passage, and then see if we can spot Jack anywhere about – or hear of him.'

They made their way very carefully up the wide main passage, off which many side galleries went. Bill held his finger over the beam of his torch so as not to make too much light. They were not yet near the cave where the children had seen the bright light and heard noises. But they would come to it sooner or later, Philip knew.

'Sh!' suddenly said Bill, stopping so quickly that Philip bumped into him. 'I can hear something. It sounded like footsteps.'

They stood and listened. It was weird standing there in the darkness, hearing the muffled boom of the great waters moving restlessly on the rocky bed of the sea overhead.

Philip thought he could hear a noise too – someone's foot kicking against a loose pebble.

Then there was complete silence. So on they went again, and then once more they thought they heard a noise, this time near to them. And Bill felt sure that he could hear someone breathing not far off. He held his own breath to listen.

But perhaps that other, hidden person was holding his breath too, for Bill could hear nothing then. It was very weird. He moved forward silently with Philip.

They came to a sudden corner, and Bill groped round it, for he and Philip had put out their torches as soon as they had heard any noise. And, as Bill reached out to grope for the wall, someone else also reached out, coming in the opposite direction. Then, before Philip knew what was happening, he heard loud exclamations, and felt Bill and somebody else struggling together violently just in front of him. Golly, *now* what was happening?

25

An extraordinary find

And now – what had happend to Jack and Kiki all this time? A great deal – some of it most astonishing and unbelievable.

Jack had not known that the others had escaped – in fact, he had not even known that they had been imprisoned. He had wandered off after the parrot, and had become quite lost. The men, as we know, had heard Kiki squealing and shouting some hours later, when they had been chasing Philip and the girls, but they had gone down the wrong passage after them and had not seen them.

So there was poor Jack, lost and terrified, with a forlorn Kiki clutching hard at his shoulder. The boy wandered down a maze of galleries, coming to more and more old abandoned workings. He was afraid that his torch would give out. He was afraid of the roof falling in on top of him. He was afraid of a great many things.

'I may be lost for ever down here,' he thought. 'I may be wandering miles away from that main passage.'

He suddenly came to a great hole in the roof above him, and realised that he had come to another shaft. 'Of course – there were quite a number of them,' Jack thought, his heart beginning to thump. 'Thank goodness – now I can climb up and get out into the open air.'

But, to the boy's dismay, there was no way of getting up the shaft. Whatever ladder or rope there had once been had rotted or fallen away – there was absolutely no way of climbing up.

It was awful to stand there at the bottom, knowing that freedom, daylight and fresh air were at the top, and yet with no means of reaching them.

'If I were a baby, I bet I'd burst into tears,' said Jack out loud, feeling something suspiciously like tears pricking at the back of his eyelids. 'But I won't do it. I must just grin and bear it.'

He gave a determined grin. Kiki listened to his words with her head on one side.

'Put the kettle on,' she said sympathetically. That made Jack give a really good grin.

'You *are* an idiot,' he said affectionately. 'Now, the thing is – where do we go next? I feel as if I am probably wandering in the same passage over and over again. But wait a minute – the shafts are all on the island itself – so I must have retraced my steps somehow, because we were all under the sea-bed at one time. As far as I remember, those shafts all connected up with one more or less straight tunnel. I'll go down here – and see if by any chance I come to the main shaft. If I do, I can go up it.'

Jack stumbled on, and came to a blocked-up part, impossible to get by. So he had to go back a good way and start out again, only to come to another roof-fall. It was very disheartening. Kiki became tired of this long journey in the dark passages, and gave a realistic yawn.

'Put your hand before your mouth,' she told herself severely. 'How many times have I told you to shut the door? God save the Queen.'

'Well, your yawn made me yawn too,' said Jack, and he sat down. 'What about a rest, Kiki? I'm getting terribly tired.'

He leaned back against the rocky wall and shut his eyes. He fell into a doze, which lasted an hour or two. When he awoke he hardly knew where he was, and felt frightened when he remembered. He got to his feet, with Kiki still firmly on his shoulder.

'Now, it's no good getting into a panic,' he told himself sternly. 'Just go on walking, and sooner or later you will get somewhere.'

It was whilst he was stumbling through the many passages that Kiki heard the noise of the men chasing the children, and shouted loudly. But Jack heard nothing, and turned off into a winding passage just before the men came up. He did not know that he was near to the wide shaft-hole – but presently he came to the big main passage, and stopped.

'Can this be the wide passage we saw on the map?' he thought. 'It may be. If only I had a brighter torch! I hope to goodness it's not going to fade out. It doesn't seem so bright as it was.'

He went down the passage, and saw some rough-hewn steps in the rock, leading upwards. Out of curiosity the boy climbed them, and came to another passage, which evidently led to yet another working. He stumbled and fell against the wall, dislodging a stone or small rock, which fell down with a crash. Jack held up his torch to see where it had fallen from, afraid that the roof was caving in.

But it wasn't. His torch gleamed on to something that shone coppery-red – a large, irregular kind of stone, thought Jack. And then he suddenly realised that it wasn't a stone – it was – yes, it must be – a large copper nugget! Golly, what a beauty! Could he possibly carry it?

With trembling hands the boy prised the nugget carefully away from its place. It was on a kind of shelf made by a crack in the rock just there. Had someone hidden it there, years ago? Or had it been placed there by one of the men working the mines now? Or was it there naturally, a real nugget in the depths of the earth? Jack didn't know.

It was heavy, but he could carry it. A nugget of copper! The boy kept repeating the words to himself. Almost as good as finding a Great Auk – not quite as thrilling of course, but almost. What would the others say?

Jack thought he had better keep out of the way of the miners more than ever now. They might take the nugget from him. It might legally be theirs, of course, but he did want to have the thrill of showing it to the others as his find before he gave it up to anyone.

The boy went back to the main passage with the nugget in his hands. He had to put his torch into his belt now, as he could not carry it as well as the copper, and it was difficult to make his way along, because the torch shone almost directly downwards instead of forwards.

'Hallo!' said Jack, stopping suddenly as he heard a noise in the distance. 'I rather think I'm coming towards that clattering noise we heard before – where the men are working. Perhaps I'm near the other children too.'

The boy crept foward. He went into a passage that turned suddenly round a corner – and there before him was the brilliantly lighted cave again. Last time he had seen it, it had been empty – this time there were men there. They were undoing the boxes and crates that the children had seen there before. Jack watched, wondering what was in them.

'I'm in the same passage as I was when Kiki flew off and I went after her,' thought Jack. 'I do wonder what has happened to the others. Golly, but it's good to see a bright light again. If I crouch here, behind this jutting rock, I don't believe anyone will see me.'

Kiki was absolutely quiet. The brilliant light frightened her after being so long in the darkness. She crouched on the boy's shoulder, watching.

There were tins in the boxes and crates – tins of meat and fruit. Jack felt very hungry when he saw them, for he had had nothing to eat for a long time. The men opened a few of the tins, poured the contents out on to tin plates, and began to eat, talking to each other. Jack could not hear what they were saying. He felt so hungry that he almost walked out to the men to beg for some of their food.

But they didn't look very nice men. They wore trousers only, belted at the waist, and nothing else. It was so hot in the mines that it was impossible to wear many clothes. Jack wished he could wear only shorts, but he knew he would not like Kiki's claws on his bare shoulder.

The men finished their meal, and then went down a passage or gallery at the further end of the cave they were in. There was no one there now. The clattering, banging noise began again. Evidently the men were at work once more.

Jack crept into the brilliantly lighted cave. The light came from these three lamps hung from the roof. Jack looked into the opened tins. There was a little meat left in one and some pineapple chunks in another. He finished them up quickly. He thought that never in his life had he tasted anything so delicious as the food in those tins.

He decided to creep over to the passage down which the men had gone back to work. It would be exciting to see how men worked in a copper-mine. Did they use pickaxes? Did they blast out the copper? What were they doing to make all that noise? It really sounded as if it came from some big machine busily at work.

He crept down the passage, and then found that he was looking into another cave. He was most astonished at what he saw. There were about a dozen men there, busy with a number of machines that clattered and banged, making quite a deafening noise that echoed round the cave.

There was an engine of some sort which added to the din.

'What strange machinery!' thought Jack, staring. 'How ever in the world did they get it all down here into the mines? They must have brought it down in pieces, and then put them together here. Golly, how busy it all is, and what a noise it makes!'

Jack watched in wonder. Were they extracting copper by means of this machine? He knew vaguely that many metals had to be roasted or smelted or worked in some way before they were pure. He supposed they were doing that. It was plain, then, that the copper in these mines was not usually found in big nuggets, such as the one Jack was even now holding.

One of the men wiped his forehead and came from the machine towards Jack's hiding-place. The boy darted away, and went into a small blind passage to wait till the man had passed. He came back carrying a mug of water. Jack waited in the little blind passage for a minute or two, leaning against what he thought was the wall. But suddenly the 'wall' gave way a little, and the boy slipped backwards. Then, putting his torch on, he found that it was no wall but a strong wooden door, leading into a cell-like place – rather like the one in which the other children had been imprisoned.

Hearing footsteps, he hurriedly went into the cell and pushed the door shut. The footsteps went by. Jack switched on his torch again to see what was in the cave.

It was stacked with bundles upon bundles of crisp papers, the same size put together and the same colours, tightly fastened together. Jack looked at them – and then he looked again, blinking his eyes in amazement.

In that cell-like cave were thousands of bundles of paper money. There were bundles of five-pound notes, bundles of ten-pound notes – there they were, neatly stacked together, a fortune great enough to make anyone a millionaire in a night.

'Now I really must be dreaming,' thought Jack, rubbing his eyes. 'There's no doubt about it. I'm in a very extraordinary dream. In a minute I shall wake up and laugh.

People simply don't find things like this – treasure in a cave underground. Why, I might be in the middle of some wonderful fairy story. It's quite impossible – I'd better wake up immediately.'

26

A bad time – and a surprising meeting

But Jack didn't wake up – and for a very good reason too. He wasn't asleep.

He was wide awake and staring at this colossal fortune in paper money. It didn't make sense. Why was it all stored here, in this cave underground? Who did it belong to? Why didn't they put it into a bank in the usual way?

'Perhaps the men working this mine are finding a lot of copper and selling it secretly, and keeping the money here that they get for it,' thought Jack. He was so lost in amazement at the sight of such a fortune piled up there in front of him that he did not hear someone coming to the door of the cave he was in.

The man who opened the door and saw Jack in the cave was even more surprised than Jack himself. He stood staring at the boy with his mouth wide open, and his eyes almost falling out of his head. Then he dragged the boy roughly out of the cell, and pulled him to the room where the machine was working.

'Look here!' yelled the man. 'Look here! I found him in the store room.'

The machine was stopped at once. The men gathered round Jack and his captor. One of them stepped forward. It was Jake.

He looked very evil and the black patch he wore over one eye made him look most peculiar. He shook Jack so roughly that the boy lost his breath completely and sank down on the ground when Jake let go of his arm.

'Where are the rest of you?' said Jake. 'You tell me, see! Who are you with? What are you doing down here? What do you know?'

Jack picked up his nugget, looked round for Kiki, who had flown in fright to the roof of the cave, and tried to think what to answer for the best. The men took no notice of his big copper nugget, which surprised Jack very much. He had been afraid they would take it away from him at once.

'I don't know where the others are,' he said at last. 'We came to the island together, two boys and two girls, and I got separated from the others.'

'Who else was with you?' demanded Jake. 'You kids didn't come here by yourselves.'

'We did,' insisted Jack. 'I say – who does all that money in there belong to?'

The listening men made some low, threatening noises, and Jack gazed round uneasily. Jake's face grew black. He looked round at the men.

'Something's up,' he said, and the men nodded. He turned again to Jack. 'Now look here,' he said, 'you know a lot more than you've told us – you've picked up something from the others, haven't you? – well, you just tell us all you know, or you may never see daylight again. See? Is that clear?'

It was horribly clear. Jack began to tremble. Kiki gave a screech that made everyone jump.

'I don't know what you mean,' said Jack desperately. 'All we knew was that someone was working these copper-mines again, getting copper, and that Bill Smugs was taking food here in his boat. That's honestly all I know.'

'Bill Smugs,' repeated Jake. 'That's what the other kids said. Who *is* this Bill Smugs?'

Jack was puzzled. 'Isn't that his real name?' he said.

'What's his real name?' suddenly said Jake, so threateningly that Jack dropped his precious nugget in a panic, thinking the man was going to strike him. It fell on the edge of Jake's foot and the man picked it up and had a look at it.

'What's this stone you're carrying about?' he said, in curiosity. 'Are you kids mad? A parrot – and a heavy stone – Bill Smugs – copper mines. You're all crazy.'

'I think this kid knows more than he's said,' said Olly, stepping beside Jake. 'What about locking him up without any food for a day or so? That will make him talk. Or what about a good beating?'

Jack went pale, but he did not show that he was afraid. 'I don't know any more than I've already told you,' he said. 'What *is* there to know, anyway? What's the mystery?'

'Take him away,' said Jake roughly. 'He'll talk when he's half-starved.'

Olly took the boy by the shoulder and led him roughly from the cave, prodding him unkindly as he did so. He led him to the same cell-like cave in which the other children had been imprisoned. Just as he was pushing the boy in, Kiki flew down and hacked viciously at the man's face with her curved beak. Olly put up his hands to protect himself, and dropped his torch. It went out.

Jack slipped swiftly to the side and crouched outside the cell in silence. Kiki did not know where he was. She flew into the cell and perched on the table there, in complete darkness.

'Now then, now then, what a pity!' she said loudly. The cell door banged. Olly had shut it on the parrot, thinking that it was Jack talking inside there. He had not even known that the bird could talk.

He turned the key in the lock. Kiki was still talking away softly, though neither Jack nor Olly could hear the words. As Olly was turning away, Jake came up.

'Did you put him in?' he asked, and flashed his torch on to the shut door.

'Yes,' said Olly. 'He's gassing away to himself in there – you can hear him – I think he's mad.'

The men listened, and Kiki's voice came clearly from the

cell. 'What a pity, what a pity!'

'He's sorry for himself, isn't he?' said Jake, and then he gave such a horrible laugh that Jack's heart went cold with fear. 'He'll be sorrier still soon.'

The men went back to the machine cave and soon the clattering, banging noises began again. Jack stood up. Kiki had saved him from a horrible punishment – poor Kiki. She didn't know she had saved him. Jack moved to the door, meaning to unlock it and get the parrot out.

But the key was gone. One of the men must have taken it. So Kiki was a prisoner, a real prisoner, and would have to stay there till someone let her out.

But anyway Jack himself was free. 'There's something wrong about all this business,' the boy thought. 'Something wrong about all that money – and those mysterious machines. The men are bad. They can't be friends of Bill's. We've made a mistake.'

He went down the passage carefully, not daring to switch on his torch. If only he could find the shaft-hole and go up it. Perhaps the others would be at the top, waiting for him? Or had they gone back home and left him all alone? Was it still day time or was it night?

Jack stumbled along passage after passage, wishing that Kiki was with him for company. He felt lonely and afraid now. He wanted to talk to somebody. He wanted to see the others.

At last he was so tired that he could not go on. He curled up in a corner of a small cave, shut his eyes and fell into a restless, uncomfortable kind of sleep. For hours he slept, tired out, his limbs getting stiff as he lay there. And Kiki slept too, in the cave, puzzled and angry, missing her master as much as he missed her.

When Jack awoke he put up his hand to feel Kiki, as he often did – but the bird was not on his shoulder. Then he remembered. Kiki was a prisoner. Because of her and her ability to talk like a human being, he, Jack was free.

He knew a lot. He knew about the hidden treasure. He

knew about those machines which were so well hidden in these underground caves for some sinister reason. He knew that the men working them were bad men. If they thought their secret, whatever it was, had been discovered, they would not stop at anything.

'The thing I've got to do, the thing I really *must* do, is to escape and tell what I know,' thought Jack. 'I somehow think I ought to go to the police. I'd like to go and tell Bill — because I think now he's not in league with those men — but I'm still not certain. Anyway, the thing is — I've got to tell *some*body.'

So once more the boy began his endless wandering in the workings of the mines. Up and down long, musty passages he went, his torch now giving him only a very poor light.

And then suddenly it gave out altogether. Jack tapped it a little. He screwed and unscrewed the bottom. But the battery was dead — no light would come from his torch unless he put in a new battery — and certainly he could not do that at the moment.

Jack really did feel afraid then. There was only one hope now of escape, and that was to find, by good luck, the shaft leading up to the open air. But that was a very poor chance indeed.

He wandered on, groping his way, his hand out before his face, carrying the nugget uncomfortably under his arm, holding it there with his other hand. Then he thought he heard something. He stopped and listened. No — it was nothing.

He went on again, and suddenly stopped. He couldn't help feeling that people were near. Was that somebody breathing? He stood in the dark, holding his breath and listening. But he heard nothing. 'Maybe,' he thought, 'the other person is holding his breath and listening too.'

He went on — and suddenly he bumped hard into somebody. Was it Jake, or Olly? He began to struggle desperately and the other person held on to him firmly, hurting his arm. The nugget dropped to the ground and hit Jack's foot.

'Oh, my foot, my foot!' groaned poor Jack.

There was an astonished silence. Then a powerful torch was switched on by his captor, and a voice said in amazement, 'Why, it's Jack!'

'Freckles!' came Philip's voice too, and he ran to Jack and gave him an affectionate slap on the back. 'Freckles! What luck to come across you like this!'

'Tufty! And Bill!' said Jack, his voice breaking in a great gasp of joy and relief. Oh, the delight of hearing a familiar voice after so many hours of lonely darkness! The joy of seeing Philip, his tuft of hair sticking up from his forehead as usual! And Bill, with his familiar grin, his twinkling eyes, and his good dependable feeling of grown-upness – Jack was glad to have a grown-up to help him. Children could meddle in things to a certain extent – but there often came a time when you had to lean on the grown-ups.

He gave a gulp, and Bill patted him on the back. 'Fine to see you, Jack. I bet you've got plenty to tell us.'

'I have,' said Jack. He took out his handkerchief and blew his nose hard. Then he felt better. 'Where are the girls?'

'Safe at home,' said Philip. 'We missed you somehow down in the mines yesterday, Jack, and we got taken prisoner, but we escaped, got up the shaft-hole, found our boat and sailed away in the half-dark. I went to find old Bill, and here he is. We couldn't come in his boat because it was smashed by someone – and Joe's boat was gone too.'

'Well – how did you come then?' asked Jack in astonishment.

'There's a way under the sea from Craggy-Tops to here,' said Philip. 'What do you think of that? We found it in an old book about Craggy-Tops. It took us ages to come. It was very weird. I didn't like it much. But here we are.'

Jack was really amazed to hear how they had come. He questioned them eagerly. But Bill had a few questions to ask Jack. 'This is all much more important than you think, Jack,' he said. 'Let's sit down. I've got an idea you can solve a big mystery for me.'

27

A lot of things are made clear

'I've got some weird things to tell you,' said Jack eagerly. 'First of all, what do you think I found? A cave absolutely chock full of money – paper money – notes, you know. Well, I should think there must have been thousands and thousands of pounds' worth there – you've simply no idea.'

'Ah,' said Bill Smugs, in a voice full of satisfaction. 'Ah! Now that really *is* news. Fine, Jack!'

'Then I saw a lot of machines at work,' went on Jack, pleased to find that his news was so intensely interesting to Bill. 'And an engine. I thought it was to smelt or roast the copper, or whatever they have to do with it, but one of the machines looked like a printing-press.'

'Ah-*ha*! said Bill, with even greater satisfaction in his voice. 'This is wonderful news. Amazing! Jack, you've solved a five-year-old mystery – a mystery that has been puzzling the Government and the whole of the police for a long time.'

'What mystery?' asked Jack.

'I bet I know,' put in Philip excitedly. 'Bill, that machinery is for printing false paper money, isn't it? – counterfeit notes – dud money. And the money, in notes, that Jack found, is stored there after being printed. It will be taken from this island and used by the crooks or their masters.'

'You've just about hit it,' said Bill. 'We've been after this gang for years – couldn't find where they had their printing-outfit installed – couldn't make out where the money appeared from. It's excellently done – only an expert can tell the difference between a real bank-note and these dud ones.'

'Bill! So the men aren't working the copper-mines then!' cried Jack, in astonishment. 'We were wrong about that. They chose these old mines, not to work any copper in them, but to hide their printing machines, and to do all their work in safety. How clever! How awfully clever!'

'Very smart indeed,' said Bill grimly. 'All they needed was a go-between – someone who could sail out to the island with food for them, and other necessities – and take away back to the Boss, whoever he is, stacks of the dud notes. Well – it was the go-between that gave the show away, really.'

'Who's the go-between?' asked Jack interestedly. 'Anyone we know?'

'Of course,' said Bill. 'I should have thought you would have guessed at once – Joe.'

'*Joe*!' cried the two boys, and in a flash they saw how everything fitted in, where Joe was concerned.

'Yes – he had a boat, and he had only to say he was going fishing in it, in order to get over to the island and back,' said Philip. 'He could go at night too, if he wanted to. Those signals Jack saw were from the men on the island – and it was Joe up on the cliff, signalling back, that night Jack met him there.'

'Yes, it was,' said Jack, remembering. 'And when he went off shopping in the car he'd take some of that counterfeit money with him, I guess, and deliver it to his bosses, who-ever they were. No wonder he would never take us out in the car with him, or in the boat. He was afraid we might suspect something.'

'Do you remember those boxes and crates down in the second cellar, behind that door he kept hidden by piled-up boxes?' said Philip. 'Well, I bet those didn't belong to Aunt Polly. I bet they were Joe's stores, waiting to be taken across to the island next time he went in his boat.

'His tales about "things" wandering on the cliffs at nights were only stories to frighten us and keep us from going out at night, and finding out anything he was doing,' went on Philip. 'Gracious, how everything fits in now, doesn't it?'

'It certainly seems to,' said Bill, in an amused voice. He had been listening to this conversation with great interest.

'Why did *you* come to this coast, to live in that tumbledown shack?' asked Jack suddenly. 'Were you really a bird-watcher?'

'Of course not,' said Bill, laughing. 'I didn't bargain on meeting a real bird-lover when I told you I was a bird-watcher. You nearly tripped me up lots of times. I had to read up a whole lot about birds I wasn't in the least interested in, so that you wouldn't suspect I didn't know much about them, Jack. It was really very awkward for me. I couldn't tell you what I really was, of course – a member of the police force, detailed to keep an eye on Joe and see what he was up to.'

'How did you know Joe was up to anything?' asked Philip.

'Well, he's pretty well known to the police,' said Bill. 'He has been mixed up in the counterfeiting of bank-notes before, and we wondered if he had anything to do with this big-scale printing that was going on somewhere, we didn't know where. We thought it just as well to watch him, once we knew where he was. He has a mighty fine way of disappearing. He's been with your aunt for five years now, as odd-job man, and nobody ever suspected he was a fellow with a very bad record. But one of our men spotted him in town one day and found out where he worked. Then down I came, this summer, to keep a quiet eye on him.'

'What a hornet's nest you've stirred up!' said Jack. 'Bill – did we help at all?'

'A lot,' said Bill, 'though you didn't know it. You made me certain that Joe was the go-between. You made me sure that it was the Isle of Gloom he kept going to. So I went there myself one day, and explored the mines a little way. That was when I dropped my pencil, I expect. But I must say *I* didn't find anything that made me suspect there were men in the mines, doing their illegal bank-note printing on hidden machines.'

'But *we* found out about it,' said Jack proudly. 'What are you going to do about it, Bill?'

'Well,' said Bill, 'last night I spoke over the radio to my

chiefs. I told them I was pretty certain what was going on here, and that I was going over to the island to rescue someone from the mines, and would they get busy, please, and begin to clear the matter up?'

'What will they do?' asked Jack, thrilled.

'I shan't know till I get back and report,' said Bill. 'We'd better go now, I think. We'll go back through the sea passage, the way Philip and I came.'

'I suppose it was Joe who smashed your boat up,' said Philip. 'He must have suspected something. I think he knew you were our friend.'

'Joe is a remarkably clever rascal,' said Bill, getting up and stretching himself. 'All the cleverer because he pretends to be stupid. Come along.'

'Bill – I want to get Kiki,' said Jack suddenly. 'I can't leave her here. The men will kill her – or she'll die of starvation or fright. Can't we go and get her?'

'No,' said Bill. 'There are more important things to be done.'

'Let's get her, Bill,' said Philip, who knew that Kiki was to Jack what a dog was to other people. 'We've only got to get out the map, find that main passage, and then slip along to the caves there. Jack will know where the cell is where Kiki got locked in. I think it sounds like the same one the girls and I were imprisoned in.'

'Well – we'd better be quick then,' said Bill doubtfully. 'And mind – no noise at all. We don't want to attract attention.'

They spread out the map, traced out where they were, and where the main passage was, and set out. It was not long before they were walking down the wide passage, silently and carefully.

Bill heard the clattering and banging noise. The machines were at work again. He looked grim and listened intently. Yes – that was a printing-press all right.

Just as they were coming to the cell cave in which Kiki was imprisoned, they heard sounds of voices. They crouched

173

against the wall, hardly daring to breathe.

'That's Jake,' whispered Philip, his mouth close against Bill's ear.

There were three men, and they were at the door of the cell where the parrot was. They were listening in astonishment. A voice came from the cell, raised high, and the words could be heard.

'Don't sniff, I tell you! Where's your handkerchief? How many times have I told you to wipe your feet? Poor old Kiki, poor, poor old Kiki! Put the kettle on!'

'The boy's gone mad,' said Jake, to the other two men. Evidently they still thought they had shut Jack up in the cave.

'Pop goes the weasel!' announced Kiki dramatically, and then made a noise like a runaway engine going through a tunnel and whistling.

'He's off his head,' said Olly, amazed.

There came a terrific screech, and the third man spoke suddenly.

'That's a parrot. That's what it is. The boy has got his parrot in there.'

'Open the door and we'll see,' said Olly. Jake put the key into the lock. The door swung inwards. Kiki at once flew out with a screech that made everyone jump. The men flashed their lamp into the cave.

It was empty. Jake turned fiercely on Olly. 'You fool! You put the parrot in there and let the boy escape. You deserve to be shot.'

Olly stared into the empty cave. It was true. Only the parrot had been there. 'Well,' said Olly. 'I expect the kid is lost for ever in these mines now, and will never be heard of again. Serves him right.'

'We're fools, Olly,' said Jake bitterly. 'First we let those other children trick us, and then the boy.'

They left the door open and went off towards the lighted cave. Jack gave a gasp. Kiki had suddenly flown on to his shoulder, and was making the most affectionate noises. She pretended to bite his ear, she made clicking noises meant to represent kisses, and altogether behaved in a most excited and delighted way. Jack scratched her head, and felt just as delighted himself.

'Now, come along, for heaven's sake,' said Bill, in a low voice. They left the passage and walked quickly away, their torches shining brightly. They had not gone very far before they distinctly heard someone else coming.

'It's somebody from the main shaft, I should think,' said Jack, in a low voice. They put out their torches and waited. The person came nearer, heavy-footed. His torch shone brightly. They could not see what he was like at all. They tried to slip back into a little blind passage, but Jack stumbled and fell, making a noise. Kiki screeched.

A torch dazzled them, and a voice came sharply out of the darkness. 'Stand where you are or I'll shoot!'

Bill put out a hand to make the boys stand still. There was something in that voice that had to be obeyed. The owner of it would not hesitate to shoot.

The three of them stood blinking there in the passage. Jack recognised the voice, and so did Philip. Who was it?

And then, in a flash, they knew. Of course they knew.

'It's Joe!' cried Jack. 'Joe, what are you doing here?'

'A question I'm going to ask *you*, all three of you,' said Joe, in a cold, grim voice. The light from his torch rested full on Bill's face. 'So *you're* here too,' said Joe. 'I smashed your boat – but I reckon you found the old way under the sea bed, didn't you? You think yourself mighty clever, all of you – but you've been just a bit *too* clever. There's a nasty time ahead of you – a – very – nasty – time.'

28

Trapped

The light gleamed on a revolver held by Joe. Bill felt angry with himself. If he hadn't agreed to go back for that wretched parrot, this would never have happened. Joe was tough. He was not likely to be fooled as easily as Jake had been.

'Turn round, hold your hands above your heads and walk in front of me,' ordered Joe. 'Ah – there's that parrot. I owe it quite a lot – well, I'll pay me debt now.'

Jack knew Joe meant to shoot Kiki and he gave the parrot a blow that surprised her very much. Kiki rose high into the air in indignation, screeching, lost in the darkness. 'Keep away, Kiki, keep away!' yelled Jack.

Kiki remained lost in the darkness. Something warned her that Jack did not want her near him. She sensed danger. She followed the little company, keeping well behind Joe, flying from place to place as silent as a bat.

The three of them were soon shut in the now familiar cave. Joe, who had shouted for Jake, locked the door himself. Then the prisoners heard them going off.

'Well, we're in a pretty pickle now, I'm afraid,' said Bill. 'Why in the world did I agree to go back for that parrot? We may all lose our lives because of that, and these fellows may escape scot-free with their thousands of false bank notes, to spread them all over the country. We really are up against it now.'

'I'm sorry I asked you to go back for Kiki,' said Jack humbly.

'I'm as much to blame as you,' said Bill, lighting a cigarette. 'Golly, it's hot down here.'

After what seemed to be an endless time, the door was opened again, and Joe came in, with Jake, Olly and two or three more men behind him.

'We just want to say a fond goodbye to you,' said Joe, his face gleaming in the lamp-light. 'We've finished up our business here. You came in at the end, Bill Smugs the cop, too late to do anything. We've got all the notes we'll ever be able to use now.'

'So you're clearing out, are you?' said Bill quietly. 'Smashing up the machines to hide your tracks – taking away all your stores and your packets of dud notes. You won't escape so easily. Your machines will be found all right, smashed or not, and your . . . '

'Nothing will ever be found, Bill Smugs,' said Joe. 'Not a thing. The whole of the police force can come to this island, but they'll never find anything they can trace back to us – never!'

'Why?' asked Bill, unable to conceal his surprise.

'Because we're flooding the mines,' said Joe, smiling wickedly and showing his teeth. 'Yes, Bill Smugs, these mines will soon be flooded – water will pour into every tunnel, every passage, every cave. It will hide our machines, and all traces of our work. I am afraid it will hide you too.'

'You're not going to leave us here, surely,' said Bill. 'Leave me, if you like – but take the boys up with you.'

'We don't want any of you,' said Joe, still in the same horribly polite tones. 'You would be in the way.'

'You couldn't be as cruel as that!' cried Bill. 'Why they're only children.'

'I have my orders,' said Joe. He did not seem at all the same stupid, grumpy fellow that the boys knew before – he was a different Joe altogether, and not at all a pleasant one.

'How do you propose to flood the mines?' asked Bill.

'Easily,' replied Joe. 'We have mined part of the passage through which you came from Craggy-Tops, under the sea-bed. When we are safely above ground, you will hear the muffled roar of a great explosion. The dynamite will blow a hole in the roof of that under-sea passage – and the sea will pour through. As you will guess, it will rush into these

177

mines, and fill them up to sea-level. I am afraid you will not find things very pleasant then.'

Jack tried to stand up to show Joe that *he* was not afraid, but his kness wouldn't hold him. He *was* afraid, very much afraid. And so was Philip. Only Bill kept a really brave front. He laughed.

'Well – do your worst. You won't escape so easily as you think. More is known about you and this gang and its bosses than you imagine.'

One of the men said something to Joe. He nodded. The boys felt certain that the time was soon coming when the sea bed was due to be blasted open – and then the waters would roar down and find their way into every nook and cranny.

'Well – goodbye,' said Joe, grinning and showing his teeth again.

'See you soon,' replied Bill, in just as polite a tone. The boys did not say anything. Kiki, out in the passage, gave a cackling laugh.

'I should have liked to kill that bird before I left,' muttered Joe, and went out of the cave with the others. He slammed the door and locked it.

There was the sound of retreating footsteps and then silence. Bill looked at the boys.

'Cheer up,' he said. 'We're not dead yet. We'll give those fellows time to get some distance away, and then I'll open this door and out we'll go.'

'Open the door? How?' asked Jack.

'Oh, I've my little way,' grinned Bill, and pulled out a queer collection of files and spindly keys. After a minute or two he set to work on the door, and in a very short time it was swinging open.

'Now for the shaft,' said Bill. 'Come on, before it's too late.'

They made their way to the main passage and then half walked, half ran towards the big shaft. It took some time to get there.

178

Just as they reached it, and looked upwards to where the faintest gleam of daylight showed, there came a curious sound.

It was a muffled roar, deep, deep down in the mines. It echoed round and about in a frightening way.

'Well – Joe spoke the truth,' said Bill soberly. 'That was the dynamite going off. If it really has blown a hole in the sea bed, the waters will even now be rushing up that under-sea passage to the mines.'

'Come on, then,' said Philip, eager to get up into the open air. 'Come on. I want to get into the sunshine.'

'I must tie my nugget round me somewhere,' said Jack, who was still manfully carrying the heavy piece of copper. 'Why – what's the matter, Bill?'

Bill had given a sharp exclamation that startled the boys. 'Look there,' said Bill, shining his torch on to the first few feet of the shaft-hole. 'Those men have gone up the shaft – and have carefully hacked away the ladder near the bottom so that we couldn't climb up, even if we did escape from the cave. They were leaving nothing to chance. We're done. We can't escape. There's no way of climbing up without a ladder.'

In despair the three of them gazed at the smashed-up rungs. Kiki gave a mournful screech that made them jump.

'Bill – I believe we might find some kind of a ladder in that big open cave where the boxes and crates of food were,' said Jack desperately. 'I believe I saw one. Shall we go back and see? I don't expect the men have done more than smash up the beginning rungs of the shaft-hole ladder – they'd know we couldn't use the ladder higher up if there was nothing to climb on lower down.'

'Are you sure there was a ladder in that cave?' asked Philip. 'I don't remember one.'

'Well – it's our only chance,' said Bill. 'Come on – back we go to find it.'

But they didn't reach the cave. They only went down the

main passage a little way and then they stopped in horror. Something was swirling towards them – something black and strange and powerful.

'The waters are in already,' yelled Bill. 'Come back. Get to the highest part. My word, the whole sea is emptying itself into the mines.'

The gurgling sound of water trickling down all the passages and into every cave was now plainly to be heard. It was a greedy, sucking sound, a sound that frightened even Bill. The three of them ran back to the main shaft at once. It was higher than the rest of the ground round about – but soon the water would reach there too.

'It will find its own level, anyway,' said Bill. 'All these shafts go down below sea-level, a long way below – and the mines will certainly fill up to the level of the sea. I reckon it will half-fill these shaft-holes too.'

'But Bill – we shall all be drowned!' said Jack, in a tembling voice.

'Can you swim?' asked Bill. 'Yes – of course you both can. Well, listen, there's just one hope for us. When the water fills up this shaft, we must rise with it – let it take us up. We can keep afloat all right, I think, if we don't get panicky. Then, when we reach the part of the ladder undamaged by the men, we can climb up. Now, do you think you can keep your heads, and, when the water comes go up the shaft-hole with it?'

'Yes', said the boys pluckily. Jack turned and looked nervously down the passage. He could see the black water in the distance, gleaming in the light of Bill's torch. It looked very horrible, somehow.

'That's the end of these mines, then, Bill, isn't it?' said Philip. 'No one will ever be able to come down here again.'

'Well, they were worked out anyway,' said Bill. 'Jack was lucky to find a nugget to take back to show everyone. It was probably hidden by a long-ago miner who forgot where he had hidden it – and years and years afterwards Jack found it.'

'I *must* take it back with me,' said Jack. 'I simply must. But I know I can't hold it and swim too. It's too heavy.'

Bill stripped off his jersey and his vest. He wrapped the nugget in his vest, knotted it, then tied a thick piece of string round it. He put his jersey on again and then hung the nugget round his neck.

'Bit heavy,' said he, with a grin, 'but quite safe. You carry Kiki, I'll carry the nugget.'

'Thanks awfully,' said Jack. 'Sure it won't drag you down under the water?'

'I hardly think so,' said Bill, who was immensely strong.

'The water's coming nearer,' said Philip uneasily. 'Look!'

They all looked. It was advancing near to the little bit of rising ground under the shaft where they stood.

'Isn't it awfully black?' said Jack. 'I suppose it's the darkness that makes it look so black. It looks simply horrid.'

'It will take a bit of time to get to our shaft,' said Bill. 'Let's sit down and rest a bit whilst we've a chance.'

They sat down. Philip's mouse ran out of his sleeve, and then sat up on its hind legs, sniffing. Kiki saw it and gave a squeal.

'Wipe your feet, I tell you!' she said.

'Now, don't you frighten Woffly,' said Philip. The three of them watched the antics of the mouse whilst they waited. The water lapped nearer, sucking and gurgling in the passages.

'It must be absolutely *pouring* down the hole in the roof of the under-sea passage,' said Philip. 'I say, Bill – will the water rush the other way too – down the under-sea passage to Craggy-Tops – and make the well salt water?'

'Well, yes – I suppose it will,' said Bill, considering. 'The well is below sea level, of course – so the sea is bound to pour into it, through the entrance in the well-shaft. That's bad, Philip. It will mean that you and your people won't have well-water any more – I can't think what you'll do.'

'Here comes the water to our feet now,' said Jack, watching a wave sweep up to them. 'Kiki, do sit still on my shoulder. Tufty, where's Woffly?'

'Down my neck now,' said Philip. 'Ooh, isn't the water cold!'

The mines were hot, so the water did feel cold – icy-cold. Philip, Jack and Bill stood up and watched it swirling round their ankles. It rose gradually to their knees. It rose above them.

The three were standing right under the shaft, waiting for the moment to come when the water would lift them up, enabling them to swim, or tread water.

'I'm frozen,' said Philip. 'I never knew such cold water.'

'It isn't really cold,' said Bill, 'but we feel so hot down here that the water strikes us as very cold. It hasn't had time to warm up yet.'

The water rose to their waists and them more rapidly to their shoulders.

'God save the Queen!' said Kiki, in a horrified tone, looking down from Jack's shoulder at the restless black water below her.

Soon Bill and the boys were lifted off their feet, and swam with difficulty on the surface of the water in the shaft. 'There's so little room,' panted Jack. 'We're all on top of one another.'

They were certainly very crowded and it was tiring work trying to keep afloat when there was really no room for swimming. The water rose steadily. Bill had taken Philip's little torch and placed it between his teeth, so that its light shone round on the shaft-wall. He wanted to see whether the ladder was still smashed, far up the shaft, or whether the men had only damaged the lower part.

He took the torch from his mouth at last. 'We're all right,' he said. 'The ladder's not smashed here. We have risen some way up the shaft with the water, and now we can get on to the ladder. I'll help you each up. Go first, Jack, with Kiki. She's getting so scared.'

Jack splashed his way to the side of the shaft where the ladder was. Bill shone the torch there. Jack clung to the rungs and began to haul himself up. Then, when he had climbed a good way up, Philip followed. Last of all Bill hauled himself up, feeling the drag of the heavy copper nugget on his neck. It had been extremely difficult to keep afloat with it, but somehow he had managed.

Up they went – and up and up. It seemed ages before they were anywhere near the top. They soon stopped shivering, and got hot with climbing. Their wet clothes stuck to them uncomfortably. Kiki talked in Jack's ear, very sorry for herself. She did not like this part of the adventure at all.

Philip's mouse didn't like it either. It had clung to Philip's ear during his stay in the water, when the boy's head had been the only thing above the surface – and now it didn't at all approve of such wet clothes. It couldn't seem to find a nice, dry, warm place anywhere.

'We're almost there,' Jack shouted down at last. 'Not far now.'

That was cheerful news. They hurried on, feeling new strength in their arms and legs now that they knew their long and tiring climb was nearing an end.

Jack climbed out first, Kiki flying off his shoulder with a glad squeal. Then he stopped in astonishment. A man was sitting quietly by the head of the shaft, a revolver in his hand.

'Hands up!' said the man, in a stern voice. 'Don't dare to warn anyone following you. Stand there. Hands up, I said!'

29

All's well that ends well

Jack stood with his hands above his head, his mouth open in horror. Had they escaped only to get caught again? He did not dare to shout.

Philip climbed out and was treated in the same way; he too was shocked and dismayed. The man with the revolver waited in silence, covering the boys with his weapon, watching to see who would come out next. Bill climbed out, his back to the man. He received the same order.

'Hands up! Don't dare to warn anyone following. Stand there!'

Bill swung round. He had put his hands up at once, but now he put them down and grinned.

'It's all right, Sam,' he said. 'Put up your gun.'

Sam gave an exclamation, and put his revolver into his belt. He held out his hand to Bill.

'It's *you*!' he said 'I was left here in case any more fellows of the gang came up. I didn't expect *you* to bob up.'

The boys stared, open-mouthed. What was all this?

'Did you get a shock?' said Bill, noticing their surprise. 'This is Sam – one of our detectives – great friend of mine. Well, Sam – seeing you here gives me great hopes. What's happened?'

'Come and see,' said Sam, with a grin, and he led the way. They all went through the pass in the hills, following the burly Sam. They came out on to open ground, and made their way towards the coast.

They came suddenly on a truly interesting sight. Lined up in a row, their faces sullen, were all the men from the mines. Joe was there too, fierce anger in his face. Two men stood near by, each with a revolver. All weapons had been taken from the prisoners.

'There's Joe!' cried Philip. Joe looked at him with a scowl that turned to surprise. So the boys and their friend had escaped! Joe was immensely surprised and racked his brains to think how anyone could have got out of a locked cave in a flooded mine and up a shaft whose ladder was completely smashed at the bottom.

'How were they caught?' asked Jack, in wonder. Kiki saw Joe and flew round his head, screeching and hooting and yelling. She recognised her old enemy, and knew he could no longer harm her.

Sam grinned at Jack's wonder. 'Well, Bill Cunningham

here,' he said with a nod towards Bill, 'he managed to tell us a good bit over the radio last night, and we put two and two together, and reckoned we'd better get going. So we got going and came over to this island as fast as we could. We found Joe's boat here, and signs of an early departure – stacks of dud notes in crates on the beach – and all kinds of other interesting documents.'

'How did you get here so quickly? There are no boats near on this coast,' said Philip.

'We've got a few fast motor boats of our own,' said Sam. 'We took two of them and came along here top speed, down along the coast. There they are.'

The boys turned, and saw two big and smart motor boats bobbing on the water near the cove, each one in charge of a mechanic. Near by was Joe's own boat.

'As soon as we spotted that the gang had wound up their business and were going to go off with their dud money, we saw our chance,' grinned Sam. 'So we posted a man at each of the shaft-holes – we didn't know which one the gang used, you see – and then, up one of them came the whole of the gang, one by one. And we got them nicely.'

'Just like you got us,' said Jack. 'That was smart work. What are we going to do now?'

'Bill Cunningham is head of this show,' said Sam, and turned an enquiring face to Bill. Bill looked at the boys apologetically.

'Sorry I had to give you a wrong name,' he said. 'But my own name is a bit too well know in some quarters to give away when I'm on a job of this sort. So I was just Bill Smugs to you.'

'You always will be,' said Philip. 'I shall never think of you as anything else, Bill.'

'Right,' said Bill, grinning. 'Bill Smugs I am. Now – what about getting these pretty gentlemen safely into the motor boats?'

The gang of fierce-looking men were pushed into the two boats. Jake still wore his black patch, but he glared so

185

fiercely at Kiki with his one free eye that Jack called the parrot to his shoulder. If looks could kill, Kiki would certainly have died under that glare of Jake's. The man was remembering how the bird had been locked up instead of the boy. That mistake had probably led to all this bad luck.

'I think *we'll* sail Joe's boat home,' said Bill to the boys. 'Come on. Let the motor boats go first and then we'll follow. Hi, Sam! Make for that house – you know – Craggy-Tops. There's a good mooring-place there.'

'Right,' said Sam, and off the motor boats went, making a terrific roaring noise over the sea. Then Bill and the boys set off in Joe's boat, and all three boats went safely out of the gap in the rocks and on to the open sea beyond.

'Well, all's well that ends well,' said Bill, as they put up the sail and set course for home. 'But there *were* a few moments when I didn't think we were going to end up as well as we *have* done.'

The boys thought so too. Philip wondered how the girls were getting on. They would be worried by now.

'I'm jolly hungry,' said Jack. 'It's ages since I had a good meal – really ages.'

'It must be,' said Bill. 'Never mind – soon be back now – then you can tuck in to your heart's content.'

The girls and Aunt Polly heard the sound of the motor boats long before they came to shore. They went out to see what was making the noise. They were filled with astonishment to see two big motor boats packed with men, and a sailing boat which looked like Joe's, all making for Craggy-Tops.

'Whatever does it all mean?' said Aunt Polly, who was still looking white and ill. 'Oh dear! – my heart will never stand all this excitement.'

The motor boats nosed to the mooring-posts in the little harbour. The girls ran down, and were amazed to see Joe among the men. They stared at them, trying to find the boys.

'Hallo, there!' called Sam. 'Are you looking for Bill What's-his-name and the boys? They're following after us in the other boat. Have you got a telephone here, by any chance?'

'Yes, we have,' said Dinah. 'What are all these men? Why is Joe with them?'

'Tell you everything soon,' said Sam, getting out of the boat. 'I must telephone before I do anything. You show me the phone, there's a good girl.'

Sam put through a call, asking for four or five motor-cars to be sent to Craggy-Tops at once, to take away the prisoners. Aunt Polly, her heart beating fast, listened in the greatest surprise. What *could* all this mean?

She soon understood when the sailing boat arrived, and Bill and the boys came into the house. They told her the whole story, and she sank back on the couch in horror when she heard what a wicked and dangerous fellow Joe was.

'As clever as a bagful of monkeys,' said Bill. 'But he's not got away with it *this* time – thanks to these four smart children.'

'It's funny,' said Jack. 'We went to the island to find a Great Auk – and we found instead a whole gang of men working at hidden printing-machines down in the mines.'

'If I'd known you were doing things like that, I'd have sent you all to bed,' said Aunt Polly severely. That made everyone laugh.

'Oh, naughty girl, naughty girl, Polly!' cried Kiki, flying to Aunt Polly's shoulder.

The cars arrived as the boys and Bill were in the middle of a most enormous meal. The men were packed into them and driven off swiftly. Sam said goodbye and departed with them.

'Good work, Bill!' he said as he went. 'And those kids want a pat on the back too.'

They got plenty of pats. The next day or two were so exciting that not one of the children slept properly at night.

For one thing they were taken to the nearest big town, and had to tell all they knew to two or three very solemn gentlemen.

'Big wigs,' said Bill mysteriously. 'Very big wigs. Jack, have you got the photograph of that pile of tins you saw on the island? Joe denies that he ever took supplies there, and we've found some empty tins in the cellar at Craggy-Tops which we may be able to identify by means of your snap.'

So even the little photograph of the tins came in useful, and was a bit of what Bill called the 'evidence against the prisoners.'

Another little bit of excitement was Jack's nugget. The boy was disappointed to hear that it was not valuable – but as a curiosity, a memory of a great adventure, it was thrilling.

'I shall take it back to school with me and present it to the museum we have there,' said Jack. 'All the boys will love to see it and handle it and hear how I got it. Won't they be envious! It isn't everybody who gets lost in old copper mines and finds a nugget hidden away. The only thing is – I'm awfully disappointed it's not valuable, because I did want to sell it and share the money between us.'

'Yes,' said Lucy, 'that would have been lovely. Tufty's share of it would have paid for his and Dinah's schooling, so that their mother and aunt could have had a rest, and not had to work so hard. It's a pity we couldn't have got a lot of money for it.'

But that didn't matter a bit, because, most unexpectedly, a very large sum came to the four children from another source. A reward had been offered to anyone giving information that would lead to the discovery of the counterfeiters – and it was naturally presented to the four children, though Bill had his share of it too.

Philip's mother came to Craggy-Tops when she heard all about the strange and thrilling adventure and its unexpectedly marvellous results. Jack and Lucy-Ann loved her. She was pretty and kind and merry, everything a mother should be.

'It's a shame your mother can't have a nice home of her own and you and Dinah with her,' said Jack to Philip.

'We're going to,' said Dinah, her eyes glowing. 'At last we're going to. There's enough money now for Mother to make a home for us herself, and stop working so hard. We've reckoned it all out. And what about you and Lucy-Ann coming to live with us. Freckles? You don't want to go back to your crusty old uncle and horrid old housekeeper, do you?'

'Oh!' said Lucy-Ann, her green eyes shining like stars. She fell on Philip and hugged him tightly. Dinah never did that, but Philip found that he liked it. 'Oh! Nothing could be nicer! We'd share your mother, and we'd have such fun together. But do you think your mother will have us?'

'Of course,' said Dinah. 'We particularly asked her that. She says if she's got to put up with two children, she might as well put up with four.'

'And Kiki too?' asked Jack, a sudden doubt creeping into his mind.

'Well, of course!' said Dinah and Philip together. It was unthinkable that Kiki should not live with them all.

'What's going to happen to your Aunt Polly and Uncle Jocelyn?' asked Jack. 'I'm sorry for your aunt – she oughtn't to live in this ruined old house, slaving away, looking after your uncle, being lonely and miserable and ill. But I suppose your uncle will never leave Craggy-Tops?'

'Well, he's got to now – and do you know why?' said Dinah. 'It's because the well water is salt. The sea did go into it, entering it from the old passage down there – so it's undrinkable. It would cost too much to put the well right, so poor old Uncle had to choose between staying at Craggy-Tops and dying of thirst, or leaving it and going somewhere else.'

Everyone laughed. 'Well, Joe did some good after all when he flooded the mines,' said Philip. 'It has forced Uncle Jocelyn to make up his mind to move – and Aunt Polly will be able to get the little cottage she has always wanted, and live there in peace, instead of in this great ruin – with no Joe to do the rough jobs.'

189

'Oh – that horrid Joe!' said Lucy-Ann, with one of her shivers. 'How I did hate him! I'm glad he's locked away for years and years. I shall be grown up when he comes out of prison, and I shan't be afraid of him any more.'

Bill arrived in his car, bringing with him a crate of ginger beer, for now no one could drink the well water. The children cheered. It was nice to have ginger beer for breakfast, dinner and tea. Bill presented Aunt Polly and Philip's mother with a most enormous thermos flask full of hot tea.

'Oh, *Bill*!' said Philip's mother, with a little squeal that Kiki promptly imitated, 'What an enormous flask! I've never seen such a giant. Thank you so much.'

Bill stayed to supper. It was hilarious especially when Philip's mouse ran out of his sleeve on to the table to Dinah's plate. That made everyone laugh. Lucy-Ann looked round at the laughing company and felt glad. She was going to live with a grown-up she would love, and children she was fond of. Everything was fun. Everything had turned out right. What a good thing she and Jack had escaped from Mr Roy all those weeks ago, and run away with Philip to Craggy-Tops!

'It's been a grand adventure,' said Lucy-Ann out loud. 'But I'm glad it's over. Adventures are *too* exciting when they're happening.'

'Oh *no*,' said Philip at once. 'That's the best part of an adventure – when it's happening. I think it's a great pity it's all over.'

'What a pity, what a pity!' said Kiki, having the last word as usual. 'Wipe your feet and shut the door. Put the kettle on. God save the Queen!'

Enid Blyton

The Castle of
Adventure

Contents

1

Now for the holidays!

Two girls sat on a window-seat in their school study. One had red wavy hair, and so many freckles that it was impossible to count them. The other had dark hair that stuck up in front in an amusing tuft.

'One more day and then the hols begin,' said red-haired Lucy-Ann, looking at Dinah out of curious green eyes. 'I'm longing to see Jack again. A whole term is an awfully long time to be away from him.'

'Well, I don't mind being away from *my* brother!' said Dinah, with a laugh. 'Philip's not bad, but he does make me wild, always bringing in those awful animals and insects of his.'

'It's a good thing there's only one day between our breaking-up days,' said Lucy-Ann. 'We shall be home first — and we can have a look round, and then the next day we shall meet the boys — hurrah!'

'I wonder what this place is like, that Mother has taken for the hols,' said Dinah. 'I'll get out her letter and read it again.'

She fished in her pocket for the letter and took it out. She skimmed it through.

'She doesn't say very much. Only that she wants our home to be decorated and cleaned, and so she has taken a cottage somewhere in the hills for us to stay in these hols,' said Dinah. 'Here's the letter.'

Lucy-Ann took it, and read it with interest. 'Yes — it's a place called Spring Cottage, and it's on the side of Castle Hill. She says it's rather a lonely sort of place, but packed with wild birds, so Jack will be very pleased.'

'I can't understand your brother being so mad on birds,' said Dinah. 'He's just as bad about birds as Philip is about insects and animals.'

'Philip is marvellous with animals, I think,' said Lucy-Ann, who had a great admiration for Dinah's brother. 'Do you remember that mouse he trained to take crumbs from between his teeth?'

'Oh, don't remind me of those things!' said Dinah, with a shudder. She could not bear even a spider near her, and bats and mice made her squeal. Lucy-Ann thought it was amazing that she should have lived so many years with an animal-loving boy like Philip, and yet still be afraid of things.

'He does tease you, doesn't he?' she said to Dinah, remembering how Philip had often put earwigs under Dinah's pillow, and black beetles in her shoes. He really was a terrible tease when he was in the mood. No wonder Dinah had such a temper!

'I wonder how Kiki has got on this term,' said Dinah.

Kiki was Jack's parrot, an extremely clever bird, who could imitate voices and sounds in a most remarkable manner. Jack had taught her many phrases, but Kiki had picked up many many more herself, especially from a cross old uncle that Lucy-Ann and Jack had once lived with.

'Kiki wasn't going to be allowed to be at school with Jack this term,' said Lucy-Ann sadly. 'It's an awful pity – but still he got a friend in the town to look after her for him, and he goes to see her every day. But I do think they might have let him have her at school.'

'Well, considering that Kiki kept telling the headmaster not to sniff, and Jack's form master to wipe his feet, and woke everyone up at night by screeching like a railway engine, I'm not surprised they didn't want Kiki this term,' said Dinah. 'Anyway, we'll be able to have her for the hols and that will be nice. I really do like Kiki – she doesn't seem like a bird, but like one of us, somehow.'

8

Kiki certainly was a good companion. Although she didn't converse with the children properly, she could talk nineteen to the dozen when she wanted to, saying the most ridiculous things and making the children laugh till they cried. She adored Jack, and would sit quietly on his shoulder for hours if he would let her.

The girls were glad that the holidays were so soon coming. They and the two boys and Kiki would have good fun together. Lucy-Ann especially looked forward to being with Dinah's pretty, merry mother.

Jack and Lucy-Ann Trent had no father or mother, and had lived with a cross old uncle for years, until by chance they had met Philip and Dinah Mannering. These two had no father, but they had a mother, who worked hard for them. She worked so hard that she had no time to make a home for them, so they were sent to boarding school, and in the holidays went to an aunt and uncle.

But now things were changed. Dinah's mother had enough money to make a home for them, and had offered to have their great friends, Jack and Lucy-Ann, as well. So in term time the two girls went to school together, and the two boys were at another school. In the holidays all four joined up with Mrs Mannering, the mother of Philip and Dinah.

'No more uncles and aunts!' said Dinah joyfully, who hadn't much liked her absent-minded old Uncle Jocelyn. 'Just a lovely home with my mother!'

Now, in the coming holidays, they were all to be together in this holiday cottage that Mrs Mannering had found. Although Dinah was a little disappointed at not going back to the home her mother had made for them all, she couldn't help looking forward to the holiday cottage. It sounded nice – and what fine walks and picnics they would have among the hills!

'Do you remember that marvellous adventure we had last summer?' she said to Lucy-Ann, who was looking dreamily out of the window, thinking how lovely it would be to see her brother Jack the day after next.

Lucy-Ann nodded. 'Yes,' she said, and she screwed up her freckled nose a little. 'It was the most exciting adventure anyone could have – but oh dear, how afraid I was sometimes! That Isle of Gloom – do you remember it, Dinah?'

'Yes – and that shaft going right down into the heart of the earth – and how we got lost there – golly, that *was* an adventure!' said Dinah. 'I wouldn't mind having another one, really.'

'You *are* funny!' said Lucy-Ann. 'You shiver and shake when you see a spider, but yet you seem to enjoy adventures so exciting that they make me tremble even to remember them!'

'Well – we shan't have any more,' said Dinah, rather regretfully. 'One adventure like that is enough for a lifetime, I suppose. I bet the boys will want to talk about it again and again. Do you remember how in the Christmas hols we couldn't make them stop?'

'Oh – I wish the hols would come quickly!' said Lucy-Ann, getting off the window-seat restlessly. 'I don't know why these last two or three days always drag so.'

But tomorrow came at last, and the two girls went off in the train with scores of their friends, chattering and laughing. Their luggage was safely in the van, their tickets were in their purses, their hearts beat fast in delight. Now for the holidays!

They had to change trains twice, but Dinah was good at that sort of thing. Lucy-Ann was timid and shy in her dealings with strangers, but twelve-year-old Dinah stood no nonsense from anyone. She was a strapping, confident girl, well able to hold her own. Lucy-Ann seemed two or three years younger to Dinah, although actually there was only one year between them.

At last they were at the station for their holiday home.

They leapt out and Dinah found the one and only porter. He went to get their luggage.

'There's Mother!' shouted Dinah, and rushed to her pretty, bright-eyed mother, who had come to meet them. Dinah was not one to hug or kiss very much, but Lucy-Ann made up for that! Dinah gave her mother one quick peck of a kiss, but Lucy-Ann gave her a bear-hug, and rubbed her red head happily against Mrs Mannering's chin.

'Oh, it's lovely to see you again!' she said, thinking for the hundredth time how lucky Dinah was to have a mother of her own. She felt grateful to her for letting her share her. It wasn't very nice, having no father or mother to write to you, or welcome you home. But Mrs Mannering always made her feel that she loved her and wanted her.

'I've got the car outside to meet you,' said Mrs Mannering. 'Come along. The porter will bring your luggage.'

They went out of the station. It was only a little country station. Outside was a country lane, its banks starred with spring flowers. The sky was blue and the air was warm and soft. Lucy-Ann felt very happy. It was the first day of the holidays, she was with Dinah's lovely mother, and tomorrow the boys came home.

They got into the little car, and the porter put the trunks in at the back. Mrs Mannering took the wheel.

'It's quite a long way to Spring Cottage,' she said. 'We have to fetch our own goods and food from the village here, except for eggs and butter and milk which a nearby farm lets me have. But it's lovely country, and there are marvellous walks for you. As for birds – well, Jack will have the time of his life!'

'It's nesting time too – he'll be thinking of nothing but eggs and nests,' said Lucy-Ann, feeling just a little jealous of the bird life that took up so much of her brother's time.

The girls looked round them as Mrs Mannering drove along. It certainly was lovely country. It was very hilly, and

11

in the distance the hills looked blue and rather exciting. The car ran along a road down a winding river valley, and then began to climb a steep hill.

'Oh, is our cottage on the side of this hill?' asked Dinah, thrilled. 'What a lovely view we'll have Mother!'

'We have – right across the valley to other hills, and yet more hills rising beyond them!' said her mother. The car had to go very slowly now, for the road was steep. As they rose higher and higher, the girls could see more and more across the valley. Then Lucy-Ann glanced upwards to see how high they were – and she gave a shout.

'I say! Look at that castle on the top of the hill! Just look at it!'

Dinah looked. It certainly was a most imposing and rugged old castle. It had a tower at each end, and its walls looked thick. It had slit windows – but it had wide ones too, which looked a little odd.

'Is it a really old castle?' asked Lucy-Ann.

'No – not really,' said Mrs Mannering. 'Some of it is old, but most of it has been restored and rebuilt, so that it is a real mix-up. Nobody lives there now. I don't know who it belongs to, either – no one seems to know or care. It's shut up, and hasn't a very good name.'

'Why? Did something horrid happen there once?' asked Dinah, feeling rather thrilled.

'I think so,' said her mother. 'But I really don't know anything about it. You'd better not go up there, anyhow, because the road up to it has had a landslide or something, and is very dangerous. They say that part of the castle is ready to slip down the hill!'

'Gracious! I hope it won't slip on to our cottage!' said Lucy-Ann, half scared.

Mrs Mannering laughed. 'Of course not. We are nowhere near it – look, there's our cottage, tucked away among those trees.'

It was a lovely little cottage, with a thatched roof and small leaded windows. The girls loved it the minute they saw it.

'It's just a bit like the house you bought for us,' said Dinah. 'That's pretty too. Oh, Mother, we shall have a lovely time here! Won't the boys be thrilled?'

There was a fair-sized shed at the side into which Mrs Mannering drove the car. Everyone got out. 'Leave the trunks for a bit,' said Dinah's mother. 'The man who comes from the farm will carry them in. Now – welcome to Spring Cottage!'

2
The boys come home – and Kiki!

That day and the morning of the next the two girls spent in exploring their holiday home. It was certainly a tiny place, but just big enough for them. There was a large old fashioned kitchen and a tiny parlour. Above were three small bedrooms.

'One for Mother, one for you and me, Lucy-Ann, and one for the boys,' said Dinah. 'Mother's going to do the cooking and we're all to help with the housework, which won't be much. Isn't our bedroom sweet?'

It was a little room tucked into the thatched roof, with a window jutting out from the thatch. The walls slanted in an odd fashion, and the ceiling slanted too. The floor was very uneven, and the doorways were low, so that Dinah who was growing tall, had to lower her head under one or two in case she bumped it.

'Spring Cottage,' she said. 'It's a nice name for it, especially in the springtime.'

'It's named because of the spring that runs down behind it,' said her mother. 'The water starts somewhere up in the yard of the castle, I believe, runs down through a tunnel it has made for itself, and gushes out just above the cottage at the back. It runs through the garden then, and disappears down the hillside.'

The girls explored the spring. They found where it gushed out, and Dinah tasted the water. It was cold and crystal clear. She liked hearing the gurgling sound it made in the untidy little garden. She heard it all night long in her sleep and loved it.

The view from the cottage was magnificent. They could see the whole of the valley below, and could follow too the winding road that led up to their cottage. Far away in the distance was the railway station, looking like a toy building. Twice a day a train came into it, and it too looked like a toy.

'Just like the railway engine and carriages that Jack used to have,' said Lucy-Ann, remembering. 'And how cross our old Uncle Geoffrey was when we used to set it going! He said it made more noise than a thunderstorm. Golly, I'm glad we don't live with him any more.'

Dinah looked at her watch. 'It's almost time to meet the train,' she said. 'I bet the boys are feeling excited! Come on. Let's find my mother.'

Mrs Mannering was just about to go and get the car out. The girls packed themselves in beside her. Lucy-Ann felt terribly excited. She was so looking forward to being with Jack again. And with Philip too. It would be lovely to be all together once more. She did hope Dinah wouldn't fly into one of her tempers *too* soon! She and Philip quarrelled far too much.

They arrived at the little station. The train was not yet signalled. Lucy-Ann walked up and down, longing to see the signal go down – and then, with an alarming clank, it did go down. Almost at the same moment the smoke of the train

14

appeared, and then, round the corner, came the engine, puffing vigorously, for it was uphill to the station.

Both the boys were hanging out of the window, waving and shouting. The girls screamed greetings, and capered about in delight.

'There's Kiki!' shouted Lucy-Ann. 'Kiki! Good old Kiki!'

With a screech Kiki flew off Jack's shoulder and landed on Lucy-Ann's. She rubbed her beak against the little girl's cheek and made a curious cracking noise. She was delighted to see her.

The boys jumped out of the carriage. Jack rushed to Lucy-Ann and gave her a hug which the little girl returned, her eyes shining. Kiki gave another screech and flew back on to Jack's shoulder.

'Wipe your feet,' she said sternly to the startled porter. 'And where is your handkerchief?'

Philip grinned at his sister Dinah. 'Hallo, old thing,' he said. 'You've grown! Good thing I have too, or you'd be as tall as I am! Hallo, Lucy-Ann – *you* haven't grown! Been a good girl at school?'

'Don't talk like a grown-up!' said Dinah. 'Mother's outside in the car. Come and see her.'

The porter took their trunks on his barrow and followed the four excited children. Kiki flew down to the barrow and looked at him with bright eyes.

'How many times have I told you to shut the door?' she said. The porter dropped the handles of the barrow in surprise. He didn't know whether to answer this extraordinary bird or not.

Kiki gave a laugh just like Jack's and flew out to the car. She joined the others, and tried to get on to Mrs Mannering's shoulder. She liked Dinah's mother very much.

'Attention, please,' said Kiki sternly. 'Open your books at page six.'

Everyone laughed. 'She got that from one of the masters,'

said Jack. 'Oh, Aunt Allie, she was so funny in the train. She put her head out of the window at every station and said "Right away, there!" just as she had heard a guard say, and you should have seen the engine-driver's face!'

'It's lovely to have you back,' said Lucy-Ann, keeping close to Jack. She adored her brother though he didn't really take a great deal of notice of her. They all got into the car, and the porter shoved the luggage in somehow, keeping a sharp eye on Kiki.

'Please shut the door,' she said, and went off into one of her never-ending giggles.

'Shut up, Kiki,' said Jack, seeing the porter's startled face. 'Behave yourself, or I'll send you back to school.'

'Oh, you naughty boy!' said Kiki; 'oh, you naughty, naughty, naughty . . .'

'I'll put an elastic band round your beak if you dare to say another word!' said Jack. 'Can't you see I want to talk to Aunt Allie?'

Jack and Lucy-Ann called Mrs Mannering Aunt Allie, because 'Mrs Mannering' seemed too stiff and standoffish. She liked both children very much, but especially Lucy-Ann, who was far more gentle and affectionate than Dinah had ever been.

'I say – this looks exciting country!' said Philip, looking out of the car windows. 'Plenty of birds here for you, Freckles – and plenty of animals for me!'

'Where's that brown rat you had this term?' said Jack, with a mischievous glance at Dinah. She gave a squeal at once.

Philip began to feel about in his pockets, diving into first one and then the other, whilst Dinah watched him in horror, expecting to see a brown rat appear at any moment.

'Mother! Stop the car and let me walk!' begged Dinah. 'Philip's got a rat somewhere on him.'

'Here he is – no, it's my hanky,' said Philip. 'Ah – what's

this? – no, that's not him. Now – here we are . . . .'

He pretended to be trying to get something out of his pocket with great difficulty. 'Ah, you'd bite, would you?'

Dinah squealed again, and her mother stopped the car. Dinah fumbled at the door-handle.

'No, you stay in, Dinah,' said her mother. 'Philip, you get out and the rat too. I quite agree with Dinah – there are to be no rats running all over us. So you can get out and walk, Philip.'

'Well, Mother – as a matter of fact – I've left the rat behind at school,' said Philip, with a grin. 'I was just teasing Dinah, that's all.'

'Beast!' said Dinah.

'I thought you were,' said his mother, driving on again. 'Well, you nearly had to walk home, so just be careful! I don't mind any of your creatures myself, except rats or snakes. Now, what do you think of Spring Cottage?'

The boys liked it just as much as the girls did – but it was the strange old castle that really took their fancy. Dinah forgot to sulk as she pointed it out to the boys.

'We'll go up there,' said Jack, at once.

'I think not,' said Mrs Mannering. 'I've just explained to the girls that it's dangerous up there.'

'Oh – but why?' asked Jack, disappointed.

'Well, there has been a landslide on the road, and no one dares to set foot on it now,' said Mrs Mannering. 'I did hear that the whole castle is slipping a bit, and might collapse if the road crumbles much more.'

'It sounds very exciting,' said Philip, his eyes gleaming.

They went indoors and the girls showed them their room up in the roof. Lucy-Ann was so delighted to be with Jack that she could hardly leave him for a minute. He was very like her, with deep-red hair, green eyes and hundreds of freckles. He was a very natural, kindly boy, and most people liked him at once.

17

Philip, whom Jack often called Tufty, was very like *his* sister too, but much more even-tempered. He had the same unruly lock of hair in front, and even their mother had this, so that Jack often referred to them as 'The Three Tufties.' The boys were older than the two girls, and very good friends indeed.

'Holidays at last!' said Philip, undoing his trunk. Dinah watched him from a safe distance.

'Got any creatures in there?' she asked.

'Only a baby hedgehog; and you needn't worry, he's got no fleas,' said Philip.

'I bet he has,' said Dinah, moving a few steps back. 'I shan't forget that hedgehog you found last summer.'

'I tell you, this baby one hasn't got any fleas at all,' said Philip. 'I got some stuff from the chemist and powdered him well, and he's as clean as can be. His spines haven't turned brown yet!'

The girls looked with interest as Philip showed them a tiny prickly ball rolled up in his jerseys in the trunk. It uncurled a little and showed a tiny snout.

'He's sweet,' said Lucy-Ann, and even Dinah didn't mind him.

'The only snag about him is — he's going to be awfully prickly to carry about with me,' said Philip, putting the tiny thing into his shorts pocket.

'You'll probably stop carrying him about when you've sat on him once or twice,' said Dinah.

'I probably shall,' said Philip. 'And just see you don't annoy me too much, Di — for he'd be a marvellous thing to put into your bed!'

'Shut up bickering, you two, and let's go out and explore,' said Jack. 'Lucy-Ann says there's a spring in the garden that comes all the way down from the castle.'

'I'm king of the castle,' said Kiki, swaying gently to and fro on top of the dressing-table. 'Pop goes the weasel.'

'You're getting a bit mixed,' said Jack. 'Come on – out we all go!'

3

Settling in at Spring Cottage

The first day or two were very happy days indeed. The four children and Kiki wandered about as they pleased, and Jack found so many hundreds of nests that he marvelled to see them. He was mad on birds, and would spend hours watching them, if the others let him.

He got very excited one day because he said he saw an eagle. 'An *eagle*!' said Dinah disbelievingly. 'Why, I thought eagles were extinct, and couldn't be found any more – like that Great Auk you always used to be talking about.'

'Well, eagles aren't extinct,' said Jack scornfully. 'That just shows how little you know. I'm sure this was an eagle. It soared up and up and up into the air just as eagles are said to do. I believe it was a Golden Eagle.'

'Is it dangerous?' said Dinah.

'Well, I suppose it might attack you if you went too near its nest,' said Jack, 'Golly – I wonder if it *is* nesting anywhere near here!'

'Well, I'm not going eagle-nesting,' said Dinah firmly. 'Anyway, Jack, you've found about a hundred nests already – surely that's enough for you without wanting to see an eagle's nest as well.'

Jack never took birds' eggs, nor did he disturb the sitting birds at all. No bird was ever afraid of him, any more than any animal was ever afraid of Philip. If Lucy or Dinah so much as looked at a nest, the sitting bird seemed frightened and flew off – but she would allow Jack to stroke her,

19

without moving a feather! It was very odd.

Kiki always came with them on their excursions, sitting on Jack's shoulder. He had taught her not to make a sound when he wanted to watch any bird, but Kiki seemed to object to the rooks that lived around. There was a large rookery in one clump of trees not far off, and Kiki would often go to sit on a nearby branch and address rude remarks to the astonished rooks.

'It's a pity they can't answer her back,' said Philip. 'But all they say is "Caw-caw-caw." '

'Yes, and Kiki says it too, now,' said Jack. 'She goes on cawing for ages unless I stop her. Don't you, Kiki?'

Kiki took Jack's ear into her sharp curved beak and fondled it gently. She loved Jack to talk to her. She made a cracking noise with her beak, and said lovingly, 'Caw-caw-caw-caw-caw . . .'

'All right, that's enough,' said Jack. 'Go and listen to a nightingale or something and imitate that! A rook's caw isn't anything to marvel at. Stop, Kiki!'

Kiki stopped, and gave a realistic sneeze. 'Where's your hanky, where's your hanky?' she said.

To Lucy-Ann's delight, Jack gave her a hanky, and Kiki spent the next minute or two holding it in her clawed foot and dabbing her beak with it, sniffing all the time.

'New trick,' explained Jack, with a grin. 'Good, isn't it?'

There were gorgeous walks around the cottage. It was about three miles to the little village, and except for the few houses and the one general shop there, there were no other houses save for a farm or two, and a lonely farm cottage here and there in the hills.

'We're not likely to have any adventures *here*,' said Philip. 'It's all so quiet and peaceful. The village folk have hardly a word to say, have they? They say "Ah, that's right" to everything.'

'They're amazed by Kiki,' said Dinah.

'Ah, that's right,' said Jack, imitating the speech of the villagers.

Kiki immediately did the same. 'Do you remember when Kiki got locked up in a cave underground, and the man who locked her up heard her talking to herself, and thought she was me?' said Jack, remembering the adventure of the summer before. 'My word, that was an adventure!'

'I'd like another adventure, really,' said Philip. 'But I don't expect we'll have another all our lives long.'

'Well, they say adventures come to the adventurous,' said Jack. 'And we're pretty adventurous, I think. I don't see why we shouldn't have plenty more.'

'I wish we could go up and explore that strange castle,' said Dinah longingly, looking up to where it towered on the summit of the hill. 'It looks such an odd place, so deserted and lonely, standing up there, frowning over the valley. Mother says something horrid once happened there, but she doesn't know what.'

'We'll try and find out,' said Jack promptly. He always liked hair-raising tales. 'I expect people were killed there, or something.'

'Oooh, how horrid – I don't want to go up there,' said Lucy-Ann at once.

'Well, Mother said we weren't to, anyhow,' said Dinah.

'She might let us go eagle-nesting,' said Philip. 'And if our search took us near the castle, we couldn't very well help it, could we?'

'We'd better tell her, if we do go anywhere near,' said Jack, who didn't like the idea of deceiving Philip's kindly mother in any way. 'I'll ask her if she minds.'

So he asked her that evening. 'Aunt Allie, I believe there may be an eagle's nest somewhere on the top of this hill,' he said. 'It's so high it's almost a mountain – and that's where eagles nest, you know. You wouldn't mind if I tried to find the nest, would you?'

21

'No, not if you are careful,' said Mrs Mannering. 'But would your hunt take you anywhere near the old castle?'

'Well, it might,' said Jack honestly. 'But you can trust us not to fool about on any landslides, Aunt Allie. We shouldn't dream of getting the girls into danger.'

'Apparently there was a cloudburst on the top of this hill some years back,' said Mrs Mannering, 'and such a deluge of water fell that it undermined the foundations of the castle, and most of the road up to it slid away down the hillside. So, you see, it really might be very dangerous to explore up there.'

'We'll be very careful,' promised Jack, delighted that Mrs Mannering hadn't forbidden outright their going up the hill to the castle.

He told the others, and they were thrilled. 'We'll go up tomorrow, shall we?' said Jack. 'I really do want to hunt about to see if there is any sign of an eagle's nest.'

That afternoon, in their wanderings, they had a curious feeling of being followed. Once or twice Jack turned round, sure that someone was behind them. But there was never anyone there.

'Funny,' he said to Philip in a low voice. 'I felt certain there was someone behind us then – I heard the crack of a twig – as if someone had trodden on it and broken it.'

'Yes – I thought so too,' said Philip. He looked puzzled. 'I tell you what, Jack. When we get into that patch of trees, I'll crouch down behind a bush and stop, whilst you others go on. Then, if there's anyone following behind us for some reason, I'll see them.'

The girls were told what Philip was going to do. They too had felt that there was someone behind them. They all walked into the patch of trees, and then, when he came to a conveniently thick bush, Philip dropped down suddenly behind it and hid, whilst the others walked on, talking loudly.

22

Philip lay there and listened. He could hear nothing at first. Then he heard a rustle and his heart beat fast. Who *was* it tracking them, and why? There didn't seem any sense in it.

Someone came up to his bush. Someone crept past without seeing him. Philip gazed at the Someone and was so astonished that he let out an exclamation.

'*Well!*'

A girl with ragged clothes, bare feet and wild, curling hair, jumped violently and turned round. In a trice Philip had jumped up and had hold of her wrists. He did not hold her roughly, but he held her too firmly for her to get away. She tried to bite him, and kicked out with her bare feet.

'Now don't be silly,' said Philip. 'I'll let you go when you tell me who you are and why you are following us.'

The girl said nothing, but glared at Philip out of black eyes. The others, hearing Philip's voice, came running back.

'This is the person who was following us, but I can't get a word out of her,' said Philip.

'She's a wild girl,' said Dinah. The girl scowled at her. Then she glanced at Kiki, on Jack's shoulder, and stared as if she couldn't take her eyes off her.

'I believe she was only following us to get a glimpse of the parrot!' said Philip, with a laugh. 'Is that right, wild girl?'

The girl nodded, 'Ah, that's right,' she said.

'Ah, that's right,' said Kiki. The girl stared and gave a laugh of surpise. It altered her face at once, and gave her a merry, mischievous look.

'What's your name?' asked Philip, letting go her wrists.

'Tassie,' said the girl. 'I saw that bird, and I came after you. I didn't mean no harm. I live round the hill with my mother. I know where you live. I know all you do.'

'Oh – been spying round a bit, and following us, I suppose!' said Jack. 'Do you know this hillside well?'

Tassie nodded. Her bright black eyes hardly left Kiki. She seemed fascinated by the parrot.

'Pop goes the weasel,' said Kiki to her, in a solemn voice. 'Open your book at page six.'

'I say – do you know if the eagles nest on this hill?' asked Jack suddenly. He thought it quite likely that this wild little girl might know things like that.

'What's an eagle?' said Tassie.

'A big bird,' said Jack. 'A very big bird with a curved beak, and . . .'

'Like your bird there?' said Tassie, pointing to Kiki.

'Oh no,' said Jack. 'Well – never mind. If you don't know what an eagle is like, you won't know where it nests either.'

'It's time to go back home,' said Philip. 'I'm hungry. Tassie, take us the shortest way home!'

To Philip's surprise Tassie turned round and plunged down the hillside, as sure-footed as a goat. The others followed. She took them such a short cut that all of them were amazed when they saw Spring Cottage in front of them.

'Thanks, Tassie,' said Philip, and Kiki echoed his words. 'Thanks, Tassie.'

Tassie smiled, and her usual, rather sulky look fled. 'I'll see you again,' she said, and turned to go.

'Did you say you lived at that old cottage round the hill?' yelled Jack after her.

'Ah, that's right!' she shouted back, and disappeared into the bushes.

4

Tassie and Button

Certainly Castle Hill was a very lonely place, for, after they had explored it, there seemed to be only their cottage on it, Tassie's tumble-down home, and a farm some way off, where they got their eggs and milk. The village lay in the valley below.

But although the great hill was almost empty of people, it was full of wild life: birds for Jack, and animals of all kinds for Philip. Squirrels ran everywhere, rabbits popped up wherever they walked, and red foxes slunk by, not seeming at all scared.

'Golly! I wish I could get a baby fox, a little cub!' said Philip. 'I've always wanted one. They're like small and lively puppies, you know.'

Tassie was with them when he said this. She often joined up with them now, and was quite invaluable because she always knew the way home. It seemed very easy to get lost on the vast hill, but Tassie could always show them a short cut.

She was an odd girl. Sometimes she would not come near them but hovered about, some yards off, looking at Kiki with fascinated eyes. Sometimes she walked close to them, and listened to their talk, though she never said very much herself.

She looked with admiration and envy on the simple clothes of the two girls: Sometimes she took the stuff they were made of between her fingers and felt it. She never wore anything but a ragged frock that looked as if it had been made from a dirty sack. Her wild, curly hair was in a tangle, and she was always barefoot.

'I don't mind her being barefoot, but she's rather dirty,' said Lucy-Ann to Dinah. 'I don't believe she ever has a bath.'

'Well, she's probably not seen a bath in her life,' said Dinah. 'She looks awfully healthy though, doesn't she? I've never seen anyone with such bright eyes and pink cheeks and white teeth. Yet I bet she never cleans her teeth.'

On enquiry, it was found that Tassie didn't know what a bath was. Dinah took her into Spring Cottage and showed her the big tin bath they all used. Her mother was there and looked at the wild girl in amazement.

'Whoever is that dirty little girl?' she asked Lucy-Ann in a low voice. 'She'd better have a bath.'

Lucy-Ann knew Mrs Mannering would say that. Mothers thought a lot about people being clean. But when Dinah explained to Tassie what having a bath meant, Tassie looked scared. She shrank back in horror at the thought of sitting down in water.

'Now you listen to me,' said Mrs Mannering firmly. 'If you like to let me give you a bath and scrub you well, I'll find a cotton frock of Dinah's for you, and a ribbon for your hair.'

The thought of this finery thrilled Tassie to such an extent that she consented to have a bath. So she was shut up in the kitchen with Dinah's mother, a bath of hot water and plenty of soap.

After a bit such agonised shrieks came from the kitchen that the children in the garden outside wondered what could be happening. Then they heard Mrs Mannering's firm voice.

'Sit down properly. Get wet all over. Now don't be silly, Tassie. Think of that pretty blue cotton frock over there.'

More shrieks. Evidently Tassie had sat down but didn't like it. There came the sound of scrubbing.

'Your mother's doing the job thoroughly,' said Jack, with a grin. 'Pooh, what a smell of carbolic!'

In half an hour's time Tassie came out of the kitchen,

looking quite different. Her tanned face and arms were now only dark with sunburn, not with dirt. Her hair was washed and brushed, and tied back with a blue ribbon. She wore a blue cotton frock of Dinah's and on her feet she actually had a pair of old rubber shoes!

'Oh, Tassie – you look fine!' said Lucy-Ann, and Tassie looked pleased. She fancied herself very much indeed in her new clothes, and kept stroking the blue frock as if it was a cat.

'I smell nice,' she said, evidently liking the smell of carbolic soap better than the others did. 'But that bath was dreadful. How often do you have a bath? Once a year?'

Tassie was extraordinary. She could not read or write, and yet, like a Red Indian, she could read the signs in the woods and fields in a way that really astonished the children. She was more like a very intelligent animal than a little girl. She attached herself to Philip and also to Kiki, and plainly thought that he and the parrot were the most admirable members of the party.

The day after her bath, she came down to the cottage and looked in at the window. She held something in her arms and the others wondered what it was.

'There's Tassie,' said Lucy-Ann. 'She's got her blue frock on. But her hair's all in a tangle again. And whatever has she got round her neck?'

'Her shoes!' said Philip with a grin. 'I knew she wouldn't wear *those* long! She's so used to being barefooted that shoes would hurt her. But she can't bear to part with them, so she's strung them round her neck.'

'What *has* she got in her arms?' said Dinah curiously. 'Tassie, come in and show us what you've got.'

Tassie grinned, showing all her even white teeth, and went round to the back door. She appeared in the kitchen, and Philip gave a yell.

'It's a fox-cub! Oh, the pretty little thing! Tassie, where *did* you get it?'

'From its den,' said Tassie. 'I knew where a fox family lived, you see.'

Philip took the little cub in his arms. It was the prettiest thing imaginable, with its sharp little nose, its small brush-tail and its thick red coat. It lay quivering in Philip's arms, looking up at him.

Before many seconds had passed the spell that Philip seemed to put on all animals fell upon the fox cub. It crept up to his neck and licked him. It cuddled against him. It showed him in every way it could that it loved him.

'You've got a wonderful way with animals,' said his mother. 'Just like your father had. What a dear little cub, Philip! Where are you going to keep it? You will have to keep it in some sort of cage, won't you, or it will run off.'

'Of course not, Mother!' said Philip scornfully. 'I shall train it to run to heel, like a puppy. It will soon learn.'

'Well, but foxes are such wild creatures,' said his mother doubtfully. But no creature was wild with Philip. Before two hours had gone by the cub was scampering at Philip's heels, begging to be taken into his arms whenever the boy stopped.

Philip's liking for the little wild girl increased very much after that. He found that she knew an amazing amount about animals and their ways.

'She's like Philip's dog, always following him about,' said Dinah. 'Fancy anyone wanting to follow Philip!'

Dinah was not feeling very fond of her brother at that moment. He had four beetles just then, which he said he was training to be obedient to certain commands. He kept them in his bedroom, but they wandered about in a manner that was most terrifying to poor Dinah.

Kiki disliked Philip's fox cub very much and scolded it vigorously whenever she saw it. But Tassie she loved, and flew to her shoulder as soon as she saw her, murmuring nonsense into her ear. Tassie, of course, was delighted about this, and felt enormously proud when Kiki came to her.

'You may think Tassie simply adores you but you come second to Kiki, all the same!' Dinah told Philip with a laugh.

'I wish Kiki would leave Button alone,' said Philip. Button was the name he had given to the little fox-cub, which, like Tassie, followed him about whenever it could. 'Kiki is really behaving badly about Button. I suppose she's jealous.'

'How many times have I told you to wipe your feet?' Kiki demanded of Button. 'Where's your handkerchief? God save the weasel! Pop goes the Queen!'

The children yelled with laughter. It was always funny when Kiki got mixed up in her sentences. Kiki regarded them solemnly, head on one side.

'Attention, please! Open your book at page six.'

'Shut up, Kiki! You remind me of school!' said Jack. 'I say, you others – I saw that eagle again today. It was soaring over the hill-top, and its wing spread was terrific. I'm sure it's got a nest up there.'

'Well, let's go up and find it,' said Dinah. 'I'm longing to have a squint at that old castle, anyway. Even if we can't go up the road that has landslided – or is it landslid? – we can get as close to it as possible and see what it's like.'

'Yes – let's do something exciting,' said Lucy-Ann. 'Let's take our tea out, and go up the hill as far as we can. You can look for eagles' nests, Jack, and we'll have a look at the old castle. It looks so strange and mysterious up there, frowning down at the valley, as if it had some secret to hide.'

'It's empty, you know,' said Philip. 'Probably full of mice and spiders and bats, but otherwise empty.'

'Oooh, don't let's go inside then,' said Dinah at once. 'I'd rather find an eagle's nest than get mixed up with bats inside the old castle!'

5

The way to the castle

'We're going up to the top of the hill, Mother,' said Philip.
'Hunting for an eagle's nest, to please old Jack. He's seen
that eagle again. We won't go up the road, so you needn't
worry – the road to the castle, I mean.'

'Take your tea with you,' said his mother. 'I shall be glad
to be rid of you all for the afternoon! I can do some reading
for a change!'

She and Dinah cut sandwiches, and packed up cake and
fruit and milk. Philip took the knapsack with the food, and
whistled to Button, who now answered his name or a
whistle for all the world as if he were a dog.

Button came running to him, giving little sharp barks. He
was a most attractive cub and even Mrs Mannering liked
him, though she said he smelt a bit strong sometimes. She
objected to Button sleeping on Philip's bed, and she and
Philip had lengthy arguments about this.

'Your bedroom's full of all kinds of creatures already,' she
said. 'There's that hedgehog always in and out of your room
now – and yesterday there was something jumping about all
over the place.'

Dinah shuddered. She never went into Philip's room if she
could help it.

'It was only old Terence the Toad,' said Philip. 'I've got
him somewhere about me now, so he won't be leaping about
in my bedroom. I'll show him to you – he's got the most
beautiful eyes you ever . . .'

'No, Philip,' said his mother firmly. 'I don't want to see
him. Don't disturb him.'

Philip stopped ferreting about his person, and put on an

injured expression. 'Nobody ever . . .' he began, but Button took his attention by trying to climb up his leg to get into his arms. 'What's the matter, Button? Has Kiki been teasing you again? Has she been pulling your tail?'

The fox cub chattered to him, and finally settled down comfortably on the top of the knapsack which Philip had slung across his back. 'Where are the others?' said Philip. 'Oh, there they are. Hi, everyone, are you ready?'

They set off up the winding roadway, narrow and steep, just wide enough to take a cart. Tassie soon appeared from somewhere, still wearing the cotton frock, though it was now torn and dirty. She had the rubber shoes tied round her waist that day. It amused the children that she always brought them with her, although she never wore them.

'Her feet must be as hard as nails,' said Jack. 'She never seems to mind treading on the sharpest stones!'

Tassie attached herself to Philip and Button. Kiki addressed a few amiable remarks to her, and then flew off over the rookery to startle the rooks with her realistic cawings. They could never get over their astonishment at this performance, and listened in silence until Kiki talked like a human being, when they all flew away in disgust.

The children went on up the road. It was very hot that afternoon, and they panted and puffed as they climbed. 'Why did we choose an afternoon like this to go up to the castle?' said Philip.

Tassie stopped. 'To the castle?' she said. 'You can't go this way. The road up above is blocked. You can only get round the back now.'

'Well, we want to see what there is to be seen,' said Philip. 'I'd like to see this landslide or whatever it is. We won't climb about on it, because we said we wouldn't. But I'd like to see it.'

'I'd like to go right into the castle,' said Jack.

'No, no!' said Tassie, her eyes widening as if she was

31

scared. The others looked at her with interest.

'Why not?' asked Jack. 'It's empty, isn't it?'

'No, it's not empty,' said Tassie. 'There are voices and cryings and the sound of feet. It is not a good place to go.'

'You've been listening to gossip,' said Philip. 'Who would be there now? There's no coming and going, there's no one ever seen about the castle! It's only the owls hooting there, or the bats squeaking or something.'

'What's the old story about the castle?' asked Dinah. 'Do you know it, Tassie?'

'It's said that a wicked man lived there once, who got people to visit him in his castle – and they were never heard of again,' said Tassie, speaking in a low voice as if she was afraid that the wicked man, whoever he was, might hear her. 'They heard cries and groans, and the clashing of swords. It is said, too, that he used to lock people up in hidden rooms, and starve them to death.'

'What a nice old man!' said Philip, with a laugh. 'I don't believe a word of it. You always get these stories about old places. I expect some half-mad old fellow came along, bought the old castle, patched it up, and lived there pretending to be an old-time baron or something. He must have been mad to live in a lonely place like that.'

'He had plenty of horses, they say, and they used this road every day,' said Tassie. 'Did you notice how here and there, in the steepest places, the road was cobbled? That was to help the horses.'

'Yes, I did notice a cobbled bit just now,' said Philip. The others were silent for a minute. Somehow the fact that the road really was cobbled here and there made them think there might be something in the story Tassie had told them.

'Anyway, that all happened years ago, and the old man's gone, and nobody's there,' said Philip. 'I'd love to explore all over the castle. Wouldn't you, Jack?'

'Rather!' said Jack. And Kiki agreed, swaying to and fro

32

on his shoulder. 'Rather,' said Kiki, 'rather, rather, rather, ra . . .'

'Kiki get off my shoulder for a bit,' panted Jack. 'You feel jolly heavy up this hill.'

'Kiki I'll have you!' said Tassie, and Kiki flew to her at once, informing her that she had better open her book at page six. Tassie did not pant and puff as the others did. She was like a goat, the way she sprang up the steepest places and never seemed in the least tired.

'Hallo – we're a good way up at last!' said Philip, wiping his hot forehead. 'Look, the road goes all strange here.'

So it did. It could no longer be called a road, for part of the hillside had fallen away and had piled itself on the road and all around. Enormous boulders of rock lay where they had rolled, and the stumps of trees showed where the moving hillside had cut them into pieces.

The children gazed over the untidy, rock-strewn landscape. 'It looks as if an earthquake had upset it,' said Lucy-Ann.

Beyond the landslide stood the castle, looking even more enormous now. The children could see how strongly built it was, and could see two of the square towers, with the long battlemented wall stretching between them.

'I'd like to go up into one of those towers,' said Philip longingly. 'What a marvellous view we'd get!'

'The castle isn't really right on top of the hill,' said Jack, 'though it looks as if it is from down below. Doesn't it look fierce, somehow!'

It did. None of the children thought it was a very nice castle. It seemed to be such a lonely, strange, sinister place. It frowned over the hillside, and was not at all welcoming. All the same, it was exciting.

'Tassie, how do we get to the back of it?' asked Philip, turning to the little girl. 'We *could* climb over this landslide bit, I suppose, but we said we wouldn't, and anyhow some of those boulders look as if they would like to go rolling over and over down the hillside if anybody gave them a little push!'

'There's my eagle again!' cried Jack suddenly, in excitement, and he pointed to a big bird that rose soaring in the air, above the castle. 'See it? It *is* an eagle, no doubt about it. Isn't it enormous? I bet it's got a nest somewhere about. Oh golly, there's another of them, look!'

Sure enough there were two magnificent eagles rising in the air. They rose higher and higher, and the children watched them, fascinated.

'How do they soar upwards like that without moving their wings?' asked Lucy-Ann. 'I could understand it if they soared downwards – glide, you know – but to go up and up and up – gracious, they're only just specks.'

'They use air-currents I expect,' said Jack. 'Must be plenty on a hill-top. *Two* eagles – and together. Well, that settles it – there must be a nest!'

'You're not thinking of taming a young eagle, I hope?' said Dinah, in alarm.

'Don't worry. Kiki would never let Jack have a tame eagle,' said Lucy-Ann.

This was true, and Dinah heaved a sigh of relief.

'They rose from somewhere behind the castle as far as I could see,' said Jack eagerly. 'Let's go round and see if we can find out where their nest is. Come on.'

They left the strange, untidy landslide, and, following Tassie, made their way to the east, climbing over the hillside with difficulty. Tassie led them to a winding little path, narrow but safe.

'Whose path is this?' said Dinah in surprise.

'The rabbits' path,' said Tassie. 'There are millions here. They make quite good little paths all over the place.'

'I can't go any further!' panted Lucy-Ann after some

while. 'I'm tired out. Let's rest and have our tea. The eagles' nest won't run away.'

Everyone thought that was a good idea. They flopped down on the grass, panting. Philip slung his knapsack round to his chest and undid it. He handed out the food, and then lay flat on the ground. Button immediately began to lick his face all over.

It was lovely to have a drink, though there wasn't nearly enough. No-one seemed very hungry, but Button and Kiki managed quite a few sandwiches between them. Tassie had a few too. She was the least tired out of any of them. She sat and scratched Kiki's head, whilst the others lay flat on the hillside.

They soon recovered and sat up. Philip heard the trickling of water somewhere near by and went to investigate. He still felt terribly thirsty. He called back to the others:

'The spring that runs past our cottage runs here. It's lovely and cold. Anyone want a drink?'

Everybody did. They got up and went to the little spring that gushed out from a hole in the hillside and then ran and leapt over the pebbly bed until it once more disappeared into the earth, to come out again further down.

The children bathed their hot feet in the cool water. Then Jack caught sight of his precious eagles again. 'Come on! We'll see where they fly down to. I wish I'd brought my camera! I could have photographed their nest!'

6

How can they get in?

They were near to the castle by now. The great, thick walls rose up, far above their heads. There was no break in them, except about sixteen feet up, where slit windows could be seen.

'It's built of the big boulders we see all over the hillside,' said Philip. 'It must have been very hard work to take so many up here to build the castle. Look – over there are some bigger windows. I suppose that wicked old fellow Tassie was telling us about liked to have a little more light in his castle than slit windows give. It's a funny place. You can quite well see where it has been patched up can't you?'

'There are the eagles again!' cried Jack. 'They're gliding down – and down. Watch them everyone!'

The little company stood and watched the two big birds, whose span of wings was really enormous.

'They've gone down inside the castle courtyard,' said Jack. 'That's where they've got their nest, I bet! In the courtyard somewhere. I simply must find it.'

'But you can't possibly get into the courtyard,' said Philip.

'Where's the gateway of the castle?' demanded Jack, turning to Tassie.

'At the front, where that landslide is,' said Tassie. 'You couldn't get over the landslide without being in danger, and anyway if you did, you'd find the great gate shut. There's another door, further along here, but that's locked. You can't get into the castle.'

'Where's the door along here?' said Jack. They went further along, turned a corner of the castle wall, and came to a sturdy oak door, flush with the wall. The wall arched over

36

it, and the door fitted exactly. Jack put his eye to the keyhole but could see nothing.

'Do you mean to tell me there's no other way into this castle?' he said to Tassie. 'What a peculiar place! It's like a prison.'

'That's what it was,' said Lucy-Ann, shivering as she remembered the story Tassie had told. 'A prison for poor wretched people who came here and couldn't get away – and were never heard of again!'

Jack was in despair. To think that two rare eagles might be nesting in the courtyard on the other side of the wall – and he couldn't get at them. It was too bad.

'We must get in, we simply must,' he said, and gazed up at the high windows. But there was no way of getting up there. The walls were far too smooth to climb. There was no ivy. The castle was impregnable.

'People would have got in before now if there had been a way,' said Philip. 'It just shows there's no way in if no one ever comes here.'

'Tassie – don't *you* know of a way?' said Jack, turning to the little girl. She considered solemnly. Then she nodded her head.

'I might know,' she said. 'I have never been. But it might be a way.'

'Show us, quickly!' said Jack eagerly.

Tassie led them further round the castle, towards the back of it. Here it was built almost into the cliff. A narrow, dark pathway led between the steep hillside and the back wall of the castle. It was almost a tunnel, for both wall and cliff practically met at one place.

Tassie came to a stop, and pointed up. The other four looked, and saw that there was one of the slit windows high up above them. They stared at Tassie, not seeing in the least how that helped them.

'Don't you see?' said Tassie. 'You could climb up the

37

cliffside here, because it is all overgrown with creepers – and then, when you get opposite that window, you might put a branch of a tree across or something, and get in.'

'I see what she means!' said Philip. 'If we could lug a plank or a bough up the side of the steep cliff here, that the castle backs on to – and put one end of it on to the windowsill, and the other firmly into the cliff – we could slide across and get in! It's an idea!'

The rest of the company received this news with mixed feelings. Dinah was already afraid of bats in the dark and narrow passageway, and would willingly have gone back into the sunshine of the open hillside. Lucy-Ann didn't like the idea of climbing the cliff and sliding across a dangerous branch that might slip, into the silent and deserted castle. Jack, on the other hand, thought it was well worth trying, and was eager to do so at once.

'Put on the light,' said Kiki earnestly from somewhere in the dark passage. 'Put on the light.'

The children laughed. It was funny the way Kiki sometimes said what sounded like a very sensible sentence.

'Let's find a branch or something,' said Jack. So they went out of the musty-smelling passage, and hunted for something to use as a bridge across to the window of the castle.

But there was nothing to be found at all. True, Philip found a dead branch, but it was so dead that it would have cracked at once under anyone's weight. It was impossible to break off from a tree a branch big enough to be any use.

'Blow!' said Jack. 'Anyway, let's go back and see if we can climb up opposite the window. If we think we *could* get in the way Tassie suggests, we might come up tomorrow with a plank.'

'Yes, it would be better to leave it till tomorrow, really,' said Dinah, trying to see the time by her watch. 'It's getting rather late now. Let's come up tomorrow with your camera, Jack.'

'All right. But we'll just see if it's possible to climb in at that window first,' said Jack. He tried to climb up the cliffside, but it was very steep, and he kept slipping down. Then Philip tried, and, by means of holding on tightly to some of the strongest of the creepers, he pulled himself up a little way.

But the creeper broke, and down he came, missing his footing at the bottom, and rolling over and over. Fortunately, except for a few bruises, he wasn't hurt.

'I'll go,' said Tassie. And up she went like a monkey. It was extraordinary the way she could climb. She was far better than any of them. She seemed to know just where to put her feet, and just which creeper to hold on to.

Soon she was opposite the slit window. The creepers grew very thickly on the cliff-side there, and she held on to them whilst she peered across at the window.

'I believe I could almost jump across to the sill,' she called to the others.

'Don't you do anything of the sort,' shouted back Philip at once. 'Little donkey! You'd break both your legs if you fell! What can you see?'

'Nothing much!' called back Tassie, who still seemed to be considering whether or not to jump across and chance it. 'There's the window – very narrow, or course. I don't know if we could squeeze through. And past the window I can see a room, but it's so dark I can't see if it's big or small or anything. It looks very strange.'

'I bet it does!' said Jack. 'Come on down, Tassie.'

'I'll just leap across and have a try at squeezing in,' said Tassie, and poised herself for a jump. But a roar from Philip stopped her.

'If you do that we'll never let you go with us again. Do you hear? You'll break your legs!'

Tassie thought better of her idea. The threat of never being allowed to go about with the children she so much liked and admired filled her with horror. She contented herself with one more look across at the window, and then she climbed down like a goat, landing directly beside the waiting children.

'It's just as well that you did as you were told,' said Philip grimly. 'Suppose you had got across – and squeezed inside – and then couldn't get out again! You'd have been a prisoner in that castle for ever and ever!'

Tassie said nothing. She had great faith in her powers of climbing and jumping, and she thought Philip was making a fuss about nothing. Kiki, hearing Philip's stern voice, joined in the scolding.

'How many times have I told you to shut the door?' she said, flying on to Tassie's shoulder. Tassie laughed and scratched Kiki's poll.

'Only about a hundred times,' she said, and the others laughed too. They made their way out of the dark tunnel-like passage, and were glad to be in the sun again.

'Well, we know what to do, anyway,' said Jack. 'We'll find a plank or something to bring up here tomorrow, and we'll send Tassie up with it, and she can put it across from the cliffside to the window. We'll give her a strong rope too, so that she can knot it to some of that creeper up there, and we can pull on it to help ourselves up. We're not as goat-footed as Tassie.'

'No, she's marvellous,' said Lucy-Ann, and Tassie glowed with pleasure. They made their way down the hillside again, finding it a little easier to climb down than up, especially as Tassie took them a good way she knew.

'It's really getting very late,' said Jack. 'I hope your mother won't be anxious, Philip.'

'Oh no,' said Philip. 'She'd know one of us would run down for help if anything happened.'

All the same, Mrs Mannering *had* been wondering what had become of the children and she was very glad to see

40

them. She had supper ready for them, and Tassie was asked to stay too. She was thrilled, and tried to watch how the others ate and drank, as she had never been invited out before. Kiki sat on Jack's shoulder, and fed on titbits that Jack and the others handed her, making odd remarks from time to time about putting the kettle on, and using handkerchiefs. Button curled up on Philip's knee and went sound asleep. He was tired after his long walk, though Philip had carried him a good way.

'You know, I half thought Button might run off when we took him out on the hillside he knows so well,' said Philip. 'But he didn't. He didn't even seem to think of it.'

'He's a darling,' said Lucy-Ann, looking at the sleeping fox club, who had curled his sharp little nose into his big tail. 'It's a pity he's a bit smelly.'

'Well, he'll get worse,' said Philip. 'So you might as well get used to it. Foxes do smell. I expect we smell just as strong to them.'

'Oh! I'm sure we don't,' thought Lucy-Ann. 'Oh dear, how sleepy I am!'

They were all sleepy that night. The long climb in the sunshine had tired them out. 'Let's go to bed,' said Philip with such a loud yawn that Button woke up with a jump. 'We've got an exciting day tomorrow, with a lot of climbing again. Don't forget to look out your camera, Jack.'

'Oh yes — I simply *must* take a snap of the eagles!' said Jack. 'Golly, we'll have some fun tomorrow!'

Then up they went to bed, yawning. Kiki yawned the loudest — not that she was tired, but it was a lovely noise to copy!

7

Inside the castle of adventure

The next day Button woke Philip by licking the bare sole of his foot, which was sticking out from the bedclothes. Philip woke with a yell, for he was very ticklish there.

'Stop it, Jack!' he shouted, and then looked in surprise across the room, where Jack was just opening startled eyes. 'Oh – it's all right – it's only Button. Button, you are never to lick the soles of my feet!'

Jack sat up, grinning. He rubbed his eyes and stretched. Then his glance fell on his fine camera, which he had put ready to take up the hill with him that day, and he remembered what they had planned.

'Come on – let's get up,' he said to Philip, and jumped out of bed. 'It's a gorgeous day, and I'm longing to go up to the castle again. I might get some wonderful pictures of those eagles.'

Philip was almost as interested in birds as Jack was. The boys began to talk about eagles as they dressed. They banged at the girls' door as they went down. Mrs Mannering was already up, for she was an early riser. A smell of frying bacon arose on the air.

'Lovely!' said Jack sniffing. 'Kiki, don't stick your claws so hard into my shoulder. I got sunburnt yesterday and it hurts.'

'What a pity, what a pity!' said Kiki, in sorrowful tones. The boys laughed.

'You'd almost think she really did understand what you say,' said Philip.

'She does!' said Jack. 'I say, what about getting a plank or something now, whilst we're waiting for breakfast – you know, to put across to the windowsill of the castle?'

'Right,' said Philip, and they wandered out into the sunshine, still sniffing the delicious smell of frying bacon, to which was now added the fragrance of coffee. Button trotted at Philip's heels, nibbling them gently every time the boy stopped. He did not dare to go near Jack, for if he did Kiki swooped down on him in a fury, and snapped her curved beak at him.

The boys went into the shed where the car was kept. They soon found just what they wanted – a stout plank long enough to reach from the cliff wall to the sill. 'Golly! It will be pretty heavy to carry!' said Jack. 'We'll all have to take turns at it. It wouldn't do to have a smaller one – it just might not reach.'

The girls came out and the boys showed them what they had found. In the night Lucy-Ann had made up her mind she wouldn't do any plank-climbing or castle-exploring, but now, in the warm golden sunshine, she altered her mind, and felt that she couldn't possibly be left out of even a small adventure.

'Mother, could we go off for the whole day this time?' said Philip. 'Jack's got his camera ready. We're pretty certain we know where those eagles are now, and we shall perhaps be able to take some good pictures of them.'

'Well, it's a lovely day, so it would do you good to go off picnicking,' said his mother. 'Oh, do stop Kiki taking the marmalade, Jack! Really, I shan't have that bird at the table any more, if you can't make it behave. It ate half the raspberry jam at tea yesterday.'

'Take your nose out of the marmalade, Kiki,' said Jack sternly, and Kiki sat back on his shoulder, offended. She began to imitate Mrs Mannering crunching up toast, eyeing her balefully the whole time, annoyed at being robbed of the marmalade. Mrs Mannering had to laugh.

'You're not going on that landslide, are you?' she said,

and the children shook their heads.

'No, Mother. Tassie showed us another way. Hallo, here she is. Tassie, have you had your breakfast?'

Tassie was peeping in at the kitchen window, her eyes bright under their tangle of hair. Mrs Mannering sighed. 'I might as well not have bothered myself to give her a bath,' she said. 'She's just as dirty as ever. I did think that she would like feeling clean.'

'She doesn't,' said Dinah. 'All she liked was that smell of carbolic, Mother. If you want to make Tassie wash herself, you'll have to present her with a bar of strong carbolic soap!'

Tassie, it appeared, had had her breakfast some time before. She climbed in at the window and accepted a piece of toast and marmalade from Philip. Kiki at once edged over to her hopefully. She liked toast and marmalade. Tassie shared it with the parrot.

The five children set off soon after breakfast. Dinah carried the knapsack of food. Lucy-Ann carried Jack's precious camera. Tassie carried Kiki on her shoulder, very proudly indeed. The two boys carried the plank between them.

'Take us the shortest way you know, Tassie,' begged Jack. 'This plank is so awkward to carry. I say, Philip, did you think to bring a rope too? I forgot.'

'I've tied one round my waist,' said Philip. 'It's long enough, I think. Button, don't get under my feet like that, and don't ask to be carried when I've got to take this tiresome plank up the hill!'

With many rests, the little party went up the steep hill towards the castle. Jack kept a lookout for the eagles, but he didn't see either of them. Kiki flew off to have a few words with some rooks they met, and then flew back again to Tassie's shoulder. She couldn't understand why Tassie carried shoes round her neck, and pecked curiously at the laces, trying to get them out of the shoes.

At last they arrived at the castle, and made their way round the great wall to the back, where the wall of the castle ran level with the side of the hill.

'Here we are at last,' said Jack, panting, and put the plank down thankfully. 'You girls coming into the passageway to watch us putting the plank in place, or not?'

'Yes, rather,' said Dinah. They all went into the tunnel-like passage, which smelt mustier than ever, after the clean heathery smell outside.

They came to where they had climbed up the day before. 'Tassie, you go up first, and tie this rope firmly to a stout creeper stem,' said Philip, giving her the rope, which he had untied from his waist. 'Then we can all pull ourselves up by it without slipping.'

Tassie climbed up the creeper-clad wall easily. She stopped opposite the slit window of the castle. She tied the rope firmly round a strong creeper stem, and then tested it by leaning forward with all her weight on it.

'Look out, silly!' shouted Philip. 'If that rope gives you'll fall on top of us.'

But it didn't give. It was quite safe. Tassie grinned down at them and then slid down, holding the rope, and landed beside them on her toes.

'You ought to be in a circus,' said Jack. But Tassie looked blank. She had no idea what a circus was.

Philip had another, shorter piece of rope. 'That's to haul up the plank with,' he said. 'Now, let's tie the plank firmly with this rope, and I'll drag it up after me as I climb up. Here goes!'

Holding with one hand on to the rope that now hung down from the creeper, and with the other to the rope that dragged the plank, Philip started up the steep cliff wall. But he needed both hands to help himself up, and had to slide down again.

'Tie the plank to my waist,' he said to Jack. 'Then I can have both hands to help myself up with, and the plank will come up behind me by itself.'

So the plank was tied to his waist, and then the boy went up again, this time pulling himself with both hands on the rope. His feet slipped, but he went on upwards, feeling the drag of the heavy plank on his waist.

At last he was opposite the castle window. He could see nothing inside the window at all, except black darkness. He began to try and clear a place to fix in one edge of the plank.

'Look out – I'm coming up too to help,' called Jack from below, and up he came, pulling on Tassie's rope. Then, between them, they managed to haul up the plank, and lift it so that it almost reached the windowsill.

'A bit more over – that's right – now a bit more to the right!' panted Jack – and then, with a thud, the plank at last rested on the sill of the narrow slit window. The other end rested firmly on a mass of tangled creeper roots, and on some stout ivy stems.

Jack tested the plank. It seemed quite firm. Philip tested it too. Yes, it seemed safe enough.

'Have you really fixed it?' shouted Dinah, in excitement. 'Jolly good! Look out, there goes Kiki!'

Sure enough, Kiki, who had been watching everything in the greatest surprise, had sailed up in the air and was now sitting on the plank, raising her crest and making a chortling noise. Then she walked clumsily across to the window and hopped on the sill. She poked her beak inside the opening. There was no glass there, of course.

'Kiki always likes to poke her nose into everything!' said Lucy-Ann. 'Can we come up now, Philip?'

'We're just making a flat place among all these roots and things, so that you can stand here safely till we can help you across,' said Philip, stamping on the creepers around. 'The cliff wall goes in a bit just here – you can almost sit down, if I

46

mess the creepers about a bit.'

'I'll go across the plank,' said Jack. But a shout from Lucy-Ann stopped him.

'No, Jack. Wait till I'm up there. I want to see you properly! I can only see your legs from down here.'

Soon all three girls were up by the boys. It was easy to go up by the rope. They watched Jack sit astride the plank, and gradually edge himself across in that position. The plank was as firm as could be. Jack felt quite safe.

He got to the windowsill. He stood up on the plank and clutched the stone sides of the narrow window. He stood in the opening.

'Golly, it's narrow!' he shouted across the plank, to where the others were watching him breathlessly. 'I don't believe I can squeeze through!'

'Well, if you can't *I* certainly shan't be able to,' said Philip. 'Go on – try. You're not as fat as all that, surely!'

Jack began to squeeze through the narrow stone window. It certainly was a squash. He had to hold his tummy in hard, and not breathe at all. He wriggled through gradually, and then suddenly jumped to the floor the other side. He yelled back.

'Hurrah, I'm through! Come on, everyone. I'm in a pitch-black room. We'll have to bring torches next time.'

Dinah went next, helped by Philip. Jack helped her down the other side. She hadn't much difficulty in getting through the window. Then came Tassie, then Lucy-Ann, then Philip, who had as much difficulty as Jack in squeezing through.

'Well, here we are!' he said, 'inside the Castle of Adventure!'

8

Up in the tower

'The Castle of Adventure!' echoed Lucy-Ann in surprise.

'What makes you say that? Do you think we shall have an adventure here?'

'Oh, I don't know!' said Philip. 'I just said it – but it's got an odd feeling, this castle, hasn't it? My word, isn't it dark?'

A mournful barking came from below. It was Button, left behind. Philip stuck his head out of the window. 'It's all right, Button. We're coming back!'

Kiki stuck her head out too, and gave a railway engine screech. 'That's just to tell poor Button she's up here, and he's not!' said Dinah. 'Kiki, you do like to crow over poor Button, don't you?'

It was very dark in the room they had jumped into. But gradually they could see better as their eyes got used to the darkness. The children blinked and tried to see their surroundings.

'It's just a big bare room,' said Jack, rather disappointed. He didn't quite know what he had expected to see. 'I suppose the whole castle's like this – full of big, bare, cold rooms. Come on – let's do a bit of exploring.'

They made their way to the door, which opened into a long corridor. They went down this and came to a lighter room, lit by one slit window and one wide one evidently added much later. This room had a big fireplace and there were still old grey ashes there. The children looked at them.

'Funny to think that people once sat round that fire!' said Dinah. They went into the next room, which again was very dark, because it had only a slit window to light it. Dinah wandered to the window, and suddenly gave such a yell that everyone jumped violently.

'Dinah! What is it?' cried Philip.

Dinah ran back to him so quickly that she bumped into him. 'There's something in this room!' she cried. 'It touched my hair. I felt it. Come out quickly.'

'Don't be silly,' began Philip, and then he stopped suddenly. Something had touched his hair too! He swung round but there was nothing there. His heart beat fast. Was there really something in the room, touching them, but invisible?

Then a ray of sunlight unexpectedly came slanting in through the slit window, and Philip gave a sudden laugh. 'How silly we are!' he said. 'It's cobwebs – look, hanging down from the ceiling! They must be years old!'

Everyone was very much relieved, but Dinah wouldn't stay in the room one moment more. She was scared – and the very idea of cobwebs touching her made her more scared still. She shuddered when she thought of the spiders that might drop on her from the cobwebby ceiling!

'Come out where it's sunshiny,' she begged, and they all went into a wide corridor, where the sun poured in at many windows. Tassie walked close to Philip, with scared eyes. She knew the old village tales, and half expected the wicked old man to appear from somewhere and take them all prisoner! But where Philip went she meant to go too.

'Look – this way leads across one of the battlemented walls to the eastern tower!' cried Jack. 'Let's go along to the tower – we'll get a magnificent view from there.'

'I feel like an old-time soldier marching round the castle wall,' said Philip, as they made their way along to the tower. 'Here we are. Goodness, it's quite big, isn't it? Look, there's a room at the bottom of the tower, flush with this wall – and there's a winding stone stair that leads to the top of the tower. Come on, up we go!'

And up they went, determined not to look at the view till they got to the highest point. The stone stair twisted awkwardly round and round, and led them straight into another room, out of which a narrow stair led them to the very roof of the tower itself.

They went up the tiny stair and found themselves on the top of the tower, its battlemented edge rising a few feet all round.

They all gasped, and gazed down in silence. Not one of them had ever been so high up before, nor had they seen such a wide and magnificent view. It seemed as if the whole world lay spread out before them, sparkling in the sunshine. Below, far, far below, lay the valley, through which curved the silver river, like a gleaming snake. What houses they could see looked like toy ones.

'Look at those hills opposite,' said Jack. 'There are hills behind those – and hills behind those too – and hills behind those!'

Tassie was amazed. She never thought the world was so big. From the vantage point of the high tower the whole country was spread like a living map before her. It was so beautiful that for some extraordinary reason Lucy-Ann felt like crying.

'What a wonderful place this must have been for a lookout!' said Philip. 'Any sentry here could see enemies coming miles and miles away. Look – is that Spring Cottage right down there, among those trees?'

It was, looking like a doll's house, halfway down the hill. 'I wish we could bring Mother up here,' said Dinah. 'How she would love this view!'

'Look! Look! There are the eagles again!' said Jack, and he pointed up in the air, where two great eagles soared to the clouds. 'I say – shall we have our lunch here, on the top of this tower, and see this marvellous view all the time, and watch my eagles?'

'Oh *yes*!' said everyone, including Kiki. She always joined in any chorus.

'Poor little Button,' said Philip. 'I wish we could have brought him too. But it was too risky across that plank. I expect he's feeling very lonely now. I hope he won't run off.'

'You know he won't,' said Dinah. 'No animal ever runs away from you, worse luck. Oh, *Philip* – you haven't brought that awful toad with you, have you? Yes, you have! It's peeping out of your neck! I just won't sit up here with a toad crawling round.'

'Now for goodness' sake don't start a quarrel up on the top of the tower,' said Jack, in real alarm. 'That stone edging won't stop anyone from falling if they start fooling about. Dinah, do sit down.'

'Don't order me about,' said Dinah, beginning to flare up.

'Where's the food?' said Lucy-Ann, hoping to change the subject. 'Dinah, you've got it. Get it out, because I'm dying of hunger!'

Keeping as far away from her brother as she could, Dinah undid the knapsack. There were two big packets inside, one marked 'Dinner' and one marked 'Tea.'

'Put the tea packet back,' said Jack, 'or we might gobble that up too! I feel hungry enough to eat all you've got there.'

Dinah divided out sandwiches, cake, biscuits, fruit and chocolate. Then she presented everyone with a cardboard cup of lemonade from a bottle.

'We've had plenty of picnics in our time,' said Philip, biting hugely into a thick sandwich of egg and ham, 'but never one in such an extraordinary place as this. It almost makes me giddy, looking out at that enormous view.'

'It's lovely to sit here and eat, looking at those hills, and that winding river down in the valley,' said Lucy-An contentedly. 'I believe that old man Tassie told us about must have bought this castle for the view! I would, I know, if I had enough money.'

They ate and drank happily. Kiki shared the sandwiches, which she liked immensely. Then she went exploring along the stone coping at the edge of the tower, climbing upside-down now and again.

The children watched her, eating their cake. Suddenly Kiki gave an alarming screech, lost her balance and fell right off the tower! She disappeared below, and the children leapt up in horror. Then they sat down again, smiling and feeling rather foolish – for, of course, as soon as she fell, Kiki spread out her wings and soared into the air!

'Idiot, Kiki!' said Dinah. 'You gave me quite a scare! Well, has everyone nearly finished? If so, I'll clear up the paper and the cardboard cups and put them back into the knapsack.'

Jack had been watching the eagles, which, all the time they were at lunch, had been soaring high in the air, looking like black specks. Now they were coming down again, gliding in large circles, their great wings spread out to catch the smallest current of air.

There was plenty of wind on the top of the hill. It blew steadily on the tower, and the children's hair was blown back all the time, as they sat facing the breeze. They watched the eagles go lower and lower.

Below them and behind them lay the inner courtyard of the castle. It was overgrown with grass and patches of heather. Gorse bushes grew there, and a few small birch-trees. The hillside had come into its own again there, and pushed up by strong-growing bushes, which had forced their way between them.

'I believe the eagles have their nest in that clump of trees over there, in the corner of the overgrown courtyard!' said Jack excitedly. 'It's the sort of craggy place they might choose! Shall we go and see?'

'Are you sure they're not dangerous?' said Philip doubt-fully. 'They're awfully big birds – and I *have* heard stories of them attacking men.'

'Yes,' said Jack. 'Well – as soon as they fly off again, I'll go and look. Anyway, we might as well go down now and have a look round. Kiki, come here!'

Kiki flew to his shoulder, and nibbled his ear gently, talking her usual nonsense. The children got up and went down the two stone stairways. Both the top and bottom rooms of the tower were completely empty. Cobwebs hung in the corners, and dust lay thickly on the floor and ledges, except where the wind blew in strongly.

'How do we get down to the courtyard?' wondered Philip. 'We'll have to go back along the wall and into the castle itself, I suppose. There must be a stairway down to the rooms below.'

So back they went, and came to the main building of the castle again. They looked into room after room, all empty. Then at last they came to a very wide stone stairway that led down and down. They clattered down it and came into a big hall. It was dark.

Something suddenly hurled itself against Philip's legs and he leapt in fright, giving a loud exclamation. Everyone stood still.

'What is it?' said Lucy-Ann, in a whisper.

It was Button, the fox cub! 'Now how in the world did *he* get to us!' cried Philip, picking the little creature up. 'He must have found some hole, I suppose, and scrambled through it to find us. Button, you're a marvel! But my word, you did give me a fright!'

Button gave some of his little barks as he cuddled against Philip's chest. Kiki addressed a few scornful remarks to him about shutting the door. She was the only one sorry to see his arrival!

'Now let's get into the courtyard and explore round a bit,' said Jack. 'Look out for the eagles, all of you!'

9

The eagle's nest

The children picked their way over the big, overgrown
courtyard. It was an absolute wilderness now, though with a
little imagination they could picture what it must have been
like in the old days – a vast stone-paved place, hewn out of
the hillside itself, with craggy pieces towering up at the far
ends.

'It's in one of those craggy places that I think the eagles
have got their nest,' said Jack, as they picked their way
across the hot courtyard. 'Tassie, take Kiki for me, will you,
and hang on to her. I don't want her interfering just now.'

Tassie proudly took Kiki, and stood still whilst the others
went towards a towering piece of rock, clothed here and
there with heather, that rose up at one end of the courtyard.
Lucy-Ann didn't particularly want to go too near to the
eagles, but she wanted to be with Jack.

'You girls stay down at the bottom of this crag,' said Jack.
'I'm going to climb up with Philip. I don't think the eagles
will attack us, Philip, in fact I'm pretty sure they won't; but
look out, in case.'

The boys were just beginning to climb when a loud,
yelping scream made them stop and clutch at one another in
fright. The girls jumped violently. Button ran into the
nearest rabbit-hole and stayed there. Only Kiki did not seem
to be frightened.

Into Tassie's mind jumped the thought that the scream
must be from one of the wicked man's poor prisoners!
Perhaps he wasn't dead, perhaps he was still there somewhere. The other children were not so foolish as to think

things like this, but the scream certainly made their blood run cold!

'What was it, Jack?' whispered Lucy-Ann. 'Come back. Don't go up there. The scream came from there.'

It came again, more loudly – a curious, almost yelping noise. Kiki cleared her throat to imitate it. What a fine noise to copy!

She gave a remarkably good imitation of the scream and made everyone jump again. Tassie almost fell over, for Kiki was on her shoulder.

'Bad bird! Naughty bird!' said Jack fiercely, in a low voice. Kiki looked at him. From her throat came the scream again – and almost at the same moment a great eagle, which must have been somewhere on the rocky crag, rose up in the air on enormous wings, and soared over the little company, looking down in amazement to see who had made such a noise.

And then, from the eagle's own throat, there came again the yelping scream the children had heard!

'Gosh – it was the eagle screaming, that's all!' said Jack, in relief. 'Why didn't I think of that? I've never heard one before. That shows their nest must be somewhere up here. Come on, Philip.'

The eagle did not swoop down to the children, but glided above them, looking down. Its interest was centred on Kiki, who feeling rather thrilled at having found such a good new noise, yelped again.

The eagle answered and flew lower. Kiki went up to meet it, looking very small compared with the big eagle. The children could plainly see the long yellowish feathers on the nape of its neck, shining in the sunlight.

'It *is* a golden eagle,' said Lucy-Ann. 'Jack was right. Look at those golden feathers! Oh dear – I hope it doesn't come any lower.'

All the five children watched Kiki and the eagle. Usually birds were either puzzled and afraid of Kiki, or angry. But the eagle was neither. It seemed intensely interested, as if wondering how it was that this queer looking little bird, so unlike an eagle, could make eagle noises!

Kiki was enjoying herself. She flew about the eagle, yelping to it, and then suddenly changed her mind and told it to blow its nose.

At the sound of an apparently human voice the eagle sheered off a little, still gazing in interest at Kiki. Finally, taking no notice at all of the children, it flew upwards to a high rock on the crag, and perched there, looking down in a very royal fashion.

'Isn't it a magnificent bird?' said Jack in the utmost delight. 'Fancy us seeing an eagle at close quarters like this! Look at its frowning brows, and its piercing eyes! I don't wonder it's called the king of the birds!'

The eagle was a truly splendid sight, as it sat there like a king. It was feathered in dark brown, except for the golden streaks on the nape of its neck. Its legs were covered in feathers almost to the claws. It watched Kiki unblinkingly.

'There's the second eagle, look!' said Lucy-Ann suddenly, in a low voice. The children saw the other eagle rising up into the air from the crag, evidently curious to see what was happening. It soared upwards, spreading out its strong pinions like fingers, the wing-tips curving up as it went. Then, quite suddenly, the first eagle tired of Kiki, flapped its enormous wings, and joined its mate.

'The first eagle is the male, the second one is the female,' said Jack excitedly.

'How do you know?' asked Dinah disbelievingly. She couldn't see any difference at all.

'The second one is bigger than the first,' said Jack. 'The female golden eagle is always the bigger of the two; bigger wing-span too. Golly, I do feel thrilled.'

'You ought to have snapped that eagle sitting on the crag,' said Philip. Jack gave an exclamation of annoyance.

'Blow! I never even thought of my camera! I was so absorbed in watching the birds. What marvellous pictures I could take!'

The two birds were now only specks in the sky, for they had soared up to an immense height. 'It would be a jolly good chance to explore this crag for their nest whilst they are safely up there,' said Jack. 'It's funny they don't seem scared of us, isn't it? I suppose they know hardly anything of man, always living up here on this hilltop.'

'I can't imagine what's happened to Button,' said Philip anxiously. 'He went down that hole and he's not back yet.'

'Probably scaring a family of rabbits out of their senses!' said Jack. 'He'll come back all right. I'm not surprised he went down a rabbit hole when he heard that scream. I'd have gone down one myself if I could! It was an awful noise.'

The boys began to climb up again. It was fairly stiff going for the little crag was steep and rocky. Its top was almost as high as the nearby tower.

On the western side, well hidden in a little hollow, Jack found what he wanted – the eagles' nest!

'Look!' he said, 'look! Did you ever see such an enormous thing, Philip! It must be six feet wide at the bottom!'

The boys looked at the great nest on the broad ledge of rock. It was about two feet high, made of twigs and small boughs, with heather tucked in between. The cup of the nest was almost a foot and a half across, and very well lined with moss, grass and bits of heather.

'There's a young one in the nest!' said Jack, in delight. 'Quite a big bird too – must be more than three months old, and ready to fly.'

The young bird crouched down in the nest when it heard Jack's voice. It was already so big that Philip would hardly have known it was a nestling. But Jack's sure eye had

57

noticed the white bases of the feathers, telling him that this was a young eagle, and not an old one.

Kiki flew inquisitively to the nest. She gave a yelp like the eagle had made. The young bird looked up enquiringly, recognized the sound but not the maker of it.

'Your camera, quick!' whispered Philip, and Jack began to adjust his camera with quick, eager fingers.

'Quick, the old eagles are coming back,' whispered Philip, and Jack gave a glance upwards. The eagles had remembered their young one, and seeing the boys so near the nest were coming down to see what was happening.

Jack snapped the camera just in time, for Kiki flew off almost immediately to meet the eagles, screaming a welcome.

'Better get down now,' said Philip, thinking that the two old eagles looked pretty fierce. 'My word, I wish we could take pictures of that young one learning to fly. It looks as if it will take off from the nest any day now.'

With the two eagles gliding not far above them the boys climbed down as hastily as they could. 'Did you get a snap?' asked Lucy-Ann eagerly, and Jack nodded. He looked excited.

'I shall have to come back again,' he said. 'Do you know, I might get finer close-up pictures of eagles than anyone has ever got before? Think of that! I'd make a lot of money out of them, I daresay, and I'd have them in all kind of nature magazines.'

'Oh, Jack – do take some more pictures then,' said Lucy-Ann, her eyes shining.

'I'd have to almost *live* up here, to take good ones,' said Jack. 'It's no good just coming up on the off-chance. If only I could spend a few days here!'

'Well – I suppose you could, if you wanted to,' said Philip. 'I expect Mother would let you, if you told her about the eagles. It would be quite safe up here, and we could bring you food.'

'Can't we *all* come and stay up here for a few days?' said Lucy-Ann, who didn't want her brother to be away from them. 'Why can't we?'

'Well – you know we can't leave my mother all alone down there,' said Philip. 'She'd think it was jolly mean.'

'Oh yes – of course,' said Lucy-Ann, going rather red. 'I never thought of that. How awful of me!'

'All the same, I don't see why *I* shouldn't come up here for a few days,' said Jack, finding the idea more and more exciting as he thought about it. 'I could make a hide, you know – and . . .'

'What's a hide?' asked Tassie, speaking for almost the first time that morning.

'A hide? Oh, it's a place I should rig up to hide myself and my camera in,' said Jack. 'Then, when the eagles had got used to it, I could take as many pictures of them as I wanted to, without showing myself or putting them on their guard. I should make my hide somewhere on this crag, within good view of that nest. Golly, I might take a whole set of pictures showing the young eagle learning to fly!'

'Well, ask Mother if you can come up, then,' said Philip. 'I'd come up and be with you, only I think one of us boys ought to be down at the cottage to help bring the wood in for the fire and things like that.'

'I could do that,' said Dinah, eager to get rid of the toad for a few days. She wouldn't go near Philip as long as he had the toad about him.

'Well, you can't,' said Philip. 'Jack will have Kiki for company and we'll come up and see him every day. Come on, now – let's explore the lower parts of the castle a bit more.'

So they made their way back across the yard into the

lower parts of the great building, expecting to see the same vast empty rooms there as they had seen above. But what a surprise they got!

10

A curious thing

They went into a great doorway, and walked across the dark hall, which echoed strangely with their footsteps. From outside came the yelping scream of the eagles again.

'I expect it was the screams of the eagles that the villagers heard year after year up here,' said Jack, as he made his way to a stout door that led off the hall. He opened it – and then stood still in surprise.

This room was furnished! It had once been a kind of sitting room or drawing room, and the mouldy old furniture was still there, though the children could not imagine why it had been left!

They stood and stared into the old, forgotten room in silence. It was such a odd feeling to gaze on this musty-smelling, quiet room, lighted by four slit windows and one wide one, through which sunlight came. It lit up the layers of dust on the sofas and vast table, and touched the enormous webs and hanging cobwebs that were made by scores of busy spiders through the years.

Dinah shivered. When the others went further into the room, walking on tiptoe and talking in whispers, she did not follow. Lucy-Ann patted a chair and at once a cloud of dust arose, making her choke. Philip pulled at a cover on one of the sofas, and it fell to pieces in his hands. It was quite rotten.

'What a weird old room!' he said. 'I feel as if I was back a hundred years or so. Time has stood still here. I do wonder why this room was left like this.'

They went out and into the next one. That was quite empty. But the third one, smaller, and evidently used as a dining-room, was again furnished. And again the spiders' webs stretched everywhere and hung down in long grey threads from the high ceilings. There was a great sideboard in the room, and when the children curiously opened one of the doors, they saw old china and pieces of silver there – or what must have been silver, for now the cruets and sauce-boats were so terribly tarnished that they might have been made of anything.

'Curiouser and curiouser!' said Lucy-Ann, quoting *Alice in Wonderland*. 'Why have these rooms been left like this?'

'I expect the wicked old man Tassie told us about just lived in a few rooms, and these were the ones,' said Jack. 'Mabye he went away, meaning to come back, and never did. And nobody dared to come here – or perhaps nobody even knew the rooms had been left furnished. It's a mystery!'

The little fox cub went sniffing round all the rooms raising clouds of dust, and choking now and again. Kiki did not seem to like the rooms. She stayed on Jack's shoulder quite silent.

They came to the kitchen. This was a simply enormous place, with a great cooking range at the back. Iron sauce-pans and an iron kettle were still there. Philip tried to lift one, but it was immensely heavy.

'Cooks must have had very strong arms in the old days!' he said. 'Look – is that a pump by the old sink? I suppose they had to pump their water up.'

They crossed over to the sink. The old fashioned pump had a handle, which had to be worked up and down in order to bring water from some deep-down well.

Philip stared at it in a puzzled manner, his eyes going to a puddle on the floor, just below the pump.

'What's the matter, Philip?' said Jack.

'Nothing much – but where did that water come from?' said Philip. 'See, it's in a puddle – it can only have been there a day or two, or it would have dried up.'

Jack looked up to the dark old ceiling, as if he expected to see a leak in the roof there. But there was none, of course! He looked down at the puddle again, and he too felt puzzled. 'Let's pump a bit and see if water comes up,' he said, and stretched out his hand. 'Maybe the thing is out of order now.'

Before he could reach the handle Philip knocked his hand aside, with an exclamation. Jack looked at him in surprise.

'See here, Freckles,' said Philip, frowning in bewilderment, 'the handle of the pump isn't covered with dust like everything else is. It's rubbed clean just where you'd take hold of it to pump.'

Dinah felt a little prickle of fright go down her back. Whatever did Philip mean? Who could pump up water in an old empty castle?

They all stared at the pump handle, and saw that Philip was right. Button began to lap up the puddle of water on the stone floor. He was thirsty.

'Wait, Button, I'll pump you some fresh water,' said Philip, and he took hold of the pump handle. He worked it up and down vigorously, and fresh, clear water poured in gushes into the huge old sink. Some of it splashed out into the puddle already on the floor.

'That's how that puddle was made,' said Jack, watching carefully. 'By the splashes of the water from the sink. But that means someone must have pumped up water here in the last few days!'

Tassie's eyes grew big with fright. 'The wicked old man's still here!' she said, and looked fearfully over her shoulder as if she expected him to walk into the kitchen.

'Don't be so silly, Tassie,' said Philip impatiently. 'The old man's dead and gone years and years ago. Do you know if any of the villagers ever come up here?'

'No, oh no!' said Tassie. 'They are afraid of the castle. They say it is a bad place.'

The five children certainly felt that it had a strange, brooding air about it. They felt that they wanted to go out into the sunshine. Kiki suddenly gave a mournful groan that made them all jump.

'Don't, Kiki!' said Jack crossly. 'Philip, what do you make of this? Who's been pumping up the water? Can there be anyone in the castle now?'

'Well, we haven't seen signs of anyone at all,' said Philip. 'And why should anyone be here, anyway? There's nothing for them to live on – no food or anything. I think myself that probably some rambler came up here in curiosity, wandered about, and got himself a drink of water from the pump before he went.'

This seemed the most likely explanation.

'But how did he get in?' said Dinah, after a moment or two.

That was a puzzler. 'There must be some way,' said Jack.

'There isn't,' said Tassie. 'I've been all round the castle, and I know. There isn't any way of getting in.'

'Well, there must be,' said Philip, and dismissed the subject, feeling that they would all be better to be out in the open air, having their tea. 'Come on – let's find a comfortable place in the courtyard and have our tea. I'm jolly hungry again.'

They went into the hot and sunny courtyard. There was little breeze there, for it was enclosed by the high walls. They sat down and Dinah undid the tea packet. There was plenty there for everyone – but all the lemonade had been drunk at dinnertime.

'I'm so thirsty I simply *must* have something to drink with my sandwiches,' said Lucy-Ann. 'My tongue will hang out like a dog's in a minute.'

Everyone felt the same – but nobody particularly wanted to go into that big lonely kitchen and bring back water in the cardboard cups.

'I know – we'll see if the spring that runs down to our cottge is anywhere about,' said Philip. 'It's supposed to begin in this courtyard, I know. It should be somewhere down at the bottom of it.'

He got up and Button went with him. It was Button who found the spring. It gushed out near the wall that ran round the castle, almost at the foot of the tower at the top of which the children had had their dinner. It was not a big spring but the water was cold and clear. Button lapped it eagerly.

Philip filled two cups and called to Jack to bring more. Jack and Tassie came up with the other cups. Jack looked with interest at the bubbling spring. It gushed out from a hole in the rock, and then disappeared again under a tangle of brambles, into a kind of little tunnel that ran below the tower.

'I suppose it goes right underneath the tower, and comes out again further on down the hillside,' thought the boy. 'It collects more and more water on the way, from the inside of the hill, and by the time it reaches Spring Cottage it is quite a big spring, ready to become a proper little stream.'

The children enjoyed the icy-cold water. They finished all the tea, and lay back in the sun, watching the golden eagles, who were once more soaring upwards on wide wings.

'This has been an exciting sort of day,' said Philip lazily. 'What do you feel now about spending a few days here, Jack – won't you be too lonely?'

'I'll have Kiki and the eagles,' said Jack. 'And all the rabbits round about too!'

'I wouldn't like to be here all alone now,' said Dinah. 'Not until I knew who pumped that water! I should feel creepy all the time.'

'That's nothing new,' said Philip. 'You feel creepy if you even see the tip of a worm coming out of a hole. Life must be nothing but creepiness to you. Now if only you'd get used to having toads crawling over you, or a hedgehog in your pocket, or a beetle or two, you'd soon stop feeling creepy.'

'Oh don't!' said Dinah, shivering at the thought of beetles crawling over her. 'You're an awful boy. Jack, you won't really stay here by yourself, will you?'

'I don't see why not,' said Jack, with a laugh. 'I'm not scared. I think Philip's right when he says it was probably only some rambler who pumped himself a spot of water. After all, if we're curious enough to make our way in here other people may be too.'

'Yes, but *how* did they come?' persisted Dinah.

'Same way as old Button came in, I expect,' said Philip.

Dinah stared at him. 'Well – how did *Button* get in?' she said. 'Find out that, and we don't need to use the plank every time!'

'Oh – down a rabbit hole, I should think, and up another,' said Philip, refusing to take her seriously. Dinah gave an angry exclamation.

'Do talk sense! Button could go up a rabbit hole all right, but a man couldn't. You know that quite well.'

'Of course – why didn't I think of that before?' said Philip aggravatingly, and dodged as Dinah threw a clod of earth at him.

'Here! Some of that went in my eye,' said Jack, sitting up. 'Stop it, you two. I know what we'll do. We'll leave old Button behind here when we go across the plank, and we'll watch and see where he comes out. Then we can use his entrance, if it's possible, the next time we come!'

'Yes – that's a good idea,' said Lucy-Ann, and Tassie nodded too. The little girl was puzzled to know how Button had got into the castle. She felt so certain that there was no way in besides the two doors, and the window through which they themselves had come.

'Come on – time to go home,' said Jack, and they all got up. 'I'll be back here tomorrow, I hope!'

11

An unexpected meeting

They went back into the castle and up the wide stone stair. Dinah felt a little uncomfortable and kept close to the others. So did Tassie. They went down the wide corridor and looked into room after room to find the one with the plank.

'Golly! Don't say it's gone!' said Jack, after they had looked into about six rooms. 'This is odd. I'm sure the room wasn't as far along as this.'

But it was – for in the very next room they saw the edge of their plank on the stone sill. They hurried over to it. It was dark in that room. They all wished heartily they had a torch, and determined to bring both torches and candles with them next time!

Jack went across first, with Kiki clutching his shoulder, murmuring something about putting the kettle on. He got across safely, and then caught hold of the rope on the other side. He helped Lucy-Ann across, then Dinah and then Tassie. Lucy-Ann slipped hurriedly down the cliffside, followed by Dinah. Tassie leapt down like a goat, without even touching the rope.

Then came Philip, and poor little Button was left behind, yelping shrilly.

'You go your own way and join us outside the castle!' called back Philip. Button jumped up to the sill but kept falling back. He could not reach it. The children heard him barking away by himself as they made their way down the tunnel-like passage into the sunshine.

'I may have to go back for Button, you know, if he doesn't come after us,' said Philip. 'I couldn't really leave him behind. But foxes are so sharp – I bet he'll come rushing after us in a minute.'

'Keep a good lookout then,' said Jack, 'because we want to know where he gets in and out, so that we can use the place ourselves.'

But it wasn't any good keeping a lookout, for suddenly Button was at their heels, leaping up at Philip, making yelping sounds of happiness and love. Nobody saw him come. Nobody knew how he had got out of the castle!

'How annoying!' said Jack, with a laugh. 'Button, how *did* you get out?'

Button couldn't tell them. He kept so close to Philip's heels all the way home that Philip could feel his sharp little nose the whole time. Button was like a little shadow!

They were all so tired when they got in that they could hardly tell their adventures. When Philip told about the puddle of water below the pump, Mrs Mannering laughed.

'Trust you children to imagine something to scare yourselves with!' she said. 'Probably the pump leaks a bit on its own. It's funny about those old furnished rooms though. It shows how the villagers fear the castle, if no one has interfered with the furniture! Even thieves, apparently, will not venture there.'

Mrs Mannering was intensely interested in the golden eagles. She and Philip and Jack talked about them till darkness fell. Mrs Mannering was quite willing for Jack to try and take pictures of the young eagle with its parents.

'If only you can make a good hide,' she said, 'and get the birds used to it, so that you can lie there and take what pictures you please, it would be marvellous. Philip's father used to do things like that.'

'Can I go with Jack, please Aunty Allie?' asked Lucy-Ann, who couldn't bear to let Jack go off by himself for even a day or two.

'No, you can't, Lucy-Ann,' said Jack decidedly. 'I'm the only one to be there, because if you or the others start messing about too, we shall scare the birds and I shan't get any decent pictures at all. I shan't be gone long! You can't hang on my apron strings *all* the holidays.'

Lucy-Ann said no more. If Jack didn't want her, she wouldn't go.

'You can come up each day and bring me food, if you like,' said Jack, as he saw Lucy-Ann's disappointed face. 'And I can always signal to you from the tower. You know we could see this house from the tower, so, of course, you can see the tower from this house.'

'Oh yes – you signal goodnight to us each night,' said Lucy-Ann, cheering up. 'That would be fun. I wonder which room is best to see the tower from.'

It so happened that it was her own bedroom that was the best. Good! She could even watch the tower from bed. 'Jack, will you sleep in the tower?' she said. 'Then I shall look at the tower when I wake, and know you're there. I'll wave a white hanky from my window when I see you waving one.'

'Oh – I don't know where I'll sleep,' said Jack. 'The tower would be too draughty. I'll curl myself up in the rug in a warm corner somewhere – or maybe clear a place on one of those big old couches. If I can get the dust off!'

Tassie couldn't imagine how anyone could possibly dare to sleep alone in the old castle. She thought Jack must be the bravest boy in the world.

'Time for you to go home, Tassie,' said Mrs Mannering. 'Go along. You can come back tomorrow.'

Tassie disappeared, running off to her tumbledown cottage and her scolding, untidy mother. The others helped Mrs Mannering to clear the supper away, and the two girls washed up, half asleep.

They went to bed, to dream of the old deserted castle, of strange cobwebby rooms, high towers, screaming eagles – and a puddle on the floor below the pump!

'That's really a puzzle,' said Philip to himself, as he fell asleep. 'But I'm too tired to think about it now!'

The next day was rainy. Great clouds swept over the hillside, making it misty and damp. The sun hardly showed all day long. The little spring suddenly became twice as full, and made quite a noise as it gurgled down the garden.

'Blow!' said Jack. 'I did want to go up to the castle today. I feel that that young eagle may fly at any time now, and I don't want to miss its first flight.'

'Have you got plenty of films for your camera?' asked Philip. 'You know how you keep running out of them just when you badly want them.'

'Well, it wouldn't be much good wanting them if I *hadn't* got enough!' said Jack. 'I couldn't buy them in that tiny village. There's only one shop.'

'You could take the train and go off to the nearest big town,' said Mrs Mannering. 'Why don't you do that, instead of staying here cooped up all day? I can see Dinah is longing to squabble with someone!'

Dinah laughed. She did hate being 'cooped up' as Mrs Mannering said, and it did make her irritable. But Dinah was learning to control herself a little more now that she was growing older.

'Yes, it would be fun to take the train and go off shopping,' she said. 'Let's do it! We've just got time to catch the one and only train that leaves the station, and we'll come back by the one and only train that returns!'

So they put on macks and sou'westers and hurried to catch the train. But they needn't have hurried, really, for the leisurely little country train always waited for anybody coming along the road.

It was twenty miles to the nearest town. It took the train a whole hour to get there, and the children enjoyed running through the valleys in between the ranges of high hills. Once they saw another castle on the side of a hill, but they all agreed that it wasn't a patch on theirs.

Button had been left behind with Tassie, much to his dismay. The children had offered to take Tassie with them, but the little girl was terrified of the train. She shrank back when they suggested it. So they gave Button to her with strict injunctions not to let him worry Mrs Mannering.

Kiki, of course, went with Jack. But then she went everywhere with him, making her remarks, and causing a great deal of amusement and interest. She always showed off in company and sometimes became very cheeky.

The children had left the train and were walking down the street, when suddenly a voice hailed them, and made them jump. 'Hallo, hallo! Whoever would have thought of seeing *you* here!'

The children turned round at once and Kiki let out a delighted squawk.

'Bill Smugs!' cried the children, and ran to the ruddy-faced, twinkling-eyed man who had hailed them. Lucy-Ann gave him a hug, Dinah smiled in delight, and the two boys banged Bill Smugs on the back.

Bill Smugs was not his real name. It was a name he had told the children the year before, when they had come across him trying to track some clever forgers. He had not wanted them to know who he was nor what he was really doing – but although they now knew his real name, he was still Bill Smugs to them, and always would be.

'Come and have lunch with me,' said Bill Smugs. 'Or have you any other plans? I really must know what you are doing here. I thought you were at home for the holidays.'

'What are *you* doing here?' asked Philip, his eyes shining.

'On the track of forgers again? I bet you're on some sort of exciting job.'

'Maybe, maybe not,' said Bill, smiling. 'I shouldn't tell you, anyway, should I? I'm probably holidaying, just as you are. Come on – we'll go to this hotel. It looks about the best one this town can produce.'

It was an exciting lunch. Bill Smugs was an exciting person. They talked eagerly about the thrilling adventure he had had with them the year before, when they had all got mixed up with copper mines and forgers, and had been in very great danger. They reminded each other of the times they had shivered and trembled!

'Yes, that certainly was an adventure,' said Bill, helping himself to apple tart and ice cream. 'And now, as I said before – you really must tell me what you are doing in this part of the world!'

The children told him, interrupting each other in their eagerness, especially Jack, who was longing to tell him every detail about the eagles. Bill listened and ate solidly, giving Kiki titbits every now and again. She had been delighted to see their old friend too, and had told him at least a dozen times to open his book at page six, and pay attention.

'What a pity you're twenty miles away or more,' said Bill. 'I'm stuck here in this district for a time, I'm afraid, and can't leave. But if I can I'll come over and see you. Maybe your mother would put me up for a day or two, then I can come up to this wonderful castle of yours and see the eagles.'

'Oh yes, *do* come!' they all cried. 'We aren't on the telephone,' added Philip, 'but never mind, just come – we are sure to be there. Come at any time! We'd love you to.'

'Right,' said Bill. 'I might be able to slip over next week, because it doesn't look as if I'm going to do much good here. Can't tell you any more, I'm afraid – but if I don't make any headway with what I'm supposed to be doing, I'll have a

71

break, and come along to see you and your nice mother. Give her my kind regards, and say Bill Smugs will come and pay his repects if he possibly can.'

'We'll have to go,' said Jack regretfully, looking at his watch. 'There's only the one train back and we've got a bit of shopping to do. Goodbye, Bill, it's been grand to bump into you like this.'

'Goodbye. See you soon, I hope!' said Bill, with his familiar grin. And off they ran to catch their train.

12

Jack is left at the castle

Mrs Mannering was delighted to hear that they had by chance met Bill Smugs again, for she felt very grateful to him for the help he had given the children in their amazing adventure the year before.

'If he comes, I will sleep in with you girls and he can have my room,' she said. 'Good old Bill! It will be nice to see him again. He must lead an interesting life, always hunting down criminal and wicked people.'

'I bet he'd have been after the wicked old man who used to live in the castle!' said Lucy-Ann. 'It will be fun to take him up there. Jack, I hope it won't be raining tomorrow again.'

But it was. Jack felt very disappointed. He was afraid that the old eagle might take the young one away. But it was no good going up the hill in this pouring rain. For one thing, the clouds were so low that they sailed round the hillside itself, big patches of moving mist. He would get lost if he tried to go up.

'I suppose Tassie could find her way up even in the mist,'

he said. Tassie was there. She raised her bright black eyes to him and nodded.

'Yes,' she said. 'I will take you now if you like.'

'No,' said Mrs Mannering firmly. 'Wait till tomorrow. I think it will be fine then. I'm not going to have to send out search-parties for you and Tassie!'

'But, Mother, Tassie could find her way up this hillside blindfold, I'm sure she could!' said Philip. However, Mrs Mannering didn't believe in Tassie and her powers as much as the children did. So Jack had to wait for the next day.

Luckily it was fine. The sun rose out of a clear sky, and not even the smallest cloud showed itself. The hillside glistened and gleamed as the sun dried the millions of raindrops left on twig and leaf. It was a really lovely day.

'We'll all come up with you, Jack,' said Philip, 'and help to carry what you want. You'll need a couple of thick rugs, and some food – a candle or two and a torch – and your camera and films, of course.'

They all decided to have a day up at the castle again, and leave Jack behind when they came back in the evening. So, about eleven o'clock, with the morning sun blazing hotly down on their backs, they began the climb up the hill.

Button came, of course, and Kiki. Kiki was to stay with Jack. The eagles evidently didn't mind her. In fact it was quite possible that they might make friends with her, and Jack might get some interesting photographs.

Carrying various things, the little party set off once more. Dinah was glad to feel her torch safely in her pocket. She didn't mean to stand in dark rooms again and feel cobwebs clutching at her hair!

They climbed in through the window as before. Button again appeared in the courtyard from somewhere, though still no one knew where. Kiki flew to the crag on which the eagles had their nest, yelping her eagle scream in what was

73

plainly meant to be a kindly greeting.

The startled eagles rose up in surprise, and then seeing the stange and talkative bird again, circled round her. Quite clearly they didn't mind her in the least. They probably took her to be some sort of strange eagle cousin, as she spoke their language!

It wasn't long before Jack climbed up to see if the young eagle was still in the nest. It was! The mother had just brought it a dead rabbit, and the young eagle was busy on the meal. When it saw Jack it stood over the rabbit with wings held over it, as if afraid that Jack would take it.

'It's all right,' said the boy gently. 'Eat it all. I don't want any. I only want a picture of you!'

He looked around for a place to make a good hide in. There was one spot that looked ideal. It was a thick gorse-bush, almost on a level with the eagles' ledge. Jack thought he could probably squeeze into the hollow middle of it, and make an opening for his camera in the prickly branches.

'The only thing is – I'll get terribly pricked,' he thought. 'Never mind. It will be worth it if I get some good pictures! I bet the eagles will never know whether I'm hiding in that bush or not!'

He told the others, and they agreed with him that it would be a splendid place, if a bit painful. The bush was quite hollow in the middle, and once he was there he could manage not to be pricked. It was the getting in and out that would be unpleasant.

'You'll have to wrap this rug round you,' said Lucy-Ann, holding up the thick rug she had brought. 'If you creep in with this round you, you'll be all right.'

'Good idea,' said Jack.

They went up to the tower-top and had their dinner there again, seeing the countryside spread out below once more in all its beauty.

'I'd like Bill Smugs to see this,' said Jack. 'We must bring him up here when he comes.'

'Where do you think you will sleep tonight, Jack?' asked Lucy-Ann anxiously. 'And will you wave your hanky from the tower before you go to sleep? I'll watch for it.'

'I'll wave my white shirt,' said Jack. 'You probably wouldn't notice anything so small as a hanky, though you can borrow my old fieldglasses and look through them, if you like. They're in my room.'

'Oh yes, I will,' said Lucy-Ann. 'I shall easily see your shirt. I hope you won't be too lonely, Jack.'

''Course not. I'll have Kiki. Nobody could possibly be lonely with that old chatterbox of a bird,' said Jack, scratching Kiki's feathered poll.

'Pop goes the weasel,' said Kiki, and nibbled at Jack's ear.

'You haven't said where you'll sleep, Jack,' said Lucy-Ann. 'You won't really sleep on one of those old sofas, will you?'

'No, I don't think so. More likely in a sandy corner of the courtyard,' said Jack. 'There's a sandy bit over there, look — it'll be warm with the sun. If I curl up there and wrap the rugs all round me, I'll be very snug.'

'I'd rather you slept out in the courtyard somehow, than in the strange old castle!' said Lucy-Ann. 'I don't like those musty, dusty, fusty rooms!'

'Musty, dusty, fusty!' sang Kiki, delighted. 'Musty, fusty, dusty, musty, fusty . . .'

'Shut up, Kiki,' said everyone; but Kiki loved those three words, and went to repeat them over and over again to Button, who sat listening, his ears cocked, and his little foxy head on one side.

'It's time for us to go,' said Philip at last. They had tried in vain to find the place where Button had got in and out, and had wandered once more all over the castle, switching on their torches, and exploring even more thoroughly than before. Only the three rooms they had seen before were furnished — the sitting room, the dining room and the kitchen. There was no bedroom furnished, which, as Philip pointed out, was rather a pity, as Jack could probably have made himself comfortable in a big old four poster bed!

Jack said goodbye to them all as they went across the plank. He held Button in his arms, quite determined to follow him and find out where he went, when he got out of the castle. He was not going to set him free till the others had gone. One by one they crossed the plank and disappeared. Their voices died away. Jack was alone.

He went down the wide corridor, down the stone stairway that led to the dark hall, and out into the courtyard, where the last rays of the sun still shone. When he came to the yard, he set the wriggling fox cub down.

'Now you show me where you go,' he said. Button darted off at once — far too quickly for Jack! By the time the boy had run a few steps after him, the fox cub had disappeared, and there was no trace of him.

'Blow!' said Jack, annoyed. 'I did mean to discover the way out you went, this time — but you're so jolly nippy! I suppose you have already joined the others now.'

Jack went to try and arrange his camera safely in the gorse bush. He had a very good camera indeed, given to him last Christmas by Bill Smugs. In his pocket were many rolls of film. He ought to be able to take a fine series of pictures of those eagles.

He wrapped one of the rugs round him, as Lucy-Ann had suggested, and began to squeeze through the prickly branches. Some of the prickles reached his flesh even through the thick rug. Kiki sat beside the bush, watching Jack in surprise.

'What a pity, what a pity, what a pity!' she said.

'It *is* a pity that I'm being pricked like this!' groaned Jack. But he cheered up when he saw what a fine view of the eagles' nest he had — and of the ledge where the eagles sat to look out at the surrounding country. The distance was perfect, and Jack rejoiced.

By making an opening in the bush on the side where the nest was, he managed to point his camera in exactly the right direction, and lodged it very firmly on its tripod legs. He looked through it to see what kind of a picture he would get.

'Perfect!' thought the boy joyfully. 'I won't take one now, because the light is awkward. But tomorrow morning would be exactly right. Then the sun will be just where I want it.'

The little eagle caught sight of the camera peering out of the bush. It did not like it. It cowered down in the nest, afraid.

'You'll soon get used to it,' Jack thought. 'I hope the old birds will too. Oh, Kiki, did you *have* to get into the middle of the bush too? There's really only just room enough for me!'

'Fusty, musty, dusty!' whispered Kiki, evidently thinking that Jack was playing a game of hide-and-seek with somebody and mustn't be given away. 'Fusty, musty, dusty.'

'Silly old bird,' said Jack. 'Now get out, please. I'm coming out too. It's certainly fusty and musty in this gorse-bush, even if it isn't dusty!'

Kiki crawled out and then Jack forced his way out, trying to protect himself from the prickly stems. He stood up, stretched himself, took the rug and went down the crag lightly, leaving his camera in position. It was clear that there would be no rain that night!

The boy read a book until daylight faded. Then he remembered about waving his shirt from the tower. So up he went, hoping he hadn't left it too late for Lucy-Ann to see.

He stood on the top of the tower, and stripped off his white shirt. Then he waved it gaily in the strong breeze there, looking down on the cottage far below as he waved. And from the topmost window there came a flash of white.

Lucy-Ann was waving back.

'He's just waved,' she called to Dinah, who was undressing. 'I saw the white shirt. Good. Now I know he's all right and will soon be curling himself up to go to sleep.'

'Why you must fuss so about Jack I don't know,' said Dinah, jumping into bed. 'I never fuss about Philip. You're silly, Lucy-Ann.'

'I don't care,' thought Lucy-Ann, as she settled down in bed. 'I'm glad to know Jack is safe. Somehow I don't like him being all alone in that horrid old castle!'

13

Noises in the night

Jack went down the stone stairways of the tower, whistling softly. Kiki whistled with him. If it was a tune she knew, she would whistle it all through with Jack.

They came into the old courtyard. There was no sign of the eagles. They were probably roosting now. But, at Jack's coming, there was a general scurrying all around the yard.

'Rabbits!' said Jack, in delight. 'Golly, what hundreds of them! I suppose they all come out this time of the evening. I'll curl myself up in that sandy corner and watch them for a bit. Now, don't you frighten them, Kiki.'

He went over to the soft sand, taking with him the thick rugs and a packet of chocolate biscuits. He curled himself up, and lay there, watching the rabbits creeping out of their holes again.

It was a lovely sight to see. There were big ones and little ones, dark ones and light ones and playful ones. Some nibbled patches of wiry grass here and there. Others leapt about madly.

Jack lay there contentedly and nibbled his biscuits, enjoying the chocolate on them. He watched the rabbits in delight. Kiki watched them too, murmuring a few remarks into Jack's ear now and again.

'I bet the eagles catch a good few of those rabbits,' thought Jack, suddenly feeling sleepy. He finished his last biscuit, and pulled the rugs more closely around him. He felt a little chilly now. The sand didn't feel quite so soft as it had done before, either. Jack hoped he wasn't going to be uncomfortable. Perhaps it would have been better to have chosen a patch of heather.

'Well, I'm too sleepy to change my bed now,' he thought. 'Much too sleepy. Kiki, move up a bit. Your claws are digging into my neck. You'd better get off me and perch somewhere else.'

But before Kiki could move, Jack was asleep. Kiki stayed where she was. The rabbits grew bolder and played nearer to the sleeping boy. A half-moon came out of the evening clouds and lighted up the dreaming courtyard.

What woke Jack he never knew. But something woke him with a jump. He opened his eyes and lay there, looking up into the night sky, full of surprise. For a moment or two he had no idea where he was.

Usually when he woke he saw the ceiling of his room — now there were stars and clouds. Then he suddenly remembered. Of course — he was in the courtyard of the old castle. He sat up and Kiki awoke too, giving an annoyed little squawk.

'I wonder what woke me?' thought Jack, looking round the shadowy yard. The moon came out again and he saw a few rabbits here and there. Behind rose the great dark bulk of the castle.

Jack felt absolutely certain that something had awakened him. Some noise perhaps? Or had a rabbit run over him? He listened intently, but he could hear nothing save the hoot of an owl on the hillside: 'Hoo-hoo-hoo-hoo! Hoo-hoo-hoo-hoo!' Then he heard the high squeak of a bat, catching beetles in the night air.

He glanced up at the tower from which he had waved his white shirt – and he suddenly stiffened in surprise. Surely that was a light he saw flash there?

He stared intently, waiting for it to come again. It had seemed rather like the sudden flash of a torch. But it didn't come again.

Jack sat and thought hard. Was it a flash? Had someone walked along the battlemented wall to the tower, and was it their footsteps that awakened him? *Was* there someone in the castle after all?

It seemed rather weird. Jack wondered what to do. He didn't really feel inclined to get up and find out what the flash was – if it *had* been a flash. He was beginning to doubt that it was now. If only if would come again, he would know.

He decided that it was cowardly to stay in his bed just because he felt a bit scared. He had better get up and make his way to the tower to see if anyone was there. That would be the brave thing to do.

'I don't feel at all brave,' thought Jack, 'but I suppose a person is really bravest when he does something although he is frightened. So here goes!'

Warning Kiki to be quite quiet, he made his way very carefully across the yard to the entrance of the castle, keeping in the blackest shadows. The feel of Kiki's feet on his shoulder was somehow very comforting.

He went into the vast hall and listened. There was not a sound to be heard. He switched on his torch, cautiously covering it with his handkerchief. The hall was empty. Jack went up the wide stone stairway, and found his way to the wall that led to the tower. He walked quietly along it keeping close to one edge, and soon came to the tower.

'Shall I go up or not?' wondered the boy. 'I don't want to in the least. If there's anyone there they can't be up to any good. *Did* I imagine that flash?'

He screwed up his courage and stole up the tower stairway. There was no one in the tower room. He crept up the stairway that led to the very top, and put his head carefully out. The moon's light was enough to show him that there was nobody there either.

'Well – I just must have imagined it,' thought the boy. 'How silly of me! I'll go back to bed again.'

Down he went once more Kiki still on his shoulder. As he came into the wide hall, he suddenly stopped still. He had heard a sound. What could it be?

It sounded like a muffled clanking – and then surely that was the splash of water?

'Is it somebody in the kitchen – somebody getting a drink of water again?' wondered Jack, feeling a prickle of panic go down his back. 'Golly, I don't like this. I wish the others were here.'

He stood quite still, wondering what to do. Then, overcome by fear, he fled out of the hall and into the moonlight yard, keeping in the shadows. He was trembling. Kiki bent to his ear, murmuring something supposed to be comforting. She knew he was frightened.

In a minute or two he was ashamed of himself. 'Why am I running away?' he thought. 'This won't do. Just to show myself that I'm no coward I'll walk into that kitchen and see who's there! It's a tramp, I expect, who knows the way in. He'll be far more frightened to see me than I shall be to see him!'

Boldly, but very quickly, the boy went back into the dark, brooding castle. Through the hall he went, and made his way softly to the kitchen entrance. He slipped inside the doorway, and then went behind the door, where he waited, listening and watching to see if any light was shown.

But there was dead silence. There was no clank of the pump. There was no splash of water. Jack waited for two or three minutes, with Kiki, perfectly silent.

He could not even hear anyone breathing. The kitchen must be empty.

'I'll switch on my torch very quickly, flash it round the kitchen, and see if there's anyone standing quietly there,' he thought. 'I can easily run out of the door if there is.'

So he took his torch from his pocket, and suddenly pressed down the switch. He flashed it to the sink, where the pump stood. There was no one there. He flashed it all round the kitchen. It was quite empty. There was no sign of anyone at all.

Jack heaved a sigh of relief. He went across to the sink and examined the floor beside it. There was again a puddle there – but was it a freshly-made one from the sink splashes – or was it the same one they themselves had made when they used the pump?

Jack couldn't tell. He looked closely at the pump, but that told him nothing, of course.

'It's a puzzle,' Jack said to Kiki, in a whisper. 'I suppose the clank and the splashing were all my silly imagination. I was frightened, and people always imagine things then. I imagined that flash in the tower, and I imagined the clanking noise and the splashing. Kiki, I'm as timid as Lucy-Ann – I really am.'

Still feeling a bit puzzled, but rather ashamed of all his fears and alarms, Jack went back to his bed in the courtyard.

It seemed uncomfortably hard now. Also he was a bit cold. He pulled the rugs round him and tried to get comfortable. He shut his eyes and told himself to go to sleep. The moon seemed to have gone now, and everything was pitch-black. Whatever he heard or saw, Jack was determined he was not going to leave his bed again that night. Let people flash lights all they liked, and pump water all night long if they wanted to! *He* wouldn't bother about it!

He was wide awake. He simply couldn't go to sleep. He didn't feel frightened any more. He only felt annoyed because sleep wouldn't come to him. He began to think about his eagles, and planned some fine camera work for the next day.

He could feel Kiki perched on his shoulderbone. He knew she had her head under her wing, and was sleeping. He wished she was awake and would talk to him. He wished the other children were with him. Then he could tell them what he had imagined he saw and heard.

At last he fell asleep, just as the dawn was making the eastern sky silvery. He didn't see it turn gold and pink, nor did he see the first soaring flight of the two eagles. He slept soundly, and so did Kiki. But she awoke at the first yelping scream of one of the eagles, and answered it with one of her marvellous imitations.

That woke Jack with a jump, and he sat up. Kiki flew off his shoulder, waited till he called her, and flew back again. Jack rubbed his eyes and yawned.

'I'm hungry,' he said to Kiki. 'Are you?'

'Fusty, musty, dusty,' said Kiki, remembering the three words she had so much liked the day before. 'Fusty, mus . . .'

'Yes, I heard you the first time,' said Jack. 'I say, Kiki, do you remember how we got up in the middle of the night and went to the tower and to the kitchen?'

Kiki apparently did. She scratched her beak with one of her feet and looked at Jack. 'What a pity, what a pity!' she remarked.

'Yes – I think it *was* a pity we disturbed ourselves so much,' said Jack. 'I was an idiot, Kiki. Now that it's broad daylight, and I'm wide awake, I begin to think I must have dreamt or imagined all that happened in the night – not that anything much did happen, anyway.'

Kiki listened with her head on one side. Jack unwrapped himself from the rug. 'I tell you what, Kiki – we won't either of us mention that flash in the tower, or the mysterious clanking or splashing we thought we heard, see? The others would only laugh at us – and Lucy-Ann and Tassie might be frightened. I'm sure it was all my imagination.'

Kiki appeared to agree with every word. She helped Jack to get biscuits out of a packet, and fruit out of a bag, and watched him take the top off a bottle of ginger beer.

'I wonder what time the others will be up,' said Jack, beginning his breakfast. 'We'll try and take a few pictures before they come, shall we, Kiki?'

14

Jack gets a shock

After he had had his breakfast Jack went to his hide. It was a lovely day. He could take some fine pictures if only the eagles were there.

He wrapped the thickest rug round him and crawled in through the prickly stems of the gorse. Kiki remained outside this time.

When he was in the hollow centre of the bush Jack examined his camera to make sure that it was all right. It was. He looked through the shutter to see if he had it trained exactly on the nest.

'Perfect!' he thought. 'That young eagle appears to be asleep. I might get a good picture when it wakes up. I suppose the other birds are soaring miles high into the sky.'

It was boring, waiting for the eagle to wake up. But Jack didn't mind. Both he and Philip knew that the ability to keep absolutely still and silent for a long time on end was essential to the study of birds and animals in their natural surroundings. So Jack settled back in the gorse bush, and waited.

Kiki went off on errands of her own. She flew to the top of the nearest tower and looked down on the countryside. She flew down to the courtyard and looked inside a paper bag there, hoping to find a forgotten biscuit. She sat on the branch of a birch tree, practising quietly to herself the barking noise that Button the fox cub made. So long as Jack was somewhere near she was happy. He was safe in that gorse bush. Kiki didn't know why he had chosen such a peculiar resting place, but Jack was always wise in her eyes.

The young eagle suddenly awoke and stretched out first one wing and then another. It climbed to the edge of the nest and looked out over the ledge, waiting for its parents to come back.

'Fine!' whispered Jack, and pressed the trigger of the camera to take the eagle's picture. The young bird heard the click and cowered down at once – but the snap had been taken!

Soon the bird recovered from its fright and climbed up again. Then, with yelps, the two grown eagles came gliding down on outspread wings, and the young one greeted them gladly, spreading out its wings and quivering them.

One of the eagles had a young hare clutched in its claws. It dropped it into the nest. At once the youngster covered the food with its big wings, cowered over it, and began to pull at it hungrily with its powerful beak.

Jack snapped it. All three birds heard the click and looked towards the gorse bush suspiciously. The male eagle glared and Jack felt uncomfortable. He hoped the bird wouldn't pounce at the gleaming camera lens and ambush it.

But Kiki saved the situation by flying down in a most comradely manner to the eagles, and saluting them in their own yelping language.

They appeared to be quite pleased to see her again

although the young eagle covered the dead hare threateningly with its wings as if to keep Kiki off.

'Open your books at page six,' said Kiki pleasantly. The eagles looked startled. They had not yet got used to the parrot talking in human language. She barked like Button, and they looked rather alarmed.

The female eagle bent herself forward, opened her cruel beak, and made a curious snarling noise, warning Kiki to be careful. She at once spoke in eagle language again, and gave such a fine scream that both eagles were satisfied. The young one fell upon its meal and ate till it could eat no more. Then it sank back into the big nest.

The female eagle finished the dead hare in a very short while. Jack got another wonderful snap whilst it was tearing up its food.

This time, except for an enquiring look in the direction of the click, the eagles took no notice.

'Good,' thought Jack. 'They won't mind the click soon or the gleaming eye of the camera!'

He spent a pleasant morning, using up the rest of his film, delighted to think of the wonderful pictures he could develop. He imagined them in nature magazines, with his name under them as photographer. How proud he would feel!

Kiki suddenly gave a most excited squawk, making the two grown eagles rise in the air in alarm. She flew into the air, and made for the wall that ran round the courtyard. Jack, peering through the back of his hiding-place, saw her fly right over the wall, and disappear.

'Now where's she gone?' he thought. 'I was just going to take a picture of her and the two eagles together.'

Kiki was gone for about half an hour before Jack saw her again. Then she came into the courtyard on Tassie's shoulder! She had heard the other children coming up the hillside and had flown to meet them. They had got into the castle in the usual way, and were now looking for Jack.

The eagles soared into the air when they heard the children coming towards their crag. Jack gave a hail from the inside of his hide.

'I'm here! Hallo, it's good to see you. Wait a sec and I'll be out.'

He crawled out with the rug round him and went down to the others. Lucy-Ann eyed him anxiously, and was relieved to see him looking cheerful and well. So he hadn't minded his lonely night at the castle after all.

'We've brought a fine dinner,' said Philip. 'Mother managed to get some cooked ham and a big fruit cake in the village.'

'Good!' said Jack, realising that he was terribly hungry. 'I've only had biscuits and fruit for my breakfast, washed down with ginger beer.'

'We've got some more ginger beer too,' said Dinah. 'Where shall we have our dinner? On the top of the tower again or where?'

'Here, I think,' said Jack, 'because the light is perfect for taking pictures this morning, and if those eagles come back I want a few more snaps of them. I've an idea they are going to make that young one fly soon. The female eagle tried to tip it off the edge of the nest this morning.'

'Kiki came to meet us,' said Tassie. 'Did you see how Button came in this morning, Jack? We left him outside, but he's here again.'

'No, I didn't,' said Jack. 'I can't see much from the inside of that gorse bush, you know. We shall never find out how Button gets in — I bet it's down an old rabbit hole. He won't be able to do that when he gets a bit bigger. Has he been good?'

'Not very,' said Philip. 'He somehow got into the larder and gobbled up all Mother's sausages. She wasn't at all pleased. I can't imagine how he can eat anything else at the moment. He must have eaten a pound and a half of sausages.'

'Greedy pig.' said Jack, giving Button half his ham sandwich. 'You don't deserve this but you're so sweet I can't help spoiling you.'

'It's a pity he smells so strong,' said Dinah, wrinkling up her nose. 'You won't be able to keep him when he's grown a bit more, Philip – he'll smell too much.'

'That's all *you* know!' said Philip. 'I shall probably keep him till he dies of old age.'

'Well, you'll have to wear a gas mask then,' said Jack, grinning. 'Another sandwich, please, Dinah. Golly, these are good.'

'What sort of a night did you have, Jack?' asked Lucy-Ann, who was sitting as close to Jack as she could.

'Oh, very good,' said Jack airily. 'I woke up once and took some time to go to sleep again.'

He was determined not to say anything about his alarms and fears in the night. They seemed so silly now, in the full sunshine with people all round him.

'You should have seen the rabbits in the late evening,' he said to Philip. 'You'd have loved them. They wouldn't come to me of course, but I daresay you'd have got them all over you! They seemed as tame as anything.'

The four children stayed with Jack till after tea. Each crept into his hide to watch the eagles. They went up to the tower again, and Jack cautiously looked round to see if there was anything different about the tower – a cigarette end, a scrap of paper – but there was nothing at all.

'Won't you come back with us tonight, Jack?' asked Lucy-Ann.

'Of course not,' said Jack, though secretly he felt that he *would* rather like to. 'Is it likely, just as I'm certain that young eagle is going to learn to fly?'

'All right,' said Lucy-Ann, with a sigh, 'I don't know why

I hate you being here alone in this horrid old castle, but I just do.'

'It's not a horrid castle,' said Jack. 'It's just old and forgotten, but it's not horrid.'

'Well, *I* think it is,' said Lucy-Ann. 'I think horrid, wicked things have been done here in the past – and I think they might be done again in the future.'

'You're just dreaming,' said Jack, 'and you're frightening poor Tassie. It's only an old empty place forgotten for years, with nobody in it at all except me and the eagles, bats and rabbits.'

'It's time to go,' said Philip, getting up. 'We brought you another rug, Jack, in case you felt cold. Coming to see us off at the window?'

'Yes, of course,' said Jack, and they all went inside the castle, their footsteps echoing on the stone floor. They went to the room where the plank reached to the windowsill, and one by one they got across.

Lucy-Ann called a farewell to Jack.

'Thank you for waving your shirt to me last night!' she called. 'And oh, Jack I saw you flashing your torch from the tower later on, too! I was in bed, but I was awake and I saw the flash of the torch three or four times. It was nice of you to do that. I was glad to see it and to know you were awake too!'

'Come on, Lucy-Ann, for goodness' sake!' called Dinah. 'You know Mother said we weren't to be late tonight.'

'All right, I'm coming,' said Lucy-Ann, and slid down the creepers to the ground. Everyone called goodbye and then they were gone.

But Jack was left feeling most puzzled and uncomfortable! So there *had* been someone in the tower last night flashing a torch! He hadn't dreamt it or imagined it. It was true.

'Lucy-Ann saw it, so that proves I wasn't mistaken as I

89

thought,' said the boy to himself as he went back to the courtyard. 'It's terribly mysterious. That clanking I heard and the splashing must have been real too. There *is* someone else here – but who – and why?'

He wished now that he had told the others the happenings in the night. But it was too late, they were gone. Jack now longed to be gone with them! Suppose he heard noises again and saw flashes? He didn't like it. It was weird and eerie and altogether unpleasant.

'Shall I go after the others and join them?' he thought. 'No, I won't. I'll wait and try and find out who's here. Fancy Lucy-Ann seeing those flashes! I *am* glad she told me!'

15

The hidden room

Jack wandered back to his hide. He felt safe there. He was sure no one would ever think of looking in the very middle of a prickly, thick gorse bush for anyone. As evening fell he felt sleepy. Should he try and go to sleep now, and keep awake later on? Could he possibly go to sleep in the hollow gorse bush?

He curled up in the thickest rug and made a pillow of another one. Kiki crawled in beside him and perched uncomfortably on his knees, her head bent to avoid a prickly bit of gorse. The eagles were not to be seen. The young one was down in the nest. Anyway, the light was now too bad to bother about photographs.

Jack managed to fall asleep. He snored a little, for he had his head in an uncomfortable position. Kiki imitated the snore perfectly for a little while, and then, as Jack made no remark about it to her, put her head under her wing and slept too.

Jack slept till midnight. Then he awoke suddenly, feeling dreadfully uncomfortable. He stretched out, wondering where he was, and was immediately and painfully pricked by the gorse. He drew his legs in again hastily.

'I'm in the gorse bush, of course,' he said to himself. 'I must have been asleep for ages. What's the time?'

He looked at the phosporescent hands of his watch and saw that it was ten past midnight.

'Hm,' said Jack, 'Just about the time that someone in the castle starts to wake up! I suppose, if I am going to do any tracking, I'd better get out of here and watch and listen.'

He crept painfully out of the bush, disturbing Kiki, who protested loudly till he made her be silent. 'I'll leave you behind if you make a row like that!' whispered Jack furiously. Kiki fell silent. She always knew when Jack wanted her to be quiet.

Now he was out of the bush, climbing silently down the crag, glad of the faint light of the moon, now a little bigger than the night before. He came into the yard and stood· listening.

There was no sound to be heard except the wind blowing fairly hard. And then Jack thought he heard the far off sound of water splashing again – and the clank of the pump handle!

He stood listening. After a while he felt sure he heard quiet footsteps on stone somewhere – was it someone walking on the castle wall – going to the tower to flash a torch again?

'Well, if he's gone to the tower, he's safely out of the castle,' thought Jack. 'I'll go in and see if I can discover any signs of him – where he hides, for instance. He must live somewhere! But it didn't look as if anyone had gone into any of those furnished rooms in the castle. So where in the world does he hide? And what about food? Gosh, it's a mystery!'

The boy stole quietly into the castle, Kiki on his shoulder. He was too excited to feel frightened tonight. Now that he was certain someone else was in the castle besides himself he was too anxious to find out about them to feel any real fears.

He went into the hall of the castle – and at once something struck him with surprise – there was a light coming from somewhere! A dim light certainly, but a light. Jack stared round him, puzzled.

Then he saw where it came from. It came from the floor – or rather, underneath the floor of the hall! The boy stepped forward cautiously. He came to a hole in the floor of the hall – there was no trap-door; it looked exactly like a hole, and yet Jack was sure it had never been there before – and up from this hole came the light.

Jack looked down. Stone steps went down into whatever was below – cellar or dungeon, he didn't know. He ran swiftly to the front entrance of the castle to see if anyone was in the tower. If there was, there would be time for him to slip down the steps and explore.

He saw a flash from the tower. Good. Whoever was there was signalling again. It would be a minute or two before they came back. There would be time to explore this curious opening. In a flash Jack was down the stone steps and then looked around him in the very greatest surprise.

He seemed to be in a kind of museum! He was in a large, underground room, with tapestries on the stone walls, and a thick covering on the floor. Round the room stood suits of armour, just as there often is in a museum. Old heavy chairs stood here and there, and a long narrow table, with crockery and glass on it, ran the length of the room.

Jack stared round in the utmost astonishment. Everything was old – but it was plain that this room was not neglected and deserted as the other furnished rooms were. There were no cobwebs here, no dust.

In the corner was a big old four-poster bed, hung with heavy tapestries. Jack went over to it. It had obviously been slept in, for the pillows were dented, and the sheets hurriedly thrown back as if someone had leapt out in a hurry.

There was a pitcher of ice-cold water on the table. 'Got from the pump, I suppose!' thought Jack. 'So that's why there are always puddles on the floor there. Someone goes for water each night.'

Kiki flew to a suit of armour and stood on the helmet, looking in through the visor as if she expected to glimpse someone inside. Jack giggled a little. Evidently Kiki thought the suits of armour were real peopole and couldn't understand them at all.

At this moment he thought he heard a noise, and in sudden fright he darted up the stone steps to the top, taking Kiki with him. He hopped out just in time, and fled to the dark shadows at the back of the hall. Then, fearing that the person whose footsteps he heard might see him by the light of the torch he was using, he went into one of the furnished rooms – the old drawing-room.

But in going inside he fell over a stool and came to the ground. The footsteps outside stopped suddenly. The torch-light went out. Evidently the person was standing perfectly still and listening hard. He had heard the noise.

With his heart beating fast Jack slipped round the corner of an old couch, and knelt there, with Kiki on his shoulder. Both were as quiet as they could be, but Jack couldn't help feeling certain that the man who was listening must be able to hear the beating of his heart!

The boy heard a cautious footstep coming into the room. Then there was silence again. Then another footstep sounded, a little nearer. Jack's hair began to prickle on his scalp and stand up straight. If the man came round the couch and switched on his torch, he would be bound to see Jack.

The boy's heart pounded away, and his forehead felt suddenly wet. Kiki clung to his shoulder, feeling the fright of her master. She couldn't bear it any longer.

She suddenly rose into the air and flew at the head of the unseen man, giving one of the yelping screams she had picked up from the eagles. He uttered a startled exclamation, and tried to beat off the bird. His torch clattered to the floor. Jack hoped fervently that it was broken.

Kiki screeched again, this time like an express train, and the man lashed out at her. He caught a feather and ripped it out. Kiki found Jack once more, and perched on the crouching boy, growling like a dog.

'Good heavens, this place is full of birds and dogs!' said someone, in a disgusted voice, deep and hoarse. The man felt over the floor for his torch and at last found it.

'Broken!' he said and Jack heard the click as he tried to switch it on. 'One of those eagles, I suppose. What does it want to come indoors for?'

Muttering, the man went out. Jack heard a curious grating sound and then there was complete silence. He did not dare to get up for a long time, but crouched behind the enormous old sofa. Kiki appeared to have gone fast asleep on his shoulder.

At last he got cautiously up and tiptoed to the door, glad of his rubber shoes. He peeped out. There was now no light to be seen shining up dimly from underground. All was darkness and silence. Jack stared at the back of the hall. Somewhere over there had been a strange opening, leading to a hidden room – an old room, so full of strange things that it looked like a museum. Maybe it was the very room where the wicked old man had hidden his guests and starved them so that they were never heard of again! Jack didn't like the thought at all.

Without trying to see what had happened to the curious opening, he ran into the courtyard and made his way back to the old gorse bush. He felt safe there. He crawled in, accompanied by groans and protestations from Kiki, and tried to settle down to go to sleep again.

But he couldn't. His mind was full of that strange room, and he kept shuddering when he remembered how nearly he had been caught. If it hadn't been for old Kiki he would certainly have been discovered. Another step or two and the man, whoever he was, would almost have trodden on him!

He wished that the others were with him. He longed to tell them. Well, they would be up tomorrow, so he must wait in patience. There didn't seem any likelihood of the hidden man coming out in the daytime. He was keeping well hidden for some reason. He wouldn't expose his hiding place by day and come out.

'How does he get food?' Jack wondered. It was easy to get water from the pump. But what about food? Well, perhaps that was what he signalled about from the tower. His torch sent messages to friends. In that case other people might come. How in the world did they get in?

'I believe this is an adventure!' said Jack suddenly, and a funny feeling crept up his body. 'Yes, it is. It's the same feeling I had last year — when we sailed away to the Isle of Gloom, the Island of Adventure, where so many things happened to us. Golly, what will the others say when I tell them we've jumped straight into the middle of an adventure again! The Castle of Adventure! Philip was right when he called it that.'

After an hour or two of thinking and wondering, Jack at last fell asleep again. He awoke to find little fingers of sunlight coming through the gorse bush, and was glad that the day had come. He remembered the nighttime happenings, and wondered if that curious museum-like room could have been real.

'Well, I certainly couldn't have dreamt a room like that,' thought Jack, tickling Kiki to wake her. 'It would be impossible!'

He crawled out of the bush and breakfasted on biscuits and plums, which the others had brought to him the day before. He sat and looked thoughtfully at the castle. Who was hiding there?

Suddenly he went stiff and looked in amazement at two men walking through the courtyard. They were going towards the castle. How in the world had they got in? There simply *must* be some way in – or had the men keys to one of the big gates or doors?

The men went into the castle. Evidently unlike the hidden man, they did not fear being seen in daylight. 'Will the hidden man tell them he thought there was someone about last night?' thought Jack in a panic. 'Will they come and look for me?'

16

Things begin to happen

Jack crawled hurriedly back into the bush again, not waiting to wrap himself up in the rug, and getting terribly scratched. When he was inside he remembered that he had left some paper bags in the courtyard below, with some apple cores in them.

'Dash!' he thought. 'If those are found they'll know there's someone here besides themselves.'

He waited in the bush for an hour or so, taking peeps at

the eagles' nest now and again. He didn't know whether to hope the others would come soon, so that he would no longer be alone, or whether to hope that they would be late, to give the men a chance to go off again without seeing them.

'If they've chosen this for a safe hiding place for some-body, they won't be too pleased to know that we are here,' thought Jack uneasily. 'I suppose we really oughtn't to have come to the castle at all. I suppose it does belong to someone – those men perhaps!'

He heard the sound of voices and peeped between the prickly branches to see who it was. It was the two men again. The hidden man was evidently not going to risk coming out of his hiding place.

Jack peeped at them. They were great hulking men, one of them with a black beard. He didn't like their faces at all. As they came near he tried to hear what they said, but they were not talking any language he knew. That somehow made things all the stranger.

Suddenly they stopped, and with an exclamation the bearded man picked up Jack's paper bags. He saw the apple cores inside, and showed the other man. The cores were still moist, and Jack guessed that the men knew they had not been there very long! He squeezed himself hard into the hollow of the gorse bush, glad that it was so thick.

The men then separated and began to make a thorough search of the castle, the towers, the walls and the courtyard. Jack watched them through a chink in the bush. Kiki was absolutely quiet.

Then the men joined up and came across to the crag where the eagles nested. It was plain they were going to climb up to explore that place too, in case anyone was hiding there.

Jack crouched as still as a mouse when an owl is near. His heart began to beat painfully again. The men came right up the crag, and gave a cry of amazement when they saw the eagles' nest with the young one in.

Evidently they did not know the ways of eagles, for they went quite near to the nest and one of the men put out his hand.

There was a whirr of mighty wings and the female eagle seemed to drop like a stone from the sky on to the man's head. He turned away, whilst the other man beat off the angry bird. The attacked man put his arms across the top of his head to protect himself, and looked up at the male bird, scared, for that too was dropping quickly downwards.

Jack could see all this, and an idea came to him. He had a marvellous view of the first man the eagle had attacked – he was still looking up, showing the whole of his face, and his neck in an open-collared shirt. Jack pressed his camera release. Click! The man's photograph was taken, though unfortunately the other man was by then looking away, and his face was hidden.

Both men heard the click of the camera, and looked puzzled. Then, as the female eagle came at them again, they hurriedly descended the crag and ran down into the court-yard. They were not going to explore up there any more. In any case they both decided that nobody could possibly hide up there with fierce birds like that around!

Jack waited in the bush, watching the eagles, who had been much upset by the visit of the two men. Soon it was plain to Jack that they meant to take the young bird away from the nest. It must learn to fly! It could no longer be left in safety if two-legged creatures came right up to the nest.

The boy forgot his fears in his interest at the efforts of the two eagles to make the young one fly. They persuaded it to the edge of the nest, and then, with a push, dislodged it on to the ledge on which the nest was built. The young bird tried to get back again, but the female eagle flew round and round it, yelping, trying to tell it in all the eagle words she knew that it must go with her. The young one listened, or seemed to listen, then turned its head away, bored.

Then, for no reason that Jack could see, it suddenly spread out its wings. They were enormous. The boy had been taking snap after snap, and now he took a splendid picture of the young eagle trying out his wings.

The youngster flapped his wings so hard that he danced about on tiptoe – and then, most superbly, he took off from the ledge, and rose into the air, with his parents screaming on either side of him. He could fly!

'Marvellous!' said Jack, and cautiously took the roll of film from his camera. 'I wonder if they'll come back. It doesn't matter much if they don't, because I've got the most wonderful set of pictures now. Better than any anyone else has ever got!'

As he slipped a new roll of film into his camera, he heard the voices of the other children. He was very glad – but where were those men?

He crept out from the bush, hardly feeling the prickles, and climbed down to join them. They saw by his face that he had news for them. Lucy-Ann ran to him.

'Has anything happened, Jack? You look very serious! What do you think! We've come up with piles of things, because Mrs Mannering says we can stay for two or three days! She's got to go to Dinah's Aunt Polly, who has been taken ill again, but she'll be back soon.'

'And she thought we might as well join you up here if we wanted to!' said Dinah. 'But you don't look very thrilled about it, Jack!'

'Well, listen,' said Jack. 'There's something odd here. Really odd. I don't know if you ought to come. In fact, as I've really taken all the snaps I need to take of the eagles, I honestly think it would be better if we all went home.'

'Go back to Spring Cottage!' said Philip, in surprise. 'But why? Quick, tell us everything, Jack.'

'All right. But first, where's Tassie?' said Jack, looking round for the little gypsy girl.

'Her mother wouldn't let her come,' said Lucy-Ann. 'When Tassie told her we were all going to stay up at the castle with you, her mother nearly had a fit. She's like the villagers, you know – thinks there's something bad and creepy up here. She absolutely refused to let Tassie come. So we had to leave her behind.'

'She was in an awful temper with her mother,' said Philip; 'worse than any Dinah gets into. She flew at her mother and banged her hard. And her mother took hold of her and shook her like a rat. I think Tassie's got an awful mother. Anyway, she can't come. But go on – tell your story.'

'I suppose – I suppose you didn't by any chance meet anyone coming down the hill, did you?' said Jack suddenly, thinking that perhaps the two men had gone.

'We saw what looked like three men in the distance,' said Philip. 'Why?'

'What were they like? Did one have a black beard?' asked Jack.

'We couldn't possibly see what they were like, they were too far away, going down another path altogether,' said Philip. 'They might have been shepherds or anything. That's what *we* thought they were, anyway.'

'*Three* men,' said Jack thoughtfully. 'That looks as if the hidden man went too, then.'

'What *are* you talking about?' cried Dinah impatiently.

Jack began his story. The others listened in astonishment. When he described the hidden underground room, Lucy-Ann's eyes nearly fell out of her head!

'An underground room – with someone living there! Oh, I know what Tassie would say – she'd say it was that wicked old man still there!' cried Lucy-Ann. 'She'd say he would like to catch *us* and imprison us, so that no one ever heard of us again!'

'Don't be silly,' said Jack. 'The thing is – *something* is going on here, and we ought to find out what. I wish old Bill

Smuggs was here. He'd know what to do.'

'We don't even know his address,' said Philip. 'All we know is that he's in a town twenty miles away. And now Mother is away too, so we can't ask her advice either.'

'Well, whether she is away or not, I think we ought to go back to Spring Cottage,' said Jack soberly. 'We have dealt with dangerous men before, and it wasn't pleasant. I don't want to be mixed up in anything dangerous like that again. We'd better all go back.'

'Right,' said Philip. 'I agree with you. But, seeing that you think all three men are out of the way, what about having a squint at that hidden room? We might find something there to tell us who uses it and why.'

'All right,' said Jack. 'Come on. Kiki, come along too. Where's Button, Philip?'

'I left him with Tassie, to comfort her for not coming with us,' said Philip. 'She was so miserable. Anyway, she'll be pleased to see us back again so soon.'

They all went into the vast hall, and the boys switched on their torches. Sure that there was no one but themselves in the castle, they made no effort to be quiet, but talked and laughed in their usual way. Jack led them to the back of the hall, and looked at the floor.

There was no hole to be seen at all. It had gone completely. The children looked about for a trap-door in the floor, but there was none. Philip began to wonder if Jack had dreamt it all.

Then his sharp eyes saw a spike made of iron set deeply in the wall at the back of the hall. It shone as if it had been much handled. Philip took hold of it.

'Here's something strange!' he began, and pulled hard. The spike moved smoothly is some sort of groove, and suddenly there was a grating noise at Lucy-Ann's feet. She leapt back with a startled cry.

The ground was opening at her feet! A big stone there was

disappearing downwards in some mysterious fashion, and then swung itself smoothly to one side, exposing a short flight of stone steps, leading down into the hidden room that Jack had seen the night before. The children gasped.

'It reminds me of Ali Baba and the Forty Thieves or Aladdin and his cave!' said Dinah. 'Shall we go down? Do let's! This is most exciting.'

There was an oil lamp left burning on the long narrow table below, and by the light of this the children saw the room. Philip, Lucy-Ann and Dinah went eagerly down the steps to examine everything. They saw the tapestries on the walls, depicting old hunting scenes, they saw the old suits of armour standing round the room, and the big, heavy chairs that looked as if they were made for giants, not men.

'Where's Jack?' said Philip.

'Gone to get Kiki,' said Dinah. 'Oh, look, Philip, here's another spike in the wall, just like the one upstairs. What happens when you pull it?'

She pulled it – and with a grating noise the stone swung up and into place, imprisoning the three children down below!

17

Things go on happening

The three children watched the great stone slide into place like magic. It was an extraordinary sight. But Philip suddenly felt worried.

'Dinah! Let me have that spike. Move away. I hope to goodness it will move the stone back again!'

The boy pulled at it, but it remained fixed. He tried to move it the other way. He jerked it. It would not move at all.

'It closes the hole in the floor, but it doesn't open it,' he said. He looked round for another spike or lever or handle – anything that he thought might open the hole to allow them to get out – but he could see nothing.

'There must be *some*thing!' he said, 'or the man that hides here wouldn't be able to come out at night. There must be *some*thing!'

The two girls were scared. They didn't like being shut up like this in an underground room. Lucy-Ann felt as if all the suits of armour were watching her and enjoying her fright. She didn't like them.

'Well, Philip, Jack will be along soon,' said Dinah, 'and he'll see the hole is shut and will work the spike upstairs in the hall to open it again. We needn't worry.'

'I suppose he will,' said Philip, looking relieved. 'You are an idiot, Dinah, messing about with things before you know what they do.'

'Well, you'd have done the same thing yourself,' retorted Dinah.

'All right, all right,' said Philip. He began to look all round the peculiar room. The suits of armour interested him. He wished he could put one on, just for fun!

An idea came to him. 'I say, I'll play a trick on Jack!' he said. 'I'll get inside one of these suits of armour, and hide. Then when Jack opens the hole and comes down don't you tell him where I am – and I'll suddenly step off one of these pedestals the armour is on, with a frightful clanging noise and scare him stiff!'

The girls laughed. 'All right,' said Lucy-Ann. 'Hurry up. Do you know how to get into one?'

'Yes. I've tried one before, when we had one at school to examine,' said Philip. 'It's quite easy when you know how. You can help me.'

Before long Philip was in the suit of armour. He had the helmet on his head, and the visor over his face. He could see quite well through the visor, but nobody would know there was anyone inside the armoured suit! He got back on the pedestal with a lot of clanking. The girls giggled.

'Won't Jack get an awful shock! I wish he'd come,' said Lucy-Ann.

'Are you comfortable, Philip?' asked Dinah, looking at her armoured brother standing quite still on his wooden pedestal, looking for all the world exactly like the others around.

'Fairly,' said Philip. 'But golly, I wouldn't much like to go to war in this – I'd never be able to walk more than a few yards! How they fought in them, those old-time soldiers, I really don't know!'

The girls wandered round the room. They looked at the tapestry scenes. They sat in the enormous old chairs. They fingered the ancient weapons that were arranged here and there. It certainly was a curious room.

'What *is* Jack doing?' said Lucy-Ann, at last, beginning to feel anxious. 'He's been simply ages. Oh, Dinah – you don't think those men have come back, do you – and captured him?'

'I shouldn't think so,' said Dinah, also beginning to feel worried. 'I can't imagine what he's doing. After all, he'd only got to call Kiki, wait for her to come to him and then follow us!'

'You know,' said a hollow voice from inside the suit of armour, 'you know, I don't believe those men we saw *were* the men from the castle. I've suddenly thought – they couldn't be!'

'What do you mean?' cried both girls, staring in dismay at the place where Philip's face was behind the visor.

'Well, think where we saw them,' said Philip. 'We saw them a good way down the hill, just above the farm, didn't we? We know there's no path up to the castle there. And now I think the matter over carefully, I'm pretty certain they were men belonging to the farm. One was that enormously tall fellow we sometimes see when we fetch eggs.'

The girls thought hard. Yes, that was where the men had been seen – just above the old farm.

'I believe you're right, Philip,' said Lucy-Ann, scared. 'And anyway, if they didn't want to be seen, it would be silly to take the farm path, wouldn't it? All the farm dogs would bark at them, and the farmer would look out.'

'Yes – and the dogs were *not* barking, or we would have heard them,' said Philip. 'So that rather proves our point. Dash! I don't believe those were Jack's men, after all. It's quite likely they never left the castle, and are still somewhere about.'

'I do wonder what Jack is doing,' said Dinah. 'I do wish he'd come.'

Jack was certainly a long time coming – but he couldn't help it! He had gone after Kiki, who had flown into the furnished room in which they had both hidden the night before – and suddenly, from the window, he had seen the three men in a corner of the yard!

'Golly!' thought the boy, 'Philip was wrong – the men he saw weren't the ones from the castle! They must have been farm workers seeing to the sheep or something. My word, I hope they're not going to that hidden room!'

The boy darted back into the hall, and went to the place where the hole should be. But it was gone, and a stone now covered the entrance to the room. He was surprised. He had no idea, of course, that Dinah had found the lever below and used it, closing the entrance.

He debated what to do. Should he open the hole and see if the others were down there? Would the men come into the hall just as he was doing it? He could hear their voices quite clearly now.

Jack darted back into the furnished room and, accidentally touching a chair as he went, raised a cloud of dust at once. He ran to the wide window and hid behind a long tapestry curtain there. He did not dare to touch it, because he felt sure it would fall to pieces in his hands.

The men were evidently still worried about the bag of apple cores. It was obvious that they knew someone was there besides themselves – and then, to Jack's dismay, he saw that they had found the pile of things the others had brought up with them that morning!

They had brought them from the courtyard and had spread them out at the entrance to the castle, looking through them carefully. Jack caught one or two words, but he couldn't understand them.

'We shall have to get out of here the very first moment possible,' thought the boy. 'We may get into serious trouble. If only I could get everyone up into the room with the plank!'

Two of the men now separated and went off into the castle, evidently to make another good search. The third man stood at the great doorway, puffing at a cigarette and apparently keeping a watch over the courtyard.

It was impossible for Jack to open the way to the hidden room, for the man at the doorway would see and hear him. There was nothing to do but wait, and hope for a chance to do it before any of the men did it themselves.

So the boy stood behind the curtain, watching and waiting. He wished Bill Smugs was there! Bill always knew what to do when things were awkward – but then Bill was a grown-up and grown-ups knew how to handle things in the right way, somehow.

The man at the doorway finished his cigarette. He did not throw the end away but carefully stubbed it out against a coin he took from his pocket, and put it into a little tin box. Evidently he was not going to leave any signs about that would tell anyone he was living there.

He turned and came into the hall. Jack heard his feet

echoing, and held his breath. Was he going back to the hidden room?

He was! He walked to the back of the hall, and felt about in the wall there for the spike. Jack, fearing that he was doing this, crept to the door of the room he was hiding in, and peered through the crack. From there he could see what happened.

The man pulled at the spike, and the stone moved with a grating sound, first downwards and then to the side. It was a marvellous piece of mechanism, very old, but still in perfect working order.

Jack's heart almost stood still. Now what was going to happen? What would the man say when he saw the other three?

Dinah and Lucy-Ann heard the grating noise of the stone as it moved, and looked up. Philip peered through his visor, hoping Jack was coming at last. But to their horror a man stood on the steps, looking at them in the greatest astonishment and anger!

He could only see Dinah and Lucy-Ann, of course. The two girls stared at him and trembled. His face was not a pleasant one. He had an enormous nose, narrow eyes, and the thinnest lips imaginable. Shaggy eyebrows hung over his eyes, almost like a sheepdog's hair.

'So!' said the man, and narrowed his eyes still more. 'So! You come here, and you go to my room. What is the meaning of this?'

The girls were terrified, and Lucy-Ann began to sob. Jack, listening, longed to push the man down the steps and break his neck! 'Hateful fellow, frightening poor Lucy-Ann like that!' thought the boy angrily, wishing he dared to show himself and comfort her.

Then he heard the footsteps of the other two men returning from their hunt. The first man heard them too and went

107

back up the stairs to the top. He called to the others in a language Jack did not understand, evidently telling them to come and see what he had found.

Philip, still hidden in the suit of armour, took the opportunity of whispering instructions to the girls. 'Don't be frightened. They'll probably only think you're two girls visiting the old castle. You tell them that. Don't say a word about me or Jack, or we shan't be able to help you. Jack's up there somewhere, we know, and he'll look out for you and get you away. I'll stay down here till I can escape myself. They won't know I'm in the armour.'

He couldn't say any more, because all three men now came down the steps and into the hidden room. One man had a dense black beard, the other was clean-shaven, but the man the girls had already seen was the ugliest of a really ugly trio.

Lucy-Ann began to cry again. Dinah was very scared, but she would not cry.

'What are you here for?' asked the shaggy-browed man. 'Now – you tell us everything – or you may be very very sorry!'

18

Prisoners in the castle

'We only came to have a look at the castle,' said Dinah, trying to keep her voice from trembling. 'Does it belong to you? We didn't know.'

'How did you find this room?' demanded the bearded man, scowling.

'By accident,' said Dinah. 'We were so surprised. Please let us go. We're only two girls, and we didn't mean any harm.'

'Does anyone outside this castle know we are here, or anything about this room?' asked the shaggy man.

'No, nobody,' said Dinah truthfully. 'We have never seen you before this moment, and we only found the room today. Please, do let us go!'

'I suppose you've been messing about here for some days,' said the man. 'We found your things. Interfering little trespassers!'

'We didn't know the castle belonged to anyone,' said Dinah, again. 'How could we know? No one ever comes here. The villagers keep away from the place.'

'Is anyone with you?' asked the bearded man, suspiciously.

'Well, you can see that for yourselves,' said Dinah, hoping fervently that none of the men would think of looking into the suits of armour standing round the room.

'We've looked all over the place,' said the third man to the shaggy one. 'There's no one else here, that we do know!'

'Please let us go,' begged Dinah. 'We won't come here again, we promise.'

'Ah – but you will go home and you will tell about things you have found here and seen here, isn't that so?' said the bearded man, in a horrid, smooth kind of voice. 'No, little missies – you must stay here till our work is done. Then, when it no longer matters, maybe we shall let you go. I said *maybe*! It depends on how you behave.'

Philip trembled with anger inside the suit of armour. How dared these men speak like that to the two girls? But the boy did not dare to show himself. That might only make things worse.

'Well,' said the bearded man, 'We have business to discuss. You may leave this room, but do not go beyond our call.'

To the girls' intense relief the men allowed them to go up the stone steps into the hall. Then the hole closed once more, and they were left alone.

'We must escape,' whispered Dinah, taking Lucy-Ann's hand. 'We must get away immediately and bring help to Philip. I daren't think what would happen to him if those men found him.'

'Where's Jack?' sobbed Lucy-Ann. 'I want him.'

Jack was not far away. As soon as he heard the stone close the hole up, and recognised the girls' voices, he darted out of the old drawing room. Lucy-Ann saw him and ran to him gladly.

He put his arms round her, and patted her. 'It's all right, Lucy-Ann, it's all right. We'll soon be out of here, and we'll get help to rescue Philip. Don't worry. Don't cry any more.'

But Lucy-Ann couldn't stop crying, though now she cried more from relief at having Jack again than from fright. The boy guided her to the wide stone stairs that led to the upper rooms of the castle.

'We'll get across the plank in no time,' he said. 'Then we'll be safe. We'll soon rescue Philip too. Don't be afraid.'

Up they went and up, then along the long corridor, lit dimly by its slit windows. They came to the room they used for the plank.

Dinah ran gladly to the window, eager to slip across to safety. But she paused in dismay. There was no plank.

'We're in the wrong room!' she said. 'Oh, quick, Jack, find the right one!'

They ran out and into the next room – but there was no plank on the sill there either. Then into the next room further on they went – but again there was no plank.

'This is like a bad dream,' said Dinah, trembling. 'We shall go into room after room, and the plank will never be there! Oh, Jack – is this a nightmare?'

'It seems like one,' said the boy. 'Come now – we're upset and excited – we'll begin at the bottom of the corridor and work our way along each room – then we shall find the right one.'

But they didn't. Room after room had no welcome plank on its sill. At the last room the children paused.

'I'm afraid,' said Jack, 'I'm very much afraid that the men discovered how we got in – and removed the plank!'

'Oh dear!' said Dinah, and sat down suddenly on the dusty floor. 'My legs won't hold me up any more. I suppose the men would never have let Lucy-Ann and me out of the hidden room unless they had discovered our way in, and made it impossible for us to escape that way.'

'Yes – if we'd stopped to think for a moment we'd have guessed that ourselves,' said Jack, gloomily. He also sat down on the floor to consider things. 'I wonder where they put the plank. It might be a good idea to look for it.'

'They've probably just tipped it off the sill and left it lying on the ground,' said Dinah, just as gloomily.

'No, they wouldn't do that, in case anyone else *did* happen to know that way in,' said Jack. 'We'd better look for it.'

So they hunted all over the place, but there was no sign of the plank at all. Wherever it was, it was too well hidden for the children to find. They gave it up after a bit.

'Well, what are we going to do, now that we can't escape?' said Dinah. 'Do stop sniffing, Lucy-Ann. It doesn't do any good.'

'Don't bother her,' said Jack, who felt sorry for his small sister. 'This is pretty serious. Here we are, stuck in this old castle with no way of escape – and Philip down below in the hidden room in great danger of being discovered. He's only got to sneeze or cough, you know!'

Lucy-Ann pondered this statement of alarm. She at once imagined poor Philip trying to stifle sneeze after sneeze.

'We've apparently fallen headlong into some strange mystery,' said Jack. 'I can't make head or tail of it. Why these men want to hide up here, I don't know. But they are ugly customers – nasty fellows, each one of them. They must belong to a gang of some sort, up to some mischief. I'd like to put a stop to it, but it's impossible as things are. The only good things about the whole affair are that the men don't know *I'm* here, and they don't know that Philip is hidden in their secret meeting place!'

'If only we could get out!' sighed Lucy-Ann. 'I know Aunt Allie is away, but we could get hold of the farmer or someone.'

'I don't see how we can possibly get out, now that our one and only way of getting in is gone,' said Jack. 'I don't think even Tassie will come up, now that her mother has threatened her with a hiding if she does.'

'We mustn't let the men know you're here too, Jack,' said Dinah. 'Where will you hide for safety?'

'In the middle of my gorsebush,' said Jack. 'That's as safe as anywhere. You girls go down to the hall and see if that room is still shut — if it is I'll slip down and go up the crag to my gorse bush. You can sit about the rocks there and whisper to me what goes on.'

'I wish we knew where Button got in and out,' said Lucy-Ann. 'If we did we might try his way. Only I suppose if it's a rabbit hole it would be far too narrow for us.'

They made their way to the hall. The stone was still in place over the hidden room. They beckoned Jack down, and he sped across the hall, out of the great doorway, across the courtyard and up the craggy, gorse-grown rock in the corner to the safety of his hiding place. He crawled in, and the bush closed round him.

The girls climbed up the rocks to be near him. From there they had a good view of everything to do with the castle. They undid a packet of food and began to have a meal, though Lucy-Ann choked over almost every mouthful. They handed Jack some food through the prickly branches of the bush.

'Good thing we brought up such stacks of food,' said Dinah. 'If we are going to be prisoners for ages it's just as well!'

'Of course, if your mother hadn't gone away she would have got worried when we didn't go home, and have sent a search party up to the castle,' said Lucy-Ann. 'It's bad luck she should have gone away just now! No one will miss us at all.'

'Sh! Here are two of the men!' said Dinah. 'Don't say a word more, Jack.'

The men gave a loud shout for the two girls. Dinah answered sulkily. They beckoned to them to come down from the crag.

'And did you find your little plank?' enquired the bearded man politely, and the other man sniggered.

'No. You took it away,' said Dinah sullenly.

'Of course. It was such a good idea of yours – but we didn't like it,' said the man. 'Now, you cannot get away, you know that. So you may stay here unharmed in the courtyard, and at night you may sleep peacefully in the big bed downstairs, for we have work to do that will take us elsewhere. But we forbid you to go up to the towers, or upstairs at all. We are not going to have you signalling for help. You understand that if you disobey us, you will be very sorry – and you will probably be put down into a dungeon we know of, where rats and mice and beetles live.'

Dinah shuddered. The very idea filled her with horror.

'So you be good girls and obedient, and no harm will come to you,' said the bearded man. 'Always be where we can see you, somewhere in this courtyard, and come when we call. You have plenty of food, we know. And there is water in the kitchen, if you pump it.'

The girls did not answer. The men walked off and disappeared once more into the castle.

'What's happening to Philip?' said Lucy-Ann, after a pause. 'Will he starve down there? I wish we could rescue him.'

'He won't starve. There's plenty of food on the table, if only he can step off his pedestal and get it,' said Dinah. 'If only we could send word to Tassie! She might get help. But there is no way of sending word.'

'I suppose Kiki wouldn't go, with a note tied to her leg, like pigeons have in wartime?' said Lucy-Ann. 'No, I'm sure she wouldn't leave Jack. She's an awfully clever and sensible bird, but it would be too much to expect her to become a messenger for us.'

However, a messenger did turn up – a most unexpected one, but a very welcome one indeed!

19

Lucy-Ann has an idea

All that day the girls hung about the courtyard, never keeping very far from the crag, so that they could talk to poor bored Jack in his hiding place. They wondered how Philip was getting on down in the hidden room. Had he been discovered?

'It's a great pity those men talk together in some language we don't understand,' said Dinah. 'If they talked in English Philip might learn quite a lot of secrets, standing there so close beside them, without them knowing!'

'Yes, he might,' said Lucy-Ann. 'I wish he wasn't down there though. I should feel so scared if it was me, hidden in armour that might creak or clank if I moved just a little bit.'

'Well, Philip won't feel scared,' said Dinah, 'He is hardly ever scared of anything. I expect he is quite enjoying himself.'

But Lucy-Ann didn't believe that for one moment. She thought Dinah was silly to say such a thing. But then, Dinah wasn't as fond of her brother as she, Lucy-Ann, was. It was bad enough to have Jack being compelled to hide in that horrid gorse bush – but it would have been far worse to have him down in the hidden room with the men, likely to be discovered at any moment!

'Cheer up!' whispered Jack, from the gorse bush, seeing her gloomy face. 'This is an adventure, you know.'

'I only like adventures afterwards,' said Lucy-Ann. 'I don't like them when they're happening. I didn't want this adventure at all. We didn't look for it, we just seemed to fall into the middle of it!'

'Well, never mind. It'll turn out all right, I expect,' said Jack comfortingly.

But poor Lucy-Ann couldn't see how. It was quite clear that they couldn't escape from the castle, and equally clear that no one could rescue them.

They had tea on the crag, the girls passing food to Jack, who was now feeling very cramped indeed, and longed to get out and stretch his legs. But he didn't dare to. When night came he would, but not till then.

The sun went down. Kiki, bored with her long imprisonment, became very talkative. The girls let her talk, keeping a sharp look-out in case the men came and heard her.

'Poor old Kiki, what a pity, what a pity! Put the kettle on, God save the Queen! Now, now, now, now, attention please! Sit up straight and don't loll. How many times have I told you to pop the weasel?'

The girls giggled. Kiki was very funny when she talked, for she brought into her chattering all the words and sentences she knew, running them one into another in a most bewildering way.

'Good old Kiki!' said Jack, scratching her neck. 'You're bored, aren't you? Never mind, you shall have a fine fly round when it's dark. Now don't start your express engine screech, or you'll bring our enemies up here at a run!'

The sun sank lower. Long shadows lay across the court-yard and then the whole of it went into twilight. The stars came out one by one, pricking the sky here and there.

The men came up the yard, two of them together. They called the girls.

'Hey, you two girls! You'd better come down and go to bed.'

'We don't mind the dark. We'll stay a bit longer,' shouted back Dinah, who wanted to walk round the yard with Jack, before she and Lucy-Ann retired to the hidden room.

'Well, come down in half an hour,' shouted the bearded man. 'It will be quite dark then, and you'd be better inside.'

They disappeared. Dinah slipped down from her perch and went silently after them. She saw them going down the steps of the hidden room. Then she heard the now familiar grating noise as the entrance hole was closed by the sliding stone.

She ran back to Jack. 'Come on, Jack,' she whispered. 'The men are down in the hidden room, and it's almost dark now. You'll be safe if you come out.'

Very glad to come from his uncomfortable hiding-place, Jack squeezed out of the bush. He stood up thankfully and stretched his arms high above his head.

'Golly, I'm stiff!' he said. 'Come on, let's go for a nice sharp walk round the courtyard. It's too dark for me to be seen now.'

They set off, linking their arms together. They hadn't gone more than halfway before something hurled itself against them out of the shadows, and almost knocked Jack over. He stopped, startled.

'What's that? Where's my torch?'

He flicked it on quickly, and then off again, in case the men were about. He gave a low cry.

'It's Button! Dear little old Button – *how* did you get here?

116

I *am* glad to see you!'

Button made happy noises in his throat, rolled over like a puppy, licked the girls and Jack, and generally behaved as if he was mad with delight. But he kept going off to the side and back again, and it was soon clear to the others that he had come to find Philip, his master.

'You can't get to Philip, old boy,' said Jack, fondling the little fox cub. 'You'll have to make do with us. Philip isn't here.'

The fox cub made a barking noise, and Kiki, who was sitting on Jack's shoulder, evidently rather disgusted to see Button appear again, immediately imitated the barking. Button jumped up, trying to reach her, but he couldn't. Kiki made a jeering noise, which would have been most infuriating to Button if he had understood it, but he didn't.

'Jack! I've got an idea!' said Lucy-Ann, suddenly clutching her brother's arm.

'What!' said Jack, who never thought very much of Lucy-Ann's good ideas.

'Can't we use Button as a messenger? Can't we send him back to Tassie with a note, telling her to get help for us, Jack? Button is sure to go back to her when he can't find Philip, because, next to Philip, he loves Tassie. Can't we do that?'

'Jack! That's really a good idea of Lucy-Ann's!' said Dinah, in excitement. 'Button is the only one of us who knows how to get out of here. He could be our messenger, as Lucy-Ann says.'

Jack considered it. 'Well,' he said, 'I must say it seems a sound idea, and worth trying. It can't do any harm, anyway. All right, we'll make Button our messenger.'

The next thing was to write a note to Tassie. Jack had a notebook, and he tore out a page. He wrote a few words in pencil and read them out to the others.

'Tassie, we are imprisoned here. Get help as soon as you

can. We may be in serious danger.'

They all signed it. Then Jack folded it up and wondered how to get Button to take it.

He thought of a way at last. He had some string in his pocket, and first of all he tied the note tightly round and round with it. Then he twisted the string fairly tightly round Button's sturdy little neck. He knew that if he made it too loose the fox cub would work it off over his head, for, like all wild things, he resented anything tied to him.

'There,' said Jack, pleased. 'I don't think Button can get that off, and the note is tied very tightly to the string. I've made him a kind of string collar, with the note at the front, under his chin.'

'Go back to Tassie, Button,' said Lucy-Ann. But Button didn't understand. He still hoped Philip would appear, and he didn't want to go back until he had seen him – or, better still, he would stay with him if he could. So the little fox cub hunted all around for Philip again and again, occasionally stopping and trying to get off this new thing round his neck. But he couldn't.

Suddenly one of the men called loudly, making everyone jump violently. 'Come in, you two girls!'

'Good night, Jack. We must go,' whispered Lucy-Ann, giving her brother a hug. 'I hope you won't be too uncomfortable tonight. Take some of our extra rugs into the bush with you, when you go to sleep.'

'I shan't go back to that beastly bush for ages,' said Jack, who was thoroughly tired of his hiding place and would have been glad never to see it again. 'Good night. Don't worry about anything. Once Button gets to Tassie, she'll soon bring help.'

The girls left him in the dark courtyard. They went into the hall, and saw the dim light of the lamp shining up from the hidden room. They went down the stone steps, and looked hurriedly round. Was Philip still in the suit of armour? They couldn't tell. All the suits of armour were standing around as usual, but whether one had Philip inside or not they didn't know.

'We're going to shut you in here,' said the shaggy man, his ugly face looking even uglier in the lamplight. 'You can use that bed to sleep in. We shall see you in the morning.'

He went up the steps, and then the stone swung sideways and upwards, closing the hole completely. The girls were prisoners once again. They stood in silence for a moment or two listening. There was nothing to be heard.

'Philip!' whispered Lucy-Ann, looking at the suit of armour in which she had last seen him. 'Are you there? Speak to us!'

'I'm still here,' came Philip's voice, sounding queerly hollow. 'But I hope I never have to spend another day like this. I'm going to get out of this armour. I can't stay in it another minute!'

'Oh, Philip – do you think you'd better?' said Dinah anxiously. 'Suppose the men come back?'

'I don't think they will – but if they do I jolly well can't help it. I'm desperate,' said Philip. 'I've got cramp in all my limbs, I'm tired out with standing so still and I've had to stop myself sneezing at least three times. It's been a most awful strain, I can tell you.'

A clanking noise came from the suit of armour as Philip began to get out of it, clumsily and awkwardly, for he felt very stiff.

'The worst of it was my toad couldn't bear being in here with me and he got out through a crack, and hopped and crawled about for all he was worth,' said Philip. 'The men saw him and were awfully surprised.'

Dinah looked about at once for the toad. She hoped it wasn't anywhere near her.

'Poor old Philip,' said Lucy-Ann, going to help. 'You must have had an awful day.'

119

'I have – but I wouldn't really have missed it for worlds!' said Philip. 'My word, I've learnt a few things, I can tell you! For instance, there's a secret way out of this room – behind the tapestry somewhere!'

'Ooooh,' said Lucy-Ann, looking at the tapestry, as if she expected to see a secret way opening before her eyes. 'Is there really? How do you know?'

'I'll tell you all about it, once I get out of this awful armour,' said Philip. 'My word, I hope I never wear it again! You wouldn't believe how hot I got inside it. There – I'm out, thank goodness! Now to stretch myself a bit!'

'And then tell us what happened in here today,' said Dinah, eager to hear. 'I bet you've got some exciting things to tell us!'

She was right. Philip certainly had!

20

Philip tells a strange story

'We'd better get on the bed, in case those awful men come back,' said Dinah. 'What will you do if they do, Philip?'

'I shall hear the grating noise the stone makes when it moves, and I'll hop out of the bed and get underneath it,' said Philip. 'I don't really think the men will suspect there is anyone here but you – they're not likely suddenly to make a search in the middle of the night!'

There was plenty of room for them all on the enormous old bed. There was an eiderdown mattress, which the three children sank into. Philip was pleased. After the hardness of the suit of armour, it was pleasant to feel something so soft.

He sat up and told his story.

'Well, you remember when you went up the steps by

yourselves and left me there?' he said. 'I was awfully angry to think those men should talk to you like that, but I couldn't do anything about it, of course. Anyway, I just stayed put for ages, and after some time all three men came down, shut up the entrance hole, and sat round the table.'

'Could you understand their talk?' asked Lucy-Ann.

'No, more's the pity, I couldn't,' said Philip. 'They had maps out, and were tracing things on them, but I couldn't see what. I almost over-balanced myself, trying to see.'

'Gracious! What a shock you'd have given those men if you had toppled over with a crash,' said Dinah, with a laugh. 'Good thing you didn't though.'

'Well, they sat about for a long time, talking and poring over their maps,' said Philip, 'and then they had a jolly good meal. They opened stacks of tins. It made my mouth water to see them.'

'Poor Philip – have you had anything to eat?' asked Lucy-Ann.

Philip nodded. 'Don't worry. The very next time the men disappeared up the stone steps and shut the hole, I clanked off my pedestal, and finished up most of what they had left. I had to hope they wouldn't notice it was gone. But I was so hungry and thirsty I didn't care. It was funny to see all the other suits of armour standing round, looking at me. I half expected them to walk up and join me in my meal!'

'Don't say things like that!' said poor Lucy-Ann, looking quite scared. She gazed with wide eyes at the suits of armour standing so silently on their pedestals, and imagined them suddenly walking off them, with a clash and a clank.

Philip laughed, and gave Lucy-Ann a pat. 'It was awfully difficult to drink,' he said. 'I couldn't tip my head back properly in that armour. I poured half of it down the inside of it, and I was terrified I'd have puddles coming out of my feet, when I went back.'

The girls couldn't help laughing. Philip always told a

story very well, making them see every detail of it.

'Well, I got back to my pedestal, feeling a whole lot better, and hadn't been there more than twenty minutes or so when the men came back again. And then an extraordinary thing happened.'

'What?' said the girls together, holding their breath.

'See the tapestry over there – the one with the dogs and the horses on?' said Philip, pointing. 'Exactly opposite where my suit of armour stands? Well, behind there is a secret door!'

He paused and the girls gazed first at the tapestry and then at Philip. 'The men talked a bit, and then one of them went to that piece of tapestry. He lifted it up and hung it back on that nail you can see. I could see everything perfectly through my visor. Well, at first I couldn't make out what the man was doing, because the wall looked as if it was made of solid stone all along.'

'And wasn't it?' said Lucy-Ann, in excitement.

'No,' said Philip. 'Part of it is only a thin slab of stone, not immensely solid and thick like the rest of the walls here, and that thin piece slides right back! Then when it had moved back, the man stepped into the square hollow place left and felt about there. On one side of the hollow place was a door of some kind, which he opened – and all three men disappeared through the door!'

'Gracious!' said Dinah. 'Where did they go?'

'I don't know,' said Philip. 'But I'd dearly like to! There's some secret here, some big mystery. Those men are up to some mischief. Why should foreigners – because two of them *are* foreigners, you can tell that by their accent – why should foreigners come to a lonely place like this, and hide and have meetings, and use secret rooms and doors?'

'Shall we see where that door leads to?' said Dinah, overcome with curiosity.

'No, don't let's,' said Lucy-Ann, who had had enough excitement for one day.

'You're scared,' said Dinah scornfully.

'No, she's not, said Philip. 'Anyway, I think it would be a mistake to mess about behind that tapestry just now. If the men happened to come back and saw that we had 'found their secret door, goodness knows what they'd do. We might never be heard of again!'

Dinah was silent. She longed to explore behind that tapestry – but she knew Philip was right. They must wait and take their time. Dinah began to tell Philip about their day with Jack in the courtyard, and all that had happened. He was very glad that Jack hadn't been caught.

'Well, that's two people those men have no idea are here,' he said. 'Me and Jack. That's good. As long as they think it's only a couple of girls they've got to deal with, they won't be so much on their guard.'

Then Dinah told him about sending Button with a message to Tassie. He listened thoughtfully, and then made a remark that sent their hearts down into their boots.

'It was fine idea,' he said, 'but it won't be a bit of good, I'm afraid. You've forgotten that Tassie can't read or write!'

The two girls stared at one another in the greatest dismay. They *had* forgotten that. Of course – Tassie wouldn't be able to make head or tail of the note. What a blow! Lucy-Ann looked very woebegone to think that her good idea shouldn't have been so very good after all.

Philip put his arm round her and gave her a friendly hug. 'Never mind. Perhaps Tassie will have the common sense to show the note to somebody who *can* read! Cheer up.'

This exchange of news took a long time. The girls began to feel sleepy. Lucy-Ann lay down on the soft bed and shut her eyes. Dinah and Philip talked a little longer and then lay down too. Philip was tired with his long day in the suit of armour, and fell sound asleep almost at once.

Dinah was awakened suddenly, two or three hours later, by the sound of the entrance hole being opened. At first she did not recognise the noise – then, very suddenly, she knew what it was. In a rush it all came back to her.

Philip and Lucy-Ann did not awake. Dinah shook the boy desperately. 'Philip!' she whispered urgently. 'Wake up! Quick, get under the bed! They're here!'

Half asleep, Philip rolled off the bed, and underneath it, just as the first man came down the steps. Dinah lay still as if she was asleep. Lucy-Ann did not stir.

The man, hearing the noise of Philip falling off the bed, stared suspiciously over into the corner where the four-poster bed stood. He turned up the wick of the oil lamp, which had burned down, and went over to the bed.

His toe almost touched Philip who was crouching underneath. The man pulled back the heavy curtains around the old bed and looked down at the girls. Dinah felt sure he knew she was awake.

He stared down at the two of them for a few seconds and then pulled the curtains back again. Apparently he was satisfied that the girls were really asleep. He did not dream that a third child was there, hidden safely under the bed!

Dinah, looking between her eyelashes, saw that there were five men there, two that she had not seen before. They spoke in a language she could not understand. One of the men she knew unlocked a big drawer in a chest, and took out a roll of maps, which he threw on the table.

Then, one after another, the maps were spread out and apparently discussed. Finally they were put back again, and the drawer locked. Then, to Dinah's excited delight, the shaggy-brown man threw back a piece of tapestry from the wall, and exposed the place where the secret door was hidden.

One of the men laid his hand on his arm, saying something in a low voice, and nodding towards the bed in the further corner.

Then he walked swiftly across the bed and drew the thick

curtains so closely round it that Dinah could see nothing more. How annoying! She did not dare to peep, because she knew if she did, she would probably be seen.

After that she could only lie and listen, wondering what was happening. She heard a sliding noise, a click, a little thud, and the sound of a key turning in a lock. Then she heard voices again. After that she heard men going up the stone stair, and peeped quickly to see who they were. They were the three she knew. Evidently the others had gone through the secret door, to wherever that led to. It was all most mysterious.

There came the familiar grating noise – and then silence. Dinah peeped out. There was no one in the room. The tapestry was replaced, and hung down over the wall again.

She called softly to Philip, and he came out from under the bed. 'Don't wake Lucy-Ann, or she won't go to sleep again,' said Philip in a low voice. 'Did you see much, Dinah?'

'Lots,' said Dinah, and told him everything. Philip listened intently.

'Five men now,' he said. 'I do wonder what they're all up to. You see, Dinah, it was much the best thing not to go messing about trying to find that secret door tonight. We'd have been properly caught if we had!'

'Yes, we should,' said Dinah. 'Philip, what *are* these men up to?'

'I don't know,' said Philip. 'If we went through that hidden door, and found out where it led to, we might learn their secret. But we must wait and take our chance, not just rush in without thinking.'

'I shouldn't think they'll come back again, would you?' said Dinah, lying down. 'Do you think you'd better sleep under the bed, in case? You made an awful noise rolling off.'

'Perhaps I'd better,' said Philip. He took one of the blankets off the bed and went underneath it, arranging himself as comfortably as he could.

125

'Are you going to stand in that suit of armour again tomorrow?' asked Dinah suddenly.

'No, rather not! I'll hide under the bed. I'm sure the men won't dream of looking for someone they don't know is there!' said Philip. 'I feel as if I never want to see a suit of armour again in my life! Beastly, uncomfortable things!'

They fell asleep again, and this time nothing disturbed them till the morning. It was impossible to tell whether it was morning or not in the hidden room, but Dinah's watch showed her that it was half-past seven.

The shaggy man came down into the room. 'You can clear out for the day,' he said. 'But keep within sight and call as I told you – or most unpleasant things might happen!'

21

Another day goes by

Jack felt lonely when the girls had gone down the steps to the hidden room for the night. He was left up in the courtyard with Kiki, and he felt bored.

'I hope the girls will be all right,' he thought. 'Oh, hallo, Button, are you still here? Why don't you go back to Tassie? You won't be able to get to Philip, you know.'

The fox cub whined and rubbed his head against Jack, asking him as plainly as a fox cub could to take him to his beloved Philip.

'Listen. You go back to Tassie with that note,' said Jack, still forgetting that Tassie couldn't read a word. 'Go on, Button. Once you get to Tassie, things will be easier for us, because when she reads that note, she will get help.'

Button stayed in the courtyard with Jack almost all night long. He didn't give up hope of finding Philip, and kept going off to hunt for him. Kiki was very scornful of him but Button took no notice of her.

The moon came up and lighted the courtyard strangely. An owl hooted, and Kiki at once mimicked it perfectly. The owl came into the yard on silent wings, to look for the one who had answered. Kiki was delighted. She kept hooting softly from one place and another, and the owl was astonished to find what seemed to him to be a perfect host of owls all over the place, calling first from one spot and then another.

Jack enjoyed the fun. Then suddenly he saw the three men standing in the moonlight, and felt glad that he had not been wandering about, for he would certainly have been seen.

He slipped away into the shadows of the great wall, and came near to the enormous door that stood facing what had once been the road to the castle. He sat down by a big bush, knowing it would hide him completely.

Suddenly he jumped violently, and stared as if he could not believe his eyes. The big door was opening! It swung slowly back without a sound, and where it had been was now a moonlit space, gateway to the outer world!

Jack half rose – but sank back again. Two men entered the castle yard, and then the great solid door closed silently behind them. There was a loud click, and then the two men passed quite close to Jack. They did not see him, for he was in black shadow. He crouched down like a toad against the earth.

The men passed and soon joined the other two. Then they all disappeared into the castle. Jack imagined they were going down to the hidden room – as indeed they were.

He waited till they had gone, and then made his way as quickly as he could to the big door in the high wall. If only he could open it! If only he could get out, and go down the hillside, even if he had to walk over the treacherous landslide! After all, those men must have come up that way.

He felt about for the handle of the door. It was a large iron ring. Jack twisted it this way and that, but the door did not open.

'That click I heard must have been the men locking it!' he thought angrily. 'It's impossible to get out. Blow it! Maybe if I'd been near enough I could have slipped out as they slipped in! It wouldn't have mattered if they had seen me because I could have run down the hillside before they could stop me!'

He sat and brooded near the door. 'I'll wait here in the shadows till they come back. Then I'll dash out with them. They'll be so taken by surprise that maybe they won't even put out a hand to me!'

So Jack sat there hour after hour, almost falling asleep. But the men did not return. Dinah could have told him why! They had gone through the secret door under the tapestry in the hidden room. The other three were somewhere in the castle.

When the eastern sky began to turn silver Jack knew it was time to return to his gorse bush. Kiki was fast asleep on his shoulder, having tired of the owl hours since. Button too had vanished.

Jack had not seen him go. He had forgotten about the little fox cub in the excitement of seeing the castle door open. He wondered where he had gone.

'I hope he's gone back to Tassie,' he thought. 'We can expect help sometime today if he has. About time too! I'm fed up with being here. Not an eagle left now, and the two girls in danger, to say nothing of poor old Philip. I wonder how he has got on. Perhaps the girls will tell me today.'

The girls came out of the hidden room about eight o'clock. The three men had gone down there and turned them out. Dinah had begged Philip to get back into the suit of armour before the men returned, but he wouldn't.

'No, I'd rather be under the bed,' he said firmly. 'One day in that horrible stiff suit is enough for me. I'd rather be caught than stand there all day again. You put me some food and drink under the bed, and I'll stay here. I can always wander about and stretch my legs when the men are not here.'

'Well – fortune favours the bold!' said Dinah, who thought that she would have felt the same if she had been Philip. 'It's a bold thing to do, to lie in hiding under the very bed the men may sleep on today – but maybe you'll be all right there. Don't sneeze, though!'

Apparently it was the men's intention to sleep the day away on the big four poster. They came down into the room and ordered the girls out. The bearded man flung himself on the bed. All the men looked tired, and the unshaven faces of the two were not nice to see.

'We'll call you down tonight,' said the bearded man, from the bed, and he yawned. 'Take what food you want from that pile of tins. There's a tin opener on the table. Now clear out and leave us. Couple of little nuisances!'

The girls grabbed a tin of sardines, a tin of salmon, one of peaches and one of apricots, and fled up the stairs. No sooner had they reached the top than the hole was closed by the stone.

'Sleep well!' said Dinah mockingly, and then the two girls went in search of Jack. He was under his gorse bush, wishing they would come.

'Jack! Are you all right? You can come out for a bit because the men are safe down in the underground room!' said Lucy-Ann. 'Do you want some sardines – or peaches? We've got both.'

'Hallo!' said Jack, delighted to see them. 'Is it really safe for a bit? All right, I'll come out and we'll squat behind this rock here. I'm longing for something to eat. Didn't you bring biscuits with you when you came yesterday?'

Dinah found the tin of biscuits, and they had a comic breakfast of sardines, biscuits and peaches, washed down by ginger beer. Still they all enjoyed it thoroughly, and exchanged their news eagerly.

Jack was intensely interested to hear all that Philip had told them. 'A secret way behind that tapestry!' he exclaimed, his eyes gleaming. 'But *where* does it lead to?'

'Goodness knows – into the hillside somewhere, I suppose,' said Dinah, dipping a biscuit into peach-juice and sucking it.

'Wait now – what side of the hidden room is the secret door in the wall?' asked Jack. 'Oh – opposite where Philip stood at the back – well, let me see – that means that the door would lead into the hill at the back of the castle. At the *back* of the castle! How funny! I wonder if there are dungeons there or something?'

'Oh dear – do you think the men are keeping people prisoners and perhaps starving them to death?' said Lucy-Ann, at once. 'Like that wicked old man did. Oh, Jack, you don't suppose that old man is still alive, do you, living like an old spider in his castle, still doing wicked things?'

'Of course not,' said Jack. 'Haven't I told you he's dead and gone years and years ago? Don't get such wild ideas into your head, Lucy-Ann. Now let me think a bit. Don't interrupt.'

He nibbled his biscuit and pondered again. 'Yes, I think I'm right,' he said. 'That door under the tapestry must lead underground through the hill at the back of the castle. I'd like to go down that passage and see what is there! I bet Philip will sooner or later!'

'I hope he'll be sensible and keep under the bed,' said Lucy-Ann. 'With men wandering in and out of secret doors and things, he might easily bump into one of them and be caught.'

'Did Button leave you last night?' said Dinah suddenly. 'Where is he?'

'Yes, he went at last,' said Jack. 'But where I don't know. I only hope he's found Tassie by now, and she has seen the note.'

'Philip says it won't be any good, that note,' said Lucy Ann mournfully. 'We forgot that Tassie can't read.'

'Blow!' said Jack. 'Of course she can't. What silly-billies we are!'

'Silly-billy, silly-billy, silly-billy,' at once chanted Kiki, pleased. 'Pop goes the silly-billy!'

'You'll go pop in a minute if you eat any more peaches,' said Jack. 'Is the tin empty, Dinah? Put it away from Kiki, for goodness' sake. She's been tucking in like anything while we've been talking.'

'Poor old silly-billy,' said Kiki gloomily, as Dinah removed the tin and tapped her smartly on the beak.

'What are we going to do today?' said Lucy-Ann.

'Well, what *can* we do except wait?' said Jack.

'And hope that Tassie has the sense to show our note to someone,' said Dinah. 'Surely she would do that? She knows she can't get to us herself – or she *would* know, if she came, and saw the plank was gone!'

The day passed slowly. There was nothing to do, not even an eagle to watch. 'Wish I could do a spot of developing,' sighed Jack, feeling in his shorts pocket for his precious rolls of film. 'But I can't. I'm just longing to see how the eagles have come out.'

There was nothing to read. The girls wandered round a bit and wondered whether they dared to go up into the tower, and try to signal from there. But who would see? No one but Tassie, and she would not know what to make of the signals.

'Anyway, if you *did* go up into the tower, you might be badly punished by any of those men,' said Jack. 'It's not worth risking it. We must just wait in patience for Tassie to send help.'

131

The day passed at last and night came. The men yelled for the two girls to go down into the secret room again. They said a hurried goodnight to Jack and went. There was no question of disobeying the men. All the children were afraid of them.

Jack did not hide in his gorse bush. When it was dark enough he went down to the spring near the bottom of the wall, to get a drink. He dared not go into the kitchen for one, in case he bumped into one of the men, or they heard the pump clanking.

He bent down to the spring – and then listened in amazement. A most curious noise was coming from the little tunnel into which it disappeared.

'Oooph! Ow! Ooooph!' A scraping, dragging noise could be heard too. Something was coming up the tunnel. Jack stepped back in great alarm. Whatever could it be?

22

Tassie is very brave

Then Jack heard the unmistakable sound of Button yelping, and he knew that part of the noise must be made by the fox cub. He bent over the tunnel, and flashed his torch on to see down its narrow mouth.

He saw a white face staring up at him, and he jumped. It was Tassie's. She was lying still for the moment, but began to wriggle again when the light flashed on her.

'Tassie! What are you doing? Tassie!' said Jack, in a low but most astonished voice.

Tassie didn't answer. She squeezed herself up a bit more, until her head and shoulders were outside the tunnel. Then Jack gave her a pull and she came out at once. Button followed, looking very forlorn. Tassie had him on a lead, and he couldn't get away.

Tassie sat down and gasped painfully. She put her head over her knees, which were drawn up, and seemed quite unable to speak a word. Jack flashed his torch over her. She was soaking wet and unspeakably dirty. Mud streaked her face and arms and legs.

She was shivering with cold and fright. Jack made her get up and go with him to the crag. He put her behind a rock, and fetched the rugs. He made her strip off the soaked dress she wore, and cover herself from head to foot with a couple of rugs. Then the boy sat close to her to warm her. Kiki perched on her shoulder and pressed against her cold cheek. Soon Tassie's breath grew more even, and she turned to look at Jack, trying to summon up a faint smile.

'Where's Philip?' she whispered at last.

'With the girls,' said Jack, not wanting to tell her everything at once. 'Don't worry for a minute or two. Get your breath back. You're exhausted.'

He sat with his arm round her, feeling the pounding of her heart shaking her body. Poor Tassie! How had she managed to get so exhausted?

But she soon recovered, as her body grew warm. She pressed against Jack. 'I'm so hungry,' she said.

Jack fed her with biscuits and salmon from the tin. Then she drank the rest of the peach-juice, whilst Kiki copied the gulping noises she made.

'Now I feel better,' she said. 'What has been happening, Jack?'

'Well, suppose you tell me a few things first,' said the boy. 'And keep your voice low. There are enemies about.'

This was news to Tassie. Her eyes widened and she looked round, scared. 'Is it that wicked old man?' she whispered.

'Of course not,' said Jack. 'Tassie, did Button take you our note?'

'Yes,' said Tassie. 'But, Jack, I gave my mother the slip and

133

came up here yesterday to spend a few hours with you – and oh, Jack, the plank was gone. Where's it gone?'

'That's just what *I* should like to know!' said Jack grimly. 'Well, what did you do then?'

'I went back home,' said Tassie. 'And I was worried about you. Then this morning Button came to find me, and I saw his string collar, and the letter someone had tied to it.'

'Go on,' said Jack.

'Well – I couldn't read it,' said Tassie, with tears in her voice. 'And there was nobody to ask. My mother was angry with me, and Mrs Mannering had gone away. I didn't like to go to the farm with it – so I suddenly thought I would make a lead for Button, and when next he went up to the castle to look for Philip, I would go with him, and find the way he went.'

'That was clever!' said Jack admiringly. Tassie felt pleased.

'So I found an old dog lead,' she said, more cheerfully, 'and I fastened it to his collar, and I went wherever he went that day. He was awfully angry about it. He kept trying to bite the lead, and he almost tried to bite me too!'

Jack patted the little fox cub who was lying quietly beside them. 'He didn't understand what was happening,' he said. 'Well – he brought you up here at last, I suppose?'

'Yes. After he had wandered for miles on the hillside, and almost worn me out, going up and down, up and down!' said Tassie. 'When it was dark he decided to come and look for Philip again – and he shot off like an arrow then!'

'I bet he did,' said Jack. 'Poor old Button – he must wonder where Philip has gone to!'

'Well, he dragged me behind on the lead,' said Tassie, 'and brought me all the way up beside the spring. Below the castle it goes into a narrow sort of tunnel – terribly narrow in parts – and oh, Jack, it goes right underneath the wall! Think of that! And comes up the other side!'

'Did you really wriggle all the way?' said Jack, in amazement. 'What a marvel you are, Tassie! But didn't the water pour down on you all the time?'

'Oh yes – it nearly choked me sometimes,' said Tassie. 'And it was so icy-cold! But most of the way up the spring the tunnel wasn't too bad – it was through rock, and it had worn it away, so that the water ran in a kind of channel in the rock, and there was space for me to wriggle up more easily. It was at the beginning and at the end, where it comes up in the castle yard, that it was so narrow. Once I thought I was really stuck! I couldn't go up and I couldn't go down – and I thought I might have to stay there for ever, because no one would ever know where I was!'

'Poor Tassie!' said Jack, giving her a hug. 'You're a very brave girl. Wait till Philip hears about this! He'll think you are wonderful.'

Tassie glowed with delight. She hoped Philip would be pleased with her. She had come to help them. And now, in her turn, she questioned Jack eagerly, wanting to know everything that had happened to her four friends since they had left her.

Jack told her the story. She listened in alarm and astonishment. Philip hiding in a suit of old armour – down in a hidden room – the girls prisoners there – cruel men wandering about furtively, nobody knew why – secret passages – why, it was like a dream! But at least here was Jack with Kiki, safe and sound!

'Could you wriggle down the tunnel with me, and we'll fetch help?' said Tassie.

'That's just what I thought of doing,' said Jack. 'I think I'd better go tonight, Tassie, and not wait to take the two girls. Anyway I'm afraid there would be more risk of someone getting stuck in that watery tunnel. I'd better go and get help as soon as possible. You'd better stay here and tell the girls what has happened. You can hide in my old gorse bush till they come tomorrow morning.'

Tassie sighed with relief. She did not in the least want to go back down that terrible way again. She would dream about it all her life long! Neither did she really want to stay in the courtyard alone for the night, but Jack said he would leave both Kiki and Button with her, and they could sleep in the gorse bush all together.

'So you be brave and do that,' he said. 'Maybe you'll see Philip tomorrow too. He *will* be surprised to hear your adventures!'

Tassie, still clad in the rugs, went with Jack to the place near the wall, where the bubbling spring ran into the beginning of the tunnel. Jack marvelled how anyone could wriggle down much less wriggle *up*, with water splashing into his face all the time.

'Now, you go straight back to the bush with Button and Kiki, wrap yourself up warmly in the rugs, and go to sleep,' said Jack. 'Don't let Kiki see me disappearing down here, or she'll want to follow me.'

So Tassie obediently went back to the gorse bush and crawled inside. She curled up in the rugs like a little animal, with Button on her feet and Kiki perched on her middle, waiting for Jack. Tassie hoped Kiki would not fly off when she found Jack did not come. She might make a dreadful noise if she found he had disappeared!

Jack crawled head-first into the cold water. He wriggled into the tunnel. It smelt damp and nasty. He dragged his body down, using hands and elbows to lever himself along. It wasn't at all pleasant.

'I wish Button had found some better way of getting into the castle and out!' thought the boy. 'How *could* Tassie have crawled up, with the water splashing into her face half the time? She's really a heroine!'

When he had got down some way, the rather earthy tunnel gave way to hard rock. Jack thought he must be

136

under the wall by now. The tunnel widened out considerably, and the boy sat on a ledge to rest. He was worried about his rolls of film. He had wrapped them up very carefully in a sou'wester one of the children had brought up to the castle, and had tied the strings round tightly. It would be too sickening if his precious films were spoilt.

He began to shiver with the cold, for he was now soaked through. As long as he was dragging himself along the tunnel he was warm, for it was very hard work – but as soon as he stopped, the cold got him, and he shook like a leaf.

He went on again. It was quite dark, and he could only feel his way along. He went on wriggling down the watery passage, glad when it was wide and high, anxious when it closed in on his body, and made it difficult for him to get along.

It seemed hours before he reached the outlet, but at last he was there! He dragged himself out, and sat panting on a patch of soft heather. He hoped that never in his life again would he have to crawl through a tunnel like that! He was sure that if the girls had been with him, someone would have got stuck with fright, and would not have been able to go either up or down, after a while. It was just as well that he had decided they must not all use this way of escape.

He began to shiver, and he stood up, his knees shaking after his long ordeal underground. He was not as exhausted as Tassie, but he was almost tired out.

'I shall get an awful chill if I don't get warm,' he thought, and he set off down the hill, glad of the bright moonlight.

He stumbled along, looking eagerly for a sight of Spring Cottage as he at last dropped down into the lane that led to it. Yes – there it was, black with the moonlight behind it, its roof silvered and shining.

Then suddenly Jack stopped. He had seen something that struck him as odd.

'There's smoke – smoke coming from the chimney!' he

said to himself, and he leaned against a tree. 'What does that mean? Can Aunt Allie be back? No, Tassie would have known. Well, then – who has lighted the kitchen fire? Who is there? Oh, surely one of those wretched men hasn't gone there to find out something about the girls?'

He crept near to the cottage. He came to the little garden. There was a light shining out of one of the windows!

Jack tiptoed to the window, anxious and puzzled. He looked cautiously in. Someone was sitting in a tall-backed armchair that had its back to Jack. Was it Mrs Mannering?

A cloud of smoke suddenly came from the chair – thick blue pipe-smoke!

'It's a man,' whispered Jack to himself. 'Whoever can it be?'

23

A few surprises

Jack stayed at the window, shivering. If only the man would get up – then he could see if it was one of the men he knew at the castle. But how dare he get into the house like that!

Jack made up his mind to creep into the house and peep through the crack in the kitchen door. Then he would be able to see who it was sitting in the armchair. So, still shivering, as much with excitement as with cold, he stole round to the other side of the house, where his bedroom window was. If it was open, Jack knew he could climb the tree near by and slip inside.

It *was* open – just a crack. But Jack remembered that the catch was very loose, and he could probably put in his hand and jiggle it off the iron peg that held it down. It was a casement window and would open very wide to let him in.

He stumbled over a bucket or something outside a door, and stopped still, wondering if the man inside had heard anything. Then on he went to the tree, and climbed it quickly.

He slipped his hand inside the crack of the window and jiggled the catch. It dropped, and the window swung open. Jack cautiously climbed inside, and stood there, hardly daring to breathe.

He made his way into the dark little passage between the bedrooms, and stood there, waiting for a moment before he ventured down the rather creaky, winding stairs. Then he began to go down, one step at a time, hoping to goodness they wouldn't creak too loudly.

There was a bend in one place, and Jack meant to stand there quietly before he went on – but no sooner had he got there than someone leapt on him, caught his arms, and jerked him violently down the last four stairs! He fell, and all the breath was bumped out of his body.

Whoever had jumped on him stood up and then pulled him roughly to his feet. Then he was propelled swiftly into the lighted kitchen, and he looked at once to the armchair to see who was there.

But it was empty! Whoever had sat there must have heard him, and lain in wait for him. Jack turned to face his captor, wriggling, fully expecting to see one of the men from the tower.

The two stared at one another in the very greatest surprise, and stepped backwards in amazement.

'Bill Smugs!'

'Jack! What on *earth* are you doing creeping in like this? I thought you must be a burglar!'

'Golly! You've bruised me properly,' said Jack, rubbing himself. He began to shiver violently again. Bill looked at his soaking clothes and pale face, and pulled him to the fire, on which a kettle was boiling merrily.

'What *have* you been up to? You're dripping wet! You'll

get a frightful chill. Where are the others? When I arrived today to ask Mrs Mannering if she could put me up for a night or two, the house was shut, and there was no one here!'

'Well, how did you get in, then?' asked Jack, enjoying the warmth of the fire.

'Oh, I have my ways,' said Bill. 'I thought you must all have gone picnicking, so I waited and waited for you to come back – but you didn't. So I decided to spend the night here by myself, and make enquiries somewhere tomorrow to see what had happened to you all. Then I heard mysterious sounds, decided it was a burglar – and caught *you*!'

'Well, I looked in at the window, and couldn't see who was sitting in that chair, so I thought I'd creep in and have a squint round,' said Jack. 'Oh, Bill, I'm glad to see you. We're in danger!'

'What do you mean?' said Bill, astonished. 'Where are the girls? And Philip?'

'It's a long story, but I must tell you from the very beginning,' said Jack. 'What about a hot drink whilst we are talking, Bill. I could do with one. That kettle's on the boil.'

'I was about to make the same remark myself,' said Bill. 'Hot cocoa and biscuits for you, I think! I'm glad you've stopped shivering. By the way, where's Mrs Mannering? Don't tell me she's in danger too!'

'Oh no – she's gone off to look after Philip's Aunt Polly, who is ill again,' said Jack. 'She's all right.'

Bill made a jug of hot cocoa and milk, found some biscuits, and gave them to Jack, who was now feeling a lot warmer. He had stripped off his wet things, and was sitting in a dressing-gown.

'I don't feel I ought to waste time like this, really,' he said, 'as the others are in danger. But I'll have to tell you the whole story, and then leave it to you what to do.'

'Go ahead,' said Bill.

So Jack began, and Bill listened in the greatest interest and astonishment. He burst into laughter at Philip's idea of hiding in the suit of armour.

'Just like old Philip! What a good idea! The men would never guess anyone was hiding there.'

He grew serious as the tale went on. He pulled at his pipe and kept his eyes fixed on Jack. His ruddy face grew even redder in the fire-light, and the bald top of his head gleamed and shone.

'This is an extraordinary tale, Jack,' he said at last. 'There is a lot more in this than you know. What were those men like? Describe them. Was there a man with a scar right across his chin and neck?'

'No,' said Jack, thinking. 'Not one of them as far as I know. I took a jolly good snap of one man, though – when they were at the eagles' nest. You know I told you I had my camera poking out of the gorse bush to snap the eagles. Well, I snapped him when one of the eagles flew at him. I snapped both men, as a matter of fact, but one unfortunately had his face turned away.'

'Have you got those snaps?' said Bill eagerly.

'I've got the films,' said Jack, and he pointed to the tightly rolled up sou'wester on the table. 'They're in there. They're not developed yet, Bill.'

'Well, whilst you have a good sleep, I'll develop them,' said Bill. 'I see you've got a little darkroom fixed up for yourself off the hall there, where you meant to do developing – you've got everything necessary there, haven't you?'

'But – but – oughtn't we go right back and rescue the girls?' asked Jack.

'I shall have to drive over to the town where you met me the other day,' said Bill, 'and collect a few men, and arrange a few things. If these men are doing what I think they are, then we stand a good chance of roping them all in together. I

141

don't think they will harm the girls at all.'

'What are the men doing?' asked Jack curiously. 'Are they anything to do with the job you said you were on, Bill?'

'Can't tell you yet,' said Bill. 'I hardly think so – but I shall soon know.' He paused and looked at Jack.

'What children you are for falling headlong into adventures!' he said. 'I never knew anyone like you for that! It seems to me I'd better stick close to you all the year round, and then I shall have a good chance of sharing them!'

He put Jack on the sofa, arranged rugs over him, turned down the lamp, and went off into the little darkroom with the films. Jack had shown him which roll contained the snap of the man.

Jack slept peacefully, for he was tired out. How long he slept he didn't know, but he was awakened by Bill coming into the room in the greatest excitement, holding a film.

'Sorry to wake you, Jack – but this is a marvellous thing!' he said, and held up the film to the daylight, which was now coming in at the window. 'You have snapped this man perfectly – every detail is as clear as could be. He's the man with the beard – but just look here! He is holding his head up, and the whole of his neck is exposed from chin to chest, because his collar has flapped open. What can you see?'

'A mark – like a long scar,' said Jack, sitting up.

'Quite right!' said Bill. He took out a notebook from his pocket, slipped a snap from it and showed it to Jack. 'Look there – see that scar on that man's chin and neck?'

Jack saw a clean-shaven man in the photograph, his chin and neck disfigured by a terrible scar.

'That's the same man, though you wouldn't think it, because in your snap he wears a black beard, which he has probably grown lately. But the scar on the neck still gives him away, if his collar happens to be open – and it was, in your snap! Now I know for certain what those men in the castle are up to. I've been looking for this fellow for six months!'

'Who is he?' asked Jack curiously.

'His name, his *real* name is Mannheim,' said Bill, 'but he is known as Scar-Neck. He is a very dangerous spy.'

'Golly!' said Jack, staring. 'Were you after him?'

'Well, I was detailed to keep an eye on him and watch his movements,' said Bill. 'I wasn't to capture him because we wanted to know what he was up to this time, and who his friends were. Then we hoped to rope in the whole lot. But Scar-Neck is a very clever fellow with an absolute gift for disappearing. I traced him to the town where you met me – and then I lost him completely.'

'He went to the castle!' said Jack. 'What a wonderful hiding place!'

'I should rather like to know the real history of that castle,' said Bill thoughtfully. 'I must enquire into its ownership. Do you know what is on the other side of the hill, Jack?'

'No,' said Jack, puzzled. 'We've never been there. Why?'

'I just wondered if you had heard anyone talking,' said Bill. 'I can't tell you any more now. My word, I am glad I bumped into you the other day, and came on here to look you up!'

'So am I, Bill,' said Jack. 'I simply didn't know what I was going to do! Now you're here, and I can leave the whole thing to you.'

'You can,' said Bill. 'Now I'm off in the car to the town, to do a little reporting on the telephone there, and to collect a few friends, and one or two necessary things. You go to sleep again till I come back. I promise you I won't be a minute longer than I can help.'

Jack settled back on the sofa again. 'I don't think I've caught a chill after all,' he said. 'What a lucky thing for me you had a fire, Bill!'

'Well, there was nothing else to boil a kettle with!' said Bill. 'So I had to light one. No, I don't think you're going to get a chill either. You'll be able to go up to the castle with me when I come back, and show me the way.'

'But how will we get in!' called Jack, as Bill went out to get his car. There was no reply except the sound of the car being started up.

'I can leave everything to Bill,' thought Jack. 'Golly, I wonder what will happen now!'

24

Kiki gives a performance

Up in the castle courtyard Tassie passed an exciting night. She had tried to go to sleep in the middle of the gorse bush, and had fallen into a doze, when Kiki began to get restless. She dug her claws into Tassie, and woke her up.

'Don't, Kiki,' said Tassie sleepily. 'Keep still, do!'

But Kiki was waiting for Jack, and couldn't make out why he hadn't come back. She began to murmur to herself, and Tassie reached out a hand and tapped her on the beak.

'Be quiet, Kiki! Do go to sleep! Button is as good as gold.'

There was a sound in the courtyard outside. Kiki put her head on one side, and listened. She thought it was Jack.

'Put the kettle on!' she cried joyfully, and scrambled out from the bush. 'Put the kettle on!'

There was an astonished silence in the yard below. Then a torch was switched on, and its powerful beam swept round. But Kiki was behind a rock and could not be seen.

Two men were down in the yard. They had heard Kiki's

voice, and, not knowing there was a parrot about, they thought it was someone talking.

'Wipe your feet!' called Kiki. 'How many times have I told you to wipe your feet?'

The men began to talk together in low voices, planning to capture whoever it was calling in such a loud voice. Kiki began to realise that it was not Jack down there, and she was disappointed and cross.

'Pop goes the weasel,' she said in a mournful voice. One of the men stooped down in the darkness, felt about for a stone, and sent it whizzing in Kiki's direction. The parrot would certainly have been killed if the stone had hit it. But it missed by about an inch.

Kiki was startled. No one had ever thrown a stone at her in her life. She spread her wings and flew up to the wall behind the men.

'Naughty boy!' she said reprovingly, 'naughty, naughty boy!'

The men gave cries of fury, and swung round, trying in vain to see who was now on the wall. They thought there must be two people now, one up on the crag, and the other on the wall.

'You come down,' said one of the men threateningly. 'We've got you covered! We're not standing any more of this nonsense!'

'Fusty, musty, dusty!' chanted Kiki, and then flew down into the courtyard, just behind the men. They were in darkness and so was she.

Kiki growled like a dog, and the men jumped in fright. The sound was just behind them.

'There's a dog about too,' said one of the men. 'Look out! Shoot, if you like!'

The frightened man pressed the trigger of the revolver he was carrying, and the sound of the shot cracked out in the night, making Tassie, in the gorse bush, jump almost out of her skin. Button, too, leapt with fright and ran out of the bush.

He still had his lead on. He ran down into the courtyard, and his lead dragged after him. As he ran by the men the lead touched one of them, and he fired again. Button yelped, though he was not hit, and the man switched on his torch. He caught sight of the cub slinking away.

'Was that the dog?' he said. 'It's a mighty small one.'

Kiki was enjoying herself. She flew to a tree near by, and began to mew. She could mew just as well as she could bark. The men listened to this new sound in the greatest surprise.

'Cats now,' said one. 'I can't understand it! There never seems anything here in the daytime. Is it children having a joke?'

'God save the King, silly-billy, silly-billy,' said Kiki from the tree, and went off into one of her cackling laughs. Then she clucked like a hen, and finished up with an eagle's yelping scream. It was a very fine performance, but the men didn't like it at all.

'Let's go back inside,' said one of them nervously. 'This place is bewitched. It's all voices and noises but nothing much to show for them. Let's go back.'

Kiki let off one of her express train screeches, and that finished the men completely. They ran for the castle as if an engine was about to run them down! Kiki laughed again, and her cackle sounded very eerie in the dark courtyard. Even Tassie felt frightened, though she knew it was only Kiki.

There was peace after that. Kiki, after flying round a little while to look for Jack, came back to the old gorse bush and struggled inside to join Tassie.

The little girl was glad of her company. 'Button's gone,' she said to Kiki. 'I expect he's gone down that watery tunnel

146

again. Now, Kiki, settle down and go to sleep. I'm so very tired.'

This time Kiki did settle down. She put her head under her wing, gave a little sigh, and went to sleep. Tassie too slept, and there was complete silence except for the trickling noise made by the spring in the corner of the yard.

Tassie was wakened by Dinah and Lucy-Ann. They had passed quite a peaceful night down in the hidden room, undisturbed this time, with Philip on the floor under the bed. He was getting very tired of living underground, and wanted to make a dash for it with the girls. But Dinah persuaded him that that would be dangerous for him, and make things even worse for them. So, grumbling, he had resumed his place under the big bed, where the girls had also put a good supply of food.

'Jack!' said Lucy-Ann, in a low voice, as she came to the bush. 'Jack! Are you there?'

Jack was not there, of course, but Lucy-Ann didn't know that. Tassie awoke and sat up, pricking herself against the bush.

'Jack!' said Lucy-Ann again, and parted the bush to see inside. 'Oh – *you*, Tassie! How did *you* get here?'

Tassie grinned. She was feeling quite all right again after a night's rest. Her face looked dreadful. It was muddy and scratched, and her hair was a wild mass of muddy tangles. She had put on her old dress once more.

'Hallo,' said Tassie. 'I came to help you. I got your note, but I couldn't read it. So I came up to see what it was all about. But the plank was gone. So I found out where Button came in and out, and came with him!'

'Did you really?' said Dinah. 'Where did Button get in, Tassie?'

Tassie told her. The girls listened in surprise. 'How could you crawl up a horrid, wet tunnel like that?' said Lucy-Ann, shuddering at the thought. 'Tassie, you are marvellous, you really are! I could never do that, I know I couldn't.'

'I don't believe I could either,' said Dinah. 'It was wonderful of you, Tassie.'

Tassie felt pleased, and smiled at the two girls. It was nice to be praised like this.

'But where's Jack?' asked Lucy-Ann.

'Gone down the tunnel to get help,' said Tassie. 'He said I was to tell you he was sorry to go without saying goodbye, but he thought it best to go at once.'

'Oh,' said Lucy-Ann, her face falling in dismay. 'I wish he hadn't gone without me.'

'Well, you know you've just said that you couldn't possibly go down that tunnel,' said Dinah. 'I'm jolly glad you came up, Tassie, so that Jack knew the way to escape. He'll get help and bring somebody up here, I'm sure. That's good!'

'But how will they get in?' asked Lucy-Ann.

'They could bring a plank again, couldn't they?' said Tassie.

Kiki joined in the conversation. 'Don't sniff,' she said amiably. 'Where's your handkerchief?'

'Oh, Kiki was so funny last night!' said Tassie, remembering, and told the two girls what had happened. When she described how the men had shot at Kiki, Lucy-Ann looked alarmed.

'Gracious! They are very dangerous men!' she said. 'I don't like them. I want to escape too. I think I'll crawl down that horrid tunnel after all, Dinah. You come too, and Tassie as well. We'll all go.'

'What, and leave Philip all alone here?' cried Tassie indignantly. 'You go if you like, but I shan't.'

'Yes, of course – we can't leave Philip,' said Dinah. 'Oh, Tassie, do come and wash your face. It's simply awful. You look like a sweep. And your clothes! Gracious, they're filthy, and all in rags.'

'I couldn't help it,' said Tassie. 'It was awful in that tunnel. I kept getting caught on things. I'll come and wash if you think it's safe.'

'Well — I suppose it isn't, really,' said Dinah, thinking about it. 'The men might come out and see you, and know you're not one of us two. We'll bring you some water, and you can clean yourself up, outside the bush.'

'Then we'll all have breakfast,' said Lucy-Ann, who was hungry.

It was difficult to get Tassie clean, because all they had to bring water in was an empty ginger beer bottle and a cardboard cup. But by means of a couple of handkerchiefs and the water, she did manage to clean her face and hands a bit. Then they ate breakfast.

Kiki ate breakfast with them. Of Button there was no sign. They thought he must have gone down the tunnel some time in the night, and was probably with Jack again.

'Look — there are the eagles back again!' said Dinah suddenly. Tassie looked round with interest, for she had not seen them that morning. The three birds came dropping down to the ledge, and sat there, looking regally out on the courtyard.

'The young one flies as well as the older birds now, doesn't he?' said Lucy-Ann, and threw him a biscuit. But he didn't even give it a look! He continued his impassive stare, appearing to be frowning deeply.

'I wish Jack was here. He would like to snap them all together like that,' said Lucy-Ann. 'His camera is still in the bush, but I don't like to use it. I suppose it's all right there if it rains, Dinah?'

'It doesn't look as if it will rain,' said Dinah. But Tassie disagreed.

'It feels stormy,' she said. 'I think there will be a thunderstorm, and maybe torrents of rain. I hope we shan't be here,

149

on the top of the hill, if there is a storm, because it would be a frightening sight. The thunder rolls round and round the top, and the lightning seems to run down the hillside!'

'I expect we'll all be rescued before the storm comes,' said Dinah. 'I'm expecting to see Jack any time now – bringing us help of some sort!'

25

At midnight

Jack slept peacefully again for some hours. He did not wake till Bill returned in the car. With him were four 'friends'. Jack thought they looked pretty tough. It was plain that Bill was in authority over them.

Bill came into the kitchen, leaving the men outside. 'Hallo!' he said. 'Awake at last? Do you want a meal? It's gone one o'clock.'

'Gracious, is it!' said Jack. 'Yes, I feel jolly hungry.'

'You get up now and put some clothes on,' said Bill, 'and I'll call one of my men in to fix us up a meal. I don't expect Mrs Mannering will mind if we make free with her kitchen today.'

'Are we going up to the castle soon?' said Jack, gathering the dressing-gown round him, and preparing to go upstairs to his bedroom.

'Not till tonight,' said Bill. 'The moon won't be up till late, and we plan to go just before midnight, whilst it is still dark. I've no doubt one or other of those men keep a lookout during the daytime.'

'Oh – the girls will be awfully tired of waiting for us, all day long,' said Jack.

'Can't very well help it,' said Bill. 'It is most important

that we get in without being seen.'

Jack went up and dressed. It was terribly hot, though the sun was behind sulky-looking clouds. He felt out of breath, though he had done nothing at all.

'Feels like a storm,' he thought. 'I hope it won't come today. It might frighten the girls up there all alone.'

There was a scampering of clawed feet on the stairs, and into his bedroom came Button, his brush waving behind him, his sharp eyes fixed on Jack as if to say 'Well, well, how you do get about, to be sure! I never know whether to find you up at the castle or down here – but I wish I could find old Philip!'

'Looking for Tufty, are you?' said Jack, patting the fox cub, who immediately rolled over like a dog. 'Hey, Bill – did you see our fox cub?'

'Well, a small tornado swept into the kitchen and up the stairs,' called back Bill, 'but I didn't see what it was! Come on down with him.'

Jack went down, carrying Button, who licked his nose rapturously all the time. Bill thought he was fine.

They had a meal together, and Bill asked a good many questions about the castle and the men, and the hidden room, which Jack answered as clearly as he could. He was certain that Bill meant to enter the castle somehow, and capture the men – but he couldn't see how it was to be done.

'They looked pretty dangerous fellows,' he said to Bill. 'I mean – they're probably well armed.'

'Don't worry – they won't be the only ones,' said Bill grimly. 'I know Scar-Neck of old – he doesn't usually leave anything to chance. He must have been pretty fed up when he found the girls in his precious hidden room! I guess their being there has made him hurry up his plans a bit, whatever they are.'

Jack began to feel excited. 'This adventure is boiling up,' he said, in a pleased tone.

151

'Yes. And somebody is going to get badly scalded,' said Bill.

Jack developed his other films. The snaps came out marvellously! The eagles stood out well, almost every feather showing clearly. The baby eagle was the star turn. Its poses were perfect.

'Look at these, Bill,' said Jack, thrilled.

'My word – they're really striking!' said Bill admiringly. 'You ought to get those taken by any first-class magazine, Jack. They would pay well for them too! You'll soon make a name for yourself, at this rate.'

Jack felt proud. If he could make a name for himself through the birds he loved, he would be happy. He wondered how Kiki was getting on without him. How disgusted she would be when she found that he was gone! Never mind – Tassie was there, and she was very fond of her.

The day dragged a little. After tea Jack felt sleepy, and Bill told him to have a nap.

'You had an awful night – and as we shall want your help tonight, you'd better sleep for a few hours. Then you will be wide awake.'

So Jack curled up on a rug in the garden outside and slept. It was hot and sultry there. Bill's men, who had sat playing cards with one another all day long, and had hardly spoken a word, removed their coats, and then their shirts. It was almost too hot to breathe.

Jack awoke again before it was dark. He went to find Bill. 'Oughtn't we to start now?' he said. 'It takes a bit of time to get up the hill.'

'We're going as far as we can by car,' said Bill. 'These fellows are tough, but they don't like mountain climbing! We'll follow the road till we get to the landslide, and then climb the rest of the way.'

Just as it got dark they all piled into Bill's big car and set off up the hill. The car seemed to make rather a noise, Jack thought, but Bill assured him it wouldn't be heard at the castle.

'The only thing that worries me a bit is having Philip down in that hidden room,' said Bill. 'If there's a rough house down there – and I rather think there may be – I don't want kids mixed up in it.'

'Well, really – Bill – it was us kids who got *you* mixed up in this adventure!' said Jack, most indignantly.

'Yes, I know,' said Bill, with a laugh. 'But it rather cramps our style to have you around just now!'

'Bill, what are you going to do?' asked Jack, with curiosity. 'Do tell me. You might as well!'

'I'm not quite sure,' said Bill. 'It depends on how things turn out. But roughly the plan is this – to get down into that hidden room tonight, when the girls are there, we hope, and the men are not. . . .'

'Set the girls free!' said Jack. 'And Philip too, can't you?'

'Yes – if Philip will condescend to scoot off with the girls!' said Bill. 'But we want him to show us the secret way under the tapestry first, and I have an idea that he will want to come with us then!'

'I bet he will,' said Jack. 'So shall I, I don't mind telling you! I'm not going to be left out of this now, if I can help it.'

'I want to find out where that secret door leads to,' said Bill. 'I think I know, but I want to make sure. And I want to learn a few things without those men at the castle knowing it. It was a pity they spoke in a language Philip couldn't understand or he might have learnt what we want to know!'

'Well, how are *you* going to learn it, then?' asked Jack.

'Same way as Philip might have!' said Bill, with a laugh. 'Put myself and the men into those suits of armour, and listen in to the conversation!'

'Gosh!' said Jack, thrilled. 'I never thought of that. Oh, Bill – do you really think you can do that? Can Philip and I hide too?'

'We'll see,' said Bill. 'I thought it was a mighty good idea of Philip's to hide in that armour, I must say, even though it was only for a joke at first. Now – here we are at the landslide, surely?'

They were. They all had to get out, and Jack now had to lead the way. He found the narrow rabbit-path they had so often used, and led the men along it, using his torch as he did so, because it was not easy in the darkness to pick out the right path.

They all walked in dead silence, in obedience to an order from Bill. Button the fox cub ran at Jack's heels, suddenly hopeful of seeing Philip. An owl called near by and made them all jump.

It was so hot that everyone panted, and rubbed wet foreheads. Jack's shirt stuck to him. There was a rumble of thunder far away in the distance.

'I thought there was a storm coming,' said Jack to himself, wiping his forehead for the twentieth time, to stop the perspiration dripping into his eyes. 'I hope the girls are safely down in that underground room. Then they won't hear the storm. But I suppose they'll have to leave poor little Tassie up in the courtyard, because they won't dare to let the men see her. Or Kiki. I hope they're both all right.'

They went on upwards, and at last came to the great castle wall. Jack stopped.

'Here's the castle wall,' he whispered. 'How are you going to get into the castle, Bill?'

'Where's that other door you told me of – not the big front door that overlooks the landslide, and which the men came in by – the other, smaller door, somewhere in the wall of the castle?' asked Bill.

'I'll take you to it – but I told you it was locked,' said Jack. He led Bill and the others round the wall, turned a corner, and came to the door.

It was very stout and strong, made of solid oak, set flush

with the wall. The wall arched above it, and the door arched too. Bill took out his torch and flashed it quickly up and down the door, coming to a stop at the lock.

He beckoned to one of the men. The fellow came up, and brought out an amazing collection of keys from his pocket. Deftly and silently he fitted first one and then another into the keyhole. Not one of them turned the lock.

'No good, sir,' he whispered to Bill. 'This isn't an old lock – it's a special one, fitted quite recently. I shan't be able to open it with any of my keys.'

Jack listened in disappointment. Surely this did not mean that they would have to batter the door in? That would certainly give warning to the men.

Bill sent for one of the other men. He came up with a curious thing in his hand, rather like a small can with a thick spout. Jack stared at it, wondering what it was.

'You'll have to get to work on it, Jim,' said Bill. 'Go ahead. Make as little noise as possible. Stop if I nudge you.'

A sizzling noise came from the can, and a jet of strong blue flame shot out from the spout, making Jack jump. The man pointed the spout of flame at the door, just above the lock.

Jack watched, fascinated. The curious blue flame ate away the wood completely! What kind of fire they were using Jack didn't know, but it was very powerful. Quietly the man worked with his can of flame, holding it steadily over the wood that surrounded the lock. The flame ate away a gap at the top of the lock. It ate away the side of it. And then it ate away the wood below the lock.

Now Jack saw what was happening to the door! The man had managed to isolate the lock completely, so that the door would swing open easily, leaving the lock behind! The boy thought it was a very clever idea.

'Now to go in,' said Bill, as he swung the door slowly open. 'Everyone ready?'

26

Going into hiding

They filed in silently. The last man shut the door, and wedged in a bit of wood by the lock to keep it from swinging. The courtyard was beginning to get light, because the moon was rising, though it was behind the clouds most of the time.

'I'll just go and see if Tassie is under my gorse bush,' whispered Jack. 'We'll have to find out the latest news from her, and she'll have to escape with the girls too, as soon as possible. She can guide them back to Spring Cottage.'

The men waited in the shadows with Bill whilst Jack went over to the crag. He climbed up to the gorse bush. A loud voice hailed him.

'Put the kettle on! How many times have I . . .'

'Shut up, Kiki,' whispered Jack, in a panic. He heard someone stirring in the bush and called in a low voice.

'Is that you, Tassie? It's Jack, back again!'

Tassie crawled out of the bush, full of joy, for she had been feeling frightened and lonely.

'Oh, Jack! Did you come up that awful watery tunnel like I did? Did you get help?'

'Yes – Bill Smugs is here – with some of his men,' whispered Jack. 'You and the other two girls must go down to Spring Cottage. Philip and I are going to wait and see what happens – if Bill will let us!'

'But how can you get the girls?' asked Tassie. 'You know they are down in the hidden room, with Philip.'

'Easy,' said Jack. 'We'll just pull the spike in the wall at the back of the hall, and get them out! Then, Tassie, you and they must hurry off as quickly as you can.'

156

'I'd like to stay with Philip,' said Tassie obstinately. 'And anyway, there's going to be a dreadful storm. I don't want to go down the hillside with thunder and lightning all round me.'

'Well – you'll have to do as Bill tells you,' said Jack. 'Maybe you'll get down before the storm comes. Are the girls all right, Tassie?'

'Yes, but rather tired of it,' said Tassie. 'Oh, Jack, Kiki made a simply awful noise last night after you had gone, and the men heard her – and they shot at her! I was really frightened!'

'Golly!' said Jack. 'I'm glad *you* weren't hit, Tassie! You might easily have been wounded.'

'The girls went down into the secret room when the men called out to them this evening,' said Tassie. 'But they asked them all kinds of questions, in horrid, rough voices. They couldn't understand Kiki talking last night, you see, and thought there must be someone else here that we hadn't told them about. So, in the end, Dinah had to tell them it was Kiki the parrot – and after that they didn't worry them any more.'

'Come on – we must go over to Bill, and tell him all this,' said Jack. 'The men are waiting over there, look – Bill's men, I mean, of course!'

The moon struggled out as the two went over to the little group of silent men, so they kept in the shadows, fearful of being seen. It wouldn't do to give the game away to any watcher just at this critical moment.

'Where are the other men?' whispered Jack to Tassie. 'Do you know? Are they down in the hidden room – or wandering about the castle anywhere?'

'As far as I know they're not about the castle anywhere – or in the courtyard,' said Tassie. 'They may be down in the hidden room though. Won't you have to look out, if you press that spike and open the entrance?'

157

'Yes, we shall,' said Jack. 'Now here's Bill Smugs, our friend, Tassie. This is Tassie, Bill, the girl I was telling you about.'

Bill put a few questions to Tassie, and she answered them shyly. It rather looked as if the men were down in the secret room. Well – they would get a shock when the stone swung back, and they saw who were at the top of the steps!

'Now listen,' said Bill. 'You are to work the lever that opens the entrance to the secret room, Jack. One of my men will watch you, to see how you do it, in case we want to use it again. As soon as the entrance is open, I and the others will stand at the top and shout down to the men below to come up. We shall, I hope, have them covered with our revolvers!'

'Golly!' said Jack, a prickle of excitement running up and down his back. 'Look out for the girls, Bill. They may be scared stiff!'

'I can yell to them to keep out of the way,' said Bill. 'You leave things to me. I promise you the girls won't get hurt. We'll have them up the steps in no time – and you, Tassie, must take them straight away down the hill to Spring Cottage. Understand?'

'I'd like to stay with Philip,' Tassie still insisted.

'Well, you can't,' said Bill. 'You'll have Philip back with you tomorrow. Now – you all understand what's to be done?'

Everyone did. Quietly they all moved forward towards the great black hulk of the castle, lost in black shadows. The moon had gone behind thick clouds. A rumble of thunder came on the air again, still far away.

They stepped silently into the hall. Everyone but Tassie was wearing rubber shoes – Tassie, as usual, was barefoot. She hadn't even got her shoes tied round her neck or waist this time. She had hidden them, for her mother had threatened to take them away from her.

Jack slipped quietly to the back of the hall with one of the

158

men. Tassie showed Bill the entrance to the underground room. He and the others waited there whilst Jack pulled back the spike in the wall. A grating noise was heard – and once again the stone swung back, and then sideways. A yawning hole appeared, with stone steps leading downwards.

The light from the lamp shone upwards. Bill stood at the top of the hole, listening intently. There was no sound at all from below.

Jack tiptoed up to him. 'Maybe there are only the girls and Philip there,' he whispered. 'Perhaps the men have gone off somewhere, down the secret way behind that tapestry.'

Bill nodded. He sent his voice rumbling down the hole. 'Who's down here? Answer!'

A small voice came back. It was Dinah's.

'Only us. Who's that?'

'Dinah! It's me and Bill Smugs!' called Jack, before Bill could stop him. 'Are you alone?'

'Yes,' came back Dinah's voice, lifted in excitement. 'Is *Bill* there? Oh, good!'

Jack ran down the steps, and Bill and the others followed, one man being left at the top on guard. The first thing Bill did was to find the spike in the wall down below, and close up the hole. He waited a moment, and then the man at the top, as arranged, opened it again. Bill wanted to make sure he could get in and out as he pleased!

Lucy-Ann flew to Jack and hugged him tightly, tears pouring down her face. Dinah grinned at Bill, and tried hard to stop herself hugging him. But she couldn't. She too was so relieved at seeing them both.

'No time to waste,' said Bill. 'Where's Philip?'

'Oh, Bill, he's gone!' said Lucy-Ann, turning to him and clinging to his arm. 'When we got down here tonight he was gone! And we don't know where or how. We don't know if the men caught him, or if Philip went off by himself, or what. He didn't leave a note or anything. But we think maybe he explored that secret way under the tapestry.'

'Bill, the men are coming back soon,' said Dinah, suddenly remembering. 'I heard one of them say to another, in English, that they were to have their last meeting here tonight. So they may be back here any time, because this is where they meet, and where they keep their maps, or whatever it is they look at so carefully.'

'Where are the maps?' asked Bill at once, and Dinah nodded towards the locked drawers.

'In there. But they keep them locked up. Bill, what are you going to do? Isn't this a mystery?'

'I'm beginning to see daylight,' said Bill grimly. 'Now look here, Dinah – you and Lucy-Ann are to go with Tassie straight away down the hill to Spring Cottage, and you are to stay there till we come. Do you understand? You can go out of that side door in the wall, which is now open. The man I have left upstairs will take you there safely and see you out. Then you must go at once.'

'But—but . . .' began Dinah, not liking to go without Philip.

'No buts,' said Bill. 'I'm in command here, and you do exactly as you're told! Now – off you go! We'll be with you tomorrow!'

Dinah, Lucy-Ann and Tassie went obediently up the steps and out of the entrance hole. The man at the top went off to the door in the wall with them, and saw them safely out on the hillside. 'Sure you know your way?' he murmured, for he was quite sure *he* wouldn't know his way down the dark hillside! But Tassie did. She could almost have found her way with her eyes shut, she knew it so well, and was so sure footed.

The girls disappeared into the night. The man returned to his post. The entrance to the secret room was now closed. Below, Bill, Jack and the others were hurriedly getting into

160

the suits of armour. Bill meant to attend the next meeting of Scar-Neck with his men! Jack was glad to see that they all had revolvers! The men said very little. They were the least talkative people the boy had ever known.

Jack was made to stand in the suit of armour right at the back of the hidden room. Bill didn't want him too near, in case, as he said, there was a really rough house! The boy was shaking with excitement.

Kiki was not down in the room. Tassie had carried her firmly up the stone steps, screeching with annoyance at being parted from Jack so soon again. But it would not be possible to have a talkative parrot down there – she would certainly give the game away.

But Button the fox cub was there! Nobody knew it, of course. The fox cub had curled himself up under the bed, where Philip had hidden, glad to smell the familiar smell of the master he loved. Jack had forgotten all about him.

Soon all the suits of armour were standing once more on their pedestals round the curious museum-like room. Only three of them were empty. All the others were filled, though one of the men, a great big fellow, complained bitterly that his didn't fit him at all.

'Now – silence,' said Bill. 'Not a word from anyone. I think I heard something!'

27

The adventure boils up

But it was not anyone – it was a peal of thunder so loud that the noise had penetrated even down to the underground room.

'I hope the girls won't be frightened,' said Bill, thinking of them scurrying down the hillside in the darkness. 'I wonder if it's raining.'

'They'll be all right with Tassie, I think,' said Jack. 'She will know places to shelter in. She won't be silly enough to stand under trees or anything like that. There are a few little caves here and there in the hillside. Maybe they'll use those till the storm is past.'

Silence again. It was astonishing how so many people, all standing rather uncomfortably in suits of armour, could manage to do so without a single creak or clank!

One man cleared his throat, and the sound was strange in the hidden room.

'Don't do that again, Jim,' said Bill. There was dead silence once more. Jack sighed softly. It was unbearably exciting to stand hidden in armour, wet with perspiration, almost panting with heat, waiting for the other men to come.

Then suddenly, sounding quite loud, there came the noise of a door being unlocked. Then the tapestry on one wall shook – and someone lifted it up from behind!

Everyone stiffened inside the suits of armour. Eyes peered through the visors. Who was coming?

A man came out from behind the tapestry, and folded it back, hanging one end on a nail, so that others following could come into the room easily. Jack saw an opening behind, leading into the wall. From it came soft-footed men, one after the other – and with them they brought Philip!

The shaggy-browed man came first. Then came the bearded man, the one Bill called Scar-Neck, dragging Philip. Scar-Neck had the neck of his shirt closed, and Jack could see no sign of the tell-tale scar.

Philip was putting on a bold face, but Jack knew he was feeling scared. After him came three more men, all ugly fellows, with sharp eyes and stern mouths. They came into

162

the room, talking. They left the secret way open, and Jack wondered where it led to.

Philip's hands were bound behind his back, so tightly that the rope bit into his skin. Scar-Neck flung him into a chair.

It was soon clear that Philip had only just been captured. Scar-Neck rounded on him almost at once.

'How long have you been in the castle? What do you know?'

'I was here with the girls,' said Philip. 'I hid under the bed. You never looked there. I wasn't doing any harm. We only came to play about in this old castle. We didn't know it belonged to anyone.'

'Get the girls,' growled Scar-Neck to the shaggy man. 'Bring them over here. We'll cross-question the whole three of them. To think that a parcel of kids should waste our time like this!'

The shaggy-browed man went over to the bed, where, he imagined, the two girls would, as usual, be sleeping. But when he pulled back the curtain, they were not there! He stared, and then roughly pulled off the blankets and rugs.

'They're not here!' he said, in an astonished voice. The bearded man turned at once.

'Don't be a fool! They must be here somewhere! We know they can't get out of this room once it's shut.'

'The boy may have let them out from above,' said the shaggy man. Scar-Neck swung round on Philip. The boy was amazed that the girls had gone, but he was not going to show it.

The shaggy man hunted under the bed – but it was plain to everyone that the girls had gone. Scar-Neck spoke roughly to Philip.

'Did you let them out?'

'No,' said Philip. 'I didn't. I was hiding here, I tell you, under the bed. I wasn't at the top.'

163

'Well – who let them out, then?' said the shaggy man, and his brows knitted together so that they almost hid his sharp eyes.

'Now – you tell us everything!' said Scar-Neck, and his voice was suddenly ugly and threatening.

Philip said nothing, but stared defiantly at the man. Scar-Neck lost his temper, raised his fist, and gave Philip such a blow on the side of the head that the boy fell off his chair. He picked himself up.

Jack, beside himself with anger, saw Philip's left ear glow bright scarlet, and begin to swell.

'Now will you talk?' said Scar-Neck, his voice growing with rage. The others looked on, saying nothing.

Still Philip said nothing. Jack felt proud. How brave he was! Then, to his horror, the man took out a revolver and laid it on the table beside him.

'We have ways of making sulky boys talk,' he said, and his eyes gleamed with rage.

Philip didn't like the look of the shining weapon. He blinked a little, and then stared at Scar-Neck again. But still he said nothing.

What would have happened next if there hadn't been a sudden and surprising interruption, nobody knew! But all at once, like a stone from a catapult, Button, who had slunk under a chair on the far side of the room when the men arrived, shot out and threw himself on Philip.

Everyone leapt to his feet, and Scar-Neck caught up his revolver. When they saw that the newcomer was only a fox cub, they sat down again, feeling angry at their sudden fright.

Scar-Neck was furious. He lashed out at the cub, and sent him rolling to the ground. Button bared his small white teeth.

'Don't hurt him,' said Philip, in alarm. 'He's only a cub. He's mine.'

'How did he get down here? When the girls got out, I suppose?' growled the shaggy man.

'I don't know,' said Philip, puzzled. 'I tell you, I really don't know how the girls got out, nor how the cub got in. It's as much a mystery to me as to you.'

'If this kid is telling the truth, we'd better finish up and get going,' said the shaggy man, sounding rather anxious. 'There must be others about, though goodness knows we've kept a good enough watch. Let's settle up our business and go.'

A rumble of thunder came down into the secret room again. The men looked at one another uneasily.

'What's that?' said the shaggy man.

'Thunder, of course,' growled Scar-Neck. 'What's the matter with you? Getting nervy just because a bunch of silly kids are playing around? What they want is a good beating, and I'll see this boy gets it before we go, anyway, even if those girls have gone!'

Button curled up quietly at Philip's feet. He was afraid of these men. Scar-Neck nodded to one of the others, and he got up. He went to the drawer where the documents were kept, unlocked it, and drew out the sheaf of papers there. He put them in front of Scar-Neck.

Then began a long discussion in a language that Philip did not understand. But Bill understood it! Bill could speak eight or more different languages, and he listened eagerly to all that was said.

Philip sat listlessly on his chair, his wrists hurting him, and his left ear now twice its size. He could not even rub it because his hands were so tightly tied behind his back.

Button licked his bare leg. It was comforting. Philip wondered where the girls had gone. How had they got out? He was glad to know they had probably escaped. Had help come? Had Jack managed to find someone? Would they rescue him too?

He wished he was standing safely inside the suit of armour he had hidden in before. He glanced round at it, and then stared in the utmost amazement.

Surely eyes were gleaming behind that visor? Philip had extremely good eyesight, and it so happened that the rays of the lamp shone directly into the visor of the armour he was looking at. It seemed to Philip as if there were real eyes behind it, not the usual hollow space.

He glanced at the next suit of armour, and saw what he imagined were eyes there too — and the next one! He felt terribly scared. Had all these suits of armour come alive all of a sudden? Who was inside? He could see that most of them were filled. He began to tremble.

Scar-Neck noticed him and laughed. 'Ah, so you are beginning to be afraid of what may happen to boys who interfere in somebody else's business! Maybe you will talk soon!'

Philip said nothing. He began to think clearly, and it was soon plain to him that it must be friends inside the armour, and not enemies. How silly of him to be scared! But it really had been an eerie feeling to see gleaming eyes looking at him from behind those visors.

'So that's how it is the girls have gone,' he thought. 'Now I understand. Jack did get help — and they've had the idea of doing what I did — hiding in the armour to see what is happening! Well, I mustn't give them away, whatever happens! I wonder if one of them is old Freckles.'

Feeling very much better now, the boy gave another look round at the armour. He did not dare to stare too hard, in case one of the men followed the direction of his look and saw what he saw.

Another rumble of thunder came down into the room, louder this time. The air was almost unbearably hot down there, and the men in the armour had hard work not to gasp. Perspiration ran down their bodies, and they longed to shift their positions a little. But they dared not move.

Bill was listening intently to all that was being said, though Philip could not make out a single word. Papers were spread out on the table, but Bill could not see what they were. They looked like blueprints of some sort, details of machinery perhaps. It was impossible for him to see.

Scar-Neck rolled them up at last. Then he turned to Philip.

'Well, our job is done. We shall not have the pleasure of seeing you or your friends any more. But before we go we shall teach you what it means to spy on us! Where's that rope?'

'Don't you dare touch me!' cried Philip, jumping to his feet. Scar-Neck took the rope.

Then, to his unutterable horror, one of the suits of armour walked off its pedestal, held up a stiff and clanking arm, at the end of which shone a wicked-looking revolver, and said:

'The game's up, Scar-Neck. We've got you all!'

The voice sounded hollow. Scar-Neck and the others stared in the utmost dismay; and then looked round at other suits of armour, which were also coming alive! It seemed like a bad dream – but a dream that had too many revolvers in it!

'Hands up!' said Bill's sharp voice.

Scar-Neck began to put his hands up – but suddenly he turned, took hold of the oil lamp, and smashed it on the ground. In a moment the room was pitch dark!

28

A terrible storm

Bill gave a cry of rage. Then Jack heard his voice. 'Get under the bed, Jack and Philip, quick! There may be shooting!'

The boys did exactly as they were told. They dived for the bed, Jack clanking in his armour. Philip lay there panting, wishing his hands were not tied. Jack got stuck halfway under the bed.

What was happening in the room they didn't know. There were shouts and panting and groans – but nobody did any shooting. It was too dark to risk that in case friend shot friend. It sounded to the boys as if men in armour and men without were rolling on the ground together, for there was a tremendous thudding and clashing.

Suddenly there was a grating noise, and the boys knew the entrance above was being opened. But who was opening it, their side or the other? Philip had no idea how it was opened from below, though he had often tried to find out, for obviously there must be a way.

Then he knew that Scar-Neck or one of his friends must have opened it, as a way of escape, for he heard Bill's voice shouting up to the man he had left above.

'Tom! Look out! Shoot anyone coming up!'

Tom sprang to the top of the steps, but he could see nothing down below. He could only hear the groans and clanks the boys could hear. Then up the steps crept one of the men. Tom did not hear him, and suddenly he felt a blow that sent him sprawling. It was Scar-Neck trying to escape. In the fight he had lost his revolver or he would certainly have shot Tom.

Before Tom could get up and catch him, he was gone –

and yet another man was on top of the surprised Tom, falling over him. Poor Tom got another blow, and his head sang. Then the shaggy-browed man kicked him savagely and disappeared too.

After that Tom didn't know what to do – whether to stand at the top of the steps to prevent anyone else coming up, or to go after the escaping men. But as he hadn't the remotest idea where they had gone, he chose the first course.

Down below things were going badly for the three men left. One of them was completely knocked out. Another had given in because Bill had sat on top of him so firmly that there wasn't anything else to do. And the third man had tried to escape down the secret way behind the tapestry, but was now being forcibly brought back by Jim, who was yanking him along with many muttered threats.

Bill at last found a torch and switched it on. The oil lamp was smashed beyond repair. It was fortunate that it had not set the place on fire. By the light of the powerful torch Bill had a look round.

The man he had been sitting on was now in the charge of someone else, and was looking extremely sorry for himself. He had a black eye and a very large lump on his head. Bill looked odd. He was still wearing his armour, but he had taken off the helmet so that his bald head, with the thick hair at each side, rose up startlingly.

The two boys came out from under the bed. Bill had to tug at Jack to set him free. Jack got out of the hot armour as quickly as he could, and freed Philip's hands.

Bill's face wore a look of utter disgust. He could see that the two men he most wanted to catch – Scar-Neck and the shaggy-browed man – were gone. He called up to Tom.

'Are you there, Tom?'

'Yes, sir,' came back Tom's voice, rather subdued.

'Have you got the two who came up the steps?' shouted Bill.

'No, sir. Sorry to say they bowled me over and got away, sir,' replied Tom, even more subdued.

Bill muttered a few rude names for the unlucky Tom. 'Come on down here,' he said. 'What a fool you are, Tom! You had a wonderful position up there – you could have stopped a whole army getting out!'

'Well, it was so dark, sir,' said Tom. 'I couldn't see a thing.'

'Well, you've let two of our most important men go,' said Bill grimly. 'That's not the way to get promotion, you know. I wish I'd put someone else up there now. I suppose those fellows are well away down the hill now. I've no doubt they've got their own powerful car well hidden away somewhere, ready for an emergency, and will be the other side of the country by tomorrow night.'

Poor Tom looked very sheepish. He was an enormous fellow, and the boys thought he ought to have been able to capture two enemies single-handed! They were in a terrible state of excitement and wished that they had been able to capture Scar-Neck themselves.

'Tie up these fellows,' said Bill, curtly nodding to their captives. Jim began to do it very efficiently and soon the men sat like trussed fowls, sullen and tousled, frowning into space.

'Now we'll have a look at those papers,' said Bill, and one of his men went to spread them out before him. Bill bent over them.

'Yes – they've got everything here they wanted to know,' he said. 'That fellow Scar-Neck is about the cleverest spy in any country. I bet he felt mad to leave these behind. They are worth a fortune to him, and are of untold value to the country he was spying for.'

One of the men rolled them up. As he did so a terrific roll of thunder echoed all round. Everyone looked startled.

'What a storm!' said the man called Jim. 'Was that lightning then?'

It was, flashing down even to the underground room. It had flashed almost at the same moment as the thunder crashed.

'Storm's about overhead, I should think,' said Bill. 'I don't think we'll venture down the hillside ourselves till it's over.'

'Aren't you going to see where that secret way leads to?' asked Jack, in disappointment.

'Oh yes,' said Bill. 'Tom and I will go, whilst the others take the prisoners down the hill – but we'll wait till daylight now, I think.'

The storm grew worse. Philip tried to tell Bill what had happened to him that day, but he had to shout at the top of his voice, because the thunder crashed so loudly overhead.

'I was so bored I thought I'd go down the secret passage myself and see where it led to,' shouted Philip. 'So when the men had gone up the stone steps after a good long sleep here, I slipped out from under the bed and went into that hole in the wall there. The men had left it open, just as you see it now, with the tapestry hooked back, and the stone slid from the opening. It goes right back, as you can see. Well, there's a door in the side of the opening. . . .'

The thunder interrupted him again and he stopped. Everyone was listening to him with interest, except the surly prisoners.

'The door there was locked, but someone had left the key in the lock,' went on Philip, when the thunder had died down a little. 'So I unlocked it. The door pushed backwards and I found myself in a narrow passage.'

'Wasn't it dark?' asked Jack.

'Yes, but I had my torch,' said Philip. 'I put it on, and saw my way quite well. The passage went downwards, at first between walls of stone – must have been the foundations of the castle, I suppose — and then I saw that I must have come out from under the castle, and was going through a tunnel hewn out of the solid rock.'

'And I suppose it led you out on to the hill on the other side?' said Bill. 'And you looked down on something rather interesting?'

'I never got as far as that,' said Philip. 'I heard one of the men coming some way behind me, and I thought I'd better hide. So I climbed up on to a narrow ledge near the roof of the passage just there, and lay quite quiet.'

'Golly!' said Jack. 'Did he pass you?'

'Yes. But he was looking for me,' said Philip. 'You see, I'd forgotten to close the door that led into the secret passage, and when the men came back, they noticed it, and got puzzled. So they sent someone down the passage to see who had opened the door.'

'And they found you?' said Bill, but his words were lost in another crash of thunder.

'When the man found I wasn't anywhere in the passage he came back,' went on Philip. 'But evidently the chief man wasn't going to let me wander about there, and he and everyone else came down the secret way then. And, of course, they soon found me lying on that narrow ledge, and dragged me down.'

'What happened to you then?' asked Bill. 'You weren't taken back to the hidden room, because the girls wondered where you were when they came down that night.'

'No. They tied my wrists together, and my ankles too, and just left me there in the passage,' said Philip. 'They said as I seemed to have a liking for the passage, I could stay there till they were ready to bring me back and question me. So there I stayed till at last they did fetch me. They untied my ankles so that I could walk — and brought me to the hidden room, as you saw.'

'Poor old Philip — a nasty experience,' said Bill.

'Golly, I *was* scared when I saw your eyes gleaming at me through the visor of the helmet, Bill,' said Philip. 'I had the fright of my life! But I soon realised you must be friends.'

The thunder was now so noisy and continuous that it was no use talking. They all sat in silence, thinking what a tremendous storm must be going on outside on the hill.

'I'm just going up to have a squint out of the front door,' said Bill. 'It must be a fine sight, this storm.'

'We'll come too,' said the boys. So up the stone steps they went, and down the hall to the open front door of the castle.

They stopped in awe just before they got there. The whole countryside lay cowering beneath the worst storm they had ever seen. Lightning tore the sky apart continually, great jagged forks that ran up and down from the top of the sky to the bottom.

The thunder was like nothing they had ever heard, it was loud and so overwhelming. It never stopped! It rolled round and round the hillside, like terrific guns bombarding an enemy.

And the rain! It poured down as if great rivers had been let loose from the sky. No one could go out in that, for they would surely be battered to the ground!

'It's a cloud burst,' said Bill. 'The sky has opened, and let down a deluge! I've never seen anything like this, except once in India. I should think Scar-Neck and the other fellow are having a pretty bad time of it out on the hillside.'

'Anyway the girls had plenty of time to get down to Spring Cottage,' said Jack. 'They'll be safe at home, I hope. Good gracious – what's that?'

29

The secret passage

As Jack was speaking, there came the most tremendous clap of thunder he was ever to hear in his life. It made him jump violently and cling to Bill. It was the loudest noise he had ever heard.

With it came a flash of lightning that lighted up the hills around for miles upon miles. There they were, unbelievably clear and somehow unreal, for half a second. Then they went back into pitch darkness again. But a queer feeling ran through all three when the flash came.

Bill suddenly pulled them back a little. 'I think the castle has been struck!' he said. 'Yes, it has – look!'

One of the towers, lit up by the next flash, was seen by the two boys to be in the act of falling! In a second it was gone as darkness came back again. Then, through the insistent thudding of the rain, came the sound of the crashing of stone upon stone, as the tower fell to the ground.

'The storm is absolutely on top of us!' shouted Jack. 'Let's go back to the hidden room, Bill. I'm afraid. I felt that flash of lightning, I'm sure I did. Bill, the thunder is in the courtyard, it is, it is!'

Bill was almost inclined to believe that it was, as it rolled round in rumbling crashes. Then another flash came, and once more the three felt a queer shock, as the lightning seemed to flash through them.

'I believe if we hadn't got rubber-soled shoes on we'd have been struck dead!' thought Bill suddenly. 'Gosh, the castle has been struck again – this time the main building. It will be in ruins if this goes on!'

He hustled the boys back to the steps that led to the

hidden room. Down they went, and then paused in awe – for now it seemed as if the castle itself was falling!

Hurriedly Bill pulled at the spike that shut the entrance. He felt he would like to have solid stone between him and the storm now. With relief he saw the stone slide sideways and upwards, and the entrance was closed.

Almost immediately there came a terrific sound of falling stone, crashing on to stone below, and the room shook.

'The castle is falling on top of us!' cried Philip, and he went pale. It really sounded as if it was. Bill thought part of it must again have been struck by lightning, and have fallen inwards. He wondered if what they heard was the floor above falling down into the hall! It sounded like that.

More crashing noises came, not made by the thunder, and then comparative silence. No one spoke for a while.

'I can see how that landslide happened,' said Bill at last. 'A storm like this could easily cause undermining of the road, and a landslide would result. I shouldn't be surprised if there was another one tonight. I should think even more of the road will be destroyed.'

'That rain was so terrific,' said Jack. 'I've never heard anything like it. I bet the poor girls are scared, down in the cottage by themselves.'

'Yes – I wish we were with them,' said Bill. He took a glance at the captives. They looked very frightened. What they could hear of the storm and the falling of the castle was evidently filling them with forebodings as to what might be going to happen next!

'You know, I've just realised that I'm awfully hungry,' said Philip suddenly. 'I've had nothing to eat since I wen⁺ off by myself to explore that secret passage.'

'You must be famished!' said Bill. 'I feel pretty hungry myself too. There seems to be a nice pile of tins over there. I think it might while away the time a bit, and make us forget this awful storm, if we attacked the contents.'

Jack and Philip examined the tins. They chose one tin of spiced meat, one tin of tongue and two of peaches. They opened them, and put generous helpings on to the plates stacked on a side table.

Bill found drinks. It was so hot that the beer he found in bottles was more than usually welcome to the men. The boys feasted on ginger beer and lemonade, both of which were there too.

Everyone felt better after the meal. The storm seemed to be dying down. Bill glanced at his watch.

'Half-past five!' he said, with a yawn. 'I didn't think it was so late. Well, as the storm is dying, maybe we could get out into the courtyard for a breath of air. It will be daylight now. I can perhaps see my men off down the hillside with their prisoners.'

'Yes. I'm dying for a breath of air,' said Philip, whose face was bright scarlet with heat. 'How do you open the entrance, from down here, Bill?'

'Up there by the ceiling,' said Bill, and showed Philip how. There was a hidden lever there. He pulled at it – but it did not move. He pulled again.

'It won't budge,' said Bill, surprised. 'Here, Tom, you try. You're as strong as a horse.'

Tom took his turn, but he could not move the lever either. The stone would not move an inch from the entrance, to unblock it.

Then both Bill and Tom tried together. The stone moved an inch or two – and then stopped. No further efforts made any difference. It wouldn't move any more.

Bill went up the steps as far as he could and tried to peer through the crack, but he could see nothing at all. He came back.

'I'm afraid part of the castle has fallen in on top of the entrance,' he said. 'The lever is strong enough to move that heavy stone, but we are not strong enough to shift whatever is on top of it by pulling hard. We can't get out.'

'We'll have to use the other way then, the passage I went down yesterday,' said Philip, nodding his head towards the opening behind the tapestry.

'Yes,' said Bill. 'I only hope that hasn't done any slipping and sliding too! Still, you said it was made out of the solid rock, didn't you? It should be quite all right.'

It was steadily getting hotter and hotter in the underground room. Button, who had retired under the bed during the fight, now came out and rolled over on his side by Philip, his pink tongue hanging out like a dog's.

'He's thirsty,' said Jack. 'Give him a drink.'

'There's nothing except ginger beer left,' said Philip, and poured some out on a plate. Button was so thirsty that he drank it all up, then sat down and licked his mouth round thoughtfully, as if to say, 'Well – that was certainly nice and wet – but what a strange taste!'

'We shall all be cooked if we don't make a move,' said Bill. 'Come on – we'll try our luck this way. I'll go first.'

He went into the hole in the wall, and pushed at the door there. It opened. Bill went through, shining his torch in front of him.

The two boys followed. Then came the three men with their captives, who were now very subdued indeed. They had not uttered a word for a very long time.

The passage was narrow, but fairly straight at first. Bill's torch showed that it was built in the stone foundations of the castle itself.

'It's likely that there are dungeons built down here too,' said Bill. 'It's a strange old place. There are probably more hidden rooms as well. The old legends about the place talk of more than one room.'

After a while the stone of the tunnel walls turned to solid

rock, uneven of surface. The air was surprisingly fresh. It was deliciously cool after the oven-heat of the room they had left behind.

Now the passage wound about a little, as if to follow the vagaries of the rock. Bill thought part of the passage was artificial, and part natural. It was plain that it went straight through the top of the hill, in a downward direction.

In some places it sloped quite steeply, and they all slithered a little. Then they suddenly heard the noise of water!

They stopped. Bill looked back at Philip. 'Water!' he said. 'Did you see any before when you came down here?'

Philip shook his head. 'No,' he said. 'It was all quite dry. We haven't yet come to the ledge I hid on.'

They went on, puzzled – and suddenly they saw what made the noise! The deluge of rain soaking down into the hillside was trying to get away somewhere, and was running down in a torrent, underground. It had found a weak place in the wall of the passage, and had poured down into it. It was now running like a river down the tunnel, making a roaring, gurgling noise.

'Goodness!' said Jack, peering over Bill's shoulder, and seeing the rushing water by the light of his torch. 'We can't go down there now!'

'It's not very deep,' said Bill, looking at it. 'I believe we shall be able to wade along all right. It's lucky for us that the passage goes downhill, not uphill, or we should have had the water pouring to meet us!'

He put his foot into it, and found that it was about knee-deep. The current was fairly powerful, but not enough to sweep anyone from their feet, though they had to take care to keep their balance.

They all waded into the torrent. It was cold and the coolness was welcome to them. Splashing through the water they went on their way again. Button was curled tightly round Philip's neck. He hated the water.

They went on a good way. Then Philip pointed up to a rocky ledge near the roof of the passage. 'That's where I hid,' he said. 'See? It was quite a good place, wasn't it? Nobody would have found me if they hadn't really been looking for me.'

They went on past Philip's ledge. The water was a little deeper now, and stronger, because the passage sloped more steeply just there. It was slow going. Jack, who was getting very tired, thought it would never come to an end. He liked adventures, but he began to feel he would rather like a rest from this one.

All at once the passage began to slope down very steeply indeed, so steeply that the torrent made quite a waterfall! Bill stopped.

'Well, I don't see how we can get down here, unless we just slide down in the water!' he said. 'Ah, but wait a minute – I believe there are stone steps leading downwards. Yes, there are. We shall be all right if we don't let the water rush us off our feet!'

He went first, very cautiously, feeling for the steps with his feet. The boys followed, equally cautiously, Jack almost being rushed off his feet once or twice by the surging fall of water.

Suddenly Bill put his torch out – and daylight appeared in front! The stone steps led out on to the opposite side of the castle hill – they were there at last!

Bill leapt out of the water and came out of a narrow opening in the hillside, almost completely covered by brambles. 'Well – here we are!' he said. 'Safe after all!'

30

The other side of the hill

The boys came out of the hole too, and they all stared at the sight below them. They were on a very steep hillside, with an almost sheer drop beneath.

Directly below was what looked like a farmhouse, with out-buildings on the slope of the hill. All around the place was barbed wire, rows upon rows of it. There was plenty just below where they stood, too.

There was a copse of trees behind the house, and in the middle was a clear space. A curious looking machine stood in the centre of this clearing. It was large and shining. To anyone down at the farm or near by it must have been completely hidden in the trees – but viewed from above it was very plain to see.

'What is it?' asked Jack, gazing at it in the clear morning sunlight.

'Not even I know that, Jack,' said Bill. 'It is one of our own country's secrets – something being worked on by our greatest military scientists.'

'And that's what Scar-Neck the spy was after?' asked Philip.

'That's what he was after,' said Bill. 'He got wind of it – found out where the tests were being carried out in secret – and discovered to his delight that there was an old castle on the other side of the hill for sale.'

'Gosh! Did he buy the castle then?' asked Jack.

Bill nodded. 'Yes. I made it my business to find out who the owner was. Scar-Neck had not bought it in his own name, or course – he was far too clever for that. He bought it in the name of an Englishman – called Brown. A man supposed to be interested in old buildings. But I soon found out who was behind Brown.'

'Aren't you clever, Bill?' said Jack admiringly.

'No,' said Bill. 'That kind of thing is easy in my job. I knew Scar-Neck was probably after this secret of ours, but I couldn't for the life of me see how he could find out anything. As you can see, it's very well hidden up here at the back of the old farm – and well protected by barbed wire, which is quite probably mixed up with other wire that is electrically charged.'

'Well – how did he get the secret then?' said Philip.

'By wonderful photography, and by making a way right under the wire down to the machine itself, I imagine,' said Bill. 'Look – do you see signs of digging there? Well, I imagine Scar-Neck and his friends did a bit of burrowing, like rabbits, right under the wire, and came up safely inside the enclosure.'

'Wouldn't anyone see them?' said Jack.

'Not from this side,' said Bill. 'Nobody would guess anyone would try any tricks from up here. It would seem impossible to get here, it's so steep!'

'And nobody knew about the passage in the castle that led right to this side of the hill!' said Jack. 'How did he find it out?'

'Got old plans of the castle, I expect,' said Bill. 'The old fellow who had this castle last was quite mad, as you no doubt gathered from the curious things he did. He made all kinds of hidden rooms with curious contrivances, and lived in a romantic world of his own. Scar-Neck found the hidden room we know extremely useful, and the secret passage a perfect godsend! It actually came out above the very secret he had been sent to find out!'

'He's a brave man,' said Philip.

'Yes – most spies are brave,' said Bill. 'But this particular one is a most unpleasant fellow, heartily disliked even in his

181

own country. He will double-cross anyone, not excepting his dearest friend. Well – I'm afraid he's got away this time. But thank goodness he's left the plans of our secret behind him in that hidden room!'

'So he can't do any damage, I suppose?' asked Philip.

'Not unless he remembers everything in his head,' said Bill. 'He has a marvellous memory, of course, so maybe he will do us some damage even now.'

'I hope he won't,' said Philip. 'I do so wish we had caught him, Bill – and old Shaggy too. I didn't like either of them at all.'

'These three we have got are only ordinary toughs, ready to do anything beastly for money,' said Bill. 'I have let the real culprits slip – and I shall get a rap over the knuckles for that! Serves me right – I had a wonderful chance of catching them. I should have guessed that Scar-Neck might smash that lamp.'

Everyone had been glad of the rest and fresh air. Now Bill got up and looked down hill. How could they get down without being torn to bits by the barbed wire? No one felt inclined to wriggle down the tunnel Scar-Neck had made below it.

Bill saw someone about below. He gave a hail, and the man looked up, evidently overcome with surprise to see so many people standing high up on the hillside.

'Who are you?' he yelled.

'Friends!' shouted back Bill. 'Is Colonel Yarmouth there? I know him, and would like to talk to him. But I can't get through this wire.'

'Look!' said Jack suddenly, and pointed to a beautiful camera standing under a thick bramble. 'That's how they got their pictures! With that! It's one of the finest cameras I've ever seen. It hasn't been hurt by the deluge either – it's got a waterproof protection. I expect that camera you gave me is ruined now, Bill. It was in the gorse bush and had no protection at all. I left it there, unfortunately.'

'What a pity!' said Bill. 'Well – maybe I can arrange for you to have this one instead – as a little return for letting me in on your adventure, Jack!'

Jack's eyes gleamed. What pictures he could take if he had a camera like that! It must be one of the finest in the world.

Another man now came out in the grounds at the back of the farm-house below. Jack had expected a colonel to be in uniform, but he wasn't.

'Hi, Yarmouth!' yelled Bill. 'Don't you know me?'

'Well, I'm blessed!' floated up the Colonel's astonished voice. 'I'll send a couple of men up to make a way down for you.'

So, in a fairly short time, a way was made for them through the rows of barbed wire which was promptly repaired again behind them. They went down to the farm-house, slithering and almost falling down the steep descent.

The Colonel and Bill disappeared into the house, to talk. The others waited patiently outside. Jack and Philip lay down on the heather and yawned. They both fell asleep at once!

After a while the Colonel and Bill came out and snapped out a few orders. Three of his men took away the captives and they were put into a whitewashed room near by, which looked as if it had once been a dairy. The door was shut and padlocked.

'That's got rid of *them*!' said Bill, pleased. 'Now we'll get back to Spring Cottage. I'm afraid we'll have to go down to the bottom of the hill, take the road there, and then make our way up the other side to the cottage. There is apparently no other way to get there.'

The boys, awake now, groaned. They really didn't feel like any more walking. Still, it had to be done.

'What about the maps, or whatever they were, we left behind in the hidden room?' asked Jack.

'Oh, we can easily get those. One of the Colonel's men will go up through that passage and get them as soon as the water has stopped,' said Bill. 'And the three prisoners will be sent down sometime today under guard, to be dealt with later.'

'I suppose the adventure is over?' said Philip. 'Quite finished?'

'Well – there are a few loose ends to tie up,' said Bill. 'We must just see if we can find any trace of Scar-Neck and his friend in any of the districts near at hand. Scar-Neck will probably cut off his fine beard – but if he does that he shows his scar, unless he can paint it out. We may get on his track again and catch him. That would really be a most satisfactory finish, wouldn't it!'

'We'll have to go and get your car too, won't we?' said Jack, remembering. 'We left it at the beginning of the landslide.'

'So we did,' said Bill. 'My word, I hope it hasn't been swept away by that deluge of rain – or buried in another landslide!'

'I want to know what happened to the girls too,' said Philip. 'I'm hoping they all got back safely before the storm really started. It seems ages since I've seen them!'

They went on down the hillside, guided by a man from the farmhouse. He was extremely interested in their adventures, but wasn't told much beyond that they had got caught in the castle in the storm, and had had to find their way through an old passage.

Button was now running at Philip's heels, happy to be in the open air. Even he had played his part in the adventure, for he had shown Tassie how to get in and out of the castle without using doors, gates or windows!

They came to the bottom of the hill and took the road there. Then they came to the lane that led up to Spring Cottage.

'There it is at last!' cried Jack, and sprinted up to it. 'Hi, girls, here we are! Where are you?'

31

The end of the castle of adventure

There was a shriek from the cottage. It was Lucy-Ann of course. She came flying out of the door, her eyes shining, and flew straight at Jack. She almost bowled him over in her joy at seeing him again.

'Jack! You're back! And Philip! Wherever did you get to? We were awfully worried about you!'

Dinah and Tassie came running out too, exclaiming in pleasure. 'Were you all right in the storm? We got so worried about you! Tassie's been up the hill and she says half the castle has fallen down the hill!'

'Were *you* all right in that storm?' asked Jack, as they all went into the little house. 'We were very worried about you three girls having to go down the hill in that awful deluge! Did you get home before the storm really broke?'

'Well, the rain had begun, and there was thunder rolling round nearly all the time, but no lightning,' said Dinah. 'We were soaked by the time we got here. Tassie wouldn't let us rest for even a minute on the hill – she kept saying that there would be another landslide – and she was right!'

'Good old Tassie,' said Jack. 'She just got you back in time. I simply can't begin to tell you what it was like up in the castle!'

But he did tell them, of course, and they listened with their eyes wide open in horror. What a night!

'Where's Kiki?' asked Jack, looking all round. 'I thought she would be here to greet me.'

'She keeps flying off to look for you,' said Tassie. 'But she comes back. She won't be long, I'm sure.'

She wasn't. In about ten minutes' time she was back, sailing through the air, shouting loudly to Jack.

'How many times, how many times, how many times, fusty, musty, dusty, Jack, Jack, Jack!'

She flew to his shoulder and pecked his ear lovingly. Philip put up his hand to his left ear which was still swollen.

'Don't you fly on to *my* shoulder and peck *my* ear,' he said to Kiki. 'It's not ready for pecking or nibbling yet!'

The girls got breakfast for everyone, and talked nineteen to the dozen, happy at having the boys and Bill. Bill sent his three men up the road to find his car.

'And now,' said Bill, when they had finished eating, 'what about a sleep, boys? I'm tired out!'

Jack was almost asleep as it was, and Philip kept yawning. So the boys went up to sleep on their beds and Bill put himself on the couch in the kitchen. The girls went out into the garden to talk.

They had to put waterproofs down on the grass because it was so wet. The day was lovely now, with not a cloud to be seen. It was fresh and cool. The stormy heat had completely gone.

They lazed there, chattering, with Kiki joining in now and again. Button was asleep on Philip's middle upstairs. Kiki was not sleepy, so she did not go with Jack, but contented herself with taking a look at him now and again through the window, to make sure he was there.

'There's someone coming,' said Dinah suddenly. She sat up and looked.

'It's Bill's three men,' said Lucy-Ann, lazily.

The men came into the garden. They looked serious. 'Where's the Boss? We want him,' said one.

'He's asleep, so don't disturb him yet,' said Dinah.

'Sorry, missie, but I'm afraid we must disturb him,' said

the man. 'We've got news.'

'What news?' asked Lucy-Ann. 'Have you found the car?'

'Yes,' said the man. 'But we'll tell our news to the Boss, missie.'

'Well, he's in the kitchen,' said Dinah.

The men moved off to the kitchen. They woke Bill, and the three girls heard them telling him something in urgent, serious voices. Bill came out, and the girls looked enquiringly at him.

'What's up, Bill?' asked Dinah. 'Have they found your car – and is it smashed up, or something?'

'They've found my car all right,' said Bill, slowly. 'And they've found something else too.'

'What!' asked the three girls together.

'Well, apparently Scar-Neck and his friend went off over the landslide quite safely, and then found my car standing where we left it,' said Bill. 'They must have got into it and turned it round – and then the deluge struck them, and another landslide began!'

'Are they – killed?' asked Dinah.

'Well, I imagine so,' said Bill. 'We don't know. The landslide caught the car and took it along. It dumped it upside-down in a gully, where these men found it – with Scar-Neck and the other fellow inside.'

'Can't they get them out then?' asked Dinah, rather pale.

'The doors are jammed,' said Bill. 'Have you got a wire tow-rope, or any good strong rope that won't break? If you have, we'll take it and try to get the car the right way up. Then we may be able to open the roof and get the men out.'

Dinah fetched some wire rope from the shed. She gave it to Bill in silence. None of the girls asked to go with the men. This seemed a terrible ending, even to two bad men.

They waited impatiently for the boys to awake, and when at last they came down, yawning and complaining of feeling hungry again, the girls ran to tell them the news.

'Golly!' said Jack, startled. 'Fancy them finding the car like that! They must have thought it was a bit of luck. And then another landslide catches them – what a frightful shock they must have had!'

Bill came back some hours later. The children ran to meet him.

Bill was smiling. 'Neither of the men is dead,' he said. 'Scar-Neck has concussion and is quite unconscious and rather badly hurt. The other fellow has a broken leg, and was stunned too. But he's come round.'

'So you've captured them both after all!' said Philip. 'Well done, Bill!'

'What about the car?' asked Dinah.

'Looks wrecked to me,' said Bill. 'But I don't mind that. I reckon I shall be handed out a new car when my chief knows I've got Scar-Neck and his friend to pass over to him. It's quite a scoop for me – though I'd never have stumbled on to their secret if it hadn't been for you children!'

'Well, we'd have been in a pretty pickle if *you* hadn't turned up,' said Jack. 'Whatever will Aunt Allie say when she comes back and hears all that has happened since she has been gone?'

'She'll say she can't turn her back for a day or two without us all getting into mischief!' said Philip, with a grin. 'Where are the men, Bill?'

'I sent Tom down to the village for help, instead of taking him back to the car with me,' said Bill. 'And they sent up a couple of stretchers and a doctor who happened to be down there – so they will be on their way to hospital by now, I imagine – and when they wake up, they'll each find a nice burly policeman sitting by the side of their bed!'

'Oh, Bill – what an adventure!' said Dinah. 'I never dreamt we'd plunge into all this when we first came here – and it's all happened so quickly. I hope we shall have nice peaceful holidays for the rest of the time. I've had enough adventures to last me for a year!'

'I want to stretch my legs,' said Jack. 'What about walking up the hillside, Bill, and having a look to see what has happened to the castle?'

'Right,' said Bill, so they set off up the road to the castle. But they could not go nearly so far as usual, because the landslide had come a good deal farther down, and the hillside was a terrible, jumbled mass of wet rocks, heaps of soil, uprooted trees and running streams – a desolate-looking region, indeed.

'It's horrid,' said Lucy-Ann. Then she turned to gaze at the frowning castle, higher up. 'The castle looks different. Something's happened to it. Let's climb up and see.'

So they climbed up higher, taking the little rabbit path they always used. What a difference they found as they came near the castle!

'Two of the towers have gone, and most of the walls,' said Lucy-Ann, awed. 'We can walk right into the courtyard now, over the rubble of stones. What a noise they must have made when they fell!'

'And look at the castle! The middle part of it has fallen in! It's not much more than a shell now!' said Jack, staring.

It looked almost a ruin. Philip stared hard at it. 'The middle part must have crashed down into the big hall,' he said. 'No wonder you couldn't move that entrance stone, Bill. There must be tons of fallen boulders on top of it!'

Bill looked rather solemn. He could see what a narrow escape from death they had all had. If they had been anywhere else in the castle or courtyard they would have been crushed and buried. Being down in the hidden room had saved their lives!

'Good-bye to my camera and all our rugs and things,' said Jack.'

'I'll replace everything you have lost,' promised Bill, who, now that he had actually captured Scar-Neck, was ready to promise the whole world to anyone! 'And I'll give you all a fine present each for letting me share such a grand adventure!'

'Me too?' said Tassie, at once. She liked Bill.

'You too,' said Bill. 'What would you like, Tassie?'

'Three pairs of shoes all for myself,' said Tassie solemnly, and the others laughed. They knew Tassie wouldn't wear them. She would just keep them and love and admire them – but she would never wear them. Tassie didn't need to!

'Let's go back,' said Lucy-Ann. 'I don't want to look at that ruin any more.'

'Nor do I,' said Dinah, 'but somehow I feel as if it's better as a ruin, open to anyone who cares to explore it, than as a castle owned by wicked old men, or spies like Scar-Neck. I like it better now! I'm glad to think of those musty old rooms all buried away – they were horrid!'

'Fusty, musty, dusty!' sang Kiki, in delight. 'Pop goes the fusty, musty, dusty!'

'Idiot!' said Jack. 'You *will* always have the last word, won't you, Kiki?'

Then down the hill they went in the sunshine, leaving behind them the sad, broken old castle, its roof open to the wind and the rain, its proud towers fallen.

'The Castle of Adventure!' said Jack. 'You were right, Philip – it *was* the Castle of Adventure!'

Enid Blyton

The Valley of
Adventure

Contents

1

Up in Bill's aeroplane

Kiki the parrot was annoyed. She had been left all alone for a day, and she talked angrily to herself.

'What a pity, what a pity, what a pity, poor, poor Polly! Ding-dong bell, Polly's down the well, good morning, good morning!'

Mrs Mannering put her head in at the door of the room where Kiki was sitting.

'Kiki, don't be so absurd! Talking away to yourself all day like that! The children will soon be back.'

'Ding-dong bell,' said Kiki mournfully, and made a cracking noise with her beak.

'I suppose you miss Jack,' said Mrs Mannering, coming into the room and shutting the door carefully behind her. 'He won't be long now, Kiki. You'll hear him and the others any minute. Now be a good bird and don't make any more noise.'

Kiki opened her beak, swelled up her throat and gave her famous imitation of an express train screeching on entering a tunnel. Mrs Mannering put her hands to her ears.

'Naughty Kiki, naughty! How many times have we told you not to do that?'

'How many times have I told you to shut the door, shut the door, shut the door,' answered back Kiki, and ruffled up her feathers so cheekily that Mrs Mannering gave her a tap on her beak.

'Funny old bird,' she said. 'Ah, listen — that sounds like the children coming back. They've been up in an aeroplane, Kiki! Fancy that! That's why you had to be left alone all day!'

'Jack, Jack, Jack!' screamed Kiki, hearing the voice of her owner. Four children burst into the room, their faces red with excitement.

'Hallo, all of you!' said Mrs Mannering. 'How did you like it? Was it fun being so high up in the air?'

'Oh, *Mother!* It was the greatest fun in the world!'

'Aunt Allie, I shall buy an aeroplane of my own as soon as ever I'm grown up.'

'Mother, you ought to have come. Bill piloted the plane and he was *marvellous*.'

'I wasn't airsick, Aunt Allie, though Bill gave me a paper bag to be sick in.'

Mrs Mannering laughed. All the four spoke at once, and she had hard work to make out what they said. Kiki gave a loving screech and flew to Jack's shoulder.

The four children sank into chairs and prepared to relate their day's adventure. There were Philip and Dinah, Mrs Mannering's children, dark-eyed, dark-haired just as she was, and both with tufts of hair that insisted on sticking up in front. Both Dinah and Philip were called Tufty at school. Then there were the other two, Jack and Lucy-Ann, brother and sister, who had no mother and father, and lived with 'Aunt Allie,' as they called Mrs Mannering. All four were like one family.

Jack and Lucy-Ann Trent were very alike. They both had red hair and green eyes, and were so covered with freckles that it was quite impossible to find a bit of pink skin on their faces, arms or legs. It was not surprising that Jack was so often called Freckles.

Kiki the parrot belonged to him. He had had her for years, an amusing and talkative parrot, with a gift for repeating anything she heard, and for imitating any noise, from a sewing machine to an express train. She adored Jack and was miserable when she was not with him.

Jack had a passion for birds, and Philip had a great liking

for animals of all kinds. He was wonderfully good with them, and they obeyed him and loved him in a marvellous manner. He always had some kind of unusual pet about him, which caused quarrels between him and his sister Dinah, who was scared of most animals and of nearly all insects. But now all four were thinking of nothing whatever but their glorious flight in their friend Bill's new aeroplane.

Bill Smugs was their firm friend. He and they had had hair-raising adventures together. In one adventure they had gone down old copper mines to track clever forgers. In another they had happened on a nest of dangerous spies. As Bill Smugs said, those children simply '*fell* into adventures.'

Now Bill had actually been presented with a fine aeroplane, to help him in his work. The children had been wild with excitement when he had written to tell them this at school.

'I bet he'll take us up for a flight,' said Jack. 'I just bet he will.'

'We'll make him,' said Philip. But they didn't need to make him, for he was quite willing to show off his aeroplane to them, and to demonstrate how well he could fly it after only a short training.

'Mother, we went far higher than the clouds,' said Dinah. 'I looked down on them and they didn't look like clouds a bit. They looked like a great big snow field. It gave me quite a funny feeling.'

'I had a parachute strapped to me in case I fell, and Bill showed me the ripcord I had to pull in case of danger,' said Lucy-Ann, the youngest, her eyes shining. 'But there wasn't any danger.'

'We flew right over our old home, Craggy-Tops,' said Philip. 'It was so strange, looking down on top of it. And we flew over here too, Mother, and our house looked like a toy one.'

'Aunt Allie, Bill says it's frightfully exciting flying at

9

night, and seeing the little pinpricks of lights shining up from the dark countryside,' said Jack. 'We begged and begged him to take us on a night flight, but he said he would have to ask *you*. You will say we can go, won't you? Golly! I can't imagine what the boys at school will say when I tell them about going up in a private plane, day and night.'

'Day and night,' repeated Kiki. 'Ding-dong bell.'

'She's got ding-dong bell on the brain,' said Jack. 'There's a small child next door who keeps reciting nursery rhymes, and Kiki listens and picks up bits of them. Yesterday she kept moaning about "three blind mice," today it's "ding-dong bell." Don't know what it will be tomorrow.'

'Humpy dumpy,' said Kiki obligingly.

'Humpty, dumpty,' corrected Jack. 'Not humpy dumpy.'

'Humpy dumpy bumpy,' said Kiki solemnly, and scratched her head with a claw. 'Humpy, dumpy . . . '

'All right, all right,' said Jack. 'Aunt Allie, *can* we go up at night with Bill? He's coming to ask you tomorrow, so do say yes.'

'I suppose I shall have to,' said Mrs Mannering with a laugh. 'You and Bill! So long as you don't go headlong into another awful adventure.'

'Adventures aren't awful,' said Philip. 'They are simply lovely!'

'Not to the people who aren't in them,' said Mrs Mannering. 'I feel quite ill sometimes when I think of the adventures you children have had. No more, please.'

'All right. We won't get into any more these summer holidays,' said Lucy-Ann, giving her aunt a hug. 'We won't worry you. I don't want any more adventures anyhow. I've had enough.'

'Well, if we *do* have another, we'll leave you out of it, Lucy-Ann.' said Dinah scornfully.

'No, we won't,' said Philip, giving Dinah a poke in the

back. 'We can't do without Lucy-Ann.'

'Now, don't quarrel, you two,' said Mrs Mannering, foreseeing one of their everlasting squabbles boiling up. 'You're tired now, all of you, after such a lot of excitement. Go and do something quiet till supper time.'

'Sing for your supper,' put in Kiki. The children laughed.

'You're an idiot, Kiki,' said Jack affectionately. 'Did you miss us today? Well, I was scared you might fly out of the aeroplane in fright, if we took you. But I expect you'd have been quite a sensible old bird, wouldn't you, and sat on my shoulder all the time?'

Kiki pecked lovingly at Jack's ear, and made a crooning noise. She sat as close to him as she could. The children began to talk about their exciting day.

'Wasn't it lovely going to the aerodrome and getting in on our passes, and walking up to Bill just as if we were grown-ups?' said Philip. 'And golly, wasn't Bill's aeroplane fine?'

'I didn't think it would be so big,' said Lucy-Ann. 'You know, it was funny – I sort of held my breath when we started off, thinking I'd get a funny feeling when we left the ground, like I do in a lift – and I never even knew when the wheels left the runway and we were in the air! I got quite a shock when I looked down and saw we were over the housetops.'

'It seemed awfully easy to fly a plane,' said Jack. 'Easier than driving a car. I wish Bill would let me have a shot.'

'Well, he won't,' said Philip. 'I say, wasn't it odd when we got into the air pocket and the plane suddenly dropped down without warning? My tummy sort of went up into my throat.'

The others laughed. 'Mine did too,' said Lucy-Ann. 'I'm glad I wasn't sick. It was a waste of that nice strong paper bag, but I'm glad I felt all right.'

'We went hundreds of miles, I should think,' said Jack. 'I

11

felt a bit funny when we were over the sea. It looked so enormous and so flat. I shouldn't like to fall out over that! What a splash!'

'I bet mother will say we can go on a night flight with Bill,' said Dinah. 'I could see in her face that she was going to say yes. If only we could! Bill said we could fly to his old home, land at dawn, and spend the rest of the night with him, sleeping all we liked in his two spare rooms – we needn't get up till twelve if we didn't want to. Fancy flying all night and going to bed at dawn!'

'Then we'd fly back in the afternoon, I suppose,' said Jack. 'Gosh, I'm glad we've got Bill for a friend. I do think he's an exciting sort of person. It's thrilling, too, to know that he's always on some sort of secret job, and never says a word about it – always snooping out some deadly secret. I wonder if he's on any job now?'

'You bet he is!' said Philip. 'That's why he's got this aeroplane. May have to take off at any moment after spies or somebody. Hope I'm with him when he does.'

'Well, you won't be,' said Dinah. 'Bill would never run us into danger.'

'I shouldn't mind if he did,' said Philip. 'Hallo, there's the gong for supper! I'm jolly hungry.'

'That's nothing new,' said Dinah. 'Come on – let's go and see what there is. Smells like bacon and eggs.'

They went to their supper. They were all hungry, and finished up the eggs and bacon and plum cake in no time. Kiki helped herself to the plum cake too, till Mrs Mannering protested.

'Jack! *Will* you stop Kiki picking all the raisins out of that cake? Look at the mess she's making! There won't be any cake left soon. Smack her on her beak.'

'Naughty Kiki!' said Jack, and tapped her on her beak. 'Don't eat it all.'

'How many times have I told . . . ' began Kiki, but Jack

12

was too tired to talk to her.

'Don't argue,' he said. 'I'm so sleepy I'll have to go to bed.'

Everyone felt the same – so off they went, and were soon asleep and dreaming of flying aeroplanes over the clouds, somersaulting and looping the loop in a most amazing but perfectly safe manner.

2

Bill gets his way

Bill came along to lunch the next day. He had a ruddy face, twinkling eyes and a rather bald head with plenty of hair at each side. The children rushed to meet him. Mrs Mannering smiled at him.

'You gave the children a wonderful time yesterday,' she said. 'And now I hear that you want to take them on a night flight. I can't think why you want to bother yourself with a pack of children like these.'

'Ah – you never know when they're going to embark on some wonderful adventure,' said Bill Smugs, grinning round at them. 'I don't want to be left out of it, you know. Besides, I feel sorry for you, Mrs Mannering, having to put up with them for eight or nine weeks these summer holidays – I thought it would be a kind deed if I took them off your hands for a while.'

'Well, what do you want them to do?' asked Mrs Mannering. 'Just go for a night flight, spend the night at your old home and come back the next day?'

'That was the first idea I had,' said Bill. 'But now I hear I'm due to have three or four days off – and I thought maybe you could spare the children for longer. We could fly to my old home, and then stay there and mess about a bit. There

13

are heaps of wild birds for Jack to see, and I've no doubt that Philip will find plenty of even wilder animals. The girls will enjoy the change too.'

'Oh! It *does* sound good!' cried Jack, and the others agreed. Mrs Mannering listened and thought for a moment.

'Yes – I don't see why they shouldn't go with you, Bill. I know you'll look after them all right and see that they don't get mixed up in any awful adventure again.'

'I can promise you that,' said Bill. 'There are no adventures to be found anywhere near my old home. It's a most peaceful, quiet place. Nothing doing at all.'

'Well, if you promise not to rush into danger or trouble, you can go,' said Mrs Mannering to the delighted children. 'When do you want them, Bill?'

'Tomorrow, if possible,' said Bill. 'The job I am on seems to be hanging fire at the moment, so I might as well take my few days now.'

'What's the job, Bill? Do, do tell us!' begged Lucy-Ann. Bill laughed.

'I couldn't possibly tell,' he said. 'All my work is secret, you know that. I'll tell you all about the job when it's over and done with, though. You'll find it jolly interesting.'

'We'll have to pack suitcases, won't we?' said Dinah. 'If we're going to stay a few days, I mean. We may want a change of clothes – and macks.'

'Yes, bring jerseys and shorts to mess about in,' said Bill, 'and macks too, because it always seems to rain at my home. And, Mrs Mannering, could you spare a few rugs, as I may not have quite enough blankets for so many visitors?'

'Of course,' said Mrs Mannering. 'I'll look some out for you.'

'I'll bring my lovely camera,' said Jack. 'There'll be room for odds and ends like that in the plane, won't there, Bill?'

'Plenty,' said Bill. 'Bring your field glasses too, because

14

you may want to have a squint at the different birds in the hills around.'

'Oh, it *will* be exciting!' said Jack, his eyes shining at the thought. 'I can't wait till tomorrow. Let's go today!'

'The plane's not ready,' said Bill. 'Got to have something done to her today. Anyway, my leave doesn't start till tomorrow. You get everything packed and ready, and come to the aerodrome tomorrow night. Be there at eleven o'clock sharp. I'll order a car to call for you and take you there.'

'What a time to start on a journey!' said Mrs Mannering. 'I don't know that I *al*together like it.'

'You can't change your mind now, you can't!' cried the children.

'No, I won't,' said Mrs Mannering. 'But somehow I don't feel very easy in my mind about it all. Oh, children, you won't go and do anything dangerous, will you?'

'There's nothing dangerous for them to do,' said Bill. 'I'll look after them all right. Anyone doing anything dangerous will be sent back to you, Mrs Mannering.'

The children laughed. Then Jack's face fell. 'I say – what about Kiki? She won't like me being away for some days. Can I take her with me? What about the plane – will she be all right in it?'

'You'd better put her into a basket or something,' said Bill. 'She might get scared at the noise and fly off. She'll be all right in a basket on your knee. We can't leave her behind.'

'Right,' said Jack pleased. 'Do you hear that, Kiki old bird? You're to travel in a basket – and mind you behave yourself!'

'Wipe your feet,' said Kiki, 'put the kettle on, kettle on! Poor, poor Polly!'

'Idiot!' said Jack, and scratched her poll. 'All I hope is that you don't try to imitate the noise an aeroplane makes. Your express train screech is bad enough.'

They all had a pleasant lunch and then Bill departed. The

15

children went upstairs to put together their things. Dinah put a whole packet of chocolate into her case, in case there were no shops at Bill's home. Jack stuffed a packet of biscuits into his case. He often woke up at night and liked a biscuit to nibble then.

'Better take plenty of films with you Jack, if you're thinking of photographing birds,' said Philip. 'I bet there won't be anywhere to buy them where Bill lives. It's somewhere buried right down in the country.'

Mrs Mannering came up to see what they were packing. It was a cold August, with rather a lot of rain, and the children would need a fair amount of warm things. They had put in pullovers and jerseys and macks and sou'westers. She added rubber boots too, thinking that shoes would not be of much use if they walked over wet fields.

'I've found you some rugs,' she said. 'You can each take one. They are old, but very thick and warm, and as good as two blankets. If Bill hasn't enough blankets for you it won't matter at all – the rugs will give you plenty of warmth. Don't forget to bring them back, now!'

Jack got his camera ready. He looked out his rolls of films. He debated whether or not to take one of his bird books with him, and then decided not to, because his suitcase was already very heavy.

'Everything's done now, Aunt Allie,' said Lucy-Ann, sitting on her suitcase to make it shut. 'I wish tomorrow would hurry up and come. Fancy flying in the dark in Bill's plane! I never in my life thought I would do that. I hope it's a long long way to Bill's home.'

'It is,' said Mrs Mannering. 'Now let me see – I'd better pack you sandwiches and cake to take with you for the journey, because you are sure to be hungry if you stay up all night. I'll do those tomorrow. Have you found a basket for Kiki, Jack? And what about taking some food for her?

There's a new packet of sunflower seeds come today. Put it into your suitcase.'

Jack found a good basket for Kiki, with a lid that closed down. He put it on the table. Kiki flew over to it at once in curiosity. She hopped inside and looked out comically.

'Clever bird,' said Jack. 'You know it's your travelling basket, don't you?'

'God save the Queen!' said Kiki, and began to rub her curved beak up and down the edge of the basket.

'Don't do that, said Jack. 'You'll break it. Stop it, Kiki!'

Kiki climbed out and flew to Jack's shoulder. She rubbed her beak against his hair.

'Ding-dong bell,' she murmured. 'Polly's in the well. Ding-dong bell.'

'Polly's in the basket, you mean,' said Lucy-Ann. 'Kiki, you're going in an aeroplane. Think of that!'

The day went slowly — far too slowly for the children. The next day was even slower. By the time that tea time came the children felt that night would never never come.

But when supper time came they felt more cheerful. The car was coming at a quarter past ten to take them to the aerodrome. Then into the plane they would get with Bill and off they would go into the darkness. Somehow it seemed far more thrilling to fly through the dark night than through the sunshiny day.

Ten o'clock struck. The suitcases and rugs were taken down to the hall. Jack's camera was there too, and a large packet of sandwiches and cakes. Jack wore his field glasses on a strap over his shoulder. Kiki's basket was in the hall also, but Kiki was still free. She was not going into the basket till the last moment.

'Here's the car!' cried Philip, his sharp ears hearing the engine purring up to the door. 'Come along! Goodbye, Mother! Look after yourself well till we come back!'

17

'Goodbye, Aunt Allie,' said Jack, giving her a hug. 'We'll send you a postcard. Hi, Kiki, come on – it's time you got into your basket.'

Kiki made a bit of a fuss going in. She was excited because of the excitement of the four children. It took quite a time to get her into the basket and shut the lid down. She began to shout at the top of her voice.

'Poor Polly, poor Polly, down the well, down the well, up the hill, in the corner!'

'She's mixing up Ding-dong bell and Jack and Jill and Jack Horner,' said Lucy-Ann with a giggle. 'Be quiet, Kiki! You ought to be glad you're coming with us, even if you have to travel in a shut basket!'

All the goodbyes were said. 'I don't like letting you go, somehow,' said Mrs Mannering. 'It's silly of me – but I don't. I've got an uncomfortable feeling – as if you're going off into another dreadful adventure.'

'We promise not to,' said Philip earnestly. 'Don't you worry, Mother. We'll be all right, and you'll see us turning up, like bad pennies, in a few days' time. Anyway, Bill's on the phone and you can always ring him.'

The taxi revved up its engine. It moved off down the drive, with Mrs Mannering left standing at the door, waving. The children waved back, excited. They were really off.

'Now for the aerodrome!' said Philip, pleased. 'I thought tonight would never come. What's the time? Oh, we're early. Good. Got the passes, Jack?'

'Dinah's got them in her bag,' said Jack. Dinah fished them out. They were passes that would take them into the aerodrome, and up to Bill himself.

It was a good way to the aerodrome. The night was very dark. Clouds covered the sky, and a few drops of rain spattered the windscreen.

'Here's the aerodrome at last!' cried Jack, seeing the lights through the window. 'Look at the flare-path – all lit up. Isn't

18

it fine? Don't the aeroplanes look enormous in the shadows at each side? Here, Dinah – where are the passes? We've got to show them now.'

The passes were shown to the man at the entrance to the aerodrome and the children went in.

'I'll set you down here and you can speak to your friend,' said the taxi man. 'Then I'll run on to his aeroplane and dump the luggage beside it for you. So long!'

'Now we'll find Bill,' said Philip as the car drove off. 'There he is, look! Hi, Bill, we're here!'

3

A grave mistake

Bill was talking to three or four men very earnestly. He waved to the children, a tall, burly shadow in the night.

'Hallo, kids! I'm busy for a few minutes. You cut along to the aeroplane and wait for me. Stow your cases in at the back where mine is. I'll be about ten minutes or so.'

'Right, Bill,' said Jack, and the four of them moved off to where the taxi man had put their cases, beside an aeroplane not very far away.

It was dark where the aeroplane stood, but the children could see enough to pick up their cases. They climbed up the ladder and into the cabin.

The inside of the plane was in darkness. The children had no idea how to put the lights on. They felt their way to the back of the plane and put down their things. They threw their rugs there too. Jack put Kiki's basket down carefully Kiki had been most indignant all the way.

'Humpy dumpy bumpy,' she said. 'Pop goes the weasel!'

There was a large crate in the middle of the plane. The

children wondered what was in it. Was it empty or full? It must be something Bill was taking back with him.

'It's blocking up all the inside,' said Jack. 'We can't sit down properly with that thing there. Let's squat down on our rugs at the back. We'll be quite comfortable there. Perhaps Bill will shift the crate a bit when he comes, and tell us where he wants us to sit.'

So they sat down patiently on their rugs and waited. The noise of the plane's engines went on and on, and it was impossible to hear anything else, though once Jack thought he could hear somebody shouting.

He went to the door and looked out. But all was darkness and Bill was nowhere to be seen. What a time he was!

He went back to his place, yawning. Lucy-Ann was half asleep. 'I wish Bill would come,' said Philip. 'I shall go to sleep if he doesn't.'

Then a lot of things happened very quickly indeed. Over and above the sound of the engine came the sound of shots — gunshots. That made the children sit up in a hurry.

Then another shot sounded — and then there came the noise of someone clambering hurriedly up the steps into the plane, and a man flung himself down in the control seat. Another followed, panting, hardly to be seen in the darkness. The children sat as if they were frozen. What in the world was happening? Was one of the men Bill? Who was the other — and what was the hurry? The first man took the controls of the plane, and to the children's amazement it began to taxi forwards. They were off! But why hadn't Bill spoken to them? Why hadn't he at least looked round to see that they were safely inside?

'Keep quiet,' said Jack to the others. 'If Bill doesn't want to speak to us, there's a reason. Maybe he doesn't want the other fellow to know we're here. Keep quiet.'

The plane rose into the air, its propellers making a great whirring noise. It headed swiftly into the wind.

The men shouted to one another, but the children could not make out what they were saying because the noise of the engine was so loud. They sat quiet and still, hidden from view by the big crate standing in the middle of the plane.

Bill said nothing to them at all. He didn't call out to know if they were there. He didn't send his companion along to see if they were all right. He simply took no notice of them at all. It was very queer and Lucy-Ann didn't like it a bit.

One of the men fiddled about and found a switch. He pulled it down and a light shone out just by the men, but the rest of the plane was still in darkness. Philip peeped round the crate, meaning to catch Bill's eye if he could.

Almost at once he came back to the others, and sat down very quietly. He said nothing.

'What's up?' asked Jack, sensing the Philip was worried.

'You go and look round that crate,' said Philip. 'Have a good look at the two men.'

Jack went and peered round. He came back feeling puzzled and scared. 'Neither of those men is Bill,' he said 'Golly – it's funny!'

'What do you mean?' said Lucy-Ann in alarm. 'One must be Bill. Why, this is Bill's aeroplane!'

'Yes, but *is* it?' said Dinah suddenly. 'Look where the light catches those seats, Lucy-Ann – they are red – and the ones in Bill's plane were green. I remember them quite well.'

'So they were,' said Jack, remembering too. 'Golly! We're in the wrong plane!'

There was a long silence. Nobody knew what to think about it. They were in the wrong plane – not Bill's at all! Two strange men sat at the controls – men who would probably be extremely angry when they found their unexpected passengers. Neither Jack nor Philip liked the look of the men in the least. They had really only seen the backs of their heads, and the side face of the man when he had turned to shout to his companion – but neither of the boys had felt

21

drawn to the two men.

'They've got such thick necks,' thought Jack. 'Oh, gosh this is awful! And there were those shots, too — were they anything to do with these men? They clambered into the plane in a frightful hurry and set off at once. I do believe we've stumbled into an adventure again.'

Philip spoke cautiously to the others. It was no good whispering, because whispers couldn't possibly be heard. So Philip had to speak loudly, and trust that he would not be heard by the men in front.

'What are we going to do? We *have* got into the wrong plane! That's the fault of that stupid taxi-man, putting down our things by the wrong aeroplane. It was so dark that we ourselves couldn't possibly tell which plane was which.'

Lucy-Ann sat close to Jack, frightened. It wasn't very nice to be high up in the air, lost in the darkness, in the wrong aeroplane with men that none of them had seen before.

'What *can* we do?' wondered Jack. 'We really are in a mess. Honestly, those two men won't half be mad when they see us!'

'They might tip us out,' said Lucy-Ann in alarm. 'And we haven't got parachutes on. Jack, don't let them know we're here.'

'They'll have to know sooner or later,' said Dinah. 'What idiots we are — getting into the wrong plane! I never thought of that.'

There was a silence again, with everyone thinking very hard.

'Shall we just stay here at the back of the plane on our rugs, and hope we shan't be noticed?' said Philip. 'Then, when we arrive somewhere maybe we can slip out of the plane and look for help.'

'Yes — that's the best idea,' said Jack. 'We are well hidden here, unless the men come round to the back for something. Maybe they will arrive at their destination, get out without

22

seeing us, and then we can slip out ourselves and ask for help to get back home.'

'I did want to stay with Bill,' said Lucy-Ann, almost in tears. 'Whatever will he be thinking?'

'Goodness knows!' said Jack gloomily. 'He'll be hunting all over the aerodrome for us. You know, I believe that must have been Bill I heard shouting, when I went to the door to see. He must have gone to his own plane, found we weren't there and yelled for us. Dash! If only I'd guessed that!'

'Well, it's too late now,' said Philip. 'I hope Mother won't be worried. Oh dear – she'll think we've fallen headlong into another adventure. And we promised not to.'

The aeroplane roared on through the dark night. The children had no idea whether they were flying north, south, east or west. Then Jack remembered his pocket compass and took it out.

'We're flying east,' he said. 'I wonder where we're going to. I don't somehow feel as if I'm in a plane at all, as I can't look out and see the ground far below.'

The others felt the same. Lucy-Ann lay down on the rugs and yawned. 'I'm going to sleep,' she said. 'I shall only feel frightened and worried if I keep awake.'

'It's a good idea of yours,' said Philip, and he stretched himself out on the rugs too. 'We shall be sure to wake up if we arrive anywhere.'

'Anyone want a sandwich or bit of cake?' asked Dinah, remembering the picnic packet. But nobody did. The shock of finding themselves in the wrong aeroplane had taken away their appetites completely.

Soon all of them but Jack were asleep. He lay awake, thinking hard. Had Bill been mixed up in the shooting they had heard? Were these two men anything to do with the job Bill had been working on – the 'secret' job? It might be just possible that Jack and the others might find out something that would help Bill. It was important not to let the two men know that they had some hidden passengers in their plane.

Kiki gave an exasperated screech in her basket. Jack jumped. He had forgotten Kiki. He tapped the basket and spoke in as low a voice as he could, hoping that Kiki would hear him.

'Shut up, Kiki! Don't make a noise, whatever you do. It's very important to be quiet. You hear me, Kiki? You must be quiet, be quiet, be quiet.'

'Be quiet,' repeated Kiki, from inside the basket. 'Shhhhhhhhhh!'

Jack couldn't help smiling. 'Yes,' he said, putting his face close to the basket. 'Shhhhhhhh!'

Kiki was quiet after that. She was a mischievous, noisy bird, but she would always be quiet if Jack wanted her to be. So she sat inside her basket, trying to tuck her head under her wing and go to sleep. But the loud sound of the plane's engine upset her. She had never heard such a noise before. She longed to imitate it, but fortunately she didn't try just then.

After a bit the two men changed places and the second one took over the controls. The first one yawned and stretched. He got up and Jack's heart almost stopped beating in fright. Was he going to come to the back of the plane? He wondered whether or not to wake the others.

But the man did not come to the back. He stood up for a few minutes as if to stretch his legs. then lighted a pipe. Blue smoke drifted to the back of the cabin. Jack was most relieved to see the man sit down again.

The boy soon grew sleepy too. He lay down close to the others, quite glad of his coat, for it was very cold. Soon he was asleep. Only Kiki kept awake, cracking her beak now and again, puzzled and wondering what this strange night adventure meant.

The plane flew on in darkness, passing over towns and villages, fields, rivers and woods. It passed over the sea to where the lights of ships shone dimly. Lights of the towns twinkled up, and here and there the flare path of an aerodrome shone up to the sky. But the plane did not fly down. It swept over them all, heading east, to the dawn.

Then, just before dawn, it began to cicle round more slowly. It dropped as it circled, and once banked so steeply that the children almost rolled over. It awoke them and they sat up, wondering where they were. They remembered at once and looked at one another with wide eyes.

'We're going to land. Where shall we find we are? Look out for a quick escape as soon as we get the chance,' they whispered to one another. 'Down we go – we're landing!'

4

Wherever can we be?

The aeroplane landed with a slight bump that shook the children and made them gasp. Then it ran along a little way on its huge wheels, and stopped. They had arrived.

But where? Dawn had come, and light came in at the windows, but it was not full morning yet. One of the men switched off the throbbing engines. At once a great quiet and peace came into the cabin. How marvellous not to have that enormous noise flooding into their ears any more! The children were glad.

They heard the men's voices. 'We've made good time – and a good landing too. You brought her in well, Juan.'

'We've not got much time to spare,' said Juan. 'Come on – let's get out and stretch our legs. We'll go to the hut and have a meal.'

To the children's enormous delight the men clambered out of the plane and disappeared. They hadn't even gone

25

round to the back of the crate and seen the children! Maybe they could escape and get help at once. Anyway they would be able to send word to Bill and Mrs Mannering telling them not to worry.

'Come on,' said Jack, getting up cautiously. 'Let's squint out of the window and see where we are. On an aerodrome, I hope. We'll probably see a mechanic or two, and ask them to direct us to someone in authority.'

They all crowded to the nearest window. But what a shock when they looked out!

They were not on an aerodrome at all. They were on a broad flat piece of grassland in a valley – and that valley seemed to be surrounded on all sides by towering mountains.

'Gosh!' said Jack. 'Where are we? Back of beyond, I should think.'

'We're in a valley,' said Philip. 'With mountains all round – awfully beautiful – but awfully lonely! How can we get help here? There won't be a plane to take us back, that's certain.'

There wasn't a house or any kind of building to be seen. The view from the other side of the plane was exactly the same – mountains on every side. They seemed to be at the bottom of them, in a green valley. It was very strange. Why should the men come there?

'What are we going to do?' asked Dinah. 'Do we get out – or stay in – or what?'

'Well – I don't know what you think, Philip,' said Jack, 'but I don't like any of this. I don't like those men, I don't like the way they flew off in the middle of the night after what sounded like a lot of shooting – and I don't like this lonely valley either. But all the same I think it would be a good idea if we got out and snooped round a bit. There must be people somewhere about – shepherds, perhaps – somebody like that.'

'What country are we in?' asked Lucy-Ann. 'Shall we be

able to speak their language?'

'I don't suppose so for a minute,' said Philip. 'But we'll just have to try and make ourselves understood.'

'I wonder what those men have come here for,' said Dinah thoughtfully. 'It seems a funny lonely place to come to. I don't think they are up to any good. I think it would be just as well to get out now, whilst we can, and hide, and then see if we can't find someone to help us. We can report everything to Bill when we get back.'

'That's the best idea,' said Jack at once. 'I'll be glad to be in the open air again. This plane's jolly stuffy.'

They looked cautiously out of every window to see if they could spot the two men. But there was no sign of them at all.

'Better get going,' said Jack. 'What about our suitcases – and rugs – and Kiki?'

'Don't leave them here,' said Philip. 'We don't want the men to guess we've been passengers in their plane. Take them with us.'

So the four of them left the plane and handed down their cases and rugs to one another. Kiki uttered a few words of annoyance at being lifted about like luggage, but only in a very low voice.

Soon all the children were standing outside the plane, wondering which way to go. Jack suddenly nudged Philip and made him jump.

'Look! Look over there!'

They all looked and saw a thin spire of blue smoke rising into the air.

'The men have made a fire down there, I should think,' said Jack in a low voice. 'Better not go in that direction. We'll take this path here – if it *is* a path.'

The little procession wound round some big rocks, and came to where a stream burbled down the hillside. It gushed out not far off as a spring, and became a little stream almost at once.

'We could drink from that,' said Philip. 'I'm thirsty. But

I'm not hungry yet. Funny!'

'Well, we're all a bit tired and worried and puzzled,' said Jack. 'Let's get some water into our hands and lap it up. I'm thirsty too.'

The water was cold and crystal clear. It was delicious. All the children felt better for a drink. Dinah dipped her hanky into the stream and wiped her face. She felt much fresher then, and Lucy-Ann did the same.

'The thing is to find a good hiding place for ourselves and these cases,' said Jack. 'I'm afraid if those two men start wandering about they may come across us. Where *can* we go?'

'Let's go straight on,' said Dinah. 'Up the hill here. If we keep up a little we shall be able to see the plane down in the valley and keep our sense of direction a bit. Keep among those trees.'

'That's a good idea,' said Philip, and they made their way slowly towards the trees. They felt safer among them. The men could not spot them there. On the other hand, they found that they could no longer see the plane.

'We can always spot it by climbing up a tree,' said Jack. 'I say – look there – is that a house?'

Set in a clearing was what looked like a house. But when the children got near they found that it was almost burnt out – just a blackened ruin, empty and deserted.

'What a pity,' said Philip. 'We could easily have asked help from the people who lived there. I wonder how the house got burnt.'

They went on a little higher, through a copse of silver birch trees. They saw another building a little higher up – but to their astonishment and dismay that too was a blackened, scorched ruin. There was no sign of life anywhere about it.

'Two burnt houses – and nobody to be found anywhere,'

said Jack. 'Very curious. What's been happening in this valley?'

Higher up still they could see yet another house — would that be burnt out too? They laboured up to it, and gazed on it in despair.

'Quite burnt out,' said Dinah. 'What an awful thing! What's happened to the people who lived here? There must have been war here, or something. I do wonder where we are.'

'Look — that cowshed, or whatever it is, isn't very much burnt out,' said Jack. 'Let's go over and see if the roof is still on. If it is, we could put our things there.'

They made their way to the broken-down cowshed. It seemed as if the flames had got hold of one half of it but had left the other half. The roof was almost off, but at the back was a sheltered place, with stalls where cows had once been put.

'This is all right,' said Jack, making his way into the last stall of all. 'The roof here will keep out the rain if it comes — and there are some jolly big clouds about. We can put our things here.'

'The floor's dirty,' said Lucy-Ann, turning up her nose in disgust.

'Well, we may perhaps be able to find a broom or something to get it clean — and we'll spread it with grass or bracken for a carpet,' said Dinah. 'Then, if we spread out our rugs on it, we could even sleep here. We may not be able to find anyone to help us today. We could spend the night here.'

They put their cases in the corner and draped the rugs over them. Kiki was put down on top in her basket. She gave a squawk of protest.

'Do you think it would be safe to let her out?' said Jack. 'She'll sit on my shoulder for hours now, I'm sure, if I tell her to. She must be so uncomfortable cooped up in that box.'

'Yes – let her out,' said Philip. 'If she does fly off for a bit and the men see her they won't know what she is or who she belongs to. She'll give them a fright if she begins to talk.'

Kiki was set free. She was overjoyed. She clambered out of the basket and flew to Jack's shoulder. She nibbled his ear fondly.

'Where's your handkerchief?' she said. 'How many times have I told you to . . .'

'All right, Kiki, all right,' said Jack. 'Not so loud, there's a good old thing.'

'Shhhhhhhhh!' said Kiki at the top of her voice. Then she said no more, but just sat and cracked her beak.

'Well – what are our plans?' said Philip, sitting on his suitcase. 'Shall we go exploring a bit further and see if we can find anyone to help us? Or shall we keep an eye on those men and see if we can find out why they've come here? Or shall we just stay here and hide?'

'I think we'd better go exploring,' said Jack. 'The most important thing really is to find help. We simply must get back home at once if we can. Aunt Allie and Bill will be worried to death about us.'

'This is such a lovely valley,' said Dinah, looking out of the tumbledown cowshed. 'I can't think why it isn't packed with houses and cattle and sheep. But I can't see a soul. I can't even see any smoke anywhere – except for that bit over there, where the men are. It's very mysterious. Why are all those houses burnt, and why isn't there anyone here?'

'Well, we've only seen just a bit of the valley and hillside,' said Philip. 'We may go round a corner and come on a whole village. Aren't those mountains enormous?'

'Yes. They make a ring all round this valley,' said Lucy-Ann. 'I wonder where the way out it. Mountains always have passes through them, don't they?'

'Yes,' said Jack. 'But I shouldn't care to go looking for one

30

if I didn't know the way. See that mountain over there? It's got a white tip. I bet that's snow. It shows how high it must be.'

It certainly was a beautiful valley, and the mountains that guarded it were magnificent. But it had a deserted lonely air about it, and even the few birds that flew by every now and again seemed silent and cautious.

'There's something mysterious here,' said Jack. 'You know – I believe – yes, I really do believe – we're in for another adventure.'

'Rubbish!' said Philip. 'We shall find a farm near by, get help, have a message sent somewhere, find a car road, go to the nearest town by car, and from there to an aerodrome. And I bet you we'll be home by tomorrow.'

'I bet we won't,' said Jack. Lucy-Ann looked alarmed.

'But what about meals?' she said. 'We've only got Aunt Allie's picnic packet – and few biscuits and some chocolate. We'll starve if we don't get home quickly. There's nothing to eat here.'

Nobody had thought of that. It was a nuisance. An adventure was one thing – but an adventure without anything to eat was quite another thing. That wouldn't do at all.

'I don't think we'll make this an adventure after all,' said Jack. But an adventure it was – and they were only at the beginning of it, too.

5

A little exploring

The four children went to the broken-down door and gazed out at the towering mountains around them. They seemed to hem the valley in and make it a green prison. None of the

31

children had seen such high mountains before. Clouds hung about halfway up two or three of them, and their tops showed now and again as the clouds shifted and parted.

'It's a very lonely kind of place,' said Jack. 'I bet there's all kinds of strange birds here – but I've only seen one or two so far. It's funny that those men should have known where to land in this valley – that smooth strip of grass makes a splendid landing ground. It looks as if they've been here before. But why should they come *here*? There doesn't seem anything to come for at all – no hotel, not even a cottage that isn't burnt, as far as we can see.'

'Oh, there may be,' said Philip. 'Hey, look at that little lizard! I've never seen one like that before. What a pretty little fellow!'

The lizard ran close by Philip's feet. The boy bent down quietly and his left hand caught the tiny creature by the neck. If he had caught it by the tail it would probably have snapped off, and the lizard would have run away without it.

'Oh, put it down, Philip, do!' said Dinah. 'Horrid creature!'

'It isn't,' said Philip. 'Look at its dear little feet with fingers on. Do look, Dinah.'

Dinah gave a squeal and pushed Philip away. Lucy-Ann and Jack looked at the tiny lizard with interest.

'It's like a very, very small dragon,' said Jack. 'Open your hand and see if it will stay with you, Philip.'

'Of course it will!' said Philip, who always seemed to exercise a strange spell over any creature he picked up. He opened his hand and let the lizard lie on his open palm. It made no attempt to escape at all.

'See? It wants to stay with me,' said Philip. 'And so it shall. What's your name, little thing? Lizzie? Well, of course, I might have known that.'

Lucy-Ann giggled, forgetting her worries for a moment.

What a lovely name for a lizard! Lizzie. Just like Philip to think of that.

'I'll see if I can catch a few flies for you, Lizzie,' said Philip, and went to a sunny patch where flies were buzzing. He caught one and held it in finger and thumb over the lizard's head. In a trice the fly was gone, and the lizard blinked with pleasure.

'Now I suppose you'll let the lizard live in your pocket or somewhere about you for ages,' said Dinah in disgust. 'I shan't go near you. If you haven't got a mouse down your neck you've got a toad in your pocket or a baby hedgehog crawling about you, or a few beetles. I think you're an awful boy.'

'Don't let's squabble now,' said Jack. 'We've bigger things to bother about than lizards.'

The lizard popped into Philip's sleeve. Kiki had been watching it with her head on one side. She was not fond of Philip's pets, and was often jealous of them.

'Pop goes the lizard,' she said, making one of her unexpected apt remarks. The others roared with laughter. Kiki was pleased. She swayed herself from side to side and cracked her beak.

'Shhhhhhhhhh!' she said.

'Oh, Kiki, I'm glad we brought you,' said Jack. 'Now, everybody, what are our next plans?'

'Well, we simply must do a bit of exploring and see if there is anyone living in this valley,' said Philip. 'If there is, we're all right. If there isn't – well, it's just too bad. We'll have to stay here till we're rescued.'

'Rescued! And how do you think anyone is going to rescue us if they haven't the foggiest idea where we are?' demanded Dinah. 'Don't be silly, Philip.'

'Well, do you propose to live here in this valley for the rest of your life, then?' said Philip. 'Oh, here's Lizzie again – coming out of my other sleeve. Lizzie, you're a jolly good explorer, I must say. I wish you could tell us the way out of this valley.'

Dinah went as far from Philip as she could. She simply could not bear his pets. It was a pity, because they were really amusing and friendly.

'You know, we'll have to be careful we don't get lost,' said Lucy-Ann anxiously. 'This valley and these mountainsides are so enormous. We must keep together always.'

'Yes, we must,' agreed Jack. 'And we must always be able to get back to this shed, too, because our things are here. At least we shall have shelter here, and our rugs to lie on. If only we had plenty to eat! Those biscuits and chocolate won't last long.'

'Your compass will come in jolly useful, Jack,' said Philip, remembering it. 'Look here – what about setting off now, and doing some more exploring, making this shed a kind of headquarters to come back to?'

'Yes, we will,' said Dinah. 'But let's cover up the suitcases and things with something in case those men come here and see them.'

'They won't,' said Philip. 'What could they possibly want to come snooping round an old burnt cowshed for? We can leave the things here all night.'

They went out of the shed. The sun was just over the mountaintops now, shining into the valley. The children saw the spire of smoke rising straight up from the fire the men must have made.

'So long as we keep away from that direction, we should be all right,' said Jack. 'Come on – let's take this path. It really looks as if it was once a proper path from this place to somewhere else. We'd better notch the trees here and there as we go, to make sure we find our way back.'

Lucy-Ann liked the idea of that. It reminded her of pioneers and trackers and their ways. Jack and Philip each took out his knife. They made a cut on every fifth tree until

34

they came out of the little wood and found themselves on a flower-strewn, grassy hillside.

'It's lovely, isn't it?' said Lucy-Ann, looking round at the carpet of flowers. 'I've never seen such bright colours. Look at that blue flower, Jack – it's bluer than the sky itself. And oh, look at this tiny pink flower – masses of it!'

'Shall we be seen out on this bare place?' asked Dinah suddenly. Jack and Philip looked downwards into the valley. They had been climbing up, and were now on the mountainside.

'There's the plane!' said Jack. 'And look out – isn't that one of the men walking over to it? Lie down flat, all of you!'

They all promptly lay down flat. Jack had his field glasses on and he put them to his eyes. He could now see clearly that the man was the one called Juan. He had a dead white face, black, thick, curly hair and a small black moustache. His neck was thick and his body was thick too. He disappeared into the plane.

'He's got into the plane. Wonder if he's going off?' said Jack. 'Will he leave the other man behind? He hasn't started up the engines yet.'

After a minute or two the man came out again, carrying something, though Jack could not see what it was. He walked off in the direction of the smoke. There was a thicket of trees near by and he disappeared into this.

'He just went into the plane to get something,' said Jack. 'Now he's gone again. I think perhaps we'd better go another way, because if we can see *him* he could certainly see *us*, if he looked up. See that gully over there? We'll go that way. We shall be well hidden there.'

They made their way to the gully, which was a regular suntrap. There had obviously been a way up there at some time or other. The children followed it, climbing higher. They came to a ledge that ran dangerously round part of the mountainside. Jack went first.

It wasn't as dangerous as it looked. 'I think it's all right,' he called. 'It's wider than it appears. Come on. I'm sure it leads to somewhere.'

They made their way round the ledge, and came to where the hillside gave them a marvellous view down into the valley and all around.

It was completely deserted. Not a cow or sheep or goat to be seen. A little higher up was a black, charred building that had clearly been a very large farm-house. Only the blackened beams were left, and part of the stone walls. Everything else had fallen to the ground and lay in a miserable ugly ruin.

'Another ruin!' said Jack, in awe. 'What *has* been happening in this beautiful valley? I simply can't understand it. Why should houses be burnt like this? I'm beginning to think there isn't a soul here besides ourselves and those two men.'

'I think you're right,' said Philip. 'There's no smoke to be seen anywhere, and not a single domestic animal, not even a dog. But what I can't make out is why no one has come here from the surrounding valleys to rebuild the houses and graze their cattle on this marvellous grass.'

'Perhaps there's something bad about this valley,' said Lucy-Ann with a shiver. 'I don't like the feel of it very much.'

They sat down in the sun, which was now climbing high. They suddenly felt terribly hungry. Dinah unexpectedly produced biscuits and chocolate from a bag she carried.

'I guessed we'd all be hungry soon,' she said. 'So I brought half the biscuits and choc we had with us.'

'Jolly good idea,' said Philip, pleased. 'Hey, Lizzie, come out and have a crumb!'

Dinah at once went a good distance away. Lizzie came out from Philip's open collar and ran down his front. It was plain that she meant to stay with Philip.

'Lizzie's down the well,' remarked Kiki, pecking a piece of chocolate from Jack's fingers.

'Kiki! Give that back!' cried Jack. 'Where are your manners?'

'Down the well, down the well,' said Kiki, who seemed to have got the well on her brain.

They were all thirsty after the chocolate and biscuits. 'I wish we could find something to drink – nice cool clear water like we found in the spring,' said Jack.

'Down the well,' said Kiki.

'All right. You find us a well of water,' said Jack.

'Would it be safe to have a snooze?' asked Dinah, suddenly feeling very sleepy. 'It's nice here in the sun.'

'Well – only just a little one,' said Philip. 'I should think we're safe enough here. Those men wouldn't come up as far as this.'

'You know – I think I can hear water somewhere,' said Lucy-Ann as she lay flat on her back, the sun shining on her freckled face. 'Not very near. Listen, all of you.'

They listened. Certainly they could hear something that was not the wind blowing round. What could it be? It didn't sound like the gurgling of a spring.

'We'll go and see,' said Jack. 'You stay here, girls, if you like. Philip and I will go.'

'Oh, no,' said Lucy-Ann at once. 'I'd rather come with you. You might lose us.'

So all four went off together in the direction of the curious noise. They climbed higher, and came to a rocky, stony part which was steep and hard to climb. But the noise was now much louder.

'Once we round the next corner, we'll see what it is,' said Jack. 'Come on!'

They climbed a little higher and then the path led abruptly round a crag of rock. It widened out a little the other side, and all four children stood gazing in awe at what was making the noise they had heard. It was a waterfall – but what a big one! It fell from a great height, almost sheerly down the mountainside, and cascaded far below them, fine spray rising high in the air. It wetted their faces as they stood there, and yet they were quite a good way from the mass of water.

'What a wonderful sight!' said Philip, awed. 'I've never seen such a big waterfall in my life. What a noise it makes. I almost have to shout. Isn't it grand?'

Far below the waterfall resolved itself into a winding river that curved round the foot of the mountain. The children could not see where it went to. The tumbling water shone and sparkled as it fell, and here and there rainbows shimmered. Lucy-Ann thought she had never seen a lovelier sight.

She licked the spray off her face. It formed into little drops and ran down to her mouth. 'I'm drinking the spray,' she said. 'Oh, look! – there's a puddle in that rock, made of the continually falling spray. Do you think it would be all right to drink it?'

It was very clear and sparkling. Jack tasted it. 'Yes, it's fine,' he said. 'Have some.'

They watched the waterfall for some time. Kiki was simply thrilled with it. For some reason or other it filled her with mad delight. She flew near to it, getting splashed with the drops, squawking loudly.

'It's a magnificent sight!' said Dinah, gazing at the roaring waterfall. 'I could watch it all day.'

'We'll come again tomorrow,' said Jack. 'But I really think we ought to be getting back now to that cowshed. Come on – it's plain there's nobody to help us just here.'

6

What are the two men up to?

Lucy-Ann was half afraid they might lose their way going back. But the boys had taken good note of everything. It was when they got to the wood that difficulty might have arisen, but here the notched trees soon set them right.

They saw that the plane was still down in the valley. So the men were somewhere about. It would be as well to be careful, and Jack told Kiki to be quiet. The waterfall seemed to have gone to her head, and she had been very noisy coming back, singing and squawking loudly.

'There's our shed,' said Lucy-Ann thankfully. It felt quite like home, coming back to it from that enormous mountainside. 'I hope all our things are safe.'

They went inside. Yes, their things were there, exactly as they had left them. Good!

The sun was now sliding down the sky. It was about tea-time. The children wondered whether to finish the rest of their chocolate and biscuits.

'Better not,' said Jack. 'We'll have them before we go to sleep tonight if we're terribly hungry. Oh – wait a minute – what about the stuff Aunt Allie packed for us? Haven't we still got that? We haven't eaten it?'

'No, of course we haven't,' said Dinah. 'I was saving it up. We've got so little that I thought we'd better not start on that picnic packet yet.'

'But all the sandwiches will be stale,' objected Philip, who was feeling very empty indeed. 'What's the good of that? We might as well eat them whilst they're eatable.'

'Well – we could eat the sandwiches, and leave the cake and the chocolate and biscuits for tomorrow,' said Dinah.

'But first let's get this place ready for us to sleep in tonight. It's filthy.'

'I don't want to sleep here,' said Lucy-Ann. 'I don't like it. Why can't we sleep outside? We've got our macks to lie on, and four rugs – and we can unpack some of our clothes and have them for pillows.'

'But it might pour with rain,' said Dinah.

'I could perhaps rig up some sort of roof,' said Jack, looking round at the ruined shed. 'There's some old posts here – and there's a piece of corrugated iron. If Philip gave me a hand, I could rig up the iron sheet on the old posts.'

The two boys tried to do this, but the sheets of iron was not held safely enough. The girls were terrified it might blow off on to them as they slept.

'If only we could find a cave!' said Lucy-Ann.

'Well, we can't,' said Jack, rather cross that all his efforts with the posts and the iron were of no use. 'Anyway, I don't think it's going to rain. Look at the clear sky. If it does pour, we'll have to get into the stall at the end of the cowshed, that's all.'

Their work with the posts had made them hungrier than ever. Dinah undid the picnic packet and took out sandwiches and huge slices of cake. They ate the sandwiches in silence, enjoying every bite immensely.

'Wonder what those men are doing,' said Jack at last. 'I can't see any smoke rising now. Shall I slip down towards the plane, keeping well hidden, and see if I can see them?'

'Yes,' said Philip. 'You're sure you know your way there and back? Don't get lost for goodness' sake!'

'If I do, I'll get Kiki to do her express engine screech,' said Jack with a grin. 'Then you'll know where we are all right.'

'Look in that plane if you get a chance, and see if you can spot any food there,' called Dinah. Jack went off with Kiki on his shoulder. Lucy-Ann didn't at all like him going off alone. She wished she could have gone with him, but she knew he wouldn't have let her.

'Let's get our beds ready,' said Dinah, who always liked to be doing something. 'Come on, you two – help to unpack the cases and get out something for pillows – and our macks to lie on.'

Whilst Jack was gone the other three were very busy. Soon they had a cosy-looking bed spread on the grass under a big birch tree. First there were the four macks, to keep the damp out. Then there was one big thick rug for softness. There were four piles of woollies for pillows, and finally the other three rugs for coverings.

'That looks very good,' said Dinah approvingly. 'Pull that rug a little over this way, Lucy-Ann. That's right. Philip, you're to sleep right on the outside. I won't have the lizard crawling over me in the night.'

'Lizzie won't hurt you,' said Philip, taking the lizard out of one of his sleeves. 'Will you, Lizzie? Stroke her, Dinah – she's sweet.'

'*Don't*, Philip!' said Dinah with a squeal, as Philip brought the lizard near to her on his outstretched hand. 'I'll box your ears if you dare to let that lizard touch me!'

'Oh, don't tease her, Tufty,' begged Lucy-Ann. 'Let *me* have Lizzie for a bit. I love her.'

But Lizzie would not go to Lucy-Ann, much to her annoyance. She ran up Philip's sleeve and disappeared. Little bumps appearing here and there in his jersey showed where she was.

Dinah looked up at the sky. It was quite clear. The sun had almost gone, and soon the first stars would prick through the sky. She felt tired and irritable.

So did the others. Their short night and the shock they had had were beginning to make themselves felt. Lucy-Ann felt that at any moment a violent quarrel might spring up between Dinah and Philip.

So she took Dinah off to the spring with her, and they

washed in the cold clear water, and drank. They sat there a little while, enjoying the beauty of the valley and the mountains around.

'They seem to be crowding in on us,' said Lucy-Ann. 'Coming closer.'

'How you do imagine things!' said Dinah. 'Come on — let's get back. Jack should be here soon and I want to hear what he's got to say.'

They went back. Philip had laid himself down on the coats and rugs, and was yawning. 'I was just coming to look for you girls,' he said. 'What a time you've been! Jack isn't back yet. I hope he's all right.'

Lucy-Ann felt scared. She adored her brother. She went to stand on a rock, so that she might see when he came. She turned to the others as soon as she got there.

'He's coming!' she called. 'And Kiki's on his shoulder.' She jumped down from the rock and rushed to meet Jack. He grinned at her, and Kiki flew off his shoulder to perch on Lucy-Ann's.

'I was beginning to get worried, Jack,' said Lucy-Ann. 'Did anything happen? Did you see the two men? What were they doing?'

They came up to Dinah and Philip. 'My word, what a fine bed!' said Jack, and he sank down on it. 'This is something like! I'm jolly tired.'

'What happened, Jack?' asked Philip. 'Anything?'

'Not much,' said Jack. 'I got as near to the plane as I could, but I didn't dare to go right up in case I was seen, because, as you know, it's right out in the open. I couldn't see or hear anything of the men at all.'

'Was Kiki good?' asked Lucy-Ann anxiously. 'I kept on thinking she might screech or something and draw attention to you.'

'She was as good as gold,' said Jack, scratching Kiki's poll. 'Weren't you, Kiki? Well, I thought the next thing to do would be to try and find where the men were – where that smoke came from. So, keeping as much to the bushes and trees as I could, I made my way towards the smoke. They must have lighted their fire again, because the smoke rose up quite black and thick.'

'Did you see the men?' asked Dinah.

'I heard their voices first,' said Jack. 'Then I thought it would be a good idea to climb a tree and use my field glasses. So up I shinned and came to the top of a nice little tree. Not far below me, near a tumbledown hut, were the two men, cooking something over a fire they had made.'

'Gracious!' said Lucy-Ann. 'Weren't you scared of being seen?'

'No. The tree hid me all right,' said Jack. 'And I hadn't made a scrap of noise. I got my field glasses and looked through them. The men were studying some kind of map.'

'Whatever for?' said Dinah wonderingly. 'I should think they know this part of the world pretty well or they wouldn't have been able to land so easily.'

'Well, they've come here for *some* reason, haven't they?' said Jack. 'Goodness knows what – but certainly for some definite reason. They must be looking for something or someone – and the map will probably show them what they want to know. I heard one say, "This way – and then up here," as if they were planning some sort of expedition.'

'We could follow them,' said Dinah at once. 'Then we'd know.'

'No, thanks,' said Jack. 'I'm not going mountain climbing behind those men. They look jolly tough. What I say is – let them get off on their expedition – and we'll be able to explore that hut of theirs – and the plane too. We may find something to tell us who they are and what they're after.'

'Yes. Let's do that,' said Lucy-Ann sleepily. 'Perhaps they'll go tomorrow. I hope they do. Jack can watch them with his field glasses – and when they're safely gone we can

43

do a good old snoop round.'

'There's really nothing more to tell,' said Jack with a yawn. 'I couldn't hear any more. The men rolled up the map and talked in low voices. So I shinned down the tree and came back. And here I am.'

'Let's snuggle down and go to sleep,' said Lucy-Ann. 'I simply can't keep my eyes open. We're safe here, aren't we?'

'Perfectly, I should think,' said Jack, lying down contentedly. 'Anyway, Kiki will give us warning if anyone comes near. Good night.'

'Good night,' said the others. Philip added a few words.

'Dinah, don't yell if a spider runs over you, or a rat or a hedgehog. There are sure to be plenty out here.'

Dinah gave a squeal and covered her head up at once. Then there was silence. They were all fast asleep.

7

A wonderful find

Soon the stars filled the sky. An owl hooted, and the wind whispered something in the trees overhead. But the four children did not see the stars nor hear the owl and the wind. They were tired out. They slept solidly, and though Dinah was almost smothered with the rug over her head, she did not wake or move.

Kiki slept too, her head under her wing. She was perched on a branch of the birch tree just over Jack's head. She awoke when she heard the owl, and hooted back softly. Then she put her head back under her wing and slept again.

When dawn came the children were still asleep. Kiki awoke before they did. She stretched out first one wing and then the other. She erected the feathers on her head and shook them. Then she scratched her neck thoughtfully and gazed down at Philip.

Lizzie the lizard was also awake and was running over the rug that covered Philip. She came to where Philip's feet stuck out and disappeared under the rug there. Kiki's sharp eyes watched the little moving bump she made under the rug as she made her way all the way up Philip's body and appeared by his neck.

'Wipe your feet,' said Kiki suddenly to the lizard. 'How many times, how many times have I told you to wipe your feet?'

Lizzie was startled. She leapt from Philip's neck on to Jack and stood half hidden in his hair, looking up into the trees, though she could focus nothing there. Kiki, annoyed at seeing Lizzie daring to tread on her beloved master, gave an exasperated squawk and flew down to peck the lizard, who promptly disappeared under the rug again.

Kiki landed heavily on Jack's middle and gave a vicious peck where the rug covered Philip's right leg, for she could see the moving bump there that meant the lizard was running downwards. Both Jack and Philip awoke with a start.

They stared up into the trees, amazed to see green leaves waving above them. Then they turned their heads and saw one another. In a flash they remembered everything.

'Couldn't think where I was,' said Jack, and sat up. 'Oh, Kiki, it's you on my middle, is it? Do get off. Here, have some sunflower seeds and keep quiet, or you'll wake the girls.'

He put his hand in his pocket and took out some of the flat seeds that Kiki loved. She flew up to the bough above, cracking two in her beak.

The boys began to talk quietly, so as not to disturb the girls, who were still sleeping peacefully.

45

'Gosh, I feel better now,' said Jack, stretching out his arms. 'I was so tired last night I could have cried. What about you, Philip?'

'I'm all right too,' said Philip, and he yawned hugely. 'But sleepy still. Well, we haven't got to get up for breakfast. We shan't hear any gong sounding here. Let's have another snooze.'

But Jack was now too wide awake to snooze. He slipped out from under the rug and went to wash himself at the spring. He gazed downwards and saw the spire of smoke rising up just as it had yesterday.

'Those fellows are up and about,' he said to himself. 'Must be getting late in the morning, I suppose. The sun's fairly high. Blow! I forgot to wind up my watch last night.'

Soon the girls woke up and were amazed to find they had slept soundly all the night through and had apparently not even stirred. Dinah looked to see where Lizzie was.

'It's all right,' said Philip amiably. 'She's down one of my socks. I like the feel of her tiny fingers on my leg.'

'Ugh! You're awful!' said Dinah. 'Well, I'm going to wash. Then we'll have breakfast — only cake and biscuits, I'm afraid.'

Unfortunately they were all so hungry that they devoured the cake, the biscuits and the rest of the chocolate too. Now there was no food left at all.

'We'll just *have* to do something about it — about the food question, I mean,' said Dinah. 'Even if it means eating your lizard, Philip.'

'She wouldn't make more than a mouthful, would you Liz?' said Philip. 'Hallo — what's that?'

'That' was the sound of voices. Hurriedly the four children got up, and, dragging their rugs, macks and other clothes with them, they ran quickly to the cowshed. They dumped the things into the last stall and crouched there, panting.

'Have we left anything at all out there?' whispered Jack.

'Don't think so,' whispered back Philip. 'The grass is a bit flattened, that's all. Let's hope they won't notice it.'

There was a crack in the side of the old cowshed and Jack put his eye to it. They had only just got away in time. The men were coming slowly up towards the birch trees, talking. They came to where the children had slept the night before.

The men walked right past the spot, then one of them stopped and looked back with a puzzled expression. He gazed at the place where the children had slept. What he said they couldn't hear, but he pointed to the flattened grass. Both men then walked back and looked earnestly down at it.

'What's done that?' asked the man called Juan.

'Funny,' said the other man. He had a large pink face with full lips, and his eyes looked small in comparison. 'Some animal, perhaps?'

'Why – that's big enough for an elephant or two to lie on!' said Juan. 'Shall we have a look round?'

The other man looked at his watch. 'No. Not now,' he said. 'When we come back, perhaps. We've got a lot to do today. Come on. It can't be anything really.'

They went on again and were soon lost to sight among the trees. 'I'm going to get up a tree with my field glasses and follow them with them as they go,' said Jack to the others. 'We must make certain they really are gone before we show ourselves.'

He went cautiously out of the shed and ran quickly to a tall tree. He was up it in a trice, for he was an excellent climber. He sat at the top, balanced on a swaying branch, his legs wound tightly round it. He put his glasses to his eyes.

As soon as the men came out on to the grassy, flowery part of the hillside he saw them. They did not take the same direction as the children had taken the day before, but kept on the flowery part for a long time. Jack could see them easily with his glasses. Then they took out a map or paper

47

and stood there looking at it between them.

'Not sure of their way,' thought the boy. 'Ah – now they're off again.'

The men began to climb steeply and Jack watched them as long as he could see them. Then they rounded a great crag of rock and disappeared from sight. He slid down the tree.

'Gracious! We thought you'd gone to sleep in the tree,' said Dinah impatiently. 'I'm tired of waiting in this filthy shed. Have the men gone?'

'Yes. They're far away now,' said Jack. 'It's quite safe to come out and have a look round. They didn't go the way we did. I watched them climbing very steeply up the mountain-side. Come on – let's get off whilst we can.'

'We could go and have a look inside the aeroplane now,' said Dinah. So they all hurried down to the valley, and came to where the big aeroplane stood on its enormous wheels. The four children climbed up the steps into the cockpit.

'The big crate's gone,' said Jack at once. 'I wonder how they got it out. It must have been empty or they could never have managed it between them. Look – there's where we hid the other night!'

Philip and Jack hunted all round the plane for food or information. But there was no food at all, and not a scrap of paper that would give them any idea as to who the men were or why they had come there.

They all climbed out again. 'Blow!' said Jack. 'We're no better off now! Not even a bar of chocolate. We shall starve!'

'If we could explore that hut you saw the men by last night, I bet we'd find plenty of food,' said Dinah. 'Don't you remember the men saying, "Let's go to the hut and have a meal"? Well, they couldn't have a meal without food, could they? – so the food must be there.'

This was a distinctly cheering idea. Jack led the way to where he had seen the men sitting by the campfire the night before. The fire was almost out, though it was still smouldering a little.

The hut lay near by. It was tumbledown, but not burnt as had been all the other buildings they had seen. Rough repairs had been done to it. The one window looked strong, and was hardly big enough for anyone to get in or out, if he had wanted to. The door was also a strong one. It was shut.

'Locked, of course,' said Jack, giving it a tug. '*And* they've taken the key. Who did they imagine was going to come along and take anything? They don't know a thing about *us*.'

'Let's look in at the window,' said Lucy-Ann. 'We could see inside easily.'

Jack hoisted Philip up. The boy looked inside, finding it difficult at first to make out anything, because the interior of the shed was dark. The only light came in from the small window.

'Ah – now I can see better,' said Philip. 'There are a couple of mattresses – and rugs – and a table and some chairs – and a stove of some kind. And gosh – just look at *that*!'

'What?' cried everyone impatiently. Lucy-Ann jumped up and down, trying to see in at the window too.

'*Stacks* of food!' said Philip. 'Tins and tins of it! And pots and jars of stuff! Golly, they make my mouth water.'

Jack could bear Philip's weight no longer. He set him down with a jerk.

'Hoist *me* up, now,' he said, and Philip gave him a hoist. Jack's eyes nearly fell out of his head when he saw the food, neatly piled on shelves that ran along one side of the hut.

'It's a kind of storehouse, or resthouse,' he said, jumping down from Philip's back. 'My word, if we could only get some! Why did those men take the key? Distrustful creatures!'

'Can we get in at the window?' asked Philip, and he looked eagerly up at it. 'No, we can't. Not even Lucy-Ann could get in there. Besides, it can't be opened. It's just a pane of glass set into the window frame, with no catch or fastener to open it. We'd have to smash it — and that would give away the fact that somebody was here.'

The children wandered gloomily round the shed. Then they set off to see if there was anything else to be found near by. But there wasn't.

'I suppose we'd better get back to our own shed and remove our things, and hide them somewhere else in case those men do have a look round when they come back,' said Jack. 'How I hate leaving all that food in this shed! I'm starving.'

'So am I,' said Lucy-Ann. 'I could almost eat Kiki's sunflower seeds.'

'Well, have some,' said Jack, holding out a handful. 'They're not poisonous.'

'No, thanks,' said Lucy-Ann. 'I'm not as starving as all that.'

Philip went up to the door of the shed and glared at it. 'I'd like to knock you down,' he said. 'Standing there between ourselves and a good square meal. Take that!'

To the great amusement of the others he aimed a hearty kick at the door, and then another.

It flew open. The children gasped in surprise, and stared. 'It wasn't locked, after all!' cried Jack, 'just shut. What idiots we were to think it was locked! Come on — now for a feast!'

8

Kiki talks too much

They all crowded into the dimly lighted shed. They gazed joyfully at the piles of things on the shelves.

'Biscuits! Tongue! Pineapple! Sardines! Milk! Gosh, there's everything here!' cried Jack. 'What shall we start on?'

'Wait a bit. Don't let's disarrange the shelf so much that the men will know someone has been here,' said Philip. 'Better take tins from the back, not the front. And we won't eat the fruit and other stuff here – we'll take it away with us.'

'I think,' said Jack slowly – 'I really do think it would be a good idea to take away as much of this as we can carry, in case we are stuck in this valley for some time. We may as well face the fact that we are completely lost, and cut off from the world we know, and may not be rescued for ages.'

The others looked solemn, and Lucy-Ann looked scared as well.

'You're right, Freckles,' said Philip. 'We'll help ourselves to as much as we can carry. Look, here's a pile of old sacks. What about filling a couple of them with the tins and carrying them off between us? We could take dozens of the tins then.'

'Good idea,' said Jack. 'Here's a sack for you and Dinah to fill, and here's one for me and Lucy-Ann.'

Philip stood on one of the chairs and reached his hand behind the front row of tins on the shelf. He threw down tin after tin, and the others put them into the two sacks. What a store there was in that hut!

Soon the sacks were full and almost too heavy to carry. It was nice to think of all that food waiting to be eaten. Jack found a tin-opener, too, and put it in his pocket.

'Before we go, let's have a look and see if we can find any papers or documents that will tell us something about these mysterious airmen,' said Philip. But although they hunted in every corner, and even under the pile of sacks, they could find nothing.

'I wonder what they did with that crate they had in the plane,' said Jack. 'We haven't found that anywhere. I'd like to have a squint at that too.'

The crate was not in the shed. So the children wandered out and had another good look round. And, in a copse of young trees and bushes, with a tarpaulin over them, they found about six of the wooden crates.

'Funny,' said Jack, pulling away the tarpaulin. 'Look – lots of them – all empty! What are they going to put into them?'

'Goodness knows!' said Philip. 'Who would bring empty crates to this deserted valley, hoping to find something to fill them? Only madmen!'

'Oh – you don't really think those men are mad, do you?' said Lucy-Ann in alarm. 'What shall we do if they are?'

'Keep out of their way, that's all,' said Philip. 'Come on. Did we shut that door? Yes, we did. Now, heave-ho, Dinah, catch hold of your end of the sack and we'll go back to our shed.'

Stumbling under the weight of the clanking sacks, the four children made their way slowly back to the shed they had hidden their things in. Jack dumped his sack, and then ran to climb the tree he had climbed before, in order to sweep the countryside with his field glasses, and see if the men were by any chance returning yet. But there was no sign of them.

'All clear at the moment,' said Jack, going back to the others. 'Now for a meal – the finest we've ever had because we've never been so hungry before.'

They chose a tin of biscuits and opened it. They took out about forty biscuits, feeling perfectly certain that they could manage at least ten each. They opened a tin of tongue, which Jack carved very neatly with his penknife. Then they opened a tin of pineapple chunks and a tin of milk.

'What a meal!' said Jack, sitting down contentedly on the sun-warmed ground. 'Well – here goes!'

Never did food taste so completely delicious. 'Mmm-mm-mmm,' murmured Lucy-Ann, meaning, 'This is simply gorgeous.' Kiki imitated her at once.

'Mmm-mm-mm! Mmm-mm-mm!'

No word was spoken except when Dinah saw Kiki delving too deeply into the tin of pineapple.

'Jack! Do stop Kiki! She'll eat it all!'

Kiki retired to a branch of the tree above, a large chunk of pineapple in her claw. 'Mmm-mm-mm!' she kept saying. 'Mmm-mm-mm!'

Dinah went to the spring and rinsed out the empty tin of milk. Then she filled it with clear cold water and came back. She emptied the cold water into the pineapple juice left at the bottom of the tin and shook it up. Then she offered everyone a pineapple drink to end the meal.

'Gosh! I do feel better now,' said Jack, and he undid his belt to let it out two or three holes. 'Thank goodness you lost your temper and kicked that door, Philip. We were so sure that it was locked, and the key taken.'

'Silly of us,' said Philip, lying down and shutting his eyes. 'What are we going to do with the empty tins?'

'*You're* obviously going to do nothing,' said Dinah. 'I'll push them down a rabbit hole. The rabbits can lick them out.'

She picked up a tin and gave a scream. She dropped it, and Lizzie the lizard ran out in a hurry. She had been sniffing in delight at the crumbs of tongue left there. The tiny creature ran to Philip, and disappeared down his neck.

53

'Don't tickle, Lizzie,' murmured Philip sleepily.

'I'd better keep a watch out in case the men come back,' said Jack, and he climbed his tree again. Lucy-Ann and Dinah stuffed the empty tins down a large rabbit hole.

Kiki looked down the hole at the tins in surprise, then walked solemnly down and began to tug at one of the tins.

'No, Kiki, don't!' said Lucy-Ann. 'Jack, take Kiki with you up the tree.'

Jack whistled. Kiki flew to him at once and perched on his shoulder as he climbed his tree, moving from side to side when a bough threatened to knock her off.

'We'd better bring out all our cases and things, ready to hide them somewhere better than in the cowshed,' said Dinah. 'If those men do look round here when they come back, they'll see them in the cowstall, as sure an anything!'

So the two girls lugged everything out, Dinah grumbling because Philip lay apparently asleep and would not stir himself to help them. Jack came down the tree.

'No sign of them yet,' he said. 'Now the thing is – where can we hide these things really well?'

'Down the well,' suggested Kiki, hearing the word 'well.'

'Shut up, Kiki,' said Jack. He looked all round but could think of nowhere. Then an idea struck him.

'I'll tell you where would be a jolly good place,' he said.

'Where?' asked the girls.

'Well – see that big tree there? – the one with thick spreading branches – we could get up there and pull up our things quite easily, and hide them in the leafy branches. No one would think of looking up there, either for us or our belongings.'

The girls gazed at the thickly-leafed tree. It was a horse-chestnut tree, dark and full of glossy leaves. Just the place.

'But how can we get the suitcases up?' asked Dinah. 'They're not terribly big – but they're quite heavy.'

Jack undid a rope from round his waist. He nearly always

had one there. 'Here you are!' he said. 'I can climb up the tree and let down this rope. You can slip it through the handle of one of the suitcases and knot it. Then I'll give a jolly good heave – and up it'll come!'

'Let's wake Philip, then,' said Dinah, who didn't see why her brother shouldn't join in the labour of heaving things up a tree. She went over and shook him. He awoke with a jump.

'Come and help us, you lazy thing,' said Dinah. 'Jack's found a marvellous hiding place for us all.'

Philip joined the others and agreed that it was indeed a fine place. He said he would go up with Jack and pull up the cases.

Kiki was most interested in all the proceedings. When Jack hung the rope down the tree, she flew to it and gave it such a tug with her beak that it was pulled from Jack's hand and fell to the ground.

'Kiki! What did you do that for, you bad bird?' called Jack. 'Now I've got to climb all the way down and up again! Idiot!'

Kiki went off into one of her neverending cackles of laughter. She waited her chance and once again pulled the rope from poor Jack's hand.

Jack called her sternly. She came, cracking her beak, not quite liking Jack's stern voice. He tapped her very sharply on the beak.

'Bad Kiki! Naughty Kiki! Go away! I don't want you. No, GO AWAY!'

Kiki flew off, squawking dismally. Jack was not very often cross with her, but she knew he was this time. She retired inside the dark cowshed, and sat high up on a blackened beam, swaying herself to and fro.

'Poor Kiki! Poor, poor Kiki!' she groaned. 'Pop goes Kiki!'

Jack and Philip soon hauled everything up and stowed it safely away in the forks of the big spreading branches. Then

Jack shinned up a bit higher and put his glasses to his eyes. What he saw made him call urgently to the girls.

'The men are coming! Quick, get up! Have you left anything behind? Have a look and see!'

The girls took a quick look round. They could see nothing. Lucy-Ann climbed the tree quickly, with Dinah just behind her. They settled themselves on broad branches and peered down. They could see nothing at all, for the leaves were far too thick. Well, if they couldn't see down, certainly nobody could see up. So that was all right.

Soon they could hear voices. The men were coming near. The children sat as quiet as mice in the tree. Lucy-Ann felt a terrible longing to cough and she put her hand over her mouth.

Down below, the men were making a good search of the old cowshed. They found nothing, of course, for everything had been removed by the children. Then they wandered out again and looked at the flattened grass. It puzzled them very much.

'I'll just have one more look in that shed,' said the man called Juan. He disappeared into the shed once more. Kiki, who was still up on the blackened beam, sulking, was annoyed to see him again.

'Wipe your feet,' she said severely. 'And how many times have I told you to shut the door?'

The man jumped violently and peered all round. Kiki was huddled in a corner up in the roof and he could not see her. He looked in all the other corners of the room, hardly believing his ears. He called to his companion.

'Look here,' he said, 'somebody just now told me to wipe my feet and shut the door.'

'You're mad,' said the other man. 'You can't be feeling well.'

'Pussy down the well,' announced Kiki. 'Well, well, well! Use your handkerchief.'

The men clutched one another. Kiki's voice was so unexpected in that dark shed.

'Let's be quiet and listen,' said Juan. Kiki heard the words 'be quiet.'

'Shhhhhhhhhshhhhhhh!' she said at the top of her voice. That was too much for the men. They fled out into the open air.

9

New plans

Kiki was glad to see the two men go. 'Shut the door!' she shouted after them. 'Shut the door!'

The men ran off, and only stopped when they were well away from the shed. Juan mopped his forehead.

'What do you make of *that*?' he said. 'A voice – and nothing else!'

The other man was rapidly recovering.

'Where there's a voice there's a body,' he said. 'There's somebody here – somebody playing tricks on us. I thought when I saw that flattened piece this morning that we were not alone here. Who's here? Do you think anybody's got wind of the treasure?'

The four children, hidden well in the leaves of the tree, just above the heads of the two men, pricked up their ears at once. Treasure! Oho! So that was what the men were after in this lonely, deserted valley. Treasure!

'How could anyone know what we know?' said Juan scornfully. 'Don't get nerves just because you heard a voice, Pepi. Why, maybe it was just a parrot.'

Pepi laughed loudly. It was his turn to be scornful now. 'A parrot! What will you say next, Juan?' he said with a sneer.

'Have you ever known parrots to live here before? And talking ones, too? If that's a parrot, I'll eat my hat and yours as well!'

The listening children grinned at one another. Lucy-Ann thought she would like to see Pepi, whoever he was, eating his hat. He would have to eat Juan's too, for Kiki was most certainly a parrot.

'It's somebody hiding about here,' said Pepi. 'Though how they got here goodness knows. Juan, maybe there is a cellar beneath that cowshed. We will go and find out if anyone is hiding there. He will be very – very – sorry for himself.'

The children didn't like the tone of his voice at all. Lucy-Ann shivered. What horrid men!

They went cautiously to the cowshed. Juan stood at the broken down doorway. He called loudly:

'Come out of the cellar, whoever you are! We give you this one chance!'

No one came out, of course. For one thing there was no one to come out, and for another there was no cellar to come from. Juan held a revolver in his hand. Kiki, rather alarmed at the shouting voice, said nothing at all, which was fortunate for her.

The silence was too much for Juan. He took aim at where he supposed a cellar might be and a shot rang out. BANG!

Kiki almost tumbled off the beam in fright and the four children nearly fell out of their tree. Jack just clutched Lucy-Ann in time and held her tightly.

BANG! Another shot. The children imagined that Juan must be firing blindly, merely to frighten the person he thought he had heard talking. What a pity Kiki had been in the shed, sulking. Jack felt most alarmed. He was afraid she might have been shot.

The men came out again. They stood looking about for

58

some moments and then walked near to the chestnut tree, talking.

'No one there now. Must have slipped off. I tell you, Pepi, there has been someone here – maybe spying on us!'

'Well, he surely wouldn't give himself away by telling us to wipe our feet and shut the door,' said Pepi scornfully.

'We'll come back tomorrow and search this place completely,' said Juan. 'I'm certain there's somebody here. Talking English, too! What does it mean? I feel very alarmed about it. We didn't want anyone to get wind of our mission.'

'Certainly we must search this place well,' said Pepi. 'We must find out who is the owner of that voice. No doubt about that. I'd start a good hunt now, but it's getting dark and I'm hungry. Come on – let's get back.'

To the children's huge relief the men disappeared. Jack, who by climbing to the very top of the tree could see the aeroplane, waited till he could see the two men passing by it on their way to their own hut.

Then he called down to the others, 'All clear now. They're by the plane. My word – what a shock I had when those shots went off! Lucy-Ann nearly fell off her branch.'

'Lizzie shot out of my pocket and disappeared,' said Philip. 'I say, I hope Kiki's all right Jack. She must have been scared out of her life when the shots rang out in that little shed.'

Kiki was sitting petrified on the beam when the children went into the cowshed. She crouched down, trembling. Jack called to her softly.

'It's all right, Kiki. Come on down. I'm here to fetch you.'

Kiki flew down at once and landed on Jack's shoulder. She made a great fuss of him. 'Mmm-mm-mm!' she kept saying. 'Mmm-mm-mm!'

It was dark in the shed. The children didn't like it. Lucy-Ann kept feeling there might be someone hiding in the corners. 'Let's go out,' she said. 'What are we going to do tonight? Is it safe to sleep where we did last night?'

'No. We'd better take our rugs and things somewhere else,' said Jack. 'There's a patch of bushes higher up where we'd be sheltered from the wind and hidden from view too. We could take them there.'

'I say – do you know what we left in the shed?' said Philip suddenly. 'We left our sacks of tina. Look, there they are in that corner.'

'What a mercy the men didn't notice they were full of something!' said Jack. 'Still, I'm not surprised they took no notice of them really. They just look like heaps of rubbish. We'll drag them up to the bushes, though. Our store of food is too precious to be left behind.'

They dragged the sacks to the patch of bushes and left them there. Then they debated what to do about the things up the tree.

'Let's just bring down the rugs and our macks,' said Jack. 'The clothes we used for pillows are wrapped in the rugs. We could leave the suitcases up there. We don't want to drag them about with us.'

It was now getting so dark that it was quite difficult to get the rugs and macks down, but they managed it somehow. Then they made their way again to the bushes. Dinah and Lucy-Ann spread out the 'bed,' as they called it.

'It won't be so warm here,' said Dinah. 'The wind creeps round rather. Where are we going to hide tomorrow? Those men will look behind these bushes, that's certain.'

'Do you remember that waterful?' asked Philip. 'There seemed to be a nice lot of rocks and hiding places down towards the foot. I believe we could climb down there and find quite a good place.'

'Yes, let's,' said Lucy-Ann. 'I'd like to see that waterfall again.'

They all lay down on the rug. They pressed close together,

for it was certainly cold. Dinah took a pullover from her 'pillow' and put it on.

Suddenly she gave a scream, making the others jump. 'Oh! Oh! There's something running over me! It must be a rat!'

'Well, it isn't,' came Philip's delighted voice. 'It's Lizzie! She's found me. Good old Lizzie!'

So it was. How the little lizard had discovered where Philip was nobody could imagine. It was part of the spell that Philip always seemed to exercise on wild creatures.

'Don't worry, Dinah,' said Philip. 'Lizzie is safe in my pocket now. Poor thing, I bet she felt dizzy falling down the tree.'

'Dizzy Lizzie,' said Kiki at once, delighted with the two words. 'Dizzy Lizzie.'

Everyone laughed. Kiki was really funny at times. 'Doesn't she love to put words together that have the same sounds?' said Lucy-Ann. 'Do you remember last hols she kept saying 'Fusty-musty-dusty' till we nearly screamed at her?'

'Fusty-musty-dusty, dizzy Lizzie,' said Kiki at once, and screeched.

'Don't,' said Jack. 'You're only showing off now, Kiki. Go to sleep. And if you dig your claws into my tummy like you did this morning, I'll smack you.'

'God save the Queen,' said Kiki devoutly, and said no more.

The children talked for a little while longer. Then the girls and Philip fell asleep. Jack lay on his back, with Kiki on one of his ankles. He looked up at the stars. What was the good of promising Aunt Allie they wouldn't have any more adventures? The very night they had promised her, they had whizzed off in a strange aeroplane to an unknown valley, where, apparently, some sort of 'treasure' was hidden. Most extraordinary. Most – extra— And then Jack was asleep too, and the stars shone down on the four children, moving across the sky till dawn slid into the east and put out all the stars one by one.

Philip awoke early. He had meant to, for he did not know how early the men might start hunting for the owner of the 'voice.' He awoke the others and would not listen to their protests.

'No, you've really got to wake up, Dinah,' he said. 'We must start early today. Go on – wake up! – or I'll put Dizzy Lizzie down your neck.'

That woke poor Dinah up properly. She sat up and tried to slap Philip, but he dodged away. She hit Kiki instead. The parrot gave a surprised and aggrieved squawk.

'Oh, *sorry*, Kiki,' said Dinah. 'Sorry. I didn't mean that for you. Poor, poor Kiki!'

'What a pity, what a pity!' said Kiki flying off in case Dinah sent out any more slaps.

'We'll have a quick breakfast,' said Jack. 'Sardines, biscuits and milk, I think. I saw a tin of sardines at the top of one of our sacks. Yes, here it is.'

They saw smoke rising up from where the two men were, and knew that they too were up. So they finished their breakfast quickly, and Dinah once more pushed the tins down a convenient rabbit hole. Then they ruffled up the grass on which they had been lying, so that it didn't look quite so flat.

'I think we'd better find a good hiding place for most of these tins,' said Philip, 'and take just a few of them with us to last us for today. We can't possibly lug these heavy sacks along all the way.'

'Couldn't we drop them into the middle of these bushes?' said Dinah. 'They're awfully thick. Nobody would guess they were there. We could slip back and fetch any we wanted.'

So the sacks were dropped into the middle of the bushes,

and certainly no one could see them unless they actually crawled into the very middle. Then the children gathered up their rugs, macks and odd clothes and set off. The boys carried the tins, and Jack had his camera and his glasses as well. So they were heavily laden and could not go very fast.

They took the same way that they had taken before. When they came to the grassy, flower-strewn hillside they sat down for a rest. After all, the men would hardly be following them! They would be hunting all round and about the cowshed.

Suddenly, from far off, Jack caught sight of a brilliant, twinkling flash. He lay down flat at once, telling the others to do the same. 'There's someone using field-glasses down there,' he said. 'We may not be seen if we lie flat. I just caught the flash of the sun on the eye-lenses. Dash! I forgot the men might sweep the mountainside with glasses. They'll be after us if they've seen us.'

'Let's crawl to that rock and get behind it,' said Philip. 'Come on. Once we're behind there we can get on and find the waterfall.'

10

A fine hiding-place

When they were behind the rock the children felt sure they could not be seen, and they breathed more easily. Philip looked round and about. The gully they had been in before lay a little to the left. They could reach it without being seen from below.

'Come on,' said Philip, choosing a path that put rocks or bushes between them and the valley below. 'This way.'

Up the hot gully went the children, and came to the ledge

that ran round a steep bit of the mountain. They made their way round and once more saw the wonderful view they had seen before. Above them stood the ruined, burnt-out farm-house. Lucy-Ann carefully didn't look at it. It gave her such a miserable feeling to see the blackened beams and fallen walls.

They stood and listened for the sound of the waterfall. It came softly to their ears, a continous, musical sound, like a far-off orchestra playing a simple tune.

'What a lovely noise!' said Dinah. 'Philip, shall we climb down or up now? If you want to go to the foot of the waterfall and hide somewhere among the rocks there, we ought to climb down, oughtn't we? Last time we climbed up – over that rocky, stony bit.'

The boys stood and considered. 'It would perhaps be best if we went down this time,' said Jack at last. 'Those rocks just above the waterfall may be slippery to climb down on, for they will be wet with the spray. We don't want to slip, and we're carrying so many things that we haven't free hands to use.'

So they chose a way that led downwards. Philip went first, finding the safest path he could; not that there was a real path, of course, for there was not. As they came near to the waterfall, spray blew around them, and left a fine wet mist on their hair. They were hot with climbing and the spray was deliciously cool.

They rounded a corner, and saw the whole of the cas-cading water at once. What a sight! Lucy-Ann drew a quick breath of awe and delight, and stood staring.

'What a thunderous noise!' shouted Jack, trying to make his voice heard. 'It makes me feel all excited.'

'It does me too,' agreed Dinah. 'As if I want to do a jig or a hornpipe or something. And it makes me want to shout and yell.'

'Well, let's!' said Jack, and he began to caper and shout as if he was mad. The others did the same, except Lucy-Ann. It was almost as if they were trying to outshout and outdance the tumbling, roaring water.

They soon stopped, quite exhausted. They were on a flat rock which was wet with the flying spray. They were not nearly at the foot of the water after all, but about a quarter of the way up the fall. The noise filled their ears, and sometimes the force of the spray made them gasp. It was somehow very exciting.

'Well,' said Jack at last, when they had gazed their fill at the waterfall, 'let's think about a good hiding place. I must say I don't think those men would dream of coming here to look for us.'

They all looked about for a cave or mass of rocks in or behind which they could hide. Lucy-Ann looked a little doubtful.

'I don't know if I can bear to hear this terrific noise going on in my ears all the time,' she called to Jack. 'It makes me feel a bit dizzy.'

'Dizzy Lizzie,' remarked Kiki at once. She too had been excited by the waterfall and had shouted with the others.

'Well, you'll have to put up with the noise,' said Jack. 'You'll soon get used to it.'

Lucy-Ann looked worried. She was quite sure she wouldn't get used to that thundering going on all the time. She would never, never be able to sleep through it.

The children wandered about by the waterfall, not going too near it because of the thick spray around it. They couldn't seem to find any good place to hide in at all. All the rocks there seemed to be wet, and there seemed to be no comfortable spot in which to put their things.

'Our rugs would be soaked in no time with the fine mist that hangs about the fall,' said Dinah. 'And we can't possibly lie on wet rugs. I don't believe this is such a good idea after all.'

65

Jack was climbing a little higher. He came to where a giant fern grew. It hung down like a great green curtain and was lovely to see. Jack wondered whether they could hide behind it.

He pushed aside the hanging green fronds and gave a shout at once. The others didn't hear it because of the noise of the water.

'Golly!' said Jack to himself. 'There's a cave behind this hanging fern – and it will be quite dry because the fern screens it from the spray. It's like a great thick curtain! Hey, you others!'

But again nobody heard him. Jack couldn't wait for them to pay attention to him. He went through the hanging fronds and found himself in a dim dry cave, with a fairly low roof, and moss growing on the floor. He felt it. It was dry. Probably when the fern died down in the autumn, the spray flew into the cave and the moss then grew damp and flourished well. But now it was like a soft, dry green bed.

'This is just – exactly – the place for us,' said Jack, delighted. 'Absolutely marvellous! Nobody could possibly see us here because the fern hangs down over the entrance, and it was only quite by accident I found it. It would be a most exciting place for us.'

There was a ledge running round one side of it, like a bench. 'We could put all our things there – tins and so on,' said Jack to himself. 'And when we've put our macks down on this moss we'll have a most lovely bed. I really *must* tell the others.'

It was quite time that he showed himself, for the others had now missed him and were yelling at the tops of their voices for him.

'Jack! JA-CK! Where are you? JACK!'

Jack heard their voices as he pushed aside the fern-fronds and looked out, just his head showing. Dinah and Kiki suddenly caught sight of his face peering out of the fern some way above them. Kiki gave a squawk of surprise and flew up at once. Dinah jumped.

'Look!' she yelled to Philip and Lucy-Ann. 'Look where Jack is – hiding behind that giant fern!'

Jack put his hands to his mouth and yelled at the top of his voice, trying to drown the noise of the waterfall. 'Come on up here! I've found something marvellous!'

The others climbed up eagerly. Jack held aside the green fronds for them. 'Won't you come into my parlour!' he said politely. 'So pleased to see you all.'

They passed through the green curtain into the cave behind. They called out in delighted surprise.

'What a lovely place! Nobody could ever find us here!'

'There's a soft green carpet on the floor! It's moss!'

'The roar of the fall isn't nearly so loud here! We can hear ourselves speak!'

'Glad you like it,' said Jack modestly. 'I found it quite by accident. It's perfect, isn't it?'

It was. Lucy-Ann was relieved that the thunder of the waterfall was lessened here, in the cave. Dinah was thrilled with the softness of the moss. Philip was pleased by the real safety of such a hiding place. Nobody would ever find it except by chance.

'Let's go and fetch our things from the rock where we left them,' said Dinah, who always liked all her belongings set out neatly together. 'There is plenty of room for them here. I shall put our tins of food on that rocky ledge.'

'We can only *just* stand upright,' said Philip. He went to where the green fronds hung down over the entrance, making the cave rather dark. He parted the fronds and at once a ray of sunshine fell into the cave, lighting it up well.

'We could tie back some of the fern so that we get the sun in the cave,' said Philip. 'We've got a jolly good view of the waterfall from here – and we can see everything around well, so that if anyone comes we shall spot them at once. It's fine.'

'I shan't mind living here a bit for a little while,' said Lucy-Ann happily. 'I feel safe here.'

'You may have to live here a *long* while,' said Philip. 'Well – I can think of worse places.'

'Those men would never find us here,' said Jack. 'Never!'

He tied back some of the fronds, and the children sat down on the floor for a little while, enjoying the sunshine that now poured in. The moss was like a cushion to sit on.

After a bit they all climbed down to where they had left their rugs and tins and other things. They carried them up to their new home. Dinah arranged the loose things on the rocky ledge. They looked nice there.

'We shall have a lovely soft bed tonight,' she said. 'We ought to sleep jolly well in here. It's not musty or stuffy.'

'Fusty-musty-dusty,' said Kiki at once, remembering the three words she had learnt in the last holidays. 'Fusty-musty-dusty, fusty . . . '

'Oh, don't begin that again, Kiki,' said Jack. 'We got tired of that long ago.'

Kiki flew to his shoulder, and looked out of the strange little cave. There was really a wonderful view outside – first of all, the cascading waterfall, with rainbows caught in it here and there; then beyond it the steep mountainside, and far beyond that, lower down, the green valley which stretched to the foot of steep mountains on the opposite side, towering up one behind the other.

It was about time for a meal again. All the children seemed to get hungry at the same time, and they glanced at the tins on the shelf or ledge. Jack felt for his tin-opener.

'You mind you don't lose it,' said Philip. 'That's our most precious possession at the moment, Jack – your tin-opener.'

'Don't worry. I shan't lose it,' said Jack, and began to

open a tin. Kiki watched with her head on one side. She liked these tins. They had most exciting things inside, she considered.

Soon they were sitting eating hungrily, looking out of the cave entrance to the sparkling waterfall not far off. It was nice to sit there munching away, with that lovely view outside, the soft moss beneath them, and the warm sun on their bare legs.

'We do seem to have some adventures,' said Jack. 'It's most peculiar the way we can't seem to keep out of them. I do hope Bill and Aunt Allie aren't worrying too much about us. If only we could get word to them!'

'We can't,' said Philip. 'We're stuck here all alone, with no means of getting into touch with anyone as far as I can see – except those two men. I'm blessed if I know what to do. Thank goodness we've got plenty of food.'

'We'd better go back to that bush where we dumped the rest ot the tins and fetch them along here as soon as we can,' said Jack. 'What we've brought won't last us more than today. Will you two girls be all right if Philip and I go along and get what we can? We shan't be able to bring them all at one go. We must make several journeys.'

'Yes, we shall be quite all right here,' said Dinah, giving Kiki the last bit of salmon out of her tin. 'You set off this afternoon. You can leave Kiki here to guard us.'

11

The cave of echoes

It was very early in the afternoon. The boys knew they would have plenty of time to go to the bush where their tins were hidden and fetch them to the cave. Perhaps between them they could carry one sack.

'We'd better go now,' said Jack. 'We'll have to keep a sharp lookout for those men, because they were going to have a jolly good look round, and we don't want them to spot us. Now, you're sure you girls will be all right?'

'Quite,' said Dinah lazily. She felt glad she was not going to go all the way back to the bush and then drag a heavy sack to the cave. She lay back on the moss. It was so very very soft, and springy too.

Jack slung his field glasses round him. They might be useful in trying to spot any men from far off. He and Philip slid through the green fronds of fern. Jack called back to the girls, raising his voice high.

'If you *should* happen to spot anyone near here, remember to untie the string that ties back these ferns *at once*, see?' he said. 'Then they will swing back and the cave will be completely hidden. Lucy-Ann, see that Kiki doesn't follow us.'

Lucy-Ann had Kiki on her shoulder, where Jack had just put here. She put her hand round the bird's ankles and held her. Kiki knew then that she was not supposed to go with Jack and Philip and she gave a dismal squawk.

'What a pity, what a pity!' she said gloomily, and raised up her crest fiercely. But Lucy-Ann would not let her go. She held her until Jack and Philip were out of sight. Then she lowered her hand and Kiki flew off her shoulder and out of the cave. She perched on a rock looking for Jack.

'Down the well,' she said grumpily. 'Blackbirds down the well.'

'No, blackbirds in a pie,' said Lucy. 'What a bird you are for getting things mixed up, Kiki!'

'Poor Kiki!' said Kiki, and cracked her beak loudly. 'Poor Kiki!'

She flew back into the cave. Dinah was fast asleep, stretched out on the green moss, her mouth open. Kiki flew over and put her head on one side, looking at Dinah's open mouth. Then she plucked up a bit of moss with her curved beak.

'Kiki! Don't you dare to put that into Dinah's mouth!' cried Lucy-Ann, knowing Kiki's mischievous ways. 'You're a bad bird!'

'Wipe your feet,' said Kiki crossly, and flew to the back of the cave. Lucy-Ann turned over on her tummy and watched her. She didn't trust Kiki in this mood.

The sun poured into the cave. It felt breathless in there. Lucy-Ann thought it would be a good idea to untie the fronds and let them swing together, to keep out the sun. So she pulled the bit of string that Jack had shown her and at once the ferny curtain descended, and the cave was lost in a dim green twilight, rather exciting to be in.

Dinah didn't wake. Lucy-Ann lay on her tummy again, thinking of all that had happened. The noise of the waterfall came in, rather muffled now, for the curtain of fronds was very thick.

'Kiki,' said Lucy-Ann. 'Kiki, where are you?'

There was no answer from Kiki. Lucy-Ann tried to make out where the parrot was. She must be sulking because Philip and Jack hadn't taken her with them. Silly old Kiki!

'Kiki! Come over here!' said Lucy-Ann. 'Come and talk to me. I'll teach you "Three little kittens have lost their mittens".'

Still there was no answer from Kiki, not even a squawk. Lucy-Ann wondered why. Even if Kiki sulked she would usually talk back if anyone spoke to her.

She peered towards the back of the cave. No Kiki there. She looked at the ledge on which their goods were neatly arranged. No Kiki there.

Well, where was she then? She hadn't flown out between the fern-fronds, that was certain. She must be *somewhere* in the cave!

71

On the rocky ledge was a torch. Lucy-Ann felt for it and took it into her hand. She switched it on and flashed it round the cave. Kiki was nowhere to be seen. She was not even perched up anywhere in the low roof of the cave. How very mysterious!

Lucy-Ann now felt quite alarmed. She awoke Dinah, who sat up, rubbing her eyes, cross to be awakened.

'What's the matter?' she said. 'I was having such a lovely snooze.'

'I can't find Kiki,' said Lucy-Ann. 'I've looked everywhere.'

'Don't be silly. She's gone out of the cave after Jack, I expect,' said Dinah, even crosser. She lay down again and yawned. Lucy-Ann shook her.

'You're not to go to sleep again, Dinah. I tell you, Kiki was here a little while ago – at the back of the cave – and now she's gone. Absolutely vanished.'

'Well, let her – she'll come back all right,' said Dinah. 'Leave me alone, Lucy-Ann.'

She shut her eyes. Lucy-Ann didn't like to say any more. Dinah could be so fierce when she was cross. The little girl sighed and wished the boys were back. What *had* happened to Kiki?

She got up and walked across the moss to the back of the cave. The rock was folded in on itself there, and there was a space behind one of the folds. Lucy-Ann looked cautiously into the dark space, expecting to see Kiki hiding there, ready to cry 'Bo' at her, as she sometimes most annoyingly did.

But Kiki wasn't there. Lucy-Ann flashed her torch up and down the little hidden corner, and suddenly her torch came to a stop, focused on one place.

'Why – there's a hole there!' said Lucy-Ann in surprise. 'That's where Kiki must have gone!'

She clambered up to the hole, which was about shoulder-high. It was just big enough for her to squeeze through. She expected to drop down into another cave the other side, but she didn't. The hole went upwards slightly, a round, narrow tunnel. Lucy-Ann felt sure Kiki must have disappeared into this cold, dark little tunnel.

'Kiki!' she yelled, and flashed her torch in front of her. 'Where are you, idiot? Come back!'

No sound from Kiki. Lucy-Ann squeezed herself right into the round tunnel, wondering how long it was. It was almost as round as a pipe. Maybe water had forced its way through at one time, but now it was quite dry. Lucy-Ann could not hear any sound of the waterfall once she was in the tunnel, though she listened hard. It was very quiet there.

'KIKI!' she yelled. 'KIKI!'

Dinah heard the yell in her dreams and awoke with a jump. She sat up crossly again. But this time Lucy-Ann was not in the cave with her. Now it was Dinah's turn to feel scared. She remembered that Lucy-Ann said that Kiki had suddenly disappeared. Now it seemed as if Lucy-Ann had too. The fronds of fern were hanging over the entrance, Lucy-Ann would not have pushed out through them without telling Dinah she was going out.

Dinah examined the cave well. No Lucy-Ann. Oh, goodness, now what had happened to her and Kiki?

She heard another yell, sounding rather muffled and distant. She went to the back of the cave and discovered the hidden space. She fetched another torch from the ledge and shone it up and down. She stared in amazement when she saw two shoes sticking out of a round hole about as high as her shoulder.

She tugged at Lucy-Ann's ankles and yelled at her. 'Lucy-Ann! What *do* you think you're doing? What's up that hole?'

Lucy-Ann yelled back. 'I don't know, Dinah. I found it by accident. I think Kiki must have gone up it. Shall I go up and see if I can find her? You come too.'

73

'All right,' called Dinah. 'Go on up.'

Lucy-Ann wriggled further up the narrow pipe-like tunnel. It suddenly widened out, and by the light of her torch she saw below her another cave – but a vast one this time.

She managed to get out of the hole, and had a look round at the cave. It was more like an underground hall. Its roof was very high indeed. From somewhere in its dim vastness came a mournful voice.

'What a pity, what a pity!'

'Kiki! So you are here!' cried Lucy-Ann, and then listened in astonishment to the echo that sounded immediately. 'Here, here, here, are here, and here!' cried the echoes, repeating themselves in a weird and strange manner.

'Hurry up, Dinah!' called Lucy-Ann, not liking the echoes at all.

'Up, Dinah, Dinah, Dinah!' called the echoes at once. Kiki flew over to Lucy-Ann, frightened. So many voices! Whatever could they all be?

'Poor Kiki!' said the parrot, in a fright. 'Poor Kiki!'

'Kiki, Kiki, Kiki!' called the echoes. The parrot shivered and gazed all round, trying to see who called her. She suddenly gave a loud and defiant squawk.

At once a score of squawks sounded all round, as if the cave was filled with hundred of parrots. Kiki was simply astounded. *Could* there be so many birds there that she couldn't see?

Dinah crawled out of the hole and stood by Lucy-Ann. 'What an enormous place!' she said.

'Place!' shouted the echoes.

'Everything we say is repeated,' said Lucy-Ann. 'It's weird.'

'Weird, it's weird,' said the echoes.

'Well, let's whisper, then,' said Dinah, whispering herself. The cave was at once filled with mysterious whispers, which scared the girls even more than the repeated shouts they had heard. They clutched one another. Then Dinah recovered herself.

'It's only the echoes,' she said. 'You often get them in enormous caves like this. I wonder if anyone has ever been here before.'

'Never, I should think,' said Lucy-Ann, flashing her torch all round. 'Fancy! We may be treading in a place that no one else has ever trodden in before!'

'Let's explore the cave a bit,' said Dinah. 'Not that there seems much to see, but we might as well do something whilst we're waiting for the boys.'

So they walked slowly round the great dark cave, their footsteps repeated a hundred times by the echoes. Once, when Dinah sneezed, the girls were really frightened by the enormous explosive noises that came from all round them. The echoes certainly enjoyed themselves then.

'Oh, don't sneeze again, Dinah,' begged Lucy-Ann. 'It's really awful to hear the echoes sneezing. Worse than hearing them squawk like Kiki.'

They had gone almost all the way round the cave when they came to a passage leading out of it – a high, narrow passage, between two walls of rocks.

'Look at that!' said Dinah, surprised. 'A passage! Do you suppose it leads anywhere?'

'It might,' said Lucy-Ann and her eyes gleamed. 'Don't forget, Dinah, that those men are after treasure. We don't know what kind – but it's just possible it might be hidden somewhere in these mountains.'

'Let's follow the passage, then,' said Dinah. 'Kiki! Come along. We don't want to leave you behind.'

Kiki flew to her shoulder. In silence the two girls entered the narrow, rocky passage, their torches gleaming in front of them. What were they going to find?

12

Behind the waterfall

The passage was a very winding one. It led a little down-wards, and the floor was very uneven to the feet. The girls tripped and stumbled very often. Once the roof came down so low that they had to crawl under it. But it grew high again almost at once.

After a while they heard a noise. They couldn't imagine what it was. It was a deep and continous roar that never stopped even for a second.

'What's that?' said Dinah. 'Are we getting into the heart of the mountain, do you think, Lucy-Ann? That's not the roar of a mighty fire, is it? What can it be? What is there that could make that noise in the middle of a mountain?'

'I don't know,' said Lucy-Ann, and immediately wanted to go back. A fire in the heart of a mountain, a fire that roared like that? She didn't in the least want to see it. She felt hot and breathless at the thought.

But Dinah wasn't going back now that they had come so far.

'What, go back before we've found out where this passage goes to?' she said. 'Of course not! The boys would laugh like anything when we told them. We don't often get the chance of discovering something before they do. Why, we might even happen on the treasure, whatever it is, Lucy-Ann.'

Lucy-Ann felt that she didn't care at all about the treasure. All she wanted was to get back to the safety of the cave with the green fern curtains.

'Well, you go back, then,' said Dinah unkindly. 'I'm going on!'

It was more frightening to think of going back to the cave

76

of echoes by herself than to go on with Dinah. So poor Lucy-Ann chose unwillingly to go on. With that peculiar, muffled roar in her ears she pressed on down the winding passage, keeping close to Dinah. The roar became louder.

And then the girls knew what it was. It was the waterfall, of course! How stupid of them not to think of that! But it sounded so different there in the mountain.

'We're *not* going into the heart of the mountain after all,' said Dinah. 'We're coming out somewhere near the waterfall. I wonder where.'

They got a tremendous surprise when they did see daylight. The passage suddenly took one last turn and took them into subdued daylight, that flickered and shone round them in a curious way. A draught of cold air met them, and something wetted their hair.

'Lucy-Ann! We've come out on to a flat ledge just *behind* the waterfall!' cried Dinah in astonishment. 'Look, there's the great mass of falling water just in front of us! — oh, the colours in it! Can you hear me? The water is making such a noise.'

Overwhelmed by surprise and by the noise, Lucy-Ann stood and stared. The water made a great rushing curtain between them and the open air. It poured down, shining and exultant, never stopping. The power behind it awed the two girls. They felt very small and feeble when they watched the great volume of water pouring down a few feet in front of them.

It was amazing to be able to stand on a ledge just behind the waterfall and yet not to be affected by it in any way except to feel the fine spray misting the air. The ledge was very wide, and ran the whole width of the fall. There was a rock about a foot high at one end of the ledge, and the girls sat down on it to watch the amazing sight in front of them.

'What will the boys say?' wondered Dinah. 'Let's stay here till we see them coming back. If we sit on this rock, just at the edge of the waterfall, we can wave to them. They will be so astonished to see us here. There's no way of getting to the ledge from above or below, only from behind, from the passage we found.'

'Yes. We'll surprise the boys,' said Lucy-Ann, no longer frightened. 'Look, we can see our cave up there! – at least, we can see the giant fern whose fronds are hiding it. We shall easily be able to see the boys when they come back.'

Kiki was very quiet indeed. She had been surprised to come out behind the great wall of water. She sat on a ledge and watched it, blinking every now and again.

'I hope she won't be silly enough to try and fly through the waterfall,' said Lucy-Ann anxiously. 'She would be taken down with it and dashed to pieces. I know she would.'

'She won't do anything silly,' said Dinah. 'She's wise enough to know what would happen if she tried something like that. She may fly out round the edge of the waterfall, though. Still, there shouldn't be much danger for her in that.'

The girls sat there for a long time, feeling that they would never get tired of watching the turbulence of the waterfall. After a long time Lucy-Ann gave a cry and caught Dinah's arm.

'Look – is that the boys coming? Yes, it is. They've got a sack between them. Good! Now we shall have plenty of food.'

They watched the two boys labouring up the rocks that led to the cave. It was no good waving to them yet. Then suddenly Dinah stiffened with horror.

'What's the matter?' said Lucy-Ann in alarm, seeing Dinah's face.

'Look – someone is following the boys!' said Dinah. 'See – it's one of the men! And there's the other one too! Oh, my goodness, I don't believe either Philip or Jack knows it! They'll watch where they go and our hiding place will be found! JACK! PHILIP! OH, JACK, LOOK OUT!'

She went to the very edge of the waterfall, and, holding on to a fern growing there, she leaned out beyond it, yelling and waving, quite forgetting that the men could see and hear her as well as the boys.

But alas, Jack and Philip, engrossed in the task of getting the heavy sack up the rocks, neither saw nor heard Dinah – but the men suddenly caught sight of her and stared in the utmost astonishment. They could not make out if she was girl, boy, or woman, for the edges of the waterfall continually moved and shifted. All they could make out was that there was definitely someone dancing about and waving behind the great fall.

'Look!' said one man to the other. 'Just look at that! See – behind the water! That's where they're hiding. My word, what a place! How do they get there?'

The men stared open-mouthed at the waterfall, their eyes searching for a way up to it that would lead to the ledge where the excited figure stood waving.

Meantime, Jack and Philip, quite unaware of the following men, or of Dinah either, had reached the curtain of fern. Philip pushed the ferns aside, and Jack hauled the sack up through them, panting painfully, for it was heavy.

At last the sack lay on the floor of moss. The boys flung themselves down, their hearts thumping with the labour of climbing up steeply to the cave, dragging such a heavy sack. At first they did not even notice that the girls were not there.

Not far off, some way below, stood the two men, completely bewildered. In watching Dinah behind the waterfall, they had just missed seeing Jack and Philip creep through the ferns into their cave. So when they turned from gazing at the waterfall, they found that the boys they had so warily followed had utterly disappeared.

'Where have they gone?' demanded Juan. 'They were on that rock there when we saw them last.'

'Yes. Then I caught sight of that person waving down there, and took my eyes off them for a minute – and now they've gone,' growled Pepi. 'Well, there's no doubt where they've gone. They've taken some path that leads to that waterfall. They hide behind it – and a clever place it is, too. Who would think of anyone hiding just behind a great curtain of water like that? Well, we know where to find them. We'll make our way to the water and climb up to that ledge. We'll soon hunt the rats out.'

They began to climb down, hoping to find a way that would lead them to the ledge behind the waterfall. It was difficult and dangerous going, on the slippery rocks.

In the cave the boys soon recovered. They sat up, and looked around for the girls.

'Hallo – where are Lucy-Ann and Dinah?' said Jack in astonishment. 'They promised to stay here till we got back. Surely to goodness they haven't gone wandering about anywhere? They'll get lost, sure as anything!'

They were not in the cave. That was absolutely certain. The boys did not see the hole in the fold of rock at the back. They were extremely puzzled. Jack parted the ferns and looked out.

To his enormous astonishment he at once saw the two men clambering about on rocks near the waterfall. His eyes nearly dropped out of his head.

'Look there!' he said to Philip, closing the fronds a little, fearful of being seen. 'Those two men! Golly, they might have seen us getting in here! How did they get here? We saw them safely by the plane, on our way to the bush!'

Dinah had now disappeared from behind the waterfall. She could not make up her mind whether or not the men had seen the boys climbing in through the fern to their cave. In any case, she thought she ought to warn them of the men's appearance. She felt sure that neither Jack nor Philip knew they were there.

'Come on, Lucy-Ann,' she said urgently. 'We must get back to the boys. Oh, goodness, look at those men! I believe they are going to try and get over here now. They must have spotted me waving. Do come quickly, Lucy-Ann.'·

Shivering with excitement, Lucy-Ann followed Dinah along the dark, winding passage that led back to the cave of echoes. Dinah went as quickly as she could, flashing her torch in front of her. Both girls forgot all about Kiki. The parrot was left sitting alone behind the waterfall, spray misting her feathers, watched the clambering men with interested eyes. She had not heard the girls going off.

Dinah and Lucy-Ann came out into the cave of echoes at last. Dinah stopped and considered. 'Now, where exactly was that hole we came through?' she said.

'Came through, through, through,' called the echoes mockingly.

'Oh be *quiet*!' cried Dinah to the echoes.

'QUIET, QUIET, QUIET!' yelled back the irritating voices. Dinah flashed her torch here and there, and by a very lucky chance she found the hole. In a trice she was in it, crawling along, with Lucy-Ann close behind her. Lucy-Ann had an awful feeling that somebody was going to clutch her feet from behind and she almost bumped into Dinah's shoes in her efforts to scramble down the hole as quickly as possible.

Jack and Philip were peeping through the ferns watching the men, when the girls dropped out of the hole at the back of the cave, came round the fold of rock and flung themselves on the boys. They almost jumped out of their skin.

Philip hit out, thinking that enemies were upon them. Dinah got a stinging blow on the ear, and yelled. She immediately hit out at Philip and the two rolled on the floor.

'Don't, oh, don't!' wailed Lucy-Ann, almost in tears. 'Philip, Jack, it's us! It's us!'

Philip shook off Dinah and sat up. Jack stared in amazement. 'But where did you come from?' he demanded. 'Golly, you gave us an awful scare, I can tell you, jumping out like that! Where have you been?'

'There's a hole back there we went into,' explained Dinah, giving Philip an angry look. 'I say, do you two boys know that those men were following you? They were not very far behind you. We were scared stiff they would see you climbing in here.'

'Were they *following* us!' said Jack. 'Golly, I didn't know that. Peep out between these fronds, you girls, and see them hunting for us down there.'

13

Safe in the cave

They all peeped out between the fern fronds, Lucy-Ann holding her breath. Yes, there were the two men, clambering about dangerously near the waterfall.

'But what are they doing down *there*?' said Jack in wonder. 'Why look for us there? They must have know we didn't go that way, if they were following us.'

'Well, they must have seen me waving to you from behind the waterfall,' said Dinah. 'They must think that's where our hiding place is.'

'Waving to us from behind the waterfall?' said Philip in the utmost amazement. 'What are you talking about, Dinah? You must be bats.'

'Well, I'm not,' said Dinah. 'That's where Lucy-Ann and I were when you came up the slope there to climb into the cave. We were standing behind the waterfall, and I tried my hardest to attract your attention and tell you that those two men were following you.'

'But – how in the world did you get *behind* the waterfall?'

asked Jack. 'It was an idiotic thing to do. Fancy climbing up those slippery rocks, and getting behind the water! You might have been . . .'

'We didn't go that way, silly,' said Dinah. 'We went another way.' And she told Jack and Philip all about the hole at the back of the cave that led down into the cave of echoes, and the passage that came out behind the roaring waterfall. The boys listened in the greatest amazement.

'Gosh! How extraordinary!' said Jack. 'Well, I suppose the men just caught sight of you down there, Dinah, and took their eyes off me and Philip for a minute, and lost us. We must have climbed into this cave through the fern just as they were watching you. What a good thing!'

'That's why they're messing about down there on those wet rocks,' said Philip, grinning. 'They think that that is our hiding place, behind the fall, and they want to get there and find us. They don't guess that isn't the right way. I can't for the life of me see how they can possibly get behind the water from any of those rocks in front. If they're not jolly careful, they'll get swept off by the water – and down they'll go like lightning.'

Lucy-Ann shuddered. 'I don't want to see them do that,' she said, and wouldn't peep out of the ferns any more.

But Dinah and the boys watched in glee. They felt safe up there in their fern-hidden cave, and it was fun to watch the two men slipping about on the rocks near the water, getting angrier and angrier.

Kiki was still behind the waterfall, watching them with interest. Suddenly she gave one of her dreadful cackles of laughter, and the men heard it even through the roar of the water. They looked at one another, startled.

'Hear that?' said Juan. 'Somebody yelling their heads off, laughing at us. Wait till I get them, that's all. They must be just behind the sheet of water. How *do* they get there?'

It was impossible to get behind the waterfall from above

or below. Quite impossible. The men realised this after they had fallen many times, and once almost slipped off a wet rock into the cascading water itself. They sat down on a ledge a good way from the water and mopped their heads. They were hot and angry, and their clothes were soaked.

They were puzzled, too. Where had those boys come from? Was there a whole camp of people somewhere? Were they hiding in the mountains? No, that could not be so, for they would have seen them roving the countryside in search of food. There could only be a few people. They must have sent out the boys to seek for food.

The children watched in delight. There was something very enjoyable in seeing their enemies at a loss, in being able to see their every action and yet not be seen themselves. Even Lucy-Ann had another peep now that she knew they were no longer slipping about the waterfall.

'We'd better go,' said Juan. 'If that's their hiding place they can keep it. We'd better get somebody else here to help us. We could put him to guard this place. If he sat here, he could see if anyone came up to get behind the water. Come on, I'm fed up with this.'

They stood up. Jack watched them through the fern-fronds. Were they going back to their hut, or to the plane, perhaps? Then, seeing that they were going to pass rather near to the cave, the boy hastily closed the fronds and pushed the others back.

'Keep quiet,' he said. 'They may come fairly near.'

They came extremely near. They took a way that led them right past the cave itself. The children sat as still as stone, hearing the men scrambling along outside. Suddenly the fern swayed and shook, and Lucy-Ann's hand flew up to her mouth to stifle a scream.

'They're coming in, they've found us,' she thought, and her heart almost stopped beating. The fern rustled again, and then there was quiet. The footsteps passed, and the children heard the voices of the two men saying something they could not catch.

'Have they gone?' wondered Dinah, and looking at Jack, she raised her eyebrows. He nodded. 'Yes – they were gone – but what a terrible fright everyone had had when they grasped hold of the fern to help them along! Little did Juan and Pepi dream that four silent children sat within two feet of them then.

Jack parted the fern again. There was no sign of the men. He felt sure they must have gone back, but he did not dare to go out and spy. 'Better lie low for a bit,' he said. 'We'll have a meal. I'll creep out and spy around later on. Where's Kiki?'

Nobody knew. Then Dinah remembered she had been with them behind the waterfall. They had gone back without her in their anxiety to warn the boys about the two men. She must still be there.

'Blow! We'd better go and fetch her,' said Jack. 'I don't really feel like moving just now, either – I'm really tired with dragging that heavy sack along so far.'

A voice spoke outside the cave . . . a gloomy, dismal, reproachful voice.

'Poor Kiki! All alone! What a pity, what a Kiki, poor pity!'

The children laughed, and Jack parted the fronds cautiously, in case by any chance the men were still anywhere about. Kiki clambered through, looking very sorry for herself. She flew to Jack's shoulder and nibbled his ear gently.

'All aboard!' she said more cheerfully, and cracked her beak. Dinah ruffled up the feathers on her head.

'Kiki must have flown out from behind the waterfall and come straight here,' she said. 'Clever Kiki! clever old bird!'

'God save the Queen,' said Kiki. 'Wipe your feet!'

Jack's tin-opener came out again, and a choice of tins and jars was made. There was a small tin of biscuits still to be finished, and the children chose some pressed meat to go with them, and a large tin of juicy apricots. Jack opened the fronds just a little to let in enough daylight to see by. Once again they thoroughly enjoyed their meal, and Kiki got into trouble for taking more than her fair share of apricots.

The children waited some time before they dared to creep out of the cave. When the sun was well down, Jack clambered out between the fronds, and had a good look round. There was no sign of the men at all. Jack found a high place from which, if he sat there, he could see for a good way in any direction.

'We'll take it in turns to keep watch,' he said. 'You can come in half an hour, Philip.'

They had a fine time clambering all about. They found some wild raspberries, and ate great quantities of them. They were delicious. Kiki ate them too, murmuring 'Mmmmmmmmm' all the time.

Each of them took turn at keeping watch, but there was nothing to see. The sun went down behind behind the mountains, and twilight came. They all went back to the cave.

'It will be lovely to sleep here tonight,' said Lucy-Ann, pleased. 'This moss is so nice and soft. Like velvet.'

She stroked it. It *felt* like velvet too. She helped Dinah to put down macks and a rug to lie on, and made pillows of pullovers and jerseys.

'A drink of apricot juice and a few biscuits for everyone,' said Dinah, as they all sat down on the 'bed.' She handed out the biscuits. Jack parted the fern-fronds and tied them firmly back.

'Must have a little air in the cave,' he said. 'It will get jolly stuffy with four of us here.'

'Five,' said Dinah. 'Don't forget Kiki.'

'Six,' said Philip, producing the lizard. 'Don't forget dizzy Lizzie.'

86

'Oh, I really hoped you'd lost her,' said Dinah crossly. 'I haven't seen her all day.'

They finished their biscuits and lay down. It was quite dark now outside. Their 'bed' felt warm and soft. They all snuggled down, making nice cosy places for themselves.

'I should really enjoy all this, if only I knew that Mother wasn't worrying about us,' said Philip, pulling the rug over him. 'I haven't any idea at all where we are, but it's a very beautiful place. Doesn't that waterfall sound lovely, singing in the night?'

'It's singing jolly loudly,' said Jack, yawning. 'But I don't think it will keep *me* awake. Oh, Kiki, do move off my middle. I can't imagine why you will keep perching there at night. Go on one of my feet.'

'Wipe your feet,' ordered Kiki, and flew to Jack's right foot. She put her head under her wing.

'Tomorrow Philip and I must go to that cave of echoes you told us about and stand behind the waterfall,' said Jack. 'Fancy you girls having a little adventure like that all on your own!'

'*Little* adventure!' said Lucy-Ann. 'Why, it was a jolly big one – especially when we suddenly saw that we were just behind the waterfall!'

Dinah was very much afraid that Lizzie would run over her during the night, and lay awake some time expecting the feel of her tiny feet. But Lizzie was curled up in Philip's armpit, tickling him dreadfully when she moved.

Lucy-Ann was asleep almost at once, and soon the others were too. The waterfall roared all through the night without ceasing. The wind sprang up and moved the big fronds of the fern. A fox or some other creature came sniffing up to the cave entrance, was alarmed at the smell of humans there and fled away silently.

Nobody stirred, except Philip when the lizard woke up, felt cramped, and made her way to another nice warm spot, this time behind his ear. He awoke for a second, felt Lizzie moving, and then shut his eyes immediately again, pleased with the feel of the tiny feet.

Towards morning a throbbing sound awoke all four children. It penetrated into the cave, sounding even louder than the waterfall. Jack sat up at once, surprised. What could that be?

The noise grew louder and louder, it seemed as if it was coming right down on their heads. Whatever *could* it be?

Rr-rr-rr-rr-rr-rrRRRRRRRRRRRRRRRRR!

'It's a plane!' cried Jack. 'A plane! Come to rescue us. Out of the cave, quick!'

They all tumbled out of the cave and looked for the plane. One was climbing into the air, a large shape against the sky. It had evidently come very near the side of the mountain, and had awakened them by its noise.

'A plane to rescue us?' said Philip scornfully. 'Not likely! That's the plane we came here in – the men's plane, idiot!'

14

The poor prisoner

Sure enough, it was the men's plane. The children all recognised it quite well as they watched it vanishing into the distance. It flew towards the west.

'Wonder if it's going back to Bill's aerodrome?' said Jack. 'Wonder if Bill knows what those men are up to?'

'We don't know very much ourselves, except that they are after some sort of treasure,' said Philip. 'But, honestly, what treasure they think they can find here in this place beats me.'

'Beats me too,' said Jack. 'Well – there they go! Do you

suppose they'll come back?'

'Sure to,' said Philip. 'They won't give up as easily as that. Maybe they've gone to report that there are other people here now – for all they know, after the treasure too! And they might bring back more men to smell us out.'

'Oh,' said Lucy-Ann in alarm. 'I don't want to be smelt out.'

'Do you think *both* men have gone?' asked Philip.

'I should think so,' said Jack. 'But we can go and have a jolly good look round and see. If one man is left, he'll be somewhere near that shed of theirs. He won't know how many of us there are here – he may think there are men with us, you know, and not dare to move about too much by himself.'

But when the children left the cave later in the morning and went to 'have a squint,' as Jack said, they could find no sign of either Juan or Pepi. There was no fire. It had been stamped out. And this time the shed was well and truly locked, and the key taken. No amount of shaking or kicking would open the door.

'Well, if we'd known the men were going to fly off, we might have asked them for a lift,' said Jack with a grin. 'I wonder when they'll come back – if they do come back, that is.'

'Not till it's daylight tomorrow, I should think,' said Philip. 'I expect they'll take off at night again. Let's go and have another squint at those crates.'

But there was really nothing to see. They were empty as before, and the tarpaulin was over them. The children played about for some hours, and had a meal under a tree. They went to get a tin or two from the rest of the store still hidden in the bush. Jack opened them.

After the meal Philip suggested that they should go back to the waterfall and the girls should take them to the cave of echoes, and down the passage that led behind the water. So off they went, first hiding all trace of having been near the men's shed.

But when they got back to their cave, Jack gave a most annoyed exclamation and began to feel in all his pockets.

'What's the matter?' said Lucy-Ann.

'Well, do you know what I've done? I've gone and left the tin-opener behind,' said Jack. 'Think of that! What an idiotic thing to do! I thought we might want another tin opened, so I put it down at the roots of that tree we had our picnic under – and I must have left it there. I haven't got it, anyway.'

'Oh, *Jack*! But we can't have a meal without opening a tin,' said Philip, seeing awful visions of a hungry night. 'Gosh – you *are* an ass!'

'Yes, I know,' said Jack gloomily. 'Well, there's only one thing to be done. I must go back and get it. You explore the cave of echoes with the girls, Philip, and I'll take Kiki and go back for the opener. Serves me right.'

'I'll come with you, Jack,' said Lucy-Ann, sorry for her brother.

'No, you've had a jolly long walk already,' said Jack. 'You go with the others. Anyway, I'll be quicker by myself. I'll just have a sitdown before I start back. I can always explore the cave another time.'

He sat down on the moss. The others sat with him, sorry for him, knowing how annoyed he must feel with himself. But it would be still more annoying to have to go without meals. The opener must certainly be fetched.

After about half an hour Jack felt able to start back again. He said a cheery goodbye to the others, and left, scrambling quickly down the rocks. They knew he would not lose his way. They all felt they knew it quite well by this time.

Jack had Kiki on his shoulder, and they talked together all the way. Kiki was simply delighted to have Jack all to herself. He was nearly always with the others. They talked complete nonsense and both of them thoroughly enjoyed it.

Jack arrived at last at the tree under which they had had their lunch. He looked for the opener, half fearful in case it had been removed by somebody. But it was still there, lying where he had left it. He picked it up and put it into his pocket.

'Three cheers,' he said.

'Three blind mice,' said Kiki. 'Handy spandy, humpy dumpy.'

'I agree with you,' said Jack. 'Well, we'll get back, I think. Twilight will soon be coming and I don't fancy going back in the dark. Off we go, Kiki, up the hill.'

'Jack and Jill,' agreed Kiki.

'Jack and Kiki, you mean,' grinned Jack, turning to go. Then he stood still suddenly and listened. Away in the distance he could hear a sound he knew – a familiar, throbbing sound. Rr-rr-rr-rr-rr!

'Gosh, Kiki! – are those fellows coming back so soon?' said Jack, staring into the western sky, which was still faintly gold. 'Yes – that's a plane all right. But is it theirs?'

The plane came nearer, growing larger and larger. An idea came into Jack's mind. He ran to where the men's shed was, and climbed quickly up into a tree not far from where they had their camp-fire. He spoke sternly to Kiki.

'Now, quiet, Kiki. Not a word. Do you understand? Shhhhhhh!'

'What a pity, what a pity!' said Kiki in a curious hoarse whisper, and then was silent, pressing against Jack's neck as she sat on his shoulder.

The plane roared nearer. It circled lower and lower. It dropped to the long smooth strip that made such an excellent runway. It bounced along on its high wheels and then came to a stop. Jack could not see the plane from where he was.

But he was counting on the men coming to the shed or to their fire, and he was right. They soon arrived, and Jack peered out through the leaves, nearly overbalancing in his efforts to see properly, for twilight was almost there.

This time there were four men. Jack looked very hard. He could see that one man was evidently a prisoner. He had his hands tied behind him. How strange!

He shambled along, his head bent, going from side to side a little as if he was dizzy. Now and again one of the others would give him a shove to keep him straight. They came straight to the campfire.

Juan set to work to light it. Pepi went off to the shed to get some tins. He took a key from his pocket and unlocked the door. He came out carrying tins of soup and meat.

The prisoner sat down on the grass, his head bent. It was obvious that he was not feeling well – or was he merely afraid? Jack couldn't tell. The fourth man, who was a kind of guard for the prisoner, as far as Jack could make out, sat by the fire saying nothing, watching Juan and Pepi.

At first they talked in low voices and Jack could not hear their words. They drank hot soup, and then carved up a tongue from a glass jar. They ate bread with it which they had brought from the plane. The prisoner looked up and saw them eating, but the three men did not offer him anything. He said something in a low voice. Juan laughed.

He spoke to the guard. 'Tell him he won't get anything to eat or drink till he tells us what we want to know,' he said.

The guard repeated this in some language that Jack could not make out. The prisoner said something and the guard struck him on the cheek. Jack watched in horror. Fancy hitting a man when his hands were tied! What cowards!

The man tried to dodge. He bent his head again and sat dismally there.

'He says you've got the map, what else do you want?' said the guard.

'We can't read the map,' said Juan. 'It's all messed up. If he can't explain it to us, he'll have to show us the way tomorrow.'

The guard translated this to the prisoner. He shook his head. 'He says he is too weak to walk so far,' said the guard.

'We'll drag him all right,' said Pepi, and took another piece of tongue, making himself a thick sandwich. 'Tell him he's to take us tomorrow. If he won't, he gets nothing to eat or drink. He'll soon come round when he's half starved.'

They finished their meal. Then Juan yawned. 'Me for bed,' he said. 'There's a chair for you, Luis, in the hut. The floor's good enough for the prisoner.'

The man begged to have his hands untied, but they would not allow him to. Jack felt very sorry for him. They stamped out the fire and went to the hut. Jack imagined Pepi and Juan on the mattress, and Luis in the only comfortable chair. The poor prisoner would have to lie on the cold, hard floor, with his hands still tied behind him.

Jack waited till he thought the coast was clear, then he slipped quietly down the tree. Kiki had been as good as gold all the time. Not even a whisper had come from her beak. Jack tiptoed to the hut. He peeped cautiously in at the window. A candle burned in the hut, and by its flickering light he could make out the four men. The prisoner was trying to make himself comfortable on the floor.

It was almost dark. Jack hoped he would be able to get back to the cave all right. He slipped his hand into his pocket and was relieved to find a small torch there. That was good!

He was very clever in the dark, for he had eyes like a cat. Once or twice he stopped, unable to think which way to go – but Kiki always knew. She simply flew a little way in front and called to him, or whistled.

'Good old Kiki!' said Jack. 'I couldn't have found my way without you, that's certain.'

The others were very worried about him. When darkness

fell and still no Jack had arrived, Lucy-Ann wanted to go and look for him.

'I'm sure he's lost, I'm certain of it,' she said, almost in tears.

'Yes, and *we'd* all get lost too, if we went out on the mountainside in this darkness,' said Philip. 'I expect he hunted about for that opener, saw that twilight was coming, and decided not to risk coming back in the dark. He'll be back tomorrow morning early, for certain.'

It was too dark to do anything. Dinah had made the 'bed' and they lay down on it, Lucy-Ann very worried. She was sure something had happened to Jack.

Then there came a scrambling noise up near the cave, and the fern was parted and pushed aside. All the children sat up, their hearts beating. Was it Jack – or had their hiding place been discovered?

'Hallo, there!' came Jack's familiar voice. 'Where's everybody?'

He switched on his torch and saw three delighted faces. Lucy-Ann almost fell on him.

'Jack! We thought you were lost. What *have* you been doing? And we're so hungry, too. Have you brought the tin-opener?'

'Yes, I've brought that – and plenty of news as well!' said Jack. 'What about a meal whilst I tell you all about it?'

15

A disappointment for the men

Tins were opened once more, and Kiki gave a delighted chortle at the sight of her favourite pineapple. Lucy-Ann pressed close to Jack.

'What happened to you? I can't wait to hear. Tell me quickly.'

'Let me have a bite first,' said Jack irritatingly, knowing quite well that all the others were longing to hear his news. But as he was longing just as much to tell it as they were to hear it, he soon began his story.

'So the plane's back!' exclaimed Philip, as Jack began to tell everything. 'Both men back too?'

Jack told of the four men. Lucy-Ann was distressed to hear about the poor prisoner.

'I'm beginning to see daylight,' said Philip at last. 'Somewhere in this valley is hidden treasure – maybe stuff belonging to the people whose houses have been burnt. Those two men heard about it, and somehow managed to get a map that showed them the hiding place. But they can't find it by that map, so they've got hold of somebody who knows the way.'

'That's it,' said Jack. 'He's foreign. Maybe he once belonged to this valley, and even hid the things himself. They've captured him and mean to make him show them the hiding-place. They're not giving him anything to eat or drink till he shows them what they want to know.'

'Brutes!' said Dinah, and the others agreed with her.

'Do you think he *will* show them?' asked Lucy-Ann.

'I hope he will for his own sake,' said Jack. 'And I'll tell you what I propose. I propose that somehow or other one or more of us follow them, and see where this hiding place is. The men can't possibly take everything away at once. We might be able to get help, and save the rest of the stuff being stolen by the men. It can't belong to them.'

'What do you think the stuff can be?' asked Lucy-Ann, visions of gold bars and beautiful jewels floating in her mind.

'Can't tell you,' said Jack. 'I think we're somewhere in the depths of Europe, where war has been, and as you know, plenty of treasure of all kinds was hidden in odd places by many, many people, good and bad. My guess is that it's something of that kind these men are after. They speak English, but they're not English. Perhaps from South America? Goodness knows.'

The others sat silent, thinking over what Jack had said. They thought he was probably right. But Lucy-Ann didn't at all like the idea of following the men. Suppose they discovered that they were being followed, and captured them?

'It might be best if Philip and I did the stalking tomorrow,' said Jack. 'I don't think you girls should be mixed up in it.'

This made Dinah angry, though Lucy-Ann was secretly relieved.

'You're not going to keep all the excitement to yourselves,' said Dinah. 'I'm coming too.'

'No, you're not,' said Jack. He switched on his torch and shone it at Dinah's face. 'I thought you'd be glaring,' he said. 'Cheer up, Dinah. After all, you and Lucy-Ann had an adventure yesterday, when you found the cave of echoes and the passage that leads to the waterfall. Give us boys a chance.'

'Well, it's all very well,' grumbled Dinah, but she did not press the point any more, much to Lucy-Ann's relief.

'Where's Lizzie?' asked Dinah, not liking to settle down till she was quite sure of the lizard's whereabouts.

'Don't know,' said Philip annoyingly. 'She might be anywhere. Under your pillow, perhaps.'

'She's here,' said Jack. 'Kiki's one side of my neck and Lizzie's the other, keeping me nice and warm.'

'What a pity!' said Kiki, and cackled loudly.

'*Don't!*' said everybody at once. Nobody liked Kiki's awful cackle. She put her head under her wing, offended.

All the children lay down. They were sleepy. 'Our fourth night in this valley,' said Philip. 'The valley of adventure. I wonder what will happen next.'

Soon they were all asleep. Lizzie ran across Lucy-Ann and cuddled down by Dinah, who would certainly have objected strongly if she had known. But she didn't know. So she slept peacefully.

Everyone felt cheerful the next morning.

'Really,' said Dinah, reaching down some tins from the ledge, 'I'm beginning to feel I've made this cave my home half my life. It's extraordinary how soon we get used to anything new.'

'How are we going to find out when those men are starting, and what way they go?' said Philip.

'Well, if you remember, the two of them came in this direction, not the other, when they set out with the map before,' said Jack. 'I think if we go to that big black rock we always pass on the way here, we may spot them. Then we can follow easily enough.'

So when they had finished their meal they set off cautiously to the big black rock. They crouched behind it, and Jack kept peering out to see if there was anything to be seen.

After about an hour he gave a low exclamation. 'Hallo! Here they come – all four – prisoner still with his hands tied, stumbling along, poor thing.'

The four men passed some distance away. The children saw them well. They recognised the two men they knew, and Jack told them the fourth man was called Luis. The prisoner's name he didn't know. It was plain that the poor man was giddy for lack of food and drink.

'Now, you girls stay here, see?' said Jack. 'At any rate, till we are well out of sight. Then go back to the waterfall, and keep somewhere about there. Don't get lost! Take Kiki, Lucy-Ann. We don't want her with us.'

Lucy-Ann took Kiki and held her ankles. Kiki gave such an angry squawk that the children looked uneasily after the four men to see if by any chance they had heard. But they hadn't.

Jack and Philip made ready to set off. 'I've got my field glasses,' said Jack. 'I can keep the men well in sight, while following quite a long way behind, so that they won't spot us. Cheerio!'

The boys went off cautiously, keeping to every bit of cover they could. They could still see the men far away in the distance. 'Do we need to mark the way we're going?' asked Philip. 'Or shall we be able to find the way back, do you think?'

Better mark things where we can,' said Jack. 'You never know. Mark rocks with white chalk. Here's a bit. And trees we will notch.'

They went on, climbing upwards a good way behind the four men. Soon they came to a very steep place, difficult to keep their footing on, because the surface was so loose that they slid down continually.

'I hope they've undone that poor prisoner's hands, panted Jack. 'I'd hate to do climbing like this and have my hands bound so that I couldn't save myself when I slipped.'

When they came to the end of the rough piece, the men were nowhere to be seen. 'Blow!' said Jack. 'That bit held us up too long. Now we've lost them!'

He put his field glasses to his eyes and swept the mountainside. Some way to the east and above them he suddenly saw four small figures. 'There they are!' he said. 'It's all right. I can see them. That way, Tufty.'

On they went again, going more quickly now because the way was easier. They picked wild raspberries as they went, and once stopped for a drink at a little clear spring of water that gushed from under a rock.

They did not lose sight of the men again except for a moment or two. The men did not turn round, or use field glasses at all. Plainly they did not expect anyone to follow them.

Now the boys came to a very desolate part of the mountainside. Big boulders had rolled down. Trees had been torn in half. Great ruts had been torn out of the earth and rock, and although the grass was growing everywhere to hide the scars, it was clear that some catastrophe had happened here.

'An avalanche, I should think,' said Jack. 'I guess a terrific fall of snow happened here – bringing down with it boulders and rocks of all sizes – knocking down trees and scoring those ruts. Last winter, I should think.'

'Where are the men?' said Philip. 'I can't see them now. They went round the ledge.'

'Yes. We'll have to be careful how we go round,' said Jack. 'We might easily be seen coming round there. There's not much cover in this devastated bit.'

So they went very cautiously round the ledge – and it was a good thing they did, for almost at once they heard voices and saw the four men.

Jack pressed Philip back. Just above the ledge was a bush. The boys climbed up to it, pressed against it, and parted the leaves so that they might see through. They found that they were looking down into a rocky gully.

Here, too, there had evidently been a great fall of rocks. In front of one heap stood the prisoner. His hands were now untied. He was pointing to the heap of rocks, and saying something in his rather dull, low voice. The guard translated, and Jack strained his ears to hear what he had to say.

'He says the entrance was here,' the guard said. The four men stared at the fall of rock.

'Exactly where?' said Juan impatiently, and glared at the prisoner. He pointed again, mumbling something.

'He says he didn't know there had been a fall or rock here,' said the guard. 'He says the entrance seems to be blocked up. But if you try to lift away some of these rocks, maybe you could find enough room to go in.'

Juan flew into a temper, but whether with the prisoner or the annoying fall of rocks it was difficult to say. He fell upon

99

the boulders and began to drag at them feverishly, shouting to Luis and Pepi to help. The prisoner at first did nothing but sat down miserably on a rock. Juan shouted at him too, and he dragged himself up to help, though he was too weak to do anything in the way of lifting.

He pulled at a rock, staggered and fell. The others let him lie where he fell, and went on dragging at the great stones, panting and wiping the sweat from their foreheads.

The two boys watched them. It looked impossible, from where they were, to unblock any cave entrance there. 'Why,' whispered Jack to Philip, 'hundreds of stones must have fallen there! They'll never, never be able to shift them like that!'

Evidently the men thought so too, after a while, for they gave up pulling the boulders about and sat down to rest. The guard pointed to the fallen prisoner and spoke.

'What about him? How are we going to take him back?'

'Oh, give him some food and a drink,' growled Juan. 'He'll be all right, then.'

'We'd better go now,' whispered Philip. 'They'll be starting back soon. Come on. How disappointing that we haven't discovered anything, though! I did hope we might see something of the treasure.'

'If it's hidden behind that wall of fallen stone it'll need powerful machinery to get it out,' said Jack. 'Nobody could move those bigger stones by hand. Come on, quickly.'

They set out on their way back, going as quickly as they could, glad that they had marked rocks and trees or they might have missed their way here and there.

The girls welcomed them, and poured questions on them. But the boys shook their heads most disappointingly.

'The treasure cave is blocked up,' said Jack. 'I only hope the men don't give up and leave this valley altogether. We'll be properly stranded then.'

16

Rescue of the prisoner

Some while after Jack and Philip had got back to the cave, Lucy-Ann, who was looking out between the fern fronds, gave a cry. 'I say, there's a man down there! – look, by the waterfall! Two men – no, three!'

Jack pulled the string which tied back the fronds and let them swing together to hide the cave. Then, parting the fronds carefully, he looked through.

'I might have guessed they would come back this way, to have another hunt for us here,' he said. 'Blow them! One – two – three of them. Where's the prisoner?'

'Fallen by the way, I should think, poor fellow,' said Philip, peering out too. 'He looked terribly feeble.'

The children watched the three men eagerly to see what they meant to do. It was soon clear. Luis and Juan were to go back to their hut, but Pepi was to be left to keep watch on the waterfall, to see who went in and out, and to try and discover the way that was used. The children could not hear what was said, but it was all plain enough.

Luis and Juan departed. Where the prisoner was nobody could guess. Pepi sat down on a rock that overlooked the waterfall, just about the level of the ledge where the girls had stood the day before.

'Blow!' said Jack. 'How can we get in and out without being seen? It's true he's got his back to us, but he might turn round at any time.'

Lucy-Ann began to worry about the prisoner. 'Suppose he has fallen down on the way, and the men have left him there,' she said. 'He'd die, wouldn't he?'

'I suppose so,' said Jack, feeling anxious too.

'But Jack, we can't leave him to die,' said Lucy-Ann, her eyes big with horror. 'You know we can't. I shan't rest till I know what's happened to him.'

'I feel rather like that too,' said Jack, and the others nodded. 'There was something awful about the hopeless way he sat. I'm sure he was ill.'

'But how can we find out what's happened to him, whilst that fellow down there is guarding this place?' said Philip gloomily.

Everyone fell silent. It was a puzzler. Then Lucy-Ann brightened up. 'I know,' she said. 'There's one certain way of making sure Pepi doesn't see anyone creeping out of this cave.'

'What?' said Jack.

'Well, if one or two of us got behind the waterfall and capered about a bit to attract the man's attention, he would be all eyes for them, and wouldn't notice anyone creeping out of this cave,' said Lucy-Ann.

'There's something in that,' said Jack, and Philip nodded. 'Yes, quite a good idea. Well, there's no time like the present. Shall we give a performance for dear Pepi now? You two girls could go and caper about, if you like – you are quite safe when you're behind the waterfall, because nobody can possibly get at you there, unless they go that same way as you do. And Pepi certainly doesn't know that way. Whilst you are attracting his attention, Philip and I will go off and see if we can see any sign of the prisoner.'

'Well, wait here till you see us behind the water,' said Dinah and she got up. She and Lucy-Ann disappeared up the hole at the back of the cave. The boys waited patiently for them to appear behind the waterfall.

After some while Philip clutched Jack's arm. 'There they are! Good old Lucy-Ann, good old Dinah! They're having a fine old game down there. What are they waving? Oh, they've taken off their red pullovers and they're waving them like mad – doing a kind of dance.'

Pepi caught sight of them at once. He stared in surprise, and then stood up. He yelled and shouted and waved. The girls took no notice at all, but went on capering. Pepi began to try all kinds of ways to get to the waterfall.

'Now's our chance,' said Jack. 'Come on. His eyes will be glued on Lucy-Ann and Dinah for ages.'

They crept quickly out of the cave, swinging the fronds closely together behind them. They climbed up the rocks there and soon took cover so that they could not be seen. When the girls saw that they were safely out of the cave and could no longer be seen, they left the waterfall ledge and went back into the passage that led to the cave of echoes. They had done their bit.

The boys made their way cautiously over the rocks, keeping a good lookout for the others. When they were quite a long way from Pepi, they stopped to take counsel.

'Now – should we go back to that blocked up cave where apparently the treasure is, and see if we can find the prisoner fallen by the way – or shall we scout a bit in the other direction – back to the men's hut, to see if by any chance they've taken him there?'

'Better go to the men's hut,' said Philip, thinking. 'I don't think it's *very* likely they've left him to die by the wayside. They might still want to get something out of him.'

So they made their way back to the men's hut. How well they knew the way now! They saw the smoke of the fire long before they came near, and by that they knew the men were back.

There was no sign to be seen of the two men or of the prisoner. Cautiously the boys peered through the trees near the hut. The door of the hut was shut and presumably locked. Were the men inside?

103

'Hark, isn't that the sound of the plane's engine running?' asked Philip suddenly. 'Yes, it is. Are those fellows going off again?'

They went to a place from which they could see the plane well by means of Jack's field glasses. The men were not going off – merely doing something to their plane. There was no sign of the prisoner being with them.

'Stay here, Philip, with my field glasses and keep an eye on the plane and the men,' said Jack, pushing his glasses into Philip's hand. 'Come and tell me at once if they stop their work there and go towards the hut. I'm going to peep in at the hut window and see if the prisoner is there. I'm worried about him.'

'Right,' said Philip, and put the field-glasses to his eyes. Jack sped off. He soon came to the hut. He tried the door. Yes, it was locked all right. He crept round to the window and peeped in.

The prisoner was there. He was sitting in the chair, the picture of misery, his face in his hands. As Jack looked, he heard him groan deeply, and it was such a dreadful noise that the boy's heart was wrung.

'If only I could get him out!' he thought. 'No use breaking the window. It's too small even for me to get in, and certainly that fellow couldn't squeeze out. What can I do? I can't break down the door. It's jolly strong!'

He went all round the hut two or three times, but there was absolutely no way of getting in. He stood and stared at the door, hating it. Horrid strong thing!

And then he saw an unbelievable sight. There was a nail at one side of the door, and on it hung – a key! A large key! A key that surely must fit the door. Otherwise why should it be there? It must have been put there so that any of the men could go in and out at any time without waiting for the one who had the key.

With trembling fingers Jack took the key from the nail.

He put it into the lock of the door. He turned it. It was stiff – but it turned all right.

The door swung open and Jack went in. The prisoner, hearing the door open, looked up. He stared in surprise at Jack. The boy grinned at him.

'I've come to set you free,' he said. 'Like to come with me?'

The man did not seem to understand. He frowned a little and stared even harder at Jack.

'Spik slow,' he said. Jack repeated what he had said. Then the boy tapped himself on the chest and said, 'I am your friend. Friend! Understand?'

The man evidently did understand that. A slow smile broke over his face. It was a nice face – a kindly, sad, trustable face, Jack thought. The boy held out his hand.

'Come with me,' he said.

The man shook his head. He pointed to his feet. They were bound tightly with rope, which the man obviously had not had the strength to untie. Jack whipped out his pocket-knife in a trice. He sawed through the thick strands and they fell apart. The man stood up unsteadily, looking as if he was about to fall. Jack steadied him, thinking that he would never be able to walk all the way to their cave. He seemed even weaker than before.

'Come on,' said the boy ugently. 'We haven't much time to lose.'

Jack put the cut pieces of rope into his pocket. He led the man to the door, put him outside, and then carefully locked the door again, hanging the key on its nail. He grinned at the prisoner.

'Bit of a surprise for Juan and Luis to find you've apparently walked through a locked door,' said the boy. 'I'd like to be here when they unlock the door and find you gone.'

Jack took the man's arm and piloted him away into the cover of the nearby trees. The man walked very unsteadily.

He gave a groan every now and again as if it hurt him to walk. Jack felt more and more certain that he would never be able to get to the cave.

He wondered what to do. Perhaps he could park the man in the old cowshed he and the others had found the first day they had arrived? He could put him in the last cowstall, and then fetch him the next day, when he was a little more recovered. That would be the best thing.

'You stay here a minute,' said the boy, thinking he had better run to Philip, tell him what had happened, and get him to keep guard till he got the man safely installed in the shed.

Philip was intensely surprised to hear what Jack had to tell him. He nodded and agreed to stay on guard till Jack came for him.

'The men seem to be overhauling the plane,' he said. 'Looks as if they'll be busy for some time.'

Jack helped the stumbling prisoner over to the cowshed. It took a long time to get there, because the man went so slowly.

Once there, he sank down in the stall and panted painfully. He was certainly an ill man. But there was no doctor for him – only Jack's gentleness, for which he seemed to be very grateful.

'You stay here till tomorrow, when I will fetch you to a safer hiding place,' said Jack, speaking very slowly indeed. 'I will leave you water to drink and food to eat.'

The boy meant to open a tin or two from the store still hidden in the bush. He could easily get them and leave them beside the man.

'The man tapped his chest. 'Otto Engler,' he said, and repeated it two or three times. Jack nodded, and pointed to his own chest.

'Jack Trent,' he said. 'Me Jack – you Otto.'

'Friend,' said the man. 'You – English?'

'Me English,' said Jack gravely. 'You?'

'Austrian,' said the man, pronouncing it in a curious way. 'Friend. Good friend. Why you here?'

Jack tried to explain how it was he and the others had come, but it was too complicated for the man to understand and he shook his head.

'Not understand,' he said. Then he leaned forward to Jack and spoke in a low voice.

'You know of treesure?'

'Treesure? Oh, you mean treasure,' said Jack, 'Not much. You know – of treasure?'

'I know all,' said the man. 'All! I draw you map – where treesure is. You good boy. I trust you.'

17

A treasure map

Jack's first feeling on hearing this was one of tremendous excitement. Then his face fell. He knew where the treasure was. Behind that fall of rock. What use was that? Nobody could get at it there.

'I know where treasure is,' said Jack, trying to speak slowly and simply. 'I saw you show the men this morning – but the rocks had fallen together, and they could not get into the treasure-cave behind.'

The man gave a short laugh. He seemed to understand. 'They are fools,' he said. 'Big fools. There is no treesure there.'

Jack stared at him. 'Do you mean to say – you fooled them?' he said. 'You knew that fall of rocks was there – and

107

you took them to it, and pretended that the entrance to the treasure was all blocked up? Isn't the treasure behind those rocks after all?'

The man was frowning hard in his attempt to follow all that Jack was saying. He shook his head.

'No treesure there,' he said. 'I fool Juan and Pepi. Ah, ah, how they hurt their hands when they pull – so – at the rocks!'

Jack couldn't help grinning. What a fine trick to play! Well, then – where *was* the 'treesure'?

'I draw you map,' said Otto. 'And I tell you way out of valley too. By the Windy Pass. You will go that way, you and your friends, and you will take the map to a good friend of mine. It is time now to find the hidden treasure.'

'But why can't you come with us?' said Jack. 'Surely you could show us the way, Otto – the pass – and come to your good friend?'

'I am very ill man,' said Otto. 'If I do not get doctor and – how you say it? – middisin . . . '

'Yes, medicine,' said Jack.

' . . . middisin soon, I die,' said Otto. 'I have bad heart, very very bad. I get pain very bad. I not walk far now. So you take treesure map, you good boy, and you take pass out of valley, and go to Julius, my good friend. Then all will be well.'

'All right,' said Jack. 'I'm very sorry about you, Otto. Wish I could do something. I'll do my best to get to Julius quickly and bring back help to you. Do you think you might be able to walk to our hiding place tomorrow, and hide there whilst we go?'

'Pardon?' said Otto. 'You talk too quick, I not understand.'

Jack spoke more slowly. Otto nodded. He understood the second time.

'You leave me here today, and tomorrow perhaps I be

strong enough to go with you to your place,' he said. 'We will see. If not, you must go through the pass and find Julius. I draw you map now, and I draw you also the way to the pass. Windy Pass. It is very, very narrow, but not difficult to, to . . . '

'To travel through?' said Jack. Otto nodded. He found a pencil and a notebook and began to draw. Jack watched him with interest. The waterfall appeared in the map. So did an oddly shaped rock. A bent tree came into the map, and a spring of water. Little arrows were drawn showing in what direction to go. It was really rather exciting.

Otto folded up the map. He gave it to Jack. 'Julius will know,' he said. 'He will read the map. Once he lived in the big farmhouse not far from here. But our enemies burnt it down, and all the other farms too, and took our cows and our horses, our pigs and everything we had. Many they killed, and only few of us escaped.'

'Now tell me the way to the pass,' said Jack.

Otto once more drew a map. The waterfall appeared in it. Jack put his finger on it.

'I know this water,' he said, speaking slowly so that Otto would understand. 'Our hiding place is near. Very near.'

'So!' said Otto, pleased. 'The way to the pass is above the waterfall. You must climb to where it flows out of a hole in the mountainside. There – I have drawn you the way.'

'How shall we find Julius?' asked Jack.

On the other side of the pass is a village, half burnt,' said Otto. 'You will ask anyone you meet to tell you where Julius is. They will know. Ah, Julius worked against the enemy all the time. Everyone knows Julius. He should be a great man now among his people – but times are strange and maybe he is no longer great, now that we have peace. But still, everyone knows Julius, and he will know what to do when you give him the treesure map. I will also write him a letter.'

Otto scribbled a short note, and gave that also to Jack. It

was addressed to Julius Muller.

'Now you must leave me,' said Otto. 'You must go back to your friends. If I am better tomorrow I will come with you. But my heart is bad today, so bad. Always it pains me here.' He pressed his hand over his heart.

'Well, goodbye, and thank you,' said Jack, getting up. 'I do hope you will be safe here. There is meat for you, and tinned fruit, all ready opened. Well – so long till tomorrow.'

The man smiled a tired smile, sank back against the wall of the cowshed and closed his eyes. He was completely exhausted. Jack felt very sorry for him. He must get help as soon as he could, if Otto was not better by tomorrow. He and others would get out of the valley by the pass and go and find Julius at once, whoever he was. If he was a friend of Otto's, he might be able to get a doctor immediately.

Feeling much more cheerful about things, Jack went out of the cowshed. Golly, what would the others say when they knew he had the map of where the treasure-cave was to be found – and directions as to how to get out of the valley!

Philip came running up, out of breath. 'The men have just left the plane and are walking towards their hut,' he said. 'Come on, we'd better go. Is the prisoner safely in the shed?'

'Yes. Hope the men don't go there looking for him,' said Jack. 'Come on – let's get back to the girls. We shall have been away from them for ages.'

'We must look out for Pepi on the way back,' said Philip, as they set off. 'He may have got tired of watching the waterfall and the girls capering about, and have decided to cut back to the others.'

'I say – do you know what *I've* got?' said Jack, unable to keep the news to himself for a moment longer.

'What?' asked Philip.

'A map showing where the treasure is!' said Jack.

'But we know where it is,' said Philip. 'Behind that fall of rocks we saw this morning.'

'Well, it isn't!' said Jack triumphantly. 'The prisoner – his name's Otto – he fooled them properly. He pretended the treasure was in a cave behind the fall of rocks – he knew the rocks had fallen, but he thought he could pretend he didn't know about them, and say the treasure was blocked by the landslide there. See?'

'Golly, and all the time the treasure was somewhere else!' said Philip. 'That was good work. Have you really got a map of the whereabouts of the treasure, Jack? And did you find out exactly what the treasure is?'

'No, I forgot to ask him that,' said Jack. 'But I found out an awful lot. I've got directions to find the pass that leads out of this valley – and a note to a man called Julius – and I know how these houses and things got burnt and why. Otto says if he's strong enough tomorrow he'll take us to the pass himself – but he gave me the maps in case he wasn't able to come with us. They're quite clear.'

This was really exciting news. Philip felt overjoyed. It looked as if they would be able to escape from the valley at last – and get help – and perhaps be in at the discovery of the treasure.

'Look out! – I believe I saw something moving over there,' whispered Jack suddenly, and the two boys crouched behind a bush. It was a good thing they did, for Pepi emerged from a thicket of trees and walked rapidly towards them. But it was obvious that he hadn't seen them.

Without a glance at their bush he strode on. 'I bet he's hungry and wants a meal,' grinned Jack. 'Good thing I spotted him. We'd have bumped right into him in two seconds. Well, that's good – we can hurry on now without being afraid of being seen. Gosh, I'm hungry!'

They both were. It was ages since they had had anything to eat. Thoughts of tinned salmon, sardines, tongue, apricots, peaches and pears floated before the mind's eye of both boys. They hurried as much as they could.

111

They were thankful when they pushed aside the fern-fronds and saw the girls sitting in the cave behind. Dinah had got a fine meal ready and waiting.

'Good old Dinah!' cried Jack. 'I could almost give you a hug!'

Dinah grinned. 'Pepi's gone,' she said. 'Did you meet him?'

'Almost collided with him,' said Philip. 'Gosh, I could eat a whole tin of salmon by myself. How have things been with you and Lucy-Ann, Dinah? All right?'

'Very dull,' said Dinah. 'Nothing doing at all, except a few capers now and again behind the waterfall to keep Pepi interested. You should have seen his efforts to find the way up. Once Lucy-Ann and I really thought he had been swept away by the water. He slipped and fell, and disappeared for about twenty minutes. We were quite relieved when we saw him again.'

'What about you boys?' said Lucy-Ann. 'You look cheerful. Got good news? What about that poor prisoner?'

With their mouths full the boys told of all they had done that day. The girls listened eagerly. When Jack fished the maps out of his pocket they fell on them with delight.

'A treasure map!' cried Lucy-Ann. 'I always wanted to see a real one. Oh, here's our waterfall, look! Surely the treasure isn't anywhere near it?'

'When are we going to find the treasure?' asked Dinah, her eyes shining.

'We're not going to,' said Jack, and her face fell at once. He explained why. 'We've got to get out of this valley, and find this fellow Julius. Apparently he will see to the unearthing of the treasure, whatever it is. Sorry to disappoint you, girls – but honestly, I do really think we ought to get out as quickly as we can, and let Aunt Allie and Bill know where we are. We should waste a lot of time looking for the treasure, and I think that now we've been told where to look

112

for the pass out of the valley we ought to take it, and get help for ourselves and for poor old Otto too. He's a very ill man.'

It was clear that Jack was right. Dinah heaved a sigh of regret. 'I would so very much have liked to go and find that treasure,' she said. 'But never mind – perhaps this Julius man, whoever he is, will let us join the treasure-hunt with him. We might stay for that!'

It was now almost dark. The boys were tired out. They lay down on the 'bed' which Dinah had already made, feeling very sleepy. But the girls wanted to talk, and so did Kiki. They had had a very dull day. They chattered away, Kiki joining in, but the boys could hardly find the energy to answer.

'Kiki's been in and out of the cave of echoes today, yelling and squawking for all she was worth,' said Lucy-Ann. 'She's not afraid of the echoes any more. 'You should have heard the echoes when she did her express train screech!'

'Jolly glad I didn't,' said Jack sleepily. 'Shut up, now, everyone. Get to sleep, because we've got an exciting day before us tomorrow, fetching Otto – and going to find the pass – and looking for Julius.'

'It looks as if this adventure is about to come to an end,' said Lucy-Ann.

But she was quite wrong. It wasn't anywhere *near* its end.

18

Now for Windy Pass!

Next morning the children peeped cautiously through the fern-fronds to see if by any chance Pepi was on guard again. But there was no sign of him.

'I do wonder what Juan and Luis thought when they got

back to their hut, unlocked it – and found the prisoner flown,' said Jack with a grin. 'They'll be astonished to find he went through a locked door.'

'Oh, they'll guess one of us rescued him,' said Dinah 'Won't they be wild? I do hope they don't find him in that cowshed. He might tell tales of us.'

'He wouldn't,' said Jack at once. 'He's got a nice trustable face – rather like Bill's but not so strong.'

'I wish Bill would suddenly arrive here,' said Lucy-Ann with a sigh. 'I do really. I know we have managed things awfully well, but somehow when Bill comes along I feel really safe.'

'Well, you're safe enough now, aren't you?' demanded Jack. 'Didn't I find you a jolly good hiding place?'

'Yes, fine,' said Lucy-Ann. 'Oh, look, Philip – Kiki's after Lizzie!'

Lizzie had appeared down Philip's leg, and Kiki, who happened to be sitting near, had given a delighted squawk and pecked at her – but the lizard was a little too quick. She ran into Philip's shoe.

'Stop it, Kiki!' said Philip. 'Well – now we'd better get busy.'

'Busy, dizzy Lizzie,' said Kiki at once, and the children laughed.

'Really, Kiki's awfully clever at putting the same-sounding words together,' said Lucy-Ann. 'Busy, dizzy Lizzie – I'd never have thought of that. Clever Kiki!'

Kiki squawked and raised her crest high. She rocked herself from side to side, as she often did when she felt pleased with herself.

'Vain bird! Conceited bird!' said Jack, and scratched her poll. 'You leave Lizzie alone. She's about the most harmless pet Philip's ever had.'

'Well, she's better than those awful rats and mice and spiders and beetles and hedgehogs he's had running about

114

him,' said Dinah with a shudder. 'I really quite like Lizzie, compared with them.'

'*Gracious*!' said Lucy-Ann, astonished. 'You *are* improving, Dinah!'

Lizzie and Kiki both joined in the breakfast the children had, though Kiki kept a sharp eye to see that Lizzie didn't take anything *she* wanted. When they had all finished they made their plans for the day.

'We'll fetch Otto first,' said Jack. 'Philip and I, I mean. No need for us all to go. Perhaps you two could pack up a few tins for us all to take with us when we go to look for the pass through the mountains. We shall want a meal on the way.'

'Right,' said Dinah. 'I hope you'll find Otto better. Then when you bring him here, we'll have a snack before we set out. Then over the pass we'll go, and find Julius — and somehow manage to send off a message to Mother and Bill. Maybe Bill will fly over in his plane . . . '

'And join the treasure hunt and let us help,' said Lucy-Ann. 'What a nice plan!'

It did seem a very nice one indeed. The boys set off, leaving Kiki behind with the girls. They went quickly over the mountain slope, keeping a good lookout, however, for Pepi and the others.

But they saw nobody. They made their way carefully to the cowshed. Jack left Philip on guard near by to give warning if anyone came near. Then he tiptoed to the shed and peeped in. There was no sound in there at all.

He could not see the last cowstall from where he stood. He walked softly in, stepping over the fallen rubble. He spoke softly.

'Otto! I'm back! Are you better?'

There was no reply. Jack wondered if the man was asleep. He made his way to the last stall.

It was empty. Otto was not there. Jack glanced round quickly. What could have happened?

The boy saw that the opened tins of meat and fruit that he had left for Otto were untouched. Otto had not eaten anything left for him. Why?

'Blow! Those men must have come looking for him when they found that he was gone from the hut,' thought Jack. 'And they found him here. Gosh! – what have they done with him? We'd better look out for ourselves, in case the men are on the watch for us. They'll know someone must have set Otto free, even if he has held his tongue about me.'

He went back to Philip. 'Otto's gone,' he said. 'Dare we have a squint at the hut? We might find out something then – what they've done with Otto, for instance.'

'Let's shin up that big tree we've climbed before,' said Philip. 'The one that we can see the plane from. If we saw all the men round about the plane, we'd know it was safe to go to the hut; but I don't feel inclined to run into danger if we think the men are by the hut. They might be watching for us to come again. If we're captured, the girls wouldn't know what to do.'

'All right. I'll climb the tree,' said Jack, and up he went, with Philip close behind him. He put his field glasses to his eyes to focus them on the plane – and then he gave a loud exclamation.

'Gosh! The plane's gone again! It isn't there!'

'No – it isn't,' said Philip in surprise. 'Well – I never heard it go this time, did you, Jack?'

'Well, I did think I heard a throbbing noise last night when I was half asleep,' said Jack. 'Yes, now I come to think of it, it must have been the plane I heard. Well, we've probably frightened the men away. They got the wind up when they knew other people were here – in a hiding place they couldn't find – people who rescued their prisoner.'

'Yes – and when they found they couldn't get at the treasure because a rock-fall had apparently blocked the entrance to it, I suppose they thought it wasn't much use

116

staying,' said Philip. 'So they've gone. Thank goodness! Now we can go back to the girls, and shoot off to the pass quickly. To tell you the truth, I was a bit worried about taking Otto with us, because from what you said it didn't sound as if we'd be able to go very fast with him. And if he'd had a heart attack by the way we wouldn't have known what to do.'

'I wonder where they've taken him to,' said Jack. 'Let's hope that now they find they can't get any more out of him they've taken him back to where he belongs, and will get a doctor to him.'

They climbed down the tree, and set off back to the girls as fast as they could. Now for the pass.

The girls were most surprised to see the two boys back so soon – but they were even more surprised to see they were alone.

'Where's Otto?' asked Dinah.

'Down the well,' said Kiki. Nobody took any notice of her and she screeched.

Jack explained. 'The plane's gone – and Otto's gone – so I suppose they've all gone off, disgusted at not being able to get at the treasure. Good riddance to them!'

'Hear! hear!' said Dinah, very much relieved to know that their enemies were safely out of the way. 'Well, what are we going to do now?'

'Go and look for the pass,' said Jack. 'I've got the map Otto drew. What a mercy he gave it to me! We'd never find the pass by ourselves without a map, I'm sure of that. I mean, the pass out of these mountains might be anywhere. Apparently there *is* only one pass, and that's this one – the Windy Pass. Come on, let's go. Packed up a few tins, Dinah?'

'Yes,' said Dinah. 'Now, where do we go from here? Up or down?'

'Up,' said Philip, poring over the map that Jack took from

his pocket. 'Up – to where the waterfall begins – here, look. Then we go along a rocky ledge – see, Otto's drawn it – then we come to a thick wood, look – and then up a steep bit to another ledge. Then we come to a proper road – the pass road that I suppose all the people of the valley used when they wanted to leave this district and visit another. Once we're on that road I shall feel better.'

'So shall I,' said Dinah fervently. 'It will be nice to see a *road*. We might even see somebody walking on it.'

'Shouldn't think so, as we haven't seen anyone in this valley at all except ourselves and the men,' said Jack. 'It strikes me as a bit queer, I must say, to think that although there's a perfectly good pass in and out of this lovely valley, it appears to be quite deserted. I wonder why.'

'Oh, I expect there's a good reason,' said Dinah. 'Come on, do let's go. The first part will be easy, because we've only got to keep near the waterfall.'

But it wasn't quite so easy as she thought, for the mountain cliff was exceedingly steep there, and the children had to do a lot of stiff climbing. Still, they managed it, for their legs were well used to walking and climbing by now.

The waterfall roared by them all the way. It made a terrific noise as it fell, and Lucy-Ann thought how nice it would be when they reached the top and didn't have to listen to quite such a colossal din.

After some time they came to where the waterfall began. It gushed out of a great hole in the mountainside and fell sheerly down, tumbling against huge rocks on the way. It was really a marvellous sight to see.

'Goodness, it does give me a funny feeling to see that great mass of water coming out of the mountain,' said Lucy-Ann, sitting down. 'It's so *sudden*, somehow.'

'I suppose when the snows melt, and the rain pours down, there is a terrific amount of water soaking down into the mountaintop,' said Jack. 'And it all collects and has to get out somehow. This is one way it gets out – through this hole – making a tremendous waterfall.'

'Where do we go now?' asked Dinah, who was very impatient to get out of the valley.

'We go up on that rocky ledge,' said Jack. 'Golly, it looks a bit narrow – it runs right over the waterfall! Lucy-Ann, don't you dare look down, in case you feel giddy.'

'I don't much feel as if I want to walk along there,' said poor Lucy-Ann.

'I'll help you,' said Jack. 'You'll be all right as long as you don't look down.'

They went along the rocky ledge quite safely, Lucy-Ann holding tightly to Jack's hand. Kiki flew above their heads, squawking encouragement.

'See how they run, see how they run!' she called, having apparently remembered the second line of 'Three Blind Mice.'

Lucy-Ann gave a giggle. 'We're not exactly running, Kiki,' she said. 'Oh, thank goodness the ledge has come to an end. Now we go through that wood, don't we?'

Jack looked at his map. 'Yes – apparently we go straight through. Where's my compass? I'll set it so that we walk in a straight line in the direction Otto has put on his map.'

They entered the wood. It was a pine wood, rather dark and silent. Nothing grew under the tall pine-trees. The wind blew them and they made a loud whispering noise, which upset Kiki.

'Sh!' she called. 'Shhhhhhhhhh!'

'Here's the end of the wood!' called Jack. 'Now for another steep bit to another ledge – and we'll look down on the road. Come on, everybody!'

19

A great disappointment
– and a plan

It certainly was a stiff climb again, up the steep, rather stony slope to the ledge they could see some way above. Lucy-Ann almost cried because her feet kept slipping so.

'I take one step up, and slip two steps back,' she wailed.

'Well, hang on to me, then,' said Philip, and gave her a tug up each time she took a step.

They all wanted a rest when they came to the next ledge, and to their delight they saw a patch of wild raspberries growing there. They could sit down in the canes and feast as they rested. Lovely! Kiki liked the raspberries very much indeed, and ate so many that Jack called to her.

'Kiki! You'll go pop!'

'Pop goes the weasel,' answered Kiki, and helped herself to a few dozen more raspberries.

Soon they all felt they could go on again. They were very high up now, and could see even more mountains towering behind the ones they knew. It was a most magnificent sight.

'I feel very small and lost somehow, with all those great mountains sitting there,' said Lucy-Ann, and the others felt the same. 'Come on – let's go round the ledge now. We shall soon see the road. Thank goodness this ledge isn't narrow. It's almost wide enough to take a car.'

It was not so easy walking round the ledge as Lucy-Ann thought, however, for there had been a fall of rocks there, further along, and there was a good deal of scrambling about to be done. They were thankful when they had got over the rock-fall and come to smoother ground again.

The ledge rounded a bend in the mountainside, and then, quite suddenly, the children saw the road below them. Yes, it was really a road! They stood and looked at it in delight.

'I never thought I should be so pleased to see a road again,' said Dinah. 'The road out of the valley! The road to Somewhere at last!'

'Look,' said Lucy-Ann, 'it winds up from quite a long way down. We can't see where it goes to from here, because it's hidden round the bend.'

'You can see the pass, the Windy Pass, from here, though,' said Jack, pointing. 'See where this mountain and the next almost touch? That's where the pass must be – fairly high up and awfully narrow. I bet we'll have to go through it in single file.'

'No, we won't,' said Philip scornfully. 'It's bound to be wide enough to take a cart. It only looks narrow because we're far off.'

'Come on, let's get down to the road,' said Dinah, and began to climb down to it. They were about twenty feet above it.

'I say, isn't it overgrown with grass and weeds!' said Jack, astonished. 'That shows how little it has been used lately. Strange, isn't it? You'd think the people would put their only road out of the valley into some sort of order.'

'It's jolly peculiar, *I* think,' said Philip. 'Come on – we can at least see it's a road, even if it is overgrown with weeds.'

They walked along the road for some way. It wound upwards always, following long curves in and out on the slopes of the mountain. At last the children could clearly see where the Windy Pass must be, a narrow passage between the two mountains, theirs and the next.

It was cold so high up and the wind was very strong. If the children had not been warm with climbing they would have shivered. As it was, they were all as warm as toast.

'Now – round this next corner – and I bet we shall see the pass!' cried Jack. 'Then hurrah for the way out of this mysterious valley!'

They rounded the corner. Yes – there lay the pass – or what must once have been the pass. But it was a pass no longer.

Something had happened. The narrow way between the great mountains was blocked high with great rocks and black boulders. It was impassable.

At first the four children didn't quite take it in. They stood and stared in wonder.

'What's happened there?' said Jack at last. 'It looks like an earthquake or something. Did you ever see such a terrible mess?'

'Great holes have been blown in the rocky walls on either side of the pass,' said Philip. 'Look, even high up there are holes like craters.'

They stared in silence, and then Jack turned to the others. 'Do you know what I think has happened?' he said. 'Well, when enemies were here, fighting, they bombed the pass – and blocked it. All that devastation has been caused by bombs – I'm sure it has.'

'Yes, I think you're right, Jack,' said Philip. 'It's just what it looks like. Aeroplanes must have flown just over the pass, and dropped scores of bombs on the narrow road there. It's absolutely impassable.'

'Do you mean – we can't get out?' asked Lucy-Ann in a trembling voice. Philip nodded.

'Afraid so,' he said. 'Nobody could get over that steep, high, dangerous wall of blown up rocks. This explains why people haven't come along to live in this valley yet. I suppose most of those living here were killed, and the rest escaped over the pass. Then it was blown up and nobody could come back. Those men in the plane, Juan and the rest, must have got wind of some treasure hidden in the valley, and thought they would try to enter the place by plane. About the only way to enter it, too.'

Lucy-Ann sat down and cried. 'I'm so disappointed,' she

wailed. 'I thought we were going to escape from this horrid, lonely valley, I really did. But now we're still prisoners here – and n-n-n-nobody can come in to rescue us!'

The others sat down by Lucy-Ann, feeling rather desperate too. They stared hopelessly at the blocked pass. What a terrible blow! Just as they had so hoped they would be able to escape, and get to Julius, and tell him about the treasure.

'Let's have something to eat,' suggested Dinah. 'We'll feel better then. No wonder we feel a bit dumpy now.'

'Humpy dumpy,' said Kiki at once. That made them laugh.

'Idiot!' said Philip. 'You don't care about a blocked up pass, do you, Kiki? You could fly over. It's a pity we can't tie a message to your leg and send you over to Julius for help.'

'Oooh – couldn't we do that?' said Lucy-Ann at once.

'No, silly! For one thing, Kiki would probably tear the message off her leg,' said Jack, 'and for another she'd never know who to go and look for. She's a clever bird, but not as clever as that.'

They felt a lot better after their meal. They ate it with their backs to the blocked pass. Nobody could bear to look at it.

'I suppose we'll have to go back to our cave,' said Dinah at last. 'Doesn't seem anything else to do really.'

'No, I suppose there isn't,' said Jack rather gloomily. 'What a sell, isn't it?'

They had a good long rest. The sun was very fierce, but the wind was so strong that they were never too hot. In fact Lucy-Ann went to a rock that sheltered her from the wind, because she felt too cool.

They started back after their rest. They were not nearly so cheerful and talkative as when they had set out that morning. The thought of having to stay in the lonely valley, after having such high hopes of escaping, was very damping to all of them.

Lucy-Ann looked so miserable that Jack tried to think of something to cheer her up. He thought of something really startling.

'Cheer up, Lucy-Ann,' he said. 'Maybe we'll find the treasure now, to make up for our disappointment.'

Lucy-Ann stopped and stared at him, thrilled. '*Really*?' she said. 'Oh, *Jack* – yes, let's look for the treasure ourselves now!'

Everyone stopped and thought about it for a few exciting moments. 'Well, why not?' said Philip. 'We can't get word about it to Julius, because we can't get over the pass. Those men have gone, and Otto is gone too. There's only us left. We might as well hunt for the treasure. It would be something exciting to do, to pass away the time.'

'How simply gorgeous!' cried Dinah. 'Just what I've always wanted to do – hunt for treasure. When shall we start? Tomorrow?'

'I say – suppose we really found it!' said Philip, looking thrilled. 'Should we get a share of it, I wonder?'

'What a good thing Otto gave you the map, Freckles!' said Dinah to Jack. She always called him Freckles when she felt in a very good humour. 'Let's have a look at it.'

Jack took it out of his pocket. He unfolded the sheet of paper and spread it out. Otto had marked it with compass directions, just as he had marked the map showing the way to the pass.

'See the things he has drawn or printed,' said Jack. 'See this funny shaped rock – it's shaped like a man in a cloak, with a ball-like head. If we saw that rock, we'd know it was a signpost to the treasure.'

'And what's this – a bent tree?' asked Dinah. 'Yes, but how are we to know where to look for them? We can't go wandering all over the mountainside looking for queer-shaped rocks and bent trees and things.'

'Of course not,' said Jack. 'We'd have to begin properly,

from the beginning – and the beginning is the waterfall we know. Otto drew a path from where the cowshed is to the waterfall, see – well, we can start right *at* the waterfall without bothering about the path. Then, from the top of the fall we must look for that bent tree, and walk to there. Then from the bent tree we look for this – let's see, what did he say that was? – oh yes, it's a stretch of smooth black rock – well, when we get there, we look next for a spring of water – and from there we look out for that funny shaped rock. Then somewhere about there is the treasure.'

'Golly!' said Lucy-Ann, her eyes nearly popping out of her head. 'Let's get back to the waterfall and start straight away. Come on!'

Jack folded up the map and looked round at the three excited faces. He grinned. 'The treasure won't be much use to us, cooped up in this valley as we are,' he said. 'But it will be something really thrilling to do.'

They set off once again, their minds busy with treasure-hunting. If only they could find what those men had been looking for and had not found! What would Bill say? He would wish to goodness he had been with them. He always said they fell into adventure after adventure.

When they got back to the waterfall, the sun had gone in, and huge black clouds hung over their mountain. Enormous drops of rain began to fall. The children gazed in disappointment at the lowering sky.

'Blow! said Philip. 'There's going to be a rain storm, I should think. No good going off treasure hunting in this. Better get into the cave before we get soaked. Here comes the rain properly!'

They only just got into their cosy cave in time. Then the rain pelted down in torrents, and added its voice to the roar of the waterfall.

'Rain all you like!' called Jack. 'But do be sunny to-morrow – we're going treasure hunting!'

20

Signposts to the treasure

They slept very soundly indeed that night, for they were tired out. The rain fell all night long, but towards dawn the clouds cleared away, and the sky, when the sun rose, was a clear pale blue. Lucy-Ann liked it very much when she parted the soaking fern fronds and looked out.

'Everything's newly-washed and clean, even the sky,' she said. 'Lovely! Just look!'

'Just the day for a treasure hunt,' said Jack. 'I hope this sun will dry the grass quickly, or we shall get our feet soaked.'

'Good thing we brought so many tins out of the men's hut,' said Dinah, reaching down two or three. 'Are there still some in that bush where we first hid them, Jack?'

'Plenty,' said Jack. 'I took one or two to open for Otto the day before yesterday, but there are heaps left. We can go and get them some time.'

They tied back the fern fronds and ate their breakfast sitting at the front of the cave, looking out on the far mountains, backed by the sky, which was now turning a deeper blue.

'Well, shall we set off?' said Jack, when they had finished. 'Kiki, take your head out of that tin. You know it's completely empty.'

'Poor Kiki!' said Kiki. 'What a pity!'

They all scrambled out of the cave. Things were certainly drying fast in the hot summer sun. 'Look, those rocks are steaming!' said Lucy-Ann in surprise, pointing to some nearby rocks. So they were. They looked most peculiar with the steam rising up.

'Better take some food with us,' said Jack. 'Got some, Dinah?'

'Of course,' said Dinah. 'We can't come all the way back here for food.'

'We've got to get to where the waterfall begins, just as we did yesterday,' said Jack. 'Follow me, all of you. I know the way.'

They soon stood at the top of the waterfall, and once more watched the great gush of water surge out from the heart of the mountain. It seemed twice as big and turbulent as the day before.

'Well, I suppose the underground water has been swelled up because of last night's rain,' said Philip. 'And so the waterfall is bigger and stronger.'

'Yes, that's the reason,' said Jack, raising his voice to a shout because of the noise of the water. 'Kiki, stop screeching in my ear.'

The waterfall excited Kiki, and she made a terrible noise that morning. Jack would not have her on his shoulder after a while, because of her screeches. She flew off in a huff.

'Now, what about that bent tree?' said Dinah, remembering. By this time they were standing a little way above the beginning of the waterfall. 'I can't see any bent tree at all!'

'Oh, golly – don't say there isn't a bent tree!' groaned Jack, looking this way and that, all round and about and above his head. 'Gosh, there doesn't seem to be one, does there?'

There didn't. What few trees they could see were perfectly straight. Then Lucy-Ann gave a cry and pointed downwards. 'There it is, isn't it? – just below us, on the other side of the waterfall. Look!'

They all went to stand by Lucy-Ann, and looked. She was right. On the other side of the fall, some way below them, was a curiously bent tree. It was a birch tree, and why it should have grown so bent over was a puzzle. The wind was no stronger there than anywhere else. Anyway, it was decidedly bent and that was all that mattered.

They crossed above the beginning of the waterfall, clambering over the rocks, and then scrambled down on the other side of the fall. They reached the bent tree at last.

'First signpost,' said Jack.

'No second,' said Dinah. 'The waterfall is really the first.'

'Well, second then,' said Jack. 'Now for the third – a big stretch of flat black rock – a wall of it, I should think.'

They all looked in every direction for a stretch of black rock. This time it was Jack's keen eyes that spotted it. It was some way off, and looked difficult to reach, for it meant climbing along the steep face of the mountainside, which just there was very cliff-like.

Still, it had to be done, so they set off. It was easier after the first stretch, for there were all kinds of plants and bushes firmly rooted in the sloping cliff, and these could be used as handholds or footholds. Jack helped Lucy-Ann along, but Dinah scorned Philip's help, especially as she knew he had the lizard somewhere about him.

It took them at least half an hour of stiff scrambling and climbing to reach the wall of black rock, though actually, in distance, it was not so very far. They stood by the rock, panting.

'Funny shiny black rock,' said Jack, running his fingers over the smooth surface. 'Wonder what it is.'

'Oh, never mind,' said Dinah, impatient to get on. 'What's our next signpost? This is the third.'

'A spring of water,' said Philip. 'Isn't that right, Jack – or shall we look at the map?'

'No – I know it by heart,' said Jack. 'A spring of water is next. Not that I can see one at all – though I wish I could because I could do with a drink after that hot scramble. My hands are filthy, and so are my knees.'

'Yes, we could all do with a jolly good wash now,' said

Philip. 'A good old rub and a scrub.'

'Rubbenascrub,' said Kiki, and went off into one of her dreadful cackles.

'Stop it, Kiki,' said Jack. 'I'll give *you* a rubbenascrub in a minute.'

There was no spring of water to be seen. Lucy-Ann began to look very disappointed.

'Cheer up!' said Jack. 'We may not be able to *see* the spring from this wall of rock – but we can surely find it if it's anywhere near.'

'Let's listen,' suggested Dinah.

So they stood perfectly still and listened. 'Shhhhhh!' said Kiki annoyingly.

Jack smacked her on the beak. She gave a dismal squawk and sat silent. And, in the silence of the peaceful mountain-side, the children heard the tinkle-tinkle of water – a merry, gurgling noise, cheerful and friendly.

'I can hear it!' cried Lucy-Ann in delight. 'It comes from somewhere over there.'

She leapt across to a little thicket of trees, and there, hidden deep in the flower-strewn grass, bubbled a clear spring, trickling down the hillside, a tiny stream of crystal cold water.

'It starts just up there, look,' said Jack, and pointed to a big bush. The spring bubbled out from below the bush. 'Fourth signpost!'

'Now for the fifth – and last!' said Lucy-Ann excited. 'Oooh – do you honestly think we are getting near to the treasure? It's really not *very* far from our waterfall cave. I thought I could hear the faint, distant roar of the fall when I stood listening for the gurgling of the spring.'

'I thought I could too,' said Dinah. 'Now, what do we look for next?'

'The oddly shaped rock,' said Jack. 'You know – like a man in a long cloak, with a round head at the top.'

'Easy!' said Philip triumphantly, and pointed upwards. 'There it is – quite clear against the sky!'

They all looked up. Philip was right. There stood the curious-shaped rock, easy to see against the sky.

'Come on!' said Jack excitedly. 'Up we go! Come along, treasure hunters!'

They climbed up to where the odd-shaped rock stood. Other rocks lay about, but this one was much taller, and, because of its height and shape, it stood out among the others.

'Our last signpost!' said Jack. 'And now – where's the treasure?'

Ah, yes – where was the treasure? Lucy-Ann looked about the hillside as if she half expected it to be strewn there. The others began to search for a cave opening. But nobody could find anything.

'Why didn't you ask Otto exactly where to find the treasure, after coming to the last signpost?' complained Dinah, tired and disappointed, coming over to Jack.

'Well, I didn't know *we* were going to look for it, silly, did I?' said Jack. 'I thought Julius Muller was going to take charge of the treasure hunt. No doubt if he got as far as this he'd know where the treasure was all right.'

'Well, it's most awfully disappointing to come all this way, and read the map so well, and then not find a thing,' said Dinah, who was cross and tired. 'I'm fed up. I shan't hunt any more. You can all go on looking if you like, but I'm going to have a rest.'

She flung herself down, and lay flat, looking upwards at the steep mountainside above her. It was ridged with flat slabs of rock, sticking out here and there like ledges. Dinah examined them lazily with her eyes. Then she sat up suddenly.

'Hi!' she called to the others. 'Look up there!'

They came over to her and looked up. 'See those big

ledges of rock sticking out all the way up the cliff-side?' she said. 'Like shelves. Well, look halfway up – see one that sticks out rather far? Look underneath it. Is that a hole there?'

'It does look rather like a hole,' said Jack. 'Maybe a fox-hole, though. Still, it's the only sizeable hole hereabouts, so we'd better explore. I'll go up. Coming, Tufty?'

'Rather,' said Philip. 'It doesn't look difficult. Aren't you two girls coming too?'

Dinah forgot that she was fed up, and she joined in the climb to the hole under the ledge of rock. When they got there they found that it was a very big hole indeed. It could not possibly be seen from above, for the shelf of rock stuck right out over it and hid it. It could only be seen from one place below, at a certain angle – and that was the place where Dinah had flung herself down some time back.

'Bit of luck you happened to spot it, Dinah,' said Jack. 'We might have hunted all day and never found it. I wonder if this is the entrance to the *real* treasure-cave.'

They peered down. The hole yawned below them, dark and appearing rather vast. 'Where's my torch?' said Jack, and, taking it from his pocket, he switched it on.

The children gazed down into the hole. It seemed nothing but a hole. No treasure was there. But, as Jack swung his torch a little further down, Dinah thought she caught sight of a passage further back.

'I believe,' she said, almost falling into the hole in her excitement, 'I do believe it goes right back, into a passage.'

Kiki flew off Jack's shoulder and disappeared into the hole. A mournful voice floated up to them.

'What's down there, Kiki?' called Jack.

'Three blind mice,' answered Kiki, solemnly and untruthfully. 'Three blind mice. Pop!'

'You're a fibber,' said Jack. 'Anyway – down we go to find the . . . '

131

'Three blind mice,' said Kiki, and went off into an imitation of Lucy-Ann's giggle.

21

The strange caves

Jack went down the hole first. He lowered himself right in, and only had to drop about a foot to the ground below.

'Lucy-Ann, you come next,' he said, and helped her down. Then came the others, excited and eager. Had they really found the treasure cave?

'It simply must be the hiding place for the treasure!' said Jack. 'There isn't another hole or cave anywhere. Now, let me flash my torch round a bit.'

At the back of the hole, as Dinah had thought, there was a passage – quite a wide one, and fairly high. A very tall man could have walked down it with ease.

'Come on!' said Jack, his voice shaking with excitement. 'We're getting warm!'

They followed him down the passage, Kiki sitting on his shoulder. Lucy-Ann held on to his sleeve, half fearful of what they might find.

The passage was wide and high all the way along, but wound about a little. It went downwards, and kept more or less in the same direction, for all its windings – that is, towards the heart of the mountain.

Suddenly the passage came to an abrupt end. Jack paused, and gasped. In front of him was a most extraordinary sight.

His torch shone brightly on to an unending mass of brilliant columns, hanging from the high roof of a cave. Whatever could they be?

Lucy-Ann clutched his arm and gasped too. She stared at

the shining white things. She saw that other white columns were growing up from the floor of the cave too. Some had met the hanging ones, and had joined, so that it seemed as if the cave roof was being supported by pillars.

'Jack! What is it? Is it the treasure?' whispered Lucy-Ann.

'It's icicles, isn't it?' said Dinah in an awed tone. 'I've never seen anything so beautiful in my life! Look at them hanging down – so still and white and lovely!'

'No – they're not icicles,' said Jack. 'They are stalactites – at least, the hanging ones are. They're not made of ice, either – but of limestone, I think. My word – what a sight!'

The children stood quite still and gazed their fill at the silent, beautiful cave. Its roof was as high as a cathedral, and the graceful stalactites hung down from it in dozens, gleaming in the light of Jack's torch.

'The ones growing up from the floor are stalagmites, I think,' said Jack. 'Aren't they, Philip? Do you know anything about them? I've never in my life seen anything like this before!'

'Yes – they're stalagmites,' said Philip. 'I remember seeing pictures of them. Stalactites and stalagmites. Gosh, what a sight!'

Kiki tried to say the two words and couldn't. Even she seemed to be awed by the amazing and unexpected discovery.

'Oh, look!' said Lucy-Ann suddenly, and pointed to what looked like an old, old shawl carved in ivory. 'Look – this has grown here too – it's just like a shawl – even to the pattern in it! And look at that sort of gate over there – all carved too! Surely somebody made them – surely they didn't just grow!'

'Well – they *formed*,' said Jack, trying to explain. 'You know – just as the crystals in a snowflake form. They don't grow because they're not alive – they *form*.'

Lucy-Ann couldn't quite understand. Secretly she

thought that all the marvellous hanging pillars had grown, and then got frozen in their beauty.

I thought this must be the treasure!' she said, half laughing.

'I'm not surprised,' said Jack. 'It's too beautiful for words. Fancy finding a cave like this! It's like an enormous underground cathedral – it just wants an organ to begin playing a grand and magnificent hymn.'

'There's a kind of path down the middle,' said Dinah. 'I don't know if it's just a natural path, Jack, or whether it has been made by man. Do you see what I mean?'

'Yes,' said Jack, flashing his torch along it. 'Bit of both, I think. Well – shall we go on? There's no treasure here.'

They went along the middle of the great silent hall, surrounded on all sides by the hanging icicle-like pillars. Lucy-Ann pointed out many that had joined with columns growing from the ground.

'The drops of water from the stalactites must have dripped to the ground, and made stalagmites form there, growing up to meet the column above,' said Philip. 'They must have taken ages and ages to form – hundreds of years. I say – no wonder this cave feels awfully old to us. I feel as if there is no Time here at all – no years, or days of the week or hours – just nothing.'

Lucy-Ann didn't like that very much. It gave her a strange feeling of being only a dream, and not real. She took hold of Jack's arm and was glad to feel its nice, solid warmth.

They walked slowly to the end of the enormous cave. A great archway stood there, and that too was set with stalactites, which, however, did not hang far down. The children could walk under them with ease.

'This archway is quite like a tunnel,' said Philip. His voice sounded big and hollow there and made them all jump. Kiki gave a mournful cough, which was magnified to a hollow, giant cough that startled everyone very much.

They came to another cave. The roof of this was not so high as the one before, and only small, icicle-like stalactites hung from it.

'Do those stalactites shine in the dark?' asked Dinah suddenly. 'I thought I saw something glowing in the corner over there.'

Jack switched off his torch – and immediately the children gasped. For up in the roof and over the walls there glowed thousands of tiny stars. They were green and blue, and shone and flickered in a most enchanting manner.

'Gracious! What are they?' whispered Dinah, amazed. 'Are they alive?'

The boys didn't know. They watched the shimmering flickering stars, that seemed to go in and out like elfin lights. 'Might be a kind of glowworm,' said Jack. 'Aren't they lovely?'

He put on his torch again and the roof shone brightly in the yellow-white light. The stars disappeared.

'Oh, do put your torch out!' begged Lucy-Ann. 'I want to watch those stars a bit longer. I never saw anything so fascinating in my life! They shine like phosphorescence – all blue and green and green and blue; look how they flicker off and on. Oh, I wish I could take a hundred back with me and put them on my bedroom ceiling at home!'

The others laughed, but they too thought that the shining, flickering stars were most entrancing to watch. Jack did not put on his torch again until each had gazed his fill.

'That's two simply wonderful caves,' said Lucy-Ann with a sigh. 'What will the next one be? I really do feel as if we'd discovered Aladdin's Cave, or something like that!'

A long passage, leading downwards, led out of the cave of stars, as Lucy-Ann named it.

'We found a cave of echoes, a cave of stalactites and a cave of stars,' she said. 'I like this part of our adventure. Now I'd like to find a cave of treasure.'

The tunnel they were in was wide and high like the first passage they had entered. Jack's torch suddenly shone brightly on something on the floor. He stopped.

'Look at that!' he said. 'What is it?'

Dinah bent to pick it up. 'It's a brooch,' she said. 'A brooch without its pin. The pin's gone. It must have broken and the brooch fell off whoever was wearing it. Isn't it perfectly lovely?'

It certainly was. It was a large gold brooch, about three inches wide, set with brilliant red stones, as red as blood.

'Are they rubies?' said Dinah in awe. 'Look how they glow! Oh, Jack, do you think this is a bit of the treasure?'

'Probably,' said Jack, and at once excitement caught hold of the children again, and their hearts began to beat fast. A ruby brooch, set in carved gold! What would the other treasure be? Wonderful visions arose in the children's minds and they stumbled on their way eagerly, their eyes searching the ground for any other gleaming jewel.

'If we could find a cave of jewels,' said Lucy-Ann. 'Oooooh – all gleaming like stars and suns! That's what I would love.'

'We might find something like that,' said Dinah. 'If we do, I shall deck myself from head to foot with them and pretend I'm a princess.'

The passage went on and on, still leading downwards, but, when Jack looked at his compass, he saw that he was no longer going into the heart of the mountain, but in the opposite direction. He hoped they wouldn't suddenly come out into the daylight without finding the cave of treasure.

Suddenly they came to steps that led downwards. They were carved out of the solid rock, steep, wide steps that curved as the passage curved.

'Almost a spiral stairway,' said Jack. 'Where are we coming to now?'

136

There were about twenty of the steps. Then came an enormous door, made of some kind of stout wood, set with iron studs. The children stood and stared at it.

A door! What was behind it? Was it locked and bolted? Who had put it there, and why? Was it to shut in the treasure cave and guard it?

There was no handle to turn. There was not even a lock to be seen. There were great bolts, but these were not shot into place.

'How can you open a door without a handle?' said Jack in despair. He pushed at the door, but it remained quite firm.

'Kick it, like we did the door of the hut,' said Philip, and Jack kicked it hard. But the door did not open.

They stared at it in despair. To come so far and then to be stopped by a door! It was too bad. Jack shone his torch all over the door, from top to bottom.

Lucy-Ann's sharp eyes noticed something. 'See that iron stud?' she said, pointing. 'It's much brighter than the others. I wonder why.'

Jack shone his torch on it, and saw that it was slightly bigger than the others – and also, as Lucy-Ann said, it was brighter, as if it had had some handling.

He pressed it. Nothing happened. He banged on it with a stone. No result at all.

'Let *me* try,' said Philip, and pushed Jack aside. 'Shine your torch on it closely. That's right.'

Philip took hold of the iron stud and shook it. It seemed to give a little. He shook it again. Nothing happened. Then he thought of twisting it.

It twisted round very easily indeed. There was a loud click – and the door swung slowly open. Jack switched off his torch, afraid that anyone in the cave might see them – though if anyone had been there surely they would have heard the bangs and kicks at the door.

The door now stood wide open. A dim light shone beyond, showing another cave. Lucy-Ann clutched Jack's arm in fright.

'It's full of people,' she whispered. 'Look!'

22

The treasure at last!

The four children stared breathlessly through the open door. They saw something that made them feel very creepy.

In the dim light figures stood about all over the place. Their eyes gleamed queerly, and their teeth shone in the darkness. Their arms and necks flashed and glittered with jewels.

The children clutched one another in fright. Who were these strange, silent folk, standing about with gleaming eyes, covered with jewels?

The people in the cave did not move. They did not speak a word either. Not one of them was sitting. All were standing. They stood there, some turned towards the frightened children, some turned away. Why didn't they speak? Why didn't they point to the children and say, 'Look – who's there?'

Lucy-Ann began to shiver. 'Let's go back. I don't like them. They're not alive. Only their eyes are.'

Kiki suddenly gave a squawk, left Jack's shoulder, and flew to the shoulder of one of the nearby figures, a woman dressed in clothes that glowed richly in the half-light of the cave.

Still the woman did not move. How strange! The children suddenly felt much better when they saw that Kiki did not seem in the least afraid of the queer company.

'Polly put the kettle on,' said Kiki, and pecked at the hair of the woman he was sitting on.

The children held their breath again. What would the woman do to Kiki – enchant her with her strange eyes, cast a spell on her and turn her into stone? Perhaps all these people had been turned into stone?

'Let's go back,' said Lucy-Ann urgently. 'I don't like this cave. I don't like these people, or their horrid gleaming eyes.'

Jack suddenly jumped down the step that was below the great open door. He marched boldly into the silent cave. Lucy-Ann squealed and tried to catch his sleeve.

Jack walked right up to the woman on whose shoulder Kiki sat. He peered closely at her. He looked into her wide open glittering eyes. He touched her hair. Then he turned to the horrified children.

'What do you think? She's a statue – all dressed up beautifully – with real hair – and jewels for eyes! What do you think of that?'

The others could not believe it – but they were very thankful to hear Jack's words, and to see him wandering among the crowd of still figures, apparently quite unharmed.

Philip and Dinah stepped down into the cave of figures too, but Lucy-Ann still did not quite dare to. She watched the others looking at the strange, beautiful statues, and tried to make herself join them.

At last she screwed up her courage to step down into the cave. She looked fearfully at the woman on whose shoulder Kiki had flown. Yes – Jack was right. She was nothing but a beautiful statue, with a finely-moulded face and a cloud of dark hair. She had magnificent jewels for eyes, and her glittering teeth were exquisite jewels too. Round her neck were golden chains, set with precious stones, and her waxen fingers gleamed with rings. Round her waist was the most beautiful belt that Lucy-Ann had ever seen, carved and set with shining red and blue stones.

There were dozens of these statues in the cave, some of men and some of women. Some of them carried small babies in their arms, fat, smiling babies dressed in the most exquisite clothes, set with thousands of tiny pearls.

It was the babies that gave Jack the clue to what the statues were.

'Do you know what they are?' he said. 'They are statues taken from churches somewhere in this country. This one represents Mary, the mother of Jesus – and the little baby is meant to be Jesus Himself. That's why they are adorned with such lovely jewels. People have spent heaps of money on them to make them beautiful.'

'Oh yes – and some of them are carried in processions at church festivals,' said Dinah, remembering how her mother had once described such a festival to her. 'Well, fancy – statues taken from churches! Whatever for?'

'Stolen, I should think,' said Jack. 'Stolen by people who took advantage of the troubled war-times, and hid them here – meaning to collect them when they had a chance.'

'They must be worth a lot of money,' said Philip, fingering the magnificent jewels. 'Gosh, I did get a terrible fright when I first saw them! I honestly thought they were real people.'

'So did I,' said Lucy-Ann, who had now recovered. 'I couldn't bear them to stand so still and silent. I nearly screamed with fright!'

'We were idiots not to guess they were statues,' said Dinah. 'I say – where does the light come from that lights these statues? It's only a faint sort of light, but it's enough to see them by quite well.'

Jack looked all round. 'It must be a sort of phosphorescent glow from the walls and roof of the cave,' he said. 'It's rather a greenish light, isn't it?'

'I say – there's another archway here!' called Philip, from

beyond the statues. 'Come and see. I believe there's another cave beyond.'

They all went to see. Through the archway was yet another cave, lighted with the same dim, greenish glow. In it were stacked great square, oblong or round, flat things. There were no statues at all. The children went to see what the flat things were.

'Pictures!' said Jack, as he tried to swing one to face him. 'Enormous ones! Where did they come from? Churches too, do you think?'

'Oh — picture galleries very likely,' said Philip. 'Maybe they are famous and quite priceless pictures — very old, too. Look at that one — it looks terribly old-fashioned. My word — these things may be worth a fortune — heaps of fortunes! I remember reading not so long ago about pictures that were worth two or three million pounds!'

'I didn't know there was so much money in the world,' said Lucy-Ann, startled. She gazed in awe at the dusty, dim old pictures, tracing their great carved frames with her finger.

'Some of the pictures have been taken out of their frames to bring them here,' said Jack, pulling at a roll of thick canvas. 'Look, this one must have been cut from its frame and rolled up so as to be taken away easily.'

There were about fifty rolls of canvas besides the framed pictures. Jack shone his torch on to many of the pictures, but none of the children thought the subjects interesting. So many were portraits of rather fat and stern-looking men. Others were scenes from the Bible, or from old legends.

'Well, this really is a find!' said Jack. 'I bet if those men could have found these, they would have made a simply enormous fortune selling them.'

'Of course — they were after all these,' said Philip. 'And that's what those crates were for. To pack them in. They meant to crate them carefully and fly them away little by little. What a brain wave on their part!'

'And Otto fooled them!' said Jack. 'Took them to a rock-fall and said the treasure cave was behind it – so they meekly gave up and flew off. What idiots!'

'And *we* found everything!' rejoiced Lucy-Ann. 'Oh, I wish we could tell Bill!'

'Are there any more caves?' wondered Jack, and walked over to the end of the second cave. 'Yes! Here's another archway and another cave. Books here! And old documents! Come and look!'

'Old books are sometimes as precious and as rare as old pictures,' said Philip, gazing round at the piles of enormous, heavily-bound books. 'I say – look at this one! It's a bible, but in a foreign language. Isn't it enormous? Look at the old printing!'

'These really *are* caves of treasure,' said Jack. 'Treasure from churches, libraries and picture galleries. I suppose the war-lords must have hidden them away, meaning to get them when peace came and make a lot of money out of their loot. How awful to steal things like this, though!'

'There's a little cave here, just off this book-cave,' called Dinah, who was exploring by herself. 'There is a big chest here. Oh, and another – and another! What's in them, I wonder?'

Jack came over to her and lifted up the heavy lid of one chest. He stared down in surprise at the glittering coins piled together in the chest.

'Gold!' he said. 'The gold coinage of some country, I can't tell which. I've never seen gold coins like these before. My goodness, there's a fortune in that box too – and in that chest, and that one! Fortunes everywhere!'

'It's like a dream,' said Lucy-Ann, and she sat down on one of the chests. 'It really is. A cave of gleaming icicles, or stalags— whatever you call them! A cave of stars! A cave of glittering, jewelled statues! A cave of pictures, and a cave of old books! And now a cave of gold! I can't believe it.'

It did seem extraordinary. They all sat down on the oak chests and rested. The dim greenish light still shone every-where, a kind of pale glow that did not seem to come from anywhere in particular, and yet was everywhere.

It was very quiet there. The children could hear themselves breathing, and a cough from Jack sounded startlingly loud.

Then another sound came through the stillness – a sound so completely unexpected and surprising that nobody could believe their ears!

'Cluck! Cluck-luck-luck!'

'Whatever's that?' said Lucy-Ann at last. 'It sounded like a hen clucking.'

'Must have been old Kiki,' said Jack, looking around for her. But she was just near by, sitting on another chest, humped up, looking rather dismal. She had had enough of caves. The children stared at her. Could it have been Kiki?

They listened to see if she would make the same noise again. But she didn't stir. And then the noise came once more, quite clearly, from another direction altogether.

'Cluck-luck-lurrrrrrk! Cluck-luck-lurrrrk!'

'It *is* a hen!' said Jack, jumping up. 'Making an egg-laying noise. But – a hen – in these caves! It's impossible!'

All the children were now on their feet. Dinah pointed to some steps at the back of the little cave of gold. 'That's where the noise comes from,' she said.

'I'll go up first and see if it really *is* a hen,' said Jack. 'I can't believe it.'

He went cautiously up the steps, and at the same time the clucking began again. Kiki woke up and heard it in astonish-ment. She immediately began to cluck too, which evidently astonished the hidden clucker, who got very excited and let off a perfect volley of clucks.

Jack came to the top of the steps. There was another door there, but not a very stout one. It was ajar. He pushed it open a little more, very slowly, so that he might see in without attracting attention, though he did not expect to see anything but a hen.

What he saw transfixed him with astonishment. Philip dug his fingers into his back.

'Go on, Jack – what's up?'

Jack turned round to the others. 'I say,' he said in a half whisper, 'it's awfully odd – but there's a little cell-like room up here – furnished – table and chairs and a lighted lamp! And – there's a meal on the table!'

'Come down quickly, then,' whispered Dinah. 'We don't want to bump into anyone. It must be someone who's guarding the treasure till the others come to get it. Come down!'

But it was too late. A curious, quavering voice came from the cell-like room into which Jack had peeped. A few strange words reached them – but they couldn't understand a single one. *Now* what was going to happen?

23

The guardians of the treasure

The children stood absolutely still, holding their breath. Who was there, in that little room at the top of the steps? The voice came again, repeating the words that the children could not understand.

Then to the top of the little flight of steps came a brown hen! It stood there, its head on one side, peering down at the children. 'Cluck!' it said, in a friendly kind of voice. 'Cluck-luck!'

'Cluck!' said Kiki at once.

Lucy-Ann clutched Dinah. 'Was it the hen talking before?' she whispered in amazement.

It wasn't, of course. The quavering voice came again, and to the children's surprise it sounded really frightened.

Nobody came to where Jack stood almost at the top of the steps. The boy screwed up his courage and marched into the little room.

At the other end of it, under a small archway or rock, stood an old, old man. Behind him was a woman, just as old, but more bent. They stared at Jack in amazement, and then, turning to one another, they poured out a stream of hurried words that the children could not understand at all.

Lucy-Ann wondered what Jack was doing up in the little room. Somebody ought to be with him. She went up the steps and joined Jack. The two old people stared at the red-haired freckled child, so like Jack.

Then the old woman made a crooning noise, pushed past her husband and went over to Lucy-Ann. She put her arms round her and kissed her. Then she patted her hair. Lucy-Ann was surprised and not very pleased. Who was this funny old woman who suddenly seemed so affectionate?

She called to the others. 'Dinah! Philip! Come along up! It's two old people here with their hen!'

Soon all four children were in the little underground room. As soon as the old man heard them talking, he joined in eagerly, speaking English in a strange, clipped way.

'Ah, ah! You are English children! That is goot, very goot. Once, long time ago, I was in your so beautiful country. I was in a big London hotel.'

'Thank goodness he speaks English,' said Philip. 'I say — what are they doing here, with the treasure? Are they in league with the other men?'

'Have to find out,' said Jack. 'They seem quite harmless, anyhow. But there may be others.' He turned to the old man.

The old woman was still making a fuss of Lucy-Ann. Evidently they had not set eyes on children for a long time.

'Who else is here besides you?' demanded Jack.

'Just me and Elsa, my old wife, and our hen Martha,' answered the old man. 'We guard all those things in the caves, till the day when they go back to their right homes. May that day come soon!'

'I don't believe the poor old things know that the war was over long ago,' said Jack to the others, in a low voice. 'I wonder who left them here to guard these things.' He turned to the old man again. 'Who told you to guard these things?' he asked.

'Julius Muller,' said the old man promptly. 'Ah, what a great man! How he worked against the enemy, even when they were shooting and bombing and burning in our valley! It was he who discovered that the enemy was using our mountain caves to hide away these treasures – treasures stolen from our churches and many other places.'

'Just what we thought,' said Philip, intensely interested. 'Go on – tell us more.'

'Then the people fled from our valley,' said the old man. 'Many were killed. The valley was empty, all save me and Elsa, my old wife. We hid with our hens and our pig, and no one found us. Then one day Julius Muller found us and ordered us to come here, by a way he knew, and guard the treasure – not for the enemy, no – but for him and the people! He said that one day the enemy would be defeated and would flee away – and then he and the others would come back to find the treasure – but he has not come.'

'He can't,' said Jack. 'The pass is blocked. No one can get in or out of this valley now – except by aeroplane. The war has been over a long time. But bad people are after the treasure – people who have heard it is hidden here, and have come to steal it.'

The old fellow looked scared and bewildered, as if he only

half understood what Jack was telling him. The children thought that he must have lived so long underground that his mind could not take in much news from the outer world. To him, his wife, the treasure, and perhaps his hen, were the only things that mattered.

'Do you live here, in this room?' asked Lucy-Ann. 'Where do you get your food from? Does your hen like living underground?'

'There are great stores of food here,' said the old man. 'There is even corn for Martha, the hen. When we first came here, we had six hens and our pig. But the pig died. And one by one the hens died. Only Martha is left. She does not lay many eggs now. Perhaps one in fourteen days.'

'Cluck,' said Martha in a proud voice. She was evidently proud of her one egg a fortnight.

Kiki repeated the cluck and then went off into a series of quacks. The hen looked surprised and alarmed. So did the two old people.

'Shut up, Kiki,' said Jack. 'You're showing off.'

'What is that bird?' asked the old man. 'Is it a – how do you call it? – a parrot?'

'Yes,' said Jack. 'She's mine. Always goes with me everywhere. But I say – don't you want to know how *we* came here?'

'Ah, yes, of course!' said the old man. 'It is all so surprising, you understand – and my wits are dull now – I cannot take in many things at once. You must tell me about yourselves, please. Wife, what about some food for these children?'

Elsa did not understand and the old man repeated what he said in her own language. She nodded and smiled a kind toothless smile. Taking Lucy-Ann by the hand, she went over to where tins and jars stood on a rocky ledge.

'She's very keen on Lucy-Ann,' said Philip. 'She can't fuss over her enough.'

The old man heard and understood. 'We had a little granddaughter,' he said. 'So like this little girl, with red hair and a sweet face. She lived with us. And one day the enemy came and took her away and we never saw her again. So now my wife sees her little lost one in your sister. You must excuse her, for maybe she really thinks her small Greta has come back.'

'Poor old things!' said Dinah. 'What an awful life they must have led – lost under this mountain, guarding a treasure for Julius Muller, waiting for him for ages, not knowing what had happened outside in the world! If we hadn't come, they might never have come out again!'

To the children's delight, Elsa got them a really fine meal. She would not let poor Lucy-Ann leave her side, though, so the little girl had to trot everywhere with her. Jack told the old man a little of their own story, though it was plain that the old fellow did not really follow it all. His wits were dull, as he said, and he could not really understand all this sudden news from a world he had almost forgotten.

Kiki enjoyed herself enormously. Martha, the hen, was obviously used to keeping the old couple company and pecked about under the table, brushing against everyone's legs. Kiki climbed down to join her, and kept up an interested, if one-sided conversation with her.

'How many times have I told you to wipe your feet?' she asked Martha. 'Blow your nose. Put the kettle on.'

'Cluck,' answered Martha politely.

'Humpy dumpy,' went on Kiki, evidently anxious to teach Martha a few nursery rhymes now. 'See how they run! Quack, quack, quack, quack!'

The hen looked surprised, ruffled up her feathers and stared at Kiki. 'Cluck, luck, luck,' she said, and pecked up a few crumbs.

Lucy-Ann and the others giggled at this conversation. Then Lizzie also thought she would join the company, as

148

there was plenty of food going. She ran down Philip's sleeve and appeared on the table, much to the old woman's alarm.

'Meet dizzy Lizzie,' said Philip politely.

'I say – they must think we're queer visitors!' said Dinah, keeping a watchful eye on Lizzie in case she came any nearer. 'Walking in like this – with a parrot and a lizard – and staying to dinner!'

'I don't think they are bothering much,' said Philip. 'Just enjoying the change. It must be nice to have company after being alone so long.'

When they had finished the meal, the old woman spoke to her husband. He turned to the children.

'My wife says, are you tired? Would you like a rest? We have a beautiful place to rest in, when we want to enjoy the sun.'

This surprised the children very much. The sun! How did these old people ever see the sun – unless they went through all the cave and passages to the hole that gave on to the mountainside?

'Where do you go to rest then?' asked Jack.

'Come,' said the old man, and led him out of the little cell-like room. Elsa took Lucy-Ann by the hand. They all followed the old man. He went along a broad passage, hollowed out of the rock.

'I should think most of these tunnels were hollowed out by underground rivers at some time or other,' said Jack. 'Then they took a different course, and the tunnels dried up, and became these passages, linking all the caves together.'

The passage twisted a little and then quite suddenly came into daylight. The children found themselves on a flat ledge of rock, hung about by ferns and other plants, full in the sun. How simply delicious!

'Another way into the treasure caves,' said Dinah. But she was wrong. Nobody could possibly enter the caves by way of the ledge. The ledge of rock jutted over a great precipice that fell sheer down many hundreds of feet. No one, not even a goat, could climb up or down to it. It was, as the old man said, a fine, sunny resting place – but that was all.

Martha pecked about on the ledge of rock, though what she could find there the children couldn't imagine. Kiki sat near by and watched her. She had formed a firm friendship with Martha. The children rather liked Martha themselves. She was such a nice, plump little thing, friendly and natural, and as much of a pet to the old couple as Kiki was to them.

They all lay down in the sun. It was delicious to feel its warm rays after being so long underground. As they lay there they heard something rumbling in the distance.

'The waterfall,' said Lucy-Ann. 'Fancy – we must be fairly near it, if we can hear it!'

They lay there sleepily. The old fellow sat on a rock near by, smoking a pipe. He seemed very contented. Elsa had disappeared.

'Isn't it strange to think we've found the treasure – and can't do anything about it at all!' said Dinah. 'We're stuck here. No way of getting word to anyone. And never will have, as far as I can see, till the pass into the valley is unblocked – and that may not be for ages!'

'Oh dear – don't say such gloomy things,' begged Lucy-Ann. 'Anyway, the men are gone. That's one good thing. I felt awfully afraid when they were in the valley too. Thank goodness they've gone!'

She spoke too soon. There came a familiar throbbing noise – and the children sat up at once.

'The plane's back! Blow! Those men will be about again now – and maybe they've even got the real truth out of Otto – where the treasure *really* is!' said Jack. 'We shall have to be jolly careful now.'

24

Juan finds the caves

The children held a council of war. What would be the best thing to do? Suppose the men did know the way into the treasure caves now, and came to them? They would begin to take away the treasure, that was certain.

'And we can't stop them,' said Philip. 'They are jolly tough men. They wouldn't let a pack of children and two old people prevent them from taking what they wanted. I can't think why they've come back unless it is to search for the treasure again and find it this time.'

Everyone agreed with Jack. 'If only we could escape and get news to Bill,' sighed Philip. 'But there simply isn't a way.'

The plane had not come into sight – they had only heard the sound of its engines. The old man did not seem to have heard anything at all. The children decided not to tell him, in case he got into a panic.

'What do you think it would be best for us to do?' said Philip. 'Stay here with the old couple and see if the men do come and take anything away? We can hide somewhere quite easily. Or go back to our own fern cave beyond the waterfall? I always felt safe there. And we've got plenty of food there too.'

'There's plenty here,' said Dinah. 'Let's stay here. After all, if the men do come, we can hide in that stalactite cave – there are plenty of hiding places there, behind those frozen columns. They won't see us. One of us could always be on guard there, to see who comes in or out.'

'Perhaps you're right,' said Jack. 'We must just wait and see what happens. Once the men really do find the treasure caves, there will be a lot coming and going – taking the treasure to the plane – taking off with it in the air – coming back again to fetch more – and so on.'

'Shouldn't be surprised if they bring more planes here, as soon as they've discovered exactly where the treasure is,' said Philip. 'It would be a slow business taking one or two crates at a time.'

'Lucy-Ann is asleep,' said Dinah. 'I think I'll snooze too. It's so lovely here in the sun. Those men won't be along yet, so nobody needs to be on guard in the caves.'

'It would be almost better to be on guard at the entrance,' said Philip thoughtfully. 'Then we could spot anyone in plenty of time.'

'Yes, that's a much better idea,' said Jack, settling down to snooze too. 'I'm sure the men won't be along today. The sun's going down. They'll wait till tomorrow.'

That night the children spent in the old couple's 'bedroom.' It was a smallish cave leading off from their 'sitting room,' where the children had had their meal. In the 'bedroom' was a pile of rugs, spotlessly clean, and the old people insisted on giving up this room to the children.

'We can sleep in chairs,' said the old man. 'That will be no hardship.'

The old woman covered Lucy-Ann up carefully and even kissed her goodnight. 'She really thinks I'm Greta, her lost grandchild,' said Lucy-Ann. 'I just can't stop her making a fuss of me, because I'm so sorry for her.'

In the morning, after another good meal, Jack said he was going to take first watch at the entrance to the passage that led to the caves. Philip was to take second watch, two hours later.

The boy settled himself down on the edge of the hole, under the big slab of rock that stuck out from the hillside. It was a fine sunny morning. The others thought they would go and examine some of the statues in the statue cave, and the old man said he would tell them their histories, and where they had come from.

Jack sat there, gazing out down the hillside. He could see a long way. He could see scores of high mountains around, one behind the other. The pine forests on them looked like short grass. He put his field glasses to his eye to watch the birds around.

It was a disappointing district for wild birds. There seemed to be very few. Jack swung his glasses from side to side of the hill, examining everything.

And then he suddenly got a tremendous shock. He had trained his glasses on to a bush, behind which he thought he had seen a quick movement. He had wondered if some bird or animal was hiding there.

He saw no bird. Instead, he saw the head and shoulder of Juan – and Juan was gazing steadily up at him through a pair of field glasses, just as Jack was gazing down at him through field glasses too!

Jack was simply petrified. He stared down through his glasses, and Juan stared up, each seeing the other quite clearly. So Juan had come once more to seek the treasure! Had he come to that cliff-side by chance – or had he got the same map from Otto that Jack had had?

'I've given the show away properly now,' thought Jack angrily. 'I've only got to pop into this hole and he'll know where the entrance is at once. But if I wander away on the hillside, he'll be after me. What a fix I'm in!'

Juan did not take his eyes off Jack. He knelt there by the bush, his field glasses fixed on the boy, watching his every movement.

'He can't possibly see the hole that I'm sitting on the edge of,' thought Jack. 'I think perhaps it would be best if I left this place and began to climb up the hillside. If I do, and Juan follows, he may miss the hole altogether.'

153

He was about to do this, when Philip leapt up beside him.

'My turn now, Freckles,' said Philip. 'Hallo, what are you looking at?'

'Pity you came just then,' said Jack. 'There is Juan down there, Philip – and he's got his glasses trained on to me – and on you too now! I was just about to crawl up the hillside to make him chase me, and perhaps miss this hole, when you came. Now he'll know there's a cave here and he'll be up in no time.'

'Golly!' said Philip, alarmed. 'We'd better warn the others at once then.'

'Yes, it's the only thing to do now,' said Jack, and he jumped back into the hole. 'Come on. It won't take Juan long to be up here. Blow! Why didn't I think he might be about already?'

They made their way quickly along the passage and through the many caves. They came to the little cell-like room and found the others there. Jack hurriedly told them what had happened.

'We must hide,' he said. But the old couple did not seem to take this in. They would not hide.

'We have nothing to be afraid of,' said the old man in a dignified manner. 'They will not hurt us.'

'You have plenty to be afraid of,' said Jack desperately. 'Do come and hide!'

But they wouldn't. Jack could not waste any more time in arguing, because he wanted to get the girls to safety. He hurried them off.

'In the cave of stalactites?' asked Dinah. Jack nodded. But when he came to the cave of silent statues, he paused. Wouldn't this be a better place? Suppose they all stood at the back, in the dim shadows, and posed like statues? Would anyone notice them? It was worth trying.

'Take shawls off some of the figures,' said the boy. 'Wrap them round you. Stand quite still right at the back there.'

It didn't take long to drape themselves and stand right at the back. 'Do you remember that game called statues that we used to play?' whispered Lucy-Ann. 'You had to stand quite still, or you were caught. I feel like that now.'

'Well, be sure you stand still or you *will* be caught,' said Jack. 'Sh! Isn't that somebody?'

'Shhhhhh!' said Kiki at once. Jack smacked her on her beak.

'Be quiet! Do you want to give us away, silly bird?'

Kiki opened her beak to squawk and then thought better of it. She flew off somewhere and disappeared. Jack was quite glad to see her go, for he didn't want her chattering and attracting attention to them.

A noise came from the tunnel beyond. Somebody was already there. It must be Juan.

'He's already gone through the cave of stalactites and the cave of stars,' whispered Philip. 'Now he's in the tunnel leading here. He'll be at the door in a minute. Pity we didn't shut it. He might not have guessed how to twist that iron stud to get it open.'

The door was almost closed, but not shut. As the children watched it, in the dim greenish glow of the cave, they saw it slowly pushed open. Then the gleaming barrel of a revolver came round it. Juan was evidently taking no chances.

Lucy-Ann gulped. Oh dear! She hoped the gun wouldn't go off. She didn't like guns at all.

The door was opened wide and Juan stood there, revolver in hand. He gasped when he saw the silent figures standing about, their curious eyes gleaming.

'Put your hands up!' said Juan sharply, to the statues. The statues did nothing of the sort. Juan's hand trembled. The children guessed he was feeling panicky as they had felt when they too had first seen the strange silent company.

'Wipe your feet!' ordered a sharp voice, and the children jumped violently. It was Kiki. She was sitting just above

155

Juan, on a ledge of rock.

'Who's there?' shouted Juan. 'I tell you I'll shoot if anyone moves.'

The statues didn't move – not even the four live ones.

'Who's there?' called Juan again.

'Three blind mice,' answered Kiki, and went off into a terrible cackle of laughter. It was almost too much for Juan. He backed a little, and tried to see which of the statues was talking.

'Pop goes the weasel!' said Kiki, and then began to cluck like Martha. Juan's hand trembled again. But he advanced a little, going down the step into the cave. Then he saw, as the children had seen, that the figures were only bejewelled statues, and he laughed loudly.

'Fool!' he said to himself.

'Fool!' repeated Kiki, and Juan swung round at once.

'Who's there? One of you children, I suppose. Wait till I get you!'

Kiki began to mew like a cat. The man looked for this unexpected cat, then decided it was one of the children again, playing a trick on him. Kiki flew silently to the next cave and began to talk to herself there.

'One, two, button my shoe, see how they run!'

The man took one more glance at the company of statues and went into the next cave. The children heaved a sigh of relief. But they dared not move yet.

It seemed a very long time till the man came back. With him came the two old people, evidently very frightened Juan shouted at them in their own language, and the children could not understand a word.

Then, without another glance at the statues, Juan went through the stout oaken door and shut it. The bang echoed loudly through the cave and made everyone jump.

Then they heard another sound which made their hearts

sink. It was the noise of strong bolts being shot home on the other side of the door.

Crash! Crash, crash! All three bolts were shot firmly into place. Now the door could not possibly be opened from the inside.

'Did you hear that?' groaned Jack. 'We're prisoners now. If only we'd hidden in the cave of stalactites or the cave of stars, we'd have been all right. We could have got out of the hole. Now we can't. We'll have to stay here till the men set us free – if they ever do.'

25

Philip's astonishing plan

The old couple looked panic-stricken when four of the statues apparently talked and came alive. But when the children took off their borrowed draperies and carefully gave them back to the right statues again, the old couple saw who they were.

Elsa came running to Lucy-Ann and fondled her. The old man stood trembling.

'What did he say to you?' demanded Jack.

'He said he was going to make us prisoners here, and that he was bringing others back with him to remove all our treasure,' said the old man. Tears suddenly poured down his cheeks. 'He is a bad man. Have I guarded these beautiful things all this time to let them fall into the hands of a man so bad?'

'It's sickening,' said Jack. 'We simply can't do a thing! We shall just have to stand by and watch those rogues take away everything, pack them into crates and fly off with them!'

'Let's go out to that sunny ledge,' said Dinah. 'I can't bear this gloom any more. I shall feel better when we are out there. Let's ask the old man if his wife would bring a picnic meal out there, Jack. You and Philip can help her to bring it. I can't think properly down here in the dark, with all those statues trying to listen.'

'All right,' said Jack, seeing that Dinah was on the point of tears. 'You go off with Lucy-Ann and Kiki. We'll soon come. You'll feel better in the sunshine.'

'Wasn't Kiki clever to lead the man away from us?' said Lucy-Ann. 'He *was* scared when she suddenly spoke to him. So should I have been! I should have thought it was one of the statues speaking.'

She and Dinah made their way to the sunny ledge. Dinah threw herself down there thankfully.

'I don't like this adventure any more, Dinah, do you?' asked Lucy-Ann. 'It's not so bad if there's something we can *do* – but we seem to be helpless here.'

'I like to make adventures go the way I want them to,' said Dinah rather sulkily. 'I don't like them to make me do things I don't like. Don't talk to me, Lucy-Ann. I shall snap at you. I feel cross.'

'It's only because of the strain we went through whilst we were pretending to be statues,' said Lucy-Ann.

'Don't sound so grown-up,' snapped Dinah. 'It's not that I just feel bad tempered because I want to get out of this valley and I can't.'

Lucy-Ann said nothing more. She settled down in the sun, waiting for the picnic that Jack and Philip would soon be bringing out with Elsa. Kiki sat murmuring to herself near by. Martha the hen arrived and began pecking about companionably. Kiki talked to her, and she clucked back.

Dinah forgot her bad temper when the others came out with a picnic meal. They had a good feast and then discussed all the morning's happening once more. In the middle of the discussion they heard the sound of the plane again, and this time saw it rising high into the sky.

'Why, they're off again!' said Jack in surprise. 'Why?'

'Probably to get other men along to help in removing everything, now they really do know where the treasure is,' said Philip. 'And as you suggested, Jack – they might even bring more planes.'

It was hateful feeling that they were complete prisoners. Jack and Philip went desperately to the bolted door once and tried to move it – but it was hopeless of course. The bolts were old but still very strong.

There was nothing to do, and they felt bored. They went to examine the statues more closely and to look at the old pictures and the musty old books.

The statues were loaded with magnificent jewels. Some of the figures were really beautifully made and dressed, but others were crude and garish. Each one, however, was adorned with jewels, though the children were not able to tell if all the gleaming brooches, dazzling earrings and necklaces, glittering bracelets, belts and rings were really valuable or not. Probably some were, and others were only semi-precious.

'I expect the men will strip the statues of their jewellery, and take only that, leaving the figures behind,' said Jack. 'They will crate the pictures and books.'

'Why couldn't we strip the jewels off and hide them away somewhere so that the men wouldn't get them?' suddenly said Dinah. 'I don't see why wicked men like that should have them.'

'Good idea!' said Jack. 'Come on – we'll take the jewellery now and hide it somewhere!'

But as soon as they began to remove it, the old couple flew at them in horror.

'Not do that! Ah, bad boy!' cried the old man, removing a brooch from Jack's hand.

'We only want to hide the things from those men,' protested Jack. 'They'll be back and steal these things soon.'

'They belong to these,' said the old man, waving his hand towards the statues. 'They must not be removed by anyone. It is against the law of the Church.'

The children did not try again. It was plain that Elsa and the old man would fly into a rage if they attempted to. They seemed to think that it was a very wicked and unholy act to take away any of the adornments belonging to the figures.

The long day passed at last. Nobody slept very well that night. They were worried about what was going to happen. It was horrid to feel they were at the mercy of rogues like Juan.

They were all out on the sunny ledge the next morning, early, having breakfast there. They had no meals in the caves now if they could help it.

'Listen,' said Dinah suddenly. 'I can hear the plane coming back.'

They all listened, the old couple too. The noise grew louder. It became very loud indeed. Then Jack leapt to his feet.

'It's not just one plane! It's many! Look, there's one! – circling down – and another over there! – and here comes another! Gracious! Juan's got quite a fleet of planes!'

There were four altogether. Evidently Juan meant to do the job properly. The children pictured the planes landing one by one on the long wide strip of grass at the bottom of the valley.

'Now we can expect things to happen,' said Jack. 'The whole of the treasure will be gone soon.'

'What a shame!' said Dinah. 'And we can't do a thing to stop it!'

'If *only* we could get word to Bill!' said Jack desperately. 'But there's no way out of the valley except in one of those planes.'

Philip stared at Jack a moment. Then he said something so

160

exciting that the others could hardly believe their ears.

'Yes – that's the only way out. And I'm going to take it.'

There was silence. Then Jack spoke, astonished.

'Whatever do you mean? You can't fly a plane.'

'Of course not. But I can *hide* in one!' said Philip. 'Didn't we hide, all of us, in a plane, coming here? Well, why shouldn't I hide in one *leaving* here? I bet I could hide unseen – and slip out when I had a chance, and get word to Bill about everything.'

'Philip! It's a *grand* idea!' said Jack. 'But I'll go, not you.'

'You jolly well won't!' said Philip. 'It's *my* idea! Nobody else is going to pinch such a gorgeous idea. I'm going, see?'

'I don't want either of you to go,' said Lucy-Ann. 'You might be seen. Something awful might happen to you. Don't leave us.'

'Jack will be with you,' said Philip. 'And the old couple. You'll be all right. I tell you, it's the only way to get help – to fly off in one of the planes, when the men go on their next trip. They'll have to come back two or three times to take all these things – and, if only I can get word to Bill, he can catch the men actually doing the stealing!'

'It sounds too good to be true,' said Dinah. 'I don't believe you can do it. Anyway – how are you even going to get to the plane? You know we're bolted in. Nobody can get out.'

'I shall watch my chance and slip out through that door when the men are going to and fro,' said Philip, enjoying his planning. 'Then I shall hide in the cave of stalactites and go up the passage to the hole as soon as I can. Then I'll get along back to the planes, and choose one to hop into. I don't reckon they will have left anyone on guard there, as they think we're all well and truly imprisoned.'

'It sounds easy, but it won't be,' said Jack. 'Better let me do it, Tufty.'

'Think again!' said Philip. 'This is my own pet adventure, see?'

'You might even be able to squeeze into a crate,' said

Dinah thoughtfully. 'Nobody would think of looking into a packed crate.'

'Good idea!' said Philip. 'In fact, jolly good!'

'Well, we can expect quite a horde of men here today,' said Jack. 'It will surprise the poor old couple. They will be in a dreadful state when they see their well-guarded treasure going.'

'Philip, we won't pretend that we are any of the statues today when the men come,' said Dinah. 'Only you. The men are sure to have a hunt round for us if they can't find us today, so we'd better all be found, except you. You can be a statue again, and wait your chance to rush out of the door.'

'Yes. I think I will,' said Philip. 'It may not work, but it's the only thing to do. Now – when will those men be along? It will take them about an hour and half to get here. It's half an hour since we saw the planes. I mustn't leave it to the last minute to put myself in place.'

'Better go now,' said Lucy-Ann, who was on pins and needles about the whole thing. 'We'll come with you and see that you're in a good place and really look like a statue.'

They all went down the passage, and made their way through the various caves to the one in which the statues stood. Martha the hen came too. She had attached herself to Jack now, and followed him wherever he went. She had laid an egg that morning, and the old woman had made Lucy-Ann have it for breakfast.

'Look! – there's a half-hidden ledge here not far from the door,' said Dinah eagerly. 'If you stood there you would hardly be seen, it's so dark there. And you would be near the door to creep out if you got a chance.'

'Yes, that does seem the best place,' said Philip. 'It really does. Now what about a shawl or something to drape over my head? I don't want my short hair to give me away.'

They found a very big shawl and draped it carefully round him. He went to stand on the little ledge, and everyone agreed that it was a splendid place.

'You can hardly be seen,' said Jack. 'Well, good luck, Tufty. We'll go now, and we shan't hide. We shall let the men see us and hope they'll think there's nobody else in the caves at all. If you can't escape we shall know, because you'll still be about tonight.'

'Goodbye,' said Philip, looking exactly like a statue. 'Don't worry about me. I'll be off and away soon, and I'll get word to Bill and Mother. We'll soon rescue you, don't you worry!'

26

The getaway

In about an hour's time Philip heard the sound of footsteps and then the bolts of the door were shot back. Juan's revolver appeared round the opening door again. But this time there was no Kiki to talk to him – nobody to be seen or heard except the silent company of statues.

Juan came down into the cave. Other men followed him. Philip watched them through a fold of the shawl. He hoped they wouldn't start stripping the jewels off the statues at once, or they might discover him.

The men exclaimed in wonder at the statues. They had powerful torches with them which they switched on at once. Philip was not prepared for that. He shrank back into his corner, glad of the draping shawl.

The men were a rough-looking lot, and they called out to one another in surprise as they saw the gleaming jewels on the necks and arms of the statues. Some of them grabbed brooches and necklaces at once. Juan gave a sharp order and the men replaced them sulkily.

Philip counted the men. There was eight. Otto was not among them, but that was not surprising. Juan, Pepi and Luis were there. There were two men for each aeroplane, apparently.

Juan led the way to the next cave, through the tunnel. Their footsteps echoed hollowly as they passed through. Philip wondered if they would all go on to the next cave – and the next. If so, he could slip out of the open door straightaway, and make his way down the hillside at once.

He listened. He could hear the men's voices from the next cave, where the pictures were. Then footsteps again, farther away. Then only a faint murmur of voices.

'They've gone to the cave of books – and then they'll go to the cave where the gold is,' thought Philip. 'I've plenty of time to get through the door and away.'

He dropped his shawl on the floor and went quietly to the door. He was through it in a trice. Up the winding steps he went, off to the cave of stars – then to the cave of gleaming stalactites. He began to feel safer. He didn't think there would be anyone on guard outside the hole, but he meant to be careful there.

There was nobody on guard. The hillside was empty. Philip climbed out of the hole and began to make his way downwards. Soon he was well on his way, keeping a sharp look-out the whole time just in case all the men had not gone down into the caves.

He was tired and hungry by the time he reached the men's hut. Thank goodness the door was open and there was nobody about! The boy got himself a good meal. He found a box containing bars of chocolate, and slipped some of the bars into his pocket, in case he had to go some time without food.

Then he went along to the planes. There they were, four of them, looking quite big as he walked beside them. Which should he get into?

He climbed up into the cabin of each and looked inside. In the last one there was a big heap of coats and rugs. It seemed the best plane to get into. He could pile the things over him and hide himself that way. He didn't at the moment see any chance of squeezing himself into a crate, as Dinah had suggested. Anyway, the crates were not in the plane, they were under the tarpaulins, where they had always been.

Having decided exactly what he was going to do, he had plenty of time left on his hands. He knew that the men would not be back for some time. They would be carrying heavy, awkward loads and would go far more slowly than he had gone.

He amused himself by snooping around. He went into the hut and found a coat hanging up there. He ran his hands through the pockets, thinking that any information he could get hold of might be useful to Bill, when he got to him.

There was a notebook in one of the pockets. Philip flipped over the pages. He could make nothing of it. It contained sentences in some kind of code, and plenty of numbers. Perhaps Bill could make head or tail of it. He couldn't!

He went to the cowshed. There was nothing to be seen there but the still-open tins of fruit, swarming with flies. Philip stared at them. 'Oh yes – they are what Jack left for Otto,' he thought. 'Ugh, look at the flies!'

He took a stick, dug a hole and buried the evil-smelling tins and their contents. Then he strolled off again and came to the tree where they had all once hidden. He squinted up and saw something. 'Golly, what's that?'

Then he remembered. 'Of course – we left our suitcases up there. I'd forgotten all about them. Fancy them still being there!'

He debated whether to get them down and hide them. 'No,' he thought, 'they might be found, and then the men might start looking for me. I'll leave them there.'

He kept a good look out for the returning men as the

afternoon wore on. He helped himself to some biscuits and a tin of peaches about five o' clock. Still no sign of the men.

But about ten minutes later he saw them far away in the distance. He was by the planes, waiting, ready to jump into the one he had chosen as soon as he saw the men coming.

He counted the men quickly. Yes – eight – so they were all back. He climbed up the steps and leapt into the cabin. He went to the pile of rugs and coats and got underneath, pulling them over him so that not even the toe of his shoe showed.

'Good thing it's a hot day,' he thought. 'The men certainly won't want their coats or macks.'

He heard the voices of the men. Evidently they were pleased with their successful day. Then there was a silence. They had passed the planes, and were on their way to the hut. 'Probably get themselves a meal, and then pack up the things they have brought from the treasure caves,' thought Philip. He yawned. He felt sleepy now that he was lying down.

Soon he was asleep, and he slept so soundly that he did not even stir when, some hours later, two men entered his plane. But he did wake when the propellers swung round as the engines suddenly roared out! He nearly gave himself away by sitting up in a fright.

Then he remembered where he was, and lay perfectly still, wondering if it was nighttime. He could see nothing under the pile of coats, of course. It might have been midnight or noon for all he knew.

One by one the planes took off. Philip's plane went last of all. He felt it leave the ground like a bird and then he was away in the air.

'They haven't seen me! They don't guess they've got me on board!' thought Philip, delighted. 'It was easy after all. Hurrah!'

He fell asleep again, and the planes roared on through the

166

night. Where were they going? To a secret landing-place? To an ordinary aerodrome?

The other children, who were sleeping that night out on the ledge, heard the roar of the planes as they left. It was such a hot night that they had felt stifled indoors and had begged the old couple to let them take the rugs out on the ledge.

'You will not walk in your sleep?' the old man had said. 'You might walk off the ledge!'

'Not one of us walks in our sleep,' said Jack. 'We'll be all right.'

Elsa, the old woman, had not wanted Lucy-Ann to sleep out on the ledge at all, and had almost cried when Lucy-Ann had insisted. Kiki and Martha were both there too. But the lizard wasn't. She was with Philip, sharing his adventure.

The children had had a horrid day. The men had found both them and the old couple in the 'sitting room' and had shouted at them and questioned them, and frightened them very much. The old man had told them that he had been living in the caves for a long time, guarding the treasure, and the men had jumped to the conclusion that the children also had been living there with them.

'Good thing they didn't ask us how we got to this valley,' said Jack afterwards. 'They just took it for granted that we and the old people came here together ages ago.'

The old man and woman had rushed to the rescue of their beloved statues when the men had begun to strip off the jewellery. The men had struck the poor old things and shouted at them. The old man had taken his weeping, trembling wife away, and the children had done their best to comfort them.

They had not gone near the men again, but had gone to sit on the sunny ledge, and wondered if Philip had managed to escape. 'I'm sure he did,' said Lucy-Ann. 'All the men kept together, and Philip could easily have slipped out of the cave of statues when they came to question us.'

The men had gone at last, taking with them a haul of jewels, one very precious figure, some pictures and a few old papers. Two of them carried a box of the gold between them. The children pictured their difficulties, hauling it up and down the mountainside.

The men had bolted the door behind them again, and once more the little company were prisoners. How they wondered what was happening to Philip! Had he managed to hide in one of the aeroplanes? Would he slip into a crate? When would the planes go off?

They knew that the planes had gone when they awoke in the night to hear the throb of the engines. They all sat up and listened. Kiki gave a squawk and pecked Martha to wake her.

'There go the planes,' said Jack. 'I bet Philip's in one. Now we shall soon be rescued. What a shock for Bill when he hears all about us! Do you think Bill will fly over in his aeroplane too?'

'I hope so,' said Lucy-Ann fervently. 'I'm longing to see Bill again. I sometimes feel as if we'll be in this valley all our lives.'

'Don't be silly,' said Dinah. 'Oh, Kiki, leave Martha alone. Whatever are you doing to her to make her cluck like that?'

'Shhhh!' said Kiki cheekily.

'Don't talk back to me!' said Dinah, lying down again. 'Well, I'm glad we heard those planes. Good luck to you, Philip, wherever you are!'

'Good luck!' called the others, and Kiki echoed the words too. 'Good luck!'

'Cluck-luck-luck!' said Martha the hen, sounding exactly as if she was joining in with the good wishes as well!

27

A discovery – and a fine idea

The next day the men were all back again in the four planes. They soon arrived once more at the treasure caves, going through the old books and papers, unrolling the dozens of canvases and looking at the pictures. They had gone to find the children and the old couple and had shouted at them again.

They had found out that somebody had helped himself to food from the hut, and they could not make it out. Hadn't they imprisoned all the children and the old people in the caves?

The children, of course, guessed at once that it was Philip who had helped himself to the food. But they were not going to say so. So Jack put on a bewildered air and replied quite stupidly, and Dinah did the same. Lucy-Ann sobbed and the men soon gave up questioning her.

As for the old couple, they knew nothing, of course. They did not even appear to have missed Philip. The men gave up their questioning after a while, and returned to their work.

Elsa was sad to see Lucy-Ann sobbing. She took her by the hand and led her into the 'bedroom.' She took down a picture she had put on a ledge there, and showed Lucy-Ann a space behind. Lucy-Ann stared at it.

'What is it?' she said. Then she called to Jack. 'Jack! Come here, and bring the old man. The old woman doesn't understand what I say.'

They came, and when Jack saw the yawning space behind the picture, he turned to the old man.

'What's that? A hidey-hole?'

'Oh, it is only a hole in the wall,' said the old fellow. 'My wife did not like it, so she covered it with a picture.'

The old woman poured out a torrent of words to him. He turned to Jack. 'My wife is sad because your little sister is frightened by those men. She says she can hide in this hole and they will not find her.'

'Let me see what it's like,' said Jack, and climbed into it. It was more than a hole. It was a tiny, round dark tunnel that had once been a waterway. Where could it lead to – if it led anywhere?

'It's a little tunnel!' Jack called back. 'Rather like the one that led out of our fern cave into the cave of echoes. I'll see if it goes anywhere.'

He crawled on for some way, and then it suddenly dipped down so steeply that he could have slid down it if it had not been so narrow. It ended in a hole that seemed to open out in the roof of a much bigger passage. Jack flashed his torch down. Yes, that really *was* a passage down there! He crawled back to the girls.

'Come behind me,' he said. 'I may have found a way of escape. We'll have to use a rope though.'

They crawled in single file till they came to the hole that dropped into the wide passage. Jack undid the rope he always carried round his waist. He tied it to a rock and let it drop down into the passage, then down he went.

The girls followed. Jack flashed his torch up and down the passage. 'Which way shall we go?' he said.

'I can hear a funny noise,' said Lucy-Ann. 'It's the water-fall, I do believe!'

They went down the passage towards the noise – and to their intense surprise and delight they came out on to the ledge behind the waterfall, the one on which Lucy-Ann and Dinah had capered about to hold their attention of Pepi some days before.

'I *say*! It's the waterfall ledge – and that is the passage that leads back to the cave of echoes!' said Jack. 'Would you believe it? We can get back to our old fern-cave and we shan't be prisoners in the treasure caves any more. Let's go and fetch the old couple too.'

He went back down the passage, swarmed up the rope, wriggled back up the little tunnel and came out into the sitting room. He told the old man where the passage led to. 'Come too,' he said. 'We will take you to a safe place.'

The old man laughed sadly. 'We cannot do as you do and crawl and climb,' he said. 'It is impossible. You go, and we will put back the picture over the hole and no one will guess.'

Jack went back to the girls, Kiki with him. 'Pity we couldn't take Martha too,' he said. 'I got quite fond of her. But the old people would miss her. They simply won't come with us. I think they're right, too – they'd never be able to swarm along that little tunnel, and swing down that rope – nor would they ever be able to get down into the fern cave. Come on! I'm longing to get back to our own cave. Ha ha – we've escaped after all! Won't those men be wild!'

'I hope they won't hurt those two old people,' said Lucy-Ann anxiously. 'She was such a dear, gentle old woman.'

They went down the winding passage and came to the cave of echoes, where Kiki annoyed them by squawking and screeching all the time, bringing back echoes of hundreds of magnified squawks and screeches that almost deafened them.

They got through the little drainpipe-like tunnel that led to the back of the fern cave, and dropped thankfully down to the rugs still spread out there.

'Home again,' said Jack, and laughed. 'Funny to think we feel this is home – but I really do.'

They settled down for a rest. 'Those men must have gone off somewhere in their planes last night, unloaded their goods and taken off again almost at once to get back so quickly,' said Dinah thoughtfully. 'I really hardly expected to see them in the caves today. I didn't hear the planes come back, did you?'

'No – but the wind has changed, so maybe the sound didn't blow in our direction,' said Jack. 'It's not so sunny now – looks like rain again. The wind's jolly strong.'

'We shall have to keep a look out for Bill and Philip if they come,' said Dinah. 'Philip won't know we're here, will he?'

'Do you girls mind if I go this evening and just have a snoop round about the men's hut?' asked Jack. 'You know – in case by any chance old Tufty didn't get away but got caught and is a prisoner.'

'Golly! I didn't even *think* of that!' said Lucy-Ann in horror. 'Oh, Jack, surely you don't think he got caught, do you?'

'Not for a minute,' said Jack cheerfully. 'But it would be just as well to make sure. I'd better go now whilst the men are busy in the caves. By the way, were all eight of them there, do you know?'

'I *think* so,' said Dinah, frowning. 'But I really couldn't be certain. Do you remember, Lucy-Ann?'

'No. I didn't look at them,' said Lucy-Ann. 'Horrid things!'

'I expect they were all there,' said Jack. 'Brr-r-r-r – the wind's cold today. I'll put on an extra jersey. So long, girls, I'll be back in a short time!'

Off he went, following the familiar way back to the men's hut. He did not think that Philip would have been caught, but still, he must make sure. He scouted cautiously about. The hut door was shut. He went up to it and peeped in at the window. No Philip there. Good!

'Better just pop up to the cowshed,' thought Jack. 'They might have got him tied up there.' So off he went. No – it was empty – good!

There was a sudden rush of wind such as often sweeps through a mountainside valley. A torrent of rain came down and the boy ran for a tree. It was the tree in which they had once all hidden, a good big thick one, that would keep the rain off. He crouched there whilst the wind whipped round him.

There was such a noise of wind that the boy did not hear footsteps coming behind the tree. He did not see the burly figure of Pepi there, staring in surprise at the crouched boy.

In a trice Pepi was round the tree and had got hold of Jack's shoulders. The boy gave a howl of fright. Pepi gripped him tightly.

'Let me go!' yelled Jack. 'You brute, let me go! You're twisting my shoulder!'

Pepi took up a stick and grinned. 'A little of this will do you good,' he said. 'You boys are a lot of trouble to us. Where are the others? You will tell me or I will beat you black and blue.'

'Let me go!' yelled Jack, and kicked hard at Pepi's ankles. The man gave a yelp of pain and hit Jack on the back with the heavy stick. Jack kicked him again.

What would have happened to poor Jack is easy to guess – if something hadn't happened to Pepi first! The wind howled round and shook the tree violently. Something fell from the tree and hit the raging man full on the shoulder. He dropped down at once, shouting, clutching at his shoulder. Jack sped off into the wind. He turned and looked back. Pepi was trying to get up, groaning. The wind howled again, and the big tree spat out something else that hit Pepi on the head. He fell back and did not move.

'Golly!' said Jack, staring. 'It's two of our suitcases that we left up the tree! They just blew down at the right moment. I hope they haven't killed him.'

He went back cautiously to the still man. No, he wasn't killed – just completely knocked out. Jack saw his chance at once. He took his rope and roped the man's hands firmly together, and then his feet. Then he tied him to the tree.

173

'Now you won't be able to come after me, my dear Pepi,' said Jack, taking a quick look up the tree in case the remaining two suitcases should come down. 'I suppose the others left you here on guard today, as they knew somebody had been at the food. Well, you won't be much use as a guard for the rest of the day, but never mind. The tree will shelter you from the storm.'

Suddenly such an extraordinary idea struck Jack that he stood perfectly still and gasped. Then he struck his hands together and yelled out loudly:

'I must do it, I must, I must! But have I time? Have I time?'

He began to run as fast as he could through the wind and the rain. 'Why didn't I think of it before? It those men are in the treasure caves, I can bolt the door on them, just as they did to us – and make them prisoners! Why didn't I think of it before? It may be too late now.'

He ran and ran, gasping and panting, hot as fire in spite of the wind and the rain.

'It won't be any good. The men will be out of the caves by now,' he thought. 'I may see them at any minute. Oh, why didn't I think of this before? I could have gone and bolted them in before I left Dinah and Lucy-Ann!'

It certainly was a most wonderful idea. The men would be absolute prisoners. They did not know the way out behind the picture, and would never think of looking for it there. Certainly the old people would not tell them. Oh, if only they were still in the caves!

The rain poured down. The wind blew like a gale. Fortunately it was behind Jack now and it helped him on. He was soaked through, but he didn't care.

There was no sign of the men. Jack slowed down when he came near the waterfall. He didn't want to run right into them. He began to think more calmly.

'Maybe they won't come out till the rain stops and the storm dies down. Rain would spoil the old books and papers and pictures. Yes, they'll be sure to wait. I may be in time yet. The men may even decide to stay the night there if the storm doesn't clear.'

Jack was right. The men, having looked out of the entrance hole of the caves, had seen the rain storm sweeping over the mountainside and had decided not to venture out with their treasures. They would be ruined.

'Better spend the night here,' said one of the men. 'In that room with the rugs. We'll turn the old people and children out.'

Only the old people were there. They made vague gestures when the men asked where the children were, pointing towards the passage that led to the sunny ledge. The men settled down on the rugs, and one of them got out a pack of cards. He set the lamp so that they could all see, and then began to deal the cards. The old people went into their 'sitting room,' sad and afraid. How they hoped that the men would not look behind the picture in the next room!

When Jack arrived at the treasure caves he could hardly walk through the passages. He stumbled along, past the cave of stalactites, past the cave of stars and into the first treasure cave, through the open door at the bottom of the curving stairway. He could see no men at all. His heart sank. Had they gone, then? Had he missed them?

He went cautiously on. When he came to the 'sitting room' he peeped in and saw the old couple there, with Martha the hen.

Then he heard the noise of the men in the next room. He beckoned to the old couple. They rose silently and followed him in surprise. Jack did not speak till he was well out of earshot of the men.

'Come,' he said, leading them out of the cave of statues and out of the stout door. 'I am going to bolt the men in. But I don't want to lock you in too.'

He shot all the bolts triumphantly. Crash! Crash! Crash! He'd done it! He'd done it!

28

The day after the storm

As soon as he had shot the bolts safely home, Jack collapsed. His tussle with Pepi, his long run through the wind and the rain, and the terrific excitement of making the men prisoners had been too much for him. He sank down on the steps outside the bolted door, and lay there quite still.

It was dark there. The old couple felt about for Jack in alarm. What was happening to the poor boy?

They found his torch in his pocket and took it out. They switched it on and looked anxiously at Jack's pale face and closed eyes. They tried to drag him up the steps.

'His clothes are wet,' said the old woman, feeling Jack's soaked jersey and shorts. 'He will get a chill, a terrible chill. Maybe he will die of it. What shall we do, old man?'

The old man answered her in her own language. 'We will drag him up these steps. We will make him comfortable in the cave of stars. You shall wrap him in your shawl and he shall have my coat.'

Together the old couple managed to drag Jack up the steps. How they panted and groaned. They could not get him any further than the top. The old man stripped off Jack's wet things and put his coat round him. The old woman wrapped him all round in her thick shawl. They squeezed out his wet things and hung them on the rocky wall to dry.

They were frightened. What were they going to do now? Those men were bolted in the caves with what was left of their precious treasure. How angry they would be when they discovered what had happened!

Jack soon came to himself again. He sat up, wondering where he was. He had been in a kind of half faint, half asleep. He clutched at his clothes. What on earth had he got on? A shawl? Gracious, was he dressed up as a statue again?

The old people heard him moving and switched on the torch again. They looked anxiously at him and were relieved to see that he was no longer so white.

'You are better now?' asked the old man gently.

'Yes, thanks. I'm all right,' said Jack, pulling at the shawl. 'Whatever's this?'

'Your clothes were so wet,' said the old man. 'We had to take them off to dry them or you would have got a terrible chill. You have my coat and my wife's shawl.'

'Oh – well, thank you,' said Jack, feeling rather foolish in the coat and shawl. 'Sorry I gave you a fright. But I just conked out – that run up the mountainside, I suppose. I say – wasn't it a good idea bolting those men in?'

'Ah – but what will they do to us when they know?' said the old man sadly.

'Nothing! How can they?' said Jack. 'They are on the wrong side of the bolted door, aren't they? Don't you worry, we're all right!'

He got up. His legs were not very steady, but he could walk all right. 'I'm just going to the entrance of the caves to see if by any chance that awful wind storm has died down,' he said. 'If it has, I'll make my way to the fern cave, where the two girls are. They'll be scared by themselves.'

Somehow he stumbled along to the entrance. The clouds were so low and black that it was like night outside. Rain still swept over the hillside in great torrents. It was quite impossible to go out.

'I should get completely lost,' thought Jack. 'Golly, the girls will be so worried about me! I hope they won't be frightened all by themselves. Well, it's no use – I'll have to spend the night here with the old people – but it won't be very comfortable.'

It wasn't comfortable. They found a place in the cave of

177

stars, a rounded, hollowed-out basin of rock, with only a few sharp edges. For the sake of warmth they all huddled together. Jack tried to make the old people take back their coat and shawl, saying that his clothes were almost dry.

But the old woman grew very angry when he suggested this, and scolded her husband hard in words that Jack could not understand, but whose meaning he could guess.

'My old one says that you are a bad bad boy to talk of putting on wet clothes,' said the old fellow. 'We will press close together. It is not cold in this cave.'

It wasn't very cold, it was true. Jack lay between the old man and his wife, looking up at the roof of the strange cave. He watched the curious greenish-blue stars shine and fade, flicker and glow. There were hundreds of them, most enchanting to watch. Jack wondered about them for a long time and then fell asleep.

In the morning the old people awoke first and felt stiff and uncomfortable. But they did not move for fear of disturbing Jack. He awoke at last and sat up. He saw the glowing stars above and around, and knew where he was at once.

'I wonder what the time is,' he said, looking at his watch. 'Half past seven! Gracious, I wonder what those men are doing! Are my clothes dry?'

Luckily they were. Jack put them on quickly, and gave back the coat and shawl with warm thanks. 'Now, you stay here a bit,' he said to the old couple. 'I'm just going to the bolted door to see if I can hear anything.'

He went off, feeling quite himself again now. As soon as he came to the top of the curving stairway that led down to the oaken door, he heard bangs and crashes. Ah – the men had discovered that they were bolted in!

Crash! Bang! Thud! Smash!

They were hammering at the stout door for all they were worth. How they shouted and yelled, how they kicked at that door and tried to smash it down!

178

Jack stood at the top of the steps and grinned in delight. Serve them right! They were getting a taste of their own medicine. They had locked the children in — and now they themselves were prisoners.

Suddenly there was a loud bang that made Jack jump. It was a revolver shot. The men were shooting at the door, hoping to smash the bolts.

Bang! Bang! Bang!

Jack went back a little way, afraid that a bullet might glance off somehow and hit him, though this was impossible. BANG! BANG!

The bolts could not be smashed. The men gave the door a few more blows with something then stopped. Jack ran back to tell the old couple all about it.

But they were frightened, so it wasn't much fun telling them. 'I think I'll take you to the fern cave, where the girls are,' he told the old man. 'We have food and rugs in that cave. Come with me.'

The old couple wouldn't stir out of the place they knew so well. They were terrified of the open air, of the hillside and the outer world. They shrank back and nothing that Jack could say would make them change their minds.

'Well, I shall just have to go to the girls myself, then,' said Jack at last. 'I'll bring them back here with food and rugs. We might as well all be together. Those men are no longer a danger to us. They can't possibly get out. Even if they find the hole behind that picture, I'm sure they won't get any further than the cave of echoes.'

He said good-bye to the frightened old people and went out into the sunshine. It was warm on his head and back — delicious. The sky was blue again, and the wind had gone.

He made his way to the waterfall, arriving there without any mistake, for he could follow the 'signposts' easily now. He was hailed by the girls as soon as they saw him. They were peeping out through the fern fronds.

'Jack! You didn't come back last night! Oh, Jack, I hardly slept at all, wondering what had happened to you,' cried Lucy-Ann.

'What happened?' asked Dinah, who was looking rather pale. She too had been very anxious, especially when the storm had come.

'Heaps!' said Jack. 'Marvellous news! Best in the world!'

'Gracious! Is Philip back, then? — and Bill here?' cried Lucy-Ann at once.

'No — that's not my news,' said Jack. 'Do you know what I've done? Bolted those men into the caves. What do you think of that?'

'What a *wonderful* idea!' said the girls together. 'But what about the old people?' asked Dinah.

'Oh, I got them out first,' said Jack. 'And I found Pepi back by the cowshed place, and tied him up properly. He's bound to that big tree where we once hid.'

'JACK! How marvellous you are!' cried Lucy-Ann. 'Did you fight him?'

'Well — not exactly,' said Jack. 'He caught me, and I kicked him hard. And just then the wind blew hard and a couple of our suitcases fell out of the tree and knocked him out. It was as much of a surprise to me as to him.'

'Oh — of course — we left our suitcases up there!' said Dinah. 'Oh, *Jack* — what a good thing we did!'

'Pepi must have had a most uncomfortable night,' said Jack. 'The rain and wind were his only companions.'

He told them how he had left the old couple in the cave of stars, and related the tale of the angry men trying to smash down the door.

'I can't get the old people to leave the caves,' he said. 'So we'd better take rugs and food and go back there to keep them company. They lent me their coat and shawl last night when my things were soaked. We can't leave them alone there without food or bedding.'

'Oh dear – I do like this cave so much better than any-where else,' sighed Lucy-Ann. 'Still – those old people have been very good to us. Is Martha there too, Jack?'

'Golly! – no, I'd forgotten all about her,' said Jack, remembering. 'I hope those men don't kill and eat her.'

This was a dreadful thought, and made poor Lucy-Ann quite dumb for a minute or two. Poor Martha. Surely the men would leave her alone?

Kiki, of course, was as delighted to see Jack as the girls had been. She nestled on his shoulder, making crooning noises all the time he was talking, pulling at his ear and ruffling up his hair. Jack scratched her poll, delighted to have her again.

The girls collected a few tins, and Jack piled rugs over his shoulder. Then, with Kiki flying ahead, they set off to follow the familiar 'signposts' to the treasure caves. The sun beat down hotly. It was a really lovely day.

'I wish I could draw a plan of how that hole behind the picture leads to our fern cave,' said Dinah. 'The mountain is riddled with holes and caves. I say, isn't the waterfall loud this morning? – and it seems bigger than ever. I suppose it's all the rain last night.'

They arrived at the entrance to the caves at last and went in. They made their way to the cave of stars and the old couple greeted them warmly and joyfully. The old woman was full of delight to see Lucy-Ann again, and greeted her lovingly.

'I'm hungry,' said Lucy-Ann, trying to wriggle out of Elsa's arms. 'Very hungry.'

They all were. It was a strange place to have a meal in – the cave of stars. The children watched the flickering, shin-ing lights, quite entranced by them. If only Lucy-Ann could take some home for her bedroom ceiling! She wished this once again as she watched the shining stars.

'Well, now, all we've got to do is to wait,' said Jack,

arranging the pile of rugs for everyone to sit on as comfortably as possible. 'Everything rests with Philip now. Those men evidently don't know he hid in a plane or they would have said something. He must have escaped all right. What is he doing, I wonder?'

29

A very strange journey

What *had* happened to Philip? He was certainly having a most adventurous time.

He slept under the pile of coats and rugs in the plane until dawn. Then the planes landed, and bumped along the ground on their huge wheels. Philip awoke at once.

He made a peephole through the rugs and watched to see what the two men in his plane were doing. They were getting out. What a bit of luck that they hadn't even looked round the plane, or taken a coat from the pile!

Other men outside were greeting the new arrivals. Philip sat up and tried to hear what was said. But half of the speech was in a foreign language, and there was such a babel that it was impossible to make out anything.

He glanced round the plane. One of the crates was now in it, and a tarpaulin was tied loosely round it. Philip tried to see what was in it. Packed in straw was one of the statues, evidently one that was very valuable.

Philip peeped cautiously out of the window of the plane, for now the men's voices had ceased. Where were the men? Could he slip out now and escape to get help?

He stared in surprise. The planes, and others too, were on a vast grassy plain – and in front and all round was the blue sea. All round! Well, then, they must be on some island somewhere.

He sat and thought for a moment. These men were rogues. They were doing a deal in valuable treasures hidden and perhaps forgotten during the last war; they had planes of their own – and a secret landing ground. What could be better than a lonely island, say, off the coast of Scotland?

'Then I suppose they'll have motor boats or launches of their own to get the stuff away,' thought Philip. 'A proper gang of them! I'll never get away from here without being seen – never. If it's an island – and it seems as if it must be – I'm as much a prisoner here as I was in the treasure caves. Blow!'

Then Dinah's idea came into his mind. What about hiding in the crate? That figure would be sure to be put on board a boat and shipped off somewhere to be sold. Well, couldn't he go with it?

He peeped out again to see where the men were. They were evidently having food and drink in a hut some distance off. Philip reckoned that he would have at least half an hour to get to work.

He loosened the tarpaulin a little more. He found that the crate was fastened by a hasp. He pulled it undone, and the whole side of the crate opened, like a sideways lid. Straw began to tumble out.

The figure was inside, packed loosely round with straw. Philip thought it must be the statue of some old-time saint. He looked at it closely. Could it be made of gold? It looked like it. Anyway, it didn't matter. It was going to lie where Philip had just been lying – under the pile of rugs and coats. And Philip was going to take its place.

It was not really very difficult to get the figure out of the straw, but it was heavy once it was out. Philip almost fell under its weight, though it was only about as big as he was himself.

He dragged it to the pile of rugs. He put it right underneath, and piled the things over it so that not a scrap of it showed. Then he cleared up the fallen bits of straw and pushed them carefully back into the crate.

Then he had the task of creeping into the straw himself. The statue had made quite a hole, and Philip settled down in the same place. He pulled the straw carefully round him, and dragged the sideways lid shut. But he could not fasten the hasp, and had to leave it, hoping that if the men saw it open they would simply think it had come undone by accident.

It was terribly warm in the straw. Philip began to be alarmed in case he might not be able to breathe after a time, and burrowed a little tunnel from his mouth and nose to the outside of the straw. After that he felt better.

He had been in the crate about a quarter of an hour when two men drove up in a cart. They unloaded all the planes. They carefully slid the crate that Philip was in out of the plane, and when the side swung open, fastened the hasp carefully. They did not guess for one moment that a live boy was inside, instead of a silent statue.

Philip's crate was loaded into the cart with other things. Then the cart was driven off towards the sea, bumping over ruts as it went. Philip was terribly jolted. The straw tickled and pricked him everywhere. He could hardly breathe.

But he didn't mind. He would soon be on board ship, and taken to the mainland somewhere. Then he could escape and go to the police. So he lay there patiently, trying to avoid the sharp prickles of the straw by wriggling about every now and again.

He could see nothing in the crate. He could only guess when the cart arrived at a small jetty, beside which a big launch was moored. He was carried on board and dumped on a lower deck.

Bump! Philip gasped, for he was very much shaken. Other things were dumped beside him. Then there came the sound of shouts and orders. The motor of the launch started up

184

and Philip felt the vessel moving smoothly over the water. They were off!

'These men don't lose much time,' thought Philip. 'They don't have these things on their hands very long. Wonder who buys them?'

The trip to the mainland, wherever it was, was a long one. Philip was now quite sure that the landing ground for the planes was on some lonely island. At last the launch eased into some kind of harbour and came to a stop. Men began to unload it at once.

The crate was rather roughly handled, and once poor Philip was put upside-down for half a minute. That was terrible. He thought he would have to call out. But just when he was certain he couldn't bear it any longer, he felt the crate being lifted again and put on a car or into a van, which drove off almost immediately.

After a while it stopped. Philip heard the sound of an engine whistling and his heart leapt for joy. They were probably at a railway station. Perhaps he would be put into the luggage van – or on a goods train. It would be easy enough to escape then. He had not dared to before, for he had felt certain that all the men handling the crate so far had been accomplices of the others.

He was not put on a train. He was left in a yard, along with other goods that were to go by a later train. He strained his ears, hoping to hear the van being driven off. Then, he thought, it would be safe for him to get out.

He waited for about twenty minutes. Then he began to try and wriggle out. But he could not undo the hasp. Blow!

He yelled. 'Hi! Hi! Help me!'

A porter not far off jumped in alarm. He looked all round. There was no one in sight except a solitary passenger waiting for the next train, and another porter on the opposite platform.

Philip yelled again, 'Hi! Hi! Let me out!'

The porter felt terribly scared. He looked at the waiting passenger. Had he heard the shouts too – or was it just the porter's own imagination? The passenger *had* heard them, and he was looking most alarmed.

'Somebody in trouble somewhere,' said the man, walking to the porter. 'Sounds as if he's in that little yard there.'

'There's nobody there,' said the porter, staring into the yard.

'Hi! Hurry up and let me out!' came Philip's urgent voice, and to the horror of the passenger and the porter, the big crate began to rock violently.

'There's someone in there!' cried the porter, and ran to the crate. He undid the hasp with trembling fingers and out came Philip, straw in his hair, straw down his neck, straw all over him, looking wild and terribly excited.

'I want the police station,' said Philip. 'Can't stop to explain anything to you now. Where's the police station?'

'Over there,' stuttered the porter, pointing to a small square building about a hundred yards away from the railway station. 'But— but— but . . .'

Philip left him 'but-ing' away, and sped off to the police station, thrilled at his escape. He had managed it wonderfully, he thought.

He shot into the police station and almost scared the policeman there out of his life.

'I want to report something important to somebody in authority,' said Philip. 'Who's the head man here?'

'I'm the constable here,' said the policeman. 'Who are you, and what do you want? You can report to me.'

'I want to use the telephone,' said Philip, thinking it would be a good thing to get into touch with Bill at once. 'Will you get a number for me, please?'

'Here here – you can't go using our police phones without good cause,' said the policeman, beginning to feel that this

186

straw-strewn boy was mad. 'What's your name, and where do you live?'

'My name is Philip Mannering,' said Philip impatiently. 'Don't hold me up, please. I've very important things to report to somebody.'

The name caught the policeman's attention at once. 'Philip Mannering?' he said. 'Here – are you one of the missing children? There's four been missing for days. You one of them?'

He drew a leaflet from a drawer and looked at it. He passed it across to Philip. To the boy's surprise he saw a photograph of himself, Lucy-Ann, Jack and Dinah – and Kiki too, of course – at the head of the paper, and their names and descriptions underneath.

'Yes – I'm that boy,' he said, pointing to his photograph. 'Philip Mannering. And I went to get into touch with Bill Smugs – no, his real name's Cunningham, of course – at once. It's MOST IMPORTANT.'

The policeman suddenly got very busy. He took up the receiver of the phone. He barked a number into it, which he got at once. He evidently got on to somebody in high authority immediately.

'Sir, one of the missing children has just turned up here – Philip Mannering – wants to report something to Detective Inspector Cunningham. Yes, sir. I will, sir.' He turned to Philip.

'Are the other children with you?'

'No – but they're all right – so far,' said Philip. 'I've escaped and I want help to rescue them. Can I get on to Bill Cunningham, please?'

The policeman spoke into the telephone. 'The other children are all right, but not with him. Please notify Mrs Mannering. More news to follow. When will the Inspector be here?'

The policeman put the receiver down and gazed in a very

pleased manner at Philip. To think that this exciting case of Missing Children should be reported to *his* little station!

'Where am I?' asked Philip suddenly. 'What is this place called?'

'Don't you know?' said the policeman, surprised. 'It's Gairdon, on the north-east coast of Scotland.'

'I guessed that's about where I'd be,' said Philip. 'Sorry I can't tell you anything, constable – but I think I'd better wait for Bill.'

Bill came – in his aeroplane! He landed at the nearest aerodrome, took a fast police car, and arrived at Gairdon in two hours' time. Very good going. Philip heard the car roaring up and ran to meet it.

'Bill! I knew you'd come! Oh, Bill – I've got the most exciting news for you! I don't know where to begin.'

30

Bill gets busy

Bill swung out of the car, took hold of Philip by the arm and had a good look at him. 'You're all right?' demanded. 'All of you? Your mother's been nearly off her head with worry.'

'I'm all right, Bill, so's everybody. But we've fallen right into the middle of a most extraordinary adventure,' said Philip. 'I must tell you quickly. We've got to get busy. You see . . . '

'Come into the police station,' said Bill. Philip followed the burly figure, full of relief to hear his determined voice, and to see his strong, clever face.

Soon the whole story was being poured out. Bill listened in amazement, occasionally rapping out a sharp question. When he heard how Philip had taken the statue out of the crate and put himself in its place, and was taken to the railway station, he burst out laughing.

'I never in my life knew children like you! Whatever will you do next? I can't cope with you. But, joking apart, this is a most extraordinary thing, Philip, most amazing. The men you got caught up with are the very men I'd been after for some time. We couldn't find out what they were up to – though we knew jolly well they were up to no good.'

'Really?' said Philip, astonished. 'By the way, Bill – that night we were to go with you in your plane – and got into the wrong one – we heard shots. Was that anything to do with you?'

'It was,' said Bill grimly. 'It so happened that two of the men were spotted there, and detained. They shot their way out – and that was what you heard. I nearly got a bullet in my leg. I can tell you, we shall be very glad to get our hands on them and have something to charge them with. Clever rogues! They are crooks from South America, in touch with the old Nazis, who have told them the whereabouts of many of the lost or hidden treasures in Europe. Many of them have never been found, you know.'

'Gosh – you wait till you see our treasure caves!' said Philip. 'Oh – by the way, here's a notebook I pinched from one of the men's coats.'

He handed it over. Bill squinted at it, and his eyes nearly fell out of his head.

'I say – my word! – look here – this is a code – the code the rascals use – and a list of all the people concerned in this racket – with their addresses in code! Philip, you deserve a medal. This is a first-class find. We can round up the whole gang.'

Philip was delighted at Bill's pleasure. Bill got up and went to the telephone. He made many calls, short, sharp and to the point. Philip listened but could not make much of them. He hoped Bill would soon set off to rescue the others.

189

They would be waiting most anxiously.

Bill put down the telephone receiver at last. 'We're taking my aeroplane and another, and twelve men counting myself,' he said. 'Starting at twelve.'

'I'm going too, aren't I?' said Philip anxiously.

'I think you'd better stay and see your mother,' said Bill. 'And also – there may be a bit of a dust-up, you know, when we get there.'

Philip stared at him in the greatest indignation. 'Bill! The others will be there – Jack and the rest – and you'd keep *me* out of it? Didn't I come here, didn't I . . . '

'All right, all right, old son,' said Bill. 'You shall come. Goodness knows what further adventure you'd get into if I left you behind.'

Philip cheered up at once. He took Lizzie out of his pocket and introduced her to Bill. 'Meet busy dizzy Lizzie,' he said, and Lizzie ran on to Bill's knee.

'Sounds like Kiki's make-up,' said Bill. 'Busy dizzy Lizzie! What a name for a lizard!'

'I suppose we can't get anything to eat here, can we?' asked Philip, wondering if there were ever any eatables at a police station. 'I've had chocolate to nibble at times, but that's all.'

'I was going to suggest that we should ask the good constable here to provide us with a really slap-up meal,' said Bill. 'We could go to the hotel, but you don't look very presentable at the moment – you seem to exude bits of straw from top to toe. We'll have a good meal and then give you a wash and brush-up.'

The wind got up as they ate their meal. Bill stared out of the window. 'Hope this wind dies down,' he said. 'Looks a bit stormy to me.'

Bill was right. Just before it was time for them to set off in the car to the aerodrome, the telephone rang. Bill answered it. He listened gravely and turned to Philip.

'There's a gale warning out,' he said. 'Afraid it's no good starting off yet, Philip. Very stormy weather where we want to go.'

'Blow!' said Philip, disappointed and anxious. 'The others will be so worried, waiting and waiting for us.'

'Yes, they will,' said Bill. 'But the aerodrome doesn't give out warnings like this without reason. They are apparently expecting one of those sudden gale-storms that mean a plane must fly absolutely blind. Not so funny. We'll have to wait a bit.'

Philip looked upset. It would be too awful if those men got back to the valley before they did and perhaps caught the others. And he did so badly want Bill to catch the men red-handed – wanted him to get there before them and wait for them to come again and take away the treasures.

'By the way, Bill – how do you know where to fly to?' he asked suddenly. '*I* didn't know what the valley was – or where – except that it is in Austria. Elsa and the old man told us that.'

'It's down in that interesting little notebook you gave me,' said Bill, 'together with other places where they may also find hidden treasures. Oh, that notebook told me quite a lot I wanted to know, Philip.'

Bill got out a map and showed Philip exactly where the valley was. 'It had a bad time in the war,' he said, 'and the only pass into it was bombed. It hasn't been unblocked again, as far as I know. Plans were afoot to work on it this year. A man called Julius Muller – the one you were told to get into touch with – has been trying to get permission to unblock the valley and enter it.'

'I wonder what happened to Otto,' said Philip. 'The poor prisoner, you know.'

'His address is in the book,' said Bill. 'I have already asked for information about him, I daresay I shall get some soon.'

He did. The telephone rang that afternoon and a voice

informed Bill that Otto Engler had been found outside a big hospital, unconscious. He had almost died of heart trouble, but was making slight progress now, though he could not speak a word.

'I bet those brutes ill-treated him and made him tell them the exact whereabouts of the treasure caves,' said Philp, 'and then took him and left him somewhere in the street, ill and terrified.'

'Quite likely,' agreed Bill. 'They wouldn't stop at much.' The telephone bell rang again, and Bill took up the receiver once more.

'Gale getting worse,' he told Philip. 'Have to put off our trip till tomorrow. Pity your mother's so far away or we could have dropped in to see her. I've been trying to get her on the phone.'

Philip did speak to his mother that afternoon, though it was only a three minute talk. Mrs Mannering was so relieved to hear his voice that she could hardly say a word herself. However, Philip found plenty to say, and had to stop halfway through because he was cut off.

Next day dawned fair and warm. The wind had almost gone – blown itself out in the night, which had been extremely stormy and wild. Philip had awakened once or twice and had felt glad they had not tried to fly through it, for certainly it was a very wild storm.

He had slept in a comfortable bed put up in the cell of the police station. This seemed very exciting to him. 'First time I've ever passed a night in prison,' he told Bill.

'Well, I hope it will be the last,' said Bill. 'Prison is not a pleasant place, my boy.'

Bill's car was brought to the door. It was large and bright and swift. He and Philip got in, Bill started up the engine and they roared away. Twenty, thirty, forty, fifty, sixty, seventy miles an hour and more! Philip was thrilled.

'She does go,' he said. 'Funny that a car seems faster than as aeroplane when you're in it. Much more of a rush, somehow.'

They reached the aerodrome at last. There was Bill's plane, its propellers whirring fast. Beside it was another, very like it. Eleven men stood about, waiting. They saluted Bill.

'Get into my plane,' Bill ordered Philip. 'I want a word with my men.'

He had his word and got in. Five of the men got in Bill's plane and six in the other. There was a terrific roar, and first Bill's plane took off and then the other one. They flew into the wind, circled round, rose higher and then made off for the east.

Philip gave a sigh of relief. Now things were on the move again. He would soon see the others. How glad they would be!

After some time Bill spoke to Philip. 'We're coming to that valley of yours, Philip, now – or should be. Have a look out and see if you recognise it.'

Philip looked down. 'Oh yes!' he cried. 'That's it! And look – there are four planes down there! That's where we land! You'd better look out in case the men are about and shoot!'

Bill's plane roared down lower. It swung into the wind and landed perfectly. The second plane followed suit.

The engines stopped. There was silence. Bill waited to see if anyone came running out. No, not a soul. He and the other men poured out. Philip followed.

There seemed to be no one about at all. Bill told his men to scatter and make a search before they went any further. Soon one of them gave a shout. 'Hey! There's one of them here! All tied up like a chicken!'

It was Pepi, half dead with cold and hunger. He was so

glad to be set free that he did not show much surprise at seeing so many strangers. In charge of one of the men he tottered over to Bill.

'Put him in the hut and lock him up,' ordered Bill. 'Who could have tied him up, Philip?'

'I can't imagine,' said Philip, puzzled. 'And look, Bill here are two of our suitcases – fallen out of the tree, I suppose. Funny.'

'There are still seven men to be accounted for,' said Bill. 'Right. Well, now – we'd better set off to these treasure caves. Look out, men, in case there's any ambush. We don't want to be shot up without warning.'

They set off, Philip telling Bill the way. Bill was filled with amazement to see the valley, the towering mountains, the burnt ruins . . . it seemed so extraordinary to think of the four children marooned here in the middle of such thrilling adventures.

'Can you hear the waterfall now?' asked Philip eagerly, after a time. 'I can! We're getting near.'

The men were amazed to hear the noise of the great waterfall, and even more astonished to see it. They did not say very much, for they were tough men, not easily surprised by anything. But they stood and stared for some time.

'Now – careful – because we're getting near to the cave entrance,' said Philip at last. 'Shall I go first? I think I'd better.'

An exciting finish

Jack, Dinah, Lucy-Ann, Kiki and the old couple were still in the cave of stars. They had just finished their meal, and were wondering what to do. What a pity the old couple wouldn't come outside the mountain – it was such a lovely day!

'We could easily go and sun ourselves there,' said Lucy-Ann longingly. 'There's no danger from those men. They can't get out of that locked door.'

Just as she spoke, Jack clutched hold of her arm and made her jump. 'Sh! I can hear voices.'

They all listened fearfully. Yes – there *were* voices – coming down the tunnel that led from the cave of stalactites to the cave they were now in.

'More men! Quick, hide!' said Dinah urgently. In a panic the children began to run to the other end of the cave, stumbling and tripping, their feet echoing round the big vault.

'Halt!' cried a stern voice, and a big figure stood just inside the cave. 'Stand still! Put your hands up!'

Lucy-Ann knew that voice. Of course she did. 'Bill! BILL!' she squealed. 'Oh, Bill, we thought you were never coming!'

She ran across the cave and flung herself on the surprised Bill. Jack and Dinah followed, shouting in delight. Lucy-Ann caught sight of Philip and flung herself on him too.

'Philip! Dear Philip, you did escape and get Bill!'

Philip was astonished to see the children and the old couple there. He had left them in the treasure caves. How had they got out? And where were the men?

The old couple came slowly up, half frightened to see so

many people by the light of the powerful torches. Bill was gentle with them.

'Poor frightened moles,' he said to Philip. 'Well, they will be well looked after and rewarded. Now – where are these men?'

'I bolted them in,' said Jack proudly. 'They are prisoners in the treasure caves.'

This was news to Philip – and, of course, to Bill too. They questioned Jack eagerly, and he told them how the old woman had shown them the hole behind the picture, and how they had managed to escape through it to the cave of echoes and from there to their own fern cave. Then how Jack had gone to the men's hut, and had come up against Pepi and tied him up – finally how he had got his Great Idea, and slipped back to bolt the men in.

'Well – that seems pretty good work to me!' said Bill. 'But it won't be an easy job routing them out of those caves. I wonder if we could take them by surprise from the back – get in at the picture-hole and give them a shock.'

'Oh *yes*!' said Jack. 'Of course you could. You could leave one or two of your men at the bolted door here, attracting the attention of the seven men – and whilst they are shouting and yelling at one another, the rest of your men could go in the other way and surprise them.'

'That seems a very sound plan,' said Bill, and gave some orders. He turned to Philip. 'I'm leaving two men here. Take them to the bolted door in half an hour's time, and they will then attract the men's attention. Jack, you come with me and the others, and show me the way back to your fern-cave, and through the cave of echoes to the passage that leads to the hole at the back of that picture.'

The little procession set off. The two men left behind waited for half an hour and then went with Philip to the bolted door at the bottom of the curving steps. They rapped on it and shouted.

An answering shout came from inside. 'Who are you? Let us out! Open the door!'

The men inside banged at the door and the men outside did the same. It was a perfect babel of noise. All the seven men were there, arguing, banging, demanding to be set free, and generally losing their tempers.

Meantime Bill, Jack and the others had gone to the fern-cave. They had crawled in, and found to their dismay that they had to wriggle through the drain-pipe hole at the back. One of them almost got stuck.

'I must say you children manage to get into the most marvellous scrapes,' said Bill, emerging from the hole into the cave of echoes. 'My, I'm hot!'

'Hot, hot, HOT, HOT!' said the echoes at once. Bill jumped. 'What's that?'

'That, that, THAT, THAT!' shouted the echoes alarmingly. Jack laughed. 'It's only the echoes,' he said. Kiki began to squawk, and then whistled like an express engine. The noise was deafening.

'Kiki always does that here,' said Jack, leading the way. 'Shut up, Kiki! Bad bird!'

Soon they were in the passage that led to behind the waterfall – but before they got there they came to the hole in the roof.

'Have you got a rope on you, Bill!' said Jack. 'We've got to get up here. I used my rope to tie up Pepi. If you can get me on your shoulder, and shove me up, I can crawl into the hole, fix the rope and let it down.'

It was soon done. One after another the men crawled into the hole, thinking that never in their lives had they done so much climbing, creeping and crawling. They looked at Jack in admiration. What a boy!

Jack came to the hole behind the picture. He listened. Not a sound. The men were all at the bolted door, shouting, kicking and arguing.

Jack gave the picture a push and it fell. The room was empty. He jumped down and the others followed one by one.

'Hope there's no more of this, sir,' said one of the men to Bill. 'You want thinner men for this job.'

'Better go cautiously now,' said Jack. 'We are near the treasure caves. We go straight through three and then come to the cave of statues. That's where the bolted door is.'

'Quiet now,' ordered Bill, and, treading softly in their rubber-soled shoes, the men moved slowly forward, revolvers glinting in their hands.

Through the cave of gold – through the cave of books – through the cave of pictures. Jack laid his hand warningly on Bill's arm. He could hear something.

'It's the men,' he said. 'Hark! – they must have got rocks or something to hammer at the door like that. They really will break it down, I should think, by the noise.'

Bill stepped from the tunnel into the cave of statues. Although he had been prepared for them by Philip, he could not help jumping a little when he saw them in that dim greenish glow. His men stepped silently behind him.

At the far end were the seven men. They had found a big rock and were using it as a battering-ram. Crash! It struck the door violently. Crash!

'Now's our chance,' whispered Bill. 'They have their hands full – not a revolver to be seen among them. Come on!'

The men moved swiftly up behind Juan and the others. A sharp, stern voice barked out behind them:

'Hands up! We've got you cold!'

The men all had their backs to Bill. At his voice, they jumped in surprise, and put their hands above their heads at once. Then Juan swung round, his hands still high. His eyes swept the stern group of men in front of him.

'How did you get here?' he said, between his teeth. 'What

198

other way in is there? Who locked us in?'

'No questions answered now,' snapped Bill. He called loudly to the two men outside the door.

'Hey, Jim! Pete! Unbolt the door. We've got 'em.'

The door was unbolted. It swung open and Jim and Pete looked round it, grinning. 'Pretty little play we had,' said Pete. 'Quite enjoyed it, I did.'

Jack slipped down too. The girls had been told to keep away till the men had been captured. They were with the old couple in the cave of stars, waiting impatiently.

Bill counted the men. 'All seven here. Good. And we've got the eighth all right too. Pete, take these fellows back to the planes. Shoot at the first sign of trouble. I'll stay here and have a look-see. It looks mighty interesting.'

The men were marched off, handcuffed, swearing and stumbling. Jack watched them go, delighted to think that he had had the idea of bolting them in. Bill had clapped him on the back for that.

Once the men had passed through the cave of stars, the girls came running to join Jack, Philip and Bill. They showed the astonished Bill everything. He whistled when he saw so many treasures.

'Fortunes here,' he said. 'Well, it won't be an easy task finding out where all these things came from and sending them back. Perhaps Julius Muller can help.'

'And the old couple can too,' said Lucy-Ann eagerly. 'They know the histories of most of the statues, anyway.'

The old man and his wife were collected on the way out and taken with everyone else to the planes. They made no objection now to going into the open air. They evidently thought that Bill was some Great Man Who Must Be Obeyed. They bowed to him whenever he spoke to them.

'We'll have to take them with us for questioning,' said Bill. 'But we'll return them as soon as possible – to the village where this good man, Julius, lives. He may be good enough to look after these old people.'

Everyone got into one or other of the planes. There were six of them. In three of them were the eight prisoners with their guards. In two others were pilots and the old couple. Bill's plane carried the children.

Their plane rose up, and the children looked down at the strange valley for the last time.

'Yes, have a good look,' said Bill. It will be in all the papers presently – the Valley of Treasure.'

'No, Bill – the Valley of Adventure!' said Jack. 'That's what *we* shall always call it – the Valley of Adventure!'

'I'm glad we found Martha all right,' said Lucy-Ann suddenly. 'I did like her so much. She was sweet.'

'Good heavens! Who's Martha?' said Bill, startled. 'I thought the old woman was called Elsa. Don't tell me Martha is someone we've left behind!'

'Oh no, Bill – she's sitting on Elsa's knee now in one of the other planes – she might even lay an egg there,' said Lucy-Ann.

Bill looked even more astonished. 'She's a *hen*!' explained Lucy-Ann. 'She got left behind in the caves with the men and we were afraid she might have been killed by them. But she wasn't. She hid under the table and came clucking to join us when we went to find her. You were busy looking at the gold, I expect.'

'I must have missed her,' said Bill. 'To think I haven't yet made the acquaintance of one of the ladies in this thrilling adventure. What a pity!'

'What a pity, what a pity, what a pity!' said Kiki at once. 'Cluck-luck-luck! Pop goes Martha!'

Enid Blyton
The Sea of Adventure £3.50

When Bill takes Philip, Dinah, Lucy-Ann and Jack on a mysterious trip
to the desolate northern isles, everything looks set for an exciting time.

But then Bill is kidnapped and the children, marooned far from the
mainland, find themselves involved in a thrilling adventure on the trail
of a ruthless enemy.

Enid Blyton
The Circus of Adventure £3.50

Why on earth did Bill have to bring the wimpish Gustavus with them on holiday? Neither Jack nor Kiki the parrot liked the boy at all.

But when Gustavus is kidnapped along with Philip, Dinah, and Lucy-Ann, Jack must follow them to a far away country and unraval a plot to kill the king.

The Mountain of Adventure £3.50

As far as Mrs Mannering was concerned, a peaceful holiday among the Welsh mountains couldn't possibly land the children in yet another dangerous adventure.

But soon Philip, Dinah, Lucy-Ann and Jack are up to their necks in the mystery of a rumbling mountain, roaming wolves, and a mad genius who plans to rule the world.

Enid Blyton
The River of Adventure £3.50

A river cruise through ancient desert lands will be an adventure in itself, thought Philip. Dinah, Lucy-Ann and Jack.

An Adventure it certainly is, especially when Bill disappears and the children, along with Kiki the parrot, are trapped beneath a forgotten temple where no one has set foot for seven thousand years.

Enid Blyton
The Ship of Adventure £3.50

All aboard for a quiet cruise among the Greek islands!

But when Kiki the parrot breaks a birthday present, Philip, Dinah, Lucy-Ann and Jack are plunged into another adventure: a desperate race against time – with the long lost treasure of the *Andra* as the prize.

All Pan books are available at your local bookshop or newsagent, or can be ordered direct from the publisher. Indicate the number of copies required and fill in the form below.

Send to: Pan C. S. Dept
             Macmillan Distribution Ltd
             Houndmills Basingstoke RG21 2XS
or phone: 0256 29242, quoting title, author and Credit Card number.

Please enclose a remittance* to the value of the cover price plus: £1.00 for the first book plus 50p per copy for each additional book ordered.

*Payment may be made in sterling by UK personal cheque, postal order, sterling draft or international money order, made payable to Pan Books Ltd.

Alternatively by Barclaycard/Access/Amex/Diners

Card No. | | | | | | | | | | | | | | | | | | |

Expiry Date | | | | | | |

Signature:

Applicable only in the UK and BFPO addresses

While every effort is made to keep prices low, it is sometimes necessary to increase prices at short notice. Pan Books reserve the right to show on covers and charge new retail prices which may differ from those advertised in the text or elsewhere.

NAME AND ADDRESS IN BLOCK LETTERS PLEASE:

....

Name _____

Address _____

_____

_____

_____

6/92